About the author

C R Clarke has been known as Nobby since he was a boy soldier in the British Army Air Corps. He is married with two sons and a grandson, and lives happily in Suffolk, England. He has been a stevedore, a terminal supervisor in the docks, a truck driver, a police community support officer during the Ipswich murders, as well as the store supervisor for the Suffolk and Norfolk Constabularies. His final throw at work was as a care assistant with the East of England Ambulance Service for four years until he was diagnosed in December 2018 with motor neurone disease (MND); putting an end to his ambulance career. He has now turned his skills to writing with his first book, *The De-Callen Chronicles*.

Cover artwork credit: Erline O'Donovan-Clarke

THE DE-CALLEN CHRONICLES

C R Clarke

THE DE-CALLEN CHRONICLES

Vanguard Press

VANGUARD PAPERBACK

© Copyright 2021
C R Clarke

The right of C R Clarke to be identified as the author of
this work has been asserted by him in accordance with the
Copyright, Designs and Patents Act 1988.

A CIP catalogue record for this title is
available from the British Library.

ISBN 978 1 784659 72 1

*Vanguard Press is an imprint of
Pegasus Elliot MacKenzie Publishers Ltd.*
www.pegasuspublishers.com

First Published in 2021

**Vanguard Press
Sheraton House Castle Park
Cambridge England**
Printed & Bound in Great Britain

Dedication

To Sue, my rock through hard times, and my family who are always supportive.

To the Royal British Legion for all their help and support, especially Judith.

Last but not least to the MND Association for the good work and support they give to thousands and my love to everyone living with this life-changing disease.

Chapter 1
Out of the Blue

A light breeze blew gently through the upstairs window of the little cottage that was nestled out of sight of the main road that ran through Rendelsham Forest. The thin flower-patterned curtain swayed through the early morning moonlight that illuminated the quite little room. The air was damp with the smell of freshly fallen rain on the forest floor and in the trees. In the centre of the room lay a very large black wolf, ears erect, nose twitching, smelling every particle of air flowing into the bedroom through the slightly ajar window. The wolf's senses were heightened by the proximity of the two figures lying peacefully asleep on the pinewood beds on either side of her. Both sleeping figures were oblivious to the dangerous creature so close to them. In the distance, the quiet was disturbed by the faint thud of rotor blades slapping the air as a military helicopter passed by en route to one of the many military bases in the area around the forest. The wolf stayed still, silent, her senses working to the maximum, eyes darting from one sleeping soul to the next. Quiet stillness once again descended on the room, the breeze continuing to silently and gently move the curtain. The setting moon began to give way to the rising sun; shadows began to creep into the room along the walls and floor, making their way towards the sleeping bodies. Suddenly the wolf sat up! Eyes sharp and alert, its nose sensing the change in the air. Every inch of its body was directed to a slightly different, more menacing movement behind the curtain. Not the natural breeze! Different.

The wolf sprang at the curtain in front of her; the distance covered in one bound without disturbing the sleeping bodies on either side of her. The wolf's head disappeared into the curtain; there was a quick crunch as its iron jaws closed on the assassin's body, expelling all the air from within the doomed creature, giving it no time to cry out. The wolf then returned to its previous position, but this time she had the lifeless creature trapped between her powerful jaws.

The room was silent once more; one of the figures stirred, letting out a sleepy moan, 'Phina.' The wolf placed the creature on the floor then went over to the stirring body, nestling her head against the boy. His arm came from beneath the quilt cover and wrapped around the wolf's neck. It stayed in that position until she was sure the boy was once more asleep, then she gently pulled away, letting the boy's arm slide against the side of the bed. Then she approached the second body, sniffing and listening. The boy was still asleep so she returned to the dead creature on the floor, re-assuming her watchful position. After a short time, the wolf silently picked up the lifeless body. Around her the night's shadows ebbed away, allowing the sunlight to penetrate and fill the room as she left silently through the open bedroom door.

Moving out of the room on to the landing, she stopped at the top of the stairs. Looking down to the kitchen below, she could see the log burner in the nearest corner; with the embers glowing through the glass door. Directly at the bottom of the stairs was an old leather armchair, comfortable through age and use. In the chair rested a big man. His name to the boys upstairs was Uncle Kurt; his real name was Kurt Nicolas De-Callen. He wore walking boots, corduroy trousers, and a checked shirt. He could quite easily have been mistaken for the local farm squire, which he most certainly wasn't. His face was gentle, but at the same time menacing. A scar ran from the top of his right ear, then crossed his cheek down to the corner of his mouth, where it ended at the dimple in his square chin which you could only just make it out because it was under a thick beard that Kurt had been growing for a year now. The scar was a testament to a previous heroic, but violent, life. He could be found there every night once the boys had gone up to bed. You would not be remiss if you thought he was on guard because he was and he had been for most of the boys' lives.

The wolf had also been with the boys every night. Asleep next to them, she was also on guard like Kurt in the room below. As she did every morning, the wolf began to creep down the stairs towards the sleeping figure in the chair… 'Ah… Phina, you will never be quiet enough to surprise me, young lady, not as long as I still have my wits about me. But I do admire you for your persistence.' Then he lifted his head and opened his eyes smiling at the wolf as she descended the stairs. 'What's that you have…?' Phina approached Kurt and dropped the creature at his feet; they both looked at each other, concern etched on their faces then Kurt nodded in agreement. 'Yes, I totally agree,' he said to Phina the wolf, even though she had not uttered a sound. If you had been looking closely, you would have seen Phina slightly nod her head in agreement with Kurt. With a sorrowful tone, Kurt told her, 'I am sorry to say we must leave as soon as possible… it's no longer safe here…, we must return, we knew this day would be coming one day… but I hoped the boys would be a little older before we returned. I'm not so worried about Karl, he is nearly a man. At his age I had already been in my first battle, but Tom… he's still too immature. I worry about what lies ahead for him, and Karl for that matter. Neither of them has any idea about their past or their potential future.'

Kurt picked up the dead creature from the floor. Walking over to the log burner in the corner of the room, he opened the door then picked up the fire tongs, prodding the now greying ashes which immediately sprang back to life, exposing the red embers beneath. He tossed the creature on to the red glowing layer in the centre of the burner. 'Good riddance to bad rubbish,' he murmured to himself. Green smoke erupted from within the creature just before it combusted into a bright yellow flame that turned red as Kurt threw a log onto the flames before shutting the door. 'That should keep the morning chill off,' he said as he turned to face Phina. Then, as he sat back down on the old chair, Phina came to his side. Kurt stroked her with such affection for a big man. You could see that Phina was not just a family pet, there was something more to it than that.

Karl was in his bed on the right side of the room, 'the neat side'. He woke with a lazy long yawn. Then, arching his back, he stretched out his arms before he finally gave a satisfied yawn and sat up. Looking down at the floor between the two beds, he could see the wolf lying there in its usual place, the exact position it was in every morning for as long as he could remember. Sound asleep, the wolf didn't stir. A 'come on, lazy beast, get up' came from the neat side. The wolf did not react to the goad.

'Shut up, Karl' said a sleepy voice from the messy side of the room. Tom turned over in his bed and faced the wall that was covered in a hooch pooch of military pictures mixed with Space Wars heroes and villains. The calm was immediately disrupted by a pillow thrown from the neat side of the room by a grinning Karl.

'Yes, on target,' cried Karl as the pillow struck the back of Tom's head. This got the desired reaction. Tom spun round and wearily sat up to face, if not quite seeing, his brother through sleepy eyes. Tom glared at his brother. He was just about to ball something back when his sleepy vision cleared and he noticed Karl had a finger to his lips indicating the universal signal for quiet. Karl pointed at the still sleeping wolf between them on the floor. Tom understood because they did this same thing every morning. He nodded his head, immediately forgetting the unprovoked pillow attack seconds before. Now united with his brother for another early morning attack on the contently sleeping wolf below them. Karl signalled the plan; covers back quietly… get into position… then jump. Tom nodded in agreement then Karl began a silent countdown in reverse from five, using his fingers as counters. Five-four-three. Tom pulled his covers back, both boys were ready to leap… two… Karl's hand went down indicating 'Go!' Both boys leapt from their beds at the wolf… Seconds later, the boys collided with a groan on the floor at the exact spot where the wolf had been seconds before. Pushing each other away, the realisation once again hit them both as it did every morning; they had been had duped by the wolf. They were now the prey. At that precise second, the beast landed on top of them, knocking them to the floor, winding them both. The boys groaned with laughter as the killer wolf attacked, bums were pinched with sharp fangs, all their exposed flesh was licked and slathered on by the not-so-wild beast. 'We give up! We give up!' cried the boys as the wolf devoured them.

Breathlessly Tom squealed with laughter, 'Get off you, heavy lump.' This was quickly followed by giggles and more painful laughter from both boys now lying exhausted in a mass of arms and legs. Satisfied that her prey was defeated, the wolf got up off the boys and walked from the room out on to the landing, leaving the red-faced pair panting and sweating in a huddle on the floor, their attack plan once more lying in tatters around them. Before they had time to regroup or plan another offensive, the smell hit them and the realisation shot across their faces.

'Chemical attack,' Karl shouted. Both boys fought for the door to gulp in fresh air and get away from the foul-smelling wolf fart. They fell out onto the landing floor, gasping for clean air, still laughing. At the top of the staircase, the wolf sat looking at the boys, her tail swaying contently behind her.

'She's laughing at us, isn't she,' gulped Tom.

'I think so,' his brother replied. The wolf turned and descended the stairs towards the kitchen, and then the second smell of the morning hit both boys…

'Bacon!' they both said in unison. Then crawling to the top of the stairs, they looked down. Below them, walking towards the kitchen table with a plate piled high with bacon sandwiches was their uncle Kurt. Tom went to get up but was not quick enough; Karl pushed his brother down back onto the floor before sprinting down the stairs towards the table and the sandwiches. Tom pulled himself up and bounced down the stairs after his brother. A little red faced and out of breath, Karl reached the bottom of the stairs. Seconds later, Tom thundered into the back of him sending Karl flying across the kitchen floor. Picking himself up, Karl turned to see Tom sitting at the table with his mitts wrapped round a bacon sandwich looking very innocent with a smug smile on his face.

'I'm going to get you for that you little turd,' he shouted angrily at his brother. Tom looked across to his uncle for protection, but his uncle's back was facing him as he made some egg sandwiches to accompany the bacon. Seeing this, Karl saw his chance for revenge. Tom stuck his tongue out at his brother knowing it would invoke an angry reaction, then he turned his stare at the pile of bacon sandwiches in front of him knowing his uncle would turn around at any second. Tom's attention was now on the bacon sandwiches, the mix of the smells now attacking his nostrils, but one eye stayed on his uncle, willing him to turn around before his brother reached him. His uncle Kurt still faced the cooker as Karl walked behind his brother. Sensing his chance, Karl directed a punch at the top of his brother's arm; his aim was to give his brother a dead arm in retaliation for the cowardly push from behind that had sent him flying. The impact of the punch caused Tom to scream out loudly like a little sissy. This was partly in pain but mostly it was Tom's aim to get his uncle's attention, which it did. Kurt turned to see Karl standing behind his now squirming little brother, agony etched all over Tom's face.

'What are you two up to? Karl, you can get that silly grin off your face and sit down and eat your breakfast, and you take that "I am the victim" look off your face, Tom. You know it won't wash with me, there's no smoke without fire. You're both as bad as each other.' Their uncle came and sat down them. Phina had left the kitchen and at that exact time was devouring the last of the deer she had caught the night before. The boys, now at peace, soon joined their uncle in making short work of the bacon and egg sandwiches in front of them. 'Ah, that's better,' said Kurt after finishing his last fried egg sandwich. Then he tapped his stomach in satisfaction, indicating he was full. Tom copied his uncle and tapped his blotted stomach in the same way but then he gave out a loud burp!

'Sorry,' he said with a childish grin on his face, after all he was still a child. Karl burst out laughing, followed by Tom and then Kurt joined in. This went on for a couple of minutes as the infectious laughter made Tom and Karl laugh then cry which then made their uncle laugh. Once the laughter subsided, Karl stood up, wiping away the tears of joy from his eyes and cheeks before he started to clear the empty plates away.

'Sit down, lad, I have something to tell you both. The plates can wait,' Kurt said very softly. Karl sat down with a puzzled look on his face. He looked at Tom who also wore a puzzled look. Then they both looked at their uncle. His face was drawn and serious. Both Karl and Tom thought their uncle looked sad and were suddenly concerned. Karl was aware of a strange feeling of foreboding and fear welling up inside him. He had never felt like this before, but he felt his life was suddenly changing. Something inside told him even before his uncle had uttered a word.

'Karl, Tom,' he began. Then he looked at Tom, his innocent face crushing Kurt's heart, but he continued, a solemn look now engraved on to his face, 'It's time for us to leave this place. Suffolk, I mean.' He stopped… waiting for a reaction from the boys, but there was none from the two young puzzled faces staring at him, waiting for their uncle's punch line that never came. 'It could be forever, never to return…,' he added. This was much harder than he had anticipated. After pausing, he continued, 'I have had news from our home world.' The two boys looked at each other confused, then at their uncle.

'Home world? This is our home world!' Karl exclaimed!

Kurt smiled at the boys and told them, 'This is not our home world.' Then he continued as the boys' mouths opened.

Karl laughed nervously, still waiting for the punch line. It must be a joke, it must be coming, he thought to himself, but deep down inside he knew by looking at his uncle's face that maybe the punch line might just not be funny this time.

'For the first time ever,' Kurt continued, 'we have been asked to return to our real home as soon as possible. It's time to meet the rest of your family and the people of our own world.'

Both boys laughed… but when their uncle didn't laugh… they stayed quite waiting for his next words.

'Own world, what do you mean, own world… like Scotland or Wales, is that what you mean, Uncle Kurt?'

'No, I do mean our own world, as in not this world, Earth.'

'Cool, we're aliens, like in Space Wars… Are we aliens then?' blurted out Tom.

'No, Tom, we aren't aliens. We are part of this world, sort of, but not quite. It's complicated.'

'What exactly do you mean, Uncle Kurt?' asked Karl.

'It's not that easy to explain to you now. I am not too good at that sort of thing, but my brother Tristan is. That's where we will be going. We will be leaving in about an hour.'

'Cool,' said Tom again.

'Stop saying cool, you idiot… This is serious,' snapped Karl.

'Yes, indeed it is very serious, boys, it's very… very serious and I don't have time now to explain but trust me, I promise by the day's end you will have been told everything. Now, please go upstairs and pack, one bag of anything you would like to keep, along with two sets of clothes. We will get new ones when we reach our world,' Kurt told them.

'Why can't we stay here?' interjected Karl. 'My school… my friends, everything we know is here,' he said, looking pleadingly at his uncle.

In a low, calm voice, Kurt replied, 'Because if we stay here, we will all die. Now, please go and pack, we leave in one hour. Don't worry,' he added. Kurt got up and walked out of the kitchen into the back garden. He shouted back to them,

'Don't worry about the dishes.'

Karl and Tom looked at each other across the kitchen table. 'Aliens,' said Karl, 'I don't bloody believe it.'

'Cool, special powers,' said Tom.

'I am going to knock your head off if you keep saying that,' said Karl more out of frustration than anger.

Kurt came back into the kitchen and noticed the boys had not moved. 'You are now both old enough to start this journey. I know you will both fully understand why this is happening when it is explained to you later. I know it's a bit of a shock and you don't know why, but you will by the end of the day. 'I promise you both.' He looked at the confused and worried faces in front of him. 'Now, it is imperative that we leave as soon as possible. I will guide and protect you as will the wolf... By the way, the wolf has a name, I should have told you years ago. It's not "Wolf", it's "Phina" and she comes from a noble clan of warriors and wolves.' Kurt looked at the two confused faces in front of him; he stepped forward and called the two boys to him. As they approached him, Kurt pulled them both to him and gave them the biggest bear hug of their lives.

'Is everything okay, Uncle Kurt?' Tom said from beneath the hug.

'Oh, yes, everything is more than okay. I will look after you both on your journey. No, journey is the wrong word. Adventure! Now that's the right word. Don't be afraid, you will see things you have only dreamed of, and things you have never even dreamed of or ever could imagine in your wildest dreams... believe me. At the end of this adventure, you will be with a loving family that is missing you very much.'

'Why haven't we ever heard from our families... or seen anyone, why haven't you ever told us?' Karl asked, surprised that he had a family at all.

'All will be explained to you both later, I promise you. Now, we need to move. We have no time to lose. I suspect we have been found by the people that we have been hiding from in this world over the last few years of your life. It's a little sooner than we had hoped, but I think you are both ready. What I mean is you are both big and ugly enough for what lies ahead,' laughed Kurt. 'Now go and get ready to leave.'

'What about Phina?' asked Tom a little worried

'Don't worry about Phina. She's been looking after you all your life, she will be coming with us. Now, go and get your things together.'

'Cool, Phina, a warrior wolf,' said Tom.

'Come on, idiot, let's go pack,' said Karl. As he got up, he walked behind Tom and ruffled his hair, then ran up the stairs with Tom in hot pursuit, both heading for their bedroom. Phina was outside in the woods some distance from the cottage patrolling, making sure there was nothing that could hinder their imminent departure. Halfway up the stairs Tom shot past his brother, knocking him slightly, but unusually this time Karl did not react. This time, he just steadied himself then called down to his uncle, 'Uncle Kurt, are we running away?'

'No, not at all, Karl,' Kurt replied looking up at Karl smiling. 'We are moving and reorganising to make our position stronger. If you like, putting it simply, we are going somewhere you can be better protected.'

'Protected from what?' Karl asked.

'We are going around in circles here, Karl. All will be explained later. Now, please get up the stairs and put your stuff in those rucksacks we bought last year. Come on, move, we need to get going. GO!' Kurt urged.

Karl entered their bedroom and closed the door behind him; Tom had already tipped most of his life onto his bed and was now in the process of deciding what to take and what to leave. This was not going too well, as he had more to take than he could possibly put in his rucksack. Tom looked up as the door shut, 'What's going on?'

'I don't know,' Karl replied, shaking his head and hunching his shoulders in bewilderment.

Tom questioned his brother, 'Do we have family in another world? Do you believe that?'

'No, I don't, Tom, but I do trust Uncle Kurt. I'm sure all will be revealed to us later today. If Uncle Kurt said it would be, it will be. To be honest, Tom, I have always thought our family was you, me, Uncle Kurt, and wolf. Why would we think otherwise? Anyway, we had better start packing, we are on an adventure!'

'What do we pack?' inquired Tom.

'Well... things like socks, pants, trousers, maybe a couple of things that are sentimental to you, or things you don't want to leave behind, Oh and a warm jacket or jumper. It might get cold.'

'But it's summer,' replied Tom.

'I know that, idiot, but it might get cold where we are going.'

'Do you know where we are going?'

'No!' his brother replied. 'Just stop asking stupid questions or we will never get there.'

'They're not stupid questions! I have never been away before. Idiot yourself,' replied Tom under his breath.

'Don't forget to pack your teddy bear, Tom,' Karl told him.

'I don't have a teddy bear,' his brother replied.

'I know, idiot. I was I was only kidding.'

Tom had already packed his longstanding companion at the bottom of his rucksack, as had Karl. There was something comforting about their old friends being close, even though neither boy had had a teddy bear in their bed for at least five years in Karl's case and two in Tom's. At their ages, they were ten and fourteen, they could still not leave their furry friends behind.

'Like Uncle Kurt said, don't pack too many clothes because we will get new ones where we are going,' Karl told Tom, then smiled reassuringly at his younger brother.

'That's good,' Tom replied, 'more room for my toys.' Then he rubbed his hands together in excited trepidation at the choices he now had to make.

The boys continued their packing in silence, both mulling over in their heads what had been said after breakfast. Twenty minutes later Tom announced, 'I've finished.'

Karl turned to look at his brother. 'You must be joking,' he said staring at the apparition in front of him.

'What?' replied Tom, and then a childish grin crossed his face.

'How can you seriously say that, Tom. Look at you,' Karl said laughing.

'What?' Tom reiterated. 'I don't know what you mean...' Tom was standing in front of his bed, his skateboarding helmet on his head, his rucksack on his back and protruding from the top flap was the hilt of a samurai sword. The one he had bought on his last trip to the car boot sale with his friend Simon's family. On Tom's chest, and going right down to the top of his knees, was a rather large metal breastplate which was from some long-lost bygone age of swords and glorious battles, which an army in red always seemed to have won, in the eyes of a ten-year-old boy anyway. He had found it in his uncle's shed where it had probably been left by an old soldier, long since forgotten.

Tom had asked his uncle how to get it shiny again and showing great knowledge, his uncle had explained how to do it. After that Tom had scrubbed and polished until it gleamed, and you could see your face in the old metal plate. 'It would easily have passed any sergeant major's inspection,' his Uncle Kurt had told him. Tom was very proud of that. When he had first found the breastplate, it had rested on his shoes when he put it in front of himself. He had grown a bit since then. Below the breastplate was a set of cricket pads that were strapped to a green pair of wheelies with frog's eyes peeking out.

Finally, to finish off the look were two ninja elbow pads. Tom put one leg forward and opened his arms and shouted 'Ta Rare. What do you really think? Good hay!' Tom stood there in all his glory, holding the pose.

'Where the bloody hell do you think you're going dressed like that?' said Karl amazed, looking at what his brother was wearing.

'Now, Timothy, language. I'm only young. I should not be exposed to that sort of language at my age. You have to be ready for anything on an adventure,' he added, smiling.

'Idiot. Uncle Kurt will never let you go out like that... What is it all for anyway?' he inquired.

Tom explained to his brother. 'Well, the helmet protects my head.'

'Obviously,' interjected Karl.

'Let me finish. I will use the sword to protect you, Uncle Kurt and the wolf. I mean Phina. Oh, so you don't need protecting then.'

'I'm sure Phina and Uncle Kurt will be doing all the protecting,' his brother added.

'You're so negative you know that, Karl. I will continue without interruption this time if you don't mind! The elbow pads will protect my elbows when I am diving about.' Tom waited for Karl's comment; none came. 'Good,' said Tom. He continued, 'It's obvious what the breastplate is for.'

Karl butted in, 'And I suppose the shiny breastplate is for signalling passing aircraft for help when the dinosaurs attack.'

'Now you are just being stupid; dinosaurs have been dead for years,' Tom continued, 'The cricket pads are to protect my legs from dog and dragon bites and the wheelies are to keep my feet dry.'

'Well, we will see what Uncle Kurt says, won't we, Tom,' said Karl mockingly.

'Yes, we will, Karl' replied Tom, then marched out of the room. How do cricketers walk in these? Tom thought to himself as he awkwardly made his way on to the landing.

As Tom departed, Karl remembered his bedside table drawer. In fact, he remembered what was in his side drawer. His most treasured possessions; his army knife and the SAS survival handbook that he had bought at the same car boot sale as Tom had bought his sword. Lastly, he picked up the little gold locket he had always had and did not know where it had come from. It had a small picture inside on the lid of a beautiful woman's face. Karl always dreamed it was a picture of his mother, but the fact was no one had ever said it was, he just hoped. He put the locket in his pocket and the other things into his rucksack. He left the room just in time to watch Tom clumsily descend the stairs towards the kitchen.

Kurt had seen the thing coming clumsily down the stairs and positioned himself at the bottom with Phina just in case Tom took a tumble. Phina looked on mystified at his side at the sight coming down the stairs, Kurt backed away as Tom reached the foot of the stairs. At the top of the stairs, Karl heard his uncle say, 'Nice look, Tom.'

A childish grin covered Tom's face. 'Well, thank you, sir,' he replied.

Karl looked on amazed at his uncle's reaction; he was just about to comment when his uncle carried on. 'But I don't think it's very practical, do you, Tom? I like the swords though, nice touch... he paused then continued. 'Ditch the breastplate, unless you plan to use that to signal help from a passing plane.'

'Have you been talking to Karl?' Tom asked.

'No. Why?' replied his uncle.

'He just said the same thing upstairs,' said Tom, pointing towards his brother at the top of the stairs.

'It's just not practical in a small van, Tom. I will get you some real armour when we get to where we are going,' said his uncle. That made Tom smile.

'Cool,' came Tom's reply.

'I've got my army knife and my survival handbook,' shouted Karl from the top of the stairs.

'Good lad. Does that mean we are all ready, then?' replied Kurt.

'Yep,' came the reply from both boys.

Phina had left the kitchen and was sitting outside. She watched as Karl, Tom and Kurt exited the kitchen. The boys dropped their rucksacks on the ground next to the road leading from the garage. Kurt was now opening his garage doors. Two big green wooden doors that creaked as they swung open. Inside was the van they would be travelling in to their 'yet unidentified' destination. What was inside was not just any van; it was a 1969 VW (Volkswagen Westphalia Weekender). Yellow in colour with chrome wheel hubs and bumpers, blue doors with flowers plastered all over the body. The interior was finished in ivory-coloured leather with earth tone units and carpets; a classic. Well, all apart from the flowers that is. It was not a vehicle you would be missed in; this reassured Karl because now he was sure they were not hiding or running away; not in that with all the un-miss able flowers plastered everywhere any way, he thought to himself.

The van was Kurt's pride and joy here on Earth, apart from the two boys and his beloved wolf, Phina. He had restored the van over the last six years, from a rusting hulk in the garden when he had first purchased the cottage. Now it was, without mistake, a beautiful mechanical masterpiece... that was, apart from the flowers. Because he had no mechanical background it was truly amazing. It was only ever used for the yearly camping and surfing trip, normally down to Devon or Cornwall in the West Country. Kurt gently eased his baby out of the garage and parked it next to the boys and their rucksacks. Then he went back and closed the garage doors, locking them for the last time.

'Throw your stuff in, boys, my kit is already in the Beatle.' He returned to the van and opened the side door. The boys threw their rucksacks in the back.

Tom turned to Karl and said, 'I'm sure this was light blue all over last year?'

'Yes, I'm sure you're right, Tom, and I'm sure it never had flowers all over it last year either,' replied Karl as he turned towards his uncle.

'Yes, you're right,' said their uncle, smiling, then he gave them a wink.

'Oh, well, I like it like this anyway,' said Tom.

'Come on, Phina,' Karl shouted. Phina pounded past Tom and leapt into the van through the side door. She was quickly followed by Karl and Tom who immediately started to make themselves comfortable in the back.

Kurt did one last walk around the cottage, checking everything had been secured then locked the back door. After that he lifted a stone in the front garden and turned it over to reveal a combination lock, opened it up and put the keys to the cottage inside. The stone was then returned to its original place where it looked the same as every other stone in the front garden. Kurt then got into the driver's seat and turned around to face the boys. 'Everybody ready? Got everything? Because we won't be coming back,' he told them.

Chapter 2
Encounter

'I'm ready, Uncle Kurt,' Karl replied. 'I just feel a bit bad about not telling anyone where we are going, all my friends and the school.'

'Yeah, me too,' said Tom.

'Don't worry about that, I have spoken to your headmaster and explained things to him, and he will tell all you friends at school on Monday.' This seemed to cheer the boys up,

'Can I sit in the front with you?' asked Karl.

'Yes, if you want, but if we get lost it's the navigator's fault,' replied his uncle. 'Right then, we will be off, goodbye cottage.' The VW drove down their little lane to the main road which ran through Rendelsham Forest, passed the army camp a few miles down the road then on into a little village called Melton, then out onto the A12 heading for the A14 which passed Ipswich and went west.

As they drove along Kurt told the boys, 'Do you know that Phina is one of the daughters of a great Wolf warrior from our home world? Her mother's name is "RA-PHINA",' he pronounced the words, so the boys would understand. 'You will meet her soon, as will Phina and me.'

Phina's ears pricked up as though she was listening. 'She hasn't seen her mother or her people for as long as you have been away from your family. I will tell you more tonight when we get to our destination.'

'Don't you mean "pup", not "daughter"?' said Karl.

'No, I said daughter and I mean daughter, that's something else you will learn about later,' replied Kurt.

'I'm really looking forward to it,' smiled Karl.

They carried on driving along the dual carriageway and soon the distinctive drone of the VW engine sent Karl to sleep in the front and behind him, stretched out on the ivory-coloured leather seats in the back of the van, Tom was also sound asleep. On the other long seat next to him was Phina, who was also asleep. The VW's engine hummed as it continued west. All three woke as the driver's door slammed shut as Kurt got out of the vehicle to put petrol into the now quite VW. 'Where are we?' asked Tom sleepily from the back of the van.

'It's a big supermarket, but I don't know where we are? They all look the same to me,' answered Karl as Kurt paid for the petrol and returned to the VW.

'We'll stop here and get a few bits to eat and drink for later on. We still have a long way to go,' Kurt told them. They drove out of the petrol station. As they did Karl noticed the sign, WELCOME TO DAISY SHOPPER CAMBRIDGE.

'Cambridge!' Karl shouted to Tom.

'How do you know that?' asked Tom.

'I read the sign' he replied.

The VW pulled up and parked at the back of the supermarket car park, which was when Tom started to regret putting his wheelies on because it was now mid-morning and the sun was beginning to warm up the inside of the old van. Especially his feet cocooned in the green frog eyed wheelies. He pulled the wheelies off. Immediately Phina disapprovingly lifted her head and looked at him. Tom smiled at her and ruffled her fur then he replaced them with his sandals, 'That's better.' Phina was not so sure as her sensitive nose twitched.

'I was wondering how long it would be before you changed them, Tom,' said his uncle, laughing as he smelt the smell of new rubber and sweat. 'Okay, boys, if you want to get out and stretch your legs or go to the toilet, I will watch Phina and get her a drink. When you come back, I will go and buy some bits for the rest of the journey.'

'I'm good. I can get the water for Phina while you go and get the bits if you like,' said Karl.

'Okay, if you're sure,' replied Kurt.

'Can I come with you?' asked Tom as Karl got the water out for Phina.

'It's okay, I'll stay here and look after Phina,' said Karl. 'You can take him, it will give me some peace.'

'Right then, Tom, let's get going.'

Tom opened the side door and jumped out. He was followed by Phina who jumped out, did a lethargic stretch, yawned, arching her back in the process, then gave herself a good shake. You could almost hear her say, 'That's better.'

Kurt then told Phina to get back in the van, 'We don't want to draw attention to ourselves by scaring the shoppers. You know the sort of reaction we've had in the past,' he said, looking at her.

'I'll look after her, don't worry Uncle Kurt. Can you bring me back a cold drink of pop, please, and a Cornish pasty?' asked Karl.

As Kurt and Tom set off towards the entrance to the supermarket, Karl sat back in the side door of the VW and Phina jumped in next to him. Both gazed at the throng of people milling all around them from cars and 4x4s to the shop and back. Karl started to feel quite relaxed in the warming sun so he lay back and put his hands behind his head; slowly he nodded off. Life was good…! He awoke sharply to the panicked screams of shoppers around him. He sat up sleepily, dazed, looking around trying to understand what was happening. The mayhem that filled his eyes and ears was being caused by a big black wolf running through the shoppers on her way to greet Tom and Kurt, who had just re-emerged from the supermarket entrance. A cold chill ran down his spine. He was helpless. He watched Phina bound further and further away from him. 'Phina,' he screamed after her, but it was too late. The pandemonium was now in full swing, people were running in all directions, jumping into strangers' cars, anything to get away from the beast running amok amongst them. It was a typical mass hysteria situation caused by a perceived threat that was totally unfounded. As Phina ran, she jumped easily over a car that had pulled up in front of her trying to block her passage. She landed on the other side next to a middle-aged woman, who, in sheer terror at seeing the beast descending on her from above, collapsed to the ground as Phina bounced over her.

'Phina, stop!' Kurt shouted, and she came to a complete standstill, chaos all around her.

'Why?' All she had done was run to her family. She stood and watched Kurt and Tom running towards her carrying their shopping bags.

When they reached her, Kurt told her to 'Stay close.' Then they all calmly walked back to the van, passing the glaring hysterical faces behind car windscreens and, in some cases, the faces were crying.

'Why?' She had not bitten anyone or torn a jugular out, what was wrong with these people?

'I'm sorry,' Karl said as his uncle and Tom reached him.

'Don't worry, there is nothing you could have done. If Phina wants to run, she will run. All you will be able to do is watch her disappear. It's these idiots around us that need to look at themselves. Pathetic,' said Kurt, then he turned and looked at Phina.

Tom noticed her eyes change to bright red for a couple of seconds then back to her natural blue. Phina jumped up and into the VW and glared back at the people now emerging from behind cars and bushes. Then she jumped up onto one of the seats and curled up, burying her head in a mass of fur. Kurt patted Karl on the shoulder, 'Don't worry, son, we will soon be away from people who react like this just because a wolf runs past. A truly pathetic race.'

Tom tugged his uncle's arm. 'Look!' he said, and then pointed towards a rather red-faced man striding with purpose towards them. Tom could see the man was upset and ranting something that Tom could not make out as he approached.

'You boys get this stuff in the van and close the door. I will deal with this person.' Kurt turned and advanced towards the man, Phina jumped out to Kurt's side. 'That might not help, Phina, but thank you' I'm not quite sure who or what this man is or what he wants but I am not going to take any chances with the boys here,' he told her.

The advancing man noticed the beast now next to the big man who seemed to be in control of it. Both were now bearing down on him. He also noticed that the beast and the man's eyes had just flashed red which unnerved him slightly as he slowed his pace. As Kurt and Phina approached him, the fire in his belly began to go out, causing him to slow down even more as he revaluated what he was doing. He started to weigh up his current options; he looked back towards his middle-aged wife. He could see and hear her berating him for faltering, so now he had no option but to confront the big man with the beast. As he got closer to the red-faced man Kurt could hear what he was saying, 'Bloody maniac… bloody idiot. What the hell do you think you are doing bringing a man-eating creature like that to a supermarket? Here amongst decent law-abiding people who are just trying to go around their normal daily business. You're a bloody fool.'

'Well said!' The shout came from one of the heroes behind the red-faced man who then turned around to see who had made the comment. To his relief, behind him there had now formed a small mob of men, who had either suddenly become very brave after fleeing the beast or had been unwillingly cajoled into joining him by wives and girlfriends who felt they had a grievance against the marauding beast and its owner. Spurred on and encouraged by the gathering crowd behind him, he quickened his pace once more.

Now spotting the small crowd of men and the increased pace of their leader, Kurt and Phina increased their pace and headed straight for the biggest threat! That was the red-faced man in front. Kurt took a few more steps, then, without losing eye contact with him or the mob behind him, he adopted a martial arts stance. It was, in fact, a hand-fighting Wolf warrior stance, but the man in front or the mob were not to know that, but they did notice him adopt it.

The advancing leader slowed on seeing this big man's reaction, but what he noticed even more was the big beast ready to pounce, bearing its massive fangs, which up until now no one had noticed.

Kurt held his rather menacing stance, now focused on the person closest to him. The following mob had not anticipated their leader slowing down and they suddenly found those at the front had stopped to avoid bumping into their leader in the front. Those at the rear of the mob banged into the middlemen who now pushed the men at the front, who all banged into each other. A couple stumbled ungracefully, nearly falling over. Not at all the actions of a band of heroes. It was all an undignified clutter of confusion and disarray. That's when the men at the back saw the big man's stance and their bravery faltered. Disentangling themselves from each other, they started to run away, to the disgust of their spouses and girlfriends.

Noticing the sudden thinning of the ranks behind them, the men at the front started to desert as well, until there were only three left by the time the red-faced man had reached Kurt.

'Get behind me, Phina, we don't want to provoke these people any more than we have to.' Reluctantly Phina went behind him, but kept her eyes on the four men. Their leader stopped where he thought he was at a safe distance away from the big man and the beast. His eyes darted from the big menacing man to the fangs of the big menacing beast who kept protruding her head around Kurt's back just to let them know she had not gone away.

The man was now quite unsure what to do next. He paused then, building up his confidence he said to Kurt, 'Let's deal with this like adults.' Kurt took the man's words meaning he wanted to fight him. The man moved one pace forward and was just about to say something to Kurt about apologising and muzzling his beast when he suddenly realised he was sitting on his backside with the big man towering over him… then the pain came…

He lifted his shaking hands to his face and felt around his lips and cheek, all okay, but the pain. He moved his now trembling hands towards his nose, ever conscious of the threatening man towering above him. As his hand touched his nose, he flinched and pulled his hands away as a sharp pain shot through every nerve in his body. Then he noticed the red liquid starting to cover his hands. He looked closer… realisation dawned; he was looking at his own. 'Blood! Oh, my god… you hit me, you hit me, you maniac,' the red-faced man screamed. Then he noticed the beast's breath on his face, and the pain in his nose made his eyes water. All he could see was the blurred fangs up oh so close to his face. In a moment of clarity he wondered, what the hell had just happened?

As the pain and fright screamed back into his brain, he suddenly thought, I'm still in great danger. Through the pain, he forced his shaking wobbling unsteady body to stand. Swaying slightly, he regretted doing this as the beast's fangs were now opposite his groin. He felt very exposed. Shaking with immense courage and extreme willpower on his part, he slowly turned around looking for some support from the mob behind him. His soul sank, the courage draining out of him in seconds. He started to shake uncontrollably; his shock complete as his understanding of his position smacked him round the face. He was on his own!

Everyone had fled. Fear filled his whole body; he felt like he was going to faint. He was an accountant, how had he ended up in this position?

The boys looked on in amazement and horror from within their safe vantage point in the van. They had seen their gentle uncle turn into a lean mean fighting machine, straight out of a boy's comic book. What had their uncle done? He had flown forward at great speed; the attack had been so fast they weren't even sure what he had done. But the fact was, the red-faced man was now, as Tom put it, 'on his arse in bits.' The man had been struck by a hand or foot, the boys were not sure which, but the man's nose had exploded in front of them as their uncle had struck him. Both boys watched on in anticipation, wondering what would happen next. All around the onlookers, which included the man's now silent wife and the ex-members of the mob, now watching from a safe vantage point, waited for the maniac's next move.

'Brian, please come back. I'll call the police,' his wife screamed, from somewhere behind him.

Kurt's next move never came. Seeing that the enemy was defeated, he relaxed his attack stance.

Through watering eyes, with blood streaming from his split nose, nasally the man stammered, 'What did you do that for? There was no need for that, you're a bloody lunatic.'

'Yes, I totally agree, no need for your or the rest of these people's hostility towards me, my boys and my wolf. We have harmed no one,' said Kurt. 'If you continue to threaten us, I will kill you, and anyone else that tries the same. Retreat now and I will let you live,' said Kurt.

The very pale-faced man, now petrified with fear at Kurt's deadly threatening words, said nothing. He could not speak, slowly and very gingerly, still shaking like a leaf, he turned. Looking through very bleary watery eyes, he searched for his wife and the safety of his blue Volvo estate car with the orange Dayglo band around the bumper. He really didn't care now; the pain was too much. His whole body was still trembling. Slowly he staggered off without replying to Kurt, heading in the direction he thought would be the safest path away from the mad man.

Kurt walked backwards, Phina still at his side. Both kept their eyes on the defeated man and all those around until they were at a safe distance to turn and head back to the boys in the VW.

As the defeated, bloodied and very sore man stumbled, he noticed the Dayglo strip on his bumper. He knew it had been a good idea to put that on, it had saved his life. He headed for safety, mumbling to himself as he continued to stumble towards his car and as he did, he thought, I was happy watching the snooker at home but no, she wanted to go shopping because she was bored, bloody bored. I've nearly been killed, and I am a hundred pounds worse off.

As he reached his now very excitable wife, she screamed at him, 'A lot of good you were. He made a fool of you, and another thing…'

But before she could finish, he said, spitting blood at her, 'Shut up, Alison, and give me the phone to call the police, before I do something I will regret later!' He managed to splutter, aware of the blood hitting the passenger door and her face as she sat in the safety of the car.

Back in the van, Kurt now sat in the driver's seat. He turned to face the boys who were now in the back with Phina. 'Everyone okay?' he asked.

'You were amazing,' Tom told him.

'I wouldn't say amazing, Tom, I only did what I had to do to keep you safe. Like I said, I will look after you both.'

'Did you really have to hit him though, Uncle Kurt?' asked Karl.

'I felt he and the group behind him were a threat to all of us, so I dealt with the threat in the most diplomatic way I know.'

'Diplomatic… you call that diplomatic… what would have happened if diplomacy had failed?' laughed Karl.

'He would now be dead along with any of the group that stayed to fight, simple as that.'

The boys went quiet. They had never heard their uncle speak like this before.

'Wow, I don't believe it, have you taken some he-man pills? I'm glad you're on my side, Uncle Kurt. Respect,' said Tom.

'Respect back, whatever that means, Tom. Right, we had better get going before someone calls the police,' said Kurt. 'That's if they haven't already,' he added.

Kurt turned the key in the ignition, bringing the old VW to life, then drove out of the car park as though nothing had happened, Phina hidden below window level. Inside his head Kurt was screaming, 'Damn, damn, damn, you bloody fool. You should have handled that like a human would.'

As Kurt drove down the slip road onto the A14, behind him in the store car park the bloodied and very pale-faced man was on his wife's mobile phone. He spat, 'Hello, officer, I would like to report an assault and a very dangerous animal. I was in the superstore off the A14 at Cambridge when this madman let a dangerous animal out of his van. Well, officer, I'm not too sure, some sort of beast-like hound. Yes, into the middle of the car park, the beast terrorised all the shoppers including my wife, who has a heart condition. What? No!' he said to the officer on the other end of the phone. 'No.

'No one was bitten by the beast, but many people ran away in terror. Not only that, the maniac then attacked me without provocation. He used some sort of Kung Fu. He hit me in the face without warning and knocked me to the floor. He told me he would kill me if I didn't retreat. Retreat, do you really bloody well believe that. You would have thought we were in the middle of a medieval battle ground. Sorry, officer, I am a little upset, I will calm down. Yes, I would definitely like to press charges and have an event created whatever that is? Thank you, officer. Five minutes you say? I will make myself known to the officers once they arrive. Yes, Mr Brian Whittle, 28 The Muse, Cambridge 07****5761. Thank you.' Then he hung up, satisfied with what he had just done.

.

Chapter 3
The Police

Kurt left the slip road and headed west along the A14.

'We will stop tonight near York. My brother lives near there in the country. We can stay with him there, where we will be safe. I also have a surprise for you there. I will explain to you both what is going on and why I reacted as I did when we get there.' After a couple of miles, on the other side of the dual carriageway they noticed two police cars, with sirens wailing and blue lights flashing, speed past, heading in the direction they had just come from.

'I think they are most probably for me and Phina,' said Kurt to the boys. 'Damn,' he said to no one in particular. 'Those idiots at the store must have called the police. And for what? Bloody humans.' Karl and Tom looked at each other, surprised at the wording their uncle had used. 'Bloody humans.' To them, it inferred he was not human. They remembered what he had said at the breakfast table, but they didn't really believe they were from another planet. Tom was just going to question his uncle about what he meant when Karl grabbed his attention. 'Tom,' he whispered, 'not now.'

'We will take the next exit and adopt my plan B,' Kurt told them.

'Plan B, what's that?'

'You will find out very shortly, Tom,' replied Kurt. He turned off at the next exit and drove out into the surrounding countryside away from the A14. After a couple of minutes, they came across a roadside parking area behind some trees. Luckily for them, when they drove in, a truck drove out leaving them alone. After parking the camper, Kurt turned to the boys. 'Right, boys, we have a little job to do now. Remember you thought the van was different last time you travelled in it, Tom? Well, it was, and we are going to turn her back into that.'

'How!' asked Tom.

'I will show you in a minute, but first, just in case we get surprised, I am going to let Phina go.'

'No!' said Karl, 'you can't.'

'No, you can't, Uncle Kurt!' added Tom.

'Don't worry, boys, she will be coming back to us in a while.' Kurt jumped out and opened the side sliding door and Phina jumped out, followed by Karl and

Tom. 'You boys wait here. I will be back in a moment,' he said.

Then he and Phina walked around to the opposite side of the van. Watching threw the windows, the boys saw Uncle Kurt bend down. When he stood back up, looking down at Phina, the boys noticed both his eyes were bright red. Phina jumped up and put two massive paws on Kurt's shoulders. Her eyes were also red. Then their eyes changed back to their original brown and blue. Kurt walked back around the van to them. The boys turned to face him as he rounded the back of the van. Looking at their faces, he noticed looks of concern. He asked them, 'Is everything okay, boys?'

'Err yes, we are just worried about Phina,' said Karl.

'Why did your eyes turn red?' Tom asked.

Karl glared at his brother.

'What?' said Tom as he returned the glare.

'It's okay, boys, I will explain that tonight. First, we have to quickly change the looks of this van. Don't worry about Phina, she will meet us further up the road because I am sure the police will stop us as soon as we get back on the main road. Our only chance is to be without Phina and in a different camper van, wearing different clothes, then we should be okay. Don't look so worried,' Kurt said to the boys. 'Both of you look like you have just seen a ghost. Everything is okay. I may have overreacted back there, but I promise you everything is all right. Once we get away from here, everything will be back to normal. Well, nearly anyway. I won't let anything harm you, I will get you back to your home safe. Right, boys, this is going to be quite easy. I have already planned for something like this.'

'Why would you plan for something like this?' Karl asked. Very worried now, Tom agreed with him.

'You don't know all the facts yet. As soon as we are settled at York, I will let you know exactly what is going on and why I have been acting a little strange.'

'Okay.'

'Are you both still with me here? Don't look so worried.'

'Yes, we are still with you, and we do trust you, Uncle Kurt. It's just hard not knowing what's going on,' said Karl Tom nodded in agreement.

'It won't be too long now and then you will know as much as I do, I promise.' Their uncle smiled at both of them reassuringly. 'Right let's cracking before we get discovered. I have done a few little things to the camper. The flowers peel off quite easily and I have some special liquid that when it's put on the paintwork with a rag and rubbed gently, the paint will come off, changing the camper's colour. We must try and do this as quickly as possible,' he said. 'If we remove an

30

area of the flowers first, I will start rubbing the paint off while you take off the rest of the flowers. There are some bin bags in the back of the camper that we can put all the rubbish into. After that, it will just be a matter of me shaving this beard off and changing our clothes.'

'It's a long time since we have seen you without your beard,' said Tom.

'It's only been about a year, Tom' replied their uncle. After forty-five minutes the van had changed, and they were getting into different clothes.

Kurt told them, 'I'm not too sure what people will remember of our clothes, so it's best to change.' Five minutes later, the boys had changed, and Kurt was removing the last of the shaving cream from his face. 'There we go, new me, new boys and a new VW, and no wolf, who would know? I think we are ready to continue our journey north and pick up Phina. Ready, boys!'

The boys got back into the camper and Kurt did one last check of the area to make sure any passing police car would not notice anything that might draw their eyes to the lay-by. Kurt got back into the van after getting rid of the bin bags under some other rubbish then he turned to the boys who were both now in the back. 'If we get stopped by the police, and I am sure we will be, if they ask you what we have been doing, tell them we have been camping in Rendelsham Forest and we are now going home to York. If possible, I will do all the talking. Is everyone ready to continue the adventure?'

'We are both good to go, aren't we, Tom?' Karl told him with a smile and a nod from Tom.

'Good, then let's get off.'

They headed back in the direction they had just come from an hour ago, eventually getting to the slip road back onto the A14. Then they headed west away from Cambridge. Five minutes later Tom shouted to his uncle Kurt from the back of the camper, 'There are two police cars heading this way, and all their lights are flashing!'

'Okay, boys, stay calm. They will probably pull us over because we match who they are looking for. Don't worry; I will deal with this,' Kurt said. The first police car sped past them and pulled in front of the camper, the second pulled in behind.

A sign popped up in the front police car's rear window, it read 'POLICE FOLLOW ME'. The three vehicles left the A14 and pulled into a lay-by which had a high grass bank on the verge on the left-hand side of the vehicles. Kurt could see one of the officers get out of the rear vehicle followed by a second. He immediately noticed two things; they both had firearms at their sides and they were both female. The officer in the front car stayed in his vehicle.

Kurt wound his window down as one of the officers came to his door. 'Good morning, officer, can I help you?'

'Hello, sir, do you have your driving licence on you? We are just doing some checks after an incident down the road, nothing to worry about.'

'You have guns. Have I done something wrong?' he replied.

'Don't worry about that, sir. We are looking for a dangerous animal. We are part of the Cambridge fire arms unit. Is it okay if my colleague talks to the boys in the back while I speak to you?'

'No problem whatsoever, officer,' Kurt told her.

'Please step out of the van, sir, so we can have a quick look round your van if you don't mind. We won't keep you long. Do you have any animals on board or anything that may harm us?' she asked him.

'Nothing, officer, feel free to look around,' replied Kurt as he handed the officer his driving licence.

The second officer opened the side door and asked the boys to get out, so they jumped out. 'Hello, boys. Come around to the other side of the van away from the road, so I can talk to you. That way I know we will all be safe,' said the officer. The boys went around the van as instructed to the other side and stood on the grass verge.

Kurt got out of the driver's seat and was standing at the front of the van while the first officer was now calling her operations room. 'Hello, control, this is PC370. Can I have a person and vehicle check, please?' Then she gave the operations room the details on the driving licence and the registration colour and make of the van. Meanwhile the second officer talked to the boys while the third officer sat in the front police car seemingly taking no interest in what was going on behind him.

'Right, boys, who have I got here then?' asked the second officer.

'I am Karl.'

'And I am Tom, miss,' said Tom.

'You don't have to call me miss. Tom, I'm not a teacher, I'm Jenny. Okay?' Tom nodded.

'So, where have you boys come from and who is driving you today?' she asked.

'That's Uncle Kurt, we've been camping with him in a wood,' replied Tom.

'We're on summer holidays,' added Karl.

'Having fun?' Jenny asked them.

'Yep, it's been good,' replied Tom.

'Do you have any pets?' asked Jenny?

'Yes,' replied Tom. Karl's heart sank. He was just about to say something to Tom when Tom added, 'A frog, a lizard and a mouse… but they are at home with our aunt.'

'That's nice. Any dogs?' asked Jenny.

'No! Tom is allergic to cats and dogs,' replied Karl quickly before Tom said anything else.

'Oh, that's a shame, I have a lovely dog at home, they are good fun,' said Jenny. 'Been to any superstores in the last couple of hours' she asked.

'Yes,' replied Tom.

Karl's heart sank once more. He's blown it, Karl thought.

'Oh, really where was that?' asked Jenny.

'Ipswich,' said Tom, 'the one next to the big toyshop, on the roundabout, I had a look inside, I liked that shop.'

'I bet you did,' smiled Jenny. 'Okay, boys, you stay here. I'm just going to speak to the other officer,' she told them. The other officer had finished talking to Kurt and she was now looking through the camper van. 'Anything?' Jenny asked her as she put her head in to the camper.

'No, clean as a whistle. Everything checks out, these aren't the people we are looking for. Let's get going. Call it in and we'll let these people get on their way.'

'I'll go and tell Mr Happy in the front car he can go.' PC370 Jenny walked towards the front police car to tell the officer he was no longer needed. As she got closer to the lead police car its driver's window came down, an arm came out and the hand waved, as if to say okay to the approaching police officer. Then it sped away with its lights blazing.

Ignorant sod, Jenny thought as the police car in front of her pulled out onto the A14, just missing a truck who had to react fast. Slamming his brakes on, smoke billowed from the tyres and it juddered to a stop just past the lay-by exit. 'Bloody idiot,' she said to herself, 'I will have to find out who that was.' Then she turned around and walked back to her colleague.

'Do you believe that! He just drove off, never got off his bum to help or say thanks, then nearly caused an accident. I'm going to find out who he was.'

'You know how some of them act, Jenny, when they see us, the first two female firearms officers in the force,' said the second officer.

'Yes, you're right. Let's get these people on their way.' Both officers walked round to Kurt and the boys.

'We've put your registration into the police system, so you shouldn't have any more unscheduled stops by the police. Thanks for your cooperation, have a safe onward journey.'

'Thank you, officers, we are going to have our lunch here now that we have stopped,' said Kurt.

'Have a nice summer holiday, boys,' said Jenny. Then the officers went back to their car and drove off with a goodbye wave to the boys.

'Well done, boys, I don't think we will have any more trouble from the police. I think they were happy that we aren't the ones they are looking for,' said Kurt.

'Tom, you nearly gave me a heart attack with your waffling,' said Karl.

'I was good, wasn't I,' grinned Tom. 'Let's get something to eat while we wait for Phina.'

'Sounds good to me. My mouth is really dry, I could do with a drink,' said Karl.

Back in the camper they got out the snacks that they had bought in the disastrous shopping trip earlier. As they were finishing their meal, the first police car reappeared, no lights this time. It parked behind them, no more than ten feet away from the back of the camper. They could see that the officer inside the police car was just sitting there staring at them.

'This isn't right. You two stay in here, I'm going to see what this officer wants,' said Kurt. As Kurt walked up to the front of the police car its door opened and the officer inside got out. The smell hit Kurt first; a putrid rotting stench. As the police car door closed, Kurt noticed the officer had a pistol in his hand. Kurt knew he was too far away to get to the officer before he would be shot by him. His mind started to race with options for tackling the threat in front of him then something logged into his brain, this was no police officer. The officer said nothing. Kurt noticed the officer's eyes; they were green, and that meant only one thing to Kurt De-Callen. He was a Dark assassin from his own world. Kurt was shocked. He had never seen a Dark assassin in human form before. He had only realised the assassins were here when Phina had caught one and killed it in Rendelsham Forest a week ago, and again this morning when Phina had killed one disguised as a bird. Options continued to run through his brain; the only thing that might help him was what he knew about Dark assassins from his home world. They had to change back to their original form before they could actually become dangerous and kill their victim, but they had never to his knowledge ever taken human form before. So, could the assassin now use the weapon he held in this human form? He didn't know, his only hope was the adage 'the best form of defence is attack'. It was true in his world, and he hoped it would be true in this one.

The boys had been watching everything that happened from inside the camper and Karl had decided to help his uncle! 'Tom, you stay here. I'm going to make a diversion to give Uncle Kurt a chance.'

'A chance to what? That's a policeman,' Tom replied.

'Look at his eyes, Tom. That's no policeman. Stay here,' Karl pleaded. Then Karl was gone, and the camper door was open, and Tom was alone.

Kurt hurled the door open. The assassin momentarily looked towards the boy leaping out of the camper. The assassin aimed the pistol at the boy. In a split second Kurt knew this would be the only chance he would get. A shot rang out! Kurt flew at the assassin, just as he had done at the superstore a couple of hours or so earlier. But this time it would not just be a bloody nose. In his subconscious he heard a voice screaming, 'Karl's been shot.' In that split second, he also saw a big black mass bearing down on him out of the corner of his right eye. His brain ignored that and concentrated on what he believed to be his biggest threat, the assassin. The assassin levelled its gun just as the black mass hit him. Phina's jaws gripped the green-eyed assassin's throat, her fangs mercilessly ripping its head from its body. Phina landed on the ground as the severed head rolled into the kerb face up, its dead human eyes looking skyward. Phina turned instantaneously and faced the now lifeless and headless corpse sprawled on the ground next to the police car. Kurt stopped his attack, landing with his feet either side of the body. Wisps of green air exited the body of the police officer through the hole in his neck where the head had once been attached. Luckily no traffic had passed while this had gone on, but it would not be long before some would appear.

From behind him Tom screamed, 'Uncle Kurt, Karl has been shot.'

Kurt turned to see Tom kneeling over the lifeless body of his brother, tears welling up in his eyes. Kurt ran over to Tom and the prone and lifeless Karl. Phina pulled the policeman's body around to the other side of the police car, away from any vehicles that now began to pass on the A14, then she went to Kurt's side.

'Don't touch him, Tom,' Kurt shouted, as he knelt at Karl's side. 'I don't want you to move him. I need to look at him.' Tom stepped back and sat on the foot ledge of the Campers door, his eyes never leaving his brother. Immediately Kurt noticed a trickle of blood coming from Karl's temple, 'No, no, please, no,' he said.

Phina's nose was now at Karl's mouth. Phina spoke, but Tom did not hear. 'He has breath,' she told Kurt. Straightaway he looked for a pulse, which he found almost at once, and then Karl's eyes opened.

'My head, what hit me?' he groaned.

'He's not dead,' Tom cried out, then he ran to Karl as he sat up.

'Take it easy, Karl, let me check the rest of you before you move any more,' Kurt advised him.

'He's fine, Father, I feel his strong heart beating,' Phina communicated to Kurt.

'It's a graze, Karl. It must have knocked you out. I'll give you a couple of stitches. You'll have a bit of a headache and a lump for a while, but you'll live. You'll be fine.' Kurt patted Karl on the back as he helped him to his feet.

'That was a very brave thing you did there, son. Ever do that again and I will kill you myself. Here, press this bandage against the cut and keep it there till I return. Now sit in the camper while I get rid of this body, then I'll stitch you up.' Tom and Kurt helped Karl into the camper and sat him down.

'Phina, keep a lookout while I put the body in the boot of the police car,' said Kurt. He took the keys from the police car's ignition and then opened the boot. It was full of cones, signs, lights, and other emergency equipment. He put some of the emergency equipment on the back seat to make way for the body. Then he put the body in the boot once there was a break in the traffic. Then he carefully picked up the policeman's head and wrapped it in a Hi-Viz jacket that had been on the back seat of the police car and put it next to the body. 'A peaceful rest for your soul,' he said to the jacket and the body. Then he closed and locked the boot of the police car. Kurt took the cars keys and walked over to the grass verge where he then climbed the small embankment on the other side of which was a farmer's field. As he did this, he realised there was no blood. Strange, he thought, normally there would be a lot of blood also the smell when the police officer got out of the car. No blood, that indicates he's been dead for some time, he thought. Kurt walked down the other side of the embankment and threw the keys high into the air. They disappeared into the high crop growing in the field. 'They are going to take some time to find them,' he said quietly to himself. Returning to the camper, Kurt asked Karl if he would be okay if they drove a couple of miles up the road to get away from the police car? Karl did not have a problem with that. He was still holding the bandage from the first aid kit against the graze. He was feeling better already; he told his uncle he didn't think he would need any stitches after all. Even though a few cars had sped by, none seemed to have seen anything untoward which, considering how busy the road could be, was amazing.

'Take that bandage away from your head wound,' Kurt said to him. Karl did and after a few seconds blood started to flow once more. 'Stitches, I think. Keep that bandage pressed on the wound. We won't be long.' They drove down the road for ten miles then pulled off and parked in the corner of a large service station car park. 'Phina, please stay in the van,' Kurt asked her.

Tom laughed, 'She won't understand you, Uncle Kurt.'

'You'll be surprised what she understands. Right then, Karl, let's take a good look at your war wound.' Then he inspected and cleaned the deep graze with a few winces from Karl. 'You'll be glad to know that the stitches I am using are the new stick-on type, they'll work wonders.'

As Kurt worked away, Karl asked about the green-eyed policeman 'That policeman wasn't right, was he, Uncle Kurt? They weren't just green eyes, they were very green eyes, and he had no expression on his face. He didn't even talk and there was no blood. Why?'

'You're very observant. Karl. I believe that police officer was dead I think he had been for some time. I also think he was dead when he first pulled us over, that's why he never got out of the police car or talked to his fellow officers.'

'Dead people can't drive, so how could he?' asked Tom who was listening intently to the conversation.

'Well, Tom, this is all part of what I was going to talk to you both about tonight. I'm sure a creature from our world had taken over his body, a creature I know as a Dark assassin. I never knew they could take over a human's body, but, obviously, they can. Normally they possess animals to get close to their victims, then they revert back into their original form which is a black creature about the size of you, Tom. It's normally dressed in black and has the face of a rat-like creature with bright green eyes, with clawed hands and feet. That's about all I can tell you, apart from, if they die, they turn into green mist and disappear. If that's the end of them, I don't know, but they never reappear but to be fair, every one of them in its natural form looks the same as every other Dark assassin so it could be the same one. Who knows?'

'How do they kill?' asked Tom.

'Normally they have some sort of poison dart which acts instantaneously, it doesn't give you any time to react. They also use knives and sword type weapons and now guns obviously.'

'Where do they come from?' asked Karl.

'I won't go into that now, it will take too long, but you will find out tonight when I'll explain everything. That's you done, Karl. It's only about three hours from here, so we may as well get going.'

Chapter 4
A Strange Day

They carried on north along the A1 until they reached the A64, taking it towards York. They reached their destination, turned off the main road and drove down a quiet country lane stopping at what looked like a farm entrance. Behind the farm gate was not a farm but a rather large cottage. 'Jump out, Karl, and open the gate please.' Karl did as he was asked, and the camper passed through the gate, parking at the side of the cottage. Karl closed the gate. Just as the gate clicked shut, the cottage door opened. In the doorway stood a man who Karl immediately recognised as being related to his uncle because his features were remarkably like those of his uncle Kurt.

'Hello, young man, you must be Karl, if I'm not mistaken. I'm Tristan, your uncle Kurt's brother. Nice to meet you. It's been a few years since we last met.'

'Hello, I'm sorry I don't remember, but it's nice to finally meet some family.' Tristan shook Karl's hand warmly, Karl smiled.

'Oh, I nearly forgot, Uncle Kurt and my brother, Tom are round the side, parking the camper.'

'Please come in. You're very welcome. The last time I saw you was when you were a very young child. As you said, you don't remember, it's been a while I must admit. Where does the time go?'

Just then Kurt and Tom appeared from around the side of the cottage. 'Brother, I see you have met Karl. This is Thomas.' Tristan and Tom shook hands.

'It's "Tom", Uncle Tristan,' Tom informed him.

'Then that's what I will call you from now on, Tom.'

Kurt and Tristan embraced as only brothers and old warriors could. The boys could immediately tell that the two of them were close and happy to see each other. 'So, where is the lovely Rowena?' Kurt asked his brother.

'She's gone into the village to get some vegetables for the meal that she's making this evening… and, yes, she is as lovely as ever. She grows more and more like her mother every day. You will see when she gets back from her shopping. It's quite breathtaking the resemblance, and, at the same time, quite chilling when she puts black on. Which I am glad to say is very rarely. Anyway, I am being rude, please come in. Please make yourselves at home for as long as you're here. Oh,

Kurt, can you put your camper around the back because it will be a nice surprise for Rowena. It will also allow me to get the Range Rover out tomorrow. While you do that, I will show the boys around the cottage, so they know where everything is.' Tristan led the boys into the cottage then along a hall past the kitchen. 'This will be your room, boys.' He showed them a room with two single beds; it was not unlike the one they had left behind in Suffolk that morning. 'The bathroom is at the end of the hall and the room next to yours is Rowena's. You will meet her soon; she's taking longer than normal. She should be back any minute. She's in the village running a few errands for me. Put your things in your room then come to the kitchen and I'll make some drinks.'

Kurt appeared with the boy's rucksacks. 'There you go,' he said, dropping them on the bedroom floor. 'Is everything okay?'

'Who's Rowena, Uncle Kurt?' Karl asked.

'Rowena is Uncle Tristan's ward, she's like a daughter to him. You will hear a bit more about your family later.'

'What do you mean?' asked Tom.

'You will have to wait until later, Tom, then I'll tell you all as much as I can.'

Karl and Tom followed their uncle along the hall into the kitchen. The kitchen had a big cast iron Aga cooker along one wall, with many assorted pots and pans hanging from a rack above it. Next to the Aga on another wall was a rather grand stone fireplace with wooden seats either side of a cast iron roasting handle, ideal for a suckling pig. The floor was covered in orange stone tiles and in the centre was a fair-sized utility island, again with pots and pans hanging from a rack above. The last wall had a typical farmhouse window overlooking the main gate; beneath it was the kitchen sink. The fourth wall was a folding wooden door with stained glass in every window pane. Then going through the folding doors, you came into a large dining room; the centre piece was a very large oak dining table and above it was a beautiful crystal chandelier. Behind the table were some patio doors that led to a conservatory which had a couple of very comfortable armchairs that looked out onto the garden and a fantastic view of the river Ouse. At the end of the garden was a towpath that followed the river in both directions, up and down.

'It must be serious for you to bring the princes here without letting me know, Kurt?' Tristan asked his brother.

'Yes, it is.'

Just then the boys entered the kitchen.

'Hello, boys, would you like some of my famous hot chocolate?' Tristan inquired.

'Sounds good,' Tom replied.

'Yes, please,' added Karl.

Tristan made them a drink each and the boys went and sat at the dining table. 'Your uncle and I are just going into the garden to talk about a few things. We won't be long,' Tristan told the boys.

'Uncle Kurt, can I ask you a question before you go?'

'Yes, Karl, ask away.'

'Why are we here?'

'That's one of the reasons Tristan and I are going out to talk. We must make a plan. We will explain it to you all when Rowena returns. Don't worry.'

'It just all seems a little strange, that's all.'

'It will all become clear soon,' Kurt told the boys, then with a smile, he and Tristan went into the garden.

Once in the garden, Tristan turned to Kurt, 'What's going on, Kurt?'

'I have had some suspicions for quite some time. I did send you a coded message by the humans' postal system, but I assume it's been intercepted so I decided to come here directly. I think it's time to take the children back to their father where they will be safer than here. We have finally been found!'

'What's happened?'

'In the last week Phina caught one of Labatina's spies in the forest, it was an assassin. Phina killed it. It was a roe deer; she could smell it from some distance off. As you know, the assassin changelings slowly kill their host who then begin to decay and smell. After a couple of days, you start to notice. I reckon it might well have been watching us and sending details back to Labatina for all that time. This morning it was a magpie sneaking into the boys' bedroom. Phina noticed the movement and not the smell, so the changeling had not been in the magpie's body for long.'

'That's very worrying. I understand the urgency now, Kurt. I have had no indications that anyone has found us here. Do you have a plan of action in mind?'

'I have had no communication with the gate so I'm going to follow our original protocol. If discovered, return to Elemtum where the children can be protected from Labatina's dark terror.'

'I think that's going to be the wisest move,' his brother replied.

'We must tell Rowena and the boys the truth. I've been putting it off with the boys all day. I've promised them I would tell them everything when I got here.'

'That's the most prudent thing to do. Rowena knows nothing of her past or her home world. She thinks of me as her father. It will be a big surprise for her to find out the truth.' Kurt could see in his brother's eyes that he was afraid that the time would come, and he would have to tell Rowena the truth.

'I've been dreading this day as well. We should have told them earlier, but you never know what children will tell other people.' Kurt confided in his brother.

'I must admit I've become quite close to her. It will be quite hard to tell her, but I know we must. Come on then, brother, would you like a local ale? It tastes like honey mist from our home world, it's been a while since we had one together.'

'That sounds good, brother. I must admit both Phina and I have also become very close to the boys, I treat them like my sons.'

Tristan and Kurt walked back into the cottage. Tristan took two local ales from the fridge and joined Kurt and the boys sat at the big oak table. They had been sitting there chatting for five minutes when the front door slammed, and a voice called out, 'It's only me, Dad. Whose is the campervan out back?'

As she walked into the kitchen, she noticed them all sat at the table. 'Uncle Kurt, what are you doing here? Dad, you never told me Uncle Kurt was coming to see us.'

'Princess, how you've grown, how beautiful you've become,' said Kurt. Then he stood up and walked over to Rowena and gave her a big hug and a kiss on the cheek. Rowena then went over and gave her father a kiss on the top of his head, then turned to face the two boys.

'Who are these two handsome young men?' she asked. The boys could see in front of them was a very beautiful young woman, slim built with long fiery red hair, piercing blue eyes and a lovely warm smile.

'I'm not a man, I am only ten,' said Tom.

'Well, hello, Tom who is not a man, I am Rowena. You can call me Row. Nice to meet you.'

'Hello, I'm Karl,' he said standing up, 'the not a man's my brother.'

'Well, Karl and Tom, it's nice to meet you. I'm Tristan's daughter Rowena.'

'That means we must be related, because Kurt is our uncle,' said Tom.

'I never knew about you two, and we only have a small family as it is.' Row turned and sternly looked at her father and uncle.

'We will explain it all to you and the boys once we have had our dinner. There is a lot to explain,' said Kurt.

'Okay,' Row said, walking over to each of the boys who stood up as she approached. Row gave both Karl and Tom a big hug and a kiss on the cheek. 'There, we know each other now,' she said. Both boys' faces went bright red; neither had ever been kissed by a young woman before. Row went and sat at the end of the big oak table. 'Sorry I'm late but the strangest thing just happened to me in the village. I was coming out of Fred's the butchers with the meat for the stew. Oh, that's a thought,' she added, 'I hope I have bought enough beef.

Anyway,' she continued, 'I said hello to this old woman when I was walking along the river the other day, she totally ignored me but kept watching me as I walked away.

'Well, as I was saying, I came out of the butcher's and there she was again, staring at me, so I decided to go over and find out why she has been following me.'

'How many times have I told you not to speak to strangers, Rowena,' Tristan interrupted.

'Oh, Dad, I'm sixteen, the village was full of people. I was okay. Now you've put me off what was I saying?

'Old woman,' Karl reminded her.

'That's right. I went towards her and said, "hello do I know you? We keep bumping into each other." That's when I noticed her eyes were bright green, that slowed me down a little. Then she gasped fell to her knees. Green smoke came from her mouth, then she just keeled over. I couldn't believe it. I got to her, but I had to stand back because she smelt terrible, like a really old rubbish bin that has not been cleaned out. It nearly made me puke.'

'Very lady like, Rowena,' said Tristan.

'Well, as I was saying, I was going to do CPR, but she just really stank. Like I said before, I nearly threw up. Thankfully PC Clarke was just across the road and saw what had just happened, so he rushed over… He started to gag as the smell reached him as well. "She's dead"! he told me and by the looks of it, the old woman had been for some days I don't really understand, it's very strange. Then he called an ambulance and covered her head with his jacket. PC Clarke took me to the station and gave me a strong cup of coffee, he wrote a statement for me which I signed then he brought me back here. He said he might have to come by sometime soon when you are here, Dad, just to make sure I'm okay. A welfare call I think he said it was? He told me he had never seen the woman in the village, they… the police, I mean, don't know who she is. She took a breath. What's really strange is that the doctor who turned up after the ambulance said she had been dead for several days because when he opened her mouth if was full of maggots.'

'Yuck.'

'How could she be standing there with her eyes open, and yesterday by the river? She was alive, but the doctor said she couldn't have been, I must be mistaken because she died before I saw her, by a couple of days? And what sick bastard put her in the village?'

Tom smiled at her use of a swear word in front of adults, and the fact that she never got told off. 'Cool.'

When Row had finished, she was visibly shaking and looking a little distressed. Tristan told her not to upset herself then he walked over to her and gave her a reassuring hug. He wiped the tears away that had begun to roll down her cheeks.

'It's okay, Dad, I am just being silly. Don't you worry about me. I'll go and make dinner, that will take my mind off it.' She walked into the kitchen, wiping the last of the tears from her face. Kurt followed her.

'Row.' As she turned to look at him, he took hold of her hands. 'There's been a lot of strange things happening at the moment so don't worry about it. Your dad and I will explain some things to you and the boys tonight that should set your minds at rest about this little incident, I promise. Okay?'

'Thank you, Uncle Kurt, I'm not too bothered. It's more of a shock, it's a bit weird that's all. Some sick sod must have propped her up outside the butchers. Why?'

Kurt smiled at her. 'There are some very deranged people in this world, thankfully we don't meet them too often.' He kissed her cheek then walked back into the dining room. As he left the kitchen, Karl and Tom walked in.

'Hi, Rowena, don't worry. We don't have a clue about what's going on either, we had a normal life up until this morning then Uncle Kurt told us we were leaving Suffolk and that we would never be back. Then we left and came north to meet our family, so I assume he means you, Rowena, and Uncle Tristan?' said Karl.

'You can call me Row remember? I like it better than Rowena. That sounds so formal, don't you think?'

'Uncle Kurt keeps going to tell us what's going on but there's always something that stops him telling us whatever it is,' said Tom.

'Don't worry, boys, your uncle is a good man. He just told me he will explain it all to us after dinner. 'That's good enough for me,' she said, smiling.

'Do you need any help?' asked Tom.

'You can keep me company and tell me all about your selves

'And you can tell us about you,' replied Tom.

'That's a deal then. Can you peel veg? We are having stew and I need some veg peeling,' she said. As the trio chatted away while preparing the meal, the talk drifted to family and the fact that none of them had ever seen any family other than their uncle and Row's dad. They didn't even remember anything about their parents; no photos, stories, nothing. This now dawned on all of them that this was actually a little strange, but, in the past, it had never mattered. The three of them stopped talking, each was left with their own thoughts until their uncles walked in.

'It's very quiet in here, is everything okay, you lot?' Tristan asked.

'Oh yes… just mulling over a few things we have been talking about,' Row replied.

'Was it about family?' Kurt asked.

'Yes,' replied Karl.

'All your questions will be answered after dinner. Whatever happens we will tell you everything, we promise.'

'Well, you lot, something smells wonderful in here. The smell is filling the house and making me very hungry,' said Tristan.

'It's a joint effort but it will be about another hour and a half, is that okay?' said Row

'That's fine, darling. Your uncle and I have some things to talk about before this evening so if you have finished here for a while you could all go and find the wolves,' Tristan said to her.

Row asked the boys if they fancied looking for the wolves? Did they not realise Row had a wolf as well? She told them her wolf was called Salina and that she was Phina's sister.

'Cool,' replied Tom.

Karl was just about to punch his brother for using what he thought was the most annoying word ever when Row pulled him away. 'See you in a little while,' she said as she pushed Tom forward towards the dining room with Karl following her at a safe distance from his brother.

'Don't go too far without the wolves.'

'Don't worry, Dad, we'll be careful.' The three of them left through the conservatory, down to the towpath by the river in search of the wolves.

In the cottage, Tristan and Kurt discussed what had happened over the last couple of days, and what their next move would be, and also the immediate problem of how much they needed to tell the kids later.

'Salina likes to go down the river, to the weir; the best way to get there is out the bottom gate and walk down towards the right which leads straight to the weir. She catches fish down there, so she's probably gone there to show her sister.

'Did you know that you can talk to your wolf? She will understand what you say, or rather what you are thinking, I think that's how it works?'

'No way, you're having us on,' said Karl.

'No, I'm not, you can really think to your wolf and she will think back to you. You really don't believe me, do you?'

'Well, not really. I suppose your favourite film is Doctor Doolittle as well,' laughed Karl.

'I believe you… you looked so serious when you said it,' said Tom.

'Thank you, Tom, I was being serious.'

'Okay, convince me. How do you do it then?' asked Karl.

As they walked along the river, Row explained to them. 'It's a little hard at first… First you have to clear your mind of everything, then just concentrate on your wolf, she will concentrate on you. Then you will start to feel like a wolf. I know, I know! It sounds stupid but it actually works!'

Karl looked unbelievingly at what she had just said.

'Then, as you connect with each other you will see your wolf's eyes go red.'

'I believe you, Row, I do believe you. Tom and I saw Uncle Kurt's eyes go as red as red could be. That was after he had been around the side of the campervan with Phina this morning,' Karl told her excitedly.

'We thought we were both going mad,' added Tom.

'That's what he was doing, he was talking to her and telling her where to meet us later. That's how she knew where we were,' said Karl as a light bulb came on in his head.

'How long have you been able to do this,' Tom asked.

'It's only been about a year now. My dad told me how to do it. He said it's because they are a special type of wolf, there are no others like them on Earth, so you can't tell anyone, or they will take you and the wolves away. It's our secret.'

'Do you think our uncles are aliens?' asked Tom.

'Why on earth would you say that, Tom?'

'He could have something, because our uncle said, "bloody humans" earlier,' added Karl.

'No, don't be daft. Don't you think we would have noticed something like that?'

'A lot of strange things have happened today,' Karl told her.

'Like what?'

'Well, like what happened with us at the superstore today, then changing the camper and things like that.'

'I don't know anything about that. Tell me more,' Row inquired.

Karl recounted what had gone on earlier, the encounter with the red-faced man and the police. Then he asked Row, 'What about that woman, the dead one?'

'Yes, I suppose you could have something, the weird green eyes. I'm sure Kurt and Dad will explain everything tonight.'

'You're probably right, grownups have a way of explaining things. I don't understand, maybe it's because they have been alive longer than me,' said Tom.

'You could be right there, Tom, it could all be a coincidence. Mother nature can be inexplicable sometimes,' replied Row.

'Inex... what?' Tom looked very puzzled.

'It means you can't explain something, you dummy,' his brother teased.

'He's not a dummy, Karl, it's a big word for a small boy. Isn't that right, Tom?'

'Yeh, it is. Dummy yourself, Karl,' said Tom.

'Whatever!' his brother replied.

They continued to walk along the river, happily talking away when Row said to them, 'Let's creep up on Phina and Salina.'

'You'll be lucky. We have never managed to creep up on Phina or Kurt, have we, Tom?'

'No, never.'

'Come to think of it, I've never sneaked up on Salina either.' Just then they heard splashing.

'It sounds like they're having fun.'

Then suddenly there was a piercing scream! Then a vicious snarl!

'That's not fun, it sounds like they are fighting,' said Karl. The three of them ran towards the sounds. When they reached the top of the weir, they looked down and they could see the two wolves, teeth bared, saliva dripping from their jaws.

'Look, Row, Phina has some blood on her leg. It looks like they have cornered something, but I can't see what it is.'

They ran down the side of the weir and along the bank... then they saw what it was, a figure in black.

'Salina, Phina, stop!' screamed Row.

Salina looked up at her, while her sister kept her deadly watch on the mystery figure. Salina's eyes went red. 'Row, stay back, this thing is dangerous. It means to harm you and the boys. Phina and me are okay. Stay back, we will deal with this.'

The boys thought they had heard a gentle voice in their heads saying, 'It's all right, don't move, we will deal with this beast.'

Row stood in front of the boys, using her arm to protect them. Instinctively Karl, being the eldest male present and being much bigger than Row, pulled her back and stood in front of her and Tom. Row grabbed Tom and held him tight.

'Don't do anything stupid, Karl,' she told him,

'Don't worry, I won't.'

Just then the boys once again heard a soft female voice in the back of their minds, 'Stay back, boys, it's all okay. I will deal with this with my sister. Karl, keep Thomas and Row back.'

Karl and Tom looked at each other,

'Did you hear a voice just then, Tom?' Karl asked.

'I did. A woman's voice telling me to stay back, it's all okay. Is that what you heard?' Tom replied.

'Yes, near enough, I think that's Phina talking to us.'

As the thing in black moved forward slightly in a last-ditch attempt to attack the wolves, Tom noticed something glint in the dying sunlight.

'It's got a knife,' Tom shouted to the wolves.

'Thank you, Thomas, I have already felt its blade. It will not get a second chance,' the voice said in his head, Tom could hear this inside his mind. The thing came forward out of the shadows of the weir. 'What's that? It's not human, look at its face.'

Karl and Row could now see exactly what Tom had; the thing had a hunched back and claws that were grasping the shining blade. It had two long tusks protruding from its upper jaw, the rest of the face was covered in hair.

'It's a wearied rat,' shouted Karl. What was even more noticeable were the piercing jade green eyes that darted between the wolves then at the three of them.

'Look out!' They all heard it in their minds as the clawed hand drew back and threw the blade towards the three startled youngsters. As the knife left the creature's hand, Phina's jaws clenched the arm, dragging the creature backwards off balance, and in that split second Salina was at its throat. The throw was wild.

'Duck!' Karl shouted, as he pulled Row and Tom to the ground, the knife flying over their heads and embedding itself in a fence post behind them. All three stood up and looked down as Salina and Phina slowly backed away from the thrashing creature dying in the water below the weir. Alert, both wolves watched for the faintest sign of danger from the creature as the writhing stopped and all became quiet, apart from the trickling water of the weir. In front of the astonished youngsters the creature shrivelled away until only green smoke was left drifting into the evening sky. Salina and Phina jumped up on to the bank next to Row, Karl and Tom leaving only the dark purple and black cloak floating on top of the water. The one the creature had been wearing moments earlier. Slowly the water currents pulled it down the river away from the weir.

Looking at the frightened youngsters in front of her, Salina's eyes went red and she communicated to them, 'Are you all okay? The creature is dead and gone. We will go back to the house now and let Tristan and Kurt know what has just happened.'

For the first time in his life Karl tried to think, to communicate something back to the wolves, in his head all he could think was, 'Are you hurt, Phina?' Then in his head he heard, 'It was only a graze thank you, Karl. I see you are starting to master communication with us. Believe me, I have been asking Kurt for years to let me teach you, but he said I couldn't as long as you lived as a human in this world. Well, now I believe everything has changed.'

Karl thought back, 'I think you're right, Phina.' Wow, this is great, he thought to himself.

'Let's make our way back to the cottage as Salina suggested,' said Row.

'What was that?' Tom said to no one in particular.

Phina replied to him as well as to Row and Karl, 'You need to start thinking to each other and not letting everyone around you hear what you are trying to communicate. It could save your life one day, Tom. You can all communicate with each other this way as well as well as with wolves and eagles.'

'Eagles, this day is just getting better!' said Tom aloud.

'No! Thomas, think and communicate it to me and Salina,' said Phina.

'Okay. I can't do it,' he said. 'It just comes out of my mouth.'

'Imagine you don't want everyone to hear what you are saying and think something, Thomas,' Salina told him.

This is mad, Tom thought.

'Yes. That's it, Thomas. It would be very bad if people from this world knew what you have just done.'

'I did it, I really did it, I communicated with a wild wolf,' said a highly excitable Tom.

'I wouldn't exactly say wild, Thomas. If anyone here is wild, it's definitely you, Tom,' Phina replied. Row and Karl laughed.

'You heard what I thought, then?' Tom asked Row and Karl.

'Yes, we did. I think you have some practising to do to get as good as Salina and Phina,' Row told him.

Salina howled in acknowledgement then she communicated, 'We will go and scout the way back to the cottage for you, just to be on the safe side.'

'We can no longer take things for granted, especially your safety now that you have been found by her,' thought Phina to all of them. With that, as the two wolves ran off in either direction away from them, they heard in their minds, 'Make your way back directly and as quickly as you can.'

The wolves disappeared. The trio walked along the towpath for five minutes when ahead of them two figures emerged from the dim light ahead.

A shout came from one of the figures, 'Are you all right? We've just seen Phina, she's told us everything.'

'We're all okay,' Row replied. 'This is all starting to get very weird,' Row told her father.

'As long as you are all okay, that's the main thing. Once we get home and we have had some dinner, your uncle Kurt and I will explain as much as we can.'

'We had a feeling something was wrong; you get a sense when you connect to the wolves. Our senses started to warn us about fifteen minutes after you left,' said Kurt as they approached.

Tristan then asked the boys if they were okay. Both boys nodded their heads and smiled.

'Right then, let's get home and have some of that wonderfully smelling stew that is bubbling away nicely back there, filling the cottage with some great smells,' said Kurt. After a short time, they all walked into the cottage, the mouth-watering aroma of fresh stew wafting towards them.

'That smells great,' said Tom. 'I'm really hungry now,' he added.

'Get yourselves around the table and I'll serve up. You too,' Row said as she looked at her dad and Kurt.

She didn't have to ask twice. The boys and their uncles sat at the top of the oak table nearest the kitchen,

'You've just spoken to one of the wolves, haven't you?' Kurt asked Karl.

'I have. How did you know that?'

'Phina told us all about communicating with her and Salina and also about the assassin in the weir… you all did well.'

Kurt explained to Karl and Tom that the creature was an assassin demon and that they could take the form of whatever they kill and that they can stay in that form for up to three days. After that the form they have taken begins to decay and eventually die. He also told them that the assassin would also die if they don't find another host in this world.

'That's why the old woman died in the village,' said Tristan.

'But, everyone in the village had seen her walking around. Row had even seen the old woman following her.'

'That's why it smelt so bad when Row went up to its dead form. It must have been trapped in the body for some reason and it could not get out, so by the time Row saw her in the village the assassin must have been in the body more than three days. But I'm not actually sure because I have never known one to take human form before?'

'So, where does it come from? It's not from this world, is it?' asked Karl.

'You're right there, Karl. It comes from our world, the one we will tell you all about in a short while, once we have had some food.'

'Here you go.'

Row started to place steaming bowls of stew in front of everyone.

'Hmm… That smells fantastic, Row, well done.'

'It was a joint effort, don't forget,' she said as she placed some sliced baguette on the table.

'Oh yes, how could I forget? Well done to you all. I can see you two doing some cooking once we get home, especially after tasting this.'

'I think we need a little more practice first,' said Karl.

'Don't worry, Row can train you,' added Tristan.

'I only peeled, not cooked,' butted in Tom.

'We will soon change that, Tom,' replied his uncle with a smile.

'Don't worry, little man. I will teach you how to cook as well as me,' said Row. Then she winked at him as she placed his stew in front of him.

Tom smiled and tasted the stew; it was as good as it smelt. Then Row joined them, and they all chatted as they eat the comforting stew. Once the stew had been eaten all was quiet as they all sat at the table, stuffed and very relaxed after what had been a very strange day for all of them.

'We'll let this settle, then, Row, if you and the boys don't mind, can you wash up while your uncle Kurt and I have a quick chat? Then we will all have that long awaited talk,' Tristan told them.

'Not a problem. I'm sure Karl and Tom won't mind helping me,' smiled Row, looking at the two boys.

Both boys nodded. After fifteen minutes of small talk, Row, Karl and Tom got up and took all the dirty cutlery and plates into the kitchen, shutting the sliding door between the two rooms on the way to give their uncles some privacy to talk.

'That was a little concerning, demon assassins taking the human form of a police officer and the old woman. Coming out in broad daylight too!' said Kurt.

'I have never known of that before, not here or on Elemtum. They are becoming bolder,' replied his brother.

'That was obviously the reasons Row didn't hear the old woman talk, nor the traffic cop either. They obviously can't talk in that form, or it was close to death and was using all its power to move?'

'You must remember, we have been away from our world for some time, who knows what has been happening back there since we've been gone?'

'Labatina has obviously been very busy since we departed; she and her followers could be able to do anything now.'

'I am a little concerned we are sending the children of our blood line back to potential danger. Why hasn't our brother contacted us? He must be aware of her followers' presence here on Earth.'

'At the first opportunity we must get to the gate. I'm quite concerned about the demon assassins. Don't they normally work in groups of four?' Kurt said.

'Let's see we've had one killed as a deer by Phina outside my cottage in Suffolk, and the magpie. The old woman, then the one the wolves killed at the weir, which had not taken on another form when it was killed, plus the policeman.'

'So, by my reckoning, unless they have changed tactics since we have been gone, that's five. So, potentially there are still at least three more out there somewhere. We must stay on guard, that is if they still hunt in teams of four?' said Tristan.

'As you said, that is of course as long as there were only two teams of assassins sent. If there were more, we have no way of knowing how many are out there until we encounter them,' added Kurt.

'That could be a big problem for us if we don't take measures now. We might regret it later. I know we can deal with them and they aren't the best Labatina has, but we don't know what else might be here.'

'I will go and get Phina and Salina back here for some food, then between them and us we will have to take turns throughout the night to keep the children safe.'

'While we speak to the children, the wolves can keep watch, then we'll get the kids to bed. In the morning, we will take the 4x4 north to the gate, set up camp for the night and check the gate out ready for entry back home the next morning.'

'That sounds like a plan,' replied Kurt.

Tristan left to speak to the wolves and Kurt opened the room dividers to see how the kids were getting on.

'Nearly finished, only two plates left to dry,' said Row.

'Good job. Tristan has gone to get the wolves back for their food, and then they will keep watch while we talk to you. Get yourselves a drink and sit at the table, we won't be too long.' Row, Karl and Tom finished in the kitchen then sat at the big oak table in great anticipation at what was to come.

'Where's your TV?' Tom asked Row, a little puzzled.

'We don't have one, we have a radio,' she replied.

'So, what do you do in the evening?' Karl asked.

'We listen to the radio, read, I paint and draw, mend any clothes that need mending. In the summer, I practice archery, the crossbow and a little rayzor practice here and there.'

'Rayzor, what's that?' inquired Tom.

'It's like a small cutlass; it's my dad's,' replied Row.

'Rayzor, archery, crossbow,' said Tom, eyes aglow with excitement. 'Cool.'

'Who teaches you all that?' Karl asked.

'Since I was little, Dad has taught me. He said I would never know when it would come in handy.'

'I wish Uncle Kurt had taught us things like that,' said Tom.

'Don't worry, Tom, I'm sure he will very soon. If that thing the wolves killed is anything to go by, I'm sure he will be teaching us all quite soon,' said Karl.

Just then there was a bang on the rear patio door. All three were startled and looked directly in the direction the noise had come from. Salina and Phina stood there, their red eyes piercing the black night,

'Let us in please, sorry for startling you.' The wolves were let in, then there was a lot of a fuss made of them.

'I'm so glad you're okay, Phina. You are both my heroes for what you've done today, and you were both so brave,' Row told them.

'We will never let anything happen to any of you if it's within our power to stop it. That's why we are here,' Salina communicated to them.

'You're not just here to protect us, you are our friends and we love you both,' Row told them.

'Thank you, that means a lot to us,' Phina replied.

'It's true, we do love you,' Tom said, then he gave Phina a big hug.

Tristan and Kurt walked into the dining room.

'Everything okay in here?'

'We are just being a little soppy, that's all,' said Row.

Kurt's eyes then went red. 'All okay out there?' he asked the wolves, but this time everyone could hear what Kurt was communicating.

Then the reply came from Salina for everyone to hear, 'Everything around here within a two-mile radius is very quiet.'

'If you both go and get the food I have put out front for you, then you can keep watch while Tristan and I talk to the children.'

'Did my eyes go red?' Tom asked excitedly.

'Yes, they did, Tom. That means you have to be careful when you communicate. It will make humans nervous and inquisitive if they see your eyes go red,' Kurt told him. Then he followed the two wolves as they padded into the hall. Kurt let them out through the front door. When he returned, he asked the children to sit at the table.

'I would just like to point out that I am not a child, Uncle Kurt, I'm sixteen,' Row told him.

'Sorry, Row, I forget you're a young lady. Sorry to you too, Karl, I know you are now a young man. Oh, and sorry to you, Tom. You're still a child and the odd one out, I'm afraid.'

'It doesn't bother me, I know my place,' Tom smiled.

'I'll start again, shall I, Tom? Lady and gentlemen, please sit at the table, and then we will begin. Was that okay, Row?'

'Much better, Uncle Kurt, Thank you.'

'That's good. Then what we are about to discuss may become quite heavy and hard for you to understand, so I will start off with a laugh that will relax us all.' Kurt told a joke that made him laugh, and his audience cringe. Kurt thought it was funny,

Karl had told 'a typical dad joke' that it made them laugh, except Tom who did not know what he meant by 'dad joke'.

'I've got a joke,' Tom told everyone.

'Go on then, Tom, before we start. It's got to be better than Kurt's though,' Row told him.

'It is. What's white and swings through the jungle?'

'I don't know, Tom,' said his uncle Kurt.

'Tarzan the Fridge,' Tom replied.

'That's so bad, it's funny, Tom,' laughed Row.

Karl shook his head, 'That was terrible, Tom.'

Just then Tristan appeared. 'What have I missed?'

'Don't worry, Uncle Tristan, it's not worth repeating,' Karl told him.

Tristan had been closing and locking all the doors and windows to secure the house so they would not get caught out while they were talking and let their guard down.

'Right then, let's begin,' Kurt told everyone.

Chapter 5
The Truth

'Well, where do we start? First, I think I will explain why we have not said anything up until now. We didn't want young children telling their friends all about our world because no one in this world knows about it,' said Tristan.

'What do you mean our world?' asked Karl.

'I can see by the look on all your faces that you were all probably thinking the same thing that Karl just asked me... am I right?'

'Yes, you are, Dad. I think we are all a little confused right now. You can't really blame us, can you?'

'No, I can't... I do understand what you must all be thinking. Is it all real, am I dreaming, why am I being told now? These are all questions we intend to answer for you. Let's start there then, that's as good a place as any, am I dreaming? No! Definitely not.

'Is it real? Yes!'

'Can I ask a question before you go on?' asked Row.

'No., Sorry, Row, let's explain things first then you can ask as many questions as you like, otherwise we will be here all night. Okay?' replied Tristan.

'Okay, that makes sense,' she agreed.

Tristan started. 'We all come from a world that we call Elemtum. Not Earth. It's very similar to Earth in many ways but also significantly different. We have a more advanced society than Earth does, but equal in others. We have learnt to use nearly all of our brain capacity, unlike humans who use very little of theirs. We live in harmony with ninety per cent of the living creatures in our world. The remaining ten per cent are dangerous creatures that live by instinct and kill by instinct to survive, but there is also the very small percentage of evil that has started to wage a war in our world. These people and creatures are called the Dark. 'Their leader and queen is someone we used to call a friend. She is Queen Labatina. More about her and the Dark later because this has a direct bearing on you and the reason you are here. Are you all aware of this planet and the universe?'

'I'm not,' said Tom.

'What I mean, Tom, is that you know we are on Earth, and there is a sun and a moon and it's all in a universe. Do you agree with that?'

'Yes,' replied Tom.

'Okay then, that's really all you need to know now. I will explain how our worlds came into being. What you have to imagine is a flat piece of paper, on that piece of paper is a big planet a bit like Earth, but a lot bigger with three big moons as well as two suns. Okay so far?' They all nodded. 'The paper starts to rip down the middle and one of the suns falls through with a moon, then the big world starts to fall through. As it falls, the paper mends itself and closes, cutting the world into two different sizes. Are you all still following?'

'Yes,' came the reply, but Tom still looked a little confused, so Kurt got a piece of paper and a pencil and drew him a diagram of what Tristan was talking about.

'I'm not an artist so you will have to imagine a bit.' He drew the basic shape of a torn universe, then Row had an idea. She ran into her bedroom and came back with some stick-on shapes that she gave to Kurt to help him explain things to Tom. He placed the stickers and drew some lines to show what he was talking about.

'Ah, I understand now,' Tom said. 'So, the number one bit is Earth, the sun and moon falling through the universe and the number two bit is your world on top of the universe and ours below.'

'Yes, Tom except my world is also yours, Row's and Karl's world as well. Good. I'm glad the diagram helps it makes sense.'

Tristan smiled at the three young faces staring intently at him, then he continued. 'One side of this paper is this universe and this Earth, and our world is on the other side of the paper, that's the part of the world that didn't fall through. The part of our world that fell through became Earth, as Tom has just said. The moon that fell through with the sun became this moon and this sun, but the moon that fell through with this earth died. That's why its grey. So, before all this happened and the worlds had not split, the complete big planet had no life on it, we believe! That was because with two suns near the world it was too hot for any life to develop and survive. Thanks to the rip, both suns moved their positions around the world, one sun fell and where it rested it was far enough of a distance away for the bit of the massive world that became Earth. This enabled life to develop, ending up as this world, that is Earth that we are on today. The dead moon also helped the Earth because it has an effect on this Earth, so there are tides here. There are also lots of other properties here that affect this Earth that not even the top scientists here know about or would even understand. What the moon here does for the Earth and all the creatures that live here I'm not going to explain because we would have to go too deep into that and we would be here for days. Is everyone still following what I have said?' Tristan got three nods in reply.

'So,' he continued, 'our world, sun and moons all survived the cut. They are all much bigger than here on this side, and our moons are all still alive. We even have creatures in our world that can reach the moons, without space craft. Think of our moons as being similar to Earth; they have atmospheres, water and living creatures which flourish there. Anyway, I am getting ahead of myself. When the rip was sealed it left behind threads that connected our worlds through the rip from our world and its universe to this world and its own universe.' He drew a red line from Elemtum to Earth on the drawing he had just done. 'We think that when humans started to appear here on Earth, it was around the time that people from Elemtum found the entrance to this thread. Think of it more as a pathway from one world to the other. We called it the Opening. It's now called the World's Pathway, or the World Gate. It was formed in our world after a massive ground movement which created the mountain of souls. The great forest is home to the peoples of the wolf and that's where the World's Pathway was first found. I say first found because we now know of several pathways to Earth and we are finding more. Me, Kurt, Phina and Salina all belong to Wolf clan, as do you.'

'Does that mean I am part of the Wolf people?' said Row excitedly.

'Yes and no,' Tristan told her.

'What do you mean, yes and no?' Row asked.

'I will get to that very shortly, Row, please be patient with me. I know you want to know everything, and you will very shortly.' Tristan continued, 'A descendant of the great Atta Wolf himself found the pathway and journeyed through it to Earth first, believing it to be the middle of Elemtum. Some of the greatest minds of our time travelled through and lived here on Earth for several moons of time. What humans call days.' They explored some of the land they were in and made friends with the primitive locals who at the time were observed to be able to show signs of evil. What I mean by that is what we class on Elemtum as pure evil. They were seen to hurt and kill their own people and animals for no reason except their own pleasure or greed. This is something that had never happened on Elemtum, except when the Dark started to appear. Don't get me wrong, there are some very honourable people on Earth and because of them most of this world is stable, but all over the world evil takes place. Countries and peoples are destroyed for no reason and it does not stop until the evil is destroyed by honourable people, here on Earth and on Elemtum. I am also sorry to say that some of the worst evil in this world is controlled by the false religions that are here on Earth. Religion was started by man to give the people of the world hope, which was a good idea, but evil soon infiltrated it and has killed, and tortured, millions of souls here on Earth through the ages, all in the name of greed.

'Once again, I must stress that there are more honourable people than evil here on Earth, but evil tends to hit the headlines and causes the pain here on Earth. I will also add now on Elemtum, in the form of the Dark. We now believe there is a definite link between Elemtum and Earth when it comes to evil.

'I have slightly side-tracked there. I will quickly get back to the scientists and scholars that came to Earth. At night, they realised the sky was completely different from our world's sky at night. They also realised the moon above them was dead, so they concluded that they were on a completely different planet. This planet was a new and emerging planet. The decision was taken to close and seal the opening, then it was reclassified as the pathway, with an entrance that would only allow authorised passengers. This would only be granted by the elders in Elemtum, these were headed by the then great King Atta. We didn't want to influence this new emerging planet but we also did not want the evil to spread to our world. We started to study this world but did not interfere with its development.

'The great gate pathway was later renamed the World's Pathway once again. It is a big wooden door, six times the size of a normal door and five times as thick as one here on Earth. It can't be seen by the human eye.'

'This is the pathway we hope to use to go back to Elemtum tomorrow,' added Kurt.

'So, to sum up quickly what I have told you. Our world is very similar to this one, but also very different, if that makes sense?'

'I don't quite understand that bit,' said Tom. The others kept quiet, while Tristan tried to explain briefly to Tom.

'Well, Tom, to put it simply, our world is four times bigger than Earth and we have two moons; the blue moon and red moon. They are three times bigger than the one here above Earth. Life started very similar to the way life started here on Earth, but we don't call ourselves human, we are just the people. All races, all types. Tt's a collective name for all the tribes of Elemtum. We nearly all live together in harmony, except for two exceptions, some creatures and animals who are predatory. They always have been and always will a bit like the crocodiles, lions and tigers in this world. As I said before, there are also now the creatures of the Dark Lands. They are the reason you are here now and not in the world where you were born.'

'So, if everyone lives in peace, why do we have the Dark and why are they dangerous? Why do these things want to kill us?' asked Karl.

Tristan replied to his questions. 'Well, Karl, no one is really sure why there is a Dark land. If you look at our history, which has been well documented by our scholars, there was no such thing as evil in our vocabulary until we came to Earth. Shortly after that, things started to change. I will answer your other questions in a bit, but some of them we don't know. How and why there is Dark? We don't know yet.'

'Why does that affect you?'

'I will go into that in a moment. Is it making any sense to you, Tom, Karl, Row?' he asked.

'Yes, it is, but it's so out of this world that it's hard to take in, or do I mean believe,' answered Row.

'That is exactly how I feel,' said Karl.

'Yeh, me as well. I get the how the worlds are different and how they were made. It's the believing like Row said, that's the bit I can't get at the moment,' said Tom.

'Okay, I can understand that, but just think… until today you had never seen a Dark assassin. You had never communicated or talked to any animal, let alone two big vicious looking wolves, am I right?'

'Yes, you are. Amazing as that is, it's still hard to believe we are from another planet. Are we aliens?' asked Karl.

'Technically, yes you are, but not totally. Yes, you are alien to this planet, but we are also joined to this planet. Do you understand that?'

'Yes, I think we all understand that! The point is… you have been there, we have not, or we don't remember being there, so it is still hard to believe. I am not saying it is all a lie, I just need a little time and a bit more proof… does that make sense?'

'I totally understand how you are all feeling right now, Karl, but please trust us, you will slowly see we are telling the truth. Trust us a little longer, please.'

'We do, and we will,' said Row.

Karl and Tom nodded their heads in agreement.

'Okay then, let's crack on with it. Going back to our planet Elemtum, we have forests, oceans, rivers, mountains, deserts. We even have part of our world that is continually covered in snow, much like the north and south poles here on Earth. We also have some very different trees and plants. There are similar animals like wolves and eagles. We also have totally different creatures such as lizards crossed with snakes; they are very dangerous. We have sea animals, mammals, insects and birds. I can't go through it all because there is so much, and you will be schooled in things like this when we get home.'

'School? No way, I've just finished school and I'm not going back, there is so much to do in life, I'm not wasting my life in school,' said Row, now very agitated.

'Calm down, Rowena, you are too old to go to formal scholars' lessons, as is Karl. You and Karl will learn all this through life skills. While you are both training at the warrior halls you will come across everything you will need to know to survive on Elemtum. However, you, Tom, you are young enough to join the scholars' lessons. You will only be a there a short time, about a blue moon behind, I mean, a year,' said Tristan.

'That's not fair. Why do I have to go and not Karl?' sulked Tom.

'Because, Tom, warriors start training at fourteen and Karl is fourteen. But don't get too upset, I know you and I know you don't like Earth schools, but you will love scholars' lessons. There is history. I know you like history. Geography, people studies, where you travel our world meeting the peoples of Elemtum, basic weapon studies.' Tom's face began to smile, he flashed a grin to his brother. Kurt continued, 'There are also flying lessons, diving lessons, cooking.'

'Cooking!' Tom exclaimed.

'Yes, cooking, Tom. Everyone learns to cook, also what to cook. We don't want food to kill you now, do we! You will have a big advantage over Karl and Rowena; they will have to teach themselves all this. You, no doubt, will become a much better warrior than both Karl and Rowena because of these scholar's lessons, and to top it all, only twenty per cent of the lessons are in the classroom environment, but it is no way like any school you have been to on Earth.'

Tom was now very happy, and his beaming smile indicated to everyone that he was.

'I can live with that,' commented Karl.

Tristan could now see that that everyone was once again happy with what they were being told, or at least understood what they were being told, so he continued. 'The peoples of Elemtum are one with the animals and creatures and the world they live in. When I say animals and creatures, I also mean some mammals of the sea and plants and trees. Different tribes can communicate with different animals; some can communicate with several, including creatures of the seas and oceans. The people, animals and birds all have brains that are more developed than humans and Earth's creatures and animals. That's why we can communicate with people when they are wolves, as you now know because you did it today.'

Karl, Row and Tom all missed the significance of what Tristan had said; 'people when they are wolves'. They would come across this later in their home world of Elemtum.

'We have no police or courts because we have had no crime; everyone has everything they need. If, for some reason, someone needs something, they will be given it by the people from one of our many storage halls around our world. We now have what you would call here on Earth an army. What it is actually closest to here on Earth is the United Nations, except we don't have separate nations. We are one nation with many different peoples.'

'The whole world is one nation? that's amazing,' said Karl.

'That is everyone except the Dark,' Kurt added. 'On Elemtum, we have collectives of warriors from the different tribes who can be called on to protect the towns and citadels anywhere on our world. We have always had predators which the local tribes have always dealt with themselves. But now we have the Dark and they occupy an area of the Elemtum roughly around one per cent of the world. That part of the world in the Deep South was a massive rainforest, but this is now a no-go area. One per cent may not sound much but when you look at the size of our world, it is a large area. It's the only part of Elemtum that is totally devoid of normal life as we would know it. Even the sand lands are full of life. That part of our world, the Dark Lands, only has six hours of light a day. The remainder of the time it is in total darkness.'

'Why?' asked Row.

'We don't really know,' Kurt replied. 'We had reports that when this once great natural beautiful area began to die, it became dark. A party of knowledgeable people were sent down there to investigate… They never came back. That's when we noticed the evil spreading across our world. We have managed to contain it to this one area, but they do raid other areas every now and then. It has taken a great number of good souls and brave warriors to achieve what we have so far, but it's not over.'

'I fear there are going to be bigger battles and the loss of more souls until this eventually ends,' Tristan told them. 'That's right, no one has ever come back from the Dark region. We don't really know why. All we know is that it is ruled over by the former queen of our world called Labatina Abanon. She has great significance for you all!'

'You will learn why very shortly,' Kurt told them. He continued, 'She is called the High Queen of Darkness by her followers. These are the dammed of our world. Some are hideous creatures created by evil. How and why they have been created, we don't know, but we do know they are all pure evil and without mercy. They kill everything more for pleasure than for any purpose. If they do have a purpose, we don't know what it is yet.

'Our greatest scholars are baffled by it. Evil is new to us. We have seen evil here on Earth, so maybe it has come from Earth, who knows? We have lost one of our greatest warriors to the Dark. He was seduced by Labatina and her evil and he now commands her army, small as it is. That's enough of that for now. Tristan is more knowledgeable about that sort of thing than me,' finished Kurt.

Row, Karl and Tom had listened intently, fascinated by all they heard but not really taking in how dangerous the little one per cent of the Dark Lands really was to the rest of the Elemtum and themselves personally.

'You might be thinking... why are we explaining all this to you when you are here on Earth?' said Tristan. 'Well, there are about fifty of our people here on Earth from our world. Until now, we did not realise any one from the Dark was here. No humans know of our presence here. That's one of the reasons we have never told you about our world. As we said before, we didn't want to take the risk of what a young child would tell their friends when they were playing or at school. I know you are still young, Tom, but we will very shortly be going to Great Porum, so I know our secret will be safe now. We wanted to make sure you are fully aware and understand the main danger that may face you in your world, Elemtum. Hopefully what we have told you, and will tell you, will prepare you for what's to come in the next few days.'

'Where were we born, here on Earth?' asked Tom, slightly confused now.

'No, Tom, none of you were born on Earth. You were all born in Elemtum in the capital Great Porum, then we brought you here for your own protection,' said Kurt.

'Who do we need protecting from and who are our parents?' asked Karl, who was now also getting confused.

'Maybe I should have started with all that first. Your father is King Frederick, the same as Rowena, so you are brother and sister,' Tristan told them, then paused to let the new information register. Karl and Tom looked directly at each other and then at Row, who was sitting between them. It took a second for the new information to sink in.

'Hello, big sister,' Karl said, looking at Row, a broad smile across his face, and then he stood up. Row stood up at the same time and they embraced. 'I'm so glad I have a sister, and I'm very glad it's you, Row,' Karl said, kissing her on her cheek.

'Thank you, Karl... me too,' she replied, then turned to Tom who had now stood up. 'Hello, little brother, so nice to meet you. This is becoming a really nice day all of a sudden,' she said.

'I'm glad that you're my big sister too... and that he's still my brother,' said Tom. Everyone laughed.

Then Row thought about the implications of what Tristan had said. 'Hang on, you're my dad. I'm still classing you as my dad. I don't know anyone else, even if he is my real father. I think I do remember when I was younger that there was a big man and a beautiful woman in my life, but I don't remember why. You've been my dad all my life, so inside I must have known you weren't my real dad, but in my heart, you will always be. I've subconsciously been blocking it for all these years, I think. You're the one that has brought me up, not some king on a distant planet, and I love you as my dad. I always will,' said Row. She then went over to Tristan with a tear in her eye and gave him a kiss on his cheek and a long hug.

'Hey, what's this for? Why the tears, Row?' Tristan asked.

'Because I know now…' Her voice quickened. 'I know that this is the end… the end of our life as we know it, I mean… and I don't want it to be, Dad! I don't want another dad.' She began to sob… Sniffling, she wiped the tears that were now running from her eyes. She continued, 'I just want to stay here, Dad, with you, Karl, Tom, Phina, Salina and Uncle Kurt… Why can't we just do that? Why can't we?' she sobbed and held her dad.

'Because, Row, it's now too dangerous for you and the boys,' he told her softly. 'Don't worry, you won't lose me; I will always be there for you and the boys. Yes, life will change, but it will get better, trust me… it will get better, don't worry.'

'I know, Dad, I'm just being a girl. You always say I'm too much of a tomboy. Well, here I am being a girl. I think I need a minute to do my face, is that all right?' she sobbed.

'Of course, it is. Row, your tears are messing up your make-up.'

'I don't wear make-up. How long have you lived with me?' She smiled at him between sobs and tears.

'I know, Row. I was just giving you an excuse to make yourself pretty once more and get that beautiful smile back on your face.'

Row gave Tristan a kiss on the cheek, then hurried out of the room trying not to look at anyone. She was feeling a little embarrassed and silly. On her way out, of the room she gulped between sobs, 'Sorry, everyone, I won't be long.' She left the room and headed for her bedroom. Closing her bedroom door, she flung herself on to her bed and buried her head deep into her pillows and sobbed away. She knew her life was changing, and it was out of her control. She did not like or want to feel the way she felt at that moment. She had a feeling it was all starting to get too much; she was losing control of her life. She was right; her life was changing as were the boys and they would never be the same again!

Ten minutes passed. Tristan decided to go and see how Rowena was. As he got up, the door opened, and Row came in looking fresh and full of life, even if her eyes looked a little red.

'Sorry, everyone, I think it all go a bit much especially with the old woman thing, and now all this. I just lost it a bit, it won't happen again,' she said with a smile.

'That's my princess, we will make a warrior of you yet,' said Tristan.

'I bet I could beat you, old man, at any of the warrior skills you have taught me over the years, just pick one,' Row challenged him.

'I believe you just might,' replied Tristan.

Everyone sat back down. Kurt and Tristan were about to continue where they had left off when Karl said, 'Anyway, before you continue, I agree with Row. Uncle Kurt, you are a father to me and Tom and that's how I think of you and always will.'

'Me three,' said Tom.

'Thank you all for what you have said. Tristan and I think of you all as our children and we always will. But the truth is you have a loving father in Elemtum. He sent you away for good reason. Let me explain before you come to any long-lasting conclusions. Remember you will get to know your father even though you don't remember him at the moment. He is a great man and he loves you all very much. It was very hard for him to send you away to safety with Tristan and me. He is very proud of you indeed, just as Tristan and I are. We have been keeping him informed throughout your lives.

'Now we will get to the not so pleasant stuff… your mothers,' Kurt said to them.

'What do you mean by "not so pleasant"?' asked Tom.

'Tom, what I think Kurt meant to say is this part of our history lesson is a little unhappy when it comes to your mothers. Note that I said mothers.'

'So, you mean Row, Karl and me all have different mothers?' asked Tom.

'Not quite, Tom. Rowena and Karl have a different mother to you.'

Tom looked like he was just about to cry; for once in his life, he did not feel happy anymore.

'I think Tom needs a hug from his big sister before you go any further, Uncle Kurt.' Row got up and went around the table to where Tom was now sitting. 'Tom, you are the little brother I never knew I had. Your mum might not be my mum, but your dad is my dad, so that makes you mine and Karl's little brother. Nothing has changed, Tom.' Row bent down and gave Tom a hug and a kiss.

Karl had now also walked over to Tom and for the first time in his and Tom's life Karl also gave Tom a hug and not his usual bear hug. 'You will always be my annoying little brother, squirt, so don't forget, but now you have a big sister, two uncles and a king for a dad. Not many kids have got that. Oh, and not forgetting, the two big wolves outside,' Karl said, then ruffled Tom's hair.

A smile came back to Tom's face as he stood up and gave his sister and brother a hug back. 'Thank you,' he said, with a tear in his eye. They all went and sat back down. This time Tom was now closer to Row and Karl.

'Come on, we had better push on. Not much more to tell you. It's been a very emotional day for all of us, believe me. Are you okay, Tom?' Kurt asked.

'Yes, I'm okay. I think I'm ready for anything now,' he replied, with a smile.

'I'm sorry to say, Tom, there is a little bit more bad news for you, because your mother is no longer with us. She passed away not long after you were born,' said Kurt. Everyone looked at Tom, who looked surprisingly cheerful now. Row reassuringly squeezed his hand softly.

'I'm okay, really. I've never met my mum. It's sad I never will, but I never knew her, so I have no memories. I will be all right. I've got you lot, haven't I?' he said, with a smile.

'Good lad, Tom. Your mother would be very proud of you, hearing you speak like that. She was a strong warrior and Tristan and I both loved her because, Tom, she was your mother and our sister, and we miss her every day. What keeps us going, Tom, is seeing her in your eyes every day which a great comfort to us both,' said Kurt. The room was now deadly silent as everyone, for a few seconds, was lost in their own thoughts. After a few seconds Kurt broke the silence, 'This won't get us anywhere. If everyone is happy, we will crack on... Now, your mother,' He was looking at an apprehensive Row and Karl who were now waiting on his every word, 'is Queen Labatina! She was not always evil. She was once, and I'm sure still is, a rare beauty, much like you, Rowena.'

Row could feel herself start to blush; she could feel her face warming up. 'Uncle Kurt, you're embarrassing me.'

'Well, I am being honest, Row.'

Tristan nodded his head in agreement. 'It's true, Row, you are the spitting image of her. As she did, you too are blossoming into a rare beauty the same as she did when we knew her in happier times.'

'Dad, that's not helping,' she said.

Karl and Tom next to her both had massive grins on their faces. Tom nudged his sister playfully.

'You two can pack that in,' she said, cheerfully pushing Tom into Karl playfully.

'Okay, okay, let's continue. Like I said, no one in either this world or ours could compare with her beauty.' Everyone looked at Row and grinned. Row shook her head not believing what was being said about her being beautiful.

'Give it a rest, will you?'

'Right, getting back to the serious stuff.' Tristan looked at his brother.

'Yes, getting back to the serious stuff... We don't really know what went wrong; she returned from this world then she started to behave very strangely, very distant, bad tempered, which was totally out of character for her. Next was her scientific exploration of the far south of Elemtum, the area which is now the Dark quarter. Several scientists and warriors went with her, including Lord Arthfael. Lord Arthfael had been Labatina's bodyguard throughout all her previous explorations in the both worlds. Labatina eventually returned from the expedition. When I say returned, she was actually found at the entrance to the Great Porum two years to the day she had left. She had changed.

'Her hair had gone from red to jet black, she was distant and confused, she never said a word about the missing Lord Arthfael, the scientists or the warriors. The king, the lords and scholars of our world put it down to shock after the harrowing journey she had just been on, coupled with the fact that all her companions and warriors were now missing, presumed dead. Not even her great love and soulmate, the king, could talk to her or get any sense from her. She was in some sort of trance or daze. Then, suddenly she returned to normality but with no recollection about what had happened to her during the missing two years. A year later Row was born to Labatina and the king. It was a very happy time. Just over a year and a half later, Karl was born, but things suddenly changed six months after you were born, Karl. It was reported by one of the watching warriors on the great tower at the entrance to the Great Porum that a flying creature had risen from the king and queen's chambers. On its back was a strange dark figure and Queen Labatina. The warrior reported that the dark figure resembled Arthfael, who had gone missing on the queen's fateful exploration. The king sent out scouts from the eagle flight with some of the Wolf warriors, but on returning they all reported finding nothing. Then, on one mission four Eagle warriors departed but only one returned, gravely injured. He had been found by the Wolf master, Detor Eosin. The dying warrior told Detor that they had come across a sizeable force heading towards the citadel and that it was of creatures the warrior had never seen or could have ever imagined. The warrior's death was reported to me, Tristan and the king. More scouts were sent out to track this force but not engage with it. It was reported that the force was heading directly towards Great Porum. The force was reportedly destroying and enslaving all the people it came across on its route. It was estimated the terrible force would reach the citadel within one week.'

Row and the boys listened intently to every word spoken by Kurt. 'A force was gathered over the next few days from all over Elemtum. It came from all the tribes, as well as the Wolf lords and Eagle lords who were at the fore leading the tribes. I led the Wolf tribe and Tristan the Eagle tribe. Altogether, we had around 20,000 warriors. We implored the king to stay and guard Great Porum, which is the centre of our world. If things went badly for us, he had a sizeable reserve force left behind to defend it. You have to remember that we had never come across anything like this before, so we really didn't know what to expect. We had worked out tactically that our best area for the forthcoming encounter, and possibly major battle, would be the Gransdon Plains which are two days' wolf ride away, so much quicker by eagle which would give us ample time to inform the king of the outcome and give him time to reinforce his defences if the outcome was bad for us. Our warriors formed up on the Gransdon Plains and awaited the Dark enemy. After a day, we had reports that a small force was approaching, the first signs of which were some black flying lizard-type creatures. These creatures spat acid. We lost many warriors in the air and on the ground. Eventually, after two hours we had killed all the creatures with a significant loss of five hundred warriors. Then small running creatures appeared. Not many, I might add, only around two hundred and none of them would surrender. So, we slaughtered them all with the loss of another twenty warriors. As warriors, we learnt a lot about our foes from this encounter, but unknown to us another force had attacked the capital. This force had not been detected, and again it was only a small one. We now believe the initial battle was more of a diversion to allow this small force to reach Great Porum undetected. We received a warning that Labatina on a flying beast had gained entry to the capital, killing many people and taking you, Row. Apparently, Karl, you were found under a dead Wolf warrior, who we believe gave his life to protect you. He must have lain on top of you as he died to stop the Dark and Labatina from finding you. We cannot be sure about this because we were not there, and nobody saw the abduction first-hand.'

'Oh my god, why?' asked Row.

'As I said, we think the first battle on the Gransdon Plains was totally a diversion for the real attack by your mother who wanted you and Karl, her daughter and son. The attack on the capital was the main objective, the other only a diversion so the main objective could be accomplished. A message was sent to all forces to intercept Labatina, rescue Row and capture the mad queen, if possible. If not, kill her and return you to the king. Your father was desperately worried about you. We had received reports of her progress and an ambush was arranged. Me and Tristan led two forces in the air. We had learnt that the best way to defeat the flying beasts was with airborne bowmen and Eagle warriors with spears. Raphina, Salina and Phina scouted below. Salina and Phina were your age at the time,' Kurt told her.

'Wow, that must have been frightening for them?'

'No, they had been trained and were with their mother, my life love. Here on Earth you would call her my wife.'

Tristan continued, 'We were engaged by an advanced small force of creatures which were defending the queen. We managed to defeat these quite easily, putting into effect what we had learnt hours earlier. We surrounded the queen, but she would not give up, so we killed the beast she was riding. I managed to grab you from her arms. All I remember were the hysterical screams coming from the queen as she plummeted to the ground on the dying creature. It haunts me still that that was not your mother as I had known her. I dove to the ground, guarded by some of the Eagle warriors, and handed you over to Raphina who, along with Salina and Phina and some Wolf worriers, returned you at great pace to the capital and your father.'

'Tristan followed the queen and the creature to the ground, trying in vain to rescue the queen from the stricken creature, but she was too violent. She tried to kill him as she fell,' Kurt told them.

'Eventually she hit the ground. Unfortunately, she had ended up underneath the creature which landed on top of her with its full weight. The flying lizard creature was pulled from your mother, the queen, but she was dead, or so we thought. That was not the end of it, her body was taken back to Great Porum and put in state for the people to pay their last respects and to lay any tributes to the queen that they had known and loved. Nothing more was seen or heard of the Dark army. Scouts were sent throughout the world but no trace of them was found, so for a time it was a mystery. A day before her ascension to the spirit world, her worldly body disappeared. There had been guards all around the capital and within the great hall where she had been laid. Nothing had been seen or heard throughout that night that might have been seen to be out of place. Your father was distraught, so we once again searched every corner Elemtum for her body but as time went on, several years later, after no word of your mother's body, the king fell in love with our sister. She was once Labatina's closest friend; they had grown up together. She was also very beautiful, a different beauty to Labatina, but as well as her beauty she also had an infectious smile, and sense of humour, just like you, Tom.' I do miss her,' Tristan told them, could sense the affection in his tone.

'She was your mother, Tom. Her name was Elizabeth De-Callen. As with your mother, Row, Karl, Labatina and the king were made for each other, they truly loved each other. The same went for Elizabeth and your father; he thought Labatina was dead and gone, as we all did. Elizabeth loved Row and Karl with all her heart. She loved you two as much as she loved her little Tom.'

'You know, I have had dreams about a beautifully kind blond-haired woman, now I know why,' said Row.

'I will explain the next part of the story but before I do, does anyone need another drink or the loo before I do?'

'I could do with a drink,' said Row and she walked into the kitchen. 'Anyone want a can of pop?' she shouted to them as she reached the fridge. Both Karl and Tom asked for one. Once Row had returned with the drinks and everyone had had a toilet break, Tristan continued.

'Who are Kurt and I? I am Wolf Lord Tristan Atta De-Callen, younger brother to Kurt Atta the Lord of the Wolf people. Kurt is the High Wolf Lord Kurt Atta De-Callen (Atta Wolf), my elder brother. He is the High Lord of the Wolf people and brother to the Great King Atta James Frederick of the Wolf and Eagle peoples, emperor and warrior of Elemtum. I am to the right of the great emperor and Kurt is to the left. That basically means we are the chosen warriors for the emperor; normally we are his bodyguards and most trusted. You, Rowena, are the next in line to be queen and empress of Elemtum; you are a Wolf warrior princess. Karl, you are second in line to the throne, you are a Wolf warrior prince. Finally, Tom, you are third in line and I'm sorry to say once again too young to be defined as a warrior at the moment, but the good news, Tom, is that you are the third in line, you can choose what type of warrior you will become, Wolf or Eagle.'

'Now that's cool, Tom, you can wait and see which warriors are the best, then choose,' Row told him.

'Yeh you're right, Row, I might be a Wolf warrior that flies like an Eagle,' replied Tom, with a big grin on his face.

'Knowing you, Tom, you just might be,' added Karl. That seemed to lighten everyone's mood and the princess and princes now seemed to be a little happier about their future.

'We've nearly finished,' Tristan told them. 'Since you have been away, your father and the elders of all the tribes have looked after Elemtum. All the people have turned their citadels and homelands into fortresses. This is because of the continued attacks from the Dark and their ever-massing evil forces, loyal to Labatina and Arthfael. They have started up again. Labatina had come back from the dead, I don't know why and for what end, but she and Arthfael are trying to slowly expand their empire,' said Tristan.

'So, why are we going back there?' asked Karl.

'It was decided you would be safer back in our world now, because Labatina has found you here. It would only be a matter of time until they found a way to get to you, probably by killing me and Kurt. At least back in our world the whole might of the Wolf and Eagle tribes can be trusted to protect you, as can ninety-nine per cent of the rest of our world.'

'Why would the people of Elemtum risk their lives for us?' asked Row

'You three are the future, a new hope for our world. You are the blood line of the Great King Atta Wolf and Fedora Elizabeth Eagle Queen, the greatest warriors in the history of Elemtum, whose union brought peace to our world a very long time ago. But that is definitely another story for another time. Basically, you are royalty to our world,' Kurt told them.

'We aren't royalty!' said Tom.

'You all are. You just don't realise it yet, but you are,' said Tristan.

Everyone went quite for a short time then Karl asked, 'Does anyone know why our mother turned evil? Against everyone who loved her so much?'

Tristan replied to Karl's question. 'No one really knew for sure, but they think it had something to do with coming to Earth. Somewhere she visited changed her, but along with Labatina only one other survived the expedition. Arthfael! He is the only one who knows what really happened, and that is still very much a secret. As we do not have him to ask, it will stay that way, for now anyway. It's getting late, so I think we should all retire and get some rest because we have a couple of long days ahead,' said Tristan.

'I'm going to go and check Salina and Phina, so can you boys go and get the camp beds and sleeping bags from the camper van? I think it would be better if we all sleep together tonight after what has happened today. We can move the oak table over to the corner of the room. After all, we do have two Wolf princes here, I'm sure they will be strong enough to do that. Then we will get Row's bed in here and set up the camp beds. That way we can keep an eye on each other, just in case. It will all be very snug,' said Kurt. Kurt left them and went to go outside to find the wolves when he turned and said, 'Well done, you lot. I have been very impressed with how you have all coped today. I am sorry to say there will be harder days ahead, but you are all strong and together we will deal with anything the Dark can throw at us.' He smiled and continued outside. The boys followed him and, in a short time, returned with the camp beds, setting them up and putting a sleeping bag on top of each. Then they helped Row bring her bed through from her bedroom. Once all was set up and ready, Karl realised he only had one pillow, Crap, he thought to himself, I hate only having one! He asked Row if she had any more. She happened to have three on her bed, so she was happy to give Karl one.

'Thanks, Row,' he said, then walked over to her and as he took the pillow from her, he kissed her on the cheek.

'What's that for?' she asked

'I'm just glad you're my sister,' he replied.

'That's so sweet.' Then she wrapped her arms around him and gave him a kiss back. 'Me too,' she replied.

Tom had noticed all this and, not to be left out, he dashed over to his new sister and gave her a cheesy kiss on the other cheek. 'Me three,' he said smiling. Then he dashed round to Karl and planted a soppy kiss on his cheek. 'You too, honey bunch,' he said.

Karl swung a punch at him but purposefully missed. 'Get out of here, weirdo.'

Tom ran back to his camp bed and jumped in. The camp bed promptly collapsed and Tom rolled out onto the floor. All three burst out laughing.

'You're mad as a hatter, Tom. Are you okay?' asked Row, 'I mean with everything. Your mum, dad and all that stuff?'

'I'm fine,' Tom replied, then he grinned.

Kurt walked in to see Tom sprawled on the floor next to a collapsed camp bed. 'Karl, what have you been up to?'

'Why is it always my fault?'

'To be fair, it was all self-inflicted,' Row told him.

'Tom playing the clown again?' Kurt said.

'Exactly that,' Karl added. Kurt apologised to Karl and took back the last remark he had made. 'Thank you,' Karl replied, and then he helped his brother re-assemble his bed while Kurt checked all the windows and doors making doubly sure all were secure.

'Your uncle Tristan will be sleeping near the front door; I will take the back. Salina is outside the front and Phina will be at the back. Now get your heads down and I will wake you at five, then we will all have a quick breakfast and leave,' Kurt informed them.

'What's happening tomorrow, Uncle Kurt? Row asked.

'We will be leaving in Tristan's Range Rover, heading north. It's going to be a long drive because we are going to the Scottish Highlands. We will camp there for the night then go to the World's Pathway and travel back to our world. I will explain about the gate tomorrow okay? So, get a good night's sleep and, Tom, no mucking about.' He then went over and kissed Row on the forehead, then he went over and patted Karl on the back and ruffled Tom's hair. 'Good night, all,' he said.

'Good night, Uncle Kurt,' came the replies. Kurt left them and, on the way, turned the light out and closed the door.

Then, from the now dark room, came, 'Good night, don't let the bed bugs bite,' Row said to the boys.

'Night,' replied Karl.

Nothing came from Tom; he was already asleep. All then stayed quiet. Row drifted away into a peaceful sleep, but Karl lay there in the darkness, wide-awake with thoughts of what his uncles had said racing through his mind. Then slowly, he began to fall asleep. Then he would suddenly think of something else that would wake him up, then another thought would smash into his brain and keep him awake. Finally, with the help of the comforting smell of his new sister coming from the pillow, his mind calmed and he fell asleep some hours later.

Chapter 6
The Journey North and the Pathway

Karl woke after what seemed to be only seconds, although it was in fact three hours after he had fallen asleep. The bright summer morning sun came through an open curtain, then he realised someone was talking. His eyes opened sleepily, and as he started to see through the blur, the muffled voice became clearer. He realised with a start, that Tom's face was very close to his, only inches away, then he finally understood what was being said. 'Come on, diddums, wake up.' Tom then pulled away from Karl, because he knew what would come next. An arm came from under the sleeping bag and swiped at where Tom had been moments before, but all the punch met was fresh air.

'Sod off.' Karl was not an early morning person and Tom knew it.

'I think you mean, sod off, Prince Tom, don't you, Karl?'

'I'll prince you, Tom,' said Karl, sitting up.

Row called over, 'Don't be nasty, Tom.'

Tom left his brother in peace and Row stretched her arms and yawned. 'I hate sleeping in clothes. You feel so dirty in the morning, and I must go and get a shower and change these smelly things. Would you like me to leave the shower running, Tom?'

'No thanks,' Tom replied.

Karl shouted over, 'Tom, getting a shower? You must be joking. You would have more luck finding the Loch Ness monster.'

'He's just jealous, because I'm naturally not smelly,' replied Tom.

'You can leave it on for me, please,' said Karl as Kurt came into the room looking bright, breezy and full of life,

'I hate you,' a bedraggled looking Row said as she passed her uncle on the way to the shower.

'You will have to be quick, Row, not your normal hour shower,' Tristan shouted through from the kitchen.

'Whatever,' Row replied with a smile, then she disappeared into the hall.

The smell of coffee and toast drifted through to the room from the open kitchen door. It mingled with the smell of sweaty bodies, but it made its way through to reach Karl. he suddenly sprang to life. 'Now I know what we need to do to get you up,' said Kurt. Karl replied with a grunt.

Tom finished packing away his bed and sleeping bag, then started on Karl's. 'Thanks, Prince Thomas,' said Karl as he headed for the toilet. When he had finished, Tom walked into the kitchen looking as alive as his uncle Kurt had been.

'That's what I like to see,' said Tristan as Tom bounded smiling into the kitchen, full of life. 'Cereal toast, orange, milk, tea or coffee, Tom? Only the best served here for a young prince. What would you like?' Tristan asked.

'Ah, cereal, toast, the lot for me please,' Tom replied.

Kurt looked at him. 'Hungry lad this morning, Tom.'

'I could eat a horse,' he replied. Tristan handed him a bowl of cornflakes, then two minutes later three pieces of buttered toast and a mug of tea.

As Tom finished his last bit of toast, Row walked into the kitchen. 'Morning all.'

'Morning, everyone in the kitchen replied, then Tom asked if there was any more toast, and also if there was any marmite or bananas.

'What? Together?' asked Tristan.

'Yes, it's lovely,' Tom replied.

'Sorry, Tom, I don't have any bananas or marmite.'

'Would you really have eaten that?' asked Row.

'Oh yes,' came Tom's reply.

'You're disgusting,' Row told him.

'Yep,' he replied with a grin.

Karl walked into the kitchen looking a lot more awake and refreshed than he had twenty minutes ago. 'You were quick. I've only just got out the shower myself,' said Row.

'I don't mess about,' Karl replied.

'Toast and tea or coffee?' Kurt asked.

'I think I had better have coffee,' answered Karl.

'You okay, Karl?' Row asked.

'I didn't sleep too well; in fact, I don't think I slept at all.'

'Oh, poor love, I had a great sleep,' she answered.

'Don't worry, Karl, you can sleep on the journey north; it will be a fair few hours,' said Tristan.

'I can't sleep on car journeys,' Karl replied.

'Oh really, just like you didn't fall asleep coming here then?' said Kurt sarcastically.

'Yeh, Karl, you were asleep minutes after we left our house in Suffolk,' Tom added.

Karl shrugged his shoulders to show he really didn't care then took the toast and coffee offered him by Tristan. As Karl was eating his toast and drinking his coffee, Tom finished his fifth piece of toast. Row looked at the boys and said, 'We are going to have to get to know each other better, you know. If I get in your space, just tell me to get lost, I won't be offended. I like quiet in the morning, until I wake up.'

'Tom!' said Karl.

'I like waking Karl up in the morning,' Tom said. 'He's so grumpy, it makes me laugh.'

'Okay, guys, it's time we left. Make sure you all have a sleeping bag, camp bed and pillows. Karl, Tom, can you pack them on the roof rack of Tristan's Range Rover along with our cooker and the tent from the campervan. There's a tarpaulin in the back that can go over the top, just in case it rains on our way north,' Kurt instructed. Everyone finished their breakfasts and set about getting ready to leave. The last rucksack was put on the roof rack, and Karl, who was now standing on the roof, started to unroll the tarpaulin which had elastic around all four sides. Tristan and Kurt then started to tighten and secure it. Five minutes later all was ready. Phina and Salina came round the corner of the cottage and started to eat the food Kurt had put out for them. Once they had finished, Kurt shouted as though he was in a western movie with John Wayne. 'Okay, yeh all mount up.'

Row was standing next to the boys, and they noticed she had tears in her eyes. 'Everything okay, Row?' Karl asked.

'Oh, I'm a little upset. This little cottage is all I've ever known. I'm just being sentimental; ignore me, I'll be fine,' she answered. Then she went and sat in the middle passenger seat in the back of the Range Rover. Tom joined her on the far side passenger seat and Karl jumped into the remaining seat behind the driver. The Range Rover was a lot bigger and more modern than Kurt's VW van.

'It's quite high, I've never been in one of these before,' Tom said.

'It's very comfortable as well. It won't take long for you to fall asleep if you're tired,' said Row. The back door opened and the two big wolves jumped in and curled up together, ready for the long journey and a good sleep, which they deserved, as they had been awake all night patrolling the local area around the cottage. Kurt drove out through the front gate; Karl jumped out and closed it behind them. As Karl approached the vehicle to get back in, Kurt put his foot down on the accelerator and drove off, leaving Karl behind, then he stopped. When Karl reached the Range Rover once more, Kurt did the same thing again. Karl gave up running behind the car after the third time and started to walk.

'Don't be so cruel, Uncle Kurt,' said Row. This time when Karl reached the car, Row opened the door for him.

Karl jumped in and fastened his seat belt. 'Very funny,' he said sarcastically.

'It made me laugh,' said Tom.

'It would,' replied Karl.

The Range Rover set off down the track until it reached the main road then headed towards the A1 north. The vehicle was filled with the sound of small talk to start with, but after an hour all was quiet. The rear seat passengers were now fast asleep, as were the two wolves in the back. A pillow resting against a window had Karl's head on it, Row's head was on Karl's shoulder and Tom's head was on Row's shoulder. The vehicle continued north. They drove all day, only stopping once for fuel and a toilet break, then they continued until early evening when Tristan, who was now driving, pulled off the main road on to a dirt track that led through a forest. The vehicle's headlights illuminated the track, but all around them the forest was as black as night. Above them the trees made a forest roof which was occasionally broken by the bright blue moon every time they reach a break in the trees. Everyone was now awake, woken by the jolting of the Range Rover as it bounced its way up the track. Ten pairs of eyes in the back searched the darkness outside the windows for any clue about where they were. Not that Karl, Row or Tom would have had any idea where they were if they had seen anything anyway. At long last they stopped in what they could just make out was an open area of relatively flat ground in the forest, wide enough for the moonlight to almost illuminate it in-between plunging into darkness as intermittent clouds floated across and momentarily obstructed the moon.

'Okay, you can get out and stretch your legs, but don't go too far, and stay together,' Tristan told them. Kurt went round and let Salina and Phina out who jumped down and stretched their backs then they followed the youngsters.

'I can hear a stream,' Row said, then she and Tom started to head towards the sound.

'Stay where I can see you,' shouted Kurt.

'Where are we, Uncle Kurt?' Karl asked.

'We are in the Scottish Highlands. I have been here many times. It's where our ancestors first came to Earth through the World's Pathway world passage. I have checked the weather forecast and it looks like we should have a good night tonight, but we will have to put the tent up because in the morning cold air rushes down from the nearby mountains and it can get very damp and chilly. There is also a thick fog that can come down and it drenches everything that's not covered.' Kurt then shouted out to Tom and Row to come and help Karl set up camp.

As Tom and Row came into view, Karl asked them if they had found the river? He was told by Tom that it was in fact only a small stream, which he said was very cold. 'like ice water' were his actual words.

'That's because it has come down from the mountains,' said Kurt.

'What mountains?' asked Row

'When the sun rises, you will see a mountain right in front of you. It's quite magnificent. The colours of the heather are truly breathtaking. In the distance, you will see several more. Once the tent is up you can start on the barbeque, Karl. There's two cool boxes under the tent on the roof rack. One has meat in it, the other pasta, some salad and stuff like bread and sauce,' Kurt told them. 'Tristan and I are going off to check the gate to the pathway and the surrounding area. We should be back in about an hour. Phina will stay with you and Salina will come with us.'

Tristan went over to the wolves; all their eyes went red as Tristan told them the plan.

'Right, we will see you all in a short while,' said Kurt then he, Tristan and Salina walked off into the black night and soon disappeared from view. Kurt shouted back 'Oh, I forgot, Tom, best you get that sword out, just in case dragons attack while we are away.'

'You're joking, right?' Row called back to him.

'Yes, only joking,' came the reply. 'Speak to Karl, he will fill you in on Tom's sword.'

'I could handle a dragon,' said Tom.

'Sure, you could,' Karl butted in.

'I know you could, little man,' said Row.

'I'm not that little,' replied Tom.

'I know you're not, Tom, but you will always be my little man, no matter how tall and strong you get,' said Row.

'Okay, we had better get on with this tent and get the barbeque going. Do you think you and Tom will be able to put the tent up while I will start the barbeque?' asked Karl.

'Why don't you and Tom put the tent up and I will get the barbeque ready?' replied Row.

'I don't think so, the barbeque is a man's domain,' replied Karl.

'Not in my house. Dad always got me to do the barbeques.'

'Okay, let's come to a compromise. Tom and I will put the tent up, you set up and light the barbeque, and I will cook. What do you think?' said Karl.

'Yes, I agree with that, "but" we will both cook. How about that?' interjected Row.

'It's a deal,' said Karl, a little reluctantly, but he had a feeling he would not win that one if he had pushed it too much. Karl climbed up the little ladder at the back of the Range Rover and unfastened the tarpaulin exposing the camping gear. 'Heads!' he shouted, as he threw the tent canvas down along with the poles that landed on the ground with a loud clang.

'Well, if there are any dragons around, they would have heard that,' Tom shouted up at his brother.

'Bring it on,' came from the roof of the camper. 'Here you go, Row,' Karl shouted down and passed her the two cool boxes.

'Don't you think it's really dark here? I've never really thought about it before, but it is very dark. I can only just see you up there,' said Row.

'It's because there's no ambient light,' Karl said as he climbed down the ladder and jumped to the ground.

'What's that?' asked Tom.

'I can't say I've heard that one before either,' said Row.

'Ambient light is the non-natural light that lights up the night sky. Things in a city that illuminate the night sky like the streetlights and the lights from buildings. Even though you may be in the country, you still get a little ambient light unless you are miles from any city or town. Here in the highlands, there isn't a lot of light because there is nothing nearby. That's why you can hardly see your own hands in front of you, especially as there is now a thick cloud covering the moon.'

'Oh, I see'.

'What about you, Tom, do you understand?'

'I think so,' he said.

'It doesn't matter, Tom, it's not important anyway,' said Karl.

'I've never really noticed before. I suppose it's because I've never been anywhere so far away from anywhere,' said Row. Just then the dark clouds parted, and the moon shone through, illuminating everywhere around them. 'Typical. That wouldn't have happened if we hadn't been talking about it,' said Row.

'That's better, I can see what I'm doing now,' Karl said, as he rummaged through the pole bag looking for the right poles to start the tent construction.

'What sort of tent is it?' asked Row.

'It's a dome tent. It has three separate sleeping compartments for three people, and two people can sleep in the middle bit,' said Tom.

'It's very easy to put up once you find the right poles. Lay it flat, put the poles in and up it goes, then just peg it down. We will probably finish it before you light the barbeque,' challenged Karl.

'We will see,' said Row with a smile, as she placed one of the tent poles behind the cool box. As Karl and Tom assembled the tent, Row prepared the food and made up the charcoal for the barbeque. The three of them chatted away about what might lie ahead for them and what it would be like travelling through the gate to the pathway.

'I bet there are loads of strange animals,' Tom said.

'No doubt in my mind at all,' said Karl.

'I would like to know what sort of clothes they wear? If they don't have TV, I bet they don't have fashion,' Row said.

'How do you figure that? Romans, Elizabethans, Tudors all had fashion and didn't have TV, did they?' said Karl

'You're right, I was being a bit dippy.' But more to the point, have you nearly finished? I have. I only have to light the barbeque now.'

'Nearly there,' Karl said as he climbed the ladder again.

'What's he doing?' Row asked Tom.

'There's a pole missing, and he thinks it must still be up there!' he pointed lazily towards the roof rack.

'Hey, Karl,' Row shouted as she lit the barbeque, 'I win.'

'Only because we've lost a pole. I think we might have left it back home,' he said, as he threw the last rucksack from the roof rack to the ground.

'What does it look like?' shouted Row.

'A pole,' Karl shouted back.

'What? Like this one?' she said, as she lifted it from behind the box.

'You cheat. We win by default,' Karl cried out.

'Well, that should have taught you two things,' she said smiling.

'And what are they?' Karl replied.

'Never bet me at anything, because you will always lose, and never trust a woman you don't know well.'

'I will accept the last thing, but not the first. Hopefully, we have a lot of life left to prove you wrong, Row.'

'Err, don't speak like that, it's creepy,' she said. They all stood round the barbeque watching the flames, mesmerised as they took hold.

'How long have they been gone now?' asked Tom

'About an hour so far I reckon, according to my watch,' Karl said. Eventually the flames died down and a red glow remained under a white ash.

'That's about ready, we may as well start cooking,' Row informed them.

'If you start that, Row, Tom and I will set the beds up in the tent and get it ready inside. Then I'll make sure you are doing that right.'

'Very funny,' she replied. Karl could just make out the sarcastic smile on her face in the dark.

When the tent was finished, Karl stood next to Row. 'Don't worry, Row, I'm not going to say a thing,' he said as he watched Row turn the meat.

'Best you don't,' she said, brandishing a two-pronged fork in his direction.

Tom sat down in one of the folding chairs, the type with a cup holder in the arm, and laid his head back and gazed up at the stars. 'It's strange to think we are from somewhere out there.'

Everyone looked up at the stars, just then something caught Karl's eye. 'What's that?' he said. 'Look to the centre of the moon, it's a flying man. Can you see it? Look, it's moving to the left'

'Oh yes, I can see it.'

'Oh yes, so can I.,'

'It's a bird.'

'No, it's a man.'

'No, it's an angel,' said Tom, and then the figure was gone.

'How strange was that?' said Row.

'You're telling me,' said Karl.

'We did see it, didn't we?' Tom asked.

'Most definitely,' Karl confirmed.

'It could have been superman,' Tom laughed.

'What are you lot looking up at?' came from the blackness. Startled, they stopped looking up and turned to face the voice.

'It's you,' Row said as Kurt and Tristan approached.

'I hope you're not burning the dinner?' Kurt asked.

'Oh crap, I forgot about that,' Row said, dashing to the barbeque, instantly forgetting about the flying figure that Karl now put down to a strange shaped cloud and the moonlight.

Nothing was burnt, so they all pulled up a chair and tucked into their barbeque feast. Once finished, they all cleaned up then sat around with hot chocolate, chatting about what they would miss and what was to come.

Tom told his uncles they all thought that they may have seen superman flying past the moon. Everyone laughed and then Tristan said 'You aren't actually too far off, Tom. What you saw was probably an angel looking at you all.'

'You're having us on, aren't you, there's no such thing as angels, are there?' Row asked.

'Well actually, Row, I'm not having you on, you may meet some angels tomorrow. If you can't get through the door to our world, you will be going to our world with the angels, but now it's time we all got some sleep, so the angels will have to wait till the morning,' said Tristan.

'You can't tell us that and just leave it like that,' said Karl.

'I can and I am. We all need a good night's sleep. it will be morning soon enough and then you will be all grumpy because you need more sleep.'

'That's not fair,' said Tom.

'Nothing is fair, you will soon learn that, Tom. Now, off to bed,' said Kurt. After hugs and kisses all round they all went and settled down in their sleeping bags on their camp beds. Phina and Salina stayed outside on guard duty to let Tristan and Kurt catch up on their sleep. Tom fell asleep thinking about angels, as did Row, but Karl just fell asleep.

In the morning, Karl moved over to where his sleeping brother lay, finding the zip to his sleeping bag he pulled it down, exposing Tom to the chill air.

'That's no way to wake your brother,' Row said to him as she watched him from the entrance to the tent all wrapped up in a nice warm fleece and deputy dog hat.

'It's the only way to get him up, believe me, otherwise he'll be in there all day.'

'Says you. Don't forget I saw you yesterday morning remember,' said Row.

'I hadn't had any sleep that night, that's the difference. He has slept like a log,' replied Karl.

Tom sat up and searched for the zip to close the sleeping bag. 'Leave me alone,' he mumbled, still half asleep.

'Oh, poor thing, he's still asleep,' said Row feeling sorry for her little brother. Karl grabbed the bottom of the sleeping bag and pulled it and Tom out of the tent into the chill damp open air.

'Okay, okay, I'm awake,' Tom shouted at his brother, holding on for dear life.

'Get up, Tom. The sooner you're up, the sooner we will all have breakfast then go to the gate. Then we'll be off to our real world.'

'I'll cook breakfast. It's all in a can, so it won't take long,' said Row.

Tom dragged himself out of his sleeping bag and wandered over to Row. 'What are we having?'

'All-day breakfast, Tom.'

'Okay then, can I have all-day breakfast please?'

'Can I have my all-day breakfast cold, please?' Karl asked.

'Oh no, you're joking, aren't you? Really, Karl, that's what you want?' Cold beans and sausages and stuff, really?' she asked.

'Yes, I love cold beans. I always have them cold. I think they taste better than when they're warm.'

'He's weird like that. He's always eaten beans from a can while they're cold,' Tom added.

'What about you, Tom?' Row asked.

'Warm please. Cold are disgusting.'

'Has anybody seen Uncle Kurt or my dad yet?' Row asked as she stirred the beans on the camping stove.

Karl told her he thought they went to check the gate to the pathway, so Row put theirs on to warm.

'I don't suppose they will be too long,' she said.

Tom, Karl and Row sat around chatting while they finished their breakfasts. Then their uncles reappeared. 'Everybody ready? Me and your uncle Tristan will just grab something to eat then we'll be off. Any left, Row?'

'I've left some in the pot for you. I'll just get it. You two sit down. Is everything okay?'

'The pathway is barred to us, so we have contacted the spirit angels who will be here in about an hour. So, we'll scoff this lot down and be off,' Kurt told them.

'Uncle Kurt, do you want us to take the tent down while you eat?' Karl asked.

'No, it's okay, Karl. Your uncle Tristan and I will use it again until we can get through the door to the pathway. We still don't know why we can't use the door. I have tried to get messages back to your farther, but we have had no reply which I must admit it is a little worrying.' After everyone had eaten, they set off for the gate. Kurt was leading the way and Tristan was watching the rear. The two wolves were out to the flanks. Row, Tom and Karl were in the middle of the group where they had the best protection from any unwanted attention. They walked through the heather, along the stream bank, towards the base of the closest large mountain. After fifteen minutes, the uncles stopped, and the wolves stayed out to the flanks. Row, Tom and, finally, Karl caught up with Kurt.

'It's okay, Uncle Kurt, we aren't tired yet, you can carry on.'

Tristan joined them. walking along with Karl. He had heard what Row had said to Kurt. 'We've reached our destination, the "gate", he told them.

'Where's the gate?' Tom asked Tristan. 'I can't see it.'

Row and Karl also looked around searching for the door, both a little puzzled about its whereabouts as well. 'It's right in front of you, you just have to see it,' Tristan told them.

'I can't see anything,' said Row. Karl agreed as did Tom.

'Can you see the bright purple heather at the foot of the mountain? It's right there, you're just not looking. What you need to do is block all other thoughts out of your mind, then stare at that spot,' said Kurt. 'Do you remember those pictures in the shops and the magazines, the ones that were just little spots until you stared at it, almost going cross eyed, then your brain recognised it as a picture, and you saw it? It's the same sort of thing; it's to stop the humans seeing and finding it,' he said.

'I can see it! I can see it!' shouted Tom. It's not as big as I imagined.'

'Oh yes, so can I,' said Karl. It's got a big brass handle, all dark old looking wood.'

'That's it, well done. Boys. What about you, Row?'

'I can't see a thing. Some rocks and heather, no door.'

'Do what I did, Row. Almost go cross eyed, stare and really concentrate,' Tom explained to her.

'No, it's not working,' she said. Then suddenly, 'yes, yes. I see it. I see it.'

'Karl, go up to the door and put your hand on the brass handle. It's okay, it won't hurt you,' said Kurt. Everyone watched as Karl nervously approached the door.

'It's okay, Karl, it won't bite you,' shouted Tristan. Karl reached out and clenched the handle.

As he did, a funny sensation went through his body, as though he was being searched from the inside out, then a booming voice said to him, 'Welcome, Prince Karl Atta De-Callen. It has been a long time and here you are now all most a warrior. But I am sorry, I cannot let you in for your own safety. Pl… pl… pl… please come in. No stay out, it's no… no… not safe.'

Karl felt something wet and soggy in his hand. He looked down. The door handle had turned into a bleeding heart. He let it go with a gasp of shock, then immediately he released the handle it was brass again and the bloody heart had disappeared. He stood motionless for a couple of seconds with his back to the others.

'What are you doing? Ae you going in or not?' said Tom.

'Did you not hear it and see the blood and the heart?' Karl shouted back, as he turned to look at everyone.

'No, we never saw or heard anything, Karl,' Row shouted back.

'We won't see anything, Karl. The door will only appear in one mind at a time. You will each have to approach the door to get passage. Obviously, Karl, you did not gain entry,' said Kurt.

'What did the gate say to you, Karl?' asked Row.

'It said I could not enter because I would be in danger, or that's what I thought it said. Then it said I could go in, and then it said it wasn't safe. And then it turned into a bleeding heart,' he told them.

'That's exactly what it told your uncle Tristan and me, except it never said we could go in,' Kurt told them all. 'Tom, Row, go and try the gate. You first, Tom.'

Tom did exactly as his brother had done and he got the same answer. 'Cool,' Tom said as he walked back.

Row passed him, and they gave each other a high five.

'Nope, looks like an angel for me I thinks. Said I was in danger,' Tom said as Row headed for the door.

Row returned from the door after a minute, a little longer than the other two. 'The door said something different to me, it just said, "Lady, you are welcome. Your mother awaits your return... You may enter". What does that mean?' she asked.

'That is very worrying. It probably explains why we can't get passage through the gate. If I'm not mistaken, someone or something now has control of the gate and the pathway,' said Tristan.

'Yes, I agree. It sounds like the gate is fighting with something, or some force that is trying to control it. That probably explains why there has been a sudden appearance of Dark assassins here on Earth. This is not good, coupled with the fact that we have had no communication with Elemtum for almost a week now. What in Atta's name could have happened?' said Kurt.

'Well, that means you three are in for a very unforgettable journey with a spirit angel and onward with Gabriel. That's the only way I can see you getting home,' said Tristan.

'What if home is not safe anymore? As you have said, you have had no contact with Elemtum for some time,' asked Karl.

'That is a risk we must take, Karl. The spirit angels will tell us if they know of any major problems on Elemtum. I will speak to the spirit angels and ask them to inform Gabriel about our concerns. If Gabriel senses any danger, you are to be brought back. Trust me, you will be safe with the angels and Gabriel,' said Kurt.

'I could always go through. After all, the gate said I could pass, and my mother is waiting for me,' said Row.

'Yes, I know, but your mother, as far as we know, is still evil. Who knows what would await you? No, you go home with beings we trust. Gabriel and the spirit angels, they cannot be turned, you will be safe with them,' said Tristan.

'Yes, I totally agree,' added Kurt. Just then a cool breeze tickled the necks of the boys and Row and made them shiver. 'Hello, Frances, my old friend, greetings.

You are most welcome,' Kurt said, as he looked behind his three young wards.

'Welcome, Frances, greetings to you also,' said Tristan. Then both he and Kurt momentarily bowed their heads. Karl, Tom and Row all turned in unison to see who their uncles were talking to. In front of them stood a very large thing, with massive outstretched wings. It was invisible. No, it isn't. It was clear. No, not even that. It was not there, but they could see it, the thing. Their eyes focused. It was a winged man. No, a bird man. No, a warrior with wings. No, a gentle creature with feathered arms. What was it? The three youngsters were all thinking the same. The form began to shrink in front of them until it was the size of a man and they could no longer see through it. In front of them now stood a young man, not much older than Karl, with long flowing hair, he, 'it', was covered with a shimmering light blue glow over all its body including its head.

'Greetings from Gabriel,' it said. 'Gabriel has been watching you. He has instructed me to guide you to him so that you can be returned to your home world. As your wise uncles have said, I am Francis. Behind me are Michael and Layner.'

Behind Frances, floating at head height were two ripples in the morning sky. As they looked closer, it was actually figures that they could see. 'What are they?' asked Tom.

'Frances is a spirit angle, Tom. He was once a great warrior from the Eagle people, a hawk lord. Now he is a spirit waiting to join Gabriel,' said Tristan. 'Did you notice that while he was speaking to you his mouth didn't move? That's because he has no mouth and the form you see is just a form he has created to keep you calm. He communicates through your soul, unlike the wolves that use a form of telepathy. His real form is the first one you saw; your mind could not sort out what it was because your brain has never seen anything like that before.'

'They are just amazing,' said Row, 'but if he is a spirit, how are we going to travel with him?'

'First you must communicate with the spirit. Be calm, and then the spirit will find what you wish to say. It's the same with all spirit angles. When he is in the form you can see in front of you now, you can just talk normally. He will understand you,' Kurt told her.

Karl thought of nothing, which was very hard to do at a time like this. Just as he was going to give in, he started to feel very calm. Then, he didn't so much hear as felt sound, 'Greetings, Karl, I am Michael. You will join with me for the journey. You do not have to do anything, just relax. I will come to you. It will feel like you are floating in a timeless space. You will not be able to move. Don't be scared, I will calm you. Your soul will become part of my soul. Your body will become like it is dead, because your soul will have left it. Your physical body will be carried along by my virtual spirit. You will be safe. I will keep your earthly body alive while I take you to Gabriel who will then cross the divide between this world and your home world. When you arrive in your home world, you might feel a little nauseous but that will be your spirit settling back into your body. When you awake you will be as you are now. You will be completely safe during this whole transformation, but you will not remember how you journeyed to your world afterwards. You will know from where you came and the reason you are there or how.' As Michael finished, Layner and Frances had also explained the same things to Tom and Row.

'Why don't you and Uncle Kurt come with us, and the wolves, how are they going to travel?' asked Row.

'I am too old,' he replied, 'you are young, and your souls are receptive. Ours are not, we can only use the pathway. Don't worry, we will see you soon enough. Your journey will only take seconds in your mind, ours will be a day at best, or a week at worst,' replied Tristan.

'That's not fair,' she replied.

'Life's not always fair, Rowena, you will come to realise that. Now it's time to leave. Say a quick goodbye, then the angles will take you home.'

Row hugged Tristan. 'I don't want to go, Dad. Let me stay and I will travel with you "please",' she pleaded.

'Row, look at me,' Tristan said as he lifted her head to look at him. 'This is the safest way for you all to get home. I will be with you as soon as possible. Believe me, if there was an easier way, we would do it, but there isn't, I promise.'

Row wiped the tears away from her cheeks. 'I know, Dad. I've never been away from you, and I suppose I'm just a little scared, that's all.'

'You will be fine, Row. You have your brothers with you, and they will be feeling the same, I'm sure. look after each other until Kurt and I catch up with you.' He then gave Row a kiss on her forehead. 'Go on, you'll be fine I promise.'

'Right then, if everyone is ready it's time to go,' said Kurt.

'What about our stuff, the stuff we packed back at our cottage?' asked Karl

'We will take that with us through the gate. Don't worry, we won't leave it behind,' replied Kurt.

'Who are we going to meet on the other side, I mean in our world?' asked Karl.

'I'm glad you asked that, Karl, because I had completely forgotten about that. Gabriel will take you to a place close to where my wife and son are. You will meet with my son Raif. He will then take you somewhere safe for your onward journey to your father.'

They all said their final goodbyes, then all three of them turned to face the angels who had all landed in front of them and were all now in human form and size. Row, Karl and Tom looked at the angels; they all had the same feeling inside them. 'I know you, you're a friend, but I can't think when and where I last saw you, or for that matter, who you are.' They all felt happy and relaxed, then they all heard the same thing in their minds.

'Come to me, you will be safe, you have nothing to fear.' As they walked towards them, the angels now had their wings outstretched towards them. The angels embraced them and cradled them close. A feeling of comfort and reassurance flowed through them, they were happy and contented.

Kurt and Tristan looked on, the wolves at their sides. Kurt shouted out, 'We will see you all soon, remember Gabriel will be watching over you. You will be safe.'

Row could feel herself falling into and becoming part of the spirit angel she was with. Karl and Tom began to feel exactly the same, then they all thought, 'This has got to be a dream.' Then all three disappeared into the angels and were gone from the sight of the onlookers. Then the angels disappeared, flying high into the sky with their large wings. Then they were gone.

'I hope we are doing the right thing,' Tristan said to his brother.

Phina's thoughts drifted into their minds, 'Don't doubt yourselves now, you have both done good by these children who are now heading back to where they belong. They are in the best company possible, besides yourselves. Who could you trust more to look after them than the angels?'

'You're right, Phina. Of course, you're right. The children are in good hands and we will be with them soon. Our biggest priority now is getting ourselves back home through the gate. Who knows why we have been stranded, but I am sure we will find out soon enough.'

Flying through the air inside the angels, the children could see all around them as if they were out in the sky flying on their own. They could not see the angels that held them within, but they could feel their presence. To any human eye below that happened to be searching the skies, all was clear. The three children drifted into a happy sleep, and as they did the angels told them stories of the world they were going to, so at least they would have some memories of the world that they had been whisked away from a whole lifetime ago.

The wolves and the warriors walked back towards the gate as the sun lifted into the sky and began to draw the damp air from the Scottish Highlands. 'What must be going on to stop the gate from giving us passage home? I can't ever remember a time when this has ever happened before,' said Tristan.

'I can't either. Can you remember when King Frederick took Phina and Salina's mother through the passage to bring Queen Labatina back home from her first journey to Earth, after her first disappearance?' asked Kurt.

'Yes,' replied Tristan, 'when we had to fight and kill the Dark menace warriors when they held the entrance to the passage at the gate.'

'Yes, that's right. Do you remember, at the time the gate told us that while the menace warriors held it, they controlled it and the power that held the gate could not be defeated as long as they held the entrance gate. Remember?' Kurt asked.

'That's right, I remember, the preachers had to re-adjust the gate's logic. I wonder if the gate and passage have been taken once again? If that is the case, then our warriors should be responding quite fast. But what could have happened to the garrison that was protecting the mighty gate entrance in Elemtum? They can't have taken the Great Porum on the other side.' Tristan said.

'That's the worry. Something is very wrong. Maybe they have entered the pathway from somewhere else and not Great Porum. They could be totally oblivious to what is happening.'

'You have point there, Kurt. It has never, to our knowledge, happened before. We have been away for a time, it might have just happened. I'm sure we will find out soon.'

They made their way over to the gate and Kurt placed his hand on its brass handle, 'You are in danger, Lord De-Callen, get away from the gate, fast. I can't control what is coming through the passage towards you' screamed the door, as the brass handle turned to the bleeding heart.

'Quickly, we must hide. Something is coming that the door tells me it can't control. The Dark, if I'm not mistaken,' Kurt shouted to his companions. They ran back towards the stream and up a small hill that was covered in bright purple heather. They hid behind some large boulders that shielded them from anyone coming out through the gate. It also gave them an escape route if needed. Kurt told the wolves to fan out and observe from further round the hill. 'If anything untoward happens to us, hide in the highlands until help arrives. I don't know what's coming, but I will put a kingdom on the fact that it's probably got something to do with Labatina and the Dark.'

Phina and Salina ran off to take up their positions and observe the gate and the surrounding area.

'Do you have your rayzor?' asked Tristan of his brother.

'I never go anywhere without it,' replied Kurt, producing his fighting knife. It was of a similar construction to a bowie knife on Earth but slightly larger. It had three subtle differences. The end of the blade was slightly curved, and the back of the knife was serrated. It also had been especially balanced to enhance the fighting style of its owner. Kurt smiled as the rayzor glinted in the sunlight.

Tristan also grinned as he withdrew his own rayzor. 'At least we will take the devils with us if we have to fight,' he said. Kurt and Tristan lay in their vantage point and observed the gate. Five minutes passed, then they noticed the brass handle turn and the gate slowly opened. A person wearing the uniform of a learned preacher very nervously stepped out. He stopped, then turned his head and looked back into the darkness behind the door from where he had just come. Looking on, Kurt and Tristan recognised the face of Yan Hassen, a preacher to the very young academics he had taught before they joined the warrior training academy. What worried both Kurt and Tristan was the fact that Yan looked terrified. This they knew was totally the opposite to the happy carefree preacher he normally was. Yan took a few more steps then stopped and scanned the area. Kurt and Tristan both heard a muffled shout from behind Yan. They still couldn't see who was shouting from the dark of the passage.

Suddenly Yan shouted, 'Kurt, Tristan, it's a trap!' Then he suddenly made a break and dashed in the direction that Kurt and Tristan were observing from. 'It's a trap, it's a trap. Dark vengeance,' he screamed. He was cut short when the head of a throwing lance protruded from the centre of his chest. The force of the lance hitting him knocked him off his feet and sent him sprawling to the ground where he stayed motionless, the lance stave sticking out of his back, pointing skyward. From within the passage, four Dark vengeance lancers walked out into the morning light and stood still. The lancers stood upright, scanning the area ahead of them in the direction where Kurt and Tristan lay observing them. Their black armoured breast plates were glinting in the sunlight, the rest of their bodies clothed in black leather apart from the blood red cloaks that dropped down their backs. Like all Dark vengeance warriors, they had mutilated faces and black ponytails that lay down their backs over their red cloaks. The foremost lancer walked up to the lifeless body of Yan and kicked it hard in the side. After no reaction and satisfied the preacher was dead, he stamped on Yan's back and pulled the lance from it. As he did so, he smelt the fresh blood on the tip of the lance. Grinning, he indicated to the other lancers to come forward to where he was standing. The first of the lancers to reach him knelt next to the shoulders of the dead Yan, pulled a knife from his belt and proceeded to cut the head from Yan's lifeless body. Then he raised the head high in front of the lead lancer and screamed a curdling lament to the triumphant lancer. Then he tossed the head back towards the open gate.

Quietly Kurt whispered to Tristan, 'This is a hunting party; demon dogs will come next with the…' Kurt stopped talking as two demon dogs emerged from the gate on thick spiked chains, held by the now visible Dark legion master. Behind him followed three condemned Dark warriors. Condemned because they had fled in a previous battle, now they were at the beck and call of the legion master to prove they were worthy or they would die. They were now all out in the open in front of the gate. Behind them the door closed.

'How did they get into the gate?' Tristan whispered.

'Shall we find out and avenge the slaughter of poor Yan?' answered Kurt.

'Filth! Where are you? I smell your fear. Show yourselves and die like warriors and not the little girls that you are,' the legion master shouted from the front of his warriors.

Kurt and Tristan stood up and walked clear of the boulders, so they could be seen. The demon dogs strained on their chained leashes, their teeth bared, saliva dripping onto the heather beneath them. Kurt noticed what the vengeance warriors had not. Phina and Salina had made their way to the demon warriors' right, creeping ever closer towards them.

'Surrender to us and I will let you die an honourable warrior's death, otherwise you die here and now in this foreign world, like the scum that you are. The decision is yours,' shouted Kurt.

The legion master replied, 'Ah, you show yourselves. Your death will be even sweeter than I had imagined, Wolf Lord. The queen will be mightily impressed with your heads when I throw then at her feet. Now die.' With those words, the demon dogs were released and immediately headed straight for Tristan and Kurt. Crazed with the smell of their impending feast they did not see the two wolves appear and bound towards them. The legion master screamed at the dogs, but they could only see the two warriors standing in front of them on the rise of the hill. They could taste their blood as they ran at them. Phina hit the first dog from the side, her jaws ripping a lethal gash in the dog's neck. Then she rolled over the top of the dog, still gripping on to it with all her might and power, bringing it crashing down stone dead onto the heather. Salina caught the left hind leg of the second dog, ripping its tendons, causing the leg to crumple under its own weight. The demon dog yelped out in pain. Salina held the crippled animal, avoiding its attempts to bite her. Phina moved in front of the dog as it snapped out at her, but she was just too far away from the crazed animal's jaws. Phina attacked the creature's other hind leg, totally disabling it and leaving the demon dog totally helpless. This time the dog did not yelp; its eyes burned with hate as it tried to drag itself forward.

Tristan walked calmly up to the beast. Avoiding the flaying head and teeth, he plunged his rayzor into the top of the demon dog's head, killing it instantly. Kurt moved to Tristan's side, followed by Phina and Salina.

The legion master screamed with rage at his warriors, 'Don't just watch them, kill them all, or I will have all your heads. Go, damn you.' The four condemned warriors ran towards Kurt and his companions, howling and screaming obscenities as they ran, their hammers, swords and pickaxes waving as they neared the top of the hill.

Kurt smiled and turned to Tristan and the wolves and said, 'That's his second mistake, separating his forces. They have no chance now, one warrior each, they are truly condemned... condemned to die.' Tristan took up his battle stance and Kurt followed, then they waited. As, the condemned warriors reached them, the lead warrior ran at Tristan, his battle axe swinging wildly from left to right. As he reached Tristan, the axe went above his head and with all his might he swung it down at Tristan. Anticipating what the condemned warrior was trying to do, Tristan side stepped the blow. The warrior's momentum kept him going and the axe stuck in the ground, embedding itself deep in the earth. Realisation crossed the warrior's face. He instantly knew that he had made a drastic error and that error would cost him his worthless life. Tristan swung his rayzor to his left and brought the sharp blade down on the nape of the warrior's neck. Death was fast as his head was separated from his body in one skilled movement. Tristan immediately turned to face the next aggressor as the warrior's body slumped down onto the axe that was sticking out of the ground. His head landed in the heather feet away.

Kurt ran at the second condemned warrior who was holding his war hammer in both his hands. He pulled it back, taking the hammer over his right shoulder ready for a strike at the Wolf warrior. Kurt leapt feet first at the warrior's chest, hitting him with all his weight, pushing the warrior backwards and sending his hammer flying out of his grip. It thundered into the third Dark warrior running behind him, hitting his knee, snapping it and causing him to crumple to the floor screaming. Phina then leapt on him and finished him off with her razor-sharp teeth. Kurt, standing on the second warrior's chest, took both hands and thrust his rayzor deep into the warrior's ribcage, penetrating his heart and killing him instantly. Kurt looked up to see the fourth condemned man running back towards the lancers. 'Kill the cowardly dog, he has obviously not learnt his lesson.'

The legion master shouted at the lancers as the fleeing warrior approached them. The lancer that had slain Yan thrust his lance into the fleeing warrior as he ran past, stopping him in his tracks. The warrior fell to his knees and the lancer kicked him off his lance. He fell backwards, dead on the purple heather. The lancer then drew back his lance and launched it at Kurt. Seeing what the lancer was doing and tracking the lance that was hurtling rapidly towards him, he moved slightly left and pulled it out of the air as it flew past him. Twisting fast and using its momentum, Kurt threw the lance back into the air in the direction it had come from, all with one magnificently skilled movement which was almost quicker than the eye could see. The lance flew off, picked up speed and height, flew over the owner's head, then changed its angle and dived at the legion master whose reactions were not as good as Kurt's. When the legion master realised what was happening, it was too late. The lance struck the master square in his upper chest, piercing his gold armour and bowling him backwards into the purple heather where he also died.

Now outnumbered, the two remaining lancers looked at each other in disbelief. 'Get them,' the now lance-less lancer shouted. Screaming, the second lancer ran at Kurt, then he must have thought twice about tackling Kurt because he changed direction and ran towards the now smiling Tristan. As Tristan goaded the screaming lancer, he ran towards him where the two wolves pounced on him. He stood no chance against Phina and Salina who went straight in for the kill and tore him apart. The last enraged and screaming lancer ran over to the dead legion master, snatched the sword from his dead leader's hand that was still clasped around it as testament to the speed at which he had died. Turning to face his enemy, the last lancer suddenly found himself looking up into the bright blue Scottish sky, confusion now etched all over his face. Then he felt the pain and as he noticed the rayzor sticking out of his chest, pointing skywards, the realisation struck him – he was dead! Tristan had taken his rayzor and with great precision and strength threw it towards the sword-wielding lancer. It flew through the air, hilt then blade turning as it spun. It struck the doomed lancer blade first as he turned round with his master's sword in his hand.

'Good throw, Tristan, that takes care of that,' said Kurt.

'Not too shabby yourself,' Tristan replied. 'Good work,' he communicated to the now prowling wolves. Kurt and Tristan checked all the bodies for any signs of life, there were none. Kurt then went over to inspect the legion master's body. From a pouch at the master's side, he pulled out a document that told Kurt all he needed to know.

Tristan checked that the door was now happy to let him in. 'We are clear to travel now,' he shouted over to Kurt, who held up the document from the dead master as he walked over to Tristan,

'This explains why the Dark warriors were inside the passage. They have found a way to enter it from the Dark Lands. They can enter Earth without our knowledge. Who knows how long they have been doing this.' Kurt handed Tristan the document, who looked at it intently then shook his head in disbelief, they must have found another pathway.

'Yan must have been taken captive when he travelled through the passage to meet us. We must get back and warn the elders and the king,' Tristan said. They gathered up the weapons, keeping some for their onward journey, and then they put the bodies into the passage, which would take them back to the entrance on Elemtum.

'That will totally confuse the guardian warriors at the other end in Great Porum,' Kurt said as he dropped the last demon dog on top of the bodies inside the door, then it shut. The World's Pathway re-opened, and the four companions entered the initial chamber inside the gate. Kurt asked the gate if it could sense the Dark warrior's entry point into the passage. All the gate could tell them was that they had some strange power that confused the senses of the gate at either end. It was all the gate could do to stop Kurt and his family entering earlier where they would have been attacked by the intruding Dark warriors. Once the gate had sensed that the Dark warriors travelling through the pathway it had sent a message to the warriors at the great gate to stop anyone else from travelling until it was found out what was going on and that it was safe to travel the pathway again. The gate closed behind them. Kurt, Tristan, Phina and Salina entered the inner chamber where they would travel back to Elemtum.

'Is this wise? We could be pounced on by the Dark,' said Tristan.

'Bring it on. They will get what their companions got, if they try, but I can't see how they can enter a moving inner chamber.' said Kurt.

Tristan nodded in agreement with his brother, 'They might have found a way to stop the chamber.'

'We will see, won't we, if they try,' replied Kurt.

They made themselves comfortable for the long journey, which they estimated should take them about six Earth hours to complete. Due to the appearance of the Dark warriors in the gate they decided one of them should stay awake, changing over every three hours, because no one knew if this would just be another ordinary journey through the World's Pathway or if they might be interrupted.

Chapter 7
A New Day and a New World

Karl awoke under a tree in what he originally thought was Rendelsham Forest. He turned his head and looked right, saw his brother still sleeping, then turned his head to the other side and saw Rowena. It's not a dream, he thought. Karl now knew he was not in Rendelsham Forest. He looked up and noticed a slight shimmer then heard a familiar voice that had entered his brain.

Michael the angel spoke to him, 'Don't worry, Karl, I am watching over you all until you all wake. Don't wake your brother and sister. Let their minds adjust or they could suffer memory loss. Gabriel placed you here. You are as close as we can go to the fortified citadel of Warriors' Rest. You have family there. Your cousin Raif De-Callen, Kurt's son, will find you here. I have dreamed your arrival to him, so when he awakes, he will come looking for you, so you must stay here. I will be watching over you all until he arrives. Until then, rest your body and mind. You have gone through quite an ordeal travelling with us. You have acquired a lot of information that you will slowly remember depending on the situations you are in. Now rest.'

Karl drifted back off to sleep only to be woken after what he thought was seconds by Row and Tom.

'Come on, sleepy head, time to get up,' Tom said as he gently nudged him.

Row walked over to him. 'How are you feeling?' she asked.

Karl replied, 'You should not have woken me; Michael said not to wake you because there could be brain damage.'

'It was Michael that told us to wake you, because if you sleep too much you might never wake up,' Row told Karl.

He stood up and asked Row if anyone else had appeared while he had slept. No, she had answered.

'We are expecting a cousin called Raif. He's Kurt's son.' As Karl finished what he was saying an arrow thudded into the tree behind him.

From the tree line in front of them they all heard a stranger's voice, 'Stay where you are, don't make any sudden movements or you will die.' Tom moved closer to Row and Karl. 'I said don't move, little one,' the voice shouted.

This was immediately followed by a second voice. 'Yeh, you're surrounded, aren't they, master?' said the voice.

Tom saw the shadow of a big man behind a bush. He nudged Row and Karl. They saw the figure run along the line of the bushes and stop twenty feet farther away from where he had started

From his new position, the second voice shouted out, 'You're surrounded by me and them two over there, so don't move or else. Right, master?'

The first voice spoke again, 'You're an idiot, Clomp and stop calling me master.'

'Sorry, master,' Clomp replied.

The first voice continued, 'Don't worry about the idiot running around, he won't hurt you as long as you don't try anything funny.'

'Who are you? Are you Raif? If you are, we are expecting you,' Karl shouted to the voice.

'How do you know my name?' Raif shouted back

'Michael the angel told us you were coming. Your dad, Kurt De-Callen, sent us from Earth' shouted Karl. The bush parted and a boy of similar age and size to Karl walked out and stood in plain view of them all.

'Clomp, come out,' Raif shouted. Clomp ripped up the bush he was standing behind and tossed it behind him, then walked over to Raif and stood next to him. Clomp was four times the size of Raif; his clothes all looked too small for him, his feet were massive, and he had bright red hair.

'Hello,' said the smiling Clomp.

'Hello, who are you...? You do have a very nice smile,' Row said.

'That's Clomp,' replied Raif.

'I'm Clomp,' said Clomp, embarrassed but still with a beaming smile.

'I am Rowena. This is Karl and Tom. We are from... Earth,' she said.

'You make us sound like aliens. You'll be telling them to take us to their leader next,' said Karl.

'Whatever, Karl,' she replied.

'You are all King Frederick's children, the ones that went missing with my father and Uncle Tristan, aren't you?' Raif asked.

'I'm not sure about going missing, but yes, apparently so,' said Row.

'Where's my father?' asked Raif.

Row beckoned him and Clomp to come and sit next to them. Once Raif and Clomp were seated, Row proceeded to tell the story of their last forty-eight hours, or what she thought was forty-eight hours. 'So, you should see them pretty soon,' she finished.

'I knew Father and Tristan left with you and my sisters to protect you all, but neither me nor my mother have heard anything since. We thought you were all dead, especially since it was common knowledge here that Labatina's Dark warriors were hunting for you,' said Raif.

'So, if you are Uncle Kurt's son then we are related. Cousins. You're the first real family we have ever met, apart from your dad,' said Kurt.

'You keep saying "Dad", what does that mean?' asked Raif.

'Dad is like father, it's just a little more personal,' said Row.

'Oh, so why don't you just say father and save a word?' answered Raif.

'Because that's what we say on Earth,' said Tom.

'But you're not from Earth... ain't that right, master?' butted in Clomp.

'Why do you keep calling Raif, master? And what sort of name is Clomp? I've never known anyone called Clomp before,' Tom asked Clomp.

'It's because Lord De-Callen saved my father's life at the battle of Dark Wood, so my "Dad"...,' Clomp laughed. 'That word's funny.' He smiled then continued, 'My father gave me to the lord to play with Master Raif. I look after him, he's my master. Simple.'

'I'm not your master, Clomp. You can go any time you want... master was only a title like "the little master" meaning I'm the dig master's son,' explained Raif.

Clomp smiled at him. 'I do understand now..., master,' he said.

'I give up... it's like talking to a mud wall with you, Clomp,' Raif said.

'Thank you, master,' replied Clomp. Karl started to laugh.

'What did you find funny?' asked Raif.

'Oh, it's just that on Earth we say "It's like talking to a brick wall". It means the same thing. Obviously, some things are the same, we all speak the same language, and we all look the same... well nearly the same,' said Karl.

'And this looks like a normal wood,' said Tom.

'This isn't a wood, this is a creeping forest,' Raif corrected him.

'We have forests on Earth, but what do you mean by a creeping forest? On Earth, creeping means to move slowly,' enquired Row.

'It means the same here, silly,' answered Clomp.

'What you mean? They move?' asked Karl.

'Of course, they do... that's why it's called a creeping forest... you can talk to them as well. They tell you what mood the world is in and who's been in the forest,' said Raif.

'Put your hand on one... go on, it won't bite you,' said Clomp.

'Just put your palm on the bark,' said Raif. He then took Row's hand and guided it towards the nearest tree trunk, placing it gently on the bark.

Row felt the bark beneath her palm gently move, then she had the strangest feeling. The branches were blowing in the wind, but it was all in her mind. A voice came with the wind, 'Greetings, Lady De-Callen, we have not felt you here since you were a young child. The air giving wind movers in this world are glad to see you and your brothers back where you belong. Stay free.'

Row could hear herself reply, 'Thank you and stay free, wind mover.' Taking her hand away Row said, 'That was amazing. I have never experienced anything like that before. That was magical, thank you,' she said and kissed Raif on his cheek.

Raif blushed, Clomp laughed and Karl felt uneasy that his sister had kissed this strange boy. Tom and Karl then put their hands on the trees, the same as Row had done with a similar outcome, except Karl looked a little odd when he drew his hand away. 'Don't worry, Raif, I'm not going to kiss you,' said Karl.

Raif looked at Karl. 'Are you all right? You look a little worried,' he said.

'I'm fine, I just want to get going to wherever it is we are meant to be,' he said, and then he smiled nervously at Raif.

Raif patted Karl on the back. 'Don't worry, you will get used to this world. What I've heard from the preachers about the missing world, it isn't too different to this one, just a little more violent. I hear people there even kill people they don't know for no reason. We only kill the Dark in this world,' said Raif.

'Yeh, we hate the Dark,' added Clomp.

'I'll take you back to my home. My mother will be so amazed and very happy to meet you, especially as you will be able to tell her about my father and his brother. She won't believe it… she really won't,' said Raif.

As they walked through the forest, they talked of the world they were now in, Elemtum, and of the world they had just come from that Raif and Clomp had only heard about in books and the stories that were told by the preachers. They had actually been there, on Earth. Clomp and Raif were impressed, even if Raif did not admit it to his new cousins.

'You never told us why you are called Clomp,' Tom said.

'That's easy. My father is Big Clomp, and so I'm just Clomp,' he told Tom with a grin.

'That clears that up then,' laughed Tom. As they walked, they talked and laughed but did not notice a pair of green eyes watching them. It had been watching them for some time before it scurried away, still unseen. Some things in the forest did see what was behind the green eyes. After an hour, they came to the edge of the forest.

'You had quite a journey to get to us,' said Row to Raif.

'Not really,' he replied, 'it took us half as long to get to you, but the forest has been moving away from where we came in from, so it's taking us longer to get back. You have to be careful in a creeping forest. You can ask it to stop moving, they are quite happy to do that,' he said.

Karl shook his head in disbelief. This place is mad, he thought.

As they left the forest, Row placed her hand on the last tree. She made contact and thought, 'Thank you.'

The tree replied, 'Take care, lady, you have been watched by an evil one.'

Row removed her hand and turned to Raif; she told him what the tree had communicated to her.

Clomp pulled out a large sharp bladed sword from the scabbard at his side. 'Don't worry, Lady Rowena, masters, it won't get near you, I promise.' His face changed from the happy smiling Clomp to the 'don't mess with me or ill rip your head off' Clomp.

'Stay at the back, Clomp, and keep watch until we get across the edge of the sand lands,' said Raif. Then he spoke to his new friends. 'It was most probably a Dark assassin. They have been creeping around, spying on us for some time over the last hundred moons. I don't know if you know but they can transform into other creatures. They are dangerous, but you can normally see their green eyes coming through their host's eyes if the suns glints of them at the right angle, so be watchful.'

Karl explained to Raif that they had encountered Dark assassins before, and those ones had taken over people's dead bodies.

'I have never known that before. That is very worrying.'

'That's what your dad and Uncle Tristan said,' Tom informed him.

Raif explained to them that they now had to cross the edge of the sand lands and that it would not take them too long, but there was one thing he must warn them about.

Karl butted in, 'We have only been here a couple of hours and we have encountered walking and talking trees, assassins. What's next?'

'Karl,' Row said, throwing him a disapproving look.

'What? I'm just saying what else is there on this bloody planet that might want to kill us?'

'It's okay, Karl, I understand. This is all strange, but it's our home, we just have to get used to it,' Row said, giving him a reassuring smile.

Karl continued, 'It's just that!' Then he stopped. 'It doesn't matter,' he said.

'It's okay, Karl, me and Clomp will protect you,' teased Tom.

'Tom. Row now threw Tom a disapproving glance, which Tom

acknowledged with a cheeky grin.

'It must be strange for you. I think it's strange seeing you all here, so it must be doubly strange coming from a world totally different to this. And to top it all off, this is your home world and you don't even know it. Anyway, we are only crossing a little bit of the sand lands, but this bit does have a thing called a lizsnake.'

'What…?" said Tom.

'A lizsnake. Don't you have serpents on your world?' said Raif.

'Yes, we do,' said Karl.

'Well, this is a serpent with legs and it's two people high and it's about fifteen people long from tail to head. It eats lizerats; it has a deadly bite to us and lizerats. Lizerats are the creatures that Labatina's Dark sorcerers turn into assassins,' said Raif.

'What is a lizerat?' asked Tom.

'It's part rat, part lizard. It has a rat's body, about five hands high, with lizard hands, feet and tail, and they live underground in the sand lands. They scavenge the sands for anything to eat; dead birds, fish, reptiles, rubbish, anything. There is only one colony of lizsnakes, so you don't come across them too often, but we had one go passed us on the way to you. They have bad eyes, so they smell very well, and they have been known to bite our people thinking they were lizerats. If a lizsnake comes near, you stay still, don't move, because lizerats always run. If you stay still, they will smell you, then realise you're not a lizerat and move away from you, then you can carry on. Whatever you do, don't scream. Lizerats scream when they run away, it's one of the reasons they get caught, so don't scream,' said Raif.

'I hate snakes,' said Row.

'Don't worry, no one has been bitten for several blue moons,' Raif told her.

'That's very reassuring,' replied Row with a mock smile.

'If this is the end of the sand lands, it must be massive,' said Tom.

'It looks like a desert to me,' commented Karl.

'Oh, it's not a desert. Lots of things live here. There are citadels further south and villages all over the place. There's even the sea of plenty,' said Raif.

They continued happily trudging through the sand lands, Raif leading the way with his rayzor in his hand. Clomp was bringing up the rear, with his war face on. Row and the boys were scouring the sands for the lizsnakes.

After twenty minutes' walking, Tom asked Raif why the desert wasn't hot like back on Earth? Raif's reply was that it was the winter sun, so it was cold. Tom found this funny because it was a nice summer's day here in their new world.

After half an hour, Raif stopped, put his hand onto the sand and shouted for everyone to stop moving and stay quiet. Everyone froze, especially Row who had thoughts of snakes popping out all around her followed by a gruesome, terrible death at the fangs of a lizsnake before she had even seen her new home world.

'There's one coming, stay still,' Raif shouted. Just then a sandpaper tongue came out of the sand and licked the air. A scaly spiked head followed it. It had soul-piercing eyes. The body continued to rise until it was fifteen feet above them.

Ten feet, my arse, Karl thought, as he looked up at the lizsnake. Then out of the sand came a pair of legs that came to rest either side of Tom. Row could see Tom's terrified face. She went to help him but found she was stuck to the spot. She was now shaking and was also very terrified like her younger brother. Tom looked at Row. He realised she was as scared as he was, then he turned slowly towards his brother. Karl showed no fear; he was walking towards the lizsnake.

'No!' Raif shouted at Karl, but Karl now began sprinting towards his brother. The lizsnake turned its head towards Raif as he had shouted, but now it was looking down at the animal running at him.

As Karl ran towards Tom, he shouted, 'Run to Row, now!' Karl's shouting at him shook Tom out of his frozen fear and he ran. He ran with all his might the short distance to Row who embraced him as he reached her. Tom reaching her also snapped her out of her fear. The lizsnake's head looked to Karl, then to Tom and Row, then back to the nearest animal to it which was Karl. The lizsnake opened its mouth, exposing rows of jagged teeth fronted by four massive fangs that were dripping with a yellow fluid that hissed as it hit the sand. The lizsnake steadied itself on its front legs then struck out at Karl. Row pulled Tom's head into her to overt his eyes from the harrowing site they were about to witness, as the lizsnake went to strike their brother. Tom pulled away from her. Raif and Clomp were now running towards the lizsnake, weapons drawn, but they knew they would not get there in time, to save the doomed Karl. The jagged teeth and mouth came down on Karl... but before the lizsnake could close its mouth to trap Karl, he had rolled sideways out of the mouth and was now climbing up the spikes that adorned the lizsnake's neck. Both Raif and Clomp stopped and looked on in amazement, as did Tom and Row. Karl was now on top of the lizsnake's head. The lizsnake tossed and turned its head to try and dislodge the animal now on its neck, its forked tongue lapping at Karl from side to side, every time it missed him. Not quite sure why, but something inside Karl told him to place a hand on the lizsnake's head which he did. The tongue stopped whipping around and the lizsnake's mouth slowly closed and its head became still. Not knowing what to do now, Raif and Clomp walked towards Tom and Row, keeping their eyes on the most magnificent thing they had ever seen in their short lives. Karl was actually patting the lizsnake's head; slowly, its whole body came from below the sand and rested on the ground. They looked at each other. Realising their chance had come, they started to run screaming at the lizsnake, weapons ready to cut it up.

'No!... Stop where you are!' Karl shouted at them. They both stopped in their tracks, then looked at Karl for direction. 'It's okay... he's calm, he won't hurt us... I promise.'

They looked at each other, baffled, this had never happened before. What was going on? Tom and Row could not believe what they had just seen either, especially Tom who had known Karl all his life.

'Row, stand in front of the lizsnake. By the way, he's not a lizsnake, he is a Surviyn. His ancestors came from the stars many centuries ago. They settled here and lived quite happily until the Dark took their sight because they would not bow down and become servants to them. They have now been hunted by the Dark ever since for not joining them,' said Karl from on top of the Surviyn.

'So, why do they kill my people?' shouted Raif.

'That has been purely accidental. They have been chasing the evil green-eyed beasts. They are very sorry about that because they feel your sorrow.'

'Why do you want me to stand in front of it?' asked Row.

'To prove to you that it means you no harm.'

'How do you know that it won't hurt her?' shouted Tom.

'Don't do it, Row!' shouted Raif.

'I trust Karl,' she said.

'But you yourself said earlier that you had only just met your brothers two days ago... and you now trust him with your life,' pleaded Raif.

'Yes, I do trust him, Raif.' Then she walked in front of the giant Surviyn's mouth. Everyone watched on in fear and trepidation, except for Karl who knew what was going to happen. The mouth slightly opened and the Surviyn's forked tongue came out. It slowly approached Row who now wished she had listened to Raif. The tongue slowly wrapped around Row's legs, then her waist, then her upper body, leaving only her head visible.

'What the hell is going on, Karl?' Tom shouted at his brother.

'Don't worry, he is saying hello,' said Karl.

Row was once more petrified with fear, all she wanted to do was scream out, but in the back of her mind she remembered Rafi's warning from earlier 'Whatever you do, don't scream'. The tongue gently squeezed her, then unwound and returned to its mouth. Row looked at the Surviyn's eyes; to her they were smiling, so she smiled back nervously.

'See, they are friendly. Climb up here and he will give us a ride to the end of the sand lands. Come on.' Karl encouraged them all to join him on top of the Surviyn. Tom walked forward towards the Surviyn and began to climb up to his brother. Row followed, leaving Raif and Clomp looking up at them.

'I'm not sure, I don't trust it,' shouted Raif. As he shouted, Clomp picked him up and, with protests, carried Raif to the Surviyn and deposited him halfway up the serpent. Then he started to push Raif up towards the seated onlookers above. Clomp followed him up until they were both sitting behind Row, who was sitting behind Tom and Karl who seemed to be in control of the massive Surviyn.

'Oh, by the way, his name is Sentar,' Karl said as the Surviyn pulled his second, third and fourth pairs of legs from the sand. Lastly, its tail flipped out making the total length of the lizsnake thirty feet long and fifteen feet wide. Clomp and Raif looked at each other both thinking 'We are going to die.'

Karl looked back and shouted, 'Hold on! He's told me that on land he runs quite fast. Ten feet my arse,' he said, looking at Raif. Then Sentar began to run. He ran like one of the lizards from Earth, the ones that run funnily on the hot sand. He really shifted across the sand at some speed. With their hair blowing in the wind, all of them laughed and marvelled at the speed they were travailing at. Even Row who hated snakes was enjoying herself, probably because she now knew it was no snake. Within ten minutes they had reached the end of the sand lands and Sentar stopped. One by one they climbed down from his back, until Karl was the only one left. He patted Sentar's head then Sentar lifted a front leg to make it easier for Karl to climb down as he had done for all of them. Karl was now standing in front of Sentar who wrapped his tongue around him as he had done with Row. Gently, Karl was released then Sentar turned around and disappeared under the sand. Karl turned around and faced his companions.

'That was amazing, Karl. How did you do that? If I hadn't seen it, I would never have believed it,' Raif said, clasping Karl by the wrist and shaking his arm in a warrior's hand and wrist grip.

Row went up to Karl and kissed his cheek, 'You were amazing! I knew I could trust you.' Karl's face went bright red.

'Well done, bro. Cool,' said Tom.

Finally, Clomp went up to Karl. 'Well done, Dad.' Then he slapped Karl on the back and sent him flying to the floor. 'Sorry, Dad,' Clomp said as he lifted the breathless Karl up and plonked him on to his feet.

Row went up to Clomp and said with a smile, 'Dad means father, Clomp.'

'Oh yeh, I forgot. Sorry,' he replied. Everyone laughed except Karl who was still getting his breath back.

As they went from the sand to wiry brown grass, Tom asked Karl a question. 'How did you do that... you know... calm that big snake thing Sentar?'

'What on earth possessed you to do that? You've never seen one of those things before and you jumped on the beast's back,' added Row.

Karl thought about what he was going to say next. He had to make sure it sounded right. 'I don't really know... what I mean is... it just happened. Something in my brain said put your hand on its head then something just took over and I did what I did. That's all,' he said.

'Well, it was very brave,' said Row.

'I would go as far as saying it's one of the bravest things I have ever seen,' said Raif.

'Me as well, master,' added Clomp.

'Uncle Kurt would be proud of you, Karl,' added Tom.

As they continued to walk the grass became greener and the land became hillier. 'Nearly there, just over the next hill, then you will see the fortified citadel. It's called Warriors' Rest. This was because when the war first started against the Dark it was a little camp where warriors used to rest before they carried on south. It was also where they returned from the south before continuing north. This was the last place my big brother ever saw Phina, Salina and my brother saw him here before he went off and died fighting the Dark. He was very brave He held some ground, letting a village in the sand lands escape before the Dark over ran them,' Raif said. 'That's why this place is now my home. Mostly when I'm not up in Great Porum. My mother stays here... I suppose she still feels close to my brother here. I know Phina and Salina prefer Great Porum. There's more to do there, more people, not just mainly warriors like here.'

Karl stopped walking. 'What do you mean by Phina and Salina's brother? Phina and Salina are our wolves. Is there another Phina and Salina? Are they popular names?' he asked.

'Phina and Salina, the warrior princesses, my sisters. I said when I met you, I had two sisters,' replied Raif. Everyone had stopped walking and stood still. Now Row and Tom were listening intently because along with Karl they were all now a little confused.

'I didn't click. Earlier I thought you were talking about people with the same names, not our wolves. So, you are talking about Phina and Salina the wolves, that have been with us on Earth?' asked Karl.

'Yes, of course, who do you think I'm talking about?' answered Raif.

'But you're not a wolf. How can you have two sisters that are wolves?'

'Phina and Salina are my sisters. I was very young when they left with you, my father and uncle, so I don't really know any of them,' Raif replied.

'I think we are missing something here,' said Row.

'Well, now I'm confused. What don't you understand?' asked Raif.

'I don't think they know about Wolf warriors, master,' said Clomp.

'Well done, Clomp, I didn't think of that. Have you all been told about Wolf warriors?'

'No, we haven't. We know what wolves are. Well, to be honest, maybe we don't because your wolves talk,' said Row.

'Our wolves talk, remember. We are one of them,' said Karl.

'Yes, I keep forgetting,' said Row. '

'I had better tell you about the Wolf tribe and Wolf warriors before we get to Warriors' Rest. Everyone sit down here, we could all do with a rest anyway, and I will explain,' said Raif. They all settled down and Clomp passed round the water that he had been carrying. Everyone took a good drink and relaxed for the first time in a long while.

'It's actually quite pleasant here, but you don't see many birds in the sky. In fact, I haven't seen any since we arrived,' said Row.

'They all moved further north. I don't know why it might be something to do with the Dark. The only birds you will see are eagles and they will be warriors,' Raif told them all.

'You train eagles to be warriors?' said Karl.

'Yes, and wolves, of course, at the warrior academy at Great Porum and the advance stage here in Warriors' Rest.'

'Amazing,' said Karl.

'Why? Don't you have academies on Earth?'

'Yes, of course. we do. Schools, colleges universities. All our warriors are trained in camps, with the army. The only military animals we train are dogs, as far as I am aware.' Karl told Raif.

'Don't forget killer gorillas,' added Tom.

'Shut up, Tom.'

'You have killer gorillas?' Clomp asked excitedly. 'What's a gorilla?' Everyone laughed.

'You idiot, Clomp,' Raif told him, then continued. 'You all know what a warrior is, right?' Everyone nodded 'yes' in agreement, even Clomp. 'You know what warriors are, you idiot, Clomp. I'm not talking to you.'

Clomp looked disappointed and stood up, 'I like your stories,' he said. Then he began to walk away.

'Clomp, what are you doing? I'm explaining to them, not you. You already know this stuff. Sit down and listen, but don't interrupt.'

'I don't know what interrupt does, so I won't be doing that, master,' Clomp said with a smile

'I love you,' said Row. Clomp sat down.

'What do you mean?' asked Raif.

'Not what you think, Raif, it's a term of endearment. You know, like you're lovely or funny.'

'No, I still don't understand,' said Raif.

'Don't worry, it's probably been lost in translation. Just carry on with your history lesson,' she said.

Raif continued, 'You all know what a warrior is, that's good.' Raif then glanced at Clomp, who drew an imaginary zip across his mouth and smiled. Everyone laughed, even Raif. He then explained that when life began people and creatures were one and they evolved into different types of people. 'Eagle warriors are one with the eagles, Wolf warriors are one with the wolves. Like Eagle warriors, the Wolf warrior can change into a wolf when he or she wishes. But what we did not know was if a female Wolf warrior went through the great door to the pathway to your old world if they would stay in the form they entered the pathway. That's why you only know Phina and Salina as wolves. It doesn't work with males; they can change on Earth. No one knows why.'

'So, you're telling us that Phina and Salina are humans, I mean, people from here? That's why we had a connection with them back on Earth and that's why they are a lot bigger than Earth wolves.' said Row.

'That answers a lot of questions. So, what do they look like as people?' inquired Karl.

'Phina and Salina, I have been told, are probably two of the most beautiful and fearless warriors in this world. They are also both princesses of the Wolf tribe. Our father is a Wolf prince and my mother is a Wolf princess. My mother, Raphine, lives most of her time in Warriors' Rest. She likes to live there so she can be close to the Dark that she hates, because they killed her son, my brother Stefan, as I have told you. She will never forgive them. The reason I have told you this is because you might see wolves talking with people or other wolves, and if you see the young ones play fighting, they change between people and wolf as they fight because they don't know how to control the spirit within them.'

'Are you a Wolf warrior?' Tom asked.

'Yes, I am,' replied Raif, 'as are my father and Uncle Tristan.'

'I knew there was something about Uncle Kurt,' said Karl.

'Are you a Wolf warrior as well, Clomp?' Tom asked Clomp shook his head without speaking.

'Clomp, you can talk,' said Raif.

'Thank you, master. I don't think I could have held my breath anymore,' Clomp answered, now very relived.

'Clomp, who told you to hold your breath?' asked Raif.

'Err.'

'I said don't speak, Clomp, not don't breathe.'

'But if I don't open my mouth, how do I breathe?' answered Clomp.

'Through your nose, Clomp, by dragon's breath, you can be stupid sometimes.'

'Stop bullying him, Raif, he's sweet,' said Row.

'We had better get moving; I never told anyone we were leaving this morning.' Raif stood up and brushed some grass from his clothes. Everyone else stood up and got ready to move off. 'Lead on, Macbeth,' said Karl.

'What?' Raif said, turning to look at Karl

'Don't worry, it's from our world, I mean our old world, from a play.' They continued to walk towards a long green hill in front of them. They could also now clearly see a tower that had a very large eighty-foot wall coming out from either side. In the middle of the tower was a small gate big enough to get four men abreast through.

'What's that?' Tom asked.

Raif pointed towards the tower with the walls and replied to Tom. 'That's the start of the fortified citadel of Warriors' Rest; it's the most southerly occupied outpost. Well, not so much an outpost now. Like I said, it's actually a citadel. Normally you only travel past here in well-armed groups, but I knew Clomp and me could handle anything that we might come up against.'

'Yeh, like that big snaky liz thing that Karl tamed, you mean,' said Row. Clomp sniggered behind her back and Karl and Tom had big grins across their faces.

'Okay, I will give you that one,' conceded Raif with a smile.

Chapter 8
Family and New Friends

As they approached the great wall of Warriors' Rest a voice called out behind them, 'Raif, Clomp and your companions, stand where you are.'

'Crap, its Detor Eosin; he must have followed us,' said Raif.

'Who's that?' asked Karl.

'He's the Wolf master, and I think I'm in trouble.'

The Wolf master walked towards the group; he looked a little out of breath but very menacing. He was bigger and broader than Kurt, his muscles visibly stretching his leather jacket. In his left hand was some sort of rifle and in his right a sword, very like Kurt's rayzor but a little bigger.

'He doesn't look so happy,' said Tom.

'He's not,' replied Raif.

'I have been following you two since you sneaked out of the Citadel; you have no sense at all. You don't learn, do you? Last time, if I hadn't followed, you would be dead now. Or at best in a dark dungeon, and now you find these people from who knows where, who have the power to control a lizsnake. Are you mad? They are not from our world, look at what they are wearing. Are you aware you have been followed by an assassin? Do you know why it did not attack you?' Detor shouted at them but mostly at Raif. 'Because I killed it, that's why.' His voice went down an octave. 'These people could be in league with the Dark. It went up an octave again. 'But you, Raif De-Callen, know better!' As he said it, he pushed Raif in the chest making him fall to the ground.

'No, Detor, they are the king's children. My father and Tristan sent them back from the old world,' explained Raif from the ground.

'Where is your proof?' shouted Detor.

'They told me. They told me things only my father would know. I had a dream,' he replied.

'You risked your life and Clomps, on a dream! Not just that, you put the whole citadel at risk trying to bring these people inside the walls. When were you going to tell someone? Once the Dark had crept in and murdered us in our beds, I suppose?' shouted Detor. 'Clomp, take Raif back to his room and make sure he does not leave until I have spoken to his mother.'

'Don't worry, I will go myself. I'm not a child, you forget that, Detor,' shouted Raif before storming off. Clomp ran after him in hot pursuit.

Detor shouted after him, 'You forget, Raif, I promised your father I would keep you safe, whether you like it or not. You three stay where you are, I will have no hesitation in cutting you down if you try anything. Now, where have you come from?' he shouted at them.

'There is no need to threaten or shout at us. Give me a sword and I'll teach you what happens to bullies,' Row shouted back at him.

Detor stood still, looking at her, then the boys.

'Well, I like that. I can see you have spirit and that's good,' he said to Row then he turned to Karl. 'And you, how you dealt with that lizsnake was both amazing and brave. In fact, that ranks as one of the bravest things I have seen, and I have seen a lot of very brave warriors. I am not sure who you are, but you do have the traits of the king, but that changes very little until I see or hear proof. Now, tell me, where are you from?'

They then proceeded to explain everything to Detor, who listened intently but never let his guard drop.

'I'm going to take you back into the citadel. I will be watching you closely. When we get inside, you will be guarded constantly until we can verify who you really are. Do you understand?'

''Yes, we understand, but there's no need to worry, we're are not the enemy,' said Row.

'I will decide that! Now stay in front of me and don't make any sudden moves. If you obey me, we will all get along fine. Do you all understand?'

They nodded their heads and told him he would not have any problems with them. Detor then escorted them to the gate in the tower where several armed guards joined them and helped him escort them into the citadel proper, which was behind several more walls with tall imposing towers. They entered a cobbled courtyard at the end of which was a very grand building with wide ornate stone steps leading to a very grand ornate door in an archway topped by a stone wolf. At the side of the door were a wolf and a warrior. The wolf was as big as Phina and it had on a coat emblazoned with a coat of arms. The warrior had on leather boots and a combat suit not unlike modern armies on Earth would wear but this one blended into its background. The warrior also had on a helmet with a gold visor so you couldn't see his face. He was standing at ease, was holding some sort of rifle which was only just visible as it too blended into the warrior's combat suit. Lastly, he had a rayzor at his side, just like the ones Kurt and Tristan had.

Tom looked at Karl, but before Tom could say a word Karl said, 'Yes, I know,

Tom.'

'Cool.' Tom grinned at his brother.

The door in front of them opened as if by magic. At the end of a grand hall, festooned with statues and pictures, was a tall lady dressed in what Row thought was some sort of silk that caught the light of the stained-glass windows in the roof of the hall. The lady had an elegantly shaped face and her hair was pulled back tightly into a ponytail that dropped down her back. To finish the whole look, the lady had a very thin leather band around her forehead with what looked like, from where Row stood, to be a small gold wolf's head with bright eyes. The lady's beauty and smile took Row by surprise because she was standing in what Row thought was a very masculine hall.

'Go inside,' said Detor, as he followed them in. He told the accompanying guards to wait outside. The hall's doors closed once the guards had left. The hall brightened up as the stained glass above them seemed to give out more light as the door closed. As they got closer to the lady, they noticed Raif step from behind her. Now dressed in black, he stopped and stood at her side. He also looked elegant and regal. There was no expression on his face whatsoever.

The lady spoke, 'Lord Wolf master, you may leave these children with me. I have spoken to my son and I believe what he says. These are the king's children that Prince Kurt promised he would protect; of that I have no doubt.'

'Very well, highness, but I have misgivings about them. Why would they be left on the edge of the Dark if they were so precious? Let me find more evidence to prove who they are, Highness.'

'That is not necessary, Detor. Kurt and his brother will be with us soon. I have had a message delivered this morning from the great door to the pathway. They are all returning; Kurt, Tristan, Lady Phina and Lady Salina should be with us this evening,' said the Wolf princess.

'Very well, highness, that is very good news. It will be good to see them all once more.' With a slight nod of his head to the princess and one to Raif, then finally to Row and her brothers, Detor left them.

'Come here and let me see who Kurt and Tristan have been looking after for all these many moons, please come forward highnesses.' Karl and Tom walked forward boldly, Row, a little hesitantly, followed. As Karl reached the lady, he gave a bow like Detor's and Tom followed his brother. Row watched them from behind. 'My name is Raphina Eleanor De-Callen and it is my honour to meet your highnesses,' the lady said. Then, as she gave them a perfect curtsy, Row noticed Raif bow his head at the same time. Row, Karl, and Tom all felt slightly embarrassed at the elegant lady's actions and words.

'There is no need for that,' said Row from behind the boys.

The lady replied, 'Oh but there is, your highness, you are the king's children and, as such, the future rulers of these lands. Have you not been informed of your heritage?' she asked them.

Karl replied, 'Well, yes, sort of, not fully, I mean.'

'I see my life love has been a little remiss in his duties as he cared for you,' said Raphina.

'No, he was not. He's been very good to us, and we have not needed to know,' Tom told her.

'Well, I see there must have been a good reason that you don't know. I will talk with Kurt and Tristan on their return. We will talk more later once you have all settled in. I expect you are all hungry and could do with a good clean, if you are anything like my son Rafael and the state he was in when he returned from his adventure.'

'Rafael? I thought his name was Raif?' said Karl.

Raphina replied, 'Yes that's what everyone calls him, even his father because he doesn't like Rafael, his real name.'

Raif interrupted her, 'Mother, do you have to?'

'Yes, I have to, your future king or queen is standing in front of you and they need to know who you really are,' said Raphina. 'Rafael Kurt Tristan Frederick De-Callen, son of Kurt De-Callen who is Atta Wolf, my life love and brother to the king of the Wolf people and emperor of Elemtum,' she told them.

'You should be proud of that, Raif, it's a very grand name,' said Row.

'Yes, I know, Row. I am very proud of who I am, but I like Raif,' he said.

'I'll call you Raif,' said Tom.

'And I will,' said Karl.

'Yes, and I will,' said Row with a smile.

'Thank you all,' said Raif.

'Rowena, you come with me, I will help you get cleaned up. I have just the clothes for a princess to wear. Rafael, take Karl and Thomas under your wing and get them the room next to yours. Get yourselves cleaned up and sort some clothes out for them. When you are all ready, we will meet in the dining hall, then we will get some food in to you,' Raphina told her son.

As Raif led the boys away, Raphina and Row walked off in a different direction. 'Where are we going?' asked Row.

'We are going to my chambers. You could do with a little pampering. You look worn out,' said Raphina.

'I must tell you, Lady Raphina, that I'm not very girly. I have been brought up by Tristan. I don't think I have ever worn a dress before in my life. I wouldn't know what to do with one. And make-up! I just don't go there,' Row told her.

Raphina stopped, turned towards Row, put her hands on Row's shoulders and smiled. 'I see, in front of me, a very beautiful, young warrior princess, because that's what you are. Don't be mistaken by what you see before you, I am not normally dressed like this. I am a Wolf princess and I fight at my king's side as do all Wolf people. We are all one. What you see is a grand show for special occasions. You are special and you will find that out soon enough, but first enjoy being a lady. You will be amazed at how you will feel. You will be in unglamorous clothing soon enough. Now, let's get you bathed and smelling like a real lady.'

Row smiled at Raphina then took her hand. 'Okay,' she said, 'let's give it a try and see what happens.'

Raif took the boys to the room they would be sleeping in; it was very basic with two beds that looked like water beds, a rack of some sort along one wall and a large storage room with shelves and racks for clothes. 'My room is very similar, except my rack is full of weapons and there is a heavy lump in the other bed.'

'Heavy lump? What do you mean?' said Tom.

'Clomp,' replied Raif.

'Clomp! You share a room with Clomp? Why? You're a prince, aren't you?' said Karl.

'This is training accommodation. Clomp and I are training to be warriors, and this is where we live. When I am not training, I live with my mother and very soon my two sisters, Phina and Salina, and, of course, Father, who you have already met.'

'We've only met the wolves Phina and Salina, not the woman,' said Karl.

'What's a woman?' asked a very puzzled Raif.

'I keep forgetting things are a bit different here. You have people, warriors and ladies. We have people who are either men or women, male or female. You're a man, Raif, and Row is a woman,' said Karl.

'I understand what you mean, Karl, but here all men start as male and ladies as female then everyone progresses to warriors,' replied Raif.

'So, who cooks and cleans and does all the jobs warriors don't do?' asked Tom.

'Everyone does those things, Tom. Mother cooks, as does Father. They clean, but they are also warriors, leaders, kings and queens. Even the Wolf master does these things. Everyone does, everyone is equal here. There are no low or high jobs, there are just jobs,' said Raif.

Karl stood still; he was taking in what Raif had just said to them. Then he went on to explain the system on Earth; poor people, rich people, some with nothing, some with everything. He then told Raif about the systems Earth has, how every country has different laws and religions. Some countries don't like other countries and how you get rich by working hard, or in some cases stealing.

Now it was Rafi's turn not to understand. 'So, you are saying there are lots of people who have everything and some that have nothing, people that starve to death, and people that steal and kill for greed. What sort of system do they run on Earth? It sounds barbaric,' said Raif.

'What do you mean barbaric?' asked Tom.

Karl listened to Raif's reply. 'Here in Elemtum there is no such thing as poor or rich, no one is starving and I have never heard of murder or theft. Why would there be? We are all equal. Words like murder are only ever used to describe what the Dark do, never the people,' explained Raif.

Karl could not believe it; no rich or poor, everyone had all they need. 'So, you're going to say you don't use money next,' laughed Karl.

'Exactly that, Karl. We have no need for money as you have on Earth. That just brings greed, theft and murder,' said Raif.

'So, how do you buy your food, clothes, toys and stuff for the house?' asked Karl.

The reply he got from Raif, he did not expect. 'We all work together for each other. Everything that is made is distributed to the storage facilities. If you need something, you go and get it. There is enough to go round. No one goes without, why would they?' said Raif.

'I don't see how that would work; it sounds like communism that we learnt about at school. That was a good idea, but people are too greedy, they want more for themselves and there is always someone who wants to be the leader who is richer than everyone else and he has the power,' said Karl.

Raif replied, 'It does work, Karl, you can see it all around. We have leaders, but they are that because they are the best at what they do. They are respected because of their actions, bravery, compassion all those sorts of things.'

'But you have kings and queens,' replied Karl, 'and princes who all live in big palaces or buildings, all those things that we have on Earth. That takes money to keep going, to pay the staff, the guards, the cooks. And you live in grander palaces, don't you? That big hall we were in for a start, that's as grand as anything the royal family has on Earth.

'That hall you were in is the people's hall where we place pictures and statues of our heroes. It's also where we have festivals and feasts. Anyone can enter there, it's not a home or palace. My mother and father have a dwelling next to it, as do many people. The size of your dwelling is dependent on the size of your family,' said Raif.

'I don't quite believe this. Your dad, our uncle, used money,' said Karl.

Raif butted in. 'Yes, that's because he was living in your world. It's alien to us.'

'I will believe it when I see it,' said Karl.

'You will,' smiled Raif.

'What do you mean barbaric?' Tom asked again.

'Sorry, Tom.' Karl explained what it meant.

'Can I try the bed?' asked Tom, trying to change the mood of things because he knew Karl liked an argument and he didn't won't that to happen with his new family.

'Get in it, Tom. I bet you have never slept in anything like that?' said Raif.

'We have waterbeds back on Earth, but I've never used one at home,' Tom replied.

'It's not a waterbed, Tom. How daft is that?' Raif chuckled.

'Where are the sheets or the quilt?' asked Tom.

'I don't know what you mean?'

Karl explained to Raif what a sheet and quilt were.

'You don't need anything like that. Get on, Tom, and you will find out why.'

Tom sat on the side of the strange bed, it felt warm and comforting. He pulled his legs off the floor and swung them into the centre of the bed. 'Now what?' Slowly the bed folded around him, even his head was completely covered.

Karl noticed there was no movement from Tom at all. 'Will he be all right in there? Can hc breathe?' he asked Raif.

Raif explained to Karl that the bed reacts to your body temperature, your size and mood; you enter a cocooned environment. 'It even senses all your body, including your brain. When you should get up, it wakes you. It also senses danger and wakes you.'

Karl asked Raif if he needed to wake Tom how did he do that?

Raif showed him a small green circle on the part of the bed that covered Tom's head. 'You touch that, and the bed will adjust the temperature inside with the outside as well as slowly adding any sound. It also controls the rhythm of the body, before unfolding and releasing him. That's all to stop the waking person being shocked as they emerge. Do you know he will be totally refreshed after only nineteen minutes?' Raif told him.

'But he's only been in there a minute. He won't be asleep yet,' Karl said.

'Go on then, press the green circle and we will see,' encouraged Raif, So,

Karl did.

As Raif had said, the cocoon began to unravel from Tom's body until he was in the same position that he had started in. Tom's eyes were open, and he looked as bright as a daisy, which was not the norm after he had been sleeping. 'That was nice. Have I been asleep long?' he asked. Karl started to laugh. 'What's so funny?' Tom asked, as he pulled his legs over the side of the bed and put his feet on the ground just as the door opened.

Clomp walked into the room and upon seeing Raif and the boys standing there with smiles on their faces, a beaming smile filled his face. 'Masters, I wondered what was going on in here with all the laughing.'

Raif told him about Tom and the bed then Karl tried the bed out.

After they had woken Karl from his sleep, he sat up on the bed. 'That was amazing, I've never experienced anything like that before. It was so comfortable. In fact, I will say that is the most comfortable bed I have ever slept in. Definitely the best sleep I have ever had in my life. I can't wait to go to bed tonight.'

'Tonight? What's tonight?' Raif asked.

'You know when it gets dark and everyone goes to sleep,' said Karl.

Looking worried, Raif asked him what he knew of the dark coming while everyone was asleep.

'He thinks you're talking about the Dark Dark, Karl. You know, the ones that are trying to kill me and you.'

'Oh! Yes, I forgot about them. Sorry, Raif, I didn't mean them. I meant like on Earth, the planet turns away from the sun so the furthest part away from the sun becomes dark, no light, it's called night. It lasts about ten hours, that's when people on Earth rest and go to sleep,' Karl explained.

'I see. Very strange. That's why we have those beds so we can sleep whenever we need to. It doesn't get "night". Here it is only black or night inside caves and sometimes the great forest where the trees are so dense it gets black. Then there's the Dark; where they are it is always black, so I have been told.'

Behind them a large figure entered the room. 'That's right,' boomed Detor the Wolf master. 'I know, I have been there and it's not a place I am keen to go back to.' Raif and Clomp braced up, stiff as a board.

'Stand up!' Raif shouted. Karl and Tom stood straighter than they had ever done before. Why, they didn't know.

'Relax, trainees, relax. I'm glad you two turned out to be part of us. I could see you both had something inside you. Your metal was shining through. Until tomorrow, trainees,' Detor nodded to them and left.

'What was that all about?' asked Karl.

Raif told them it was his job to oversee the training of the Wolf warriors and that he was hard but fair, the best trainer master in Elemtum. He also told them the code meant they braced up whenever a trainer or a warrior entered a room they were in; this was a mark of respect. It was done until you became his brother, a warrior, then no more.

'That will have to come sooner rather than later,' Karl said confidently. 'I don't intend doing that every five minutes.'

'You haven't even started training yet,' said Tom.

'I have,' replied Karl with a wry smile.

After washing and putting on their trainee uniforms that Raif had given them from the stores, he explained the uniform to them. 'The boots are automatic sizing for best fit and comfort; you won't even know you have them on. The combat suit has different settings; it automatically changes the temperature according to your blood temperature and the outside air temperature, keeping you at the most optimum temperature to enable you to achieve the task you are doing. It absorbs moisture so no rashes or sweating so you won't smell so you can't be found by the Dark creatures. In automatic, it also heals you if you get a wound in any part of the uniform. The advanced warrior suit has a lot more options that you will get trained in. It's like the one the guards to the hall had on which blend in to the surroundings. Oh, I forgot the boots have sticky soles so you can climb on anything and spikes that can come out to help you climb things like trees and ice. Your gloves look thin but they have the same capabilities as the uniform and can become sticky like the boots if you need it. They are also connected to you.' The boys looked puzzled. 'What I mean is, there are sensors that will recognise your finger prints through your gloves which will let you communicate to any instruments you might have or want to use. Finally, for the trainee is the helmet ours are standard; communicator, black vision, sonic light protecting. But it does not have a range finder or the interface to track the enemy and lock on to fire your weapons – that's for warriors only. Any questions?'

'When do we eat?' asked Clomp.

'Not you, dummy. I meant Karl and Tom.' Both boys nodded their heads in satisfaction. 'Okay, then try them out until you are happy with them.' The boys fiddled with their new gadgets then after a short time one of the walls came to life. On it was a life-sized image of Rafi's mother, Raphina.

'Is everyone ready for some food? If so, bring the princess to the Warriors' Hall. Row and I will be waiting for you there.' Then the image disappeared.

'That was great. Can we all do that?' asked Tom.

Raif told them about the communication portals. 'Every room that people go to regularly like halls, studies, working areas, sleeping rooms, all have a communication portal. You can tell where they are because normally next to a door there will be a small silver disc in the wall. Put your finger on the disc, think about who you want to speak to and what you want to say, then your image and message will be sent. It's as easy as that.'

'Have a go, Tom, it's easy,' said Clomp. So, Tom put his finger on the silver disc. After a few minutes, he took it off.

'Well,' said Karl, 'what did you say?'

Just then Row's image came on the wall. 'What do you mean, Tom? All we got down here was, "hello"? You need to think what you are going to say before you touch the disc, Tom, it's not a toy! See you in a minute.' Tom went a little red and felt stupid.

'Don't worry, Tom, females always pick it up quickly. I don't know why,' said Clomp.

Karl slapped Tom on the back. 'Yeh, don't worry, dummy.'

'I would like to see you try, smart arse,' Tom replied.

Then they all left the room heading for the Warriors' Hall. On the way, Karl tried to explain to Raif and Clomp what a 'smart arse' was. By the time they reached the hall they had some idea but still weren't too sure.

They entered the Warriors' Hall, which was another high-roofed hall with pictures of warriors and weapons displayed all around and, once again, the roof was stained glass. The notable difference with this hall was that it was full of people; four rows of long tables were full of warriors in uniforms, male and female, and there were children of all ages and wolves. Then Karl and Tom noticed a big brown wolf walking between two tables. As it did, it changed into a leather-clad female warrior. This happened almost without the onlookers realising; one second a wolf, the next a female warrior. Karl and Tom looked at each other, not believing what they had just seen. The female warrior turned around to face the boys. It was Raphina Eleanor De-Callen. She smiled at them and beckoned them to join her. Raif pushed them forward, and then he and Clomp sat at the end of one of the tables with some other trainees. Someone from the back of the hall shouted out, 'silence, the Wolf queen.'

The hall became silent. 'Thank you, Valmeer. It has been many years now, Warriors and children, since the princess and princes were taken away from us as babies for their own protection by my life love, Kurt Nicolas De-Callen, Wolf Lord and Prince of Elemtum. They are now back amongst us.'

Just then two female warriors lifted Row up by her arms on to the table next to the Raphina. Row was dressed as a Wolf warrior: Mohican-type boots with imitation synthetic leather trousers and a white flowing shirt; her hair was tied back and she wore a pendant around her neck that dropped down to the centre of her chest. Like the queen, she had a thin leather band around her head with a small wolf's head pinned to it that also had diamond eyes encrusted within it. Row stood there on the table, a beaming smile on her face that illuminated the whole hall. The warriors around her all cheered. Then two warriors lifted Tom up onto the same table, then Karl. The warriors all cheered once more. After a short while, it all became quiet.

'These are our princess and princes. Remember them and look after them. They are new to our... their world, so guide them,' Raphina told them all. After loud cheers, they were helped down from the table. Several warriors and children from each table then got up and walked to the end of the hall where there was another long table which was completely empty; no one was sitting at it. Karl asked the Eagle warrior sitting opposite him what was going on. The warrior told him that the warriors and children had volunteered to help set out the meal. Once the meal was laid out on the table, they would go up and take what they wanted then they return to their own table to eat the food.

'Oh, like a buffet,' Karl told him.

The Eagle warrior looked at Karl, a little puzzled. 'I'm not sure what a buffet is, prince.'

'It's an Earth word for what we are doing now,' replied Karl.

'Why buffet?' asked the warrior.'

'Why do we call people, people or eagles, eagles?' replied Karl

'You have a good point, prince. I can see I will have to be careful when debating with you, young prince,' said the warrior with a smile.

The food was brought through to the hall from an adjoining room and laid out on the empty table. The table was soon full of food that none of the new arrivals had ever seen before. Row asked Raphina if this was the norm for a lunchtime meal and Raphina had told her it was not the norm; it was to celebrate her return and that of the two princes. 'Normally we would eat in our own homes.'

'What happens now?' asked Tom.

'We eat it, of course,' replied the big Eagle warrior sitting opposite him.

Raphina whispered something into Row's ear and she passed it on to Tom who passed it on to Karl. 'Because we are princes and leaders, we don't eat until everyone else has taken their food.'

The rest of the warriors and children in the hall, bar a few who must have been leaders, got up and fetched their food back to their tables. Rowena and her brothers stayed at the tables amongst the warriors. Some of the warriors and children from each table got up and brought back plates for them. On these was a sort of bread, a bit like Earth's tiger bread. Then some platters with assorted meats, salad and vegetables appeared. Finally, flagons full of a red liquid, which they were told was the crushed berries from swamp bushes.

Tom was poured a beaker of the red liquid which he sipped cautiously. 'Um, it's nice. It tastes like cranberries and strawberries. I like this,' he said as he gulped down a cupful.

Across the table from Tom, one of the blue-eyed warriors leaned forward and said, 'Careful, young prince, you should drink that with the tangle root. It helps to break it down in your stomach, otherwise you could find yourself running to the toilet.' The warriors around them laughed.

Urgently, Tom asked him which one of the vegetables was the tangle root? The warrior pointed at something on the platter that to Tom looked remarkably like a leek. He picked one up and started to chew it; his face contorted into a picture of pure disgust as he spat it out into his hand to the obvious enjoyment of the warriors around him.

The blue-eyed Eagle warrior handed Tom a cup of water that he gulped down in one go. 'Throw it on the floor, young prince, and take a drink of this to clear your mouth. Go on, just throw it on the floor. It's okay, a grinder will clear it up,' said the warrior. Tom threw the disgusting mess in his hand on to the floor under the table and gulped down more water. 'Watch me, young prince,' said the warrior, then he bit a piece of the tangle root off and immediately swallowed the red liquid and chewed until it was all gone. 'That's how you do it. The tangle root gives you a great store of energy in your body, and you will need that when you start your warrior training, prince.'

Watching what had just happened, Karl did as the warrior had just shown; he chewed the mixture and swallowed the red liquid. 'That's not bad, Tom, try it again.'

'Not on your life, it's disgusting,' Tom replied. The warriors once again laughed at the young prince, who this time also found the funny side of what had just happened and laughed along with warriors.

After that, Tom and Karl watched what and how the warriors ate the food and followed their lead. The queen had been telling Rowena what and how to eat the food, so she had not had the same problems as Tom.

Detor walked up to their table and stood in front of Karl and Tom behind the blue-eyed Eagle warrior. He had a big grin on his face. 'I can see as well as warrior training, we will also have to train you two princes how and what to eat. It will not matter how good a fighter you become, if you die of hunger because you don't know what to eat. You will be no good to me.' Then he laughed aloud which triggered a banging of cups on the tables by the warriors and children in the hall. At the end of the meal Detor stood up and shouted for quiet, which he immediately got, then he turned to the Raphina. 'May I have your leave, with my trainees.'

'Yes, Detor, please carry on. I will send a message when Lords Kurt and Tristan arrive,' she said.

'Thank you, my queen. Wolf warrior trainees to the flying field. Eagle trainees, it's your lucky day. You have the rest of the time to practice your skills. Now go!' Detor shouted. The trainees all got up and sprinted from the hall.

Karl and Tom hesitated then went to get up, but Raphina instructed them to follow her and Rowena. In a side room off the main hall, Raphina told them they would be flying to the capital of Great Porum to meet their father. She informed them that they would be in harnesses attached to great eagles accompanied by Eagle warriors for protection. She would be flying with them on her wolf eagle which she explained were given to Wolf warriors when they were born. Because the wolf and the eagle were brought up together, they instinctively knew each other inside and out and are very close. The door opened and in came the blue-eyed warrior that had spoken to Tom when he had trouble with the tangle root.

The warrior entered and bowed gracefully towards Raphina. 'Thank you, Andor. I believe you already met Tom and Karl in the hall.'

Andor smiled. 'Yes, queen, the young prince was very amusing. I must say. I have been informed by Detor that you require an escort for the princes to Great Porum. I will have the honour of that task with my brothers of the Eagle lake flight. Arn and Alerio will be the eagles to take the princes, they are very calm. Lord Barra has chosen them to be the princes' life eagles, so it will be good for them to get to know each other.'

'I will take Rowena on my eagle; I believe there is an eagle waiting for her at Great Porum,' said the queen.

'I believe so,' replied Andor.

'Why do some warriors call you queen, Raphina?' Row asked her.

'Because I am Princess of Elemtum, but I am also the Queen of the Wolf clans.'

'So is Kurt the king?' Tom asked.

'No, it works like this. The oldest male of the Wolf clan, who is part of the royal line, is the king which is your father, Frederick De-Callen. As I am the oldest female in line, I become the queen of the clans. It's a little different from royalty on Earth, but it works.'

They all left the room and made their way out onto the flying field. All over the field were Wolf warrior trainees with the biggest eagles Rowena, Karl and Tom had ever seen. Two of the huge eagles walked over to them: proud and magnificent they stood in front of them. Andor explained to the boys and Rowena that the eagles were now trying to communicate with the boys. Karl took a step forward and the eagle lowered its head towards him. as he had done with the lizsnake, Karl placed his hand on the eagle's head, his eyes closed as did the eagle's.

Andor looked at the queen, who walked over to him and whispered in his ear, 'The prince is a sensor. I have heard stories, but I don't know of anyone who has ever met one. This must be kept a secret. Labatina can never find out, do you understand, Andor?'

'Yes, queen, I totally understand. I will inform Lord Barra when I see him.'

Karl instinctively climbed on to the back of the eagle and unfastened its harness, pushing it off the eagle's back. 'This is Alerio and he is happy to fly with me,' Karl shouted from the eagle's back.

The queen looked at Andor, a concerned look on her face.

'It's okay. He's the most confident person I have ever seen mount an eagle, especially as he has never met one before. He has the gift, I'm sure of it,' Andor told her.

Tom was standing next to Rowena. 'He's done it again. Row. How does he do it?' he asked her.

'I don't know, Tom, it is just amazing.' They both looked up at their brother in awe.

Andor's eyes went red at the same time as Alerio's and Karl's. After a minute, their eyes all went back to normal. Andor then explained to the queen, Tom and Rowena, 'They are speaking to each other. The eagle has questioned Karl's mind and he knows everything needed to fly with Karl. I have never experienced anything like this before.'

The queen shouted up to Karl and Alerio, 'Go and fly. Get used to each other and when you are comfortable and confident come back, but don't go beyond the boundaries of the citadel.'

Alerio turned around, then taking a few steps, he beat his wings and he was in the air with Karl smiling on his back. A few more long flaps and they were high in the sky, building up more height. By now, everyone on the field was watching the prince and the eagle effortlessly soaring high above them.

Five minutes later the eagle's wings suddenly came into its body like a dart. 'Oh, my god, he's lost control,' shouted Rowena. Tom looked on helplessly as his brother hurtled towards the ground on the back of the giant eagle.

'It takes a Wolf warrior a very long time to be able to do that with an eagle and that's with an eagle he has known all his life,' said Andor, looking on in amazement at the sight in front of him. When it seemed all was lost, the eagle opened its wings and turned. Picking up speed, he flew back into the air after coming within feet of the ground. For the next five minutes, the onlookers were given the most spectacular flying demonstration any of them, including the Eagle warriors, had ever seen.

Karl and Alerio returned and landed feet from Tom and Rowena, the wind from the eagle's wings blowing into them as it closed its wings. Karl stroked Alerio's head, then whispered to the eagle, jumped off and walked up to them both. 'That was truly great, amazing, and fantastic. We just clicked,' he said.

'I think there is a little more to it than that, Karl. We will talk when we meet your father' said the queen, as she and Andor walked up to them.

Andor spoke to Karl and told him to fly around and keep an eye on his brother when he flew with Arn. So, Karl got back on Alerio and they soared off into the sky. Andor went over to Tom and Rowena. 'Tom, you next. Unlike the Wolf trainees, you will have a trained eagle to fly with so let him do all the work, relax in the harness on Arn's back and enjoy the ride. He will get to know you, so after a few days we will take the harness off and you can fly with him like Karl did. Rowena, you will fly with Raphina. She will hold you so you will be safe with her and the queen's eagle is one of the best. Okay, Tom?'

Tom nodded his head then he and Andor walked over towards Arn who watched Tom's every move as he approached. 'When we reach Arn, Tom, he will lower his head as Alerio did with Karl. Go to the side of his head, near his eye and place your hand on his head. It will feel like someone is talking to you, but you might not understand so don't worry. When Arn opens his eye, he will have finished, and you should be able to climb up on to him and fly.'

'What do you mean, "should"?' asked Tom.

'In very rare cases, the eagle will not like its proposed rider. If that happens, he will push you away gently with his head, then we will have to find another eagle,' said Andor.

'Go on, Tom, you can do it,' Row said, trying to encourage her little brother.

'I'm not scared,' Tom said, then walked up to Arn's head, stood near his eye and placed his hand on the giant eagle's head. After two minutes, the eagle's eyes opened. Smiling, Tom climbed on to the back of the eagle and released the harness as his brother had done, dropping it to the ground.

'What are you doing, Tom?' Andor shouted up to him.

'It's okay, Andor. Arn told me to release it. He said I don't need it, so I did,'

Tom shouted back.

Raphina and Row ran up to him. 'No, Tom, it's too dangerous,' shouted Rowena.

'She's right,' added Raphina, 'listen to your sister.'

'I'll be fine. If Karl can do it, so can I,' Tom shouted back.

Just then Arn turned and began to run. As Arn's claws left the ground, Tom turned around and waved back at them. He promptly lost his grip and fell off the eagle's back, thumping onto the ground. Rowena was the first to start running towards him. Andor soon caught her up and Raphina, now in wolf form, passed them both. As they ran, Tom stood up and Arn came swooping down and grabbed him with his talons, pulling him high into the sky. The runners stopped and looked up to see Arn let Tom go, then dive beneath him where he landed at the exact spot he had fallen from seconds before. Arn flew straight then Alerio and Karl joined them on their right side. Both eagles were now wing tip to wing tip.

Karl gave Tom thumbs up to get a reaction from his brother and to make sure he was okay. Tom's reply was a beaming smile and two thumbs up, so Karl indicated to Tom and Arn a downward motion, indicating dive. Like something out of a World War Two fighter plane movie both eagles tilted their wings in unison and began to dive. Both eagles turned and headed low along the ground, soaring at head height just feet away from the concerned onlookers. This time Tom waved and stayed on his eagle before he and Karl flew back up into the sky once more.

'As you know, I have been an Eagle warrior all my life. I have never seen anything like that before, I am truly amazed,' Andor told Raphina and Row.

'We have some very special warriors amongst us. Are you the same?' Raphina asked Rowena.

Rowena looked on, she had only known the boys a short time, but she knew inside that she would not be able to fly like them and she told Raphina this. Eventually, the boys landed and walked over to the cheers and woops of all the on looking trainees and instructors.

When they reached Andor, he told them, 'Very impressive, young princes. You both have a gift, it's obvious.' Then Andor took them both by the wrist and shook their hands.

Row and Raphina walked up to them. Row embraced her little brother, 'I thought you had really hurt yourself. You scared me, Tom,' she said hugging him once more.

'Did you know what Arn was going to do?' asked Andor.

'Yes, he told me everything. He said I would enjoy it, and I did, it was great.

I can't wait to go up again. Row, you've got to try it.'

'No, it's okay, Tom, I will be happy with Raphina. I might try a solo flight another day,' she told him.

'Well, because you two took to flying so easily, that solves a problem. I will stay here and get things ready for the return of my love Kurt, and you, Rowena, can travel with one of your brothers,' said Raphina.

'I don't know if I am happy with that. I have seen them both fly,' replied Row. They all agreed that Row would fly with Tom who promised not to do any aerobatics. If Row was not happy with his flying, she could swap and fly with Karl or one of the young Eagle warriors who would be escorting them. They had chosen Tom because he was calmer and did not fly with as much aggression as Karl did, so Andor decided he would be better with a passenger. Raphina left them to get on with her preparations for her partner and brother's return.

Eagles and escorts assembled after collecting weapons from the armoury. Tom asked Andor, 'Why do you have wings but the other Eagle warriors don't and they have to fly eagles?'

Andor replied, 'It's all about age and maturity. After thirty red moons, the Eagle warrior goes to a sacred place on top of the red mountain, where your eagle becomes a sprit within you. Then the eagle gifts you their wings which still have all the grace and power they once had. It's the last journey your eagle and you ever do together as separate beings.'

'That's sad,' said Row.

'No, it's not, Rowena. It's a happy time because you gain all their knowledge and they gain yours. You and your eagle become one and you will be together for ever. It's a beautiful time for the warrior and the eagle,' replied Andor.

'Yes, it does sound beautiful, you're right,' said Row.

'Is that what will happen to us?' Karl asked.

'No, prince, you are a Wolf warrior so you ride your wolf. You will be separate beings all of your lives.'

'That's a shame,' replied Karl.

Andor gathered all the Eagle warriors together and briefed them on the day's assignment then he introduced them to the people they would be protecting. 'Warriors, this is Princess Rowena De-Callen and her brothers, Princes Karl De-Callen and Thomas De-Callen, the great king's daughter and young sons. I will remind you it is our duty to protect them today, with our lives if need be. Look out for the obvious dangers and anything unusual. You all know what the Dark can do, we have been living with it long enough. We will fly a V formation with scouts out front, behind, above and below. I will fly with the princess and princes in the middle. It's nothing we haven't done before, apart from the two newly winged Eagle warriors. Welcome to you and learn from your more experienced fellow warriors. This will be a return journey with the king and the Wolf lords. When everyone is ready, scouts, you will lead off, and we will form up in flight. A word for the princes; no aerobatics please.'

Both boys nodded their heads and smiled. 'Oh, I will fly as an eagle not an Eagle warrior. Is everyone happy?' Everyone nodded. 'Okay, if everyone is ready, we will depart.'

Row added, 'And I am warning you, if you do aerobatics you will both be in trouble when we land. That's if I'm not sick down your back, Tom.' That comment brought a laugh from the assembled warriors then they all dispersed, headed to their respective eagles, made a fuss of them before passing on the instructions and then climbed up and got ready to fly.

Andor took Karl and Tom to one side while Row made a fuss of Arn and Alerio, getting to know the two massive eagles. 'Karl, Thomas, listen to me carefully. WI said about aerobatics I meant. If you break formation there is a great possibility you could die. Stay tight and close to me. I am more manoeuvrable than you so don't worry about me. In an attack, your job will be to keep your sister and yourselves alive and safe. If it looks like we are losing the fight dive low, as low as Arn and Alerio dare go. They will instinctively know which way to go to get you to safety. Trust them. I will fight a rear-guard action with the Eagle warriors and catch up with you later, do you both understand?'

'Yes, Andor,' replied Tom.

'Is an attack likely then?' asked Karl.

'Not likely, but the Dark will know you are here by now, so you never know how they will react, especially as Labatina has been after you for so long, but I am not expecting anything.'

The scouts ascended into the warm blue sky where they slowly disappeared. The lead Eagle warrior approached Andor and informed him the formation was ready to leave. Andor nodded his approval. Then in front of them, he transformed from a warrior into an eagle, as Karl, Row and Tom looked on in amazement. It had all seemed so easy and gentle, not like the screaming agony of the Earth films, but then he wasn't turning into a werewolf. He lifted into the air and observed the formation take flight. Tom was in the centre with Row who was clinging to his back with all her might. Happy all was going well Andor flew slightly behind Alerio and Arn, keeping a watchful eye on the two princes who were both flying well.

The formation headed towards the northern sun, cruising just above the clouds where they could see for a very great distance. There was nothing else in the sky that could threaten them. Alerio and Arn kept Karl and Tom updated about where they were and what they were flying over. They flew over the great inland sea, the swamp lands, and the great forest. Andor flew close to the boys and Row communicated with them.

'Soon you will see the crystal domes and the old sun temple on the skyline. We aren't too far away now. We have made good time. We will be peeling off from the formation over the great central hall where we will land in the grand courtyard. I will indicate to you when it's time to dive. No fancy stuff. Remember, you still have your sister with you.'

Rowena communicated back. 'It's okay, I am really enjoying the flight. It would have been better with an in-flight film and a drink though,' she said.

Andor looked at her with a confused expression on his face; he thought 'What? I don't understand.'

Rowena smiled at him and thought, 'It's okay, I'm being stupid.'

Andor nodded his head but he was still unsure what she meant. In the distance, they started to see shapes on the horizon. As they got closer, they could make out a massive high wall with turrets, similar to Warriors' Rest but on a grander scale. Beyond that they could see buildings made of crystal. glinting in the sun. In the middle of it all was a pyramid.

Tom shouted out, 'That's the old sun temple Arn told me about. On Earth, there are things called pyramids. They were built by ancient people called Egyptians,' Tom communicated back to Arn and Alerio.

Karl added, 'It would be interesting if they have hieroglyphs the same as on Earth?'

'We will have to have a look later,' Row communicated.

As they approached the wall, they could all see the guns in the turrets following them. Then, as if they had been given an order, all the guns returned to their original positions. They flew over the wall and headed for the sun temple; beyond that they could see a big hall very like the one they had their lunch in but three times as big. Arn, Alerio and Andor split from the formation; they began to turn back towards the pyramid. Andor communicated to them that they would circle the sun temple then land in the grand courtyard. As they turned to go around the sun temple, Karl noticed that Kurt and Tristan had come out of the great hall and were walking down the steps towards the great courtyard. Arn and Alerio came in abreast of each other, then began to descend between the sun temple and a tall blue building that, to Karl, looked like it had crystal windows. Just then Karl was momentarily blinded by the glint from what he assumed was someone opening a window in the tall blue building. Then Tom felt Row's dead weight against his back. They were now feet from landing in the courtyard. Tom felt Row starting to slip off to his right. He stretched his right arm back to keep her steady, and with great effort held her on the eagle's back as Arn landed.

'There's something wrong with Row!' Tom communicated to everyone. He turned to see Row's eyes closed and her head flopped to one side. Seeing something was wrong, Kurt and Tristan ran to them and between the three of them and with the help of Arn they managed to get Row onto the ground safely.

Kurt felt for a pulse which he found, but only barely. Tristan noticed the veins in Row's neck starting to become very visible and dark green in colour, spreading from a red pin prick in the side of her neck. 'She's been poisoned. I've seen this before; it looks like an assassin's poison pellet,' said Tristan. Moments later a healer was at their side. 'It's an assassin's poison,' Tristan told her,

The healer opened her medical bag and placed what to Tom looked like dock leaves on Row's neck. She also took a small bottle from her bag that looked remarkably like something you would use to squeeze eye drops with on Earth. The healer gently pulled Row's head back, which automatically opened her mouth, then dropped four blobs of a bright yellow gel into her mouth aiming at the back of her throat. Almost immediately, Row began to cough up bright green bile. Tom noticed the healer began to take the green leaves off Row's neck which were now black, then replaced them with fresh green ones. Row was now on her knees being supported by Kurt and Tristan as her body heaved and more of the green bile came out of her mouth, tears flowing from her eyes as she retched in agony. Tom saw that the green veins were now disappearing and that the leaves the healer was replacing were no longer going as black as they initially had. Row was now retching up clear bile as a second healer appeared with a jug of red liquid, the same liquid Tom had tried at the lunch in the hall hours earlier. Row's face was now bright red and she was in a great deal of pain, crying out in agony. The second healer placed some of the red liquid into a cup and the first healer dropped a blue pill in to it followed by one drop of the yellow gel.

'Drink this, lady,' the healer said and placed the cup in Row's shaking hands. With Tristan's help, she managed to drink the liquid. After a couple of seconds, she stopped retching and started to breath normally again.

Row wiped the tears from her eyes. 'Can I have some more?' she asked the healer.

'No, sorry, lady, but you can have some of this soothing ice water; it will cool your throat and stop it swelling up.' Row gulped the ice water down, three cups in the end, one after the other. She wanted to talk but she found it too painful to do so. 'You must rest now, lady, for at least two days. Don't talk. If you try, it will only damage the cells in your throat,' said the healer.

Two warriors came over with a stretcher that floated above the ground. It looked a bit like the bed Tom and Karl had tried earlier, the only difference was that it was smaller and glowing light blue. 'What's that?' asked Tom.

'It's a healing vessel. It will help the lady to sleep. While she does, it will help heal her wounds. She has suffered a great trauma to her internal organs and her arteries. If we do not act quickly, she could still die,' the healer told him. Once Row had been placed inside the healing vessel, the healer turned to Tom and his uncles and told them, 'Hopefully, we reached her in time.' Then the healer explained that depending on the poison used she could make a full recovery, or she could become paralysed, blind, deaf or she could even have brain damage That was the worst scenario.

'But, hopefully, she will be better than new once she finishes her treatment, but we will only know when the healing vessel has finished its healing, which could take anything from one to ten days' time, depending on the internal damage. Only the vessel will know when she will be ready to come out of her sleep.'

The healer noticed that Tom was shaking so she placed a hand on him. Tom felt a calming sensation flow through him, and he stopped shaking. 'Thank you,' he said. The healer smiled at him, then turned and followed the second healer and the warriors with the vessel who now had begun heading back towards the big blue building. Tom noticed that there were a lot of warriors running around purposefully and the Eagle warriors he had flown there with were still in the air, darting from building to building around the centre of the citadel. The second thing Tom noticed was that Karl nor Alerio were anywhere to be seen. 'Where's Karl?' he asked Kurt.

'He never landed. He and Alerio turned back just before you landed. Andor went after them. Do you remember what happened, Tom?' Kurt asked him.

Tom did not know. The first he knew something was wrong was when Row's full weight came against him. Up until then, Row had been fine, he explained. Kurt's eyes went red and Tom now realised that the search seemed suddenly to centre in and on the blue building, the one that the healers and warriors and Row had just entered.

'What's that building?' asked Tom

'That's the healing centre. On Earth you would know it as a hospital, Tom,' Tristan told him.

'There's nothing more we can do here. I will go and see your father. You and Tristan head to the healing centre and check on Row. Ensure she is properly guarded,' said Kurt.

Tom and Tristan hurried of in the direction of the healing centre and Kurt headed off towards the great hall to speak to his brother, King Frederick De-Callen.

Meanwhile, unknown to Tom or the others, Karl had seen the window open and what looked like a pipe stick out of it as the eagles had approached. He had tried to shout but he was not heard, so he tried communicating but he only managed to reach Alerio who he was flying on. As they turned, Alerio had communicated with Andor who then sped after them. Karl flew to the top of the blue building where he saw what looked like a large lizard with wings; four wings to be exact. That must be evil, he thought. He communicated to Alerio, 'Can you grab that thing with your claws?'

'I think you mean talons and, yes, I can, Karl. Hold on tight,' Alerio replied. As Alerio dived for the creature, he changed position so his talons were now heading straight for the creature, and his eyes were now focused on the fast-approaching creature below him. The creature sensed something and looked up.

'Too late.' Alerio's talons slammed into the creature's neck behind its spiked head snapping its neck instantly, the body slumping in Alerio's grip. With his sharp eye and keen sense of smell, Alerio was not going to miss.

'Well done, Alerio,' Karl shouted, then he jumped off Alerio's back, landing next to the winged lizard creature.

'Stay back, Karl, I want to make sure this thing is dead,' communicated Alerio. Karl stepped back as Alerio, using his talons and beak, ripped the creature's head from its neck and the rest of its body.

'What is it?' Karl communicated.

'I don't know, I have never seen this sort of creature before,' the eagle replied.

Just then a door opened on the roof and a healer stepped out. Karl turned to look at him. 'It's all right, it's dead,' Karl said. There was no reply from the healer. Alerio turned sharply with a small jump.

'Get behind me quickly, Karl,' he communicated. Karl moved quickly behind Alerio as the healer pulled out a blow pipe from his robes and put it to his lips just as a rayzor hit him full on his chest, bowling him over. Alerio moved with speed. He thrust his big talon on the healer's head, ready to strike.

From above them, Andor descended. 'Thanks, Alerio, I knew you would be able to tell if that was a real healer or not.' Under Alerio's talon the healer was now motionless, green smoke was leaving its body. 'It's dead. That's a pity, I would have liked to talk to it,' said Andor. 'Are you okay, Karl?' he asked.

'I'm fine, thank you. Wasn't that amazing what Alerio did from that high up?

And your throw was something else,' said Karl.

'Alerio was very impressive,' replied Andor. Alerio stayed with the bodies, while Andor retrieved his rayzor from the dead healer. After seeing the green smoke, they knew that he had been possessed by a Dark assassin. Then Andor picked Karl up in his big arms and flew with him to the ground next to the entrance to the healing centre. He summoned one of the warriors now guarding the entrance to him, 'Take the young prince to his sister's side. Lord Tristan is already there with Prince Thomas,' he told the warrior.

'Thanks, Andor, I will never forget that.'

Karl and the warrior left and went into the healing centre and Andor went to inform Kurt about the assassin and the creature on the roof. The warrior showed Karl to a door that was guarded by two Wolf warriors; one was in people form, the other was a wolf because a wolf's senses are much better than those of a warrior in people form. The warrior opened the door and nodded to the prince who entered. Inside, Karl saw Tristan and Tom standing either side of a floating blue bed.

'You're safe, thank Atta for that,' Tristan said as he embraced Karl.

Tom, with tears in his eyes, went up to his brother and hugged him. 'I thought you and Alerio had been killed. I couldn't do a thing to help Row! It all happened so quickly, then blue people appeared and helped her. Now she's asleep and they don't know how she will turn out.'

'Take it easy, Tom, everything will be okay. She's in good hands,' he told his brother then hugged him. 'It will be okay, Tom, I promise.'

Then Tristan stood in front of them both. 'Tom, listen to me. Everyone I have ever known get into one of these healing vessels has always come out better than they when they went in. That stuff the healer said is what they have to say to cover their backs, just in case it goes wrong. But, as I said, I have never known it to go wrong in these things.' He touched the healing vessel. 'They are amazing. When they transfer her into the proper vessel, and not this portable one she's in at the moment, there will be no stopping her recovery, trust me.'

Karl told them both about the assassin and the creature on the roof. Then Tom told Karl what had happened when they landed and all about the healers and the healing vessel Row was now in. The door opened and the same healer that had attended Row in the courtyard walked in. 'How are you all' she asked. As the healer talked to them, Karl realised the healer had slightly blue skin and brilliantly blue eyes. The healer noticed Karl staring at her. 'You have never seen a healer before have you, young prince?' she asked.

'Err, no, sorry. No, I haven't. Was it that obvious? ... I'm sorry,' replied Karl.

'Nor have I,' said Tom.

Karl stretched out his hand to shake the healer's, but instead of shaking Karl's hand, the healer put hers on top of his. Immediately Karl felt calm as his brother had done earlier. 'You are strong, young prince, you don't need my help today, but, Lord Tristan and Prince Thomas, you look like I could help you.'

'First, how is Row doing?' asked Karl.

'It's a little early to tell, young prince, but I can tell by her signs on the healing vessel that she is content, and her body is showing no signs of long-term trauma, which is as good as we can hope for at this stage. She is strong, stronger than she makes out, I am sure of that. I feel she will do well. Rest is a great healer.' Then she explained to Karl and Tom that by putting their hands on the light blue handprint at the side of the vessel in the area of Row's head they could send good feelings and strength in to Row. Even though she was asleep she would still be comforted by it. The healer then fixed both Tom's and Tristan's sorrow with a touch from her hand and then she left. Through the door Kurt appeared, and asked how Rowena was doing. After Tristan answered him, Kurt asked that all three go to the king's chambers so the king could meet his children.

As they all made their way out of the building and they walked across the courtyard, Tom asked Tristan what their father, the king, was like. He explained to them both that the king was a big man, every bit the warrior. Looking at him, you would shake in your boots. He was the fiercest of all the warriors and his enemies hated him and trembled at the mention of his name. Tristan also told them that he was the gentlest, kindest, and funniest person he had ever met and that he loved his children and missed them every day he was away from them. 'So, don't be scared of him when you first see him,' Tristan told them.

'Why didn't he come to meet us when we first arrived?' asked Karl.

'He wasn't here, he was away talking to the nomadic Romonia people who had just sailed across the endless sea from the land of ice where they spend their winter. When you crossed with the angels, he was flying from the coast. He has only just arrived, and he is eager to see you. Oh, there is one thing I forgot to tell you. Don't be alarmed when you see him. His head is in that of his wolf form.'

'What?' replied Karl. They all stopped at the bottom of the steps leading to the great hall.

'I will explain. When he was attacked by your mother, Karl, it was the back of his head that was hit with the axe from Arthfael. He nearly died. The Wolf master called your father's wolf side out, but because of the massive trauma to his head and brain, he was turned into his wolf self before he died to save him. It did save him but the person part of the back of his head was dead and did not reappear when he reformed from wolf to person. Only the wolf part of his head stayed in the person form. If it hadn't, he would have died when he returned to his people form. Your father could go to the blue moon and be completely cured but he will not.'

'Why's that'? asked Tom.

'Because it means he will be away from our world for too long and he has vowed to stay the way he is until Arthfael is dead for killing Elizabeth. He also wants to find out the truth about Labatina. You see, he still believes Labatina is under some sort of evil curse and, until he can cure or kill her, he will stay in his present form.'

'What do we call him? Karl asked.

'Father, I presume. We will find out in a short while,' said Tristan.

The three of them walked up the steps past two warriors now standing at the entrance to the great hall. Both warriors were dressed in the royal guard ceremonial uniforms of black shiny knee-length boots, white trousers with a grey and black stripe down the side. They had black jackets on with grey buttons, cuffs and silver chain mail epilates with grey piping around the collar. On their heads, they had black helmets with a grey plume on the side tipped with red. On the front of the helmet, above the gold visor, was a fierce looking silver skull and cross bones. Both warriors had shining silver rayzors at their left sides and some sort of pistol-sized weapon on their right hip. To the boys, they looked both fierce and resplendent. Both warriors turned and followed the trio into the hall. This hall was the grandest they had seen yet. Once again, it had a high roof but this time it was painted with what the boys believed to be some sort of history.

'What does all that on the roof mean, Uncle Tristan?' Tom asked.

'That, Tom, is the history of the Wolf and Eagle peoples from the beginning of time. It shows when Wolf and Eagle became one and the people took Wolf and Eagle life lovers. The first and greatest couple were Atta Wolf, the father of the Wolf nation, and Rowena, the mother of all the Eagle people, who fell in love and joined the two greatest peoples in this world together. There are other peoples here in our world, but none are as close as the Wolf and the Eagle.'

As they walked along the great hall, Karl and Tom both looked up at the great wonders depicted on the roof. Every time the boys looked up, they saw something they had not noticed before. When they got near to the end of the hall, their attention was drawn by the voice of a female Wolf warrior standing at the end of the hall. Both boys looked at her. There was something familiar about her, but they did not know her.

'Hello, little lords,' she said.

Both boys looked at the stunningly beautiful warrior, trying to puzzle out why she looked and sounded so familiar to them. The warrior had long red hair that flowed down her back; she also had the same headband worn by Raphina and Rowena. She was wearing an elegant long red dress that touched the floor, covering her feet. Around her slim waist was a wide jewel-studded leather belt hanging at an angle. A rayzor was at her side in a silver sheath which was also festooned with bright glistening jewels. The lady smiled at them.

'Don't you recognise me? After all those years together?'

'Phina! It's Phina, Karl!' shouted Tom, He ran towards her and was embraced for the first time in his life by Phina, the Wolf warrior princess.

'What about you. Karl? You will never be too old enough for a hug from me. Come on.' She smiled.

Karl walked up to her, a beaming smile on his face. As he got closer, Phina grabbed him and pulled him in. hugging them both. All three were now crying and laughing.

'I can't believe it, Phina, you are beautiful and a woman too,' said Karl

'Thank you, Karl. Don't look so shocked and I'm not a woman, I'm a Wolf warrior princess.'

'I feel so embarrassed now about pulling your tail and fighting with you. What you must have thought of us?' said Karl.

'Don't you worry about that, either of you. On your world I could only be a wolf, but here I am a warrior and a wolf and your friend,' she said.

'Not just a friend… family,' said Tom.

Chapter 9
Dad

The door in front of them opened and another beautiful, but blond, warrior walked in. She had on a light blue dress like Phina's with the same headband, belt and rayzor.

'I see you recognise my sister,' she said.

'Salina!' Tom shouted and the hugging and crying happened once more. 'This is amazing. I can't believe it, and it's so cool,' Tom said.

Salina asked about Rowena and Tristan explained how she was doing. 'You go and see her, I'll look after the boys,' said Phina. Salina kissed the boys and left the way they had entered. 'Come on then, let's go and see your father. Has Tristan told you about his looks?' Phina enquired.

'Yes, he has, I'm not quite sure what to expect. It sounds horrible. Tom thinks he will look cool, but that's Tom.' They all walked through the door at the end of the hall, the one Phina and Salina had come through minutes earlier. On the other side of the door was a long narrow hallway that had very plain looking doors to the left and right at ten-feet intervals.

Phina explained, 'These were small rooms for visiting warriors. All in all, there are one hundred rooms that come off the great hall. At the very end of the hallway are your father's quarters for when he is here at the capital citadel.' They reached the end of the hallway where there was a very normal looking door. There was no indication that there was a great king inside. As they approached the door, it opened and in front of them were two more royal guards, dressed the same as the two at the entrance to the great hall. The difference this time was they did not let them pass.

'Please, one moment. The king has someone with him. He has asked if you would not mind waiting in here. Lord Tristan, Princess Phina, please go through to the king.' The guard stepped to one side and opened the door to his left. 'Princes, please, through here. Your father will be with you shortly, he is having council with his leaders now. He does apologise to you. They are discussing what and how your sister was attacked and the need for tighter security here in the capital.'

Karl and Tom walked through into a very comfortable looking room; the walls were decorated in warm red and green, with heavy drapes plus a large bookshelf full of books along one wall. There was a small table in the corner with a matching chair and in the centre of the room was a very large sofa covered by some sort of flower pattern, a flower neither boys had ever seen before. At the side of it on a small table were some cups and a bottle of green liquid. The boys sat down on the comfortable sofa and immediately noticed a painting on the wall opposite them.

'It's her,' said Karl.

'Who?' replied Tom.

'The woman in my picture is the woman in the locket, the one that has been in my bedside table for as long as I can remember, it's really her!'

'It can't be, Karl, you had that locket on Earth.'

'Yes, but, Tom, we come from here, so it might have come from here as well. It must have… because it's her.'

The boys stared at the picture in front of them, the face looked so familiar to Karl. Tom knew it from Karl's locket. They both wondered if she was either of their mothers.

After a while, Tom started looking around. 'I wonder what the green liquid is?' he said, breaking Karl away from his daydream of the beautiful lady in the picture.

'What, Tom?' he said.

'The green liquid in the bottles, I wonder what it is?'

'Try it, Tom, then you will find out.'

'It could be poison.'

'Don't be a plonker, Tom, who would put poison in bottles next to glasses, out in the open, in one of the king's rooms?'

'Who would try and kill our sister out in the open, in the middle of a fortified city?' said Tom.

'Good point, Tom, let's just leave it, shall we?' said Karl. The boys chatted away for what seemed like an hour; they talked about everything that had happened to them since arriving in their home world. They also talked about their father and the trepidation they both felt about meeting him. Then the door opened and Phina walked in.

'Are you two okay in here by yourselves? I'm surprised you haven't had any of the green berry juice, it's very nice and very good for you,' she told them.

'We weren't sure, Phina. It could have been anything, especially after what happened to Row,' said Karl.

'You're perfectly safe in here, this is your father's study.'

'Who's that person in the picture, Phina? I think I recognise her,' said Karl.

'You recognised her from the locket, I bet?' Phina replied.

'How would you know that?' Karl replied.

Phina explained, 'Elizabeth gave all three of you the same locket to remind you of her and to make you happy whenever you looked at it. A reminder of home but Tom lost his. Everyone thought at the time he had swallowed it because he used to put everything in his mouth then.' She told them that Rowena also had the identical locket but whether she still had it, she did not know. 'It is your mother, Elizabeth.'

'I thought it was my mother. I could feel inside me every time I looked at the picture in the locket that I knew her. I thought it was my mother,' said Karl. 'But, wait a minute, Kurt told us all that Elizabeth was Tom's mum and that mine and Row's was Labatina so why did you say our mother?' asked Karl.

Phina explained to them that even though Labatina was Karl and Row's biological mother, Elizabeth was their real mother. She had spent more time with all three of them than Labatina had. She had been their mother in every way possible throughout their all their lives until her death. Both boys were now quiet, looking at the picture of Elizabeth on the wall.

'Your father, the king, wants me to take you to him. He is in the strategy centre with Kurt and Tristan,' Phina told them.

'Can I ask a question? Why do some people call our father king and other people call him emperor?' asked Tom.

Phina explained to them that he was a Wolf warrior, in fact, he was the king of the Wolf tribe, but he had also been chosen by all the tribes and peoples of the world to rule over it as emperor, so he was both a king and an emperor. She also explained that Kurt and Tristan were princes of the Wolf tribe, because they were brothers to the king and all male brothers of the Wolf king were princes, but not all were emperors. That seemed to make sense to Karl and Tom, even though they thought it might get a little confusing for their subjects. Phina told them that it did not, because everyone knew who the emperor was and who the king of the Wolves was. Everyone knew who the king's brothers were. 'Right then, you two, let's go see your father, the great king and emperor of Elemtum.'

They left the room through another door that was concealed behind the hanging drape. Then they came to a spiral stairwell going down; it was quite narrow and illuminated by silver lights mounted along one wall also spiralling down. Karl commented that it was a little creepy. Phina informed him it was because it was actually an escape route to the strategic centre below them. They descended about thirty feet before they came across a glowing orange light that moved vertically up and down. Phina explained that it was a sensor that scanned for many different threats; it was like an X-ray on Earth, she told them. It also detected weapons, poisons, explosives, acids, chemicals and the Dark. Most Dark warriors gave off a pungent odour, even after they had washed; there were only two from the Dark that did not, Labatina and Arthfael. For some reason, they did not smell like the rest of the Dark. Then Phina explained what they had to do,

'Walk into the light but don't go through it or you will be eliminated, instantly, and we don't want that to happen to our young princes, now do we?' she told them. 'Then stand perfectly still, it will monitor your heart rate and blood pressure and also if you are sweating excessively. Next it will perform all the other checks I told you about. If you are okay, the light turns green and you can proceed to the next security check. If it finds something it senses is a potential threat, or is indeed a threat, then you will be frozen instantly. The whole process takes around three seconds, give or take a second. You go first, Karl, then your brother will see its okay and won't be too scared.'

'That sounds good to me. Go on, big brother. Oh, and by the way, I'm not scared,' said Tom.

'I knew you wouldn't be, little prince,' replied Phina. 'Go on, Karl, it won't hurt. It will be over very quickly.'

'I don't like the way you said it will be over very quickly, Phina.' Then he stepped into the orange light.

Tom watched on, fascinated, as the light went across his brother's body. Seconds later all was green, and Karl stepped out of the light and turned, smiling, to his brother. 'Come on then, little prince,' he said.

Fearlessly, Tom strode with purpose into the now orange light. Karl noticed his brother tense and close his eyes as he entered. Seconds later all was green once more, but Tom did not move. 'Open your eyes, plonker, it's finished and you're still alive,' Karl told him.

Tom opened his eyes, smiled and stepped out. 'I knew,' he said, 'I was enjoying that.'

'Sure, you were,' replied his brother, reassuringly patting Tom on his back.

Phina stepped into the light and it went immediately red and a hatch opened to the side of her. The boys could hear 'Five! Four!' Phina dropped her rayzor into the hatch which then closed, and the light turned immediately green and she stepped out of the light.

'My god,' said Karl. 'What would have happened if you had not got your knife out in time?'

Phina explained that if they had been watching her, she had already unsheathed the weapon before she entered the light. If she had still taken too long to deposit the weapon in the security box, then she would have been frozen instantly. If she had run out of the light, she would now be dead, she told them.

Now they were all stood the other side of another orange light,

'We wait for the royal guards to open the first entry door. After that we have the second scanner. This senses fear as well as all the things the first sensor checks for. It's exactly the same procedure as before. Remember, don't run out of the light. Oh yes, I almost forgot, this one also scans your eyes and a pad will come out of the wall either side of you. Place your hands, palms down, on the pads and they will check your fingerprints. Happy?' said Phina.

Both boys nodded, then the door in front of them opened and once more there was an orange light, but this time it was horizontal. Karl entered. He was immediately bathed in the orange light, then the two sensors came out of the wall and Karl placed his palms on each pad. Seconds later two metal straps came out of the pads and secured themselves around Karl's wrists. The light turned red. Karl looked back at Phina, hoping for some reassurance or guidance; there was none. Phina looked worried. Suddenly a thin jet of what looked to Tom like water shot out from all around Karl and he was instantly frozen in position.

'What's happened, Phina?' Tom asked

'He's been neutralised. Not permanently though, you will be glad to hear, but I don't know why. This should not have happened.' A transparent screen dropped between Phina and Tom and his brother. Tom didn't know whether he should laugh or cry as the door opposite Karl opened. In front of him were two royal guards and two people dressed in very similar attire to the sort of suit fireman on Earth wore when they were dealing with chemical spills. The red light around Karl disappeared and the two suited people walked either side of Karl. Then the metal wristlets returned to the pads and disappeared. Karl was then lifted up under his arms by the suited people like a cardboard cut-out in a shop. Phina reassuringly put her arm around Tom's shoulder and hugged him gently. 'He'll be all right. He will be as good as new when they defrost him. They just have to be careful they don't bump into anything or they might knock something off.' Tom looked up at her and noticed she was smiling. 'Only kidding,' she said. Tom started to laugh as he watched the suits take his stiff brother away. Phina noticed tears welling up in his face. 'It's okay, Tom, he will be fine.' Then she gave him a reassuring hug. 'We just have to make sure it doesn't happen to you now.' Tom looked up at her once more, concern etched all over his face. 'Chill out, Tom, it will be cool,' said Phina. 'Oh, I'm sorry, Tom, I couldn't resist that.' Tom started to smile and Phina wiped the tears from his eyes. 'That's better,' she said. 'I don't like your sad face.

I don't think I ever saw that face once on Earth.' Tom got another hug just as one of the royal guards reappeared in front of them and the orange light disappeared.

'We are very sorry, lady, prince. We believe because we don't have recent samples of your eyes, pictures and fingerprints it did not recognise the prince. The system was a little confused because it recognised the emperor's DNA but it knew it was not him, so it froze the prince. We are taking him to the reconstitution chamber, and he will be back with you in a while. Please follow me and I will take you to the emperor.'

Phina and the surviving king's child followed the guard along a very narrow hall. Phina explained to Tom that it was so narrow because it effectively restricted the room anyone had available to fight; you could not swing a cat or, for that matter, more importantly a rayzor or axe. Finally, they left the hall and entered a room with lots of tables and chairs in it.

'What's this room, Phina? Is it where the warriors sit ready for battle?' asked Tom.

'No, Tom, it's the dining room. You know, where we eat,' Phina replied with a smile.

They carried on through the dining room and came out at the intersection of four hallways. The guard went left and Phina and Tom followed. At the end of that hall were two more royal guards. 'These are the operation rooms, Tom. This is where all the plans for defence and operations against the Dark are coordinated. This is also where all the emergency planning is coordinated if there is a natural disaster, like floods and things like that if they were ever to happen. You could say this is the nerve centre of our world, this is where your father is.'

Tom looked up at her; she could see the apprehension on his face and even a tinge of fear in his eye and in his voice when he asked her, 'Would you come in with me to meet my father.'

'Of course, I will, Tom. There is nothing to be worried about. Your father is a great warrior but also a very gentle loving person who, believe it or not, is more nervous about meeting you than you would think.' The door to the operation room opened. Tom could see a multitude of screens on the walls and a big table at one end which was encircled with comfortable looking high-backed chairs. They entered the room. All fell quiet. All around him warriors turned and looked at the little lost boy from Earth standing in front of them.

Tom immediately noticed Kurt, who smiled broadly at him. 'Come on then, Prince Thomas De-Callen, don't you give your uncle Kurt a hug any more now you're a posh royal?'

'Uncle Kurt!' Tom shouted, and he ran to him as if they had been separated for years not just days. He was lifted up by Kurt, squeezed until he gave in with a smile then Kurt put Tom down.

'You survived your little adventure then, Tom, unlike your brother and sister, who I am glad to say are both doing well. Particularly Karl who is thawing out nicely.'

This made Tom laugh and he began to forget his nerves. Tom felt two big hands grab around his chest, just under his arms, then he began to be lifted; then he was spun around and caught again by the big hands. He now found himself staring into the eyes of a werewolf, or at least what he thought was a werewolf? 'Ahhh!' the sound came out involuntarily from his mouth as he looked into the big and menacing eyes of the wolf. The werewolf then opened its mouth and Tom saw the razor-sharp teeth inches away from his face. That's when he heard laughter around him, but he didn't dare take his eyes off the teeth.

'It's okay, Tom, it's your father.' The words came into his head; it was Phina.

The werewolf seemed to smile at him, and then he heard in his head, 'My son, how you have grown into a fine young warrior. You're not scared of your father, are you? It has been so long. It's good to have you back with me. If only your mother could see you know, she would be very proud of you.'

'Are you a werewolf?' Tom asked, as the wolf man king put him back on the floor. Around him everyone was laughing once more.

Phina came up to him and explained that he had been sending his thoughts to everyone, not just his father and it was probably because he was a little nervous and was not concentrating.

The king knelt down in front of his son and placed his big hands on Tom's shoulders then thought to him, 'I am sorry, Thomas, due to my injuries my people's brain was too badly damaged, but I was saved by being turned into my wolf form. I soon found out that, for some reason, I can reform back into my people form but my wolf head remains. I can also return to my full wolf form whenever I want. You are young and I don't want to frighten you. How would you rather see me?'

'As you are, Dad, I think you look cool. My friends will be jealous if they knew my dad was a werewolf,' replied Tom.

'"Dad"? What does that mean, Thomas? I am not familiar with the word.'

'It is an affectionate word from Earth meaning father, lord,' Phina told him.

'I like it, Thomas. You and your brother and sister can call me Dad, but no one else can,' the king told them all then a beaming smiled filled his wolf face. It was the same smile you would recognise on a dog when you play ball with it.

This brought a huge smile to Tom's face. Then the realisation hit him that maybe his new dad might not be so bad after all.

'I can see by the look and attitude of this young warrior that you have all done a good job looking after him. I am just sorry we have not done as good a job of looking after them since they have arrived here on Elemtum and for that I apologise to you, Thomas. I will also apologise to your sister and brother when they reappear. I have spent too long worrying about this world and my people and not enough about my children, and for that I am most truly sorry. I have also come to the conclusion, after meeting you, Thomas, and knowing that my brothers Kurt and Tristan are back, that they are more than capable of running things while I am away getting fixed on the blue moon.'

'What! You mean you will go and get better and become a proper human again?' Tom said excitedly.

'No, Thomas, I mean I will become a whole Wolf warrior again. I have never been, nor ever will be, human.'

He smiled at his son. Everyone laughed and Tom went red. 'Right. Brothers…, you have control. My son and I are going to see how the rest of my family are doing. Phina, you can accompany us as I need a good warrior to watch my back and I haven't seen you for so long so a good old chat is in order. What do you think, Thomas?'

'I totally agree, King Dad.'

The king chuckled at what his son had said then excused himself for two minutes while he had a quick conference with Kurt and Tristan. After that he, Tom and Phina left the command centre and headed to the surface, this time without any problems or frozen boys. They talked and laughed as they left the great hall and headed for the infirmary. Phina kept an eye out for anything strange but nothing struck her as so. They went to see Rowena first; they were told her condition had not changed, but all the signs were good. The next visit was to Karl, who they found lying in a blue gel, slowly defrosting. The healers told them that they would keep Karl sedated, otherwise he would be in tremendous pain with the extreme cold and it might cause even a strong heart like his to fail. As there was nothing they could do, they decided the next best thing to do was to go and get some food and drink. The king spoke to the chief healer about his wish to go to the blue moon for treatment. Phina, Tom and Salina, who had been with Row when they went to see her, went to the dining hall. It was a little different to the last one Tom had been in. It had some long benches or you could sit on smaller round tables surrounded by chairs; the latter option was what they decided on. What was also different was the way the food was served; it was more a cafeteria style system where you picked up a tray and went along a big glass display case that had buttons with pictures of the food inside, much like a vending machine on Earth except the food was definitely of a better standard than most on Earth. No money was involved, as money was not used and had no purpose on Elemtum. All you had to do was simply push the button corresponding to the food you wanted, the glass front opened and you placed it on your tray.

'What sort of thing did you like to eat on Earth?' asked Salina.

'I can tell you exactly what he likes,' smiled Phina. 'Burgers, sausages, chicken nuggets, chips and mayonnaise.'

'How do you know that?' Tom asked.

'Have you forgotten already, Tom? I've lived with you for almost all your life.'

'Yes, I know that, Phina, but you were a wolf.'

'Yes, that's right, Tom, but what you didn't know then was that I was a Wolf warrior, not just a wolf. I could see and hear everything you did and said,' she replied. 'The only thing I couldn't do was talk to you. I could have communicated with you and, as you know, we never did that until the last days on Earth, So, just remember I know all your little secrets.'

Tom's face went bright red as he blushed. 'Don't worry, your secrets are safe with me.' Then she gave him a wink.

'More importantly, Tom, is what do you want to eat?' asked Salina. 'There are things like burgers, sausages and chips, with some nice sauce. Do you want to try them? I will show you which ones they are.' They all walked over to the counter and Salina pointed out what she thought he would like. Tom pressed all the right buttons and ended with a mountain of food on his tray. 'I take it you're hungry?' smiled Salina.

'You will realise the longer you know him, Salina, that Tom is always hungry.' She laughed. They sat down at the round table and Tom tucked into the pile of food in front of him. He cut a piece of what looked like a burger and took a bite.

'Humm, that tastes great. It's better than the burgers at home. It has a lovely flavour. What is it?

'Do you really want to know?' asked Phina.

'Yes, it's great, I will have this again.'

'It's wild boar,' Phina answered.

Salina looked at her and was just about to say something when Phina winked and smiled, something Tom did not see.

'Ah, boar, yes, very nice,' Salina said with a smile, understanding what her sister was trying to tell her. Boar sounded a lot better than swamp cucumber slug.

Next, Tom tried what looked like a sausage; he gave the same reaction as before.

'I thought you might like that,' Phina said with a smile.

'This tastes like, ah, like, chicken. Yes, that's it, like a spicy chicken… Is it chicken?'

'No, Tom, not chicken. It's a terror shark; very hard to catch but tastes great. One of my favourites,' Salina told him.

'I don't care, it's really nice. Anyway, I think I should just eat and not know what it is.'

Phina and Salina laughed which set Tom off. After the laughter stopped, they ate their food. By now it was early evening but it was still bright sunshine outside. The door to the dining hall opened and silhouetted in the doorway was the unmistakable figure of the king with his wolf's head,

'Look who I've got with me!' he shouted.

A figure stood in the doorway as the king moved out of the way but because of the glare from the sun reflecting brightly coming off the person's clothing, they could not see who or what it was. As the figure entered the hall and moved into the shade, they could see the person was in a silver reflective suit, a bit like something an oil fire fighter would wear back on Earth. Then they realised, as the figure got closer to them, that it was Karl. He walked up to the table looking a little worn out but smiling.

'How are you feeling?' asked Phina.

'A little cold still, but okay. They told me I had to wear this absorption suit for the rest of the day until my body temperature stabilises. The healer told me the suit will turn white when it is okay for me to take it off.'

Tom started to laugh. 'You look daft,' he said.

'Not as daft as I feel,' Karl replied with a smile. Everyone asked him how he was feeling. He told them that all he remembered was walking into the light and the metal cuffs going around his wrists. The next thing he remembered was a big wolf man standing over him who turned out to be their dad. He told them they had a good talk and that he had explained his plans to get himself fixed, and also about the talk with Tom and that he was happy for them to call him dad. 'This is all very bizarre. I'm sure I am going to wake up and it's all a dream,' said Karl.

Phina told him to sit down, then went and got him a similar dinner to what Tom was eating. Karl also enjoyed the meal, finishing it all with the green liquid they would not drink in the king's study. The king joined them and the boys updated him on their lives so far. Finally, the talk turned to Rowena and the king told them that she was making excellent progress and the healers were already talking about reviving her as early as the next day if she continued to improve at the same rate. After that, the king told them that he had decided to go to the blue moon as soon as tomorrow and that he would be taking Rowena with him for further treatment. He didn't expect to be on the blue moon for more than three days if what the healers said was anything to go by. The boys were to be left in the care of Kurt, Tristan, Phina and Salina, just like the old days. To the boys, Earth now seemed a life time ago.

They finished their meal and left the dining hall, as the king and Kurt excused themselves once again to attend to other matters. Phina and Salina also had other duties to perform so Tristan took the boys to their quarters next to the king's. Each boy had his own room which was twice the size of the room Raif had shown them back in Warriors' Rest. Row had also been given a room between them. Each room had an interconnecting door. If you walked through all the doors to the right you ended up in their father's room. If you went left you ended up in Phina's and then Salina's rooms. Directly across from them were Tristan and Kurt's rooms. Tristan opened Tom's room and all three went in.

'Wow! This is big,' Tom said as he entered, 'and look it's got one of them beds, and what's this? Oh! Look at that'.

'I take it you like your new room? I will leave you to have a look around while I will take Karl to his. Are you happy with how the bed works?' Tristan asked him. Tom nodded yes then Tristan and Karl walked through into Row's room then on into Karl's. 'This is very similar to Tom's room, the difference being there is some literature Kurt thought you might like to read about this world's history, its geography, animals, reptiles and creatures, some of which are friendly and some not. Although, we will have to change that now as I hear you have tamed one of them already. You have only been here one day.'

'I didn't tame it, Uncle Tristan, I communicated with it and I found out that it was friendly.'

'So, what would you have done if it wasn't friendly?'

'I don't really know, but I'm sure I will find out one day.'

'Yes, with what's going on at the moment, I fear that could be sooner rather than later. Set your bed for first light. Do you know how to do that?'

'No,' replied Karl.

So, Tristan showed Karl what to do. He also told him to meet in the dining hall where they would discuss what would happen the next day, then left him to show Tom the alarm and tell him about the plans for the next day. Tristan entered Tom's room but he was nowhere to be seen, then he heard banging. With a smile, Tristan walked over to the back wall of the room and pressed the flashing red light on the wall. The wall parted and inside was a red-faced Tom.

'I've been in here since you and Karl left,' he said, a little flustered. 'The door shut and it would not open. There is a red light in here I kept pressing, but it didn't do anything.'

Still smiling, Tristan explained to Tom that he had walked into the sanitary unit, where he should go to the toilet and to clean himself. He explained, 'You pressed the green light that opens the sliding door. Once you enter, the door shuts and it will not open again until you perform an action, i.e. go to the toilet or have a clean. You see the mirror on the wall? Just touch it and a screen will appear... Go on, just press the mirror,' he told him.

Tom pressed the mirror and a screen came up, it said on the display:

1. Urinate
2. Defaecate
3. Clean teeth
4. Clean clothed body
5. Clean unclothed body
6. Clean clothes only
7. Clean weapons/equipment
8. Exit

'It's simple Tom. Press the one you want and off you go. There is no water used, it's all done by light which kills all the germs and gets rid of sweat and blood and things.'

'No water? That seems odd. Where does the dirt go and what about your bum? If you, well you know what I mean, how do you wipe it?'

'You will see, Tom. Have a clean before you go to sleep, press whichever one you want and it will clean you. It's really fast too.' Tristan pressed the exit screen, the door opened and they both walked back into the room. He told Tom about the alarm and where to go in the morning. 'I had better go and tell Karl about the sanitary unit. See you in the morning, Tom.' Tristan left and went back to Karl's room. Again, there was no one to be seen.

'Help! Help! I'm stuck in here!' came from behind the wall. Once more, with a smile on his face, he opened the sanitary unit and proceeded to explain it all to Karl. Tristan left Karl who set his bed to sunrise then walked through to his brother's room. He found Tom on the floor with his toys around him and his rucksack thrown in a corner.

'Where was that?' he asked his brother, who told him about the walk-in wardrobe next to the bed. He had found it when he took one shoe off and fell against the wall which then opened, exposing his rucksack and shelves full of clothing and boots and jackets, hats. It was all in there. None of it was fashionable but it was all cool, he explained to his brother. Karl went back into his room and stood at the side of the bed. There was no seal where a door should be but he did notice a slight difference in the colour of the wall. He put his hand towards it. When it was inches away, the door sensed Karl's hand was there and opened, sliding away to his right. In front of him was his rucksack which he dragged out and opened. He took all his clothes out and put them on the shelves in the wardrobe, then he found a drawer in which he placed the locket, knife and SAS survival book. After closing the door, he went over to the sanitary unit and went in. He felt an urge so he decided to try out the toilet. He pressed Defaecate. To his left a seat came out of the wall very similar to a normal toilet on Earth except that it had the seat and below that was a shelf and that was it. 'No bowl, no water.' He correctly assumed that you pooed sitting down and it dropped on to the shelf. But after that what? he thought to himself. Whenever I poo, I also wee, so where does that go? It will all splash everywhere, that can't be right? He looked at the seat. It was very clean and there were no traces of poo or wee on the floor. He had noticed a fridge type thing in his room so he went back out and opened it up. Inside were several bottles of different coloured liquid as well as what he made out to be bottles of water. He picked the bottle with the green liquid in it, one because it would show up if it splashed around and two because it was the only thing apart from the water that he recognised and was actually comfortable pouring down the loo. He went back into the sanitary unit and noticed the toilet had gone, so he went back to the mirror and chose urinate. The toilet popped out and Karl poured some of the green liquid through the seat onto the shelf. To his astonishment, the liquid seemed to instantly evaporate. Between the seat and the shelf, a yellow light came on every time the liquid hit the shelf, then it was gone.

Amazing, he thought, and he poured some more green liquid down. He was so excited by the disappearing liquid that before he knew it the bottle was empty. He was now intrigued about what would happen with a, hopefully, solid dump. He thought about the best way to do this. Would he need paper? He didn't trust the mirror because it said nothing about cleaning your bum after defaecation. To top it all, he was now getting the urge to go for a number two. Bloody hell, he thought. Do I go and ask Tristan, or do I just go for it? The only trouble is there's no toilet paper. It could all go horribly wrong.

He decided the best thing to do was to just go for it. That would be better than looking a fool in front of Tristan. The best thing to do, he surmised, was to leave the room then return so as not to confuse the system, because it was set for urinate. So, Karl went back over to the mirror and pressed 8. Exit. The door opened and

Karl left the room, then he re-entered. He went up to the mirror and pressed 5. Defaecate. The toilet popped out again, seat and shelf, no sides to them. He stood in front of it, unzipped the silver suit and pushed it down his legs, then he promptly sat down as the urge grew. As soon as he had sat on the toilet seat it all gushed out of him. That was close, he thought, I never realised it was that close.

Karl sat there with his own thoughts then in a flash he remembered what it was it was all about. The toilet had no sides. He quickly put his hands down to the back of his legs. They were dry. He was relieved. Then he looked at the floor either side of him. Nothing. He promptly stood up and looked down at the shelf; it was immaculately clean. How did it do that? he thought. He waddled over to the mirror and pressed 2. Clean clothed body. The toilet went back into the wall and the light changed to red, then blue then green and a voice said 'Clean finished'. Now, that left Karl with a dilemma. How do I check if I'm clean? he thought. I have no paper. What if there is some poo still there? This was a lot more difficult than he had first imagined.

Ah! He had an idea. He waddled as far away from the mirror as he could, which was not far enough away to see his exposed bottom. So, he jumped up to try and get a view of his bottom in the mirror. This was a lot harder than he had thought it would be, and then he stopped. You bloody idiot, he thought, they have probably been doing this for decades and I'm faffing about like a numpty. He pulled his silver suit back on, zipped it up and walked over to the mirror and pressed 8. Exit, then walked out of the sanitary unit. He walked through the adjoining doors, through Row's empty room into Tom's. The room was dark except for a light blue light coming from the bed. Tom was now happily wrapped up in it fast asleep. Good idea, Karl thought, and wandered back to his room leaving all the interconnecting doors open. They had never slept apart in all their lives. He fell on his bed, which closed around him and he was fast asleep.

CHAPTER 10
Linasfarn

Tom's eyes opened. For a split second he was unsure of his surroundings, then it all came back to him. He had never felt so rested, relaxed and awake. For the first time since he had been in his new room, he realised that light was flooding in from a window in front of him that had been a wall the night before. He was sure of that. Tom was looking out of his enormous window which went from floor to ceiling and wall to wall directly in front of him. On the other side of the window, he could see a big lake. He didn't remember that from when he had flown in, but then his mind was on other things.

'Morning, Tom. Have you had a good sleep?' Tom turned to see his brother standing there smiling. 'What a view to wake up to, hey.'

'It's amazing, isn't it? Have you got the same sort of window?'

'I have,' Karl replied. 'If you look carefully in the lake there is someone swimming in it, but they must have good lungs because they dive under the water and don't come back up for ages.'

Tom peered out at the lake; he saw nothing except water and trees. Just as he was getting bored looking at the water, he noticed a glint in the water. A green-haired girl's head and shoulders popped out and waved towards him. Tom looked behind him expecting someone to be standing there but there was just his brother and he wasn't waving. Tom waved back and the girl with the green hair was gone.

'Come on, Tom, we had better go and meet the others in the dining hall.'

'Who do you think that was, Karl?'

'I have no idea. Maybe one of the others can tell us. Whoever it is, she must be mad. That water looks freezing.'

'Talking about freezing, I've just noticed you haven't got your silver suit on. Are you feeling better?'

'That sleep really helped. It must be that temperature controlling that Raif told us about.'

The boys left the room and met Salina walking down the corridor. She asked them how they were and informed them that Rowena's condition had improved during the night. Her soul rhythm was much better. The healers were very impressed with her inner strength. The boys weren't too sure what she was talking about, but it sounded good. They all entered the dining hall and were met by their father, Kurt and Tristan. There was a lovely smell coming from somewhere and the boys were told it was something they would recognise,

'Eggs, bacon and fresh bread,' said Kurt.

'It's not, is it, Uncle Kurt?' said Karl.

'You know me so well, Karl. It's a variation on the theme you might say,' he replied.

'How varied is that?' he asked.

'The bread is bread, even better than on Earth I might add. The eggs are eggs, except they are from a swifter. That's a bit like an ostrich. And the bacon is a puff ball. That's like a mushroom but it tastes remarkably like bacon but without the fat. I think you will both like it.'

The boys were ach brought a plate of food; the bread was great, the puff ball was amazing, and the egg was very strong but they both agreed they could quite happily get used to the taste if there was some salt and pepper about, which their father said he could arrange. After the plates had been cleared, they all walked over to the infirmary to see Row. On the way, they talked about what the day had to offer for the boys. They were told they would have an easy day, getting to know the capital and the local area with their eagles and Salina. Phina had gone back to Warriors' Rest to help her mother. Kurt would be joining them later that morning and Tristan would stay here to take command while the king went with Rowena to the blue moon. They entered Row's room to find the familiar faces of the healers who had saved her life the day before.

'The good news, my lords, is that we intend to wake her from her medically induced coma in two days' time. We could possibly do it today but the poison the Dark used was very strong and we want to give her body as much time as possible to rest without feeling strained. Today, we will take her, along with the king, to Penterum in the next sail craft to leave. All being well you will see Rowena and the king back to full fitness in two days.' The healers bowed and left the room.

'Penterum, where's that?' asked Karl.

'That, Karl, is the name the healers give to the blue moon, their home.'

'What's a sail craft?' asked Tom, straight after.

Kurt explained it was like a ship, but it was a spaceship. It had sails that lifted the craft into the sky taking the craft into outer space then on to the blue moon. 'You can learn a bit more about that in the books we gave you and Karl yesterday, Tom, if you're interested?'

'I think we will both be interested in everything to do with this planet.' Both Karl and Tom agreed, then together the boys sent Row their best wishes and comforting thoughts through the panel in the healing vessel. They left Row with the healers and returned to the strategic centre through the main entrance. This was a little wider than the spiral staircase they had gone down with Phina the day before. They could all easily stand in a row and the scanners did all of them at once. This time no one was frozen. The king said his goodbyes to his sons then left them with Salina while he finished tidying up the affairs of state with Kurt and Tristan as well as a couple of other troubling issues before he left for the blue moon, Penterum, with Rowena.

Salina took the boys into one of the side rooms off the strategic operations room. In the middle of the room was a big table with a 4D projected image of the capital they were now in. 'This is a Holler map; you can program in anywhere in this world and it will bring up a 4D holographic image of the area. The size of the area will depend on the map size you will see on the Holler table. If you don't know the exact coordinates you are looking for, use the touch screen that you can pull out of the side of the table. It's in tablet format like the ones on Earth. Use it to find the area with your fingers then press the green button and, hey presto, it will be illuminated on the table for you. Go on, have a go, it's very easy. Try it, both of you.'

Karl went around to the front of the table and pulled out the touch screen. He chose Warriors' Rest. He was amazed when he thought he saw Phina walking towards the hall with her mother. 'That can't be a live image, can it?' Karl asked.

'It really is, Karl. On this planet we have micro imagers up in the outer atmosphere that cover the whole world. Each one is the size of a football. I say cover the whole world but the ones over the deep south area have stopped working. We believe that the Dark have something to do with that.'

'You know, Salina, that's what I find funny about this world. It seems so old fashioned yet is actually more modern than Earth,' said Karl.

'I think when you say old fashioned, Karl, it's all actually new, just done in a more planet friendly way,' Salina replied. 'You see, we live with this world and we look after it and everything on it, even the creatures that would do us harm, except one, the Dark. They do not kill to live like wild animals do; they kill for pure enjoyment and to do their masters' bidding.'

'Why is there so much destruction on Earth then, and things like global warming, deforestation, chemical spills, all those sorts of things?' asked Karl.

'I am probably the last person you should ask, Karl. Your best chance to get a proper answer would be to speak to one of the history preachers; they will probably have a better idea than me.'

'So, you are saying you don't pollute anything? What about your industry, which must pollute the air, the ground or water, don't they?'

'No, as far as I am aware, we do not. Everything is world friendly. The way we build, the way we use natural resources, they are replaced or regrown. When we have industrial fires, there are special filters that filter all the dangerous gases, making them harmless to the world. We don't really have massive industry; everything is built or made at a local level for local use. I think, to answer your question simply, it's down to the fact that the people here have a different mindset. On Earth, it's all about money or making things bigger. That's not the case here. We make things right the first time and we don't mass produce. There are no rich people or money. There's no greed. That's what I think the big difference is, if you ask me,' answered Salina.

'I think from what I've seen so far, I would probably agree with that, Salina,' replied Karl.

'Yes, and me,' added Tom. Tom took control of the tablet, coming across a place called Linasfarn which was shown on the map. It was an island out in the middle of the endless sea. 'What's there?' he asked.

'It's a small island where sea slugs give birth; there is nothing there except wild grass and the caverns where sea slugs hide in very bad weather.'

'Can we go there?'

'Why, Tom? It's sea drenched and windswept and very cold at this time of the year. It's not far, only a short way by eagle or boat. You would see a wilder side of the planet, I suppose, and it would improve your flying with the wind and the high waves. I am sure of that... but unless you like dark dank, damp caverns or sea slugs there's not a lot for a young boy to see or do,' she said.

'That sounds just up Tom's street, Salina. He likes caves and wildlife, but it's not for me,' said Karl. He told them it would be fine if they went on a trip to the island, he would quite happily stay with Tristan and learn about the strategic centre and read the books he had been given.

'It will be a bit difficult. It means you will have to fly, Tom, while I run in my wolf form then get hold of a boat and...'

Tom cut her off. 'No, you don't, Salina, you can fly with me and Arn.'

'I don't fly, Tom. Only male Wolf warriors have eagles, I have never learnt to fly one. Now, a wind sail is different. I can fly a wind sail, but mine is at Warriors' Rest.

'You can fly with me! Go on, Salina, you might find you like it,' said Tom.

'Okay, Tom, let me speak to Kurt or Tristan first just to make sure there are no problems with going there. If they are happy and Arn is happy taking me, then we will go.'

149

'Great, let me go and find Arn and I will tell him.'

As Tom started to make for the door, Salina shouted after him, 'Remember, Tom, no one has said yes yet!'

'Okay, I know,' Tom shouted back and left the room.

After Tom had left, Karl asked Salina about the green-haired girl in the lake. She had been on his mind since he first got up and saw her. Salina told Karl about the Taniwha. 'She comes from Selessi, which is the subterranean citadel that you can only reach by diving deep into the Jade Sea which is a two-day flight away. The only way you can be taken to Selessi is by a Taniwha. I have only ever known two people to have ever gone there and returned, your father and Elizabeth. Sometime after they returned when Tom was born this little green-haired Taniwha first visited the silver lake. That's the lake you can see from your quarters. At the bottom of the silver lake, we believe is a passage that leads to the silver citadel. It is believed that the Taniwha built it before our capital was built. It's also believed that there is a passage from the silver citadel, Selessi, to the Jade Sea. That's how the little one comes to be in the lake, but she's not always there.'

'Is "she" dangerous?'

'Not that I am aware of, Karl, we don't really know what their purpose is, they just exist like we do, I think.'

Salina and Karl left the map room and went in search of Tristan or Kurt, but they found the king instead, who told them he had come across Tom running up and down a corridor, lost, and that he had told his father what he would like to do. The king was quite happy to allow him to go to Linasfarn as long as Salina was with him and eagle scouts patrolled their route. There was no intelligence to suggest the Dark had ever been to Linasfarn, as it was further north than they had ever been reported. The king said his farewells and they walked with him to the sail craft port where they met Kurt, Tristan and Tom standing next to Rowena in her healing vessel accompanied by the two healers.

'I can go!' Tom informed Salina, who told him she had already spoken with his father. They all said their final farewells and the king boarded the sail craft with Rowena and the healers. The walkway retracted, then the craft's airtight door was closed. The craft looked like the hull of two ships welded deck to deck, one upside down. It was a golden yellow colour and had port holes all over the hull. Karl asked where the pilots sat because he could not see a cockpit or a bridge. Kurt explained to him that it was automatically controlled, the plan was pre-set, and it would follow a pre-planned route to the blue moon. Two great retaining grapples were released, and the ground started to gently shake then a low dull sound filled the air: Dum, Dum, Dum, Dum, Dum, Dum, Dum, Dum. The sound and the vibrations matched the rhythm of the beat. Karl and Tom felt the waves of sound and vibrations pound through them, then the giant craft began to float skyward; it did not fly, it floated. The vibrations and sound dissipated as the craft got higher and once it was high over the citadel two sails came out on either side and began to ripple from the front to the rear then the craft began to move forwards. At the back of the craft, a fin came out from below the tail and slowly the craft glided away into the sky.

'That was amazing. How does it fly? What fuel does it use?' Karl asked excitedly.

'Over to you, Tristan. I was never any good at things like that, but Tristan nearly entered the science and engineering college,' said Kurt.

'Yes, and the only reason I didn't was the damn Dark. I ended up battling with them instead of thumbing through documents and theory papers. But anyway, Karl, to answer the question my brother failed miserably answer you, that thumping Dum, Dum sound is the sound waves that have been intensified by a procedure I am not even going to try and explain to you. To cut a long and very dull lesson short, those waves cause lift. Then the sails come out and supply thrust and direction, as well as absorbing solar energy for power. The rippling sails are copied from a fish called the bone fish; it has a solid bony body with a hard jaw and razor-sharp teeth. It is a scavenger of the deep; it eats anything it finds. Anyway, I digress, it has fins along its body, horizontally on both sides like you saw on the sail craft. They ripple along, allowing it to manoeuvre in any direction it wishes at a moment's notice. It's very efficient and that's exactly what the sail ship does too.'

'This is the sort of things I want to learn. That and about the creatures and animals of this world,' said Karl.

'Then you need to come with me and see the people's library. It is housed in that big pyramid structure you could see when you flew in,' Tristan told Karl.

'Yeh, you can go over there and me and Salina will go flying to that island and search the caves,' said Tom.

'I don't know how much searching we will be doing, Tom,' replied Salina. Have you spoken to Arn yet?'

'I don't know where they keep the eagles,' Tom replied.

'They don't keep the eagles anywhere, they are free spirits, Tom, not pets or caged animals. They live in the north with the rest of their kin, but I know Arn is in the great forest with his brother and the eagle flight you came here with. He will stay near you until you release him. You should be able to call him. Give it a try.'

'How do I call him?' he asked.

'Communicate,' Salina told him.

So, in his mind he thought, 'Hello, Arn, are you about?' There was no reply, so he thought it again and again, still nothing. 'He's not answering.'

'It's most probably because we are in the port. It has a sonic shield around it so the noise of the craft does not interfere with the rest of the capital,' Salina told him.

'When you entered the port through the gate, that is where the shield starts. It surrounds the whole port and docking area. It's a non-intrusive shield, that is, you don't know it's there, Tom,' Tristan told him, then they all left the port and headed back to the great hall where Tristan and Karl left them and went off to the library. Tom and Salina went outside to a large grassed area.

'Try calling Arn again, Tom, he should hear you now.'

Tom thought to Arn once more. Nothing. Then he noticed a smile cross Salina's face, and he was tumbling in the air, grabbed by Arn as he had done on the training field in Warriors' Rest. Salina had seen the eagle flying in behind Tom. At speed, Arn had flicked Tom up in the air with his beak between Tom's legs then he had waited below for Tom to fall on to his back.

'Hello, Thomas, are you well? I hear we are going for a flight.'

'I didn't know what was happening, Arn. For a big bird, you're very quiet.'

'It's a good job you're not tasty, Thomas, or you could have been my dinner.'

'You wouldn't eat me, would you, Arn?' Tom said then he wrapped his arms around part of Arn's neck. 'It's good to see you.'

'No, I would not eat you, Thomas, there's not enough meat on you,' Arn replied.

Tom knew that under all those feathers Arn was smiling. He could feel it inside.

'Come on, Tom, we will go and get combat suits on. They will keep us warm in Linasfarn, especially as we might end up in a cavern if you have your way,' Salina thought up to him.

Tom guided Arn back down to the ground and jumped off. 'Be back in a mo,' Tom thought to Arn.

'What is a mo? And how heavy is it? Don't forget we are taking Salina the wolf with us,' replied Arn.

'It's an Earth saying, Arn. It means I will be back quickly, in a moment. It has no weight. Anyway, a big strong eagle like you should be able to carry me and Salina and Phina and Karl, with ease.'

'Yes, I could, young prince, but my aerodynamics would mean it would be like flying like a wolf,' replied Arn.

'But wolves can't fly, Arn.'

'That's exactly my point,' Arn replied.

Tom went back with Salina to the accommodation to get changed into their combat suits. After they were changed, they went to the dining hall and put some food in a day sack for later, then headed back out to Arn who was eagerly waiting their return. He was ready for a good flight with his soulmate and Salina. He had only flown over Linasfarn but never landed, so this was something new for him as well as Tom. Arn and his passengers lifted high into the sky above the capital then turned north and flew high over the northern plains. As they flew, the plains turned from green to brown and Tom started to notice great big six-legged animals that were covered in a woolly fur, all with four great antlers protruding from their heads. Scattered around the plain were large numbers of these animals grouped together with their young in herds of around eighty. Eighty because that was all Tom could count before they started to mingle together, and he lost count.

'What are they?'

'Buffalents,' Salina told him. 'They are grazing animal that move in big herds over the great plain. They are very placid; you can walk up to them and they will come over to see who or what you are, but when they breed, then they are very protective of their young and will charge and kill anything that comes near.' Then Salina told Tom about a band of Dark warriors on what was thought to be a probing party out to test their defences, but they came across a herd with calving buffalents. The Dark warriors attacked some of them. At the time, it was believed to be for food because when the bodies were checked for documents and maps, they were found to have no food or water. The animals charged the Dark warriors who were about twenty strong, but the buffalents wiped them out, then continued to graze. 'So, if you ever come across them with their young, don't go near them,' Salina told him.

They continued north until they reached the furthermost part of the great plain. In front of them were the blue mountains; they were actually grey but the snow on the tops dulled the grey so when the early and late sun struck them, they shone blue. As they approached the mountains, they could see white clouds rolling off the tops of the great peaks which then fell into the valleys below, pushing cold air along the valley and out on to the edge of the great plain. Up high on Arn, Tom could feel a change in the temperature. A chill went through his body and he shivered. 'Don't worry, Tom, the suit will compensate for the change in temperature and you should feel comfortable again in a couple of seconds.' By the time Salina finished talking, Tom was warm again.

Arn communicated with them, 'That is not a good sign. Those rolling clouds will bring wet and stormy weather behind them. I estimate we will have about eight hours before it hits.'

'That should work out just fine, Arn. We will be at Linasfarn very shortly and I am sure after two hours there, Tom will have seen everything, then we will head back and miss the storm. Does that sound good to you?'

Arn agreed then turned east in front of the mountains and headed towards the endless sea. He dived low over the sea, skimming the waves. Tom loved it but Salina who was more used to dry land was not as enthusiastic as the young prince. She hugged him tightly and pushed her knees into Arn's back. 'It's okay, Salina, we are nearly there. If you look ahead you can just make out the outline of the island.'

Suddenly Arn veered right, his wing tip feathers touched the white froth of the heaving waves, then he climbed fast. Salina gripped Tom harder and stuck her knees in harder. 'Arn, what are you doing?'

'Look behind you,' he replied. Salina and Tom turned their heads to see a massive jaw lined with sharp jagged teeth and four large eyes above slowly slip back into the waves; the eyes reappeared just above the waves. They were following them.

'What the hell was that?' Tom shouted, too excited to communicate.

'That, Thomas, was a terror shark. Its real name is the Blue Devil Shark. It hunts the waters of the endless sea looking for prey normally along the bottom, but when the sea gets rough it comes to the surface looking for anything in distress or a passing opportunity that we might have just been if it wasn't for Arn. Thanks, Arn, well spotted,' Salina communicated and patted his back.

They reached Linasfarn without any further nasty surprises or encounters. They landed just in from the shoreline in a clearing amongst some trees. The wind howled through the trees, rustling the leaves, adding to the noise of the waves crashing on the rocks a short distance from them. 'I didn't think it would be this noisy. There's no beach,' Tom shouted.

'There is on the other side of the island. That's where the sea slugs are, if they have not gone into the caverns with this bad weather coming,' Salina told him.

'What actually is a sea slug?' he asked.

'The closest thing that you would know, Tom, is a seal. They are very intelligent animals but because they cover themselves in green sea slim, they look like slugs. The other difference is you can communicate with them, if you know how to communicate in their tongue, which I don't. I expect your brother could though. There is one other thing! They have arms shoulders and heads, not people heads, like seal heads. I suppose the closest thing on Earth would be a seal crossed with a mermaid,' she told him.

'Wicked! So, if they are over there why are we over here?'

'Because I wanted to show you something further up ahead of us, then we can walk over some hills through another wood and we will come out at the caverns and the beach where we will see the sea slugs.'

'What about Arn?' Tom asked.

'Don't worry about me, Thomas, I am going to fly around looking for some fish to eat out at sea. Just call me if you need me and I will return,' Arn communicated, then he flapped his massive wings and he was in the air and gone.

'Take care, Arn,' Tom communicated to him.

Salina and Tom started on their walk and very soon they reached some gently rolling green hills. Even though the hills were gently rolling, the wind rushing over them was not. Snug inside their temperature-controlled suits, they barely noticed it blowing all around them. When they reached the tallest of the hills, Salina pointed out a small copse nestled at the bottom of the hill.

'That's what I wanted to show you, Tom.'

'What? More trees?'

'No, not the trees, Tom. It's the things hidden amongst the trees,' she told him.

Tom was intrigued about what it was. Salina would not let on what she was talking about, as she did not want to ruin the surprise. They walked down to the copse. Standing on the edge, Salina turned to Tom and said, 'In here are things you will recognise; it's a shame Karl is not here, he would be fascinated by them.'

Now even more intrigued, Tom was eager to go in and have a look at what was behind the trees. They pushed their way through the trees and bushes that were barring the view of what was within. Finally, they pushed through to some stone pillars, on which were writing and pictures that looked familiar to Tom but he could not put his finger on why. The pillars held up a stone roof that was covered with hanging vines, Salina parted them and beckoned Tom to walk through, which he did closely followed by Salina. Inside was very dark; Tom could not see a thing.

From her day sack Salina pulled out a small round ball no bigger than a tennis ball. she gently said, 'Light' and the small ball illuminated the dark. In front of them was a large room.

'That's Stonehenge and a pyramid! That's one of the Inca pyramids and I've seen those pictures before!' as he pointed to designs carved on the walls and stone objects on the floor which were about three feet high. 'They are on the ground in

Argentina or Peru or Mexico, I'm not sure where. How did they come to be here?'

'These stone models are older and obviously a lot smaller than the ones on Earth. No one knows why they are here or who put them here; it's one of our mysteries. I thought you might like to see them.'

'That means someone from Earth or someone from here has been world travelling a long time ago.'

'Yes, that's right, Tom and we are none the wiser about who it might have been.'

'Could both worlds have been visited by aliens, as there are no records of these things in our records anywhere? Karl would have loved these; he will be sorry he missed them.'

As they walked around the brightly illuminated room having a closer look at all the stone replicas (or were they originals?) Tom went into the centre of Stonehenge. 'You're not allowed to do this on Earth, Salina. They have a rope around it to stop you getting near them. Uncle Kurt, Karl and I have been to the real one on Earth.' He went quiet and knelt down, putting his hand towards the base of one of the stone carvings, then stood up. 'There's wind coming from underneath this one, the one on its side that's fallen over,' he shouted over to Salina. Tom bent down again and put his hand at the bottom of the stone. There was definitely wind coming from beneath it. Salina walked over to him and bent down to feel for the wind. As she did, the ground around them and the stone gave way! Tom and Salina fell twenty feet and landed on a pile of mud that had been piled up almost into a v shape. Tom rolled one way, Salina another and the stone slid between them both. Picking up speed the stone slid to the bottom of the mud pile, but unlike Tom and Salina who rolled to a stop, the stone carried on moving at speed. It slid across the ground and smashed through the rock wall in front of it and disappeared into black air. Salina hurried over to Tom who was getting up and brushing himself down.

'Are you all right, Tom, that was quite a fall? It's a good job this pile of mud was here.'

'I'm fine, Salina. I think this suit helped.'

'It will have, they absorbed the power of the impact when you fell. But the most worrying thing is why this mound of earth is here? It's not old, this is freshly dug mud. Why is it here? There is no hole from where it came. Strange!'

As Salina stopped talking, they heard some shouting coming from somewhere inside the hole the stone had left. They both went over and were about to look through when Salina held Tom back. 'We don't know who or what is down there, Tom, stay back.'

Salina got down on her belly and crawled forwards to the hole. Peeking over the edge, eighty feet below her bodies were rushing about and at the centre of all the rushing Salina made out the outline of a very unhappy Dark menace centaur. He looked up at the hole the stone had made. Salina pulled her head back, but she understood the orders the centaur was barking out. 'We had better move, Tom, the Dark is below us and I think they are unhappy about the stone landing amongst them. By the sound of it, the mutt in charge of them is sending them up here. Come on, let's look for a way out. They have never been known to be so far north before. I wonder what they're up to?'

At the other end of the small cavern, they were now in was a passage, quite small but big enough for a person to run through. Off to the side was a small shaft in the ground big enough for Salina to get in. Where it would lead, they did not know but it was better than staying where they were. 'I will put Earth money on the Dark charging up this passage so I think we will try the shaft. Are you game for that, Tom? You're not having too much luck since you have been in Elemtum, are you?'

'I've been all right, Salina, it's my brother and sister that have had the bad luck. You know, it still sounds strange when I say sister.'

'It will do, Tom, your new life must be strange. New world, new family. Anyway, we had better stop chatting and get out of here. I will go first, follow me, Tom.' Salina slipped into the hole and Tom followed her. They were both glad when it changed from a hole into a tunnel. They crawled along on knees and elbows, then down through the damp cold muddy tunnel. After about ten feet, they came to a junction. One route continued straight on, the other bent round to the right.

'My gut instinct says right. I have learnt that taking the harder route, Tom, inevitably turns out to be the easiest and best way to go.'

So, they both went right. After another ten feet, the tunnel became wider and higher until they were both able to walk along it. 'You can see that someone has been digging along here. Look at the marks in the side of the tunnel, so why did they stop?' Salina wondered.

'Maybe there was something wrong with it?' said Tom.

'Yes, you may be right but what? That's what worries me,' she replied.

'Maybe it just got too hard for them, so they stopped?'

'That's what I like about you, Tom, you always look on the bright side. I think you're a bit of an optimist at heart.' They carried on along the tunnel then it started to descend a little more steeply, so they had to use the sides of the tunnel to steady themselves and grip onto to stop them sliding down the tunnel.

'Why don't we just slide down? It would be a lot quicker,' Tom suggested.

'Yes, a lot quicker and a lot more dangerous. There could be anything at the other end of this... rocks, a drop or the Dark. We are doing just fine, Tom, no need to rush.'

Back in the library, Karl was having a much more sedate time. He was sitting at a very large table surrounded by shelves full of books. In front of him, spread around on the table were several books that had caught his eye after Tristan had explained to him how the library was set out. He had been looking at the illustrated encyclopaedia of the Dark army. The biggest bunch of misfits, deviants, sociopaths and criminals that must have been dragged from the deepest and most desperate parts of this world, he thought. The book reminded him of one he had had on Earth, *The uniforms of World War 2* (in colour).

Someone must have got very close to get all the detail, he thought. He carried on looking through the book and stopped at the Dark menace centaur. The page read: This Dark menace warrior leads a force of hybrid Dark warriors, which can be a mixture of several types of Dark menace warrior or even of Dark creatures. It is believed the hybrid warriors are the fiercest of all the Dark warriors because they are the furthest from the original form of each species. This is because they carry two or more *alleles of the same gene. The centaur can take many forms but stands out because it is the loudest and most animated of the Dark warriors, normally a cross of one of the recognised leader forms and a creature. The picture depicts a centaur which is a cross of a Dark legion master and an acid lizard. Note this hybrid does not possess wings, unlike some that have been found. (If possible, kill any hybrids found on the battlefield). They obviously don't like them then; they look particularly nasty, Karl thought to himself, then turned the page and found lizsnake. Karl started to read: This reptile is known to be deadly to all peoples, Eagle and Wolf alike. It is thought to be in league with the Dark but up until now there has been no proof nor has it ever been seen in the company of any Dark creature. 'Rubbish, I will have to get that amended.'

Meanwhile, Tom and Salina gingerly made their way down the steep tunnel until they started actually climbing down, all the while looking for safe foot and hand holds. Eventually they reached the end of the tunnel which stopped at an eight-feet-long passage down to another tunnel. Salina indicated to Tom to stop and be quite while she listened for any sign of movement below them. They stayed quiet for several minutes, nothing. So, Salina lowered herself through the gap and dropped silently on to the ground. To her horror, directly in front of her was a Dark warrior with his back to her. He was standing to attention, obviously guarding the tunnel junctions beyond him. She did not dare move a muscle. 'Stay still and silent, Thomas, Dark warriors ahead,' she communicated to him. She knew the warrior would not detect her by smell because the smell coming off it was worse than a decaying puff ball mushroom and they smelt something dreadful when kicked. So, she opted for stealth. Silently she edged towards the warrior until she was inches away.

He was still oblivious to her. Then she sensed danger behind, so quickly grabbed the warrior's chin and the side of his head and twisted sharply with all her strength, instantly breaking its neck. With one sleek movement, she lowered its body to the floor and spun round to confront the danger behind. What confronted her was Tom on the back of a spreadeagled Dark warrior whose head had been caved in by a boulder that was lying next to him. Tom got up as Salina made her way to him, 'Well done, Tom,' she whispered.

'It was nothing,' he replied.

'No, that was a very brave thing for a boy your age to do.'

'No, really it was nothing,' he replied. 'The rock I was standing on gave way as he walked past the hole and it fell on his head and I fell on top of him,' he said, grinning.

'From what I've heard from Kurt and Phina, only you could do that, Tom.' She then ruffled his hair, smiling. She was growing fond of the young prince.

'We had better get going and find a way out. I'm sure someone will miss these two soon. Let's move.' They went to the junction and Salina judged the best thing to do was head away in the opposite direction to where the Dark warrior had been heading. They hurried off into the dark tunnel, ending up in a large cavern scattered with stalagmites and stalactites. Behind them, they now heard shouts of alarm, so quickened their pace. 'They must have found the bodies.'

They clambered over freshly fallen rocks and dodged between the stalagmites. Everything was damp and wet; the rocks were covered with a layer of slippery moss. They stumbled and slipped their way along the cavern, Tom in front, Salina turning regularly to see if they were being followed. She could hear the sounds of pursuers but saw no one. When she looked back, Tom was gone. She called his name but there was no answer. She stopped moving and listened. What she did not know was that Tom had missed his footing, slipped on one of the moss-covered rocks and banged his head, falling between the rocks that Salina had just passed. All she could hear was the sound of Dark warriors some distance off. She began to search the area where she had last seen Tom. Stopping once more, she heard the ever-nearing sound of the Dark warriors, then a very faint moan. Stumbling towards it, she came across Tom between two boulders 'Tom, can you hear me? Are you all right? Tom!

'No,' came the reply. 'I slipped and banged my head. I feel a bit funny, dizzy.' Salina helped him up from between the boulders and sat him on a broken boulder next to them. Conscious of the Dark warriors closing in on them, she looked at his injury. The skin on the side of his forehead to the left of his right eye was flapping down; he was losing a lot of blood. Tom could feel the wet sensation dripping down his cheek,

'I'm bleeding,' he said, dazed.

Lying, Salina told him it was only a graze and she pulled a gauze dressing from one of her combat suit pockets and peeled a layer off one side. She pushed the flap back to its proper position, applied the patch and then placed the gauze dressing on top of the wound.

'These are self-selling, Tom, so they will stick to your head and stop the bleeding, then they start to heal the wound. You will be fine. How are you feeling, Tom? Do you think you can carry on?'

'I think I will be okay. I don't feel dizzy any more. I remember where we are now. How close are they?'

'Don't worry about them, Tom, they are not close enough to worry about. Come on, let's get going and try and find a way out of here.' They continued to slip and slide deeper into the cavern. The light got dimmer and dimmer the further in they went. It was apparent to Salina that this was turning into a major tunnel system going deeper and deeper underground, and she could still hear the Dark in the background, hunting them. Finally, they came across two narrow paths at the end of the cavern, leading in opposite directions.

'I think we've lost them,' said Tom, as he tenderly touched the dressing on his head. It didn't feel sore any more. Whatever Salina had put on it had worked and worked quickly. Salina was still worried about the little prince because she knew how dangerous head wounds could be, but he seemed all right. He was talking which was a good sign. She asked him if he was thirsty which he was, so she gave him some green berry juice that would refresh him and give him some energy that would help him immensely. They stood on flat ground for the first time in what seemed like a very long time. They stood in silence looking at each other, both listening for the sound of their pursuers. Nothing was heard.

'I should have just stayed reading books with Karl,' Tom said, tears welling up in his eyes. Everything was getting a little too much for him.

'You've been amazing, Tom,' Salina told him, then gave him a tender hug and wiped the tears from his cheeks. 'You're safe with me, Tom, I won't let any harm come to you.'

'I'm not crying, Salina, it's all the grit in the air down here,' he told her.

'I know it is, Tom, I'm getting some in my eyes too,' she said, smiling at him. Tom had no idea of the dire situation they were now in. They were being chased by the Dark who would undoubtably kill them both on sight. They were in a cave system that had never been explored before. And they kept going down, which is not good if you are trying to get out of a cave. They had limited food and water, no rope and, threateningly, there was a storm brewing above that could end up flooding the whole cave system. Salina just did not know how this would end; wolves weren't used to going so deep into the ground and she was getting very worried, but she would not let Tom know this. They looked both ways down the path; neither gave any indication as to which way they should go. 'What I will do, Tom, is scout each direction in turn and find the best one for us to go. I'll do it in my wolf form. I will be quicker and my senses are much better. We must find somewhere for you to hide while I'm gone. It won't be for long,' she promised him.

Slightly down the left-hand trail they came across a hole in the ground that was partially covered by a boulder, big enough for Tom to hide in and the entrance was away from the path so any Dark warriors that might pass would not see him. 'I will have to change out of this combat suit,' she told him, 'because, unlike the other clothes we have, these do not have the right molecular structure to change when we turn into our wolf form.'

'You can't run around naked, Salina, not in this damp wet cave. What if the Dark catch you?'

'Tom! I will be a wolf covered in fur.'

'Oh yeh, I forgot you're a wolf.'

'Now, get in your hole like a good boy,' she said jokingly. 'And no peeking,' she warned him. Tom blushed but in the dark Salina could not see. Tom got into the hole while Salina undressed. 'Here you go, Tom,' and a bare arm passed down her boots then the day sack and finally her combat suit. Tom blushed once more because as the combat suit was passed down Tom had a glimpse of Salina's breast; he immediately turned his head away, feeling embarrassed. Then he felt a warm breath on the top of his head and he looked up and was slightly startled by the wolf looking down at him. 'Are you okay, Tom? I can sense a rise in your heartbeat and blood pressure,' she communicated to him.

Tom's face went bright red once more, and then he mumbled, 'I'm fine thank you, Salina.'

Salina then communicated, 'Be quiet and still. I won't be long.' Then she was gone.

Salina ran off into the black and Tom was worried because he had forgotten to say 'take care'. Then the vision of Salina's naked breast filled his mind; he had never seen a real naked woman before and he became worried that Salina might read his mind when she returned so he tried to think of something else and that made it worse.

What did get him thinking about something else was hearing a noise, then a voice saying, 'They're round here somewhere, I can feel it. You go that way and I will go this way. Hey, remember, whoever brings the head will have Arthfael's favour.'

Then Tom heard feet shuffling away. He had an urge to go out and make sure they had gone, but then another thought rushed into his brain. 'It could be a trap. What about Salina? She doesn't know.' Now Tom was worried and frightened. Is it my head they want? But I'm only ten. It can't be, he thought.

Salina heard the oaf running down the path towards her, so she leapt up onto a rock slightly higher than head height and waited. As the Dark warrior ran towards her, she waited for the exact moment to pounce and she knew where to strike, his neck. He could not scream, he would be dead in seconds, and he was. Salina jumped off the lifeless body still only just attached to its head. He had been heading back towards Tom, so now she took more care. Reaching Tom's hiding hole, she continued down the opposite path. Tom was unaware she had passed.

'Take care, Salina, there are Dark warriors all around us. I can hear them,' he communicated to her.

Further down the path she came to a junction. She could hear the sound of someone running down the left path, so she let him go. She went down the right one where the air became damper and she sensed water. Water must go in and out, she thought, so she decided that would be the way she would go with Tom. She ran back to Tom's hole and turned back into her people form, now feeling a little exposed because she knew the Dark were close. She gently called down, 'Tom, I'm back. We must go. The Dark are all around. Pass up my suit.' Tom's hand came out of the hole clutching her combat suit, but his eyes were averted and closed. Salina took the suit and quickly pulled it on. 'It's okay, Tom, you can come out now.' Tom passed her boots out then Salina helped to drag him out of the hole. Quickly they ran down the path heading for the water Salina had sensed. Eventually the tunnel started to fill with a gentle breeze.

'Air flow, that's a good sign, Tom. If air is coming in that might be our way out,' she told him. They continued running and came out of the passage into a large lake inside a big cavern. At the far end they could see light. 'That's our way out, Tom.' They looked across the calm black velvet water towards the light, life rushing through their bodies once more. A drop of water fell from one of the stalactites above and plopped into the velvet water sending ever-increasing circles across the lake. Eventually they faded away and the lake was still and silent once more. Tom put his hand into the water. It was icy cold,

'How are we going to get across that?' he asked. 'It's freezing.'

'We swim, Tom. It's not too far. You can swim, can't you, Tom?' she asked.

'Yes, I can. I got a swimming medal at school. I can swim ten lengths.'

'Impressive. How far is that?' she enquired.

'About,' Tom thought, 'to that light over there.' He asked her if she thought the water was good enough to drink and she told him she thought it would be because it would have been filtered through the ground above when it come down, or it would have come from an underground source that should be equally as fresh, so it should be fine.

'I will try it first, Tom.'

She scooped some water up in her hand. It looked clean, so she had a taste. It tasted a little of metal but she put that down to the water running through the ground. 'It seems fine, Tom.'

Tom cupped his hand and scooped up some water and drank from his hand. 'It tastes okay,' he told her, and took a few more mouthfuls. 'I think I'm ready to try and cross now.'

So, they both lowered themselves in the icy water. The icy cold took their breath away. 'Bloody hell, it's cold,' he cried out.

Salina swam behind Tom so she could give him some support if he needed it. 'Breathe steadily, Tom. Your combat suit works in water too. It will soon start to warm you up and keep your body temperature normal. Start to swim. I'm behind you. The suit will also help you float.'

They swam towards the light and their potential escape route. Tom's breathing became steady as the swimming also became easier. Salina was watching his every stroke as well as occasionally looking behind her for signs of the Dark. When, after fifteen minutes, they had reached what Salina thought was the middle of the lake she looked behind her and noticed figures emerging from the tunnel they had just come from. Lights started to flash in their direction and she could hear animated screaming and see lots of waving arms. She also noticed that none of them got into the water. Why? Ahead of them, in the direction they were swimming, there was no one that could impede their escape.

'I keep touching things with my boots and hands,' Tom shouted back to her. Salina had not noticed anything but maybe Tom's arms and legs had been deflecting whatever it was away from her.

'Things like what, Tom?' she shouted back to him.

'I don't know. Things,' he replied.

Salina swam to his side and told him she would take the lead for a bit. They carried on swimming. Something brushed her foot, then her hand brushed something, so she grabbed at it and pulled it out of the water in front of her. To her disgust, it was a severed hand. She tossed it away and started to survey the water for any signs of anything that would be capable of doing that to a swimmer. Then her mind raced. Terror shark, she thought.

'Keep swimming, Tom. Not far now. Don't worry about the things in the water, there only some dead fish. You're doing well.' She looked back and noticed the Dark warriors had still not got in the water after them. They know something, she thought to herself, not far now.

From above they both heard a clicking sound CLICK, CLICK, CLICK.

It got louder, then there was a shrill scream.

'Stay very still and quiet, Tom.'

He trod water as quietly as he could. Looking up, they both saw a black shape moving along the cavern roof, then it began falling towards them, two yellow eyes looking down at them.

'Get ready to dive, Tom,' Salina shouted. As the thing got closer, wings came out from the black shape, it changed direction and started to glide towards the Dark warriors that were still screaming and flashing their lights on the bank of the lake. Suddenly they noticed the black beast was heading for them. They dropped their lights and began to scatter, two of them running into each other.

It was now too late for them; the beast climbed, then dived at them. Salina calmly told Tom to carry on swimming to the furthest bank and the light that was now only a length away.

The beast landed claw first on top of one of the warriors on the ground. On the end of its wings were two claws; one of them came down and grasped the warrior's head then it ripped it from his body, slinging it high into the air where it came splashing down into the lake. It started to bob, then slowly sank as it filled with water. The second warrior tried to crawl away, but the beast hopped onto him leaving the headless body behind. The beast dug its claws into the warrior's back; they could hear the screams as they swam. The flesh was ripped from it and thrown on the ground around the screaming warrior. Then an arm was ripped off and the screaming stopped. The arm ended up in the lake like just like the head had done. A leg followed, then the beast lifted the lifeless torso in the air, flying back towards Salina and Tom. It dropped the lump of flesh into the lake and dived towards the swimmers nearly at the other side. Salina looked back and noticed that the rushing beast was gone. They reached the other bank and Salina helped

Tom out of the water then she pulled herself out.

'I think that was a little more than ten lengths,' Tom told her.

'You did well, Tom. Now, let's get out of here before that beast comes back. I didn't see where it went.' They moved away from the water's edge. Ahead of them they could now see light, sky and trees.

Chapter 11
New Friends

'We did it!' shouted Tom, as he ran towards the light and the outside entrance to the cavern.

'Stop!' shouted Salina. Tom turned to look at her. From outside the cavern one of the black beasts swept in through the entrance. 'Tom, look out!' Salina screamed, but it was too late. The beast's claws skewered Tom's shoulder, then he and the beast were gone into the black of the cavern above the lake. Salina ran back to the edge of the black water, but they were nowhere to be seen. Distraught, she stared up into the black, then came back to her senses and started to look for a way up inside. That was not feasible; she felt utterly useless. She ran to the entrance and looked up; she was looking at a very large mountain. She moved further back amongst some trees and looked up again. One hundred feet above her, she could see a black cave entrance with what looked like white animal droppings on the ledge. That must be where it came from, she thought to herself. I must try and get some help. No. Poor Tom, I must try and find him. I can't give up hope that he's still alive, he has to be. She put her hand up to her eye, something was happening that had never happened before, an involuntary tear.

Salina knew there would be no help because she did not recognise the mountain above her. She assumed this was part of a world under the world she knew. It may be a forgotten land, or one they just didn't know about. There was nothing to do now except climb, so she did. She pulled on a pair of gloves from a leg pocket then had a quick look around. There was no apparent danger, so she grabbed at the lowest boulder, then a rock and a ledge. She continued, gradually climbing higher and higher. Half an hour later, she was just below the opening she had seen from the ground. Looking around her, there were still no signs of any danger. The beast must have scared the Dark warriors away, but knowing the Dark they would return in force and destroy the problem. That's when Salina began to think. 'Maybe the thing that took Tom hated the Dark. There could still be hope for Tom.'

With great inner strength, Salina leapt from the position she was in, twisting in mid-flight. High above the ground, she stretched out and grasped the ledge above her and swung into the rock face with a thump. Steadying herself, now hanging at arm's length, she called on all her reserves of strength and from that position she pulled her whole body up until the top half of her body was above the level of the ledge. With one last massive effort, she flipped herself onto the ledge where she lay motionless, totally exhausted. She rolled onto her back and looked up to the sky; above her was a bright blue sky with cotton wool clouds lazily drifting by. For a minute she forgot herself, then the stark realisation of why she had just climbed halfway up a mountain smashed like a fallen tree back into the forefront of her mind. 'Tom!'"

Salina rolled back onto her stomach, pushed herself on to her knees, then stood up. In front of her was the entrance to the cave that she had seen from below. The floor was covered in white and black droppings that she assumed had come from the beast. She carefully walked forward into the dark cave conscious that she was silhouetting herself, she started to hug the cave wall, as she cautiously made her way deeper inside. As she got further in, she started to hear a faint clicking sound that started to resonate around the cave and into her sensitive ears CLICK, CLICK, CLICK, CLICK, CLICK. It was constant and getting louder so she made herself one with the cave wall and became deadly silent and still.

Out of the gloomy dark, a large black figure clawed passed her out onto the ledge where she had just come from. The creature stood up; its body was the size of two warriors standing on each other's shoulders and four abreast. It unfolded two leathery wings that stretched out nearly blocking all the light from the entrance of the cave. On each wing tip was a claw as well as the two large sharp claws on its feet that had mercilessly stabbed into Tom's body more than half an hour earlier. Seeing the beast fully stretched out in its menacing pose made Salina thankful for her odour-eating combat suit. Then realisation hit her. The beast had not seen her pushed into the cave wall. Was it blind?

The creature then flung itself from the ledge into the air. It dropped out of Salina's view then its massive leathery wings lifted it into the sky and it came back into her sight for seconds and then it was gone. Surmising that the creature that had taken Tom had just left she now rushed down the cave into the dark. She knew this was against all the tactics and theories she had ever been taught, but this was different. Tom, her prince, was in there somewhere.

She started to smell rotting flesh, so she stopped running and continued to proceed more cautiously. As her eyes became accustomed to the dark, more became clear. She realised she was now in another cavern, not the one she had been in with Tom. As she moved slowly forward, she started to stand on pieces of dead animals. No, not animals, warriors and creatures from the dark. Then she noticed a leg, then an arm, scattered around the cavern floor. She searched the ground for Tom but thankfully she found no sign of him or anything that he had been wearing. As she searched, a lump of flesh slammed down right next to her. It had come from above. She looked up. Looking back at her were eight pairs of yellow eyes! She froze. Above her one of the beasts opened its wings and glided down, landing quite gracefully in front of her, its wings outstretched, staring and clicking at her. Then another landed behind to her left and another to her right. Salina contemplated turning into her wolf form but by the time she had removed her combat suit and boots she would be dead. All seemed lost. I never thought my end would be like this, she thought to herself, then she decided to go out with a fight.

She slowly moved into an attack stance when a shout came from above. 'Tearmoss!' the voice shouted.

The beasts backed away then lifted up into the dark from where they had come, washing Salina with wind and dust stirred up from the ground as their large wings beat them into the air. Salina looked upwards for who or whatever was behind the voice. From the black above, a winged figure descended, landing in front of Salina. The figure in front of her did not resemble the beasts with the leathery wings. It was totally different; was elegant and very feminine. In front of her eyes, Salina saw the wings fold almost out of sight behind the figure. It was, without a doubt, female. The female was covered in a thin layer of fur that did not hide her slender body shape and most startling of all were her brilliantly sparkling blue eyes. Its head was most definitely beautiful. It reminded Salina a picture she had seen of a beautiful Irish singer on Earth who had shaved her hair off. She could not remember her name, but she had been beautiful as well. An innocent beauty. But this winged beauty had slightly pointed ears and a thin layer of fur covered her head.

'I have been watching you since you entered the nursery. You are a wolf and your young companion smells very much of human, but he is also a wolf and an eagle. What do you want here?'

'I come only to find and take home my young prince from this place and all its dangers. Do you have him? Is he safe?' replied Salina.

'We have him, and he is safe and unharmed.'

'But I saw one of those creatures impale him on their claws and take him away.'

'That is true, but he is now safe and well and those creatures are our young, doing what they must to protect themselves.'

'What do you want? What are your intentions?' Salina asked.

'More to the point, wolf, what are yours?' the creature replied.

'My intentions are simple. Find my prince and take him home to his family.'

'Are you in league with the foul-smelling evil ones who have started to plague our home?' it asked.

'You mean the devils we call the Dark, who also plague my world and are trying to kill us all. That's the reason my prince and I are here with you now.'

'If that is the case, then you are welcome here. We are a peaceful race who came here from the stars before your kind set foot on this world. I am Zuzza Zell and I am the daughter of the Queen Lessi Zell. What you see around you is the nursery where we look after and train our young until they are old and wise enough to take their place at our side in the form you now see me. This is called Zell. We are Zell. 'Let me take you to my city. Can you fly?'

'No, not without a craft,' Salina replied.

'I will call one of the young to take you. The entrance is only a short distance up, and I will meet you there.' Zuzza's wings unfolded and she flew straight up into the black.

Moments later, one of the young descended and landed in front of Salina. She noticed in its right wing claw it held what looked like an apple-sized melon. The young Zell hopped within reach of her and gently handed her the fruit. Salina accepted it with a smile and a slight nod of her head. The Zell watched her intently, obviously waiting for something to happen. Salina took a bite of the fruit; it was juicy, tasty and sweet, and reminded her of something she had tasted on Earth. A very sweet pear, she thought. She stepped forward and patted the Zell on its chest to thank it for the fruit. The Zell jumped back and seemed to start choking. Unsure what to do, Salina looked on, praying the beast would not die in front of her. That would be all she needed now. The Zell continued to choke. It was then Salina realised the Zell was not choking, but regurgitating.

'But what?' Then one of the pear-tasting fruits came out of its mouth and plopped onto the floor next to its feet. Oh, I wish I had seen that before I ate the last one, she thought. The Zell kicked it towards her, so she picked up the now slimy fruit and placed it in her day sack. She smiled at the Zell and pointed upwards. The Zell flapped its wings, lifted into the air, hovered over the top of her, then its feet and claws came down either side of her and gently grasped her below her arms and she started to rise beneath the Zell. It flew straight up, up past where the rest of the young had been looking down at her. Further up there were clean and comfortable looking nests; each had a mounted tray next to it with fruit and some sort of raw vegetables on it, as well as water. Finally, at what must have been towards the very top of the inner mountain, they came to a ledge. This had been made by skilled hands. At the back of the ledge was a massive door made of some kind of metal that glistened in the bright light that shone on it from either side. The Zell placed her on the ledge and flew back down, leaving Salina alone. In front of her the big metal door slid open. Salina was blinded by a brilliant white light that came from within the door. Gradually it faded.

Once Salinas's eyes had readjusted, she saw the figure of Zuzza, bathed in light. 'Please come in,' Zuzza said and gestured for her to enter. Once Salina had entered, the door slid shut behind her and she was standing in a large hanger painted bright white. She adjusted her eyes once more. There were no signs, no pictures, nothing at all, just a very large empty hanger. 'I can see you are wondering what this is for. It's very simple. It's big enough to get all the young Zells in if needed, and that's all.'

'I just wondered. After the dark foul-smelling cavern, it just surprised me. So different.'

'That area is not how the young ones normally live. They normally live slightly higher until the change happens, then they come inside and start to live their lives like real Zells and they are given their names. There is a reason it smells, and you no doubt noticed how the young dealt with the evil ones? Did you also notice that the young ones did not eat their vanquished?'

'Yes.'

'They ripped them limb from limb and there was a reason for that.

'What reason?' Salina asked.

'To scare the evil ones in to coming no closer. We don't eat meat, but they don't know that, and that's how we want it to stay until we come up with a strategy to defeat them and send them back from where they came.'

'My world... is that what you mean?'

'Yes, if that's where they come from.' Zuzza took Salina through the hanger by a small normal size door into a smaller room with some very large coloured buttons on one wall.

'How do the young get any further, with a small door like that?' asked Salina.

'They don't,' replied Zuzza, 'not until they change. Would you want those great lumbering young ones hopping and flying around your home until they were trained?'

'No, I suppose not,' replied Salina, managing a smile.

Zuzza pressed one of the buttons and almost instantaneously the same door slid back open. Salina looked back at the now open door, but instead of the white hanger there was now a long corridor lined with light blue strip lights. Surprised, Salina looked back at Zuzza who was now dressed in a plain blue shirt which hung down to below her waist on top of some black tight leggings and shiny black knee-length boots. Even more surprising was the fact that Zuzza now had a person's face; black hair tied in a ponytail and a pretty plain face that smiled at her.

'How did you do that?'

'How did I do what? Get us here? Or do you mean change my appearance?' Zuzza answered.

'Both. I am very impressed; did we go up? Or down?'

'We did neither,' Zuzza answered. She went on to explain to Salina as they walked that when the door closed, the structure they were in travelled to the desired location in the city. But they stayed within the structure and did not move. Could they change like Salina could change from wolf to person? Many lives ago they lived on Earth deep within the Amazonian jungle in South America. As man developed, they moved back to the original base they had come from in 'the stars'. That base was the place they were now. She told Salina they watched Earth develop and head on a course to self-annihilation. So, unable to stop it, they left. They also watched the Wolf and Eagle tribes; they developed totally differently to Earth. They concluded that every creature lived in harmony on her world. That was until the evil appeared. The evil that they had detected had come from Earth and from what Salina said, it seemed to be the same evil they were now dealing with. This information Salina found very interesting.

'So, where are we actually now?'

'We are in my world, Salina. You fell in from the part of your world that is connected to mine, and you entered my world through one of the tunnels the Dark had excavated. Before they came, that area had just been rock and mud. That was all that was between our worlds and we coexisted happily. 'Somehow the evil Dark found our world. The water people told us they entered our world through the island above. Some of the water people were killed by them, so they warned us to take care. We did not realise how dangerous they would be.'

'Who are the water people? I have not heard of them before.'

'I believe you call them sea slugs.'

'Ah yes, not a very enduring name, I must admit, but with our two princes and princess back in our world, I have a feeling things like that will change,' said Salina. They reached the end of the corridor. The door opened, and they entered into a city underwater. 'I did not expect this. How wonderful is this? What stops the water from coming in? It just seems to float above and around you.'

'We have a sea cell dome; it's made from water and a substance called croll. When croll is bound together with water and air it makes a solid shield around whatever you want to protect.'

'That is amazing. There is so much I would like to find out about you, but first can you take me to my little prince?'

They walked through the city streets. It was clean and bright, a total contrast to the dark cavern the young were in. Zuzza explained that everything Salina could see had come from the sea then rendered with a compound, also from the sea, that coated the object and made it strong, strong enough to build with. 'Most of the buildings you see are made with sand and stone that has been mixed with the compound, put into moulds to set then erected into whatever we want to build. The final stage of the build is to render the surfaces and there you have it. Obviously, there is a little more to it than that; windows, glass, power, it's all from the sea. It's probably not apparent to you yet, but over time we have evolved from creatures of the air to creatures of the sea.'

They entered a building that was called The Adjustment Centre.

'What is this building, Zuzza?'

'The Adjustment Centre is where the young are brought after the change. They spend their first cycle here, not just here, this is their centre of operations, while they adjust to their new life before they become part of our society and re-join their families. The way we have evolved from a winged creature to an aquatic creature has taken a very long time and we still haven't finished.' Zuzza told Salina the cycle of life for the Zell. 'They are born in the dark as little winged ells. The next five cycles are spent in the cavern and outside flying in the air and the forest around the mountain. Finally, the ones you encountered are nearly Zells; they are finishing the fifth cycle. Very shortly, the hanger door will open, and the young Zells will come inside. Unlike today there will be bars along the walls that they will attach to and their old body will die and will be left hanging. The new reborn Zell will break out of its old shell and will be as I am today. They will come here and their training will continue. We help with their adjustment from winged, free creatures to a creature whose movements are more restricted and everything in life will be harder, then we introduce them to water and the sea.'

Salina and Zuzza walked into the building. It was very clinical, much like the infirmary Rowena had been in. Zuzza put the palm of her hand against a black panel in the door in front of them. The panel turned white and the door opened. Inside was another room but this time it had a high ceiling and all that could be seen were vines, bushes and trees. There were walkways leading off in several directions, each a different colour. 'This is the first place the young Zells come to. They are slightly confused about what they are after leaving their old body. It also comes as a shock that they can no longer fly, so this area is meant to calm them and surround them with things they are comfortable with, the trees and the woodland surroundings, that they have lived with all their lives so far.'

Salina noticed eyes watching her from the treeline.

'Ttast! Come out! That is not how you greet people, is it?' Zuzza said.

From the treeline a young man Karl's age came out with his head bent, obviously very nervous. 'Ttast, this is Salina. She comes to us in peace from the world above.' The young man lifted his head and looked at Salina, 'That's it. Look at whoever you greet in the eyes. Show them you are not scared. You are a proud Zell. Remember that,' said Zuzza. The young Zell smiled and started to cough. 'No, Ttast, you don't do that anymore. Remember, you eat food now, there is no need to regurgitate food as a welcome offering. A shake of the hand will suffice.'

'In my culture, we grasp each other's wrists. Let me show you,' Salina told the young Zell. She grasped the young Zell's wrist in the Wolf and Eagle warriors' shake. The young Zell's smile broadened, and he seemed a lot happier.

'Do you know where the young wolfling is?' Zuzza asked him. He nodded his head and started to show them when Zuzza called him back and told him to speak and not just nod as he had done. She told Salina it was all part of their training and that this particular Zell had only been in the centre two days and still had a lot to learn.

'The youngling is at the back near the fountain; one of the older Zells gave it a buoyancy bell,' Ttast told them. They followed him through the greenery, along a yellow path until they reached the fountain. In front of them, Tom was playing with something in the water.

'I had forgotten he is still a young child. Seeing him there, he is so fragile in this world, I mean our worlds,' Salina said. Tom heard Salina's voice and swung round.

'Salina!' he screamed and got up and ran to her. She lifted him up and spun him around. They both laughed with joy which Zuzza noticed, realising the bond between them must be strong. It confirmed to her that Salina had been telling the truth and that it had been a good decision to save the Wolf child. Salina put Tom down; he was no longer wearing his combat suit but a black boiler suit. It was much thinner and more comfortable to wear than a normal Earth boiler suit. Salina checked his shoulders; no sign of any damage whatsoever.

'I didn't like to think about what had happened to you, Thomas. I did think I would be taking your body back to your father. I am so overwhelmed at seeing you. It's amazing. How did they fix you so quickly?'

'I don't remember. All I remember was the pain. I was so scared, then a black flying dog took me to a big white room where they covered me in stuff like seaweed. After that, I remember nothing until a mermaid took me out of the water and I was fine. I had some food, which was nice then a big man gave me this.'

Tom lifted the bell-shaped object out of the water; it had two pipes sticking out of it. 'You blow these pipes and it sinks. Blow them again and it rises. It reminds me of a submarine I had as a kid.'

'You're still a kid, Tom,' Salina said and gave him a hug. Salina asked Zuzza how they fixed Tom so quickly. Zuzza told her they put some very fast regenerating algae on Tom, then one of the water people took him away. When they brought him back, he was fine.

'We don't know what they do. But it works, and we trust them.'

'Oh, I almost forgot, Salina, I also remember seeing the green-haired girl from the lake behind where we slept. Me and Karl saw her. It was her family that made me better. Her name is Tanibeth. She and her family are very nice.'

'You saw who? Tanibeth?'

'Yes, that's right. The girl with the green hair from the lake.'

'I know of this girl. She is their leader's daughter. All I know is that the water people take the sick away with them and when they bring them back, they are fit and healthy. It was the sea people that give us the algae for our first aid packs,' Zuzza told Salina.

Far, far away on another world, Arn fought the torrents of wind and rain that were lashing him and the island of Linasfarn. Below him the trees were bent almost double by the force of the storm hitting the island. Arn battled on through the deluge of rain that pounded him, threatening his ability to say in the air. All his feathers were now drenched in rain making it almost impossible for the great eagle to fly. He knew he had to make land or he would very soon fall from the sky.

Karl turned another page and looked in wonder at the illustrations in front of him., Omanian, the desert tribe that lives underground, away from the harsh environment of the desert. The picture showed a person in brown boots and brown combat suit, wearing gloves and goggles but also something Karl recognised from Earth as a headdress worn by the Arab peoples on Earth. In the book it said it was a traditional sand-shielder.

The library door opened, and Tristan walked in, a very concerned look on his face. 'Karl, we think Salina, Arn and Tom may be in trouble. The eagle patrol that was in the area of Linasfarn did a sweep of the area but they had to return due to the freak storm that appeared over the area. They could not find any trace of Arn, Tom or Salina. To add to that, the area on the surveillance images has disappeared. We have no coverage of the whole area. We are getting a small force together to go and investigate once the weather allows. We may have to take hover vessels to get to the island if this weather continues. We will put an airborne force on standby to follow us when they can. Both Kurt and I think it would be good training for you if you would like to come with us.'

'Too right,' Karl replied, then got up very excited, leaving the books as they lay on the table. He and Tristan headed back to the strategic centre. Karl took a detour to his room to put on some rough terrain clothing because he was going on a rescue mission, not a fighting mission. He met Tristan and Kurt minutes later in the strategic centre. As well as Karl and his uncles, there were Wolf and Eagle warriors and there were also several types of people Karl had never seen before. Some of the people wore combat suits. Some were obviously scholars; they had that teacher look about them. Others were definitely accountants or council officials, Karl thought to himself. Karl was fascinated by the different combat suits in the room. His eye caught that of a young warrior who must have been around Row's age. She was wearing a bright blue combat suit but something about it was different. For one, it was made of a different material. The warrior in blue looked over at Karl and smiled. Karl smiled back at the warrior. Her green eyes sparkled, and something compelled him to go and talk to her.

'Hello, I'm Karl.'

'Yes, I know, prince. I am Hollie from the water company and I must listen to the briefing. If you are on this mission, I think you should as well.'

Karl thought to himself, she's a bit pushy for someone that works for a water company.

'Right then. Water company, before the main landing on Linasfarn you will deploy and do a reconnaissance of the sea surrounding our landing area, then go ashore and secure the local area around the landing point. The main force will move through you inland. Make sure you have your friendly forces tag working when you land so we can see you when we land. After that, you will be on call in case we come across anything that suits your special abilities. Happy with that, Hollie?' Kurt told her and the assembled warriors.

'Yes, sir, on it,' she replied and started to leave.

'Good luck, specialist leader, on your first mission, I'm sure you won't need it,' said Kurt.

'Thank you, sir,' she replied and left.

Karl was amazed. Specialist leader? he thought. Someone is pulling my leg. The briefing finished and everyone left apart from Kurt and the council officials, who started to set up the command room with the preachers.

'Who are they?' Karl asked Kurt, indicating the people that were left in the room.

'They are the tacticians and support specialists. They are made up of the older warriors, preachers, engineers and communication specialists. Many of them perform other roles until they are needed here to perform their mission roles, as they are today. Very important people, Karl. Some of them perform this role because they have been wounded or injured and can no longer stay in combat units; they are an experienced and valuable asset we are lucky to have.'

'So, what do they actually do?' asked Karl.

'They monitor the battle zone; arrange the logistical needs at the time, casualty evacuation, re-supply, communication, overwatch as well as battle planning and intelligence. The way we work, it's either me or Tristan who will watch over the command centre and the other will be in the battle zone. Normally your father would be here, but it's a hell's own job persuading him to stay here.'

Karl had many more questions he wanted to ask but Kurt told him they had better make their way to the shuttle bay that would take them to the seaport to join the mission. On the way out, Kurt took Karl via the combat store and got him a combat helmet, a rayzor and his intelligent weapon – only a pistol-sized one to be used for his own personal protection until he was properly trained on the bigger weapons.

They made their way down to the shuttle bay and bordered the troop shuttle waiting for them. On board were around one hundred warriors who had been selected for the mission, including Hollie who winked at him as she put her helmet on. The shuttle left the docking port and travelled at speed along a vacuum tunnel. Karl could feel a gentle throb like the one he had witnessed when his father had left on the sail craft for the blue moon, so he assumed the same principals were being used to lift and propel the craft he was in now. As they sped along, Kurt instructed Karl on the use of his combat helmet, the proper one, not the training one Raif had told him about. Then Kurt instructed him on using the PPUSI (Personnel Protection Unit Small Intelligent) that he now had in a holster on his thigh.

Once the training had finished, Karl took his helmet off and asked Kurt a question, 'Specialist leader Hollie, who is she?'

'Hollie was last year's top cadet; she is so good that your father put her into one of the toughest teams we have as one of their unit leaders. The water company are water specialists, a bit like SBS or navy seals on Earth, only better. If you look at her helmet, it is slightly different from ours because it is also a breathing apparatus. What she is wearing is enough for her to complete any underwater mission. Hollie and her team do not need air tanks, flippers and all the other things Earth special forces need.'

'Is she a Wolf or Eagle warrior?' Karl asked.

'Neither. She is from the mountain people. Normally they specialise in mountains and rough terrain, but she has a natural talent for swimming and combat. Her tactical awareness is superb.'

'Two minutes to seaport' came over the internal shuttle communicator. Everyone got ready to disembark from the shuttle. It came to a halt, two side doors slid open and the warriors left the shuttle. A short walk and they were at the quay. Moored in front of them was a fast assault craft; it was covered in silver panels and it looked more like a submarine than a ship or boat. The side of the assault craft opened revealing a small hanger that had some wheeled and tracked vehicles inside. Kurt explained to Karl that the silver panels were part of the craft's stealth system and that it could change the craft's whole signature and make it blend into its surroundings so it became almost invisible. As long as no hatches were opened that would break the stealth. He also explained that the combat suits Hollie and her team were wearing also had a similar system, like the one they had seen in the combat suits of the guards at the top of the steps that blended into the building behind them. The craft was also submersible and that was how Hollie and her team would deploy to the island, unseen from above. Not only that, the crossing to the island would be quicker underwater, out of the rough sea and wind above.

'Can I ask a question, Uncle Kurt?'

'Ask away, Karl.'

'Why are we going so heavy handed, all these warriors, when this is probably just a simple search and rescue mission?'

'That would have been the case, Karl, if all the surveillance cameras had not gone out in the whole of that area.'

'That could just be the bad weather,' said Karl.

'The only problem with that, Karl, is that the cameras are well outside the area the weather is affecting. You have to remember they are on the outer limits of the planet, before you enter space, that is not affected by the weather system. That is our major problem. That and the fact that Salina would have contacted us by now if everything was okay. We just don't know what is going on, so we can't take any risks, especially because your brother and Salina are out there somewhere.' They entered the craft and the water company stayed in the hanger sorting out their kit while the rest of the warriors went to the warriors' seating area.

Kurt took Karl up to the command deck of the craft and introduced him to pilot who showed Karl the craft's systems and how it was flown. 'Don't you mean sailed?' inquired Karl.

'No definitely not, young prince. This craft flies through the water, it doesn't sail, and it has no sails,' the pilot informed Karl. The pilot opened the forward viewing portal telling Karl he could take the craft to sea. He showed Karl that all the safety lights were on, indicating the craft was sealed for submersible operations. All compartments had also confirmed all was in order. They went over to the navigation screen and put in the route the craft would take to get to its water company deployment area, the rest of the flight would be manual. Karl sat next to the pilot who told him what to do. He pressed the display screen and released the mooring grapples that slid back into the quay, then he pressed 'depart on rails'. There was a slight jolt as the rail clamps attached to the underside of the craft, then 'manoeuvre to sea' was pressed and the craft started to move forward at some speed. He was told that if it was an emergency departure everyone on board would have to be strapped into seats, or they would suffer significant injuries from the g-force as they shot forward leaving the dock and reaching the sea in thirty seconds, compared with four minutes attached to the rail. The rail would automatically detach from the craft when they reached the outer sea, then all Karl would have to do was press 'navigate 1' and the craft would navigate to its first way point, or press 'navigate all' and it would go to manual. Karl pressed 'navigate 1' because the route had been entered. The craft started to submerge and then it began to dive. Now it was just a matter of watching the systems and warning panels then acting accordingly. Karl thanked the pilot and excused himself to go and find the water company to wish them luck on their mission.

Kurt winked at him and said, 'She will eat you alive, Karl.'

'What! Uncle Kurt, I'm interested to see them get ready, their pre-deployment routine.'

'Of course, you are, young prince,' Kurt replied, with a smile.

Karl went red and hurried away. As he entered the main hanger, he stopped and observed the water company, Hollie was going through their immediate action drills, what to do in case of different things happening. Actions on getting lost, engaging the enemy, rendezvous points. Extraction points, everything you could think of that could go wrong was covered as well as everything that should happen.

'Right, team, remember we are the best. Let's show them how things should be done. Final kit check and we will be there. Oh! And remember, "Fight hard and die well".' The team nodded and went about their final preparations.

Karl walked over to Hollie and smiled. 'Everything ready, Hollie?'

'Yes, everyone's drills are slick. They all know what they are doing. Can I ask you something, prince?' She didn't wait for him to reply. 'As a neutral observer, did you think I was a little over the top with the fight hard bit?'

'Firstly, Hollie, I'm Karl not "prince" and second, I thought you were very professional and inspiring to your team. Thirdly, I wish I was going with you, instead of being here with Uncle Kurt.'

'Don't wish too much, Prince Karl. Kurt tends to end up where the action is, and you never know, you may be in the water company one day taking orders from me,' she said with a wink in her eye. 'Oh, and if I were you, Karl, I would get myself a combat suit instead of the exploration kit you have on. You won't last two minutes in battle with that lot on.'

'I didn't realise we were going into battle,' responded Karl.

Just then one of the craft's crew entered the hanger and shouted, 'One minute to deployment point.'

'Okay, team, let's get it together!' Hollie shouted.

'Good luck, Hollie,' said Karl.

'I don't need luck, prince, I have a good team but thank you anyway,' she smiled. Hollie and her team strapped their weapons to their bodies, donned their helmets and moved over to a hatch in the hanger floor. A panel next to the hatch turned red and Hollie nodded to her team. then the light went green and the hatch opened revealing sea water. One, two, three, four of the team were gone, then Hollie, five, followed by six, seven, eight and Karl was left alone in the hanger. He had a great urge to follow and be number nine. The hatch closed, and Karl turned and headed back towards the door that led back to Kurt and the pilot. As he reached the door it opened, and Kurt stepped through.

'Did the team get off okay?' he asked Karl.

'Yes, they were away with no problems; I would have loved to go with them.'

'That's good to hear, Karl, but it takes a lot of training and dedication to become that good. You never know, you might even be part of a team like that one day.'

'That's what Hollie said,' Karl replied.

Behind Kurt came the rest of the warriors who had embarked with them. They began to get into the vehicles that were in the hanger; the rest of them checked their equipment and were given final orders. Karl asked Kurt how they would deploy from the craft. He was told that if it was all cleared by the water company, the craft would fly onto the beach they had selected, and everyone would disembark through the same side door they had entered. They were expecting no resistance, so it should be quite simple; the warriors had practised it many times.

'What about me? What will I do?' Karl asked.

'You, Karl, will be at my side while I am leading the warriors forward. You will watch my back and I will watch yours. Are you happy with that, prince?'

179

'Happy! Extremely, thank you.'

'Just remember what your helmet can do for you and use your weapon wisely and you will be fine. I shouldn't really let you come with me. One, you're the king's son, and two, you don't have a combat suit on. But I know in normal clothes it is very exhilarating, you feel more exposed but that makes you more aware. My first combat was in normal clothing when I was surprised by some mountain tigers, when I was just a little older than you are now. All I had was a rayzor, but I remember how alive I felt to this day You will feel vulnerable, but stay by my side and you will be safe. I don't think this little manoeuvre will come to anything but you never know. I know you have courage, the Wolf master saw you with that lizsnake, so you should be fine. Come over here with me and see how Hollie and her team are doing.'

Karl walked over with Kurt to a screen he had not noticed before; it was in the corner of the hanger near where Kurt and the warriors had entered. Kurt explained that it was the tactical operational map and that it showed all combat forces on the ground. In this case, only Hollie's team who showed up as eight white dots moving towards the island. At that moment, there were no red dots indicating enemy positions. Each symbol on the screen indicated the units on the ground. Karl noticed that next to Hollie's team of white dots was a number one. He was told that Hollie's team was Water Company No One.

Hollie slowly came to the surface; she was confident her head would not be seen because the waves were crashing around her and onto the beach. The sky was grey, and she could see the clouds tumbling in the turbulent sky above. Perfect weather for reconnaissance. Any enemy would probably have themselves tucked up inside out of the appalling weather. That was if there was any enemy. She expected this to be another where very little happened. She crawled along the seabed, keeping her body submerged, but her weapon at the ready under the waves. Off to her left the section second-in-command popped his head up and did the same as Hollie. With her infra-red sensor on, Hollie scanned the beach. Nothing. Then she looked at the treeline. Nothing. Then, as she was just about to emerge from the water, she spotted a figure walking just inside the treeline. It had a weapon in its hand.

Hollie spoke to her team, the command centre on the ship, and to the strategic centre back in the citadel. She informed them of the possible enemy figure in the treeline and told her team to get ready for a possible encounter. She moved forward on her belly, staying as low as possible, focused on the moving figure. She had to identify it, for all she knew it could be a friendly, but they were unaware of any friendly people on the island except Tom, Salina and the sea slugs, and the figure she could see was none of them. She silently crawled closer. Through the bushes and trees she caught sight of a face, scared and demented looking, typical Dark foot warrior, the lowest of the low and the brainless of the bunch. Hollie pulled a throwing knife from the top of her boot, not standard issue but a favourite of Hollie's and she was good with it. The foot warrior turned and walked back the way he had just come. As he passed the gap in the trees where she had first seen his face, she let the knife fly. The foot warrior fell to the ground. The sound of him falling into a bush was masked by the howling wind and colliding trees and bushes all around them. Suddenly from behind the bush a demon dog leapt out at Hollie. Totally shocked by the surprise attack, Hollie was slow to react. From behind her, one of her team took aim and the dog fell dead next to her. Before Hollie could get up, three of her team were around her. In her intercom she heard, 'Sorry, boss, I knew you had him, but I haven't had a kill for a while, so I thought I'd have that one.'

'Thanks, that's never been known before. A basic grunt with a demon dog, as far as I know.' (Some of the war phrases used on Earth, had made their way to Elemtum. Humans were good at things like that, grunt). Hollie looked up and all around her the water team was now in defensive positions. Well trained, she thought. I must buck up.

'You're right, Hollie, that has never been seen before. The Dark obviously like to keep us guessing,' one of her team mentioned. The second team now came ashore without any further encounters. They also went into a defensive position; both teams now went silent and observed in a complete circle.

On the craft, Kurt ensured his assault force was ready to deploy. They waited for Hollie's signal to proceed. What everyone did know now was that the Dark were the furthest north they had ever been reported, and that Tom and Salina could be in very serious danger, if not worse.

Arn had landed safely and he had taken cover under some trees, near to where Tom and Salina had fallen and entered the structure that ended up leading them to the tunnels and eventually through an open thread to the Zells' world. Arn could smell the Dark. They were close. He tried contacting Tom and Salina but got nothing, but he did get a reply from Kurt and Karl, who asked how and where he was and if he had Tom and Salina with him. They informed him that, strangely, they could not see him on the tactical map. They also let him know what was going on and where they were. They would bring the assault craft on to the beach. If it was safe, he could meet them there. If not, he was to stay where he was and wait for them to reach him. They believed Hollie and her water team where not too far from him. Arn stayed where he was as he knew the Dark were close and he did not want to give his position away if he could help it.

Tom had been given his repaired combat suit back. He and Salina, along with Zuzza, had gone to the Zells' command centre, where they had been told of some developments near a thread on Elemtum. The thread that they believed the Dark had somehow found. On the wall of the command centre was a large map split into three sections. One section showed the city they were in and the surrounding waters. The second showed the mountain the young Zells were in, broken down into levels showing the positions of the Dark and the proximity of them to the young Zells. The third screen showed the world above the sea and the island of Linasfarn. On that screen they could see red dots indicating live people (Hollie's team). Nearby were red dots with a black circle around them, which one of the command staff explained, indicating dead. On a monitor next to the big screen was a picture of a silver ship under the water off Linasfarn. They were trying to identify if it was a threat to them when Salina told them it was one of her craft and that it would be pose no threat. She explained that most probably the red circles were water warriors who had just killed the two black encircled red dots that were most probably bodies of Dark warriors they had just dispatched. What was more worrying for Salina was the fact that she could see a sizeable force of red dots emerging from a cavern that was heading towards the water company, who at that point were unaware of their presence. Salina asked the Zells if there was any way they could get a message to their people to warn the water company about their possible impending doom at the hands of the much larger force. They told her they had an underwater passage that led to her world, the same passage that the green-haired girl used to cross from their world to hers. The Zell also told her of a force that could deal with that number of Dark heading for Hollie.

'The young Zells. They are fearless, strong, and I know the Dark are terrified of them,' one of the commanders told her.

'But they will never get there in time. Or the water company might take them for Dark creatures,' Salina replied.

'We could ride them, and then our warriors would see the young Zells are on their side, especially when they see us attacking the Dark warriors,' said Tom.

'That's an idea, but we would never get there quickly enough to be any good,' replied Salina.

'That may not be so,' butted in the Zell commander. 'It looks like your assault craft is moving in to support your water warriors. 'Look.' The commander pointed to the large screen. They could see the large dot speeding towards the smaller red dots that were now turned green, because the Zells now classed them as friendly. 'That other force inside the assault craft will not be enough to beat the much larger

Dark force, but it will give them a much-needed breathing space as long as they fight well. That will give you and the young Zells time to come to their aid!' the commander told her.

'Come on, Salina, we have to do it.'

'You're right, Tom, but I don't want you to fight. As soon as we get there, land near the assault craft and get inside.'

'Yes, okay! Now, let's get going!' he urged.

Hollie could see no reason why she could now not call the assault craft in. With nods from her team, she did so. 'Assault one, company one, you are clear in. Be aware there may be hostiles in the area, so be prepared to fight. Water company one will move forward, and scout the area ahead, then we will wait for your arrival, out.'

'Okay, one, let's move. Watch your backs, assault one is on the way.' The water company broke cover and started to stealthily patrol forward, as the assault craft sped towards the beach.

'Company one, confirm you are clear of the beach, we are coming in.'

'Company one clear,' Hollie replied.

Over the intercom came 'Brace! Brace! Brace!'

In the hanger on the assault craft, everyone braced themselves for the deliberate collision to come. The assault craft came out of the sea, sliding at speed up the beach to a standstill. Either side of the craft, stabilisers came out of its hull to keep the craft upright. On the top of the hull a turret came out with two sonic weapons pointing menacingly out of it. They started to sweep the area around in front and above the craft. They were all automatic and had a deadly range of up to a mile for anything in the air or on the ground. The side door opened and the fighting vehicle inside the hanger raced out, heading for a pre-designated fire position, to give maximum support to the warriors deploying from the craft at speed. It headed away from the craft to set up all-round defence until the last warriors had left the craft and come ashore. The stabilisers on the assault craft's sides began to operate like legs pushing the it off the beach, where it was at its most vulnerable, back into the water where it would wait and give support if needed.

His heart pumping, the adrenalin surging through his veins, Karl had followed his uncle out of the craft behind the vehicles leading their mighty warriors. Karl's first combat and he was only fourteen; he felt exhilarated and scared all at the same time, but he felt safe with Kurt powering forward next to him and the warriors behind.

'Stop, stop, stop!' came from Hollie and her water company. 'Contact! I repeat, contact!'

There was a short pause then through their helmets everyone could hear sonic weapons being fired. Then 'Damn, they're still coming!'

'Command, water company one, we are pulling back under a massive assault from Dark warriors flooding out from a large cave in front of us. There are too many for us to be effective. I have lost one of my team already. If I don't pull back, we will all die!' A chill went through everyone listening to the strong but calm broadcast. 'We are conducting a fighting withdrawal to give you time to reboard the craft. We will be able to hold for about five minutes. Out.'

Then Kurt came over the communication channel, 'Well done, water company one. Pull back to our lines and we will defend this area. We will defeat the Dark on the beach. We are better off together.'

'But, sir.'

Kurt cut her off. 'No buts about it, Hollie, bring your warriors back to our lines. And that's an order! Assault force one, prepare to receive water company one. Give them all the supporting and covering fire we can and prepare to defend our area aggressively. Out!'

Zuzza, Salina and Tom raced through the Zell city back to where they were transported back to the white hanger. From there, they went through to the young Zells' cavern where there were only two young Zells to be seen.

'Where are they all?' Tom shouted, as they ran to the lip of the ledge.

'Mount the two Zells. They have been harnessed for you, then follow me. The young ones will know what to do,' shouted Zuzza, then she leapt from the ledge.

Salina looked down and saw that Zuzza had turned into the small winged creature she had first met hours before on the cavern floor. One by one, the two Zells landed on the ledge. First Tom then Salina got on to their respective Zell who then flew down and out to the entrance to the cavern that Salina had climbed up to on her search for Tom. They joined Zuzza, but still Tom could see no other Zells.

'What do we do now?' Tom asked.

'We fly to the sea, which is a short distance away over the forest, then we will dive into the water and come out on your planet near to Linasfarn. Don't worry, the young Zells are excellent swimmers. They glide through the water just as they do the sky.'

'How will we breathe?' Salina asked.

'The Zells can store a lot of air in their lungs, so they will be okay. You will have a breathing mask. Look on the back of the harness. In that small bag is the mask that has a pipe which is attached to a small bottle of air. As soon as you put the mask on, it will supply you with air. Enough for the journey through the water.'

Tom and Salina both tried their masks on. Happy that they worked, they let them hang round their necks then tightened the straps ready for when they entered the water.

'All we need now are the young Zells,' said Salina.

Zuzza let out a high-pitched screech, then five loud clicks and in front of them three hundred Zells lifted up into the air and hovered above the forest.

'Bloody hell!' cried Tom, 'I never thought there were that many.'

'The Dark warriors will run in terror,' said Salina. 'I have seen what one of them can do. I would hate to think what three hundred will do.'

Zuzza, Tom and Salina all lifted above them and led the young Zells over the forest. They could now see the sea glistening in the sunlight ahead, Tom put his hand on the Zell he was riding and thought, 'Hello I'm Tom, can you hear me?'

'Greetings, Wolf boy Tom. I am Velum Zell. Thank you for talking to me.'

'I hope I don't offend you, but are you a boy or a girl? I'm sorry I don't know,' asked Tom.

'I am neither a boy nor girl, I am a young Zell. When I become a proper Zell, I believe I am to be a female,' Velum replied. 'Get ready, Tom the Wolf prince, we are about to enter the sea. Keep low and hold on.'

In front of them, Zuzza and Salina and her Zell dove into the water. Tom bent low as if he was on a fast motor bike and pulled his mask on just as Velum hit the water. Tom felt an initial rush of cold water, then his suit kicked in and he began to warm up instantly like he had done in the lake. He tried to open his eyes but all he everything was blur and his eyes stung so he closed them for the rest of his underwater journey. He did not know whether he was up or down, going left or right, but his ears popped. It was like going down a water slide with your eyes shut. Ten minutes later he could feel Velum rise, then he was out of the water, climbing high.

In front and below them there were scenes of total mayhem. Warriors were grappling with Dark warriors in deadly hand-to-hand fighting. By the look of it, Kurt, Karl and Hollie were still holding off the Dark, but only just. The rain had stopped but the wind was still quite fierce. Salina told Zuzza to hold the young Zells where they were, and she and Tom would go down and warn Kurt about his unexpected ally in the sky. Salina and Tom flew low across the sea Salina thought hard and sent out a message to anyone listening.

'This is Salina De-Callen and Prince Thomas. We are flying in coming behind the assault craft any moment. We are riding two big black winged creatures that are here to help with a small army. I need Lord Kurt to make himself known. I have good news for him.'

As they passed the assault craft, the turret followed them but did not fire. It meant at least the weapons' officer on the craft had heard Salina.

'Salina, it's great to hear from you. Is Thomas safe?'

'Yes, father, he is with me and he's fine. I have three hundred winged creatures called Zells that are fierce warriors from the sky and they are here to help you. They are led by one of their princesses, Zuzza Zell. We are going to attack the Dark at the cave and stop them. Thomas will land and stay with you. I will fight with the Zell.'

As Kurt communicated with Salina, Karl noticed a Dark warrior break through the thinly defended line and rush full bore at him and Kurt. In front of him, lying on the ground, was a dead water company warrior with his hand holding a rayzor and at his side was a sonic rifle. Karl dashed forward and retrieved both. He lifted the rifle to his shoulder and squeezed the trigger. He felt a kick at his shoulder as the sonic beam shot out. It flew over the Dark warrior's head. Angry because he had missed, Karl ran at the advancing warrior. His options were now very limited because the Dark warrior was so close. All around him hand-to-hand combat raged. Karl ran at the warrior full pelt and threw the rifle at the warrior's head. The Dark warrior instinctively ducked and took his eye off Karl who leapt off a dead Dark warrior's body into the air slightly above the attacking warrior. As he went past, Karl swung the rayzor down on the exposed neck of the Dark warrior, slicing deep into the tissue nearly severing the Dark warrior's head, enough to stop him in his tracks. With adrenalin pumping, Karl rushed forward to plug the gap the Dark warrior had got through. It was obvious to him that the warriors he was going forward to help were working in teams of two; one firing weapons, the other slicing the enemy down with their rayzors when they got too near.

Tom and Salina held their position above and back from Kurt. Below and in front of them a Wolf warrior fired a weapon at an attacking Dark lancer who fell twenty feet in front him. The Dark warrior tried to get up, wobbled, and fell back down. Then it got back up on its knees drawing a sword from its belt. Adrenalin still coursing through his veins, Karl dashed forward faster than he had ever done before and leapt at the Dark lancer who brought his sword back to strike the wolf. But he was too slow and Karl tore into the lancer's neck and did not let go until it was dead. Around him, more lancers and condemned men tumbled down, felled by his own warriors' sonic rifles. From above, Tom had noticed the wolf dash forward killing a Dark warrior, but what the wolf did not see high above him was Arthfael ordering more of his Dark warriors to snatch the prince. He knew Prince

Karl to be one of Queen Labatina's top priorities.

Tom saw some of the Dark warriors gathering into a small squad. Suddenly, they started to run en masse towards the wolf. Tom looked again for the wolf but all he saw was his brother standing over the dead lancer.

Karl was a little dazed by what had just happened. He remembered running, but not really remembering; it did not make sense. Then he realised he was in front of his lines. He saw Kurt running through the gap he had just come through. Behind him several warriors racing towards him. Then he smelt the stench of the Dark warriors. He turned as a net flew over him. Several Dark warriors pulled the ropes attached to the net and started to drag the now fighting Karl back towards the approaching Dark warriors. The more Karl fought, the more he became tangled in the web-like net. Around the net, the Dark warriors pulling the net were joined by more Dark warriors whose job it was to protect the warriors pulling the net. Some of the Dark were afraid; it showed in their eyes. They had seen the Wolf lord at their fore and he was deadly in battle. That was one thing the lowly Dark warriors knew, but they continued to surge forward until clashing headlong into Kurt and his warriors. Swords and rayzors flew, screams could be heard above the din of the battle raging around them but the numbers were taking their toll and Karl was being dragged, kicked and punched ever deeper into the Dark-held territory.

Kurt knew he had no chance at the moment to save Karl but if he did not pull back to their line, they would be overrun by the Dark.

'Fall back,' Kurt shouted over his helmet communication system as he swung wildly at anything that came within his reach. He and his warriors slowly pulled back, leaving none of their own behind, dead or alive. As they reached their line, the rows of Dark warriors in front of Kurt started to fall. The assault craft commander had pushed his craft up the beach and through the treeline and was pounding the Dark warriors with his turret weapons. His craft was now stuck, so they had no means of escape but the fire power it was giving to the Kurt and his warriors was excellent, giving them all time to breath for the first time since the battle had begun. From behind slightly raised shields, the weapons' officer fired anti-personnel balls at the Dark warriors. Like anti-personnel weapons on Earth, they decimated the forward ranks of the Dark still standing.

Tom saw the trouble his brother was in and communicated it to the Zells. He also asked one of the other Zells close to him to follow them and help him get his brother back. His quick plan was for the two Zells and Tom to race down, attack the Dark warriors dragging Karl away, then Tom would jump off his Zell and get Karl out of the net. Once he'd got Karl onto the second Zell, they would all fly away to safety. Easy, he thought.

Very quickly, another Zell flew down to them and they raced off to Karl's rescue. Salina had gone down to help Kurt and had given Tom implicit orders to stay where he was. Salina and her Zell helped Kurt and the last of his warriors get back to their lines. One of the Eagle warriors pointed skywards and Salina looked up. Tom shot past her, high into the sky, then started to descend

'Stop, Tom!' she shouted and communicated, but he was not listening

Tom and the two Zells swooped down on the warriors dragging Karl away. Tom's Zell dived at the warriors pulling the net, grabbing one with its feet claws, ripping his hands free from the net and lifting him screaming into the air. The Zell then let him go, where he fell to his death amongst some of his fellow Dark warriors, killing or injuring them. The second Zell attacked the warriors that were trying to protect the ones dragging Karl away, decimating their ranks. The other warriors, having already come across the massive black flying beasts, started to run. Some of their leaders screamed at them and cut them down. Two of the fleeing warriors slayed their leader who had tried to stop them. The last remaining warrior holding the rope to the net looked up to see Tom's Zell descending at speed towards him. He dropped the rope and ran but he didn't get far. Tom's Zell landed on top of him, skewering his body to the ground. Tom jumped off Velum and ran towards his brother amongst the dead bodies of the recently departed Dark. Tom could see Karl was still in the net.

'Karl, Karl,' his little brother shouted. Karl looked up, totally exhausted from his struggles to free himself and the beating he had received for his efforts. The end of the net was only held closed by the ropes that had been pulling it, so Tom loosened the rope enough for Karl to claw his way out and shakily stand up with the help of his brother.

'Thanks, Tom, I'm glad you're safe, I thought I was a goner. What is that big bat thing you were on? I saw bits through the net. They must be friendly, aren't they?' Karl asked.

'They are. They are Zells. It's a long story. I will tell you later. One of them is for you to ride.'

Velum hopped over to them and told them to climb up quickly. The Dark creatures were coming back, and it looked like there were more behind them. They got on the two Zells who lifted into the air. That's when Karl and Tom saw how close they were to being captured again. Arrows, spears and bolts whizzed past them as they rose out of range. Behind them, the sky blackened as three hundred Zells descended onto the advancing Dark hordes. Destruction rained down on them from above.

Back at Kurt's lines, he and his warriors watched in awe and amazement at the magnificent spectacle that they witnessed. More Dark warriors came from the cavern and were decimated on the field of death until nothing was left of the Dark from the cavern. Any Dark still in the cavern were now too scared to come out, if any were still alive at all. The Zells flew around the battlefield looking for movement, but there was none.

Karl and Tom flew back to their lines and met Salina flying towards them. Behind her, they could see squadrons of Eagle warriors coming over the sea towards them. The wind had died down significantly, and from above shafts of sunlight started to beam through parting dark grey clouds onto the death covered landscape as the weather front passed through.

'Thomas, Karl, follow me to the ground. Kurt wants a word with you both.'

'Crap,' said Tom.

Karl said nothing; he was still a little dazed. The Zells landed behind Kurt who was thanking Zuzza for all they had done; they had most definitely saved them all. Karl and Tom thanked Velum and the other Zell then went over to Zuzza who was now in her people form. Tom and Karl thanked her, giving her a heartfelt hug. Zuzza was quite surprised by the hug; they did not do that, but she found it very comforting. Salina thanked Zuzza for all she had done to help them then Zuzza left to collect the twenty dead young Zells that had paid the ultimate sacrifice for a race of people they did not know. This did not go unnoticed by Kurt and his surviving warriors.

The commander of the eagle force landed and spoke to Kurt. Their first task would be to guard the entrance to the cavern, ensuring no more Dark warriors surprised them. After that they would all collect their fallen warriors then check all the Dark for maps or documentation that might explain why they were so far north and how they had got there. The final task was to stack the Dark dead in several piles, due of the great number they would have to be disposed of all together. Normally a specialist team of warriors would arrive within hours with a unique cocktail of natural plant acids that would completely dissolve one hundred stacked bodies in an hour quite efficiently.

Two more assault crafts arrived and pulled the beached assault craft back into the water, where some of the crew inspected the underside for any damage just in case as the craft was not exactly designed to do what it had done. It was widely acknowledged that what the commander of the first craft had done was outstanding; it had helped save many lives. Teams of warriors went about the task that warriors and fighting armies have done throughout the centuries under the leadership of their commanders, leaving Kurt to deal with the two princes.

'Thomas, were you not told by Salina to stay where you were, out of danger?' Kurt asked very controlled and calm.

'Yes, Uncle Kurt, but...' Tom was interrupted.

'No buts, Tom. What you did was irresponsible and dangerous. You are ten years old, and you will do what you are told. Do you understand, prince or no prince?' Tom looked at Kurt indignantly. After all, he had just saved his brother and he was getting told off, that couldn't be right. 'Do you understand I asked, Tom?' repeated Kurt.

Salina looked at Tom; she knew what he was thinking and gave him a supportive smile.

'Yes, I understand, Uncle Kurt, and I will not do it again.' He thought for a second then said defiantly, 'I don't actually mean that I would do it again.'

Kurt looked at the young prince. He could see the defiance in his eyes. 'What you did was very brave, Tom, but you need to think before you act. But I will say this: sometimes hasty and impulsive things, although rash and dangerous, can be very heroic and, without doubt, you saved your brother's life... You are a very courageous and brave boy. If you manage to live long enough to be a warrior, you will be absolutely incredible, I am sure of that. But please listen to me, I want you to become that warrior prince, but if you continue to do things like that you will never fulfil your destiny, Thomas.' Kurt went up to Tom and gave him the warrior's handshake, then a big bear hug, more out of relief than anything else. Even though Tom knew he had been told off, he beamed with pride. Salina ruffled his hair and Karl gave him an enormously brotherly hug.

'Thank you, Tom, you were very brave today. You saved my life and I owe you,' said Karl.

'Now to you, Karl. What I said to Tom applies to you as well but there is a difference... You are turning, so your body is in a mess right now. I bet just recently you have been feeling stronger and running just that little bit faster, mood swings, rage. Am I right?'

'How did you know?' Karl replied.

'Your wolf has emerged; you just don't know how to control him yet.'

'That's true, Karl. I saw a wolf run from where our warriors were fighting and kill one of the Dark warriors out on the battlefield. Then, when I looked again, you were standing there alone,' Tom told him excitedly.

'That is the turning, Karl; normally you are taught and prepared for the turning. It was thought you were too young to turn. Females normally turn around sixteen years and males around eighteen years, so at only fourteen you have turned very early. You are the youngest anyone has ever turned, as far as I am aware, that is,' said Kurt.

'I'm a wolf now?' Karl said excitedly. Seconds later a young wolf stood before them. 'I feel strange,' thought Karl. Everyone around received his message.

'Cool,' said Tom.

The wolf looked at him. 'What's cool, Tom?' it asked.

'You being a wolf... sit, boy,' Tom said, and patted Karl the wolf on the head.

The wolf snapped at him. 'Not funny, Tom,' it thought.

'Remember, Tom, his whole body is changing, so he will not be the brother you know for a few days. Take care with what you do and say, or you could lose that hand,' smiled Salina. Tom pulled his hand back and put them in the side pockets of his combat suit, out of Karl's reach.

'How do I get back to being me?' asked Karl.

Kurt explained that until he learnt to be his wolf, he would not be a young person until that side of him was under control. Karl felt an overwhelming desire to bite his brother's leg.

'Why do I want to eat Tom?' asked Karl. 'I'm not a werewolf, am I?'

'No, you aren't, Karl. What is happening is your young natural instinct to hunt and kill your food is starting to emerge but that does mean is that we will have to put a muzzle on you, just so your brother will survive the night,' said Kurt.

'He's joking, aren't you?' thought Karl, looking at Kurt.

'You are joking, aren't you?' Tom said, also looking at Kurt.

'I'm afraid not. Boys. I mean boy and wolf,' Kurt chuckled.

'Father! I don't think that's appropriate, do you?' said Salina.

'You're right, Salina, but we had better get a muzzle quickly. Until then, we will make one out of rope until we get back to the citadel,' Kurt said, trying to be serious.

'Until then I will go and take this combat suit off and transform into a wolf. That should calm Karl down and I will take him for a run and get rid of some of that energy and mischief he has building up inside,' said Salina. She walked over to some of the trees that were still standing and took her suit off, then Salina the wolf reappeared. Walking back to them, she thought to Tom, 'Can you get my clothes and take them back with you to the craft when you go?' Tom's face went bright red and he rushed off to get the clothes.

'What was that all about? It looked like you embarrassed the boy, Salina,' said Kurt.

I will tell you later, thought Salina who then went over and rescued a warrior and his boot from Karl's jaws.

'Come with me, young wolf, I will take you for a run and we may find something to quench that appetite you now have.'

'Take care, Salina, there may still be the odd Dark warrior around. Our warriors are combing the island, so you will not be far from help if needed,' shouted Kurt.

The two wolves ran off along the beach Tom returned with Salina's clothes, still glowing red. Kurt and Tom walked back towards one of the waiting craft. As they went to board, Tom had a familiar feeling. It was Arn; he had found them. Looking a little bedraggled for a mighty eagle, he landed next to them. Tom ran to him. It was clear to everyone present they were both overjoyed to see each other.

'What happened to you, you look terrible?' asked Tom.

'I got caught up in that storm. I have been sheltering on the other side of the islands. I have been feeling all kinds of emotions. What have you been doing, Tom?' Arn asked.

'It's a long story, Arn; I will tell you all about it when we fly home.'

'Fly home, Thomas? I'm not too sure about that,' commented Kurt.

'He will be safe with me, Kurt, you know that. If you want a little more reassurance, send a couple of Eagle warriors back with us. I have some listening to do, I think,' communicated Arn.

'Okay, but no deviations,' replied Kurt who then ordered four Eagle warriors to escort them back to the citadel.

Tom and Arn took off, escorted by the warriors, and headed out to sea. Tom started to tell Arn his amazing story. They left the clean-up and exploration of the cave to the newly arrived warriors.

Kurt boarded the craft to see Hollie sitting on a seat, a little worse for wear, with a dressing on her head, blood on her cheek and her arm in a fracture sling, slowly mending. 'Good to see you, Commander Hollie,' Kurt said.

'I'm only a leader, sir,' she replied.

'Not any more, Hollie. You were magnificent out there. You lead with bravery and courage. Your actions were exemplary.'

'You can say that again, Lord Kurt, she saved my worthless ass twice today,' shouted over one of her water company.

'But I lost four warriors, sir,' she said, with a tear in her eye.

'You did, Hollie, but I've lost many more and every one of them fought and died with honour the way they would have wanted to go. It was through no fault of yours or mine. you must always remember that. This war is not our doing, and neither were these brave warriors' deaths. Now, think no more about it and rest. We will honour our dead another day.' The craft door closed, then departed the island of Linasfarn heading back to the citadel with what the history books one day called, 'The Heroes of Linasfarn'.

Kurt left her and returned to the beach to organise the reinforcements and the clean-up operations that would soon start taking place.

Kurt knew that the island had cost them all so much and changed some of them forever!

CHAPTER 12
Life-Changing Events

Karl felt strong as he ran along the beach at speed with a beautiful wolf at his side; he could run for ever. He had never felt this alive in all his life. As a boy, he would be panting by now but today, he had no such worries. He felt powerful, he sensed everything around him including Salina's heart next to him. She darted ahead of him; he increased his pace and caught up with her effortlessly. For the first time in his life, he was really alive. Nothing could stop him, the wolf blood powered through his veins. He was now a noble creature. For the first time since leaving Earth, he felt like a prince.

They ran and ran until they reached a large wood where Salina told Karl to stop to get his breath and calm his breathing and heart rate. She was sure that they would find something to hunt inside the wood ahead. It had been a long day and even though his people body was battered and bruised, his wolf form was not and it did not take long to lower his heart rate and steady his breathing. He could smell everything around him. His eyesight was sharp, as was his hearing. Even a leaf landing he could hear and instantly see where it had fallen.

'So, when we catch this pray, do we eat it?' Karl the young Wolf prince asked.

'Only if you're hungry,' replied Salina. 'I am, so I assume you will be too. We only kill what we need and no more. We don't kill for the fun of it, that's your first lesson.' They walked silently into the wood, the branches swaying gently above them. The tail end of the storm dying above them.

Karl's ears were full of noise. 'I can't hear a thing now,' he told Salina.

'This is your second lesson; concentrate on what is around you, separate the noises you hear. Put the noise of the wind and the branches to one side and listen for the rest of the sounds. The living forest.'

Karl concentrated and found he could actually separate the sounds in his head; dampen one sound down and heighten another. He could never do that as Karl the boy. He put the wind and the bristling branches and leaves in one corner, then listened intently to the quiet side of his mind He could hear nothing.

'Listen, Karl, do you hear? Do you hear it?' asked Salina.

Karl could hear nothing, so she told him about the different wavelengths of sound. If he scanned them, he would hear the gentle movement inside the woods and if she was not mistaken, it was an old leaopole deer. A leaopole deer was very much like a muntjac deer on Earth, she told him. He was still none the wiser. Then he picked it up, small movements. He recognised the deer's footsteps. One of the four steps is different, he thought to himself.

'If you listen carefully, Karl, you can hear that the deer is lame in one leg,' she told him.

'I thought there was something different about what I was hearing. It just didn't sound right, and it wasn't in rhythm. Do we have a plan of attack?' he asked Salina.

She told him the plan was to stalk the deer. Karl would make his way behind it and Salina would advance on a frontal attack, more of a diversion than an actual attack, but she would bring the deer down if it got close enough. The idea was to drive the panicked deer towards Karl who would ambush it as it ran towards him. Either it would fall prey to him or it would turn and flee back towards Salina. Either way it would be heading towards its eventual death.

Karl crept around the area where the deer was grazing and positioned himself behind his unsuspecting prey.

Salina howled her intention that the hunt was on. The howl was a warning to Karl to get ready but it was also to panic the deer, which it did. It ran in totally the opposite direction to the howl it had heard seconds before, straight at Karl as planned. Salina wanted Karl to make the kill. He needed to kill it to release the built-up overpowering craving he had. All young wolves had this initial craving for the kill, but once they had killed as a wolf, they would never get that craving again. Modern Wolf warriors only hunted as a last resort, there was no need to anymore.

Scared, the deer ran straight towards Karl who patiently waited. He was ready to pounce and bring the deer down. He caught sight of the panicking deer leaping through the bracken in the woodland, then there was thud and the deer fell from his sight, but what Karl did see was a lance sticking up above the bracken. He kept his quiet position and observed the direction the lance had come from. Out of the undergrowth from Karl's right came a Dark lancer. Karl communicated to Salina what he had seen.

So, why didn't the Dark lancer react to my howl? she thought.

Karl knew the reason why. As the lancer got closer to him, he had no ears; it looked like they had been hacked off. Karl leapt out of his hiding place and pounded onto the startled lancer's chest, pushing him over onto his back. Karl the wolf went for his neck, ripping it open. There was no sound because when the lancer's mouth opened to scream, Karl noticed that he had no tongue. Karl felt the lancer's weak grip on his fur as he held tight to his foe with his full weight on his chest. It wasn't long before the struggle stopped, and the lancer was dead.

Salina appeared and told Karl to follow her. Together they would search the local area for any more Dark warriors.

On the blue moon, Rowena had awakened from her coma and was sitting up being checked over by the healer who had accompanied her on her journey from Elemtum. The healer was worried that Rowena had awoken from the coma by herself. Normally the healing vessel would gradually wake the patient as their illness or wound healed. But Rowena had awoken by herself without making her condition any worse. After some tests and a complete scan, the healer declared Rowena fitter and healthier than she had ever been, but they still wanted her to relax and sleep for another twenty-four hours before she should get up. Rowena insisted on going to the toilet by herself. After that, her next priority would be to get something to eat and drink. The healer helped her up. At first Rowena was a little unsteady but once she got her senses back, she insisted on the healer letting her go, because, as she put it, 'I'm not an invalid, I can manage.' Rowena stumbled then walked out of her room into the attached toilet. 'It's okay, I know how to go to the toilet,' she told the healer as they entered. So, the healer left her alone and patiently waited outside. Minutes later the door slid open and Row stood there very embarrassed. 'Sorry for having a go at you, I don't know what came over me.'

'It's okay, it's a side effect of coming out of the healing vessel too quickly. Don't worry about it, I was expecting it, lady.'

'Thank you for that. Can you tell me where the toilet is? This is an empty room.'

The healer smiled and showed Row the mirror and how the system worked.

In a room not too far away, her father was now in a healing vessel, but this one was much more elaborate than the one Rowena had been in. Her's had been the equivalent to A&E on Earth, her father's was for deep trauma care. He also had a specialist Wolf healer present just in case of any unforeseen circumstances. At that present time all was going as planned and the emperor king would be better than new in a day or so.

Rowena had no idea where she was, so while she ate the healer informed her about her missing days and what had gone on. Rowena could not believe she was on a moon, so the healer opened a window in her room so she could look out on the moon. The first thing she noticed was the light blue sky. The blue moon was nothing like the grey desolate moon above Earth, this one was alive and very blue. The healer explained to Row that there was a lot of water on the moon as well as great forests; she also told her that if you stayed on the blue moon your skin took on a blue pigment like the healers who were all born on the moon. If you were born on the blue moon, you became a healer and that was that. The healing power came from the blue, and the blue was a magnificent sight at the core of the moon, it was said. The healer had never seen the centre of the moon, but she knew and told Row that Gabriel made this moon to heal the worlds and the healers were the chosen race to do just that; heal any world they come into contact with.

On the wall a very serious looking healer came on the internal communicator, 'All class ten and above healers not on essential duties please report to the docking bay immediately. Trauma casualties from Elemtum will be arriving within the hour.

'I must go,' said the healer to Row, 'if you need anything press the red button on the healing vessel and someone will come to you.'

'What's going on?' asked Row.

'There must have been a battle down on the planet. I will know more when we get down to the docking bay. We have not been informed of any pre-planned battle, so it must be an unexpected encounter,' replied the healer.

'Can I come and help?' asked Row.

'Sorry, lady, you are not well enough for such things. Once you have regained your strength, maybe then but until then get yourself better. After that, if you still want to help, then we will see.'

'I would like to help when I can. I would love to learn how to help and heal people,' Row replied.

The healer smiled and gently helped Rowena get back into the healing vessel because she had started to feel weak after her short walk. Rowena fell back asleep and the healer left her and headed to the docking bay.

Back on Linasfarn, Karl and Salina had completed a search of the local area. They had found nothing except several butchered animals and sea slugs that the Dark warriors had obviously been eating. Salina decided that because of the unexpected Dark warrior they had just encountered returning to their own forces would be the most prudent thing to do in the circumstances until the whole island had been searched and secured. They ran back to beach and informed the new commander of their encounter then boarded one of the assault crafts that was returning to their home port. Salina stayed as a wolf to keep Karl calm, because she knew until he mastered his wolf feelings and controlled them, he would not change back into a person. The longest she had known anyone to change back was her father. She had been told it was only because he wanted to stay a wolf for ever. It had been told by generations past that if after a week you had not changed back to your people form you would stay a wolf for ever. The old Wolf master had managed to scare Kurt back to being a person when he told him he could not become a Wolf warrior if he stayed just as a wolf. He would be shunned from their world and he would have to be sent to Earth to live his life amongst the native wolves there. That did the job and Kurt had transformed back into a boy after the Wolf master had left. Salina did not think they would have that problem with Karl. High above, Tom and Arn flew in the clear cloudless sky. Around them flew Eagle warriors for protection. Tom had said goodbye to his new friends the Zells and he promised them that he and his brother and sister would visit them soon. Zuzza had given Tom a small shell the size of a whistle. She had told him to go to the lake behind his quarters, blow it and the green-haired girl would come to him and take messages to the Zells and likewise they would give her any messages for him. The whistle was securely zipped up in his combat suit; he intended to find a chain and attach it once he had got back to Elemtum.

Karl was now curled up next to Salina inside the assault craft heading back to the seaport. Back on Linasfarn, Kurt was organising the reinforcements he had received into scouting and search and destroy teams to comb every inch of the island. Earlier he had said thank you to Zuzza and the Zells who had returned to the sea on their way home. There had been talk about opening a land corridor to their world, but it was agreed that the planning for that would best be done in the future once things had settled down, if at all.

Kurt set up his command post inside the first assault craft. Extra sensors and monitors were set up around it out to three miles that would give them notice of any attack. That was three miles up and three miles at ground level. He knew their biggest challenge would be to search the caves and the tunnels the Dark had excavated. Luckily, due to the tunnels that had been found in the sand lands two years ago a specialist tunnel unit had been formed from the miners of the northern mountains who had mined the mountains for hundreds of generations. There was nothing they did not know about mining and tunnels and now thanks to the Wolf warriors they were also superb tunnel fighters. Forty of them had been seconded to Kurt for the exploration and search of the tunnels on Linasfarn. That task would not start until the morning to give the northern miners as much rest as possible because tunnel fighting was hard and very strenuous, although the miners would not tell you that because they were tough northerners. The real reason it would not start until the morning was that the northern miners were also big drinkers. They brewed a local beer called grog, and always partook the night before they did anything strenuous. The mining leaders were strong individuals, and they could keep their teams in line if they had had too much grog, which they did quite often.

It was not unusual to see several of the miners with broken noses and black eyes before they started their operations. Because they were good at what they did, a blind eye was turned by the leaders of all the tribes they worked with.

Observation posts were set up all over the island once the surface had been searched toughly. Now all that was left were the tunnels. It was thought that the Dark had tunnelled to Linasfarn and had not landed from the sky nor from underneath or across the water. If they had, they would have been detected. The warriors settled down. Those that could slept or did administration for themselves and their equipment, the rest did their duties and observed or waited in quiet or guarded areas depending on what orders they had been given. In Kurt's command centre, people made plans for the following day's operations. All the wounded and dead had been accounted for; the dead were on the way home to be honoured and cremated together as was the way of the warrior on this world. The wounded that needed serious treatment were now close to the blue moon, the rest were in the infirmary being taken care of. It was a matter of pride that any injured warrior that reached an infirmary or a sail craft to the blue moon would live.

Tom and Arn had landed in the citadel with the Eagle warriors after an incident free flight. Arn left to go home with his fellow eagles and Tom made his way down to see his uncle Tristan and get some food because he was now feeling very thirsty and unbelievably hungry after his adventure. Karl and Salina had docked and were now in the shuttle heading back to the citadel. All was now quiet. Was this the calm before another storm? Nobody would know until the next morning when the northern miners started their missions. Until then a good rest was the order for the remainder of the day. The wounded warriors started to arrive on the blue moon then, professional as ever, the healers dealt with every patient depending on the triage that had been done during and after the battle, with the injured continuing to be cared for during the journey to the moon. Before long sixty warriors had been treated and were all now in intensive healing vessels.

Rowena's healer returned to check on her; she found the princess still fast asleep, so she was left to sleep until the morning.

Karl and Salina had finally arrived in the citadel where Salina changed back into her people form in the privacy of her own room. She then woke the curled-up wolf outside her door and walked with Karl back to his room. She opened the door to the room and Karl jumped onto the bed. After Salina had spoken to Karl about the plan for the next day, which was to try and get Karl to change back to his person form, then back to wolf until he had mastered the transition process, she said good night and left.

The doors between Karl's, Row's and Tom's rooms were still all open. Karl padded through Row's room into Tom's and found Tom fast asleep in his bed. Karl looked at his sleeping brother then jumped up and curled upat the bottom of Tom's bed and fell asleep, dreaming of running and transforming from wolf to boy.

Tom woke to find Karl fully clothed, curled up at the bottom of his bed.

Rowena woke on the blue moon to see her healer looking down at her. 'How are you feeling this morning, lady?' she asked.

'Please don't call me lady. I'm Row. I don't like lady. Please just Row.'

'You had a restless night.'

'Yes, I know. How I know I don't know, if that makes sense? I dreamt I was a wolf running through a wood with Karl and Tom. At one point, I was howling in the moon on top of mountain and then flying with my brothers but we weren't on eagles, we were eagles. All very strange.'

'Have you ever turned into your wolf form, Rowena?' the healer asked her.

'No, never. Why?'

'Last night you transformed several times into a white wolf, then back to your people form. Has one of your brothers gone through the change?'

'Not that I am aware of, but there was something funny with my dreams. When I ran with Karl and Tom, Karl was a wolf and Tom was not. Odd, don't you think?' Row asked.

'It has been known that with siblings when one transforms the other senses it and transforms as well. Your brother Tom is still very young, so he can't turn into a wolf yet.'

'But I saw him as an eagle. He flew with me and Karl. What does that mean?' Row asked.

'I don't know, lady, but maybe your father will. He is now out of intensive care and he is recouping in a normal healing vessel several doors away.'

'My father is here, on the blue moon? Has he been hurt in the battle you told me about yesterday?'

'No, lady.'

Row looked at her sternly,

'Sorry, Row! Your father came here with you. He decided to get himself back to normal for you and your brothers. He has been in an intensive care vessel for the last two days. It has gone well. He is back to his normal self once more. All he needs now is rest. But having known your father for some time now, he will be up and out of here as soon as he can. The first thing he said when he woke up this morning was "How is Rowena?"' That brought a smile to her face, she had never met her father, so she was quite keen to go and see him. The healer convinced her that it would be better if she had some breakfast first, that would give her father time to have his. That would give them strength for the coming day that would most probably be a very busy one, knowing the king.

Row told the healer that she was ready for some food, so the healer took her out into the fresh air and across a courtyard that was in full bloom with flowers and plants that she had never seen before. They arrived at the far side of the courtyard where under what looked like coconut matting was a healer who was barbequing some food from a big golden tray. 'We traditionally have grilled fish for breakfast here on the blue moon. It is very good for you and it sets you up nicely for the day. Try the blue fish with the red eyes; it's very nice and it comes from are biggest lake called the wise man.'

'That's a funny name for a lake. Why is it called that?' asked Row

'As far as I am aware, it's because it will take a wise man to get to the bottom of the lake. We have nothing here that can go that deep,' replied the healer.

'Can I ask you your name? You have been very kind to me over the last few days and I would like to call you by your name.'

'My name is Paccia Septima. I am the sister of Theon Septima and I have an adopted sister called Nerilla who also helped you on the day you were attacked,' the healer told her.

'Well, Paccia, it is nice to meet you and I am most grateful to you and Nerilla for all you have done for me. I now hope we can all be friends.'

'I would like that very much, princess,' Paccia replied.

'If you continue to call me princess or lady, this will be a very short-lived friendship, do you understand!'

'Yes, sorry! I will remember I promise.' Paccia laughed along with Row. After the laughter had stopped, Paccia said that she had never had a Wolf friend before and Row replied that she had never had a blue friend before, which set them both off laughing again. 'We must eat,' said Paccia, 'You need to keep your strength up. Go on, try the blue fish.'

Row was handed a blue fish on a dish with a fork. She pulled the skin back and pulled some flakes of fish away with the folk. She gingerly placed some of the fish in her mouth. For a couple of seconds there was silence, and then the flavour filled her mouth.

'Hum… that's lovely. It tastes like, let me think, let me think,' she said to herself. 'Yes, I've got it. Langoustine, that's like a lobster on Earth. Oh, I'm being daft, aren't I? You haven't been to Earth, have you? Stupid me,' she continued. 'Well, it's really nice, I could quite happily eat this again.'

Just then a loud voice boomed from behind her, 'If I'm not much mistaken, the beauty with the flame red hair is my daughter!'

Row turned and faced a tall distinguished looking man with a beaming smile. Her first thought was, a better-looking George Clooney's brother is my father.

'My, my, what a beauty you have turned into, Rowena De-Callen. The last time I saw you, you were a very small little girl. But look at you now!'

Row was a little unsure what to do next. She had been told about her father and she was expecting to meet him. Finally, she now was, but what should she do?

Her father answered it for her, 'Well, isn't my daughter going to give her father a hug then? You can never be too old for that. What did Tom call me? Oh yes… give your dad a hug?'

As Row looked into his eyes and saw love and genuine happiness, something inside her clicked and she ran to the father she had forgotten. She kissed his cheek and held him tight. 'You look fine. I was told you were having a serious operation?'

'I'm as tough as old boots. It takes more than a traitor to keep me down and it was the thought of you being hurt and your brothers full of life that convinced me I had better get myself sorted out. Well, now I am thanks to these marvellous people.' He lifted his arm and gave a sweeping gesture that included all the healers around them. 'We will never be separated again.' He looked down into his daughter's eyes and realised how much she looked like his first love Labatina. It made him smile but it also sent a chill down his spine which he was not expecting. 'You look like the spitting image of your mother.' After a few seconds he continued, 'I had better get some of this fine fish down me to keep me going. We have lots to talk about and some brave warriors to see. I have been informed there was a battle on Linasfarn where your brothers showed exemplary courage. For one as small as Thomas it shows they are made of better stuff. I am very proud of them both. Anyway, we will have enough time to talk of such things later. Let's eat. Try the blue fish, they are fantastic.'

'I've tried some, and yes, they are really fantastic. I will have some more with you, Dad. Do you know Paccia?' she asked her father.

'Of course, I know Paccia. Her father is a dear friend to me, I have known her since she was tiny. When I heard she was the healer looking after you, I knew you could be in no better hands. Yes, I know Paccia.' He went over to her and gave her a tender kiss on the cheek, 'And how is my second daughter?' he asked.

'I am very well, even better for seeing you back to your normal self. In fact, you look better than new,' Paccia replied.

'Do you know, Rowena, that Paccia has been banging on at me to get myself sorted out after the attack, but it took you and your brothers to finally get it done. I should have listened to her. Now, not only do I have to deal with her but you and your brothers too. I have no chance.'

They all laughed then the king went between Row and Paccia. He put his arms round their shoulders and walked with them to the food counter where they had more blue fish and chatted away like long-lost friends.

Tom gently shook his brother. Gently because he remembered what his uncle Kurt had said to him when he had been annoying Phina the wolf when he was a lot younger than he was now. 'Let sleeping wolves lie, Thomas. One day one will wake up and bite your hand off.' Now that his brother had just become a wolf very recently, he shook him gently remembering Kurt's words. Karl's eye's opened and he looked at Tom, unsure of where he was. He slowly sat up and looked around.

'Tom!'

Tom patted Karl on the head and said, 'Little wolfy not sure where he is, does wolfy want a bone?'

Karl brushed his brother's hand away and asked what day it was.

'The day after yesterday, you know when you became a wolf, remember?'

'Oh, that's okay then. I thought I had a dream. So, I was a wolf then?'

'Yes, you were, Karl, and you went for a run with Salina, while me and Arn flew back here. Remember?'

'I remember and I think I killed a Dark lancer as well, if I remember rightly.'

'No way. What? As a wolf you mean?'

'Yes.'

'Cool,' Tom replied. They went and got washed before making their way to the dining hall where they met Tristan and Salina.

'Ah you're a boy again. Good, that saves me a job,' said Salina. 'Do you think you can change at will now?' she asked.

Karl shrugged his shoulders. 'I don't know, I haven't tried.'

'Go on then, try now,' Tristan urged him. 'Just think "I'm a wolf". That's all I do.'

In front of them Karl turned into his wolf form and then back into his people form.

'Well done, Karl, you're a quick learner. Get yourself some breakfast because I have some news about your sister and father,' Salina told him. The two boys raced off and got themselves some food and returned to Salina and Tristan.

'Your father and sister have fully recovered. They have met each other, after that they went together to see the injured warriors. They will be back just after lunch. Isn't that good news?' said Salina.

'That is good news. Just think, for the first time in our lives we will actually be with all our family,' said Karl.

'Oh, one more thing. In fact, two more things. I have been asked to tell you something from your father,' Salina told them.

'You mean Dad,' Tom butted in.

'Okay, Tom, just for you. Your dad has said during the night Row turned into a wolf and back again and neither of you are to go anywhere until your dad and sister get back. He doesn't want you getting into any more trouble, especially you, Tom. He said you were too young.'

'I'm not too young, I saved Karl's arse yesterday,' Tom answered.

'You did not save my arse,' replied Karl, then the two of them got into a slanging match until Tristan stopped them.

'You both did very well yesterday. Your dad wants you both to know he is very proud of you. Now, less of the arguing. If you have enough energy to argue, I have just the thing to use that energy up,' said Tristan.

'We haven't got a lot of energy, we are still quite tired from yesterday,' replied Karl. Tom backed him up and agreed with him wholeheartedly.

'It's just an Earth thing.' Both boys knew they had already been earmarked for something horribly sweaty, they were sure of that. As they finished their breakfast, the Wolf master walked in with Phina who had returned that morning with him from Warriors' Rest. They walked over to the table.

The Wolf master bowed his head sharply and said, 'Princes.' The boys smiled and nodded back to him.

'Wolf master, I hope you are well,' Tom replied.

Phina looked on with a smile.

'I am very well, young sirs, but a little worried about both of you. I watched some of the surveillance footage of the battle yesterday. The tricks you two got up to, how you both survived, I will never know. You must have charmed lives. But just in case that charm wears off, I have obtained the help of two of the best rayzor fighters on the planet. They are going to teach you a few lifesaving moves this morning,' he said with a big smile.

'Great,' replied Tom, 'that sounds cool.'

Karl had other thoughts apart from cool. Ahh, he thought to himself, he knew if the Wolf master was involved it probably wouldn't be pleasant.

'I will have to leave you in their capable hands, because I have got to go to Linasfarn to relieve Lord Kurt, but I will be getting a full report from the warriors on how you get on. If I feel you are not up to the required standard, I will be seeing you both again very shortly, so do well. Now I must leave.' He bowed his head once more then Tristan got up and walked out with him. After the Wolf master had gone Phina gave both boys and Salina a hug and kiss then she joining them for breakfast.

'He didn't even tell us who our instructors would be. Do you know something? That bloke scares me,' said Karl.

Phina told the boys that when she was little, he scared her as well but when you got to know him, he's a real softy.

'Yeh, and I believe that,' replied Karl.

They all finished their breakfast then Phina asked them all about what they had got up to the previous day. She was aware of the battle but not the part Tom, Karl and Salina had played in it. She was amazed when she learnt what they had done. Because she had not seen any of the surveillance footage, she was unaware of Tom and Salina's adventures in the caves or with the Zells. The talk gradually turned to the rayzor training the boys would be doing that morning. Salina and Phina old the boys it would only be basic stuff the warriors would teach them, especially as Tom was so young. But it would be enough to get them familiar with the rayzor, enough to save their lives. Karl asked if they knew the warriors that would be teaching them.? They said they knew the warriors very well and that it was about time the boys went and got changed into their combat suits because the warriors would be meeting them outside in the courtyard in fifteen minutes. They would then be taken to the armoury where they would get a balanced rayzor that would be theirs until they grew bigger, then they would need resizing and re-balancing. Excited but very nervous, the boys left Phina and Salina and returned to their rooms to change. Back in their rooms the boys shouted to each other about what they thought they might be doing and who the warriors that would be teaching them were. Fully dressed in their combat suits, boots and gloves, carrying their helmets, they made their way out into the courtyard where they found Salina and Phina standing talking.

'You won't need your helmets,' Phina shouted to them as they came down the steps. She told them to leave them on the steps, they would be safe there. The royal guard would watch them.

'But what if the warriors say we need them?' asked Karl.

'We are the warriors that will be teaching you and I say you do not need them. Happy?' Salina said.

'But the Wolf master told us the warriors were the best rayzor fighters on the planet,' said Karl.

Tom kicked him. 'Dumb ass,' he said. 'They are the best. Why do you think they were sent to guard us on Earth?'

'That's right, Tom' replied Phina, 'but unbeknown to us then we could not transform back into our people form on Earth.'

'Ah, it all makes sense now,' said Karl.

'Good, I'm glad about that,' said Phina.

'You sound a little serious,' Tom interjected.

'That's because I am serious, Tom. This training can be the difference between life and death, along with the fact that you both seem to find it easy to get yourselves into trouble here, the sooner you learn the better. So, to that end, the first thing we need to do is warm our muscles up before we start. Off you go, boys, three times round the courtyard. Last one back does twenty hand pushes. Go on, off you go. Salina and I have already warmed up. Go!'

The boys looked at each other then started to run. After the first lap it was neck and neck then slowly Karl pulled away from his brother until on the last lap Karl was a full half lap ahead of his him. Karl ran triumphantly back to Phina and Salina.

'Well done, Karl, now get down and give me thirty hand pushes,' said Phina.

'But you said the winner didn't have to do any,' argued Karl.

'No, Karl, I said the last one back did twenty. I said nothing about how many the first one would get. For arguing, it's now forty,' said Phina.

When Tom reached them, Salina showed the boys what a hand push was. She got down on her belly, spread her legs wide, placing her hands under her chest, then she lifted her body up by extending her arms. It was a bit like a press up but with your legs wide and your arms under your body.

'You're joking,' said Karl.

'If there is one thing you will learn today, it will be to keep your mouth shut and do what you are told. Now, down and that's now fifty,' said Phina. There was now no sign of a smile on her face whatsoever. Karl was just about to say something back, but thought better of it. He got into position and did one hand push, then another; he continued until he had done twenty, then collapsed in a heap on top of his hands. After doing five, Tom had done exactly the same. Sweating and panting the boys lay on the ground. 'Okay, well done. For a first time, that wasn't bad, either of you. Now the serious stuff, the rayzor! We will walk to the armoury and get you sized up for your weapon. Keep swinging your arms as we walk, taking deep breaths.'

The four of them walked out of the courtyard back towards the sail craft port but just before the entrance to the port they turned left and headed back towards the strategic centre. Finally, they ended nearly back where they had started from.

'Why have we walked all that way to end up... Sorry, I'm doing it again, aren't I?' said Karl, as he realised he could be heading for another beasting if he continued.

'Well done, Karl, at least you are realising when and where you should speak, and yes there was a reason we did that. It was to bring your heart rate back down,' Phina told the sweaty prince walking by her side.

Karl smiled and nodded his head in confirmation that he knew what Phina was saying. They came to a big steel door to the left of the steps the royal guard were on; both boys thought it was funny that they had never noticed the door before. Phina told them that was because they had no need to notice it before. They had not entered it before as they had not entered or noticed the other hundreds of doors in the citadel. Going through the door they encountered another door which took them into a room with a sensor in it that scanned each of them just as the scanners in the strategic centre had done. Once past the sensors, a door opened that led into a corridor full of tall steel mesh cages. Behind each were different types of weapon, swords, rayzors, rifles, pistols and many more weapons that neither of the boys had ever seen before, not even in the countless Si-fi movies they had watched on Earth. Each cage had its own door and held around six hundred weapons. The cages stretched on either side for one hundred metres at the end of which was a stable type door that had the top half open. From inside, the boys could hear hammering and drilling sounds echoing out along the cage-filled corridor. They had reached the door when Karl noticed it had a light red glow about it; he was just about to touch it when Phina pulled his hand away.

'If you don't want to lose it, don't touch it,' she told him. Then she went on to say, 'A word of warning, boys. Don't ever touch anything on this planet if you don't know what it is, because it may just kill you,' Phina had her serious face on which the boys had never seen that before but they understood the messaged it told them.

'You know, on Earth there would be a health and safety sign telling you not to touch the light or it could cause death,' Karl told a confused Phina and Salina.

'Why on earth would you want to tell your enemies not to touch the light? It defeats the object of having the light, does it not?'

'You're right, Phina, but we did not know, I nearly touched it!' Karl told her.

'You do have a valid point there, Karl, but anyone that should be here would know. Admittedly I did tell you a little late but that's because I forgot you are new to this place, so I apologise.'

Just then the door's red glow turned green and a large man appeared in the top half of it.

'Boys, meet Clomp senior; he is the royal armourer. Master armourer these are Princes Karl and Thomas. The latter likes to be called Tom.'

'Nice to meet you, masters. My son has told me all about you and your strange ways. Come inside and I will sort you out with a rayzor each.' The boys entered the workshop followed by Phina and Salina. Clomp senior took them over to a machine which he explained measured their body's height and muscle mass and picked the right rayzor for them. Before being asked Tom stepped forward in front of the machine.

'Okay, Master Tom, stand inside the machine and grip the two handles and put your feet on the marks on the floor.' Tom did as he was instructed. 'Close your eyes, master, and the machine will scan you all over. If it doesn't like you, it will turn you into a Dark monster, then kill you!' Clomp senior started to laugh. Tom opened his eyes. Clomp senior looked at him, 'That's just my little joke.' He smiled. Tom closed his eyes once again and the machine hummed gently for about a minute then it was all over. 'Okay, master, you can come out now. Second master, you can get in.'

Tom got out and Karl got in. On the way in he looked at Clomp and said, 'I know I'll be turned into a Dark monster and killed.'

'No,' replied Clomp. 'Because you are bigger it just kills you,' he said, smiling. 'Not really, just another joke.'

'I would never have guessed!' replied Karl sarcastically, before he entered the machine.

'I can see you have still got a lot to learn, young prince,' interjected Phina. Karl looked at her; he knew just what she meant.

'I'm sorry, master armourer, that was uncalled for and I apologise,' said Karl.

'No need, Master Karl, I can be a little silly sometimes.'

'Don't you apologise, Master Clomp, I was out of order with that reply and I apologise to you,' replied Karl.

'No, master...' Clomp started.

'Clomp, accept the apology or we will be here all day,' Salina butted in.

'Sorry, lady,' Clomp said.

'Not a problem, Clomp, but could you please measure him!' she replied with a smile.

Clomp senior did as instructed. Before long, both boys had been measured and were now eagerly waiting for the master armourer to return from his storeroom with their rayzors. Clomp senior returned with the two very shiny weapons; both were in proportion to the boys' bodies because of the measurements his machine had taken. He placed one on a work bench then called

Tom to him. 'Now, Master Thomas, here is your first rayzor. You will note that it is the length of your arm, from shoulder to your largest fingertip.' Then he reversed it and gave it handle first to Tom. 'Be very careful, master, it is very sharp and, until you start warrior training, if you need it sharpening just bring it back to me and I will sharpen it for you. You should be able to balance the blade on the tips of your fingers. If you can't, then it's not balanced properly. Go on, have a go.'

Tom held the blade in his left hand by the hilt and balanced it on the four fingers of his right hand. He let go with his left, it balanced perfectly. A smile of pride filled Clomp senior's face as he watched Tom easily balance the blade. He flipped the blade up and caught it with his right hand; everyone looked at him amazed.

'When did you learn to do that?' Karl asked him.

'I don't know, I just did it. It felt, well, easy, I mean.'

'You could be a natural, Tom. Every now and then you come across natural rayzor fighters. Salina, Kurt and I were all naturals, it obviously runs in our blood line,' Phina told him as Clomp senior handed a leather sheath over along with a studded belt.

'I made these especially for you, master. Don't worry, Master Karl, I have made the same for you, but they are different so you won't mix them up. See, Master Thomas, yours have eagles on the belt and wolves on the scabbard and yours, Master Karl, are the other way round.' Clomp senior then handed Karl his rayzor who also balanced it perfectly, flicked it up and caught it as his brother had done.

'I see we have a couple of naturals here. Now, we will see how good you are at using them, won't we?' Salina told them with a cunning smile on her face. The boys returned rather nervous smiles then they turned to the master armourer.

'Thank you, Master armourer. The belts and scabbards are most excellent, and the rayzors are superb. You obviously have a lot of skill, I am honoured to receive these from you, thank you,' Karl told him.

'Yeh, me too. Thank you very much, they are all very cool,' added Tom.

Clomp senior blushed; he was overwhelmed by the boys' kind words. Nobody had ever thanked him as nicely as that before. He could feel that the words were all genuine; he liked these two new princes.

They left the armoury and went back up to the courtyard where they would be practising with the rayzors. Once back in courtyard, Phina told Karl to remove his rayzor from its sheath, which he did as Clomp had done, then he handed it over to her. 'First things first, I will explain the parts of the fighting knife to you;

essentially a rayzor is a traditional and very affective fighting knife. It's actually a cross between a knife and a small sword. Tt is said that the great wolf himself Atta had a favoured sword which he liked so much that when he broke it he decided to make himself a better one, one that he could use to defend himself from some of the larger predators that were around in his day and that was how the rayzor was born. It hasn't really changed since that day.' Phina then went on to explain the parts of the rayzor and the way they could be used in a fight. 'I will name and show you the parts,' she told them then she pointed to each part. 'At the end of the blade you have the pointy bit called the tip,' Phina pointed to that part and Karl and Tom laughed.

'We know that bit,' said Karl, 'it's pretty obvious.'

Phina continued with a smile. 'From the tip along the top of the blade this curved bit is called the top swage edge, taper ground, the blade narrows slightly with a gentle curve and this is called the spine depression. Are you both still with me?' she asked them.

'Yes' replied Karl.

'Yes, but do we have to remember the names of these bits?' Tom answered, looking a little worried.

Phina answered. 'For you, Tom, this is an introduction to the names only, but if you remember them it will help you later.' Then she looked at Karl. 'You must remember them. As a trainee warrior, you will be expected to know this.' Karl nodded his head and Tom laughed.

Phina continued. 'Next, this flat bit past the spine depression is called the flat heavy spine area for impact and it adds weight to the rayzor. I will explain what all the parts are for in a moment. Then at the back of the heavy spine we have a cross guard sticking up, a sharp curve called the thumb rise which leads to the full tang handle and on the end, we have a small pommel with a spike. Is everyone still happy with what I have said so far?'

'Completely,' replied Karl. Tom just nodded his head and smiled.

'We will see later, won't we?' smiled Salina, then Phina continued.

'Underneath the spike and pommel, we have the handle with finger grooves then a small spike and a dark insertion that is a line cutter followed by the chisel edge. From the chisel edge we have long staggered serrations and lastly a cured blade that goes back to the tip and is called 30 Circumferential centre metres of hollow ground main blade. I used centimetres because I knew you would both understand that measurement.' Then Phina pulled two pieces of paper from her map pocket. 'There you go. I am good to you both. I have drawn it for you to make it easier for you to remember.' Then she handed them a drawing each. 'I am not an artist so take it or leave it.'

'Now, we will practice the hold or grip.' Phina returned the rayzor to Karl. 'Take hold of your rayzor by the handle, put your fingers instinctively around finger grooves. We call this the hold. This is a stable hold position which you easily fight from, using the pommel and spike with a backhand strike or jab. By putting your thumb on the thumb rise, you quickly turn it into a stabbing weapon utilising the tip of the blade or even the cross guard. The top edge and hollow ground main blade are both razor sharp and are used when slashing or hacking in either direction. The chisel edge is good for punching your attacker and the two small spikes either side are quite damaging when used this way. You can also punch with the spine depression or the flat heavy spine, both very destructive especially in the face with the weight of a blow behind it. The staggered serrations cause a jagged wound and can also be used as a saw. Finally, the line cutter cuts line, rope wire and can come in very handy. Questions, anyone?'

Neither Karl nor Tom had a question and were ready to have a go.

'Right then. Karl, you come with me over here and, Tom, you go with Salina. We will demonstrate a move, then you follow, then practice. The first thing we will teach you is the hold and the different stances you should adopt for different situations you may encounter. Then we will get a little more advanced. We won't get too deep on the first day. This is basically an introduction to the weapon. We will do this for a couple of hours until the movements become instinctive.'

The boys went to their allocated areas which was only a few feet from each other but far enough away that they would not hit each other when they started to swing their rayzors around. They started their drills and very quickly got into the swing of things. Soon they were whirling around, slashing, cutting and stabbing at thin air. From a distance, it looked like the boys and their instructors were engaged with each other in an elaborate knife dance. This went on for an hour then they stopped, sweating, panting and ready for a drink. A quick energy boost, then the dance went on. Three hours later, looking very masterful in their actions, tired and worn out, they all stopped.

'That was quite hard work,' gasped Karl.

'It certainly is,' replied Salina. 'Just imagine doing that for a couple of hours in a hand-to-hand battle. It is very draining. That's why those sorts of battles don't last too long, it is literally exhausting. The only bonus to the rayzor is that it is quite light compared to the Dark's handheld weapons.'

'Well done, both of you. That was four hours continuous hard work and you both lasted, especially you, Tom. I am impressed with both of you. Now, go and get yourselves cleaned up and we will meet you in half an hour in the dining hall.'

Phina and Salina were very impressed with their two young protégés.

'What about the rayzors? Do we take them back to the armoury?' asked Tom.

'They are yours now. Yours to look after. Remember, Tom, Clomp senior will sharpen yours whenever you want, but you, Karl, I will teach you how to sharpen yours after we have had some food. Now off you go. Well done, both of you.' The boys walked back to their rooms, and after washing they both flaked onto their beds. Tom fell asleep straight away but Karl could not. He lay thinking about the massive change in his life that had happened. A few days ago he was a normal boy with a normal brother. Well, nearly normal, he thought and they lived in sleepy Rendelsham Forest. He wasn't sure if he was happy now or not. It had all happened very quickly; he hadn't had time to think about it.

Rowena and her father had visited the wounded warriors to thank them, as well as everyone who could be thanked for all the help they had given the wounded. They were now on their way back to Elemtum, heading for Great Porum where her brothers were. There was a steady hum inside the sail craft as it glided away from the blue moon. She was starting to get to know her father again and she liked him, which was a good thing. She had also made a new friend, her healer, who sat beside her also returning to the citadel. As she sat there, she was troubled. Was she happy? She had been taken away from a happy life and thrust in to this world. It felt to her now that she had been dragged away from that happy life and was now thrown into a life she did not understand, one that she did not particularly like. Or was it because she had been separated from her family; Tristan the only father she had ever known, and her new brothers that she had grown to love in the short few days they had all been together? It had all sounded so promising, their new world, but, in fact, she found it strange and very dangerous. With these worries on her mind, she fell asleep dreaming of Earth as the craft carried her to her new home.

Karl had fallen asleep; he dreamt he was back on Earth with Tom and Rowena. where they were all very happy. That's all he could remember when he was awoken by the sound of shouts and gun fire. He sat up in his bed and began to fully wake up. On the communication wall Salina appeared, 'Karl! Tom! Both of you stay together. Phina is coming for you don't go out until you are with her. The citadel has been breached by the Dark and we don't know how. Keep your rayzors at hand.' Then her image was gone.

Karl thought he could hear a noise outside his window. As he went by the window wall, the view, normally tranquil with the sight of the trees and the lake, had totally changed. There were masses of Dark warriors coming out of the lake with some sort of breathing apparatus on their faces which they were discarding as they hit dry land. There were also a couple of seaborne vehicles, tracked submarines to be precise, that had been destroyed by some of the royal guard that were fighting valiantly. Off to Karl's left, the royal guard were fighting a withdrawal action, slowly moving out of Karl's sight. Karl had not noticed a demon dog staring at him. Watching all the mayhem in front of him had drawn his attention away from what was right in front of him. His first inkling of the fact that he was in very real danger was the window exploding as the demon dog smashed through it. Instinctively Karl put his hands up to shield his face. Luckily for him, the demon dog was a little disorientated after crashing through. Startled, Karl found himself pinned to the floor by the foul-smelling dog. Even more luckily, his hands were now under the beast's throat, pushing its flaying, snarling, snapping head away from his face. The dog's saliva was falling on to his face making the experience even more disgusting. Karl knew it would only be a matter of seconds before the dog would get free and would rip his throat out. He wrapped his legs around the hindquarters of the dog and held tight. He could feel sweat dripping from his face, at least he hoped it was sweat. 'Tom!' he screamed from beneath the beast. There was no reply. He could feel the demon dog's claws ripping into his chest through the thin clothes he had put on after getting himself clean earlier. It was easy to ignore the pain with the dog's teeth gnashing away inches from his nose. His arms were starting to fail him. He knew he would soon be at the dog's mercy which, in this case, would be none. He started to fear for his brother, who was not as strong as him. He would most surely be next on the demon dog's list to kill. 'Tom!' he shouted once more. Nothing. Then it crossed his mind that maybe Tom was already dead. That made him mad and gave him a sudden burst of energy and strength. With all his might, he heaved with his right arm, released his right leg from around the dog, only to swing it back round when he heaved. The effect was to twist his body with such force that he pushed the demon dog over, ending up pinning the dog upside down under him. He felt a rage against the beast for what it and its kind were doing to him his family and his people. Before he realised it, he had changed into his wolf form. Now the wolf was on top of the dog and he could see fear in the dog's eyes as he savaged its exposed throat. At that second, he was conscious of two things; one was the door to his room opening, the second was a Dark warrior climbing through the window. It was easier to go forward, so he decided whoever it was coming through the door would get some wolf for good measure, then he hesitated.

Tom came into his mind, then he heard, 'Karl, it's Phina. I am coming in.'

Karl decided to keep hold of the demon dog until it had stopped fighting. He hoped Phina would be quicker than the Dark warrior behind him at the window.

Phina was in fast. Past him and the now dead demon dog, she thrust her rayzor into the demon warrior's chest, deep into his heart. The warrior crumpled, half in half out of the broken window, momentarily blocking the Dark warrior behind him. Karl now got off the dead demon dog and transformed back into his people form then ran through Row's room towards Tom's shouting to Phina, 'I've not heard anything from him, I've been shouting but no reply.'

Phina thrust her rayzor past the dead warrior in the window taking out the Dark warrior behind, then she turned and followed Karl after picking his rayzor up from beside his bed. On the way she closed and locked the doors giving them a few extra seconds.

Fearing the worst, Karl entered Tom's room and came to a complete stop when he saw the sight on Tom's bed. Phina raced in behind him. She also came to a complete stop. In front of them on top of the bed was Tom's body. They both started to laugh. Tom was fast asleep.

Phina handed a stunned Karl his rayzor. 'You might need this today. Don't leave it lying about and don't stab your brother with it,' she said. Behind them came screams and the sound of a door being hammered down. 'Quickly, wake Tom, we need to move fast,' said Phina.

Karl touched the wake button at the side of the bed.

'What? What's going on? Why did you do that?' Tom said as he got up from his undignified waking, then he saw Phina. 'What's up?'

'We are being attacked,' Phina said calmly so as not to alarm Tom in his sleepy state. 'We need to get down to the operations room fast. That's where you will be safest until we find out what is going on. Follow me and stay close. Karl, stay at the rear. Use your rayzor if you have to. Now, let's go.'

Then there was a bang on Tom's door. A royal guard called to them to hurry. They were holding the Dark warriors back, but they would have to start a fighting a withdrawal very soon. Phina carefully opened the door to be met by Steven the senior guard commander of the day. 'Quickly, Phina we must go now,' he said.

Phina rushed out into the hall. Tom followed, instinctively picking up his rayzor as he left the room. Karl came last. He turned to look back. He could see the guards hacking and slashing with their rayzors. Because of the confined space they were fighting in, they had the upper hand, but it would not last for long.

They ran down the narrow corridor into the dining room that was empty until one of the side doors burst opened and in strode a Dark Mangoul warrior. It reminded Tom of one of those American wrestlers he had seen on satellite TV back on Earth. It had big hairy feet, and around its waist was a rough studded leather belt, hanging from it were shrunken heads attached to it by chains. If it wasn't for that, the Mangoul would have been completely naked apart from the fact that it had numerous pierced rings all over its body that were all connected by chains. These too were adorned with more skulls of other types of animals, all hanging grotesquely around it's body. Its body was also covered in scars. The head was mainly a set of sharp teeth with the top covered by small spikes. 'I wonder what his stage name is?' Tom joked.

'Mangouls are no joking matter, Tom,' said Phina as she walked in front of the boys. 'Karl, take Tom down to the strategic centre. I will keep this one back.'

'No, Phina, I am not leaving you here with that,' replied Karl as he strode in front of her.

'You will do as you are ordered, Karl, and that's an order. Now go!' she shouted. The Mangoul raised its arms then started to beat its chest, at the same time giving out a piercing shrill scream that froze the blood. 'Now will you go, Karl!'

'Definitely not!' shouted Karl as he ran heading straight for the Mangoul. Phina made a grab for him but missed, then to her surprise Tom ran past her after his brother.

'Ahhhhhh,' Tom shouted as he ran, waving his rayzor above his head.

The Mangoul stopped screaming and started to laugh at the boys running at him.

Phina shouted, 'Come back,' as she started to run after them. Karl ran at the Mangoul who took up a very aggressive stance, widening his legs to make himself more stable. He lifted high the big hammer that he held in two hands, the one that he was going to use to squash the two little annoying people that were running at him. Karl saw the Mangoul's move. He quickened his pace, then seeing his chance he slid between the Mangoul's legs. Not knowing where the annoying child had gone, the Mangoul twisted its upper body to see where the little one was. Karl was now on his knees, facing the Mangoul. He sliced the back of its knees with his rayzor. The Mangoul crumpled to his knees but made no sound, blood gushing from the disabling blows.

As he ran, Tom was not sure what he was going to do but it no longer mattered as suddenly he was lifted into the air backwards and then thrown. He skidded on the floor until he ended up where he had started his run from.

'Phina!' he shouted, annoyed as he got back up.

'Sorry, Tom, you're too small,' she shouted back at him. The Mangoul tried to batter the child behind him with his hammer but Karl easily avoided the blows with one well-timed swipe of his rayzor. The Mangoul's right arm that held the hammer smashed to the floor. This time it did scream out. The killing blow was administered by Phina as she thrust her rayzor into its head… for a second all went quiet, then the Mangoul's eyes glazed over, and it went crashing down on to its back where Karl, still behind it, raised his weapon ready to take off the head. 'There's no need for that, Karl, its dead,' commented Phina.

Adrenalin now pumping through his veins, Karl lowered his rayzor then looked down at the dead body at his feet. Phina walked over to the open door, closing and locking it; she could see no one in the hall beyond. She turned around seeing both Karl and Tom staring at the dead Mangoul. She walked up to Karl, putting her hand on his shoulder. 'Are you okay?' she asked.

'I don't really know,' he replied. 'All that seems to have happened since we got here is people getting hurt or killed. Is that all that happens on this bloody planet? Is it always like this?' he asked.

'Both of you listen to me,' said Phina. 'I don't know what's going on at the moment… But I can assure you both it's not always been like this. Hopefully one day soon it will return to how it was. Now, let's get down to the strategic centre before we have any more surprises.' As she finished talking, the door that led towards the strategic centre burst open. Both Karl and Phina lifted their rayzors instinctively, Tom was a little slower.

In front of them stood Tristan with four of the royal guard. 'Thank Atta for that! We have been worried. All the accommodation areas have now been overrun as well as all around the central lake. Get below quickly. We are regrouping. We need you safely below,' he said to the boys.

Karl was just about to respond but Phina was quicker. 'Below, Karl, now! We will talk later.'

Karl knew he would get an ear bending for what he had done but he didn't give a damn. Why should he, he thought, if it wasn't for him that thing would have killed them all. He was starting to get a bit fed up with this world and the people in it.

They made their way down into the strategic centre behind all the security where they would be safe. The air was full of communications; situation reports were coming from different areas around the citadel all saying they were fighting substantial numbers of Dark warriors. Thankfully casualties had so far been light, but even that was a worry because a large number of their forces were still mopping up on Linasfarn.

Back on Linasfarn, Kurt and a sizeable force were preparing to return as fast as they could to the capital, leaving only a skeleton task force with some miners to finish on Linasfarn. It could be a fatal decision to split his force but all the analysis pointed to the fact that the Dark had been defeated on Linasfarn and they were very unlikely to return in any great number soon.

Tristan briefed everyone on the situation as he knew it at that point. 'As you can see, the princes are safe here with us thanks to Phina and the royal guards.' He continued, 'The initial onslaught…'

There was a loud metallic smash as Karl threw his rayzor on the floor; the whole strategic centre went quiet apart from the constant battle chatter coming over the loudspeakers. Everyone looked in Karl's direction. 'I don't need people to die for me, I can look after me and I'm fed up of being treated like a child on this damn planet!' he shouted, then turned and started to walk off towards the map room. Phina went to grab his arm but Karl shrugged off her grip. 'Leave me alone, Phina, I want to be by myself,' he told her, then walked off into the empty map room where he sat down, putting his head in his hands. It was all getting a bit too much for him.

'He will be all right,' Phina told the room, 'it's all been a bit of a shock for him, I think.'

Tom walked off without saying a word, joining his brother in the map room.

When the door shut Tristan continued. 'You may want to give that back to the young prince,' said Tristan, as Phina picked up the discarded rayzor. She nodded her head. Tristan continued, 'Right, the situation is this: Dark warriors came out of the central lake about an hour ago. Thanks to the alert royal guard they were seen almost immediately, and the alarm was raised. They have come ashore in vast numbers. From where, we don't know, but after the debriefing from Kurt yesterday, we know that our world and another world apart from Earth are connected, the one Salina and Prince Tom literally stumbled across. By the way, has anyone heard from Salina… Phina?'

'Nothing since we did the rayzor training with the princes,' she replied.

'After this update, Phina, can you try and track her down?' Phina nodded and he continued. 'The Dark forces have split into three separate groups; one went directly for the accommodation where the princes were, another headed directly to the infirmary and a third tried to open the battlement gates. Up-to-date reports say each part of their attack force was around two hundred Dark warriors and several demon dogs within each group. The third group is now, as I speak, trapped between the inner and second battlement walls and they are slowly being picked off. The local command tells me they will have destroyed that force within an hour. So, that means they are now nearly all wiped out. The second group have been defeated on the second level of the infirmary and I am sorry to say we have lost several healers as well as around thirty warriors who were patients on those two levels. Lastly, we have about a remaining eighty or so Dark warriors roaming above us who are being tracked down. In all, it is estimated we have lost about sixty warriors to this action not including the wounded in the infirmary and the healers, so not a good day. We are regrouping, consolidating, then we will carry out a final clearance of these Dark bastards. After that, we will have to try and find out how they got here and why our sensors did not work. It's almost the same as Linasfarn. They must have found some way of turning the sensors off. The only vulnerable area that we did not know about was the bottom of the lake but once all is safe here, we will get a water team down there to see what's going on. It has only been a red moon since we last checked the bottom of the lake. All was normal then. Finally, the king and his daughter are still airborne, coming back from the blue moon. He has been fully informed. He is as mad as hell that he has missed another fight. He will stay airborne until we can confirm the citadel is once more secure. Okay, think that's it from me. Unless you have any questions please carry on.' Tristan walked over to Phina. 'What's up with Karl?' he asked.

'I don't know,' she replied. 'I hope it's just the wolf transformation. He was not trained to deal with the changes that his body would go through. I think it would be best to leave him with his brother for the time being. I think they have both seen a lot of death and violence in the last few days. It could well be that. Remember, they were brought here from a comparatively safe world. Now that you look at it, they were thrust headfirst into this madness. They are still two young boys with no training whatsoever, but they have both performed magnificently. You should have seen them just before you came in, Tristan. They had no fear when it came to dealing with that Mangoul. I had to pull little Tom back.'

'That could be the problem, Phina. They have no fear and they should have!'

'You know, Tristan, they could both be suffering from battle shock.'

Tristan agreed with her making a note to get Row and a healer to talk to them both, then he told her that Kurt would also be a wise warrior for the job. The boys liked him, and he knew them. Phina agreed and then set about the task of finding her sister.

Up in the sail craft, Rowena knew something was wrong by the way her father and the other warriors on board were reacting. She asked Paccia if she knew what was going on. Paccia told her what she had heard, that there had been an attack on the citadel, and a slaughter in the infirmary. Row was shocked. Where have I come to? she thought. It's like being in the Middle Ages.

Seeing Row was getting upset, Paccia hugged her, assuring her it would all be all right, that this world was not as bad as it seemed at that moment. Paccia's comforting embrace calmed Row down. Now feeling relaxed, Row asked about her brothers but Paccia had heard nothing about them, so Row walked over to her father. 'What's going on, Dad? Is everything okay down there?'

Her father held her by her shoulders and told her things were bad down at the citadel. Greater Porum had been attacked through the great lake in the centre, and that many people had died. He told her he was very worried because the last thing he had heard was that the Dark had sent a sizeable group of Dark warriors into the accommodation where the princes had been. Tristan was personally leading a team to find them. The only good news he had was that Tristan believed Phina was with them. Then a shout came from the front of the craft, 'Lord, Tristan is on the communicator. He has an update for you.' The king left Row with a smile. She returned to Paccia who held her hand which immediately calmed Row down once more.

'My brothers and Phina are missing. They were at the point where one of the main attacks struck,' she told Paccia.

'Can you feel your brothers are in danger?' she asked Row.

'I can sense they are both very troubled, that's all. So, they must be alive,' she replied.

'Then that is a good thing, Row,' said Paccia.

Her father returned with a smile on his face. 'Very good news. Your brothers are both fine. They are safe in the strategic centre. By all accounts, they both accredited themselves magnificently.' He then hugged both Row and Paccia. The relief could be seen on his face but he quickly returned to the strong leader that he was.

'See, you knew they were both okay, didn't you?' Paccia told Row as she tenderly squeezed her hand.

King Frederick went forward to the pilot. 'Take us down,' he told him.

'But, lord, it's not safe. Greater Porum has not been secured yet. Lord Tristan has…'

The king interjected, 'With all respect, is Lord Tristan the king?

'No, sire.

'That's right, I am! The day the Dark stop me doing anything will be the day I die. If today is that day then so be it. Now get me down there,' he told the pilot as he gently patted him on the back. 'Good lad.' He walked back into the hanger deck where everyone cheered. 'Oh, I didn't realise you could all hear that,' he said.

'We couldn't help hearing, Dad,' laughed Row, 'but I'm glad we are going down, I hate being stuck up here.'

'Don't worry, Rowena, I will protect you when we land,' said her father.

From the hanger deck forty warriors roared, 'And we will, princess.' Rowena went bright red and sat back down next to Paccia.

'Oh my god, I'm so embarrassed,' she told her friend. She stayed there until they landed.

'What do you mean the king's landing? We haven't secured the citadel yet,' shouted Tristan in the strategic centre.

'You know the king,' replied the communications officer.

'I do that; get some warriors to secure the dock.' The operator informed him that they had three eagle squadrons approaching; one would escort the king, the other two would secure the landing site.

'Good. Finally, things are starting to happen.' Tom looked at his brother sitting with his head in his hands. He had never seen Karl looking so down before, not even the time at the Christmas fayre when he had won a prize and it turned out to be an abacus. 'Are you okay?' he asked, not expecting to get a proper answer just a grunt.

To his surprise, Karl lifted his head and said, 'How are you feeling, Tom? Do you like it here?'

'Of course, I like it here, don't you?'

'To tell you the truth, Tom, I don't really know anymore. I don't know if it's something to do with turning into a wolf, or all the people that have died, maybe the fact that Row was hurt, you've been hurt, and these Dark people are trying to kill us every minute. Or the fact that I miss Earth and our old life. I don't really know, that's the problem, Tom.'

Tom thought for a moment. 'You see, I look at things differently. I love the fact that we have all these people around us now, we have a dad who's a king, we have a sister, we are princes, we have a cool cousin, and that's just to start with. Oh! And we have big eagles that we can fly. You can turn into wolf. How cool is that? We have guns, swords, we have done more exciting things since we have been here than we ever did on Earth. Now we have proper family and...!'

'Okay, Tom, I get the message. But why don't I feel like that? ... I should!'

'I think it's got something to do with you turning into a wolf, if you ask me,' said Tom.

'I think you might be right, Tom,' replied Karl, now with a hint of a smile on his face.

'Come on, let's go and see if there's anything we can do to help.' Karl nodded in agreement. They got up and walked back into the main operations room. As they entered, they saw Phina just about to leave.

'Phina, where are you going? Do you need a hand?' shouted Karl. She replied that they had better speak to Tristan first. They had just got a message from their father. Tristan told them that their father and sister were landing. 'The king has given me instructions not to let either of you out of my sight until he gets back, especially Tom because he feels you are too young to be getting yourself into the trouble you have been in.'

'I could do with a hand looking for Salina. Karl would be quite handy, especially as he can now transform into a wolf… he could be my sniffer dog,' she said with a smile that brought a smile to Karl and Tom's faces. 'That's better.'

'Tom, you stay with Uncle Tristan. I'm off to help Phina,' said Karl then he walked off towards her.

'That's not fair.' replied Tom

Tristan shouted after them, 'If the king asks, I haven't seen you, understand?'

'Thanks, Uncle Tristan,' Karl shouted back then he and Phina left. Tom folded his arms and looked utterly miserable.

Chapter 13
The Clean Up and Discovery

'Don't worry, Tom, you can help me. I've got to do an aerial search using a sky lark; it's a bit like a drone on Earth but we fly it from over there.' He pointed at a door that had 'sky lark' written on it; he and Tom walked over to and went inside.

'Wow, it's like a computer game!'

Inside the room was a three-hundred-and-sixty-degree screen. In the middle was a chair and a console. Tristan explained that the sky lark was a small remote-controlled bird, so small that no one would take any notice of it but it had the power to see and zoom in and look at something a thousand per cent clearer from thousand metres than a person's eye. It could also hear through an invisible laser at up to three thousand metres. 'It's not a real bird but even looking at it close up it looks like one. It's very simple to fly. That sliding switch is its speed throttle; forward fast, back slow, dead centre and it will stop and glide unless you press the hover button. You see that raised pad to the right of the speed throttle? If you look at it from above, it has four arrows on it; that is left, right, up and down. Very simple to use. Everything else is controlled by a little computer.' He then explained to Tom that the little lark was on the roof and that all he had to do was hover it then go forward and he would be away. He would be looking through its eyes. If it got too close to anything a warning buzzer would sound and the direction pad would vibrate only in the direction of that object. 'Have a go, Tom,' said Tristan, so Tom sat in the seat, adjusted it to suit him, then nothing happened.

'How do you turn it on?' he asked.

'Ah yes, good point, Tom,' Tristan replied. 'You see the green button? Press that and all the screens will come alive and the lark will activate. Press the blue button, which is the hover button, with that button on then when you throttle forward it will hover higher and get lower when you throttle back. Once the hover button is turned off it will fly, but remember to push the throttle forward first, before switching the hover off.' Tom pushed the green button and the screens came to life all around him, then he pressed the blue button and slowly increased the throttle. The picture on the screens gave the impression that he was rising. A big grin filled Tom's face.

Outside, Phina and Karl spoke to one of the searching warriors heading to update Tristan on the situation. They had cornered some Dark lancers and Mangouls around the armoury area but they would not surrender so they were going to be terminated very shortly. The lake had been surrounded but nothing had come out of the water for an hour now. The warrior headed down to Tristan while Karl and Phina headed out into the courtyard. They could not recognise the courtyard they had been in earlier. Mess and destruction lay all around them. Some armed warriors were collecting the bodies of their dead friends and fellow warriors; all with as much dignity and care as possible. Once all of their comrades had been taken care of, then the Dark dead would be taken away and burnt in a massive pyre. The Dark had been known to come back to life, but not when they had been burnt. They stood and surveyed the scene in front of them with much sadness.

Karl turned to Phina. 'Where do we start looking?' he asked. She replied the last place she knew she was going was to the armoury so that's where they would start their search. It was strange that Salina had not made contact with anyone. It was not like her. They made their way across the courtyard dodging dead Dark warriors, then went round to the back of the great hall to the entrance to the armoury. The entrance was surrounded by dead Dark warriors, Mangouls, lancers, condemned men as well as several demon dogs, all looking like they had been slain by a sword of some kind, because each dead warrior or dog had big open wounds as though a mad man had attacked them all. In front of the bodies were two Wolf warriors and four Eagle warriors.

'Have you done this?' Phina asked them. Each shook their head and pointed towards the armoury door that was still shut tight. In front of the door was another pile of Dark warriors.

'So, who did this? Do you know?' asked Phina.

'A great noble warrior, who was actually never a warrior but he fought like a wild thing,' said one of the Eagle warriors. He then went on to explain that there were still some Dark warriors about that had been playing dead then leaping up as someone went past. They had not checked all the bodies yet, so it was still unsafe. Phina told him she had her rayzor and a very sharp boot knife so she was not worried.

'But the prince, Phina,' the warrior said.

'Don't worry about the prince, he is more than capable of defending himself,' replied Phina, then she and Karl made their way through the bodies. After Phina's comments to the warrior, Karl was suddenly very confident, happy and he felt ten feet tall until one of the Dark grabbed Phina's leg as she went past. Karl had seen the hand grab her and even before Phina turned to look down Karl was on the

223

Mangoul and had cut its throat with a knife from his boot.

'I can see you are becoming a real warrior and you have never been trained. Impressive, Karl, you must be a natural.' she told him.

'You knew he was still alive! I could hear his heart beating, so I am sure you could as well?'

'Yes, I could. I just wanted to know if you could and what you would do about it. You did exactly what I thought you would.' They made their way towards the armoury door where they came across the brave warrior who had slain all of the dead Dark around them.

'Oh my god, Phina, it's the master armourer, Clomp senior.'

Shocked, Karl knelt down and checked for a pulse; there was none. 'You know, I only met him once. He was such a nice person, just like his son, he must have fought like a man possessed, a great warrior. Look at the circle of dead Dark warriors around him, but why did he come out of the armoury? He was safe in there; they would never have got in.'

'Something made him come out,' said Phina, then she got on her communicator and spoke to Tristan. She asked him to open the armoury door by overriding the master armourer's code. When he asked why she told him the sad news about Clomp senior. They both new Little Clomp would be devastated as would be his wife, normally the happiest jolliest person on any planet. It would be hard times for them both and they would need all the support they could get.

'It is a truly sad day,' was Tristan's final comment, before he overrode the armoury security code.

The door slid open and in front of them on the floor, propped up against the wall was an unconscious Salina. Phina rushed to her side and checked her pulse. It was weak but she knew she was alive because she could faintly hear her heartbeat. Salina had a broken lance embedded in her ribs and several slash and stab wounds to her arms and legs. She also had a swollen cheek, a cut lip and a bleeding nose; she had taken a good beating. On her communicator she called for a healer fast, but worryingly she was told that all the healers were attending to the large number of casualties. No one would be able to get to her for at least thirty minutes.

Just then she heard the king's voice. 'Phina, I have just docked. I have Paccia and Rowena with me. We are making our way directly to you. We will be there in three minutes.'

Salina regained consciousness. 'He saved me. They surprised me. Clomp saved me! He dragged me in here and went back out. Is he okay?' she whispered.

'Don't talk, save your energy. Help will be here very shortly,' replied Phina.

'Is he okay?' Salina insisted.

'You are talking about Clomp, aren't you?' asked Phina.

'Yes,' she replied.

'Sorry, he's dead, but to his honour he fought well and took about twenty of them with him. He died well!' Phina told her sister. Salina smiled as a tear welled up in her eyes.

Behind them they heard Paccia telling them to stand back and give her room. Paccia rushed past them and started to take Salina's vital signs. She was followed by Karl's dad who looked like he wanted to rip someone's head off. He gave Phina a warm hug and a smile, then the same for Karl but this time he added a warrior's handshake then slapping his back.

'I have been hearing good things about you, son,' he said. Then he told Phina, 'I will leave Salina in your and Paccia's capable hands. I am going to take Karl with me and do a check of the citadel. I have some warriors from the sail craft who are craving revenge, so we will check the areas then I will be down in the strategic centre if you need me, Phina. Paccia, we are evacuating all the wounded back to the blue moon. The sail craft is being readied as I speak. Take Salina with you when you have stabilised her. Come on, Karl, you can tell me what you have been up to since I have been away.'

Rowena had appeared behind them with a healing vessel. She placed it next to Salina. 'How is she?' Row asked Paccia.

'We need to get her into the healing vessel; I will tell you what I'm doing because I know you are interested in healing.' Row went to work helping Paccia, and a concerned Phina helped where possible. She was reassured that Salina would get the best treatment possible and as long as she survived being put in the healing vessel, she would survive and would be back with them all before they knew it.

At that point Karl and his dad left. Outside, Clomp's body had been moved away from the Dark dead and was now covered a sheet.

Above them soaring through the sky, keeping an over watch, was a flight of Eagle warriors plus two eagles. One of the eagles broke away from the flight and dived directly at Karl and the king of wolves.

'Dad, its Alerio! He's my eagle. I've not seen him for a few days,' shouted Karl.

'He will be missing you, son. Remember you connected with him and he will be part of you one day. Go and fly with him, I will get one of the Eagle warriors to fly with you.' Above them the second eagle also began to dive but it was heading for the courtyard. Karl left his father and ran to one of the open spaces nearby where Alerio had landed. As he ran towards his eagle, he could see in Alerio's eyes that he was overjoyed to see him. The eagle was stepping from one foot to the other almost in a welcome dance. Karl reached him and was thrown up on to the eagle's back by Alerio's beak and head. Karl lay on the eagle's back with his arms partially around its neck.

'I've missed you,' he told Alerio.

'And I you... I smell you have changed. There is a strong smell of wolf on you.'

'Is that a problem?' Karl asked.

'No, not at all,' replied Alerio. 'If anything, it will make us a lot stronger when it comes for us to become one. Now let's fly and you can tell me what you have been doing since we last met.' They were just about to lift off when they heard a scream of joy from their right and when they looked up into the sky, flying directly above them were Tom and Arn. Arn had been calling to him as he circled above and Tom had heard it through the sky lark. Tom had not even flown the bird, but he made his apologies to Tristan who understood because he knew the bond between a person and their eagle. Tom had rushed out of the strategic centre into the courtyard with royal guards chasing after him. Arn had been waiting there for him. Karl and Alerio joined the now gliding Arn and Tom. Both boys had beaming smiles. In Karl's head, he now realised he was in the right world, this is where he belonged, the change in his life was for the better, he was sure of that. All his worries for the time being floated away behind him as the eagles soared through the sky followed by their Eagle warrior escorts who were having trouble keeping up.

As they swooped and dived in the sky, they heard Row say, 'I am leaving again, I'm going back to the blue moon with Salina. Paccia is teaching me some of her healing skills so I won't see you for a couple of days. I'm sorry, I wanted to spend some time with you all but I promised Phina I would look after Salina until she is well again... then we will all be together. Fly with us for a while. We are behind you, take care, I love you both.' The boys and their eagles turned and flew alongside the sail craft that had now lifted and was steadily getting higher and higher. They could see Row waving at them through one of the port holes. They stayed with it for several minutes until they had to peel away because the air was starting to get harder to breath and fly in. Above them was black and stars and below them was blue and white. They had never been so high in all their lives but they weren't scared, they felt safe with their eagles. 'Bye, take care, you two,' Row called to them as they fell out of from her sight.

As they descended back into blue and white, they met up with the four eagle escorts that they had left behind as they climbed with Row and the sail craft. 'Your father has asked us to fly with you to Linasfarn and meet up with Kurt and some of the miners. Prince Thomas, he wants you to come along because he wants you to speak to your friends the Zells. He wants us to speak to the green-haired girl and her tribe to find out if they know anything about the Dark and the lake attack,' ne of the Eagle warriors thought to them both. He added, 'Lady Phina will be with lord Kurt who will both act as your bodyguards while you are there.'

'Another adventure,' Karl shouted across to Tom who smiled at the thought of seeing the green-haired girl and the Zells. They flew low along the ground then out to sea just as Tom and Salina had done days before. An hour later they were flying over Linasfarn. The beach that the warriors and Karl had landed on days earlier was now empty but over by the old artefacts where Tom and Salina had fallen through there was now accommodation and some command boxes along with a surrounding wall that was well guarded by heavily armoured towers. 'That must be where Kurt and Phina are,' communicated Karl to Tom and the warriors. They landed inside the tower compound. Karl and Tom said goodbye to Arn and Alerio who were going to go sea fishing for their dinner, so they went to find Kurt and Phina.

It turned out that they were early; Phina and Kurt had not yet arrived. So, they made their way to the dining box to wait. Inside they met one of the leaders of the mining team who told them all about the tunnel hunting and exploration they had been doing. They had found all the tunnels that Tom and Salina had been through, plus some of Salina's handiwork with the Dark warriors. They had made contact with the Zell who wanted to see if a tunnel from their world to the surface of Linasfarn could be created so there could be mutual cooperation between their world and Ardania, along with the mutual security it would bring. This was one of the reasons why Kurt was not there; he had gone back and spoken to the king about the logistics that would be required for that to happen. A tunnel that had also been found that had been sealed from within but the miners had broken into it which then led them to another underground cavern with a second lake. Around this lake the Dark had built docks and moorings for some sort of vessel or submarine, one of which was still moored there. It was the same as the crafts that had come out of the great lake at the centre of Great Porum.

It was the lead miner's best guess that this was where the attack on the citadel of Great Porum had been assembled and embarked from. So, there was a great possibility that this lake may lead to the great lake in the centre of the citadel. He also added that one of the miners had seen a mythical sea beauty with green hair, as one of the miners put it. The woman was watching them when they had first entered the cavern and made their way to the lakes edge.

'Was it a young girl or a woman?' Tom asked.

'That was no girl,' replied the miner with a wry smile.

'How does he know?' asked Tom.

'Trust me,' said one of the Eagle warriors, 'if any person on this planet can tell if it was a girl or not it would be a miner!' Everyone around them laughed and the miners slapped each other's backs.

'It's true,' said one, laughing. 'We know a female when we see one.' Once the laughter had died down, in the corner hidden by the miners was Zuzza Zell. She had gone to see the miners when they entered the young Zells' cavern and she had come to talk to Kurt about the proposed tunnel. She quickly made her way over to Karl and Tom past the staring miners.

'Zuzza,' Tom said as she approached, 'it's nice to see you again. This is my brother, Karl, and these are our friends. They are Eagle warriors.'

Karl was immediately attracted to Zuzza.

'You look a lot better than when I last saw you, Karl,' she said to him.

'I must apologise I did not have the honour of meeting you last time, I was a little bit engaged at the time,' said Karl in fluent Zell.

'That was very impressive, Karl. When did you learn to speak Zell?'

'I don't know Zell,' he replied.

'Then, that is even more impressive. You must have the tongue,' she said to him. Karl looked at her, puzzled. He'd had someone say this to him before but he could not remember who.

'What does that mean?' he asked her. She told him about the ancient stories amongst her people that told of the coming of the four: one tongued, one gentle, one brave and one Dark. Together they would bring all worlds together or they would rip all worlds apart. 'Yes, but what does that mean, Zuzza? I don't understand,' replied Karl.

One of the Eagle warriors told Karl that on their world it meant you had the ability to talk or communicate with all conscious living things.

'But I can't do that,' Karl replied.

Then Tom butted in, 'You spoke to the lizsnake creature, didn't you? You had never met one of them before.'

'Yes, I suppose you might have something, but I can't believe it myself.'

'It's okay,' said Zuzza, 'it's only an old story. No one really believes it.'

'We believe all those sorts of stories,' said the miners' leader. 'There's always some truth in them, you mark my words. They're not just made up, it's more serious than that,' he said and was immediately backed up by his nodding and grunting miners.

One of the Eagle warriors shouted over the din, 'There are more things to worry about than whether old stories are true or have some hidden meaning. Our biggest worry right now is finding the damn Dark and how they infiltrate our land without our knowledge. That's more important right now.' Everyone stopped talking and nodded their heads.

'Come on, lads, we've been in the light too long, we will start to shrivel soon. Let's get back down there, we will see your lordships later... lady.' The leader nodded to Karl and Tom then Zuzza. They all left, muttering about bad backs and miners' coughs, their leader telling them to give up the whining or they would get no grog that night. That did the job and the whingeing stopped. All that could be heard was their big boots marching off and the odd clang of a spade or a shovel.

'That's better,' said Zuzza. 'Those people make me nervous and they're a little bit smelly.'

'I agree with you there, lady,' said one of the warriors. They all sat down and talked about this and that. The Eagle warriors were amazed at how the two boys had handled what were known as two of the most difficult and stubborn eagles in the kingdom. Karl and Tom could not believe what they were hearing about their eagles, they had it all wrong. Karl was more interested in talking to Zuzza. He was fascinated about where she came from and how they had gone from bats to people. They talked for a while then Kurt and Phina arrived with the Wolf master, much to Karl and Tom's dismay. They greeted everyone and told the princes about Salina's condition and the good news that they had just received that she was now stable.

The miners' leader reappeared in the doorway. 'My lord,' he said, 'me lads have dug their hearts out and sweated out two people's bodies worth of blood and them there tunnels is all safe to travel down without any bits falling on your royal heads, thanks to your Wolf lot,' He took a breath, 'who have secured everything. You can now all go down and start your parlaying with the big black bird creatures and the lot that live in the sea. Pardon my description, me lady, but I'm not quite sure what you lot is called yet,' he said tipping his helmet towards Zuzza.

'Don't worry about me,' said Zuzza. 'What we are called for your information, Master miner, are Zells,' Zuzza said with a smile.

'That's what I like about you miners, straight to the point. Well done and tell your lads there will be barrel of their favourite grog waiting for them from me when they finish tonight,' said Kurt.

The miners' leader tipped his helmet to Kurt. 'Your lordship is most kind and my lads will drink to you and yours' health tonight.' Then he told them to follow him and he led them to the second cavern and lake. They're journey down was a lot more comfortable and less bruising than Tom's and Salina's previous journey. There were now proper stairs with railings down lighted and encased tunnels. At every junction were signs telling which junction it was and the distance to the next junction or area of interest, i.e.: cavern, lake, etc. They also had the name of a miner at the bottom. No one was really sure whether that was because he had made the sign or dug the hole, not even their leader knew. At one point they all got into some wheeled carts on rails pulled by a pulley system, by cart, it was actually a bucket with benches in it. This part of the tunnel started off with lights but ten feet in the light these abruptly stopped. Phina and Tom had noticed the sign above them just before the light disappeared and it read: Keep your bony arms and legs inside the confines and don't nod your head or it may come off. The signs were one after the other, broken down into two words per sign with the last being slightly bigger with three words just to labour the point. All were just above head height and the last finished as the light disappeared. This made Tom laugh and it made Phina a little dizzy as she found herself straining her neck back to read them as they whizzed past. In the darkness of the tunnel, it was just like being on a roller coaster back on Earth, Tom thought as his senses went wild being buffeted left and right, up and down. Cold damp air rushed past them. Tom and Karl both loved it. Everyone else was ready to murder the miners' leader if they ever stopped and got out alive. Eventually, the carts all came safely to a halt and a smiling miners' leader jumped out of the front cart.

'Sorry, everyone, I forgot to mention the black tunnel. We thought you light-dwelling people would be too scared to get in the carts if you could see what was coming.' He laughed nervously as he saw a very unhappy Kurt and Wolf master vacate their cart. He added, 'You will all be glad to know the rest of the way is on foot.'

'That was great,' said Tom. 'Did you like it, Karl?' he asked.

Karl replied, 'It was all right, nothing exciting.' Normally Karl loved fairground rides and theme parks but now he was conscious that Zuzza was watching him. In front of Karl and Tom, Kurt now briefed all those assembled about the plan. They would make their way to the second lake; some of the young Zells were already there as well as some of their people not in their winged form. Between them, they would guard the lake because that would be where their small party would camp for the night. All in all, there were Kurt, Karl, Tom, Phina, the Wolf master and four Wolf warriors. Zuzza would go back to her young Zells for the night because they were still hyped up after the battle they had taken part in against the Dark with their new friends, the Wolf and Eagle people. In the morning, Zuzza and some of her people would return with breathing apparatus like those Tom and Salina had used on the backs of the young Zells when they had flown through the sea to Linasfarn.

They made their way to the lake through another renovated and lighted tunnel where the miners' leader left them to return to his men to tell them about the grog from the Wolf lord, then help them drink it. In the cavern, more sleeping pods had been erected along with a dining pod, like the one they had met the miners in earlier.

Kurt told Phina that he had been updated about her sister Salina; she was doing well but she had lost her little finger on her right hand. It could not be saved, but it could be regrown once she had recovered from the wounds that had been inflicted on her. He pulled out a note tablet and turned it on. 'Salina is a strong person. She received eight puncture wounds to her chest and back as well as deep lacerations to her arms, legs and head. There was also part of a lance embedded in her chest,' Kurt told them all. 'The healers tell me she will make a full recovery.'

'Do we have any idea what all these attacks are about yet?' asked Phina.

'No is the simple answer,' replied Kurt. 'Relatively speaking, the Dark is a modern phenomenon, which all started after the disappearance and reappearance of Queen Labatina, but since the boys and Row have returned it has all kicked off again. We know it is public knowledge that Labatina wants her son and daughter back, but what made the change in her and how were the Dark creatures and warriors created? Still no one knows what her end game is.' He continued, 'Let's get these accommodation pods comfortable then we can get our heads down. It's been a long day and I'm sure it will be another one tomorrow.'

Kurt and the Wolf master took one pod, while Karl, Tom and Phina shared another one. Phina shared with them so she could keep an eye on them; to stop them getting up to anything and so she could protect them. The remaining warriors were sharing another bigger one because two of them would patrol for four hours then two of the other warriors would take over and so on until the morning.

Zuzza said good night then she walked to the lake's edge watched by Karl where she turned into her winged Zell form. In front of him, her clothes dissolved to be replaced by a fine layer of black velvet. His initial thought was that she was turning into a cat woman but then she lifted her arms horizontally and, between her arms and the side of her body, black leathery wings appeared. She shook them and stretched like a ballerina before a performance. She gracefully leapt into the air and beat her wings, slowly disappearing into the dark recesses of the cavern ceiling.

'Wow,' Karl said quietly to himself, 'I still don't know how old she is.' He turned round to find Phina watching him.

'Did you know she is a princess, Karl?' she asked him, 'and she's around the same age as Rowena.'

'Thanks, Phina.' He smiled at her then made it known that he was ready for bed by yawning and stretching his arms. He did not want to get into a conversation about Zuzza with Phina. She was no fool and told him that she was also tired and would be heading to her bed also. As Karl walked past her, he leant over and gave her a kiss on the cheek.

'What's that for?' she inquired.

'It's just thanks… thanks for everything… that's all. Thanks.' Then he walked off towards his accommodation pod. Phina smiled then followed him. Inside the pod, Tom was already asleep on his air bed, tucked up in his temperature-controlled sleeping bag. Karl and Phina got into their bags and shuffled around until they were comfortable then Karl asked Phina if she actually knew what was going on the next day? As far as she knew, they were going to dive in the lake with Zuzza and some of her people because she had told them that there was a passage that led to Selessi which was the world of the Taniwha, the people who the little green-haired female belonged to. There was also one that led to Zuzza's inner lake which led to her world. Really, the only unknown thing was what they would find at Selessi. Slowly the stress and strains of the day faded away, sleep overtook them; they were both well away and fast asleep in minutes.

Tom had a dream that night. The green-haired girl, Tanibeth, visited and warned him that going to her world would mean they would run into a trap. Bad people were waiting there for them. Her people were a peaceful race and they wished no one harm. The reason they had moved from the world above was because they found that world to be too violent and now beings from that world had invaded theirs which had now been attacked without provocation. The last of her people who had not been killed were now being kept in the gathering hall in the centre of their city. She also told him that there must be at least one hundred of the bad people in her city and, as far as she knew, now the leader that headed the initial attack was not with them, they were running amok; unchecked and out of control. At that moment the surviving Taniwha were still alive. Lastly, she told him that she would guide them, she would meet them under the lake, then he woke up to the sound of Phina and Karl talking. 'Is it morning already?' he asked.

'Yes, Tom, time to get up. You had a good sleep,' said Phina.

'But I can see it's still dark,' he said sleepily.

'Dumb ass, we're in a cave,' Karl replied.

'Oh yeh, I forgot,' replied Tom.

'Leave him alone, Karl… He's just woken up.' Phina had only just woken up too and she was not in the mood for an argument.

'Eh! What's that?' exclaimed Tom as he gingerly picked up a piece of red seaweed from the side of his sleeping bag. He lifted it in the air. 'Karl, are you trying to be funny?'

'Nothing to do with me,' Karl replied. 'I literally got out of my sack two minutes ago.'

'Phina?' said Tom.

'No, not me, Tom,' she replied.

'Do you know, that's weird. I had a dream about that little green-haired girl last night and now I find this.' He waggled the seaweed and got splashed with water, salty water at that. 'It hasn't been out of the water long,' he said, 'it's dripping wet.'

'Let me see,' said Phina. 'That is strange. Why is it here? Someone must have dived into the lake to get it and very recently. I will show Zuzza when she appears and ask her if she recognises where it could be from. It is a little worrying that someone has got in here. Luckily, they must be friendly. I will speak to Kurt and the guard.' Phina left them as Karl and Tom sorted their beds out then made their way to the dining pod where they met a very rough looking miners' leader, who tried to convince them that he was fine even though his eyes were glazed and he stank like a brewery. Apparently after he had left them, he had proceeded to teach his men to drink like a true miner which ended up lasting all through the night until an hour ago when he took the cart ride back down to them. He was now sat drinking copious amounts of the red juice and muttering, 'Never drink, boys, it's wicked. Never drink, mark my words, never drink.'

Phina advised him that his best course of action would be to go and jump in the lake and have a swim. He thought that was a good idea and left the dining pod. As Kurt walked in all that could be heard was the splash of water and then, 'By the beards of the ancient miners, this is cold!'

'That's what I like to see, a bit of gumption in the morning. Who is that?' he asked.

'That's the miners' leader.' Tom informed him.

'Well, I never. Those miners always amaze me and I was only saying I expected him to turn up this morning worse for wear. I told the Wolf master that he would most likely challenge his men to a drinking competition and here he is fit as a warrior and swimming laps of the lake. Good, like to see it. Don't get me wrong, I would not have minded if he never turned up at all today. He is not needed. He and his miners have worked their hearts out over the last few days.'

Tom, Karl and Phina all looked at each other, close to bursting out with laughter but they all managed to hold it in. The Wolf master walked in and suddenly none of them felt like laughing any more. He nodded good morning then went and sat by himself in the corner of the dining pod. Phina and the boys sat at a table with some of the Wolf warriors. Kurt went and sat with the Wolf master, who looked like he would rather be on his own but you don't tell someone like Kurt to go away. One of the Wolf warriors walked out and a short time later came back in with a stack of boxes the size of an egg box. He placed one in front of all that were seated, getting a thank you from everyone except the Wolf master who just grunted. Kurt asked the Wolf master if everything was okay and he replied that he was just in the mood to be by himself, so Kurt excused himself and went and sat with the rest of them leaving the Wolf master to be by himself. The boys shrugged off the Wolf master's behaviour and looked at the boxes in front of them. Tom picked his up, turned it around then upside down. Finally, he shook it, then sniffed it. He was baffled about what it was. 'It's obviously got some sort of breakfast inside,' said Karl as he watched his brother.

Kurt explained to them that it was heated rations that were used when away from civilisation. 'They all pack flat. You push gently on the longest sides and they pop into boxes,' he told them. 'Then you see the little red tab on the side?' Both boys had. 'Pull that, wait a minute and there you have it, a warm breakfast.' The boys pulled their red tabs and waited. Karl could feel his box warming up, so could Tom except Tom's was starting to smoke.

'Is that normal?' he asked.

Hurriedly Phina replied, 'No it's not, Tom, throw it on to the floor in the corner fast!' Tom did just that. He hurled it into the corner where everyone watched it expand and balloon out, steam started to puff out of the corners of the box then it collapsed in on itself and that was that. The steam from the box now made the pod smell like breakfast, which encouraged everyone else to pull their tabs. But Tom was now without breakfast which was soon rectified when the Wolf warrior brought him another one. Gingerly he pulled the red tab. This time all seemed to go as planned and he ended up with a warm breakfast.

'Scrambled eggs and bacon,' Karl said.

'No, not quite. Remember what we had the other day?' said Phina. 'Well, it's the same stuff only in a box that has been hydrated and warmed.'

'It still tastes nice,' Tom said as he put forkfuls of it into his mouth as though he had not been fed since he arrived on the planet. The boys found that what seemed like a small amount at the start was actually very filling and more than enough for breakfast. Everyone was chatting about this and that, waiting for Zuzza to return. Tom told Kurt about his dream, the wet red seaweed and the warning from the girl with the green hair. Karl was sitting facing the Wolf master and he noticed that for someone who wanted to be alone, he was taking great interest in what Tom was saying.

'Yes, very interesting. Phina told us briefly a little earlier. I want to know now if anyone has been playing a joke on the young prince and placed that seaweed on his bed?' Everyone stayed quiet. 'Good, as I suspected there is probably a bit more to this. You should never underestimate dreams. We will see if Zuzza knows the weed and where it's from.'

'My lord,' said the Wolf master, 'you're not really going to take this boy's dream for anything other than a young adolescent prank? We cannot be side-tracked by this; we have a serious task ahead of us.'

Angrily, Kurt answered the Wolf master, 'I will remind you that the boy you referred to is a prince of these lands and he is my king's son I have already asked if anyone had been playing around and I am satisfied that something has gone on, and it is worth investigating further. I don't know what's wrong with you this morning but you had better snap out of it before we start this operation.'

'I apologise, Kurt, and to you, young prince. I am obviously wrong. Now, if you will excuse me, I am going to make sure that all my equipment is ready for the forthcoming operation. I advise you all to do the same.' It looked like the words were going to choke the Wolf master and he left without another word.

'I have never seen Detor act like that before. Something must really be bothering him,' said Kurt. 'I will go and see what's got his back up.'

'No,' advised Phina. 'He's a leader. He needs to deal with whatever it is and get on with the job at hand. Let him stew. We all need a bit of time alone every now and then. We have all known him for a lifetime, he's a good warrior and I have no concerns and I'm sure you don't either, Father.'

Kurt nodded in agreement and suggested that the Wolf master could be due for some rest or home leave. The only problem was his family had been wiped out by the Dark. He had lived on the other side of the sand lands and when the troubles first started, he had been away with King Frederick when his village had been attacked. Some of the villagers had been killed, the remainder disappeared. This included his whole family, no trace of them had ever been found. Seconds later, Detor Eosin reappeared.

'My old friend, I must apologise, I don't know why I feeling so strange. I think it might be that I have been thinking about my family quite a lot lately and seeing the young princes with you brings back memories of my two boys who would be the princes' ages now. I must be a little jealous or maybe just sad. Please forgive me, all of you.'

'There is nothing to forgive, old friend. As long as you are all right, that's all that matters to any of us.' Kurt walked up to Detor and embraced him warmly, warrior to warrior, then returned to the table and made room for Detor to join them. Now, with smiles all round, they continued to talk about nothing in particular, just anything that came into their minds at that time. Karl wondered when Zuzza would return. Tom talked about all the cool stuff he had seen, or wanted. Phina talked about when the two boys were young and about her sister. Detor talked about his boys and family and the next half hour generally continued like that until Zuzza appeared and Karl's face lit up.

She bowed gracefully and addressed them all with the Zells' normal morning greeting, 'Suck in life.'

'What does that mean?' asked Phina. Zuzza explained that it basically meant live well and to the best of your ability. Phina liked that and made a note to use it. Zuzza was in her black flying form and Karl was transfixed by her beauty and definite female shape.

'Hello, Karl,' Zuzza said but Karl did not even hear her.

Phina nudged him and communicated, 'You're staring, Karl.' That brought Karl back to reality.

'Sorry,' he said.

'Sorry for what, Karl?' Zuzza replied. Karl's brain could be seen working and thinking fast about what to say and do next when Phina jumped to his aid.

'What Karl was going to say was sorry for interrupting you, but do you know what and where this is from?' She held up Tom's red seaweed. Zuzza smiled and told them all that it was red sea blossom and she asked if they had a container of some kind that she could use to put the salty lake water in. They did not, so she took them all out the box to the lake side. They gathered around her and she placed the red weed in the water. Seconds later, it transformed into a beautiful blossoming flower of bright red and pink. When she pulled it out of the clear water and held it up, it slowly returned to a red weed. They were all amazed at its transformation then Zuzza told them that the Taniwha females used them for everyday decoration when they swam the seas, normally placin it in their hair or linking it together to make belts or chains.

'See, I'm not making it up, the girl did bring it to me.' Tom went on and explained to Zuzza about his dream.

Just then the king appeared. 'What's all this about a dream?' he inquired.

Tom ran to him. 'What are you doing here, Dad?' he asked.

After a hug, he told them that he did not want them to have all the fun and that Tristan was starting to bore him with logistic matters so it was time to leave Great Porum and have some fun. Tom Told him about the dream and the red seaweed.

Zuzza told them all, 'It could have two meanings; one, the bearer loves you if it is a red blossom, or two, she needs your help. I would guess as you don't know her it probably means she needs your help and the dream was her way of telling you. Taniwha females are telepathic but they have to be close and I would say she was next to you,' Zuzza told Tom and the others. That all now made sense to all and they decided, except Detor, that was that. They would look for the green-haired girl and see if they could help. It may, in fact, help them in the long run, Kurt told them all. Zuzza told them that the girl Tanibeth was a sea maid or sea person who had once lived on Earth until they were driven out. Karl and Tom found this information amazing; she was a mermaid. They didn't stop to think how mermaids got from Earth to Elemtum.

The king asked if everyone was ready, then Zuzza called up to the roof of the cavern. What looked like the roof of the cavern started to move, not just move but fly down to them. Thirty Zells landed around them, only five of which were young Zells and much bigger than the adult Zells who, like Zuzza, were people size. Ten came forward and bowed to her. The plan was for the five strong young Zells to pull the ten of them through the water by means of wrist straps that would trail behind them, two to each young Zell. Zuzza would lead the way with five of her adult Zells the remaining twenty would scout ahead and act as a defence around the main body as they were pulled through the water. Karl went to his father, Kurt and Phina joined them. 'I can see by that look, Karl, that something is on your mind,' said Kurt.

'Tell us what's on your mind; out with it then, Karl,' said his father. Just then Tom joined them.

'Does anyone else wonder about things like, what Zuzza just talked about?' They all looked at Karl puzzled. He continued, 'What I mean is, how are the mermaids getting from Earth to here or wherever it is they are? I mean, there must be more threads from Elemtum to Earth, maybe one from deep in one of Earth's oceans that has never been discovered yet by man or us? And how did the Dark get from where they are to here or to where the Taniwha are? Do you understand what I am saying?'

'Yes, I think I'm getting it,' replied his father. 'You might very well have something there. It's an area we have never really looked at before, but you do have something that may well help us define what has actually been happening.'

'We definitely have to establish how all these new worlds are connected. I believe from what Zuzza said, about travelling from her world to ours via the sea and the Dark breaking into their world from the land, there must be some interconnecting parallel worlds that touch and are not connected by strands. We may have been travelling from planet to planet without realising it, who knows?' said Kurt.

'I think the Zells and the Taniwha can help us find some answers. That's why it's now very important to help the Taniwha,' said Phina. They all agreed and then they got together with the rest of their party. Zuzza went through some of the actions they would take if they came across the Dark or any other occurrences that might face them once they dived. They all agreed on their contact drills and Zuzza passed that on to her Zells. Finally, all assembled were ready to dive. The young Zells lifted effortlessly into the air, then five of the Zells attached a strap to each one of their legs. As this was happening, Karl, Tom and all the warriors present donned their helmets. Phina helped Tom and Karl and showed them the settings they would need to go underwater. She also told them that as soon as the helmet was set to water the combat suit, gloves and boots would all seal and become watertight. The boys noticed when they put their helmets on, they now had the proper warrior's fighting helmet with all the attachments as standard, infra-red, weapon zeroing, night-sight targeting, to mention just a few. Their father came over and put his arms round them both.

'I thought you deserved these. You both seem to have a natural ability, so I am sure you can deal with all the added features. Just remember to stay behind me and Kurt. "Behind", understand?' he emphasised sternly. Both boys nodded but behind the nods were mischievous smiles. Their father patted them on the back and told them to take care. The young Zells landed in the water. The four Wolf warriors attached them to their belts then wrapped some of the loose straps around one wrist. The young Zells then dived beneath the water and the four warriors followed. Next were the king and Kurt followed by Tom and Karl, and finally Detor and Phina took the plunge. Zuzza had left ahead of the first two young Zells with the adult Zells except four who followed Detor and Phina as the rear guard. The initial dive was in darkness. Karl and Tom and the others with helmets on could see in the dark but only the Zells around them and the dark green shapes that indicated the sides of the cavern walls under the water. As they went deeper, they could see a wall of total dark green except far below where there was a large half circle of light green that indicated light. As they got deeper and closer to the light, it was obvious that this was a tunnel that had been drilled through from outside into the bottom of the lake that led to caverns above. There were definite drill marks on the rock wall, blatantly obvious to everyone. This had been drilled by a machine of some sort and it was now clear to everyone that's how the Dark had entered Linasfarn. As they went through, they came into a field of tall slowly swaying seaweed. Karl estimated the weed to be at least ten feet high. The seaweed gave way to a brilliantly clear light green sea. Now the boys could see Zuzza way up ahead but it looked like she and her Zells had stopped. The boys had enjoyed their swim, or rather their glide, through the water behind the young Zells especially in their watertight combat suits and helmets. Tom moved over, touched Karl's arm and pointed up. Above them, swimming side by side in unison, were two terror sharks, seemingly oblivious to the swimmers below them. As the boys continued, they felt a slight buzz and their head up display stopped for a fraction of a second then continued as normal. They reached the others who were all looking down into a dark trench at least a couple of miles wide and which stretched left to right as far as they could see.

'That looks deep,' communicated Karl. 'I don't think our helmets will stand the pressure down there,' said Kurt. Zuzza glided over to them and Karl communicated with her. 'Is that where we have to go?' he asked.

Zuzza replied to Karl's question. 'The city of Selessi is down there. The young Zells can't swim down but the adults can. What about you?' she asked.

Kurt told her that no one there knew if the helmets and suits would be able to stand the extreme pressure down there.

'Once you get down, it's not a problem because the city is encased in a field of some sort of electricity or some sort of electric field that creates a dome around the city. When you enter the dome, the atmosphere is normal, as it is up on Elemtum.'

'The big question is, can we make it down there?' Karl replied. They had all heard what Zuzza had said, no one really knew the answer. Kurt seemed to think the helmets and the suits would be okay but he wasn't sure about the boots and gloves and whether or not they would be the weak point that would make the suit and helmet fail in the extreme pressure of diving deep. They decided the best course of action would be to go back to their start point and contact Tristan in Great Porum. He could find the answer for them. Time was of the essence but dying trying to help was not going to happen and the king would not risk a single life trying it out, he told them,

They had lost too many good people over the last few days and years and he was not going to needlessly waste anyone else's life. 'If there are better options at hand, and in this case there are, we will take them.' They turned round and all headed back through the tunnel back to the lake and eventually back to the cavern lake that they had left thirty minutes before.

Rowena and Paccia had reached the blue moon with Salina whose condition had not changed but had stayed stable. The healing vessel had been doing its job correctly, so all signs were good. The condition of the other fifteen seriously injured warriors was just as good apart from one of the healers who had passed away but none of the other healers on board seemed worried about the loss of one of them. Paccia had been with the healer as she died as had Row. The dying healer knew she was drifting away and she had asked Row to hold her hand as she passed on. Row had done as she had wished. As the healer passed away, a strange feeling came over Row; she became very happy and relaxed. She would swear afterwards that the healer had spoken to her as she had held her hand and told her to use her gift wisely. After the healer's death, the other healers including Paccia smiled at Row every time they saw her. But not one of them would tell her why. They docked on the blue moon and the casualties were efficiently discharged from the craft and taken to the intensive care vessels that would speed their recovery. After that, only time would help them. Time is indeed a great healer, thought Row as Salina was transferred into her second more permanent intensive care vessel.

'There is nothing we can do here now,' said Paccia. 'You can spend the evening with me and my father; our home is a short distance from here. I will get you something comfortable to wear after that we can go for a refreshing swim. Does that sound good to you?' she asked Row, who totally agreed and said it would be nice to get away from death and suffering for a while. They left Salina in the care of one of the other healers and set off on the walk to Paccia's home. The buildings of the blue moon were totally different to Elemtum; it was more like a cross between ancient Rome and the Renaissance. There were no high-rise buildings except the massive infirmary with its extensive grounds next to the sail craft dock; both were new buildings less than ten years old. The rest of the city was no more than three stories high. Each window had shutters and there was lots of green vegetation wherever you looked. Every now and then there was a grand fountain or small pond and small streets lined with trees that looked like willow; every other one was in bloom with all the bright colours of the rainbow but pastel. The small intermingled streets looked cobbled but they were not; it was an illusion. As they walked arm in arm, Paccia told Row that her father had visited Earth many years ago and was impressed by the old architecture. So, the city was changed from being very functional, to being both beautiful and functional, Paccia told Row. The trees had been engineered so that every other tree would be in bloom, week after week. They walked for ten minutes and came to a grand three-storey gothic mansion straight out of a Bram Stoker novel, except it was cream and lilac in colour and surrounded by green lawns. They walked along an ivy-covered walkway up to a big dark brown door that would have been at home in an English country church. Expecting it to open outwards, Row kept her distance and stood back. Instead, the door slid to the left and disappeared into the wall. Row started to laugh. Paccia looked at her, puzzled.

'What was funny?' she asked.

'I'm sorry, Paccia, I just expected it to open out and when it slid sideways! Well, it just took me by surprise and made me laugh.'

'Okay,' said Paccia, still not understanding why Row had laughed. They stepped into a large hall with a massive chandelier hanging from a high ceiling. On each wall were big gold framed pictures of very impressive blue people. In the middle of the hall was a large circular table on top of which was a crystal figure of a beautiful woman clothed in a toga with bare feet. 'That is a likeness of my mother. Also, if you look at it, depending on the light, the crystal turns blue,' Paccia told her.

Row noticed that there were no doors leading from the hall, only a winding staircase. 'Please,' Paccia said, indicating to Row to go up the stairs so she did, followed by Paccia. At the top of the staircase was another large picture. This time it was of two people, one female and one male. The female was again very beautiful and next to her was a light blue male in a white military type uniform. Something about the woman made her stop and stare; the beauty was hauntingly familiar to Row.

'That's my father at the warriors' ball before the Dark appeared. He loves that picture. Do you recognise the female, Row?' she asked.

'I have seen her before but I don't know where. Is she your mother?' Row asked.

'It's your mother, Row, Queen Labatina.'

Row was mesmerised. She had never seen a picture of a true likeness of her mother before, well, not that she could remember.

'She's so beautiful, I couldn't really see it in the crystal figure. Why would she want to become so evil?' asked Row.

'No one knows. If we knew that, maybe we would stop the horror that is going on at the moment.'

Row then asked why her father was with her mother and not her own mother. Paccia told her that healers did not take partners for life, and because Row's mother and her father had grown up together, they were the greatest of friends. It had been the worst day of her father's life when he had found out what Labatina had become, she told Row.

'Come on, Row, we can't stand here looking at old pictures all day. Let me show you to your room,' said Paccia. They passed a door that Row was told was the door that led to the living and dining area, then proceeded up some more stairs on to a balcony that had a beautiful view of a rather big tree lined lake. Row could see people swimming in it under the warm sun that was now high in the sky.

'That look's good,' said Row.

'Once you're settled, we can go down for a swim if you like?'

'That would be great,' replied Row, and then Paccia took her through one of the doors to the left of the balcony.

'The door to the right is to my father's office and his bedroom,' Row was told.

Through the door was a small study; the walls were covered in shelves containing books on herbs and medicine. This was Paccia's study. They carried on through another door into a large bedroom.

'Oh my god, a "bed"!' Row shouted. 'It seems ages since I slept in a proper bed.'

'This is my room,' said Paccia. 'Yours is through the interconnecting door. You will be glad to know there is also a replica of a human bed in there too. My father loves the humans and the way they live, as you will no doubt have gathered by what you have seen around our home'.

'So, your father has been to Earth?' asked Row.

'Oh yes, many times. He's actually there now, collecting samples from the Amazon region.'

'How does he get there?' Row asked but Paccia didn't really know.

'He just goes there whenever he wants,' she said.

'But he's blue. Doesn't he get noticed?' asked Row.

'No,' Paccia replied, 'he takes pigment pills that make him look human. They last a week.' She walked Row through into the spare room where she would be staying. It was very similar to Paccia's; a four-poster bed, bedside table, wardrobe, carpet, mirror, lamps, a small dressing table. It would not have looked out of place in a well-to-do Victorian England home. 'Get those things off and we will go and have a swim. There are some casual clothes in the cabinet, pick what you like. I will be back as soon as soon as I have changed,' said Paccia.

Row opened the door of the wardrobe and looked inside. It was full of very thin kaftan and ancient Roman leotards and toga-type dresses, very nice but not the sort of thing Row had ever worn before. She pulled a few out and held them against herself as she looked in the mirror. They were all rather short but then she came across a long toga-type dress, flowing white with shoulder straps and a red ribbon that crossed the chest and separated the bust. It did not show too much cleavage so she opted for that one. She got out of the clothes she had been wearing since she left the blue moon the last time she had been there. She had not noticed before that it was now covered in blood splatters; that's when she started to feel a bit grimy. She looked around for somewhere to put her dirty clothes. In the end, a pile on the floor was the best option for now. She dropped the dress over her head and it fell down, the hem stopping just below her bottom. The crossed straps had got in a tangle. Row heard the door open and was in a quandary as to what to do, standing there almost naked.

'It's only me,' called out Paccia 'Stay still, I will sort you out,' she told Row. She sorted the straps out and pulled the dress down past Row's hips where it fell to the floor. Red-faced, Row's head popped out the top of the dress. Paccia sorted the red straps out so they fell properly across Row's body. Then to Row's horror Paccia put her hand between the straps under the dress' material and moved one of Row's breasts so it fell squarely to the side of the strap. 'There,' she said as she stepped back. 'Row, you look stunning in female clothes.'

'You can't just do that to someone, Paccia!'

''Do what?' Paccia asked.

'Touch my boobs,' Row replied.

'Sorry, Row, I don't know what "boobs" are.'

'They are my breasts. "Boobs",' Row emphasised.

'Why?' Paccia asked.

'Because they're private. Not unless I ask you to… It's my personal space,' smiled Row, a little embarrassed.

'But I'm your friend and a healer. What's wrong? I washed your breasts when you were unconscious.'

'Okay, Paccia, I don't need to know any more. It's just not the thing to do on Earth.'

'But you're not on Earth, Row. I can't see the problem.'

'It really doesn't matter. Really, let's just leave it, okay?' said Row.

'If I have offended you, I am sorry, I did not mean to.'

'I was just shocked; I have never been touched there before,' said Row feeling herself going red. 'Let's go for that swim,' she said, and started to leave the room.

'Sorry, Row, I didn't realise. I will ask next time I touch your body, particularly your breast,' Paccia told her as they left the room. They walked through Paccia's room and out onto the balcony. They walked down the stairs to the first level then to another spiral staircase out to the back of the house onto a well-manicured lawn. They walked underneath a sunny, cloudless sky to a wooden jetty at the bottom of the garden that went twenty foot out into the lake. At the end was a ladder to could climb back up out of the water. At the halfway point of the pier were two loungers with soft long cushions.

'This is beautiful,' said Row, 'but we didn't bring any swimming costumes or towels.'

'You are confusing me today, Row. What is a swimming costume?' Paccia asked.

'It's something you put on to go swimming in.'

'Why would you put something on to go swimming in water? Your clothes will get wet,' questioned Paccia.

'It's not the fact that they get wet, they are meant to get wet. It just hides your bits as well,' said Row

'Your bits of what?' asked Paccia, confused.

Then Row mimed putting her hand and arm across her body to show she was trying to hide her female bits, 'Bits,' she said.

'Oh, I see what you mean now. We are back to your boobs again.' Paccia nodded. 'I understand you, you're a little embarrassed about your body.'

'No! You're not getting it. There are just some bits of your body strangers should not see. Do you understand?'

Paccia told her not to worry, everyone bathed in the lake naked. There was no shame in it. 'Why would you want to hide your body? It's natural, why would you?' she said.

Row looked around. She spotted naked people of all races. All naked, all without a care in the world that their bits were out everywhere.

'Okay,' said Row, 'just don't tell my dad or Tristan.'

'Why? They come here whenever they are on the blue moon. The waters have healing qualities, so don't worry about them.'

'We don't have any towels.'

'We don't need any. We will lie here until we dry,' said Paccia as she pulled her dress over her head and walked to the end of the pier. Noticing a friend, she waved to the person in the water, then dived in.

Oh well, thought Row as she pulled her dress over her head and dashed to the end of the pier, jumping straight in feet first. All she could think about was, everyone is staring at me, but it all disappeared as she hit the lukewarm, velvety water.

Splash, plunk, plunk, splash, splash plunk were the sounds as Karl and Tom hurled pebbles into the lake. 'Did you see that, Karl? Seven,' said Tom.

'Rubbish, that was only five,' Karl replied.

'Karl.' A shout came from inside the dining pod, it was Kurt.

'I had better go and see what they want. I will be back in a mo to beat your measly five,' said Karl.

Tom corrected him. 'Seven!' he shouted back as Karl walked away.

'Whatever,' came the reply just before he disappeared into the pod.

Inside the pod there was now a communications screen on one of the tables. Karl could see Tristan on it. He was telling all assembled, Kurt, the king, Detor, Phina and the Wolf warriors, that they had dispatched specialist water teams to them. Hollie and two other teams had dived down into the great lake in the centre of Great Porum and, according to Hollie, she was following a massive submerged tunnel towards what she believed somehow was the Jade Sea. Another team was now on Linasfarn and would be with them very shortly.

The king was asked if he could return to Great Porum to meet the world elders to discuss strategy and the next move in the war against the Dark. He was going to leave with Detor and the four Wolf warriors. Phina would stay with Kurt and Karl and Tom as well as some Wolf warriors who were coming down from the surface. Once the water team arrived, they would be given better diving suits that they knew would be safe at great depths. Kurt would stay in command, while Karl and Phina would go with the water team for the experience. That brought a grin to Karl's face. The king took Karl to one side and told him to take care and no heroics. Karl told him not to worry as he had learnt a lot in last few days and was in no rush to get back into battle.

The king, Detor and his warriors left to travel back to Great Porum. Kurt and Phina were pouring over some underwater maps that didn't make sense; they called Karl over to have a look to see if he could see anything with his young mind that they may have missed.

Tom was sitting at the edge of the lake, kicking the water with his waterproof boots. He had got bored of throwing pebbles and stones by himself. He stopped kicking and stayed still testing his boots to see if they leaked under water, forgetting he had just swum thirty minutes underwater in them with no problems. Daydreaming, he gazed into the water directly below him. Slowly he noticed two oval light blue lights coming towards him. The lights were mesmerising but not enough to keep his feet in the water. He pulled his feet out of the water but continued to watch the lights. They soon became two blue eyes. He made out a face, then green hair came into view along with a smile with glowing white teeth. It was Tanibeth. Her head popped out of the water and looked around. No one else except Tom was there to observe her. As she stared into Tom's eyes, he noticed she had red, green, blue and yellow blossoms platted into her hair. Around her neck was a necklace of polished shells and pearls. Tom looked down at the necklace and realised her shoulders and arms were bare, she had little fins on her elbows and her chest was covered in shiny green and blue scales carried on down into the water. Every now and then he saw the glint of a green blue and silver tail gently moving backwards and forwards, highlighted by the light from the spotlights that had been placed around the water.

'You're a mermaid!' said Tom quietly.

In his head he heard, 'No, I am Tanibeth, a Taniwha. What is your name?'

'I am Tom De-Callen, a prince of Elemtum,' he communicated trying to impress her. She smiled and held her hand out to him.

'Have you come to help me, Prince Tom?' she asked him.

'Yes, if I can,' he replied as he took her hand and slipped into the water next to her.

'Come with me. I will keep you safe in the water. You can help me.' She started to pull him under the water.

'My helmet! I can't breathe under the water,' he hurriedly told her.

'You can,' she answered and came close to him and kissed him. As she did this, Tom could feel something going down his throat it wasn't unpleasant and it didn't make him gag. He was quite calm. When she stopped whatever it was that she had done, she pulled away and smiled at him. 'Come with me, it's okay now,' she communicated and pulled him under the water. He did not struggle. Under the water he opened his mouth! It did not fill with water, then he opened his eyes but his vision was blurred and he felt uncomfortable. He could feel himself starting to panic until Tanibeth calmly rested her hands on his shoulders. 'Open your eyes, Tom.' He did as she asked. Tanibeth put her fingers up to her eyes, wiped away tear drops and then wiped each of Tom's eyes with a tear drop. Seconds later he could see as clear as day.

He smiled at her. 'Thank you, this is amazing.'

She pulled him deeper and deeper. He went willingly. At the bottom of the lake, she stopped and removed his boots with a very sharp shell. Tom could feel the cold water now and it slowly travelled up the legs of his combat suit sending shivers through his body until it had travelled the complete distance of his inner suit and he was now getting cold. Tanibeth could see he was getting cold so she told him she would make him warm once they swam through the hole into her world. She pointed at the now visible tunnel in the rock that Tom had swam through earlier. Tom nodded his head, then took her hand and she led him through the tunnel. On the other side in the lighter clear water, they found themselves amongst the tall seaweed then they stopped.

'You don't need this thing that you are wearing. It is only holding you back,' she communicated to him.

'I can't take it off, it's all I have on,' he told her. She told him she would give him skin to stay warm and help him swim. 'How?' he asked. Tanibeth took the sharp shell from a small bag at her waist, carefully cut up one of the combat suit's legs and around the top of the leg. The combat suit material floated away and slowly sank. Now Tom's right leg was bare. Tanibeth then rubbed her hand along her tail. She showed Tom her hand covered in the green, blue red and yellow scales. Gently, she rubbed her hand along Tom's calf, around his shin, over the top of his foot, between his toes and on the sole of his foot. Instantly wherever she touched was now warm, and slowly the pigment on his leg changed colour. A rainbow of colour rippled along his leg, glinting as if caught by particles of sunlight from above. As Tom watched his leg turn, she cut the other leg of the suit off and did the same again. Slowly Tom's right leg was covered in the same scales that covered most of Tanibeth's body. Bit by bit, both legs became covered and before he knew it or could do anything about it the skin and scales joined together until Tom too had a tail.

Tom felt the warmth rise past his groin then up to the lower part of his belly. Tom started to think, am I turning into a fish?

Tanibeth laid her soothing hand across Tom's cheek. 'Don't worry, Tom, you will go back to how you were when you leave the water,' she told him. When he heard this, he began to relax as she took of the last of his combat suit off with the sharp shell. 'There you are, Taniwha like me,' she told him then placed her necklace around his neck. She smiled at him, then Tom kissed her on the cheek and she kissed him back.

Karl was inside the pod looked at the holographic maps that Kurt and Phina had in front of them. He asked them to explain the maps to him, so Phina did just that. Turning the tablet showed different angles of the map. She brought up the map of Linasfarn and gave the device to Karl. He turned it and orientated it until he could see the top of the island. He moved in to where Tom and Salina had first fallen, then looked down on the island from above. He could see the island was surrounded by sea, which it was. He panned out. He could see the coast, then going north he went across the sea to the mountains then south all the way to the desert lands.

'It all looks okay to me,' he told them. 'What's the other map of?' he asked.

'I've put the view on to Linasfarn but inside so we can see the tunnels Salina and Tom went through all the way to the miners' cart ride and the lake we are now at.' Phina pointed to the side of the lake, showing the pods they were now in. 'The picture mode is at its highest, so the closest thing you would know, Karl, would be similar to a powerful X-ray on Earth, except the picture is real, not the black and white picture you see in a hospital. Do you understand?' she asked him.

'Yes, I do. I don't know how it works yet but I assume these maps are here and now. Real time, I mean, not photographs that have been enhanced of a previous time?'

Kurt answered Karl's question. 'They show real time "now". Look at the changing time on the corner of the devices. See the date?' he said, 'under that is the time.' Karl looked at the date on both devices; they matched the exact date and time that it was at that second.

'How are these pictures taken?' he asked.

'By our sensors in the sky,' said Kurt.

'We asked Tristan earlier to set the sensors in this area to their maximum. That's why we can see through the ground to where we are now. Don't ask me how it works, you would have to ask him or one of the boffins back at Great Porum. All I know is that the picture through the ground is separated and put back together in a fraction of a second showing what we can see now. A perfect 3D picture of inside the island at the precise area we want. Like I said, don't ask me how it is done.'

'That's amazing, Uncle Kurt. can I have a play?'

'By all means, Karl, you can't do any damage to it so have a good look.'

Karl dived the map picture into the lake right down to the bottom and to the passage that led out into the map. He could see the contours of the sea bed stretching for miles. 'That looks fine, too,' he said. Then he went through the tunnel in the rock at the bottom of the lake they had swam through earlier. As he did so, he noticed a jump in the time at the bottom of the screen. It had jumped forward by twelve hours. Strange, he thought, so he went back through the tunnel to the bottom of the lake. The time jumped back twelve hours to the time it was in the pod. He did it again, the same thing. 'Kurt, Phina, come and watch this. I just want to make sure I'm not doing something wrong here.'

Kurt and Phina came and looked over his shoulder. 'Watch,' he told them then he proceeded to move the picture as he had done before. 'Look at the time as I go through the tunnel. Look! Did you see that the time jumped?' He went in and out several times.

'I think you may have found something,' Kurt told him. Phina agreed. They looked at the two monitors together.

Karl moved the picture through the tunnel one more time but only on the device he was using did the time change. He scrolled down to the bottom of the lake and went through the tunnel. 'There. Look at the map coordinates. All I have done is go through the tunnel. Look at the coordinates, they are now thousands of miles from our position as well.'

'That brings up another quandary. If it changes by twelve hours and the distance also increases, does that mean when we dived through the tunnel, we went forward in time twelve hours and moved thousands of miles in the blink of an eyelid? So, if that is the case, why did only thirty minutes lapse by the time we returned as it should have due to the distance we travelled? If what we are seeing is to be believed, it should have been twelve hours and thirty minutes by the time we returned. But we had no sense of travelling thousands of miles, as you would have done in a known pathway, don't you think? said Phina.

'I see what you are saying, Phina, and I agree. Let's give it to Tristan and the boffins to think over.'

'It must be a thread like the one to Earth. So, Salina, Tom and the Zells must have travelled to us on the day the fight with the Dark happened so the time must be adjusted when we travel through it' said Karl.

'There must be many of these around the planet and the Dark have found some, which explains this place and the appearance of the Dark here and at Great Porum,' Kurt concluded. Tristan acknowledged that he had heard and understood all that had been said and it would be passed to the king and the world elders and they would ask the scholars to investigate.

While Kurt and Tristan talked, Karl decide to go back out to Tom. Outside the pod, Karl could not see Tom anywhere. He looked behind the pods to make sure Tom was not mucking around. Still no sign of him. Karl shouted out his name. Nothing, so he went back into the pod and told Kurt and Phina. They all came out and searched the area. Still nothing. 'I'm going down to check the lake,' said Karl.

'I'm coming with you,' Phina told him. Kurt would wait until water team two arrived then they would all look. Kurt told them to go no further than the tunnel to the sea. Phina and Karl grabbed their helmets and jumped into the water. They swam slowly down, stopping every now and then to make sure Tom was not bobbing around. Eventually they reached the lakebed. At the point they reached the bottom, they found Tom's cut up boots.

Through the helmet communicator Karl asked Phina, 'Why Tom would cut his boots off?' She was as baffled as he was, it just didn't make sense. 'That's not right,' he told Phina as he held one of the boots up to her. They decided to go as far as the tunnel to the sea. After that they would decide whether to return to the surface or go a little further in. They continued to swim towards the tunnel and the light coming from the sea.

Above them, water team two had arrived and Kurt was briefing them on the forthcoming operation, and now the search for Thomas De-Callen, the king's son. After the briefing, as the team got its kit together ready for the dive, one of them started to take holographic images of the cavern and the lake. These were sent directly to Tristan. On their way down, the team would be fitting better signal conductors from the surface of Linasfarn to the bottom of the lake and beyond. One of the water team warriors set his kit up to send the pictures to Tristan. The warrior handed Kurt the portable monitor so he could look at the pictures he had taken and was now sending. The time caught his eye and the coordinates were correct at that point.

Chapter 14
Strange Times

Karl and Phina decided to swim to the end of the small tunnel leading to the sea. Once through they looked out into the tall seaweed in front of them. Nothing caught their eye until they started to swim up to get a better view of the area. As they got higher, Phina drew Karl's attention to some dark material in-between some of the seaweed and tall grass. They swam down to it. As they got closer, they could make out the leg of a combat suit, a small one at that. Karl's heart sank. As he got closer, he realised there was nothing in the suit. On further inspection, they found another cut off leg, then the rest of the suit.

He's naked, they both thought. How is he breathing? Has he been taken? It was too surgical for a terror shark. They did not know the answer to any of these questions, so they decided to do a search of the area up to the trench.

Back on dry land, Kurt and the water team operator had sent all their data back to Tristan who had several boffins on standby to decipher it. Once Kurt and the operator had sent the information, they suited up in the deep-water suits that had been brought to them by the water team which were more than capable of standing the deep-water pressures that they expected to find down at the bottom of the trench.

Hollie and her two water teams had followed the tunnel that had been cut through the rock at the bottom of the Great Lake in Great Porum. Steadily and carefully, they probed deeper and deeper through the tunnel. At one point her underwater navigation equipment went haywire so they continued blind using the old-fashioned water compass which made them take extra care and proceed at a slower pace. It did not restrict them too much because in the tunnel they could only go backwards or forwards. There were no other exits they could take. After half an hour of swimming, they came out into clear water. Above them they could see light penetrating the surface of the water. It was not tidal, so they were not likely to be in a sea. She knew it was not a cavern or a cave because there was too much light. It must be another lake, she thought. She took one of her teams slowly to the surface. The top of Hollie's head down as far as her eyes slowly surfaced. She gently treaded water turning through one hundred and eighty degrees then looked up. All around was sloping rock leading to a big hole in the middle. Above her was sky. She realised they were inside what looked like a dead volcano. She returned to her original position. To her front she could see a stone quay and two of the submarine type craft moored to it, but no guards anywhere and no signs of life. It could be a trap, but she was going to continue. With her hands under the water, she gave the teams below the signal to move. Around her three more heads pierced the still water without making so much as a ripple. Silently they moved forward towards the quay. The four below watched underwater for any signs of danger, ambush or a surprise attack from behind which was highly unlikely as they had just travelled there by that route and had seen nothing.

Once Hollie's team reached the stone quay, the second team's heads came out of the water and they watched Hollie and her team scale the quay until they were lying flat on top of it. Still there was no sign of life. Hollie and her team got under cover where they could watch the second team exit the water. Now all eight were scanning the area for any signs of a threat. There were still none. They spread along the quay; one had scanned the two submersible crafts, but there were no readings of life or movement inside. In front of them were large wooden crates like the twenty-feet steel containers that can be seen at any dock on Earth which are regularly used to convey goods from town to town or country to country. These crates were also scanned with similar results. Passed them was a mixture of buildings, only a handful, five to be precise. They looked like they had been used as some sort of workshops. These were surrounded by scraps of metal, bits of engineering and wood. The area looked like the aftermath of a battle but there were no bodies, and nothing was burning. The whole area looked like it had been left in a hurry. Slowly, both teams moved forward towards the buildings. One by one, they searched the buildings but found nothing of any significance. It was blatantly obvious that the previous occupants did not use toilets of any description; on every floor were piles of faeces and puddles of urine.

While one team went out to the boundaries and secured the outer perimeter, Hollie and her team went to clear the last building. As they got near, the stench of death filled their nostrils. Cautiously they went forward. The door to the building was slightly ajar; the stench of rotting flesh that engulfed their nostrils was overpowering. The closest warrior opened the door then stood back, turning his head away from the door and quickly pulling down the visor on his helmet to seal it. Fresh filtered air quickly filled his nostrils, but he could still taste and smell the putrid odour of death. He gestured to the others to do the same. 'Put your helmets to purified air,' he told them. 'Whatever is in there, has been there a while,' said the warrior. 'I'm going to pull the door wide open. Be ready for whatever is in there.' The other warriors readied their weapons, ready for whatever could be in there, 'just in case'. The Dark had been known to ambush warriors by hiding behind the dead, so they would not take any chances.

The warrior swung the door open and the other warriors, including Hollie, had their weapons raised ready to fire. In front of them, two bodies rolled off a stack of bodies behind the door. These were the bodies of two females; they could only just make that out, as they had been grotesquely mutilated. From what tribe or people, they could not tell, but they all knew they would have died horribly at the depraved hands of the Dark. Hollie scanned the bodies. As she did, everyone heard scraping. There was a slight movement of one of the bodies to the back of the room. Hollie picked up a small heat signature then a small hand rose above the corpses at the back. The lead warrior navigated his way over the bodies, trying not to stand on heads if possible. As he got closer, he looked down and there was a very small gap… in it was a little girl, naked like the rest of the corpses but alive. The little girl looked up at the menacing and threatening looking warrior… she screamed and did not stop. She went as rigid as a board. The warrior was suddenly confused about what to do next; he looked back to Hollie as the only female there for help.

'I'll deal with this poor soul,' she told the warrior who nodded and slowly made his way back over the dead bodies, backwards out of the building, thankful that he was now out of the building and not standing on the dead any longer. Hollie walked carefully towards the child who still had her eyes closed and continued to scream. Gently, she put her right hand on the child's bare and bloodied shoulder. The child immediately stiffened, stopped screaming, opened her eyes wide and stared at the face now in front of her. Hollie smiled at her. She had removed her helmet and given it to the warrior who had first found the little girl. With her helmet off, the girl's reaction was instant. She leapt at Hollie. Her arms went around Hollie's neck and her legs wrapped around her waist, then the child buried her head in Hollie's shoulder where she held on for dear life. This was the second time in a week Hollie had been surprised since joining the water team. She was now at a loss about what to do, so she put her arms round the girl and carried her out of the stinking, blood-drenched building. The warriors carefully placed the two bodies that had fallen out when the doors were opened back into the building and closed the doors. There was nothing else that could be done for them on that day; cremation would be arranged at a different time.

The warriors steadily searched the remaining area and found nothing, but they did find some clothes suitable to dress the child in. Hollie settled the child down and gave her some energy blocks out of her backpack which the child eagerly devoured. While she chomped on the blocks, Hollie checked the child over. Apart from a few small cuts and bruises, she seemed okay. What was in her head was another matter and until she started talking no one would know what had happened to her or the others. Hollie and her water team were now left with a problem; what to do with the child. The trauma she had been through meant she had to be treated gently. Their mission could not continue until the girl was taken out of harm's way by people who were trained to help her. The warriors set up a defensive perimeter while two scouted the local area ahead. They followed drag marks and footprints which took them away from the buildings towards an opening in the old volcano wall. They reported back to Hollie who told them to continue and scout around outside the volcano. If they made a contact, they should make their way back to the defensive perimeter being set up. Hollie took the child to the water's edge and began to clean the blood from her face. When the child's face was as clean as a whistle, she noticed there were no cuts on it. She cleaned the girl's arms and legs; under the black dirt and the dried blood her skin was also clear. The only marks that Hollie found were around the child's neck as though someone had tried to strangle her. Hollie clothed the child and as she did, she saw a green glint her eyes. The child's face started to turn from a frightened little girl into something else, something menacing. Evil eyes started to search Hollie's face, moving down to her weapons. Then her head twisted, and the little girl's eyes searched each warrior in turn, taking in their positions and weapons. Hollie stood up and walked slowly backwards, away from the child. Quietly, she spoke into her helmet as she placed it back on her head, 'Stand to, the child is going wearied; I think there could be a little more to her.' Two of the warriors closest to Holly came over and lifted their weapons, aiming them at the strange child. In front of them, the girl's eyes had changed to jet green.

'Look at her hands,' said one of the warriors. The girl's nails started to extend, turning into claws. At the same time, her mouth began to widen, sharp pointed fangs filled her mouth. Saliva now dripped from the mouth of the once pretty little girl as a snarl crossed her face turning her into some sort of evil creature like nothing that any of them had ever seen before. The creature ran at the nearest warrior which happened to be Hollie. The creature leapt at her; teeth bared, saliva flying in every direction. It moved with great speed, taking Hollie aback. Her reactions as far as her weapon was concerned were slow, but her defensive reactions were quick. She timed the move perfectly. As the creature's teeth loomed large in her vision, saliva splattering onto Hollie's visor, she lurched forward, headbutting the creature straight in the mouth. The creature careered backwards. As Hollie lifted her head, pieces of the creature's destroyed teeth bounced off her and her helmet, scattering about as the creature, now sprawled on the ground, screamed with pain and anger. It bounced back up, hysterical, and ran at Hollie once more, but this time she and the other two warriors were ready. Three blasts from their weapons blew the creature sideways, spinning to the ground where it stayed motionless. In front of their eyes the creature turned back into the lifeless body of the now dead little girl.

Tom and Tanibeth had swum together into the abyss where she showed him a concealed entrance which would lead them to Selessi avoiding any unwanted watchers in the city below. Tanibeth put her hand on a limpet and a rock rolled away revealing a shimmering bubble that covered the entrance. Tanibeth swam into the bubble, then stepped through into a chamber. Tom followed. Once inside, she told Tom that he would turn back into his normal form and to that end she handed him what looked like a pair of pyjamas to put on as he changed, otherwise he would be naked. Tanibeth put a top on and told Tom to turn around to save any embarrassment. Slowly the fish scales faded away and they turned back into people. The flowers in Tanibeth's hair turned into red seaweed which she took off and placed on a rock shelf along with her necklace and pearls.

Tom called to Tanibeth behind him, 'Are you dressed?'

'Yes,' she replied and they turned and looked at each other.

Tom smiled at the young girl of his own age now in front of him. 'I didn't recognise you with your clothes on,' he said, joking.

'That's because you have never seen me in this form before, Tom. But my head has not changed, so why don't you recognise me?'

'Don't worry, Tanibeth, it's Earth humour.'

'I don't understand,' she replied.'

'It doesn't matter, I was trying to be funny,' said Tom.

'Oh! Will you be doing that a lot?' she asked.

'No, I don't think I will,' he replied, feeling a little awkward. Trying to change the conversation, Tom told her, 'The clothes feel and look like pyjamas; they are very comfortable.'

'I don't know what pyjamas are,' she replied.

Tom explained that they were things you went to bed in on Earth, but still she did not understand so Tom gave up and asked what the plan was from there on. She told him that the secret tunnel led into the city of Selessi where they would sneak in and free her people who had all been locked up by the evil ones.

'Will you help me free them?' she asked.

'Yes, I will,' Tom replied immediately, with a smile. He had forgotten his dream from the night before when he awoke to the red seaweed.

'Are you sure? It will be very dangerous,' Tanibeth emphasised.

'I'm not scared. Let's get going,' he urged.

'Thank you, Tom, you are very brave.' Then she kissed him on the lips. Tom blushed. She took Tom by the hand and led him down the partly illuminated tunnel. As they went further in, Tom's ears popped. 'We must be going deep,' he told her.

'Yes, outside normal people would be crushed to death… but you and I will be fine because we can both turn.'

'Do you mean I will get that mermaid stuff when I want,' asked Tom.

'No, Tom, it's Taniwha not mermaid. That's what the humans used to called us, and, yes, if you want to and you are in water, you can now turn and be a "mermaid", as you put it.'

'Cool beans,' replied Tom. 'That means I'm a fish, soon I'll be a wolf, and someone told me I'm also an eagle. I think that's about it; I don't really need to turn into anything else now I've got all the bases covered.'

'You're strange, Tom! Half the time when you speak, I don't have a clue what you are speaking about.' They both laughed then Tanibeth became serious. 'From now on, Tom, we will have to be quiet because we will be going close to the walls of my city. The evil ones are on the other side and I don't want them to hear us.'

Tom whispered to her, 'What is the plan?'

'I don't really have one. Sneak in get to my people, let them out, we all escape, your people turn up and kill all the bad people, all of them.'

'Hmm, sounds simple, but I bet there will be a little more to it than that,' replied Tom quietly. They continued in silence deeper and deeper down the tunnel. The tunnel was well lit, whoever built it probably had this sort of scenario in mind; t to be used either to escape the city or, as they were doing, sneak back into it.

After twenty minutes, they had reached the end of the tunnel. In front of them was another bubble. They walked into it. Tanibeth explained to Tom that there was a moving rock which was the entrance. In front of that was a hanging garden that would shield them from any prying eyes when the rock moved. 'Are you ready, Tom? When we get through just follow me,' she told him. She pressed a similar shell as she had before and the rock in front of them opened silently. In front of them now was a wall of green interlaced with flowers of red, green, blue and yellow.

For a second, Tom was taken aback by the beauty in front of him. Behind them the rock returned to its original position. No turning back, Tom thought. Tanibeth led Tom by the hand from behind the wall of green and colour between some pillars adorned with flowers and waterfalls. Above them was a roof of green. Around them were benches and chairs to relax on while admiring the beauty of the garden, which they did not have time to do. They moved along a wicker-covered tunnel to its end and stopped.

Tom could see white buildings in front of him; each one had some sort of sea or water picture on it. Dolphins, whales, octopus, sharks and old sailing ships, but mostly creatures he had never seen before, although some he had. He remembered he had seen them in books, so they were obviously from their time on Earth. Wherever he looked there was something different made by lots of different coloured shells. What struck him next was how quiet it all was and very neat. It did not look like the Dark menace had rampaged through this city; it was all very strange.

'Come on,' Tanibeth whispered, 'it's not very far now. You see the courtyard over there?' She pointed in its direction. Tom followed her extended finger and saw the courtyard. Behind it was a magnificent building with grand pillars reaching up to an arch. But what was odd was behind the pillars Tom noticed a very small door which looked out of place in the grand building.

Something doesn't seem right, he thought but his mind was put at rest when Tanibeth smiled at him and pushed him gently back behind the wicker. Not more than thirty feet in front of them, two Dark lancers walked past. Once they had moved away, she told Tom that she had been watching them and that they had about twenty minutes before they came back again.

'So, we must run,' she told him, taking his hand. They ran to the courtyard, across its open space where he felt very exposed. It felt like a thousand eye were watching him cross it. At the other end, they ran up the grand steps and behind the big pillars where they stopped to catch their breath. All they could hear was their deep breathing; Tom was convinced the whole city could hear his beating heart pumping away in his chest. Very quickly their breathing was back to normal. After a quick check back across the courtyard they walked to the small normal sized door and stopped.

Tom and Tanibeth looked around, all was still quiet. He noticed a tear run down her cheek. 'Are you all right? Is something wrong?' he asked.

Tanibeth tenderly touched his arm then gave him a kiss on his cheek. 'I'm just so grateful for the sacrifice you have given to my family.'

Tom looked at her. Sorrow filled her face. He took her by the hands and quietly said, 'I would do anything for you and your family, so don't worry.' Ten slowly, carefully, quietly, he opened the door and they went through. On the other side, Tom saw people dressed in the same sort of clothes as he was. They all looked terrified.

From the front of them someone shouted, 'No! Tanibeth, you didn't!'

Tom was confused. He turned and looked at her; she had floods of tears in her eyes. Tom sensed someone behind him, then before he could turn to look, he felt pain, his sight dimed, and he could feel himself falling.

Just as he blacked out, he heard, 'I'm sorry, Tom.' Then the crying faded away...

Phina and Karl waited for a while then turned around, making their way back to the cavern and the lake they had left earlier to wait for the water team to get their pressure suits for the deep dive they would have to do to try and follow Tom's trail. They had searched the area around the entrance to the sea near the trench. Finding no sign of him, they assumed he must have somehow been taken down deeper. When they got back to the surface, they could see that the water team had already arrived and were suited ready to go. Kurt was not with them because he had been urgently recalled to the king's side in Great Porum, leaving Phina and the water team to find Tom and look after Karl. After a drink and a quick snack to build their energy back up, Phina and Karl had changed and were ready to go.

Back in the water, they were soon through the tunnel and into the tall seaweed. They headed across the seabed towards the trench. As they approached the top of it, a submersible craft, hidden by masses of seaweed, came out ahead of them. It turned sharply away from them. Behind it were winged lizard-type creatures, all with Dark warriors astride them. The lead warrior was a female. All in black, her red hair was flowing behind her in the water; she had a crazy smile on her face. The creatures gliding behind the submersible craft all kept pace with it. They continued to move away, oblivious of the watching eyes. The water team watched without reacting. If only they had known who was aboard and if Labatina had only known that her son was so close. The Dark warriors and the craft moved away, completely disappearing from the view of Karl, Phina and the water team who stayed hidden on the seabed between the waving seaweed and water plants.

'Did you see who that was, Phina?' said Karl.

'Yes, Karl, I did! It was your mother, Labatina.'

'That was her? My god, she looked nasty, I'm glad I'm with you guys. She gave me the creeps,' replied Karl, showing no emotion whatsoever.

When they were sure there was no more Dark warriors in the area, they made their way to the end of the trench and looked down. They could see through the gloom to the gently flickering light of the city of Selessi. There was no sign of any more Dark warriors so the team started to descend towards the city. Slowly, lights and the mysterious city below started to come into view after twenty minutes of descent. Now at the base of the dome that surrounded the city of Selessi, they searched for a way in. Karl, Phina and two of the water team went in one direction around the dome; the remainder of the water team went the other. Karl tried peering in to see what was on the other side, but the dome's surface became hazy and he could make nothing out except lights shining somewhere in the dome. After an hour of searching to no avail, the two teams met up on the other side of the dome.

'Nothing,' said one of the warriors from the second water team. Phina agreed with him. They were stumped as of how to enter the city.

'It can't be that hard to get in. The Dark did,' said Karl.

'I think they may have had help,' replied Phina.

'I think we are being watched,' said Karl. 'I can feel it in the hairs on the back of my neck.'

'You could be right, prince,' said one of the water team. 'My helmet sensor is picking up movement and a rapid heartbeat to our left amongst the sea grass.'

'Put your weapon on incapacitate and fire at it. That will give us time to get whatever is spying on us,' said Phina. The warrior lifted his weapon, aimed and fired; the sonic wave shot forward, parting the grass and hitting the person hiding there. They all swam towards the body which now lay motionless on the seabed between the grasses.

'It's the little girl from the lake, Tanibeth. What's she doing here?'

'This is her home, Karl. She should be able to get us in.' Phina then indicated to the water team to revive the child.

'More importantly, Phina, why is she hiding from us?' said the leader of the water team. They gathered around her just to make sure she could not escape if she tried. Karl went to her and cradled her head in his arms; slowly Tanibeth's eyes opened and even in the water Karl could see she had tears in them. She kept miming the word sorry over and over to him until Phina approached. Tanibeth then closed her mouth, fearful of what would now happen to her.

'It's okay, Tanibeth. It's me, Phina. We have met before. Do you remember? I ran with you on my back the first time you left the lake,' she communicated to her.

Tanibeth nodded yes then Phina asked if she could take them into the city? At first, Tanibeth did not want to but then she relented when Karl started to ask her about Tom. Her eyes now bursting with tears, she nodded and took them over to the dome and placed her hand on it. Where her hand touched a bubble appeared and she stepped in, beckoning them all to follow. Once inside the bubble she pressed its inner wall and it opened and they walked into city. From a small pouch on her back Tanibeth pulled some of her clothes out and put them on as she changed back to her person form. She stood up and ran to Phina, gripping her. The little girl's face was bright red, streams of tears now flowed from her eyes.

'I have been so stupid, Phina. The Dark deceived me. Now all my people are dead, and Tom has been taken by the Dark queen.'

'What do you mean?' shouted Karl 'Tom has been taken where?'

'Karl, that is not necessary. Look at her, she's petrified and scared stiff,' said Phina.

'What have you done?' asked Karl.

'It's okay, Tanibeth,' said Phina. 'We will not hurt you. You are safe with us. Tell us what has happened.'

'I was swimming towards the lake when the Dark ones appeared. They stopped me and told me they had entered my city and held all my people as captives and unless I returned with them to the city, they would all be killed. I took them back to my city and went in with them. They kept the dome open and hundreds of them flooded in. I had let them into the city; it's entirely my fault, I didn't know.' She began to cry again, Phina calmed her down and told her to continue. 'They went from structure to structure, ripping everyone from their homes and putting them all into the sacred hall. Then their queen arrived and asked who the leader was. A Taniwha called Cetus came forward. He is not the leader, but he said he was. She said to show they meant business, because they knew he was not the leader, she cut his head straight off.' Then Tanibeth stopped talking as the horror of that day came back to her. Tears welled up once more. Phina hugged her, reassuring her that she was now safe. She began to calm down once more. She continued shaking as she spoke, holding back the tears that broke through now and then. 'The queen told the evil ones to take the head and the body to Serberus. I don't know what that is, but she said he would be hungry.' Tanibeth began to cry once more.

'Please, Tanibeth, continue. Please, we need to know what has happened to Tom,' Karl pleaded.

Tanibeth sniffed, then wiped her eyes. 'I am sorry,' she said. She paused then, when she was ready, she continued. 'The queen told me she would kill me and all the people of Selessi unless I bring the Earth child to the city. If I did that, she would not hurt him, and the city would be spared. I had no choice. I found where Tom was and I went to him in his sleep. The next day he came with me back to the city.'

'So why were Tom's clothes on the seabed?' Karl asked.

'I thought if I gave him the gift I have, that he would be able to escape once they had him and the city would be spared! We are not violent people. What was I to do?' she sobbed.

'So, when did they take Tom?'

'Not long before you came,' she replied. 'We went into the sacred hall; they were waiting for Tom behind the door. They hit him over the head and took him away.' She started to cry once more. 'Then they killed all my family and the people of the city, because she said I had brought the wrong person. She said she did not want the whore's son, but her own.'

'Karl.'

'She was very mad. I got out by hiding under a dead body then when they left, I escaped the city. That's when I saw you coming so I hid. I didn't know who you were. I am so sorry. I really like Tom and his people. I'm so sorry.' Then she became inconsolable and the tears flooded out. The realisation hit her she was the last of her kind. She was all alone and she had done something unforgivable.

'We won't be able to communicate from down here, so we will have to get to the surface and let everyone know what has happened. More importantly, get a search underway for Tom,' said Phina. They had a quick search for any living Taniwha but found none.

While they did this, Karl sat and talked with Tanibeth. He told her that he did not hold her responsible for anything that had gone on that day and that he knew the pressure she must have been under to save her people. They would get Tom back, he was sure of that. Tom was lucky, one of life's survivors. He could fall in poo and come out as fresh as a daisy carrying a gold coin he had found in it, so he would be okay, he was sure of that. He hugged Tanibeth and told her he would look after her, she would become part of his family. He also told her not to worry about Tom, he would understand. Nothing would bring her family back now and that would be something she would have to come to terms with herself. Everyone at Great Porum and on the blue moon would help her to deal with that. Tanibeth stopped sobbing, weakly smiling at Karl. By then, the searchers had returned. Not a living soul had been found, so it was time to leave.

Tanibeth opened the dome for them and they all left. Back in the water, Tanibeth pulled the trousers from her tail and placed them back in her little pack along with her top then she darted off ahead of them to make sure all was clear. Slowly, too slowly for Karl, they made their way to the surface where Tanibeth was waiting for them. She told them they she had encountered some Octavians. They were very fast, she had told them what had happened and they would look for the evil ones they were seeking. They went in the same direction the submersible craft Labatina had gone in.

On the surface, they communicated with the strategic centre. Karl's father swore he would kill every Dark creature if Tom was harmed. A call went out to the peoples from all tribes to come together to deal once and for all with the Dark. They also heard from Hollie who had seen a very large winged lizard leave the sea and rise into the air, heading south. There was some one riding it but from her vantage point she could not make out who it was or if they had Tom. There had been no sign of a submersible craft which gave everyone hope that they could catch them. If Tom was not with them, they could find out where he was. The search was now on for the craft.

Hollie's water team had come across a sea slug that told them of a passage back to the Jade Sea where it had seen a metal underwater-ship go south. With the help of some sea slugs, Hollie and her two teams were now being pulled south by the sea slugs in the direction they had seen the metal sea craft go. The two separate teams were told by Tristan that they were hundreds of miles apart and Phina's team was hundreds of miles from Linasfarn, so they must be travelling through passages in time and space like the one to Earth, only starting and finishing on Elemtum.

Tanibeth knew of the passage the sea slugs were talking about; it was one of three she knew about. That one the one she used to get to the great lake and there another that was well south that she had never travelled to. Tanibeth left them floating; she departed to get them some help in the form of the Octavians she had met earlier. She returned half an hour later accompanied by dangerous looking octopuses, but these had fins sticking out from their bodies on two sides. 'Don't be scared, they are very inquisitive. They will smell you and feel you with their tentacles; they will not hurt you.'

Tanibeth spoke to them in some sort of guttural bubble language which they responded to, then they approached Phina, Karl and the water team. One by one the Octavians gently felt and smelt their way around every person, probing, touching, stroking. Then there were lots of bubbles and the Octavians all came together in a mass huddle. Tanibeth went to them, then shortly after a lot of stroking of heads and bodies she returned to the floating group. 'They are happy to help; they will wrap a tentacle around your hands and pull you along. Make sure everything is well secured because we will be travelling very fast underwater. Is that okay?'

Phina thanked Tanibeth then informed the command centre who were happy with the plan as it was the only one that they had at that time. Then she went over to the largest of the Octavians and stroked its head-body. With great care, the Octavian curled a tentacle around Phina's waist and lifted her out of the water. A tongue came from its body and slathered across the front of her helmet then gently put her back in the water.

'It was a good job I had my visor down,' she told everyone through the communication system. The plan was to take the passage that Tanibeth knew went south. Hopefully, they would meet up with Hollie and her teams if all went to plan and the passage came out where they hoped it would. This was at the point the Dark had entered from their home base or very close to it. Tristan had done some calculations; he believed they would be going in the right direction if his assumption about the southern passage was correct, which Tanibeth believed it was. But she was only a young Taniwha, so nobody really knew if she was right about the tunnel but it was the best they had at that moment.

One by one the Octavians picked one of the team and took them by the hand, then they were off under water, travelling at some speed which took everyone by surprise except Tanibeth because she had swum with the Octavians before. It was strange to see; they glided through the sea, their fins rippling, tentacles outstretched behind them, slightly moving their fins and tentacles to change direction. Gills at the top of their bodies opened, letting in water which was then expelled at tremendous speed at the other end. That plus the action of the fins propelled the Octavians forward. Even dragging their passengers did not hinder their progress.

Hollie and her teams were having similar success. The sea slugs were excellent swimmers, not as fast as the Octavians although faster than a top Olympic athlete but they could also keep that speed up for a much greater length of time. One water team member was on the back of each sea slug. Not only that, but they were having intelligent conversations with the sea slugs as they swam. No one realised until then that you could communicate with sea slugs via thought as you could with people. Hollie found out something that may become very helpful in the future; sea slugs, or Serpennorse as she was told was their proper name, believed that there was a sea passage from this planet to the planet that had broken away before life had begun. There was an old wise Serpennorse that had left on his life journey that had known of such a passage, but he could be anywhere and he would not return until his life was near to his ancestors. Then he would impart his gained knowledge and disappear. Hollie tapped that into her onboard computer to remind her to let Tristan and the king know about this the next time she met them.

Lying on a sun lounger with a cool drink in her hand, oblivious to the danger Tom was in and the drama that was unfolding for Karl and Phina, Rowena relaxed in the sun, talking to Paccia. Having swum naked and now lying next to her, soaking up the rays, life once more felt good. She was looking forward to the meal Paccia had promised to make for her later; she had enjoyed the morning fish so much that the blue moon speciality was now on the menu for the evening. Until then, it was relax, relax, soak up the sun, swim and relax. After all what she had been through since arriving, she deserved it. Slowly, she began to fall asleep.

Suddenly she awoke with a start! She could feel someone's hand running along her body. She sat up to see Paccia standing over her. 'What are you doing?' she exclaimed.

Paccia looked at her, puzzled. 'Applying screening lotion to your body otherwise very shortly you will burn. My blue skin prevents this but yours is pale. You will burn. Am I doing something wrong again?' she asked.

'Yes! I mean no. Well, what I mean is, it's nice of you to think of me and to start applying screen. It's just that, well, it's my private space and unless I ask you to do it, don't or speak to me and tell me first. I nearly had a heart attack. Do you understand?' Row asked her.

'Well, not really,' replied Paccia. Row quickly pulled her dress back on just as another healer turned up.

'Forgive me, Paccia, I have been sent to fetch you. I went to your home. As you weren't there, I knew you would be here. We have to prepare for a possible impending prolonged battle. The king's forces are going to all come together to search for the Dark. There has been some trouble on Elemtum.'

'Are my brothers involved?' asked Row.

'I have no word of them. I believe they are safe with the king and Lady Phina,' the healer replied.

'If your brothers were in peril, I am sure we would have been informed by the king,' said Paccia.

'You're right, Paccia. No point getting worked up over nothing. I'm sure after some of the adventures Karl and Tom have been on, the king and Kurt will not let them out of their sight.'

'I am sure that is the case, lady,' said the healer.

Paccia told the healer to return to the infirmary where she would meet everyone to get the emergency stores and trauma kits ready. The healer departed. Paccia and Row gathered their things together then walked back to Paccia's home. Row told her she would cook something while she was away setting things up. Paccia agreed. When they got back to her home, Row was shown where the preparation and cooking room was. They even had some human cookbooks that had been used to make new recipes using Penterum and Elemtum food. She could use these to help her. Paccia told Row those books were in her father's room where she would find his library and the cook books. She could help herself to them. She also told her that there was an A to Z food complimented book that told you the name of the food from these worlds and what the equivalent would be on Earth. Enter the Earth food name and it would tell you the equivalent food on these worlds. Paccia left Row and changed into her medical clothing. When she returned, Row was now in Paccia's father's library searching the spines of the books for something that looked like it could be a cookbook, especially the A to Z.

'Have you found anything?' she asked.

Row turned and smiled. 'No, I have just started looking. Any idea where they could be? This is a big library.'

'No, I'm sorry, Row, I would be as lost as you in here. The only subject I know the whereabouts of is herbs to stop bleeding and that's only because my father gave me it to read. After he left for Earth, I put it over there, next to the books on herbs. I know I will be wrong when he returns because he would probably have put it in the blood area.' Paccia laughed, then asked Row if she would be okay by herself?

'Yes, it will take me quite some time to find what I am looking for, then find the stuff to make the dinner. There will be enough to keep me busy, thank you. Oh, and over dinner I will talk to you about personal space. That should be fun,' said Row.

Paccia answered with a smile and said, 'Sounds like fun.' Not really knowing what Row was talking about, she then said goodbye and turned to leave.

'If you hear anything about my brothers and my family, will you let me know?' Row asked.

Paccia turned around and walked back to her. Holding both Row's hands tenderly, she told her 'Of course, I will, straight away. Don't worry, we would have been informed if anything was wrong. This is just alerting us to a probable battle where there might be casualties. So, don't worry, we have done this many times before.' Paccia lent forward and kissed Row on the lips then stroked her cheek with her hand.

The kiss and touch sent a tingle through Row's body. She was at peace and happy in that instance, then Paccia was gone. That must have been some of her healing powers crossing to me, thought Row. Smiling, she turned and looked at the shelves of books in front of her.

Where do I start? she thought.

She spent an hour searching then came across a book called the Olde World Farmhouse Kitchen Cookbook, (everything a new housewife needs to know to keep her husband sustained and happy). This made Row laugh. God, it must be an old book, she thought and looked at the print date. 1947. 'That is old,' she said to herself.

She thumbed through the recipes and stopped at *Tripe* (a cheap and easy meal for your man that will keep him coming back for more). This also made Row laugh and she put the book aside for reading later. She knew she must be in the right area, so continued looking. Then she found Earth recipes using Elemtum ingredients. She had a quick flick through. It looked promising, so she kept the book. She read the author's name; Labatina De-Callen. 'Oh my god, that's my mother, the mad bitch!' she said aloud. There was no picture of the author on the sleeve like on Earth books which was a shame, but in any case, it was what she needed, she thought.

Then she collected the happy sustain your husband book and left the library, closing the door behind her. Row had a look around the house and found no store of food, but she did find a nice little nap sack that would come in handy when she found out where to get food from. It was also handy for carrying her two books because she was going to the infirmary to find Paccia to get directions to a food store. She left the house with the nap sack and headed back towards the infirmary. As she got closer, she saw a sail craft heading for the docking station.

Surely the battle has not started already, she thought to herself. She quickened her pace. When she was feet away from the infirmary, a voice she would recognise anywhere shouted over. Row turned to see Tristan running towards her. As he reached her, he said, 'Well, that was easy, I thought I would have to go searching the blue moon for you.' He kissed her on the cheek as he hugged her.

'I have missed you.'

'It's only been a day, Dad' replied Row, 'and I have missed you to be fair. I feel a bit out of place being up here. It feels like I'm missing out on everything.'

'That why I am here to get you and take you and any recovered warriors back to Elemtum.'

'Is something up?' she asked.

'I am afraid there is. Row. It's Tom. As far as we are aware Tom is now in the hands of Labatina and the Dark.'

'Oh, my god!'

'We don't honestly know whether he's alive or dead,' he told Row. They left together and made their way back to the sail craft where they were soon joined by around one hundred warriors who were now well enough to return to Elemtum. The main door to the craft closed and they were soon in the air heading home. Tristan told Row about the circumstance of Tom's abduction and what Phina, Karl and Hollie were doing to try and find him. Row was totally shocked; she could not believe what was happening.

This bloody world, will it ever give us peace? My poor brothers, she thought to herself as tears started to swell in her eyes. She wiped them away, sniffed and dug deep.

Chapter 15
The Escape

Tom woke with a sore head; he could feel dried blood on the crown of his head. He rubbed it softly. He could feel the swelling. I must have been hit from behind, he thought. Suddenly he became aware of his foul-smelling surroundings; the air was damp and sticky. Around him he could see bare black rock, damp with water trickling down from above. He looked around. Spiked steel bars were the most prominent feature of what he assumed to be a cell; the remainder of the cell was pitch black. Slowly, he got up and stumbled forward. Getting his balance, he straightened up and grabbed the steel bars to steady himself. He lent against the bars and looked out into a dimly lit passage slightly illuminated by two burning torches which were an equal distance apart from each other, separated by about ten feet, Tom guessed. Then his mind drifted to what he remembered. The first thing that shot into his brain was hearing the word sorry repeatedly. He remembered the voice; it was Tanibeth. His brain could not compute why she was saying sorry. Then a chill ran down his spine, he had a recollection of a dark figure in the periphery of his view before all had gone black. A horrible thought crossed his mind. Surely Tanibeth had not betrayed him and handed him over to the Dark. The realisation hit him. She must have. Why? he thought then tears filled his eyes. He backed up, slumped against the damp rock and buried his hands in his head. He cried quietly at that moment. Fr the first time since he had arrived on Elemtum, he felt his proper age, alone and very frightened.

'No point crying, boy, crying won't save you.' Tom immediately stopped crying and lifted his head from his hands. Wiping the tears from his eyes, he investigated the darkness from where the voice had come. He could see nothing except black. Then there were two bright yellow eyes with blue irises and jet-black pupils. They blinked then they were gone.

'Who's there? Tom called out.

'Not who, boy. I am a what. A what that would have eaten you back on Earth. That is where you're from, isn't it?'

'How do you know that?' replied Tom.

'I can smell you, boy, that's how.'

'What are you then? Come forward so I can see you,' asked Tom.

'You come forward, boy, I have no legs.'

'I'm nearly a warrior, I'm not a boy,' said Tom.

'Don't make yourself older than you are. You will be old soon enough, then you will wish you were young again and your life will have passed you by. Don't wish yourself old, boy, it will come soon enough.'

'Sorry, I didn't mean anything,' replied Tom then he walked gingerly forward.

The yellow eyes stayed fixed on him then Tom remembered what the eyes had said. 'I would have eaten you back on Earth.' Tom stopped in his tracks.

'Why have you stopped, boy?' the eyes said.

'You said you would have eaten me back on Earth. What's stopping you eating me now?' asked Tom.

'I don't eat boys or humans anymore. I'm not what I was,' it replied.

'Can I trust you?' said Tom.

The yellow eyes started to laugh. 'Do you know that what you just said was very stupid? "Can I trust you?" You can't, idiot. You don't know me, do you?' Tom knew exactly how stupid it was as soon as he said it. 'Come forward, boy, I'm playing with you. I won't eat you.'

Tom continued to edge forward. step by step. His eyes were now becoming accustomed to the dark. In the corner he saw what looked like a... panther! As he got closer, a hand grabbed his ankle. Tom shrieked and tried to pull away, but the hand held him firm.

'Stop the squealing, boy. You will bring them down, then we will both get a beating.'

Tom stopped, and the hand let go. 'I'm Blacky,' it said.

'Are you a panther?' asked Tom.

Blacky told Tom that he was once a panther living in the rainforests of South America back on Earth. 'That's when I would have eaten you, boy,' he told Tom.

'You can call me Tom.'

'Okay then. Tom, sit next to me and we will keep each other warm. I will tell you how I managed to get here. Then you can do the same and we will know each other.' Tom sat next to Blacky. 'Well, boy... sorry, Tom, what a mess we have got ourselves in. You recently and me, well, that was some time ago and, to tell you the truth, I'm actually not sure how long I have been in this bad place.

'How can you talk? If you're from Earth, panthers on Earth don't talk, do they?' asked Tom.

'They can talk, Tom.'

Tom looked into the face of the panther. Apart from the staring yellow eyes, he could not make out if Blacky was teasing him. 'You're right, Tom my boy. On Earth I was a normal panther. A proud fearless one I might add,' added Blacky.

'So, what happened to you?'

'You're a sharp lad, Tom. Don't miss a trick, do you?'

'Hardly hard to miss, Blacky. You have no legs, a panther's body, a head that can talk and arms,' said Tom. 'You would have to be blind to miss it.'

'Ah but you see, Tom, these arms aren't mine. They belong to someone else. You're right, I don't have my legs right now, but I will get then back. That is, of course, if I don't die first which is actually very likely.'

'So! How did you become like you are then?' Tom asked.

'Now that's a long story. As we don't have anything else to do, I will tell you the short one. Before you were obviously born, I was roaming my rainforest... content. I had just eaten my kill and it was getting near mating season, so I was out searching for that ideal panther. You know what I mean, lad?' Tom saw Blacky wink.

'No, not really,' Tom replied.

'Oh, you're that young, are you?' he said.

'No, I'm not young. I'm nearly a Wolf warrior.'

'I will try and remember that in future, young Wolf warrior,' Blacky said sarcastically.

Tom did not mind; he had made his point.

Blacky continued. 'Well, if I remember properly it was any lady panther. To be truthful, there weren't that many around.' Blacky laughed. 'Anyway, I digress. I felt a pain in my shoulder. I knew something wasn't right, so I ran. The next thing I remember I am on a steel table and a human woman was stroking my fur. Then I was gone again. The next thing I remember is having no memories of being a panther, but I also knew I was a warrior from a strange land. When I looked down, I saw a panther's body and upon looking in a mirror I saw a panther's head, but I knew inside here.' He tapped his head. 'I'm a warrior, a great fearless warrior but somehow in a panther's body. How did I know it was a panther's body? I had never seen a panther before in my life, but inside this head,' he tapped it once more, 'in here, I am both warrior and panther. I lived with that beautiful woman for several years. I suppose you could call me her pet, now I think about it.' he said. 'Then things began to change. An evil man came on the scene and I think he resented the attention I received from the woman. Who, by the way, was a queen, Queen Labatina from Elemtum. I know that much... anyway, I digress again. The evil man must have hated me because the queen slowly changed; she was definitely manipulated by this person and for the worse I can tell you. Soon I found myself with human arms and human legs. He experimented on me. When I awoke from his latest experiment, he was there in front of me, so I attacked him and left him with a nice scar to remember me by. I would have killed him, but someone stunned me and the next time I awoke I was chained and all around me were animals and creatures with different warrior parts. We were all one big experiment to try and make the greatest warriors ever, but it didn't quite work. Many of these poor creatures went mad or disfigured themselves and were taken away until I was the only one left. One day, I escaped from my chains when the shackle holding me to a wall failed and I pulled them from the wall and escaped the laboratory. I went in search of the evil man. I never found him, but I did find several demon forms that I killed until, finally, I made my way out into a big black forest. Out there I felt alive, but they sent evil creatures after me, creatures I had never seen before. I made it out on to a great green plain but that was my downfall. They swooped from the sky, big acid spewing dragons with hideous warriors astride them. They would have surely killed me but a black-clad-masked woman stopped them and I was thrown in here where I have been for some time now. They used acid to burn my warrior legs off, I think, because when I woke up here, they were gone. But I will tell you this, Tom.' Blacky paused for breath. 'On the rare occasions I have been out of this cell, I have seen there may be a way out of here when I'll get rid of these useless arms and get my own legs back. You just watch me, I'll be out of here like a shot. One day I will get them back and have them put back on this old battered body, then I will be happy.'

'I will help you, Blacky. We just need to get out of here, that's all,' said Tom.

'That would be a nice dream, lad, but I don't think it will ever happen. Even if I would like it to, the reality is different to my dreams of freedom. Enough of that. Anyway, Tom, it was very good of you to offer to help but I think we might meet another fate before that dream will come to fruition,' he said.

'I'm lucky,' said Tom. 'I've got out of many scrapes since I have been here.' This made Blacky laugh.

'Bless you, young Tom, you have guts and I'm sure you mean what you say but…'

Tom butted in, 'We will get out and I will get you your legs back, I promise.' Then he stood up, walked to the steel bars and shook them with range. In front of Blacky's eyes, Tom turned into a wolf.

Karl, Phina and the water team had been going at some speed for nearly an hour when Karl picked up a heat signature and told the others. They called the strategic centre to see if any friendly forces were in the area but all they got was static on their communicators.

Hollie held tight to her sea slug; they were travelling like dolphins surfing the waves. After half an hour, as the slug left the water, her heat sensor in her helmet made out a heat mass in the water that she judged to be about ten miles away. They were closing in on it fast. She told the rest of the team that their best option was to get close under water then leave the slugs and recce the heat signature she had received. At that point, she could not make it out, so they would approach it very cautiously.

'It has disappeared,' said Karl into his helmet to everyone.

'Get ready for action. I think they must have seen us and gone underwater. Two of you stay on the surface in mutual support and keep watch up top. Everyone else down with me.'

Tanibeth and the Octavians went away from them. Phina did not want them getting hurt and if whatever it was did not see them, they could still escape. They set their weapons to lethal, dived and waited for the encounter.

Hollie got closer. As she did, she felt something strange inside her, something familiar, something that made her smile and she did not know why. 'Everyone hold fast, I'm going forward alone.'

'No way, boss!' her second-in-command snapped at her.

'Yes, way,' she replied, 'and that's an order. I have a feeling these are not the enemy.'

'How can you say that for certain, boss?' said her second-in-command.

'Because I can feel it,' she said. 'Keep all-round protection; you know the drill. I will report back very shortly. Trust me!' Hollie left them and swam towards the heat source.

Karl also felt strange. 'Someone is coming. I know they are friendly,' he told Phina 'I sense no danger.'

'What do you mean, you sense no danger?' she asked.

'I just do. I just know. It was the same with the lizsnake, I just knew, that's all.'

'Okay, everyone change your weapon setting to NL,' she said. NL meant incapacitate, non-lethal. They all changed their settings as a figure emerged from the gloom.

'It's Hollie, I would recognise that shape anywhere,' said Karl.

'Really, Karl, you don't say. How are you so knowledgeable?' said Phina. Karl could feel his face reddening inside his helmet.

'It's okay,' Hollie called back to her teams. They started to advance towards her position.

Hollie did a scan and found the frequency for Karl and the teams with him.

Then she told her own team so they could all communicate.

'Well, if isn't Prince Charming and his merry men,' Hollie commented.

'Careful, Hollie, or you might get a clout. Phina is one of my merry men, as you put it,' replied Karl.

Hollie quickly responded, 'Sorry, Phina, I didn't notice you there.' Phina and Salina were Hollie's idols. Even though they were much older than she was, they had proven themselves many times to be superb warriors and it was her ambition to emulate them.

Reassuringly Phina replied, 'Don't worry, Holl, I'm not going to get upset, so don't worry.'

Hollie swam up to them and trod water.

'How come you know of Prince Charming and his merry men?' Karl asked Holly.

'My mother had travelled with your mother and she brought back some Earth fairy stories and read them to me when I was young,' she said. Then there was a shout in their ears.

'Terror shark!'

The last of Hollie's water team members who was swimming towards them was suddenly pushed out of the water in the jaws of a massive terror shark. Before they could react, the shark hit the water, sending white waves and spray all over the remaining teams treading water. Then it was gone with the warrior in its mouth.

'Look behind you!' Tanibeth shouted. Then she swam at the group treading water and jumped over all of them. High above them they saw the scales on her body sparkle with a multitude of colours reflecting in the sun, and then she dived into the water with a little splash and was gone. They all then saw the fin of the second terror shark turn and dart after Tanibeth.

'Can she swim faster than that shark?' called Karl.

'I don't know,' replied Phina. They all set their weapons to kill. Some of the team went under water, the remainder stayed afloat all watching out for terror sharks.

'We all need to get out of here.'

On cue, several sea slugs appeared. 'I am never going to call you sea slugs again,' said Phina.

The leader of the Serpennorse group approached her. 'We have found the craft you are searching for; it is an hour's swim away. There is land there and we could see a very large dark forest just in from the shoreline, about fifty feet from the water.'

'Can you take us?' asked Phina.

The Serpennorse shock its head. 'We can only carry nine, but we have called the Octavias back and they will be here soon. They sped away when the terror sharks appeared as they are no match for them.'

'In that case, Hollie, Karl, myself and six of the water team will go with you now. The remaining team members will wait for the arrival of the Octavians and catch us up.'

Hollie sorted her teams out then they were off but not before Karl asked one of the team to ask one of the Octavians to search for Tanibeth.

'What a way for a water specialist to die, especially Sam, he had so much experience,' Hollie told Karl.

Overhearing her, Phina gave her some advice. 'Try not to think too deeply about it, Hollie, or you will go mad. I have lost count of the warriors that have died fighting with me. Every one of them was as good as Sam. You will get hardened to it. You can't bring them back, just think of the good times as you remember them.'

After that neither Karl nor Hollie said a word, but they were both thinking different things. Karl about his brother and Hollie about how she was going to tell Sam's life partner.

Phina and her group got on the Serpennorse and they splashed off leaving the remaining warriors treading water and keeping up their all-round defence. Those left knew they would not lose another warrior like that; they were determined.

Tristan and Rowena left the sail craft dock and made their way down to the strategic centre where they were met by the king and some very learned people in robes all looking very knowledgeable. Frederick gave his daughter a long embrace. 'By Atta, it's good to see you so well, Rowena. It is so good to have you close once more. All I need now are your brothers to return where I will be keeping them under lock and key. After what has happened to you, I bet you would rather be back on Earth now, don't you?'

'No, not at all, Father,' Row told him. She noticed the king had a faraway look in his eyes. 'You're thinking about Tom, aren't you, Dad?'

'You know me already,' he replied. 'I am worried, about you, your brothers, Phina, Salina, Hollie and all the teams out there. My heart weighs very heavy now.'

Row clasped her father's hand. 'We all feel it, Dad, you're not alone. The sooner we get Tom and Karl back and safe with us once more, the happier we will all be.' Tears filled their eyes. Row wiped hers away with her sleeve then her father's. 'Come on, let's get everyone back.'

'You are wise beyond your years, Row. Let's get to it.' He turned to face all those now assembled. 'Right, everyone, thank you for getting here so fast. I believe the time is now right to strike at the Dark and destroy them. I want plans made up for the invasion of the Dark quarter and the total destruction of this evil once and for all. That's the first point. Secondly has anyone received any updates from Phina, Karl, Hollie or the water teams? I would also like an update from the blue moon about how the preparations are going before we start the next phase. We will need the healers more than ever in the next few days.'

Tristan informed him that the leader of the healers, Gebhuza, was returning from Earth, where he had been for the last two months, to ensure everything possible would be done by the healers before the battle that was sure to follow. Kurt was also returning from Linasfarn and should be with them very soon

'Good.' Then the king explained why the preachers were here. He was talking about the people in robes, the greatest minds on Elemtum. Information from Kurt had been sent to them regarding what was below Linasfarn and the abnormalities in readings that had been gathered. Some of the information had been sent back by the Zells. 'I am going to wait for Kurt to arrive. I think it is important that he listens to what the preachers have to say because it will be a major factor in our planning. So, until then, people, please relax or go and have something to eat. We will re-assemble back here in one hour. Thank you all.' Then he turned to Row and Tristan. 'Can you take Row to her quarters to freshen up and change into a combat suit. You never know what will happen next. Can you run through the suit with her too, Tristan? I want her to have a side arm and a rayzor.'

Row and Tristan left but did not head for the rooms Karl, Tom and Row should have shared. Instead, they headed for a set of rooms within the strategy centre. The room layout was very similar to the one now in ruins above them that she would have had. Once again, Row's room was in the middle and her brothers' rooms were either side as they had been above. Tristan did not need to show her how to operate the toilet, she had already been locked in the empty room with the mirror at the infirmary on the blue moon. He showed her how to open the sliding door to the walk-in wardrobe, the personal armoury and store where her personal equipment was kept. Once she had change into an all-round combat suit that was good for all most any combat situation, Tristan showed her how to operate the different functions of the suit, helmet, gloves and boots. He knew she could handle the rayzor because she had grown up with one as a child. He only had to familiarise her with the handheld weapon. It was just a little bit different to the one he had trained her with on Earth. It fired pulses and not bullets and it could be lethal or non-lethal. She asked what the doors were either side of the room. He told her that to the left was Tom's room and the right, Karl's.

'Can I have a look?'

'There are your brothers, they won't mind.'

Row opened the door to Tom's room and walked in. On shelves around the room were all the toys from his rucksack that he had brought from Earth. Seeing them, Row realised how young her baby brother was and the danger he was now in. Tears welled up in her eyes. Tristan said something to her, but she did not reply so he walked round to her and saw the tears.

'What's wrong, Row?' he asked, now very concerned because she didn't cry that often. Row then started to cry.

'Oh, Dad, he's so young. Why would anyone want to harm him? If they knew him, they wouldn't hurt him.'

Tristan held her, trying to calm her. 'It's okay, Row. We will get him back, I promise.'

'Will we, Dad? Will we really get him back? You've seen what the Dark do to people. They just destroy. What chance has a little boy got?'

'I know how you feel, Row. We will do everything in our power to get him back. I, nor any one on Elemtum, will stop until he is back with us. I promise you that.'

Row looked up into the face of the one person she had known all her life. She was comforted by his words because she knew he meant it. She stepped back and wiped her eyes. 'That's it, that's the last tears until I see Tom and Karl again.' She smiled at Tristan. At that moment, she longed to go back to what they once had back on Earth, then that thought was gone. She knew that would never be her life again. She turned and walked back into her room; Tristan followed her.

'Do you want to look in Karl's room?' he asked.

Row shook her head and said, 'No, I don't think so. I'm feeling quite hungry. Fancy something to eat?' she asked.

Tristan did fancy some food, so they left Row's room and headed for the dining hall. Most of the people from the earlier strategic centre meeting were there, standing in groups with the people they felt most comfortable with discussing what academics and warriors discussed.

The shaking of the bars had brought the attention of one of the Dark warrior guards. In his new wolf form Tom had retreated to the dark shadows of the cell that could not be seen from the bars. The Dark warrior came to the bars. Slurring, he screamed for whoever was making the noise to come forward. The warrior could only loosely be called a warrior; he was very overweight and smelly, he also limped on a damaged leg. He spat his words out. It looked like he had a few teeth missing either through not cleaning them or someone had probably knocked them out.

'It was the boy, you oaf,' shouted Blacky.

'Where's the boy?' the warrior spat.

'He escaped,' Blacky shouted back.

'If you've eaten him, I will slice you up,' shouted the warrior now in a rage as he fumbled for the keys to open the cell door. A legless cat with human bits was no match for the warrior and the oaf knew that because he often went in and beat Blacky just for a laugh when he was bored. The cell door opened and he limped towards Blacky, a club raised ready to strike the hapless cat thing grinning in the corner. He closed in on the cat. From the blackness of the cell, two bright blue eyes appeared. They raced towards, him then he was dead. The oaf was not quick enough to react to the pouncing wolf.

Tom the wolf had pounced onto the oaf's chest, knocking him over. Then his fangs ripped at the warrior's jugular vein. Between shock and the massive loss of blood, the warrior died very quickly. Tom did not let go until the guard was dead. He then turned and looked at the strange creature now in front of him; he recognised the panther somewhere in the back of his memory, so he did not attack it.

'There's a good boy, Tom,' Blacky said, trying to get the measure of the young wolf. He was not attacked so that was good, he thought. Recollections of helping the panther creature returned to the wolf and he walked over to Blacky and allowed him to pull himself onto his back.

'Go, Tom, go. Get us out of here!'

They ran off into the dimly lit passage, Tom's senses now heightened, sniffing, stopping to listen every now and then, sniffing, stopping, listening for the faintest sound. They reached a corridor junction. Nothing. So, on Tom ran. Blacky held on to Tom's fur with all his might; he did not want to be left behind now. Tom could hear sounds behind them but nothing in front of him, so he picked up speed. As he ran, he noticed some large wooden and steel doors on every side of the damp corridor. He knew inside would be some poor soul existing until he was killed. He made a mental note to come back and let everyone go, but for now he ran until he came to another corridor junctions and stopped. 'Any ideas, Blacky?' he asked.

'Go right,' Blacky responded, 'that way I am sure leads to the arena.'

'Arena?' Tom replied. 'Why on earth would we want to go there?'

'Because, Tom, there will be no one there unless there is a fight on. That brings them all together to watch the gore, then it's a bad place to be. I know it will be deserted. These cells lead all the way to the arena, so prisoners can be dragged to their deaths for the amusement of the Dark and the fat guards don't have to travel too far. And the best bit of all, Tom… you can get to the outside world from there.'

Tom went right until they got near the end of that particular corridor. Here Tom could smell and hear life from the other side of the open door that was adjacent to the steel gate that led out into the arena. Blacky told Tom that was the guard room where the gate keys were kept, Normally, there would be three guards with weapons.

'Any ideas?' Tom asked.

'Normally this time of day they will be asleep because there was a fight this morning and if Labatina and the Wolf general were happy they would pay their warriors with venom, which is an alcoholic liquid, very potent. As long as the alarm is not sounded, I am sure you could sneak in and take the keys.'

'It sounds too easy,' said Tom.

'Yes, it does. I'm a little concerned that the warrior we got past earlier has not raised the alarm. It could be a trap.'

'It most probably is,' replied Tom. 'But I will tell you this, Blacky, I would rather die escaping than in a cell waiting to die.'

'You are right there, young man, sorry, wolf. It will be a pleasure to die at your side, so it will.'

'Me too, Blacky, but I'm not writing us off just yet.' Tom, with Blacky on his back, gently padded towards the open door. Slowly he pushed his nose around the corner. What Blacky had said was true. The three Dark warriors were fast asleep. Tom noticed a key on the floor at the feet of one of the inebriated warriors.

'That's too easy, Blacky. It's a trap! Tom thought.

'Well, then shall we fall into it and see where it takes us?'

'Okay.' He stealthily crept in, bending down in front of the warrior with the key at his feet. Blacky leant over and picked it up with one of his people hands. Still there was no reaction from the warriors. Nothing. Tom backed out into the corridor, Still nothing.

'Right then, young Thomas the wolf, take me to the gate and we will see if this key works.' Tom walked forward sniffing, listening. Still no sign of life. Blacky stretched and put the key in the lock, then turned it. There was a loud click, then nothing.

'Push the gate,' said Tom, and he helped Blacky by putting all his weight against the gate as Blacky pushed it. It swung open with a very loud creak and a bang as it slammed against the wall. Once more there was nothing. Tom walked through onto the sand-covered arena floor expecting something to happen. Still there was nothing. 'It might not be a trap,' said Tom.

'Don't relax yet, Tom; it still doesn't seem right. It was too easy. Look over directly in front of us.' In the gloom, Tom made out two massive wrought-iron gates.

That is definitely the exit, Tom thought to himself. He wasn't sure if he should run fast or walk slowly. Blacky heard Tom's thoughts.

'Run fast, Tom; never walk to your death.'

So, Tom ran... halfway across the arena floor he could feel his heart pounding in his chest then he came sliding to a sudden halt. The trap they knew was coming was sprung.

Suddenly lights blazed down on them. Tom looked around, but everything had now disappeared due to the light dazzling them. For several seconds he was blinded. Gradually his sight came back to him. Above the main gate that would have led to their freedom was a balcony and behind a bright light was a dark figure that he could not make out due to the dazzling light behind him. Then a familiar voice boomed out around the arena.

'I will enjoy watching you both die because you have been a thorn in my side.'

He can't be talking about me, thought Tom. I've only been a short time... I think?

'I believe he is talking about both of us,' said Blacky.

The voice continued, 'I have wanted to slap you since the first day I met you.'

'I know that voice. It's the Wolf master, I'm sure of it,' Tom thought to Blacky.

Then around the arena all the lights came on and it was slowly filling with silent Dark warriors. The spot lights turned off. Then Tom could see his tormentor. It was Detor Eosin, the Wolf master.

Tom went to shout why, but all that came out was a howl but that was good enough because the Wolf master understood, and he started to laugh.

'Pathetic,' he shouted. 'Now you will die, as my lady wishes.'

From behind him came Labatina, red hair flowing down across her bare shoulders. Tom noticed she was adorned in Dark tribal art from head to toe. It looked like she was completely clothed but she wasn't.

'Nice to see she dressed for the occasion,' said Blacky.

Then Labatina spoke. 'I will bath in your blood, little bastard, then I will wash away you and your mother for good. Then it will be the time of the Dark for Elemtum and the hidden worlds. I will rule them all alongside my son and daughter who will soon come to me… It is their destiny.'

'I am no bastard. I have a mother and father. My father is the king of wolves and the emperor of Elemtum and together my family, including my brother and sister will save you, Labatina, and kill that traitor standing next to you, so bring it on!' Tom shouted, now back as a boy with Blacky on his back.

Labatina laughed. 'Mighty words for one so small and far away from his family. Don't forget, little boy, that the family you talk of is also my family and you have no part in it. As I speak, they head this way to join me.' The now full crowd roared and the massive gates in front of them started to open. In strode five Dark Mangoul warriors all with a vast array of menacing and deadly looking weapons. The crowd erupted once more. Queen Labatina raised her arms and the arena fell silent. She looked down at the five warriors and pointed to Tom with Blacky on his back.

'Kill them and make it slow!' she screamed. The Mangoul began to run at them. Then Tom heard in his head a reassuring voice. Tom, again a wolf, turned and ran the way he had just come from leaving the Mangoul behind him, no match for the speed of a young wolf.

'What are you doing, Tom?' Blacky shouted in his head.

'It's okay, Blacky, we are going to be saved,' Tom told him.

The boy's gone mad, the panther thought, as a dark shadow descended on them. With a jolt, Tom was in the air and Blacky was hanging on once more for dear life. Two talons had wrapped around the little wolf, avoiding Blacky, lifting them both up into the blue cloudless sky watched over by the blue moon. Tom could hear the queen's screams then Detor Eosin barking his orders trying to order his troops to pursue. But Arn, Tom and Blacky had the advantage. All available Dark warriors were in the arena and it would take them some time to get to the flying lizards outside the arena. By then, they would be long gone.

'Arn, how did you find me? How did you know I was here?' thought Tom.

'We are together, Tom, we are one. I will always be close.' Then he did a roll and tossed Tom and a screaming Blacky into the sky as he had done on that first day. When Tom landed on Arn's back, a boy again, but this time he also had the strange beast, Blacky, behind him. Tom snuggled deep into the feathers on the great eagle's back. Moments later he was asleep. It had been an exhausting day for a small boy, but now he felt safe. Arn flew fast and high, much higher than a flying lizard could go. He headed for the sun and the blue skies he could see over the horizon. Once settled, Blacky spoke to Arn and explained his predicament and how he had come to meet Tom as Arn flew on.

Chapter 16
Death and Deceit

After an hour, Kurt arrived back from Linasfarn so everyone returned to the strategic centre where it was all quite apart from some of the operations staff talking to teams out on the ground. The king started speaking, 'Thank you all for being patient. As you can see, Kurt is now amongst us. Welcome back, brother. Now, we can start the briefing by the preachers. Please carry on.' The king indicated to them to start.

'Hello, everyone. Some of you know me, but for the benefit of the others, I am Samee Diocesan...' She paused as though she was waiting for a reaction; there was none. After all, she was not talking to academics but warriors. Tristan smiled because he had been at university with Samee and he not only knew her personally but very intimately as well. They had been very close at university for five terms. She continued, 'I have overseen the think tank which has been studying time and the relationship with our worlds, including Earth and Penterum. When Tristan sent me the data from below Linasfarn, it added to my theory about multiple time layers within Elemtum and, for that matter, our sister planet Earth as well.'

The warriors looked at each other. 'What do you mean by multiple time layers?' asked Kurt.

Samee blushed when she realised who was talking. She had asked to be combat trained when she was young just after leaving university, 'just in case' she had put it at the time and Kurt happened to be the one who taught her. They too had become very close, long before Kurt had settled with Raphina. It seemed she became close with most men she met and, why not, she was single. She did have the brain the size of a planet that did attract warriors, it has to be said. The blushing died down as she answered his question. 'We all know what happened when the Earth and its moon fell away from Elemtum. Well, my theory is that when it fell away, time itself fractured leaving different layers of time within our world and the Earth. I have never been to the Earth, but I am almost positive this is the case there too. So, what I am saying is, if you had a cross section of Elemtum, you would see that there are many different layers that have long since died and been covered over. We all know that is how we get minerals and such things. Well, there are also layers of time trapped within our worlds. Each layer has one or two points at which it can be accessed. For example, when the Zells came to your aid, they used a trapped time pathway. We knew nothing about them or the pathway until they arrived with the gallant Salina and Prince Thomas.'

One of the warriors butted in. 'The prince is too young for you, Samee!' Everyone laughed, including Samee.

She responded, 'Yes, thank you for that. I can see I have a reputation. Now, can we continue?'

The king also spoke. 'Yes, this is a serious briefing, save the humour for afterwards, please.'

It all went quiet. Samee continued, 'As I was saying, when the Zells came to your aid, they had come through a crack in time. These cracks are everywhere. In the sea off Linasfarn and below Linasfarn. The ones we know about we call threads; the world pathway to Earth and there is a time fracture that we have recently been made aware of below the great lake. We now know that this one that leads to the Jade Sea, from there to who knows where? So, I am convinced there are others. Think of them as superhighways to worlds or parts of planets that may only take us seconds to get to without realising, as was the case with the bottom of the lake at Linasfarn. So, to finalise, in essence what I am saying is we have worlds within worlds that we are only starting to learn about. For example, the Zells' home. We have superhighways in time. While you are in them, time is different, maybe seconds, days, years ahead or behind. We won't know that until we study the ones we know about and discover any others that there might be out there.' Just as everyone thought she had finished she continued, 'The amazing thing is the Zells' world could be light years away in distance yet it only took minutes to enter ours from theirs.' She took a breath. 'The other amazing thing is your body does not change when you travel through these time fractures or, as I like to call, them time pathways. It's mind blowing when you sit and think about it.'

'A form of time travel,' said Row.

'Yes, exactly,' said Samee 'How did you know about that? she asked.

'I lived on Earth. It's in fiction books, in films and TV shows,' said Row.

'Yes, yes, I will have to speak to you afterwards. Some of these stories could be closer to the truth than Earth realises. By the way, who are you?' She looked at Tristan who had his hand on Row's shoulder. 'Is she yours, Tristan?' Samee asked.

'The king's daughter,' he replied to the relief of Samee. She smiled at Row and winked at Tristan. 'I will have to talk to you after as well... there I'm finished, lord.' She nodded to the king.

'Thank you, Samee, I will have to talk to you after as well,' said the king.

'I will look forward to that,' she replied.

The king responded very quickly, 'To talk about your theory.' Samee smiled and nodded her head once more.

The king continued, 'So, we must conclude that the Dark have found some of these time pathways and have been using them to their advantage.'

'Lord, may I?' said one of the learned preachers.

'Yes, please, Minister Changoff. If it has a bearing on all this, then please do,' said the king.

'I have been studying time along with Samee, although we are not close.' Samee blushed once more but was intrigued about what her mentor was about to say. 'I study time and history, I agree wholly with Samee. Everything she has said is correct, but I will now add another dimension. I have two main points. I am now convinced that parts of time trap evil and, if you come across it, you too become evil, as long as all the factors are there. After a lifetime of studying this here and on Earth, I believe it was the ancient people, the first to inhabit Earth, who first found these time cracks and, somehow, they managed to turn them on and off. I also believe they travelled the Earth and developed the art of high-speed interplanetary travel. They even visited Linasfarn before their end came.'

'Why did their end come?' someone asked.

'I don't rightly know, to be truthful. Anyway, the time pathways that they used enable them to travel through Earth and I believe they reached Elemtum, by mistake landing on Linasfarn. They did not realise this was another world. Something happened and it all stopped and was forgotten. I believe something wiped them out.'

'Do you mean the pathway to Earth could have been known to ancient peoples of the Earth, like the ancient people of Egypt? I lived on Earth for several years, so I know some of the people of Earth think things like the pyramids were made by people from space but I guess they did not realise they were in space at the time, just another island. Also, I have been told it could have been people from all over the world that found the time pathways or why would there be the different miniature models from different parts of Earth in one place, i.e. Linasfarn?' Row asked?

'Yes, as you have rightly said but not our pathways to Earth, the threads, but the time pathways that we are finding now.'

'Well, the young warrior female is right. The pyramids are one example of their culture, as is Stonehenge. The Mayan temples are another, as are the Inca temples and there are several more that I will not bore you with at this time. The main activity on Earth was centred around what Earth people now think is a myth, but one such place was Earth's capital city. Its name was Atlantis. If you can come across and speak to the older of the Selessi people, their ancestors lived there long after the original ancient peoples had gone. Likewise, the ancient man moved into the structures left behind by them and used them as their dwellings which grew into their future empires but the people in the know either died or moved away'.

'Ah, we have some sad news about the Selessi people. It seems they have been wiped out by the Dark,' Tristan told everyone assembled. 'We know of only one survivor. She is, at present, with Phina and Prince Karl; her name is Tanibeth.'

'Oh, my goodness, that is a great loss to our world,' Changoff told everyone. He was genuinely distressed by the news.

Kurt asked him about his second point.

After he recovered, he continued. 'Oh yes, my second point... Well, my second point is that I believe these time pathways, or some of these pathways, hold the essence of evil and those, as I said before, whoever is touched by it and is at the time in the right state of mind... well, I believe the Earth term for it is they go mad. If they are mad and are touched by this, they become homicidal and very destructive maniacs. I will give you an Earth example... Adolf Hitler. He was a lowly unintelligent below average man of the times, but he went on to rule an intelligent hard-working country and nearly a world. What happened to him to make him that man? I believe he came across a pathway or someone that had knowledge of such a thing. We all know of the horrors his regime committed. There are many in Earth's history, and now there is one in ours and, I'm sorry to say my lord, it is Labatina... I believe she came across one such pathway on her travels of the Earth. When the Dark comes through evil, builds up. It seems to seep out slowly but slow enough for the world's population to deal with, as I said, Hitler, Stalin, etc. Our world is now touched but it does seem a much quicker escalation because there is a strong power behind it focused on one or two souls here. Labatina for one, but I don't believe she is working alone. I might add a touch of hope that every civilisation I have studied has always defeated this evil and then it festers until another host appears and off it goes again on its path of destruction and death until it is once more stopped.'

'So, are you saying this too is Elemtum's future, going from one evil episode to another, generation after generation?' asked the king.

'I fear it may well be, lord' replied Changoff. The king thanked him for his words. Samee told all assembled that she believed all that Changoff said was most probably true.

'Well, there we have it, people, this could be a long war which may never end. Best we all get our heads together and come up with a plan and quickly if my son is to be saved, as well as our way of life,' said the king.

Karl, Phina and the water team members with them were now within sight of the submersible craft. It had been beached and was partially on its left side; there was no obvious sign of life. The beach was golden sand; the blue green sea made an idyllic picture postcard view, but it was spoiled by a thick dark jungle fifty metres beyond the beach. They swam directly behind the craft, in line with it, making it hard for anyone observing them from the land in front. It would soon be night, so the plan was to wait out at sea, then at dusk come in and occupy the submersible until dawn. There would be a forward observation post (FOP) just inside the jungle, amongst the vegetation. Two members of the water team would man that to give early warning of any danger, and if need be, hold the ground while the remainder of the team get to the water then they would cover the FOP's extraction. If the remaining water team members arrived, they would set up a second OP and the remaining team members would enter the submersible. Unbeknown to Karl's group, the Octavians had got back to the remaining water team and they mistook the instructions they were given because Tanibeth was not there to properly translate. So, the water team and the Octavians were now heading to a point some ten miles north of Karl's group's location. Night began to fall, and the team moved up to the submersible where they stealthily made their way to the jungle's edge after waiting some minutes to make sure there had been no reaction to their arrival. Carefully, they patrolled one hundred metres into the jungle. They found the tracks of the Dark leading into the jungle but there were footprints on the ground that did not match Tom's. So, either he was carried or he was taken off before the submersible beached or he was never on the sub. After half an hour, the FOP was set up and the remainder of the group retreated to the submersible. Hollie was one of the water team in the FOP. more because she had only ever done one OP in her training and this was the real thing, so she wanted the experience. Toby was the second team member with her; he was a water team veteran with years of hardened battle experiences behind him, he was just the person to mentor and guide Hollie which she was more than happy about. Back in the submersible one of the water team set up a high frequency dish to try and contact the water team still at sea, but unless they too had set up a dish they would not be able to contact each other. There was not a lot Karl or Phina could do because the water team had all the security and observation posts covered, so they decided to get their heads down and try and get some sleep. The inside of the submersible was quite large so there were plenty of areas to sleep, including six bunk beds that they decided to occupy for the night. As Phina had told Karl, 'any fool can be uncomfortable'.

They went to bed and tried to get some sleep. For what seemed an age, they tossed and turned. Eventually, after two hours, they had both fallen asleep, still blissfully unaware that Tom had escaped earlier with Arn and was safer than they were. There was no real plan to what they were doing, they were just doing. They all felt the need to try and get as close to Tom as they could. If possible, the new plan was to rescue him. What seemed like minutes after they had fallen asleep, a gentle hand shook them awake; it was Hollie.

'Good morning, have you had a good sleep?' she asked them. They had what seemed like a very quick one, they replied. Hollie had taken turns with Toby, so she had managed to get four hours which was not bad compared to Karl and Phina's six hours. The FOP had been changed over during the night and they had received an update from the other water team who had confirmed that they were now ten miles from Hollie's location and would be patrolling through the night to get to them.

Tom, Blacky and Arn were now safe in Warriors' Rest. Blacky was with a healer who was seeing what they could do for him and Tom was having some breakfast with Raif and his mother, Raphina. A message had been sent to the king about Tom's arrival and his rescue by Arn, but so far, they had been unable to contact Karl, Phina and the water team to inform them of the good news and recall them to safety. They were amazed that he had managed to escape from the depths of the Dark's clutches. Arn was a hero; he was being pampered for the daring rescue he had undertaken on his own. None of the Wolf warriors believed Tom had turned into a wolf at such a young age and they were all still coming to terms with the fact that the Wolf master was a traitor. That information had been sent directly to the strategic centre. Warriors' Rest was a strange place to be in at that time. There was elation that Tom was safe and disbelief that the Wolf master was a traitor. Many questions were floating about how long and why, constantly on every one's lips, except Row. She had never liked him; she had always thought there was something not quite right about him. There was even more good news when the blue moon reported that Salina had regained consciousness and was doing well. She had to be all but restrained to stop her returning to join the fight.

As Tom and Raif talked, the door opened and in walked Clomp with his normal cheery grin on his face. He saw Tom sitting there, his face beamed. 'Master Tom, you're alive. I was going to come and save you, but Master Raif stopped me.' Clomp bounded over to Tom, bodily lifted him from his seat and gave him a huge hug which Tom thought was more of a bear hug. When Clomp put Tom down, he told him he was sorry about his brave farther but Clomp was still jolly. He told Tom the king had personally told him that his father had slain twenty Dark warriors until he was overrun and killed. Clomp told Tom the king had said to him, 'Your father was a great warrior. He died well. with honour. There is to be a statue erected in his memory. Not only that, the king wants me to become the master armourer… me a master. Tom, can you believe that?' said Clomp. Tom was happy for him; he liked Clomp and they laughed about the stupid things that had happened since his arrival.

Clomp joined them for breakfast and they continued talking about what they had done since they last met. It was very obvious to Clomp, Raif and his mother that Tom had been in the thick of things since leaving them. Raphina had been informed by Kurt that their youngest daughter Salina was now doing well. They would all be together very soon as the king was bringing everyone down from Great Porum to make Warriors' Rest his new operational centre so he could be closer to the enemy, meaning less distance to travel to kill them all.

Raphina forbade Raif and Clomp from taking Prince Tom outside the citadel's walls. If they did, Clomp would not become a master armourer and Raif would have to face his father's and the king's discipline. They promised to keep Tom safe and, with the words of Raphina ringing in their ears, 'That poor boy has been through more than anyone of his age should suffer in a lifetime and he's only been here a couple of days.'

As they left the dining hall, they met Blacky being pushed in a wheelchair by one of the healers. He told them excitedly that they would take him to a place called the blue moon and grow his legs back and it would only take three days. He was over the moon, literally, and very excited because the sail craft that brought the king and his operations staff here would then take him and some of the other wounded warriors up to the blue moon. The next time they would see him he would be a panther again. He added that he had decided to keep the brain he presently had just, so he didn't eat Tom. Tom was very grateful for that and they all wished him well as the excited parts of the panther were wheeled away.

A Wolf warrior came over to them and addressed Raphina. 'My lady, I have a message from the king and Lord Kurt De-Callen. The prince is to be kept with you. A healer who is a specialist in the wolf transformation process will be over shortly to give the prince an in-depth medical. They are concerned for him because it has never been known for one so young to transform into its wolf state.'

Raphina thanked the warrior then turned to Tom. 'Prince Thomas De-Callen, you will stay with me until the healer arrives, Raif, Clomp it looks like you will not be getting the young prince into any more trouble. I will tell you now, young Master Clomp, the king has arranged for you to become an apprentice to your father's apprentice. He will teach you all you need to know so you can become the next master armourer, so go and find him and start your training. I was going to tell you later, but as I'm taking Tom with me now, you may as well shoot off.'

'Thank you, Lady De-Callen. See you later, Tom, Raif.' Then he was off, the quickest anyone had ever seen him run in his life. Before Raphina could say another word, Raif had answered her next question.

'Yes, I know, Mother, go and practice my rayzor drills again,' he said and, as he did, his shoulders dropped, gloom crossed his face.

'Don't be like that, Raif De-Callen. Pull your shoulders straight. Stand like a warrior, not a spoiled child.' Raif straightened up. 'That's better. What I was going to say was go and speak to the Master gunner. Tell him I think you are ready to be taught how to fire the turret guns.'

'Really?' he replied, then he went up to his mother, kissed her on the cheek then ran off towards the inner battlements. As he did so, he shouted back, 'See you later, Tom. Watch they don't put a needle up your bum. They like to do things like that.' Then he was gone.

'What does he mean "put a needle up my bum"? I'm not letting anyone put a needle up my bum,' he said, determined not to let it happen.

Raphina reassured him that Raif was only joking and nothing of the sort like that would happen. Reassured, Tom went with Raphina to the infirmary to await the healer's imminent arrival with his father. At the infirmary, they were greeted by the duty healer who told them they were honoured. The great healer Gebhuza Septima had returned from Earth and he would come and check the prince over to ensure he had not been damaged by his early transformation. Tom could not understand why anyone had to inspect, check, prod, do anything to him. He was fine and had never felt better in his whole short life. Raphina tried to convince Tom that his transformation should not have happened so early in his life and that he needed to be checked over to make sure he was all right internally. But Tom would not have it, especially when he found out the great healer was also one of Queen Labatina's closest friends and her fellow explorer. 'Just meet him, Tom. He's a nice person, a great healer. The best in fact,' said Raphina.

'Okay, but if I don't like him, I'm off,' he emphasised. They sat waiting, talking for almost an hour when the door opened and in walked a healer in a human in a very tight jump suit, too tight for his rather large belly. He also wore walking boots with a cravat around his neck. Tom noticed he was half blue and half normal skin coloured. 'Why are you half blue?' Tom asked before anyone had said a word.

The healer responded, 'How delightful. The little chap speaks his mind. Excuse me, Lady Raphina, so nice to see you once again. Radiant as ever.'

'Thank you, Gebhuza Septima. Charming as ever but you know I don't like that sort of thing.'

'Yes, my lady, remiss of me to forget.

'I don't like him,' said Tom. 'He's not real, he's a liar.'

Gebhuza walked towards Tom. 'Don't worry, Prince Thomas, it's probably something to do with the early change you have been through. Young one's should not become wolves as young as you have.'

'What would you know? I'm not staying for this idiot to fiddle with me,' shouted, Tom as he pushed Gebhuza away from him. Surprised, Gebhuza fell directly backwards, landing bum first on the floor,

'How dare you, you little imp?'

Raphina, who had been sitting, stood and tried to stop Tom as he ran towards her, away from Gebhuza who was looking for something or someone to help him up off the floor. Tom was off, running straight at the window.

'Stop that brat,' Gebhuza shouted at Raphina, who glared at him then returned her gaze to Tom who was now leaping at the closed window.

'No, Tom, stop, we are six levels up,' she shouted as she lunged for him, just missing the back of his foot then he had smashed through the window. He was gone! He began to fall. Shards of glass splintered around him, falling earth bound. Raphina, now at the window, watched Tom fall. Then, before her eyes the young Wolf prince became an eagle. His wings outstretched, he caught the air and, with one mighty beat, Tom's direction changed. He was now flying skywards as the shards of glass smashed to the ground ten feet below him. Around the front of the infirmary, passers-by instinctively looked up to where the smashing glass had come from. They saw the sixth-floor window that was shattered with Raphina now watching the eagle now soaring skyward.

'Tom, come back. You don't have to have the check-up, I promise' Raphina shouted after him but it fell on deaf ears. Tom was not listening; he was flying high, he wasn't in any mood to come back. A little disorientated, he just flew; he didn't know where he was going, he just flew.

'What are you gaping at, you idiot? It's your fault he's gone. Go and get him!' the now red-faced blue and white healer shouted at Raphina.

'Tom is right. There's something not quite right about you, I have always thought that,' Raphina shouted back at Gebhuza. Then she pushed him back down on the floor as he tried to get up.

'I have never been so insulted in my life. Your king will hear of this and that child needs a good lashing and an in-depth medical evaluation; he's not normal.'

Raphina walked quickly away as a warrior and a healer appeared at the door asking if everything was all right. Gebhuza knew he was no match for Raphina; she was very strong, intelligent and quick-witted. He would not go after her. He knew he would probably end up back on his backside with a black eye and a fat lip. The warrior and healer helped him up, then he stormed off, pushing his rescuers aside. He was heading for the king; he could not let this incident go unpunished.

'Bloody idiot,' Raphina muttered under her breath. Then she ordered a warrior to go to the eagle flight leader and ask him to come to her at her dwelling. 'If anyone can find him, Arn will.' The warrior had left for the eagle flight when the warrior and healer who helped Gebhuza up approached Raphina.

'I have never seen Gebhuza act like that, but I must admit he has been very short tempered towards us lately. I don't know what's happening to him. Can I tell you something strange, Lady Raphina?'

'Yes, of course you can, Shannon; we have known each other for many years.'

'I don't like to talk behind the great healer's back but when he brushed passed me, I felt a chill strike my soul. I have never had that before in my life, lady, not from a healer.'

'That's a bit of a coincidence, Shannon. Prince Tom was very upset when Gebhuza walked into the room. He called him not real and a liar. He did not like him and responded by leaping out the window. Now that's not a normal reaction for a child, is it?'

'Most definitely not, lady. That child sounds as though he was scared by him, definitely, and with you here the prince should have stayed quite calm. I just don't understand.'

Tom headed south. Something told him to go south. Why he did not know. Was it because he had just escaped from the Dark in the south? His heart was beating ten to the dozen and for some reason he was very angry about something; he did not know what. As he flew south, he started to feel calm then sensed he was being watched as a black shadow fell over his wing. He looked up. Above him now were Arn and Karl's eagle Alerio. They swooped down, gliding either side of him.

'You are rightly troubled, Thomas. We both felt pain and danger from within the great so-called healer. He is hiding something,' communicated Alerio.

'Follow us. We are going somewhere safe where you will be able to calm down. You have destiny. There is an old prophecy we need to tell you about. Follow us, you are safe with us,' Arn told him.

The three of them began to turn and climb then Alerio broke away. 'Thomas, stay close to Arn and don't be scared. You have a destiny, as does Karl who will need my help very shortly, so I must leave you both now, but we will be together again in a different place.' Alerio turned away from them and headed south. They turned north.

'Where's he going?' asked Tom.

'He has a destiny with Karl, as I have a destiny with you,' replied Arn. They continued to climb and headed north-east.

Through the advanced secure communication system, Karl, Phina and the water team received the news the mission was scrubbed as Thomas had returned and promptly disappeared in the form of an eagle. If seen, his location was to be reported back to command. If possible, caught and returned to his father at Warriors' Rest. Hollie and Phina decided to stay put and await the arrival of the second part of their water team which was heading their way. Then they would all leave the area and return to the lake at Great Porum.

'Bloody hell, what has he been up to? Did you know he could transform into an eagle?' Karl asked Phina.

'Your brother's biological mother was one of the last from a mythical people who were closest to the soul of the planet. What I mean by that, was that they sensed the planet and all living things on the planet. It was believed, although never proven, that there was a bit of their souls in every living thing on this planet and they were particularly close to the eagles. It was said in the old writings that were discovered some time ago that Tom's mother's people could form into any living thing. So, unlike you, whose mother is a Wolf and father is the king of wolves, you can only form between people and wolves. In theory, your brother could potentially form into any living thing.'

'So, where are the people of Tom's mother? You are talking about Elizabeth, aren't you?' Karl confirmed.

'Yes. It was said only the females of their people had this connection with the world and the males were fearsome warriors. Then a plague hit the people that no one knows where it came from. Anyway, it decimated her people.' Elizabeth and her father, Jacob, survived but they only because your father, the king, rescued them after the eagles told him of a people that were being exterminated by a savage plague that killed only them. Elizabeth was brought up with Tristan and Kurt, much as you and Tom were. She became their sister and they truly loved her, Anyway, your father and Elizabeth fell in love and became soulmates. She had helped him get over the loss of Labatina. As you know, your father was seriously injured in the attack by the Dark, Elizabeth was killed. What you didn't know was that her father was also killed on the same day. He was the last of his people, that is apart from Elizabeth's child, Tom, you and Row's half-brother.'

'Didn't you say that it was only females that had these powers?' asked Karl.

'Yes, that's what we thought,' replied Phina.

'Bloody hell, my brother never does anything by half does he. I remember Tristan and Kurt told us back on Earth that Elizabeth was their sister. It all makes sense now.'

The communications warrior interrupted them, 'Phina, the FOP is reporting movement and a lot of it from several different areas, all advancing on their position, Hollie has told them to return to our location. They are bugging out ASAP.' They all put their helmets on and readied their weapons.

The FOP returned to Hollie, telling her they had better move fast or they would be surrounded. Their only way out would be back into the sea. But they would have to move immediately. Phina and Karl, along with the warriors inside the craft, came out and everyone got behind the craft for protection. Hollie told her team to get in the water and cover them. She and Phina would hold the Dark off, giving them time to get away. Her team and Karl refused. Phina ordered Karl to leave, but Karl said he outranked Phina as a prince of the king. Then their argument was interrupted by the voice of the Wolf master. 'Give up and you will not suffer the fate of your unfortunate water team.'

From within the jungle foliage something was thrown out and landed twenty feet in front of them. It was the severed head of one of the water team who had been patrolling towards them. Then one by one the heads of the rest of the team were thrown onto the sand.

'Bastards,' Hollie said under her breath. 'That's it all, of you get in the water. I will hold them off.'

Phina was standing behind Hollie. She brought the hilt of her rayzor up and struck Hollie on the back of the neck, stunning her. She fell to the sand. Phina turned to the water team gathered around them. 'Take her with you. This is my destiny. Tell her I'm sorry but it's not her time yet.' The team obeyed and dragged Hollie into the sea, out of sight of the Dark, behind the craft. 'Karl, you go with them,' she told him.

The Wolf master's voice echoed out from the jungle line once more. 'Give up and you will be treated fairly... Answer me!' he screamed after a long wait for a reply.

'Yeh, like hell we will,' said Phina. Then she shouted back, 'Come on then. You and me end it now. If I win my team goes unharmed, if you win you can do what you like.' There was silence from Detor Eosin; he was obviously thinking about what she had said. Unknown to him, her team had already gone and she was playing for time.

Detor Eosin replied, 'You and me, Phina… come out and I will meet you and kill you. It would be a shame because I did like you and your sister. What a waste.'

Angered by the remark, Phina walked out from behind the craft knowing she was the only one left. She would draw the fight out giving Karl and the water team a bit more time to escape. Out in front of the craft, the traitor was nowhere to be seen. She knew she was a better fighter than he ever was, so she relished the chance to fight and kill him. The rest of the Dark would probably slaughter her afterwards then that would be that. She was not scared; she relished the opportunity to die as a warrior with the added satisfaction of killing Detor Eosin.

'Coward,' she shouted into the jungle. Then the Black jungle parted and Detor Eosin stepped out and walked towards her then stopped. Unknown to both, a wolf was watching them from the top of the craft, hidden by the small conning tower. Detor lifted his arm and waved for her to come towards him.

'Come on, Phina, meet your fate,' he shouted.

Phina started to walk towards him, lifting her rayzor, eyes focused on the traitor's face. Detor Eosin lowered his arms just as a lance came flying from within the jungle. Phina did not see it until it passed close to the Wolf master. She knew she had lost. She did not have the time to react quickly enough but the wolf saved her. The wolf had seen the lance flying towards her. It leapt between her and the lance. The lance struck the wolf in its left rib; the force of the blow sent the wolf and the lance into Phina, bowling her over. The Wolf master did not move. Getting up, Phina went to the dying wolf now lying on its side. The spear had snapped and the last desperate breaths of life were ebbing away. She looked into the wolf's dimming eyes and saw Karl.

'Oh no, Karl, not you!' She pulled her helmet off and cradled the wolf's head in her arms. His breathing had stopped. Phina knew the prince was dead. Gently she placed his head on the sand and stood up. As she looked up the handle of Detor Eosin's rayzor struck her across the head, knocking her out. Behind him swarms of Dark warriors streamed out of the jungle and gathered around the two bodies. Several of them prodded the dead wolf with spears and knives, several started to rip the combat suit from Phina's unconscious body.

'Stop!' Detor shouted. 'Leave the Wolf princess alone, she is mine. Tie her and take her back. If the queen sees you stabbing her son, she will not be happy with you. Leave him alone! Where is the lancer that threw the lance that killed the queen's son?' The crowed went silent, then a strong voice broke the silence.

'Lord, you told me to throw the lance at the princess. I did not know the queen's son would leap out. She would not blame me for that,' said the lancer.

'Grab him,' Detor ordered. The Dark warriors around the lancer took hold of him. There were so many hands that he could not move. He floated, manhandled aloft the screaming Dark warriors towards Detor until he was finally above the lifeless body of the wolf.

'See what you have done! You will become one with the Dark!'

'No, lord, you will become one with the Dark when I tell the queen you ordered me,' shouted the lancer.

'Too late, prince slayer. Think of me saving you from the wrath of the queen. At least this will be quick.' Detor smiled as he slowly drew the sharp blade across the now struggling lancer's neck. The baying crowd released him. As he fell to the ground, writhing, he grasped at his neck, his fingers entered the gaping wound where bubbles of blood frothed from the gash. Large eyes pleaded for help then Detor lifted his rayzor and the lancer's head fell onto the sand next to the body of the lancer. The head and eyes stared at the lifeless body of the Wolf prince.

'Drag that thing away from the queen's son and find something to put the wolf in so we can present him to his mother,' Detor shouted. 'Oh, and if any one of you filth mention any of this to the queen, I will personally make your life a living misery until you die a terrible death. Do you all understand?'

The Dark warriors looking on all nodded then brought a tarpaulin out from within the craft and rolled the wolf into it. A Mangoul warrior lifted it onto his vast shoulder and waited for Detor's next command. The remainder searched for the rest of the water team. None were found. 'Take the craft and search the waters for the cowardly water team. Don't come back until you find them,' screamed Detor. Then he went back into the jungle with the dead Wolf prince and the unconscious Phina. Some way out at sea the water team had seen what had happened and, with saddened hearts, feeling helpless they too left with the unconscious Hollie. They all knew there would be hell to pay when she woke up. A mile out to sea they met the sea slugs and Octavians who, between them, took the water team away from the area before the Dark warriors had decided who the doomed crew would be to take the submersible out to look for the water team scum.

The dead wolf and the unconscious Phina were carried through the dense jungle along a once well-used path. In ancient times, it was used by the wolves to get to the ceremonial arena for the week of battle where wolves and people pitted themselves against each other in an ancient Olympics. Some of the events have not changed from the ones on Earth except someone usually died at the end of each discipline. For instance, in the javelin, warriors stood a certain distance away and threw the javelins at each other. If they missed after the first round, then they walked two paces towards each other and tried again. The warrior on the receiving end had to stay still when he or she was not throwing. The first one to draw blood was the winner. Then they would advance to the next stage, but more often than not the javelin would go through the opponent, killing them. But it had been known for people to complete in many games without injury. But as Tristan put it, Elemtum became civilised and those barbaric games were stopped. Now the barbaric Dark were using the arena so in theory it had returned to its original use. Detor and his Dark warriors took a day to fight through the jungle until they reached the arena which was the temporary home of the Dark away from their main base deep in the south on the border of the ice waste lands. Detor was not looking forward to telling Labatina her son was dead, but he had come up with a story that Karl had been killed by mistake by one of the water team when he went to Lady Phina's rescue. Of course, he had done all he could to save the young prince, even turning him to a wolf like he had King Frederick, but he had been too severely injured to save. He went into Queen Labatina's temporary quarters where she was drinking with Lord Arthfael. The queen's bodyguard questioned Detor about what was wrapped in the canvas sheet he was carrying. He told them he had to show the queen; it was not dangerous and he was allowed passage to the queen. Arthfael moved a little away from her but not far enough that he could not react if she was in danger or if anyone else approached.

'Ah, Detor, you have returned from your little adventure. Did you kill all the king's warriors?' Arthfael asked. Detor ignored him; they did not see eye to eye.

'What have you brought your queen?' Labatina asked.

'My queen, I am sorry to say that what I bring you, you will not be pleased to see.' Arthfael stood and went over to Detor. There was no love lost between the two warriors. Arthfael pulled his rayzor out and put it to Detor's neck. Detor could not react because he still held Karl's body.

'Upset the queen and I will feed your innards to the queen's pet and hang your carcass high on these arena walls.'

'Arthfael, leave Detor. You know he is one of our most trusted lieutenants. There is nothing he can show me that will upset me.' Arthfael lowered his rayzor then went and stood next to the queen. Detor could see excitement dancing around in Labatina's eyes; she was expecting the bloodied corpse of one of her mortal enemies.

'You will not like this one, your majesty. Please brace yourself for a shock,' said Detor then gently lowered the canvas bundle onto the floor in front of the queen and Arthfael. He then unfolded the bundle, revealing the contents.

'It's a dead wolf. So what?' said Arthfael.

'It's not just any wolf, it's the queen's son, Karl, killed by the water team just before they fled. They knew we would not pursue them and leave the queen's son unattended.'

The queen did not say a word. She undid the gown she was wearing, letting it fall to the floor leaving her completely naked in front of the two warriors. Then she transformed into her wolf form; not the white wolf she used to be but a jet-black one with piercing red eyes with a small patch of white fur above her heart. Labatina went over to the dead wolf, sniffed the body, overcoming the pungent smell of the lancer's blood that had contaminated the body. She detected a smell she remembered from somewhere in her distant forgotten memory. She knew this wolf. Its smell, even in death, was familiar to her. She had loved this wolf. She knew it inside. What Detor had said was true and she howled. She howled for over an hour. Both Arthfael and Detor left her and instructed her exterior bodyguard not to let anyone near the queen until they returned. The whole arena could hear the sorrow in the wolf's lament and it scared them because the retribution would be swift and bloody, and they did not know who it would be directed at.

Suddenly all went quiet. Arthfael and Detor ran back to Labatina's quarters. She was now back in her people form, wearing all black. She was standing with the dead wolf in her arms. 'If I am really evil why I can't I bring my son back to life? It's because I am not evil, and I have been tricked. Since my poor son was brought to me, his smell rekindled thoughts that have been hidden for a life time. Why am I here? Why is he dead? Where is the king?' Labatina asked them. They looked at each other, both now worried.

'You are not well, my queen. You need to rest. Give me your son. I will ensure he is sent to his ancestors with humility and grace,' Arthfael told her.

Detor added, 'We will build a pyre in the centre of the arena; you will be able to watch Karl ascend to his ancestors from this room. Rest and I will inform you when the ceremony will take place.' He then walked up to the confused queen and took the dead wolf from her.

She tried to resist but Arthfael reassured and calmed her, then took her through to her bedroom and sat her on the bed. 'Rest, my queen. You must be strong enough to see Karl ascend to your ancestors where you will be re-joined when you too become a spirit.'

Labatina felt strange; she didn't know why. She was not the strong, determined queen of darkness anymore. She was confused and willingly lay down and went to sleep. Visions of babies and young children flashed through her mind as did time frame pictures of the dead and dying, mutilation and evil spirits. Her master, the lord of darkness, came to her and told her she was being weak and she would be destroyed if she did not return to the Dark. This went on for several hours while she battled her demons.

Arthfael and Detor had sent a message to the Dark master to return to them because the queen was failing; he would know what that meant. In the meantime, the Dark had built a funeral pyre and Karl's wolf form was placed on top. This was the traditional way for all Elemtum warriors to go to their ancestors; the fire would release their soul and it would ascend to meet those that had passed before. The Dark had adopted the same practice, because generally they had a lot of bodies to get rid of, normally of their own forces.

Detor informed Arthfael that the ceremony could begin. He was told to wait for the signal from the queen. Then Arthfael went to the queen's quarters, Detor followed him. Labatina was still asleep; she was in some sort of coma induced by her brain to stop any damage to the Dark within. Also unknown to the queen at that time, Arthfael had administered some drugs into her arms that the Dark master had left for such a case as this. They knew she would not be waking soon.

Arthfael and Detor took her by the arms and lifted her to her feet. Arthfael held her head to look like she was holding her head up. The final touch was a black veil over her head so the Dark warriors below would not get suspicious and see she was asleep. They dragged her to the balcony, held her upright, opened the shutters, showing her to the warriors below. A wild cheer erupted; they all chanted her name until Detor lifted his free hand for silence. The he shouted out for all to hear. 'The queen wishes that you send her son to his ancestors.' All went quiet and the chosen warrior, trembling, threw a lit touch onto the pyre that burst into life because they had thrown tar over some of the wood to ensure it lit. Behind the trembling warrior, four other Dark warriors grabbed him and waited for the fire to take hold. As the flames licked around the wolf's body the trembling now screaming warrior was tossed onto the inferno. His job was to act as a bodyguard to the ascending soul. The rest of Elemtum did not do this part of the ceremony.

By now, the queen had been laid back on her bed. Arthfael and Detor then went back to the balcony and listened to the screams of the burning warrior as lances pushed him back into the fire as he tried to get away from the flames. The rest of the assembled warriors who had now circled around the pyre, chanted and stamped their feet as the flames went higher. Karl's wolf form could now not be seen from the balcony.

'Good, that's one of the brats gone. Now just two more to get rid of,' said Arthfael. Detor nodded his approval as they turned to walk back into Labatina's chambers. Arthfael closed the blinds and, as he did, Detor drew his rayzor and held it to Arthfael's neck, pushing him up against the blinds, stopping him from reaching his own rayzor.

Calmly Detor spoke, 'If you ever lift that rayzor towards me again, Arthfael, I will kill you. Do not use me as a pawn in your games with the queen or you could end up out there on top of your own pyre. That's if you are lucky.' Then he pushed him a little more against the blinds, digging the rayzor into his neck drawing a little blood just to make his point. Arthfael was no match for the Wolf master and they both knew it. Detor lowered his rayzor, slowly backing away from Arthfael. When he was far enough away, he turned and walked out of the room. Arthfael felt his neck and looked at the blood on his hand; it was then he decided the Wolf master had to die.

Outside, some of the Dark warriors started to point skyward into the night sky. A black shadow was descending towards the flames. As it got nearer to the flames, the warriors could make out an eagle, talons pointing down wings flaring as it closed in on the fire. It seemed to the Dark warriors that it too had been engulfed by the flames. Then moments later, burning wood rained down on the watching Dark warriors who started to run away in all directions to the lambasting of their leaders. Then from the fire the eagle lifted out of the flames and climbed skyward, not a single feather was alight. Hanging limp in its talons was the wolf, also untouched by the fire.

The eagle climbed higher and higher then from the crowd below someone screamed out, 'Don't just stare at it, you morons, kill the bloody thing.' Detor had left the main building to see the eagle rising from the fire. It took him several seconds to realise what was happening then he exploded at the lack action from the warriors staring at the eagle and the body of Karl disappearing into the black night. There was total confusion; none of the Dark warriors had weapons with them. You never went to a cremation with weapons you didn't need to, but in this case they did. One of the two lancers who had been prodding the dead burning warrior back into the pyre vainly and ineffectively lifted and threw his lance after the departing eagle but it had no force or direction and landed in the fire at the top of the pyre which was now well alight.

Detor went up to one and stabbed him in the back with his rayzor. 'Throw this idiot on the fire, you are lucky you are not going with him,' he screamed at the second lancer. 'Get the lizards. Go after them, I want the eagle dead and the dead wolf back here. Go, you idiots, don't just stand there. Go!' He called one of the Dark legion masters to him. As he approached, Detor struck him with his rayzor and decapitated him with one blow. Then he screamed at all the Dark warriors watching, 'That fate awaits anyone who fails me. Now get them!' He kicked the head into the flames, more in frustration at the idiots around him, knowing the eagle would get away with the body. By the time the first flying lizard with its Dark rider left the ground Alerio was long gone and was now beyond their reach with his soulmate, Karl. Detor knew that Karl's dead body had been lost and he didn't much care either. The queen was in no fit state now and Arthfael would get a slap very shortly if he did not watch out. He was very angry. He knew just what he needed to calm himself down… Phina!

Arthfael came down from Labatina's quarters. 'What's going on? What's all the shouting about?' he asked, then saw the decapitated body 'What did he do to upset you?'

'He got in my way and he was an idiot,' replied Detor then barged passed without saying another word. He made his way to the same cell Tom and Blacky had been kept in. This time outside the cell, well away from the bars, were two Dark warriors staring in at Phina. She was sitting with her back to the wall with her arms holding her knees up in a sitting position, staring at the warriors watching her making a mental note of every move they made.

Detor told the guard to open the cell and follow him in and to be ready for anything. The cell door creaked open. Phina stood up, ready. 'Grab her,' Detor ordered the two guards. They rushed at Phina. The first to reach her flew backwards, holding his groin in obvious agony, Phina had directed a disabling blow with her foot. The second warrior guarded against this but not for the blow to his shin that snapped the bone sending him reeling in agony. Detor drew his rayzor.

'Phina, we can do this the easy way or the hard way.' He called for more guards who were just around the corner because he was expecting this sort of reaction from Phina. Dark warriors arrived very quickly and entered the cell, forming a semi-circle around Phina. 'Now, Phina, if you want to do this the hard way, we can do it the hard way with the help of these gentlemen.' Detor made a sweeping motion with his rayzor, indicating the Dark warriors drooling around him.

Phina laughed. 'Gentlemen!' she said.

'I have known you and respected you for what you are, a great warrior. But I have also watched you and I know you have been looking at me because you too appreciated a skilled warrior who is your superior. Together we would be a force to reckon with. Arthfael is a fool who lusts after the queen; he does not know what I know about her. Now I am going to have you whether you like it or not. You need to understand that I am the Wolf master and you will be my soulmate, like it or not. I don't want to, but I will get these warriors to hold you down and I will have you, then I will let them have you. Then every warrior out there will have you until you are nothing but a Dark warrior's whore. That's if you survive, of course. Or we can become one and fight side by side as life loves. The choice is yours,' he told her.

Around her the Dark warriors leered and smiled, looking her up and down hoping she would decline his offer.

'Since you put it so nicely, Wolf master, I must accept your second offer. Tell these filthy vermin to go and I will show you what a Wolf warrior princess can do for such a great warrior.'

Detor looked at her and thought to himself, this is a trick, surely? Then he looked at her once more. He wanted her. The Dark warriors will only be around the corner; I am much stronger than she is, he thought, trying to persuade himself. He had convinced himself that he could deal with anything Phina could try and throw at him. 'Okay, I will give you a chance. Any funny business and the second part of my deal will happen. You only have one chance,' he told her.

Phina smiled at him. 'I am no match for you, Wolf master, and I can see the sense in your proposal, but you cannot have me with these vermin watching, ogling us.'

Detor agreed and ordered the Dark warriors to leave them but to wait around the corner until he called. The unhappy warriors left the cell and went back to the position they were in moments ago, dragging the two warriors that Phina had dealt with earlier, and locking the cell door on Detor's orders.

He walked up to her and stopped just out of arm and leg reach. She smiled at him but did not say a word. Then she bent down and removed one boot, then the other. Her hands returned to the neck of her tattered combat suit; she grasped, the zip pulling it down until it was level with her hips. Detor could see the curves of her breasts. Excited, he went to take a step towards her but she put a hand to stop him. Staring at her, he started to believe he was going to have this beautiful creature. Then she took hold of her suit, pulling the left shoulder down then stopped and did the same to the right, pulling the suit down to her waist revealing the perfectly formed upper female figure of the most beautiful warrior princess in all of Elemtum. Detor was now getting very excited, truly believing he was going to have the female of so many of his dreams. Phina continued. She pushed the suit over her hips, then bent slightly and pushed it down to her ankles where she flicked it away, leaving her completely naked. She stood in front of him in all her perfect beauty. Nothing was hidden from him. She was now just a naked female; a very beautiful naked female and Detor could not believe this was happening. He could not control himself anymore. He walked over to Phina, took her head in his hands and kissed her. She responded passionately as his hand quickly went down excitedly. Then she whispered, 'Take your clothes off.'

He fumbled with his jacket and threw it on the floor. Then his shirt quickly came off so he was bare chested. He undid his belt and his rayzor fell to the floor, loudly echoing down the corridor. One of the warriors came running around to see a naked Phina behind Detor. Her head turned to look at the warrior as did Detor's.

'I don't need your help. All of you go to the guard house. Come and get me in an hour… now go!' he shouted. The warrior shuffled away, collected the rest of the warriors and they moved to the guard house, not wanting to annoy the Dark Wolf master. He turned his gaze to Phina, kissing her once more but this time she pushed him away.

'Your trousers. You still have your trousers on.' He smiled and fumbled with the buttons so Phina undid them for him, pulling them down to his ankles.

'That's better,' whispered Phina. 'Now we can really get to know each other properly.' Detor smiled. This time she kissed and caressed his chest. He was right, she did like him. He could see his future with her, it was all coming true. Phina kissed his shoulder, then his neck, putting both her hands on the sides of his head, then she kissed him mouth to mouth. She had him now. With a swift sharp surgical movement, she twisted his head sharply with great force, breaking his neck, killing him instantly. Holding him so as not to let him fall, she lowered him to the floor then dragged him to the dark corner of the cell, the same corner in which Tom had not been able to see Blacky. Phina then went up to the bars of the cell and shouted down the corridor. Five warriors ran up, stopping when they saw the naked Phina standing there. 'Detor wants some grog. The rest of you can go and have some grog on him. He is now in a good mood. I will wake him when you return and maybe…' She stopped talking and looked at the warriors. She pointed at one of them. 'And you can come back and join us,' she said smiling. All the warriors looked at the lucky one with disbelief. Phina smiled. 'Don't worry. Over the next few days, if you are good, you can all come and play,' she said. Excitedly, they ran off. Minutes later the singled-out warrior came running back with a small barrel of grog and three mugs. He stopped at the cell bars and looked at Phina, still naked.

'You have the keys,' Phina said. Realisation hit the warrior smack in the face. He turned around and started to run back then stopped, returned, handing the mugs through the bars, placing the barrel on the floor outside the cell. He then turned around and headed back to the guard house for the keys.

The guard house was empty. The warriors were all now in the makeshift tavern drinking grog on Detor's tab. The warrior serving did not hesitate to give them the grog because who would lie about that. Detor would have then disembowelled for disobeying him. After all, the warriors would not lie because they would soon be dead if they did.

The lucky warrior ran back to the cell and opened the door, stepping inside. Phina kissed him and told him to go over and wake Detor and give him some grog. The warrior filled a mug and went towards Detor's body. He was now in front of her. this was her chance. She quickly went up behind him. Pulling the rayzor from its sheath she drew it back just as the warrior turned to see what was going on behind him. It was the last thing he ever saw. The surgical strike took his head from his body. The head dropped to the floor then the body followed, both landing next to the dead Wolf master.

Quickly she dressed in her tattered combat suit and put her boots back on. She took Detor's belt and rayzor then carefully made her way to the guard house. The gates were open; she sneaked through, checking her way was clear and slowly made her way around the arena until she reached the main arena gates.

As she made her way towards them, she heard a shout from behind her, 'You, warrior, where are the guards?'

Phina did not turn to face the person whose voice she recognised as Arthfael. She moved into the shadows to try and keep her appearance hidden but she could hear Arthfael approaching ranting, 'You insolent dog! How dare you ignore me, turn and look at me,' he shouted. Phina lifted her arms to gesture she did not understand. 'Where the bloody hell did they get this one from?' he muttered to himself as he got closer. Phina felt his hand on her shoulder trying to turn her to face him so she obliged. She spun round to Arthfael's total surprise.

She smiled at him and said, 'Traitor!'

Then the palm of her right hand swiftly came up and struck him on the nose, pushing his nostrils up, shattering the dorsum, sending bones back into the root of the nose. He screamed out in pain and crumpling to the ground with both hands feeling for his nose but the instant he touched it he was in agony as a sharp pain shot into his brain. His hands were covered in blood. Watery eyes looked up at Phina just as she finished with a direct full force right boot to his groin which brought no sound from Arthfael. He fell sideways, the pain of the kick and the shattered nose making him faint and he lay helpless on the ground. Phina looked down at the miserable excuse for a warrior, deciding to finish him there and then. Just as she was about to stamp on his head to crush his skull, a lance bounced of the wall next to her, clattering against the ironwork of the main arena gate. Phina decided there and then that she could deal with him later. It was now time to go.

She knew she had to get over that gate before any more Dark warriors appeared, so she began to climb it. A quarter of the way up, she felt a hand grab her foot then the assailant tried to pull her off the gate as he shouted alarm. This one is quite strong, she thought to herself as she held on to the bars and swung her body round, aiming a kick at the side of the lancer's head. It stuck as aimed and the lancer crumpled to the ground, out cold as another lance struck her back. Luckily the lance was going sideways so did not penetrate but it still had some force behind it and it hurt. She thought to herself, that's going to leave a bruise.

She climbed higher over the gate spikes on the top then leapt the twenty feet to the ground on the other side, rolling as she landed to absorb the force of the jump. As she did, a dagger flew past where her head was seconds before. She looked back to see a bloodied Arthfael at the now slightly ajar gate. Next to him were several rather worried looking guards who she recognised from the cell earlier. Ignoring them all, Phina sprinted for the jungle. She hoped it would be some time until the Dark warriors would find her, if ever! She ran two hundred metres then entered the jungle. Just inside she stopped and took off her boots and combat suit. Then, turning into her wolf form, she began to run Her senses now heightened, she had a better view of her way ahead. She could hear no one behind her so she continued to run until she hit a small clearing where she looked up and saw the stars. Now she knew which way to run and she did just that. Every so often she would stop and listen. Nothing. She carried on. After two hours, she came to the edge of the jungle at a sandy golden beach. She followed the beach north. Now she was able to pick up the pace and run unhindered. She ran at a steady pace for three hours, expecting to be attacked at any time until the jungle to her left started to thin and disappear. In front and around her now was sand. She believed she had just entered the sand lands. This too brought its own problems. Before long, it would be light. She was sure the Dark would send up air patrols to find her, so she had to find somewhere to hide before it became light.

She knew the Omani people lived here but she could kick herself. She had had the opportunity to meet them in their underground city, but she had volunteered to go to Earth with Salina instead. She picked up the pace again to try and cover more ground until morning, then she could rest hopefully after finding cover on the way.

Chapter 17
Revelations and Sorrow

In her room, Rowena was totally unaware of Karl and Phina's fate. She was aware that Tom had returned to Warriors' Rest and assumed it would only be a matter of time before Karl returned with Phina. Wanting a little time to herself, she decided she would take her mind off things by reading the cookbooks she had got from Gebhuza Septima's library on the blue moon. Row retrieved the books from the knapsack she had borrowed and as she leafed through the Elemtum and Earth food book she came across a document tucked between some of the pages. This was followed by several more as she held the book by the spine and shook it. She opened one and read the handwritten document.

5th day We have been taken to a witch doctor. I have spoken to the human spiritualist. He has told me that they know of a plain that they can reach on another planet for spiritual guidance. They have a root they boil and drink to reach that plain. They believe Labatina is a voodoo queen spirit from that plain. Ss, she is going to try it tonight! I am getting very close to her so I am not too sure whether she should take the drink or not. Maybe it might loosen her up and make her a bit more receptive towards me because I feel she does not have the same feelings for me. I am going to get a sample of all of these Earth native plants and vegetables they use. I believe it's hallucinogenic, which could actually work in my favour. I have made liquor that I will mix with it that should have the desired effect. After that I will just have to find a solution for her beloved life partner, the king.

Oh my god. I wonder if Paccia has seen these? I wonder if Dad has seen these? I bet he hasn't, Row thought to herself. She dropped the document to one side, unfolded another and read on.

1st day We have travelled to Earth from the southern pathway. I told Labatina not to tell anyone because that would just complicate things and our research could be stopped. We are in a country called South America in a town called Brazil. I have paid a very happy local one gold coin to take us into the interior so we can search the jungle for herbs that we do not have on Elemtum. Labatina is worried about sneaking away especially as she is leaving Rowena and Karl with Elizabeth and does not like the fact that she is lying to Frederick. I have told her to think of the end result and the medical breakthroughs that will happen because of the sacrifices we are making securing these specimens that will not only benefit her children but everyone on Elemtum, the blue and red moons.

2nd day We have had a hard journey through this jungle that I have been informed is a rainforest. We are a day away from the area I want to look at. Some people from Elemtum have been here before and they are the ones that told me about a spiritual human who has the knowledge of all the medical herbs and medicines that we do not possess on the blue moon or Elemtum. I am happy to be with Labatina, she is good company and a kinder person I have never met. It is starting to rain so I will stop.

Row put the documents down and picked up another one, and read on.

7th day Labatina is still unconscious; she has been strange since she drank the potion. I may have put too much of my formula in and it has reacted to the voodoo potion. I feel eternal shame at what I have done to Labatina; she was in a vulnerable state and I took advantage of her. She did not resist because when I had finished, she was unconscious. She was like a rag doll. I don't know what came over me, she is a beautiful female and I have broken my healer's vow. I feel great shame but I am the only one who knows and I will now dedicate my life to keeping her safe. Have had thoughts of suicide but I can't do it. I don't have the courage and it would leave Labatina vulnerable and alone in the confused state she is in.

Rowena was full of rage and was just about to rip the paper up but resisted. How could he? He's an eminent respected healer, the greatest by all accounts. I bet sis daughter knows nothing of this. How do I tell her? Do I tell her? What about Dad and Karl? What do I do? All these thoughts whizzed through her head. She did not know her mother but she was once a good person and, by the sound of these documents, she was turned by someone who should have protected her. She could be changed back though, she thought. As far as I am aware, no one has ever seen her kill anyone, I'm sure! There were two more documents on the pile that she had not read. She hesitated then she picked another up and continued reading.

12th day She has been raving and trying to kill me. I don't know whether it's because she has realised what I have done to her. I could not help myself. Her beauty is unsurpassed. She bewitches me and she was just lying there. Oh my. All that is good, what have I done? I don't recognise the person I have become. She was awake the last time and just stared at me, no sound no reaction. If she remembers, I will have to silence her. The king would kill me. The humiliation of being found out. I couldn't live with myself. The shame.

20th day She is totally mad. Another voodoo queen performed a ritual on her and she calmed down. There must be something in this voodoo cult, it seems to be working. The voodoo queen has told me things are difficult with her soul because the spirits have told me she is with child. She only has forty something days until she gives birth. I am totally shocked Labatina is having a child. I don't know what to do. I may have to kill them both I am so confused. If the king finds out, how will I hide? They will come looking for us if we do not contact Elemtum soon.

'Oh my god. So, who or what happened to the child? Wait, depending on timescales, there are no bloody dates in these entries,' Row spoke to herself. She dropped that document and picked up the last one. Her hands were trembling and her heart was beating. She began to read.

Have passed. My story worked. The king thinks Labatina is deep in the jungle doing research and cannot return to Elemtum until… The next part of writing had smeared, water must have got on the ink and the only word she could make out was the name for the blue moon, Penterum. Why would he mention the blue moon? She went down to the next readable text.

She remembers nothing, not even having the child. The voodoo queen has it now and they are going to look after it until I return then I will get rid of it. Labatina's mind is not how it was… she is cruel… then kind. She has bursts of pure evil. She killed a dog with her bare hands yesterday; she ripped its throat out, and she is too powerful for me. I can't get near her. She is deranged. The voodoo queen has told me she is pure evil. Something that has happened to her, has sent her in her travels to hell and back. (Note to self, research hell that everyone in this village talks about.) I am reassured that Labatina has no idea what I have done to her. My life can continue. I am so relieved and that means I don't have to commit murder. I think Labatina will need special mental care and treatment, but I must be careful I do not want her memories to come back.

We are returning to Elemtum. Once Labatina is back in Great Porum, I will be returning to Earth to deal with the child if the people of this village have not killed her.

Her. It's a girl, he killed a girl. Row was shaking with anger as she stood up and gathered the papers. What do I do now? He has to pay but who do I tell? Row thought for a while then decided it should be Raphina. She was calm and cool headed and she knew Raphina would know what to do. Maybe she would also know about voodoo. Someone must know. There might be something that could be done to help her mother. Rowena was now convinced her mother was under some sort of spell from the voodoo people on Earth, all thanks to Gebhuza Septima the so-called great healer. Oh my god, what will Paccia think? It will be horrible for her to find out that her father is the one that has caused all this and done what he has to my mother. Poor Paccia. Then a thought smashed into her brain. Who is

Paccia's mother? What if Gebhuza Septima had not gone back to Earth and killed the child? What if he took the child back to the blue moon; she would be my half-sister, related by a rapist, Oh my god!... Oh my god! Row did not know what to think, she would have to tell Raphina. Just then, there was a knock on her door. Row hid the papers and opened the door. It was Kurt.

'Hello, Row, sorry I have not been to see you, I have been very busy, I am so sorry about Karl, I loved that young man as though he was mine. I will avenge his death.'

'What are you talking about, Uncle Kurt?' He then explained what had happened to Karl and Phina. Row was disbelieving. 'That can't be true or I'm sure I would have felt something! No, you're wrong, Uncle Kurt,' she replied.

The tears welled up in her eyes. Kurt could see she was in pain. He comforted her as the tears ran down her face. She had felt strange inside all day long, even before she had read the letters. She felt that now a part of her heart and soul had died with him. 'I never used to cry, Uncle Kurt. Do you believe that?' Row told him. After pulling herself together and stepping back from his comforting embrace, she looked up into his eyes. Kurt held her hands and said, 'Yes, I do, Row. Do you remember as a little girl I took you to those wild apple trees, and you fell and grazed your arm? You never cried then, not until I put that mustard paste on the graze then you cried and I don't blame you. That was horrible stuff but it didn't half work.'

Row began to laugh at the memory of that day. All the others she had had back then flooded through her memory, and then she became very sad again.

'I know what's wrong, Row,' Kurt told her as he saw the change in her expression.

'No, you don't, Uncle Kurt. It's all gone! I was so happy back then and when I met Karl and Tom, my life seemed fulfilled. I always knew there was more than what there was back then, but I just didn't know it would end in such heartbreak here. Do you know you are the first person I have spoken to about all this? I feel so alone now. And poor Tom, what about him? Does he know his brother is dead? He too could be dead.' She started to cry and held her uncle close once more; her world seemed to be falling apart. Kurt hugged her and held his own tears back.

'We can't think like that, Row. We have to be strong for Tom and for the memory of Karl. All our efforts must now be put into finding Tom, saving Phina and retrieving Karl's body so he can be sent to the spirits in a way that befits a great warrior.'

Just then Raphina came into the room. 'Is everything okay? Kurt, Row?'

'Rowena is justifiably upset. The last couple of days have taken a toll on her and she just needs a bit of love and support from us until things settle down.'

Row turned and looked at Raphina. 'I've found something else out as well.' She hesitated then continued. 'I wanted to tell you, Raphina, but its's also important that you hear this as well, Uncle Kurt. It's terrible and I think it could be the underlying problem that has caused this entire episode,' Row told them. Slightly puzzled, Kurt and Raphina sat down with Row who took the documents from her knapsack and held them in her shaking hands.

'You must promise me, Uncle Kurt, you will not shoot or start killing people after you read these.'

'I promise,' Kurt replied.

Row told them where she had got them from and how she discovered them. Then she handed them to Raphina in day order so it would read a little better than when Row had first read them. After Raphina read one, she gave it to Kurt. Row could see their expressions change as her's had done. She could see the disbelief in their faces, then the anger.

'I never trusted that animal; I knew something was not right with him. Tom noticed it as soon as he met him. He sensed something when he met him, he knew something… I don't know how, but he knew,' said Raphina. After some time, Kurt put the documents down, his face was twisted with anger.

Raphina went up to Row, she embraced her and held her as her tears flowed once more, now happy she would not hold the dreadful secret alone anymore. 'You can stay with Kurt and me, if you like, until you get yourself settled and Tom comes back.'

Row thanked her but said that she may have to stay with her father once he had been told. They both understood.

'I tell you both now I will hunt that bastard down and when I find him, he will suffer for all the suffering he has caused in this world. The king must see these and we must search the rest of his home. There has to be more. Maybe there's an explanation for the Dark there?' Kurt told them as he passed up and down the room. 'We have to tell the king!'

'Maybe there's a cure for my mother?' interjected Row. They could both see an expression of hope on her face.

'Maybe, Row, we just won't know until we get some answers,' Raphina replied.

Then they all sat down together and talked. They all agreed, even though it would pain him greatly, the king must know. They made their way to the operations centre that had been set up for the forthcoming actions against the Dark which were to be launched from Warriors' Rest. Entering the building, they came across Tristan so they showed him the letters and explained it all to him. Next, they entered the operations room and asked King Frederick if they could speak to him privately. The king went with them to a side room, unaware of any new problems. He was a little perplexed as to why his daughter, sister and brothers all looked concerned and needed to speak to him in private. It had been decided Raphina would tell the king; she would stay the calmest of all of them and hopefully her calm would soothe her brother. Raphina told Frederick of the documents Row had found and what they contained. The king took all the information in very calmly. He took the documents and read them carefully. He turned away, walked up to a table that was against a wall and slammed his fist down on it, the documents still clenched in it.

'I knew it…' he said as he turned to face his family. 'I knew there was something behind how Labatina had acted over the last few ages… she is under some sort of spell, witchcraft or whatever that voodoo potion is he talks about. Who knows?' He went over to Row, held her hands and looked into her eyes.

'This means we may get your mother back. I know her, the gentle caring loving person she was. Yes… I knew it. This must all stay a secret between us. No one else should know. We need to make sure Gebhuza Septima stays unaware that we know because I want to take him alive. That way we may be able to extract all the information from him regarding what has happened to Labatina. Does everyone agree?' They all nodded in agreement. Then he asked Tristan, Raphina and Kurt to wait for him outside because he wanted to speak to Row. The three of them left then he asked Row to sit down next to him.

'Are you really okay with this, Dad?' she asked.

'No! Between you and me, I want to find that piece of scum and push my rayzor into his guts and pull it out through the top of his head, but there will be time for that later. What we must do now is play the happy family as though we know nothing of this. When Tom and Phina are back and we have Karl's body, then you, me and Tom are going away to relax and get to know each other better. I know a lovely place where your mother and I used to go. We will camp under the stars as we did back then. It will be just what we all need. We can run as wolves, get back to our ancestors.'

Row interrupted him, 'Dad, don't get ahead of yourself. Don't forget there will be a lot of water under the bridge before we can even think about that sort of thing.'

'Yes, you're right… I'm thinking too far ahead. I just wanted to get that thought out of my head, what he's done to her… to us'! he paused and looked at Row's face. 'Just like your mother.'

He gently squeezed her hand, then stood and kissed the top of her head. Row stood and gave him a hug only a daughter could. Neither wanted to break the embrace because then they would be back to reality and they really didn't want that just yet. 'This will never do. Let's get back to the others. We have plans to make.' Frederick pulled away and Row looked up to see tears in his eyes.

'It will be all right you know, Dad. I just know it; I have felt it since I was born.' The king smiled and they walked hand in hand to the door. He smiled at his daughter once more and she smiled back at him, then wiped the tears from his eyes. 'There, you're the king and I'm a princess. We can't let our subjects see us crying, now can we? They might think something is up.' She smiled at him and they walked through the door back to reality. Waiting for them, Kurt, Tristan and Raphina were now poised over the map table. The king and his daughter walked over and asked what they were looking at. Kurt told him they thought they knew where they were holding Phina and Karl. Samee had loaded a new set of maps; they had not been verified but they had been made up from the calculations she had made about the cracks and where they were located on Elemtum. Or, rather, where they thought they were. The ones they had been told about by people who had travelled through them which included fresh information from the Zells and the sea slugs. They had plotted Hollie's position, where Karl had been killed and Phina taken. Tom and Blacky had told them about the place they had been held and Kurt could remember something that he had been told when he was a young trainee warrior by the then Wolf master.

Centuries ago, when the wolves had fought tournaments to the death, it was done in the deep south in a coliseum that had been built a day's walk into the southern rainforest. What Hollie had called a jungle, Tom and Blacky had described perfectly and Kurt had looked it up in old manuscripts. He now knew where it was. 'That gives us a location. What about a plan with objectives?' asked the king.

'We have a small team that will go in, recce the area then we will get in there in force and bring Karl and Phina back. With the information that team brings back, we can make a proper plan to attack it and destroy this Dark once and for all,' Tristan told them all as he swept his hand over the map indicating different points to his recce plan.

'Good, so who's the team?' asked the king.

Kurt answered him, 'Hollie and two of her teams will do the recce. Andor and a flight of his best Eagle warriors along with a ground force led by me will do the assault.'

'Hum… I'm not sure, Kurt,' said the king.

'It's okay, because I haven't finished yet. Paccia and three healers, Zuzza and ten young Zells as well as Sentar the leader of the lizsnakes and some of his clan. Four troops of my favoured Wolf warriors, as well as some miners to blow the place from the face of the planet. Lord Willacox is up for that, big style. And before you reject it, Frederick, just hear out the plan.'

'Okay then tell me the plan,' said the king.

'And I'm going too,' said Row.

'We will talk about that later,' the king told her.

Then Tristan told him the plan was in their heads so it would take him, Kurt, Raphina and some of the operations specialists to put it into a format everyone would understand and that would take some time.

'So, why bother with the recce? Just go in and wipe them out,' said the king.

'I would be a fool to let any of your troops go into a pre-planned battle without doing a recce first. You just don't know what could be there. You must remember when we went into battle and found those acid firing flying lizards. We don't want something like that to happen again, now do we?'

'I see where you're coming from and I totally agree, but you must remember, time is of the essence, if we want to get Phina back alive. This plan needs to be on the table in hours, not days,' the king emphasised. 'Come back to me with your plan as soon as possible, and it needs to be a good one if I am going to be responsible for possibly sending warriors to their deaths.'

'It will be, lord,' Tristan replied.

'What have I missed?' A voice came from the back of the room, when they turned… there stood Salina as fit and healthy as she had ever looked with a smile across her face.

'Planning to kick the Dark off the planet, I hope?' she said as she walked over to her smiling family assembled in front of her. Everyone was overjoyed to see her back amongst them.

'Where's Phina? I went via the boys' accommodation and it was in bits. All their stuff has gone.'

'Yes, we had to move them after the Dark attack,' said Tristan.

'You don't know, do you?' said her mother.

'I don't know anything that's happened,' said Salina. Kurt went to her and held her by the shoulders.

'Karl is dead and Phina has been taken by the Dark.'

Salina was totally shocked and stunned. She had not been told by anyone. 'That's why everyone has been so quiet… I knew something was wrong… When? How?' she asked.

'Come back home with me and we will explain everything to you. Row. you come too. Kurt, Tristan, Frederick, you are all welcome to come and share a meal with us later if you get some time,' said Raphina. They thanked her and told her they would come along in a while if they got the plan sorted. So, Raphina, Salina and Row left the king and the others who would follow later.

Chapter 18
Life

Phina ran on now sensing the night would end soon and that what happened in the next hour would seal her fate, she was sure of that. She slowed her pace and began to search for a concealed hiding place but she knew if none was found she would have to try and bury herself before light if she had any hope of evading the Dark chasers she knew would now be on her trail. Stopping, she changed back to her people form and began to look around her in the black night. She could see in the distance the light of a new day slowly creeping across the desert towards her. She spotted out of the corner of her eye the black silhouette of a mound to her left. She cautiously made her way towards it, conscious now that time was not on her side. As she approached, the mound the sand beneath her feet started to crunch under every step. Warning bells rang in her head but she still did not realise the danger she was in until the ground beneath her cracked and fell away below her. She crashed through the surface and tumbled down into blackness out of control. Now, not conscious of whether she was up or down, she tumbled back as powdery sand started clogging her eyes, nose and mouth. For a split second helplessness rushed over her, fear tugged at her until she realised she was no longer falling. She waited for the last of the sand to stop moving. She also sensed she was the right way up but could feel the sand packed in around her. She could still move her hands and arms, which she did, thrusting them up, grasping for air. At full stretch she was still cocooned in the sand but it was not dense enough to stop her breathing. She knew that with every breath she inhaled more sand particles and, eventually, she would die. Phina moved her body, her arms and legs, feet and hands, to try and make space around her but every time she did that the space was immediately filled with more sand. She could also feel herself slowly sliding downwards.

Is this how it ends? she thought to herself. Now totally calm, her brain raced for a solution to her ever-increasing predicament.

Tom and Arn had flown on after leaving Alerio some hours ago, flying ever higher. Tom was happy and content, trusting his soulmate to take him to somewhere safe, where he would be joined by Karl and Alerio later, he was sure. But where this safe place was Tom did not know. He asked Arn.

'We are going to the eagle's spiritual home, a place where Eagle warriors only go when they become one with their eagle. If we will be welcomed there, I am not sure but something within me tells me that's where we must be to wait for Alerio and Karl.'

They flew on, ever higher, until in the morning light Tom saw a massive mountain looming from the black night in front of him. As the morning reached the mountain, Tom could see it shimmered red and as he looked up it disappeared into cloud. 'Are we going up there?' he asked Arn.

'Yes,' he replied, 'and further still to the red moon,' he told Tom. Alerio was now four hours behind then cradling the lifeless body of Karl gently in his talons. Hour by hour, Alerio's strength was ebbing away; eventually he would plummet to the ground unless he reached the red moon in time. By the time the king and his brothers had returned to Kurt's home, a plan was in place for the next day. Salina had been updated on everything that had happened while she helped Raphina prepare some food. Eagerly, Raif ran to the door to let his father and uncles in. He had a question he wanted to ask them all. Kurt embraced his son. 'By Atta, Raif, you are nearly a warrior. Has it been that long since I last saw you?'

'I am a warrior. I am trained and ready to fight at your side,' Raif replied.

'Nearly trained,' his mother butted in.

'Yes, you have a lot more to learn yet, little brother,' added Salina with a smile.

Raphina pulled her son away. 'Let your father and the king enter our home, Raif. You can ask them all the questions you like after dinner,' she added.

Everyone was finally seated and the generous meal was now in front of them. Kurt, Tristan and the king asked Raif about his training and the trouble he had been up to while his father was away. Raif explained that it was not trouble but adventures he had with Clomp. After much laughter, the meal was finished, Raif was sent to bed with a promise that his father would listen to the proposal his son had in the morning. As Raif went to bed, the morning light had already illuminated Warriors' Rest and the start of a new day had already begun but there was still much to talk about for those who remained.

Above her, Phina could feel pressure pushing down on her. Someone or something was directly above her. That's when she realised she was entirely without any clothing. She had to take the combat suit off when she became a wolf; she hadn't really cared in the dark and alone but this was not the best position when about to be discovered and may have to fight. She stayed completely still until she coughed as the sand filled her nose and mouth but it did not matter. Above her, he already knew she was there. His long tongue slipped into the sand

314

and made its way down to Phina. Feeling around her, it slowly entwined her. She could feel some pressure around her body where what she thought was a snake had wrapped itself around her. She expected to be pulled into the creature's mouth any second. She felt herself rising, then air filled her nostrils and she managed to expel some of the sand from her mouth and nose then start to breathe once more. Suddenly she thought, turn back to a wolf and the snake might get confused. It will be my only chance to escape. So, she did. As she changed, so did the grip of the tongue until she was in her wolf form but she was still securely held.

Then she heard a voice. 'Well, what do we have here? A Wolf warrior, if I am not mistaken,' the voice said. 'Now, will it be male or female? Friend or foe?'

Through watery sandy eyes, Phina the wolf could make out a figure in robes the colour of sand in front of her. It was a female with jet-black flowing hair which went below her shoulders. Across her mouth and nose was a red scarf in total contrast to her drab brown and yellow robes. Blue eyes flashed from above the scarf, beautiful, but at the same time menacing and alert. In her hands she held a spear. At her waist was a wide brown leather belt with a crude metal D shaped buckle with a curved blade in a sheath at her side. 'Turn back into your people form or you will not be released,' she called to Phina. Not sure whether the female warrior in front of her was a friend or enemy she knew her options were limited so she returned to her people form. Phina could not see what creature held her in its tongue's grip, nor was she sure if she wanted to. 'Sentara, release the Wolf warrior but stay on guard until we are sure who she is.' said the robed female who stood watching Phina's every move, one hand on the hilt of her weapon and the other on the spear. Sentara unwound its tongue from Phina, leaving her standing in semi-darkness in front of the lizsnake and the robed warrior.

Surprised, the warrior asked Phina a question, 'Do you normally roam the sand lands totally naked or are you mentally deranged?'

Phina replied that she was neither roaming or mentally deranged. In fact, she was a warrior princess who hours earlier had escaped from the clutches of the Dark queen and her sociopaths, which was why she found herself in this position. She had been wearing a combat suit that would not allow her to change form and run away faster. Her name was Phina De-Callen, daughter of Kurt De-Callen and niece of the emperor of Elemtum.

'Well, that explains everything then. I am Abla, a warrior of the Omanian tribe, and you have fallen into one of Sentara's rat traps. Luckily you are now safe and amongst friends.' She unfastened her belt and removed the outer robe she had been wearing and handed it to Phina.

'I can't take you back to my people like that. To be naked is a private matter and only your mother or lover should ever see you like that.'

'Thank you, Abla, I am very grateful for your help. Do you have any communication with Warriors' Rest to the north so I can let my people know I am safe and let them know what has happened to their prince?'

'We can help you. Climb up onto Sentara with me and he will take us to my people where you will find help... and some clothes,' she added. They climbed up and Sentara hurried along, entering sand tunnels at some speed. Phina could feel fresh air blowing through the tunnels which became lighter and bigger as the lizsnake ran along them. Around her, every now and then, multi-coloured lights flashed, but because of Sentara's speed she could not see what they were. Phina could sense they were now travelling downwards. They started to descend until she could see light up ahead. As they got closer, she realised it was a large door whose frame was surrounded with lights. As they approached it, it seemed to float open in front of them. There had been no word or gesture from either Abla or Sentara Once through the door Phina was surprised. Around her was all clinically white. Suddenly she felt dirty and out of place. Sentara stopped and she and Abla climbed off the lizsnake's back. Abla bowed to Sentara and patted the side of his head. Sentara nodded its head, turned and ran off back down the tunnel. Phina noticed that they were the only two people in the large room. Abla explained to Phina that this was a sterile area where they would be cleaned and checked for any abnormalities.

'Abnormalities?' Phina asked. 'What do you mean?'

'Things have a habit of attaching to you nowadays,' said Abla.

'What do you mean?' Phina asked again.

'We have had two desert warriors return from foraging in the sand lands. They fell ill. Then after the surgeons did an autopsy on one of them, they found creatures that had been burrowed into them.'

'Creatures? What? Living creatures?' Phina asked.

'Exactly that. They would have turned the warriors into some sort of Dark warrior so the surgeons told us. As it was, one of them died and the other is no better than a vegetable. He is fading away very fast. They tried to remove the thing, but it did not go well. It was too attached to his internal organs. If they had continued, he would have died. Personally, I would have preferred if he had. He is my youngest brother.'

'I'm sorry to hear that,' replied Phina. She was genuinely sorry and Abla could see it which confirmed what she had already thought when she first met Phina. Ahe was an ally and probably a friend.

Tom and Arn landed on the very top of the red mountain, high above the clouds that cut the top of the red mountain from anyone looking up from below. From where they were, the clouds were half a mile below them. This was a big mountain, a special mountain. On the way up Tom expected it to be very dark up past the clouds. He had never been so high before in his life. It was not dark at the top; in fact, it was very light. In front of them was a very old building, the sort of building that on Earth would have had a lot of graves around it. A mausoleum type structure but not as grand as the type of thing an English gentleman of the Victorian era would have put himself and his family in when they died. Around it, and creeping towards them was a very low-lying fog, a fog that was only ankle high. 'What's this place, Arn?'

'It's where we become one with our soulmate. One day, Tom, you and I will ascend here and meet Kathleen, the mother. She is the mother of all eagles, the great eagle soul, the one that cares for us when we ascend. We all have memories of her from birth, then the only other time we meet is when we become one together. That will be at the end of our life when we ascend to the red moon.

'What will happen then, Tom, is I give my soul to you and we live together on this planet. I will go to Mother Kathleen and she will take me to live in paradise on the red moon through this portal in front of us.'

'What? As eagles?'

'No, Tom, as beings, living free beings with no danger, life with friends and family forever.'

'That does sound good,' replied Tom. 'But what happens to my family, Arn?'

'We will eventually meet them all there, Wolf and Eagle; it is the planet of the souls and peace at the end of our life. In the future, I will grow weak. We will come here together, then we will become one. I will enter you and be one with you for the rest of our lives until you die. Then we will separate again and continue the rest of our existence on the red moon. My body will stay here at this place with the help of Mother. You will return to your family with me accompanying you for the next part of our life, in this world. We will be together. It can be changed if you don't want it, then I will ascend to the red moon alone. Thinking about this may be what happens because you can now change into an eagle of your own free will. So, I am not sure what will happen.'

'Cool,' replied Tom with a beaming smile. He wasn't frightened anymore about this place that initially felt strange to him.

'Oh, I don't mean cool that you will be alone on the red moon. I will want to be with you'

'Thank you, Tom. You will, one day.' replied Arn.

Arn and Tom's attention shifted from one another to a figure emerging from the old building. A calm fell over them as the figure neared. Arn bowed his head and thought to Tom, 'Bow your head. Its Mother Kathleen.'

Tom was not sure what to do so he knelt on one knee and bowed his head. He had to use all his willpower to stop himself looking up at the figure but something in his mind said, don't look at her, she might turn you to stone or something, so he kept his head bowed. Mother glided towards them, hovering in the thin veil of fog. Arn felt a hand on his head then heard a familiar voice that he did not remember where it came from. 'Why are you back, Arn? Your soul is still young. I have been watching you. It is not your time but I know what your brother will ask me and for that I am glad you are here to help me bring them safely to me.'

Then Tom felt a hand upon his head. 'You are young and strong willed. I see why Arn has chosen you, little lord. But you will not ascend with Arn, you have your own eagle soul.'

Tom answered her, 'Yes, Mum, I'm young and I come from the Earth to here, I mean, Elemtum umm, that's because I come from here, Elemtum, I mean. I was born here not Earth.'

'Thank you, Thomas De-Callen, I am well aware of you and where and what you and Arn have been doing since you joined.'

'It's okay, Tom, you can lift your head and stand up,' thought Arn to him. Tom lifted his head up then stood up, there was no one in front of him. He turned to look at Arn. Mother Kathleen was standing by Arn's side, smiling at Tom. Sometimes when Tom looked at her, she was whole... no, he could see through her but she was still there... whole. Strange, he thought.

Then Kathleen spoke. 'So, you have come here to help your brothers.' she said.

'Brothers?' replied Tom.

'Yes, brothers. Karl and Alerio,' said Kathleen.

'Oh yes, I keep forgetting Karl has Alerio as well,' answered Tom.

'Well, Thomas De-Callen, I am Kathleen, mother to all the eagles and I know Karl and Alerio are near and they need our help.'

'What do we have to do to help them?' asked Tom

'I feel Alerio is weakening. His soul is keeping Karl's soul with him and it is taking a lot from him. Both of them are fading fast so we need to help them.'

'We will all come together and send our energy and Mother's special energy to them,' Arn told Tom reassuringly.

'We must come together. Come to me, Thomas, and you, young Arn. We must act now or it may too late for them,' said Kathleen. Tom went to her as did Arn; Mother put her arms around Tom and placed a hand on Arn. They were all together as the fog lifted and surrounded them. The fog was not cold or damp, wet or freezing, it was comforting… part of them. Tom was relaxed; he had probably never been this relaxed before in his whole life, not even in his bed. Not as relaxed as this. Both Arn and Tom felt energy and hope leave them but the fog compensated their loss. It was strange as the energy and hope left them. They could feel it leave but the fog replaced it so they gave more. How Tom did not know or care, he and Arn just gave. They sensed the energy, hope and love slide down the side of the red mountain, down and down past the cloud that surrounded the red mountain and continued down. Down to the struggling Alerio, weighed down by Karl's soul that was getting heavier and heavier. He feared he would have to give up and they would fall to their deaths together. As young as they were, he could not carry on much longer. His reserves of everything were nearly all gone.

Tom could not move. He was in a sort of daze but it was a good daze. He was happy and he knew what was going on. He knew he was saving his brother and Alerio.

Alerio was flagging. Karl's body and soul were now like flying with a ten-ton weight. He knew he could go no further. he felt himself start to fall uncontrollably. He had never felt this sensation before but he would not let his soulmate go, no matter what. Then the fog reached him and surrounded them. He could feel his fall stop; he was being held by something safe and energising. Alerio and Karl were lifted. The effort he felt before was gone, the heavy burden was no more. He felt Mother for the second time in his life, and his brothers Arn and Tom. They had saved them, he knew that, and soon it would be his turn to save Karl. He knew that too. He had always known it. Fire shot through his body and soul. He beat his wings and lifted higher and faster than he could ever have done, even without Karl. It was a culmination of the help from above. A spark from Karl's soul helped him. It made him fly. The power from his wings lifted them and the fog disappeared. He now knew he would reach the summit and Mother.

Tom could feel Karl getting closer. He was only just there. This brother was very dark or was it that he was now in a very dark place? Tom started to realise he was no longer in a daze, that Arn was at his side and Kathleen had gone, or had she? In front of the old building was a circle of fog, swirling around something that Tom could not make out until he saw a glimpse of Kathleen. Yes, it was Kathleen, the mother. Then Alerio came swooping in over the lip of the summit. Below him, held firmly, was the limp body of a wolf that Tom knew was Karl. Tom went to move but Arn held him back. That's when realised he was in the air above everything that was going on below.

'Be still, Tom, let her save him.' Tom stopped and watched in silence. The big eagle moved closer to comfort him.

Alerio gently came to a hover and placed Karl's body into the swirling fog and landed next to Mother. Inside the fog seemed to become denser, hiding them from Tom and Arn. Worried, Tom looked up at his soulmate who reassuringly gently bent his head in a calming nod.

The fog swirled but there was no sound. This went on for five minutes or so. Tom did not have a watch so he was not sure, he would comment later to his father. Then there was a bright light that made Tom and Arn close their eyes. This then travelled at lightning speed into the old building through two arched doors just as Tom opened his eyes. He had not noticed the doors before. The doors closed and the fog was gone. That's when Tom noticed his brother on the ground. He looked back to the doors but now the building was gone. Karl was the only thing left on the ground below Tom and Arn.

Karl lay motionless below them where Alerio had placed him; there was no Alerio or Kathleen, they had disappeared.

Tom heard Arn, 'We have been privileged, Tom. We will never see Kathleen the mother again. Not, that is, until we become one or ascend.'

Tom did not really hear what Arn had said, he just looked at his brother. 'Is he dead?' Tom asked nervously through tear filled eyes.

'Go and see,' Arn replied with a smile, if eagles could smile. Tom slowly approached his brother's body. After sensing the dark place his brother had been in as he had arrived, Tom was not sure what or who he would find. He could see no signs of life. Nothing, no twitch, nothing. He stopped and looked back at Arn who urged him on with another nod. 'Go on, it's okay,' he told him encouragingly. Tom stopped over his brother and looked down; no rise or fall of Karl's chest ed life, still nothing. Tom knelt next to him; he just looked until he heard Arn in his head, 'Touch him.'

So, Tom, now a small boy, did. He placed his hand on Karl's chest and the reaction was instant; his chest lifted. There was another brilliant light that made Tom close his eyes once more. Karl gasped, opened his eyes and smiled at his little brother, 'I was wondering how long it was going to be before you came over.'

'You could see me?' Tom asked, surprised.

'No, I could feel you,' Karl replied. He sat up, then stood with Tom's help.

Tom blinked and Karl was gone. He turned to look at Arn and Karl was standing next to him. This is strange, he thought. Looking at Karl, he realised he was also looking at Alerio. Or was it Karl inside Alerio? Tom was not sure. He blinked and there, next to Arn, was a smiling Karl, strangely different but still the same Karl.

'All right, Tom, what's up?' Karl asked.

'Ah, it is you, Karl. It is you, isn't it?' Tom asked.

'Yes, Tom, it's me. I'm okay, me and Alerio.'

'Alerio? Where's Alerio?'

'He's here with me… in me, part of me,' replied Karl. 'See.' Then in front of him, Karl was now Alerio then Karl again.

'You were dead?'

'I didn't know I was dead,' Karl replied and smiled.

'Everyone thinks you are dead.'

'Well, I had better change that, hadn't I.'

'You are alive, aren't you?' said Tom, as he walked towards his brother.

'Course I am, idiot! See.' and he hit Tom on the arm.

Tom stared at his brother, oblivious, for the first time in his life, to the punch Karl had given his arm. Karl put his arms around his brother and held him tight, the emotion was too much for them both, tears filled their eyes as Arn looked on feeling as they did. All was very quiet.

'I'm back, Tom, … thanks to you, Arn, Alerio and Kathleen the mother… Back.'

After a short time, Tom pushed his brother away. 'You have become very soppy since you became a zombie,' Tom laughed.

Karl smiled. 'It's good to see you and Arn again, Tom. It seems like I have been away for ever!'

'So, what happened? How did you come back to life? And where has Alerio gone?'

'Alerio is part of me now, Kathleen the eagle mother told me the only way I would live was if Alerio's soul and spirit entered me there and then, years ahead of the time when we would normally have joined together. So, that's what Alerio did.'

'So, is Alerio dead now?' asked Tom.

'No, he's in me and I am in him. We are together until we ascend to the red moon where we will live for the rest of time. You and Arn will join us one day, unless of course you and Arn get there before us. Alerio gave up his freedom to save me but he gets it back now and then.'

'What do you mean?' asked Tom.

'Watch,' replied Karl. 'Stand back.'

Tom moved to Arn's side. 'What's he doing?' Tom asked.

'Watch, Tom, my brother is taking over.'

Tom watched his brother turn from Karl to Alerio and he didn't even realise when the change took place. One minute it was Karl, the next Alerio. In front of them, Alerio lifted into the dark sky with the stars behind him, the wind from his powerful wing strokes blew into Tom's face and made him close his eyes. 'They're both alive, aren't they?' Tom asked.

'Yes, they are, Tom, and it's time for us to leave. We can't stay here any longer. We don't want to meet any departing souls on their journey home to the red moon,' Arn told him then called out to Alerio to return, his shrill call reaching high into the dark sky. Alerio returned and landed next to them.

'I'm ready,' Alerio told them.

'Do you mind if I fly?' Tom asked.

'You can fly with both of us and if you get tired you can ride on the back of whoever you want; I will not take offence, we are all brothers now, Tom.'

Tom changed into his eagle form. He had to concentrate really hard as it was not second nature yet but he changed and the two big eagles watched the little one lift into the sky where they joined him. 'Remember, flying this high is very dangerous. The thermals up here can play havoc with you. One minute you have lift, the next nothing, so stay with us and if you lose the lift glide down under control until you find the next thermal. That's what we will be doing until we reach about three thousand feet when we will convert to normal flight back to Great Porum,' Arn told Tom.

'So, we are basically falling under control?' replied Tom.

'Yes, you've got it in one, little brother, you learn quickly,' answered Alerio. Or was it Karl? Tom was not quite sure.

As they left that place no one had noticed that the old building had returned to the top of the red mountain; it was now covered in grass and honeysuckle covered the ground around the building. The three eagles flew to the edge of the summit and dropped out of sight, diving down, flying close to the red mountain side which, from that close, did not seem red at all. They disappeared quickly into the cloud that surrounded the mountain one thousand metres below the summit. Tom focused on the mountainside and the eagles either side of him. He felt exhilarated and full of life as he shot past the green and red vegetation clinging to the mountainside. He stayed close to his brother. He would not let him go again.

The Dark and their leaders knew that after the death of the emperor's son and the escape of the Wolf princess that it would not be long before the enemy would come to the arena in force so they moved. They moved deeper into the jungle, underground to their lair where they were safe and well-guarded with more warriors than the emperor could ever dream of. But the queen was not well, she was not right; she was not her Dark self so Gebhuza Septima would have to be summoned to find out what was wrong because Arthfael did not. Detor Eosin was dead. Even though he had been an irritation to Arthfael, he'd had some properties the Dark lord would miss. He had not expected the little scouting party of Dark warriors to encounter the water team or Phina and the prince but, in the end, it had worked out well. Yes, they had lost a lot of warriors on the attack on Great Porum but that had been acceptable. He had nearly had the Wolf princess but he had been a fool; he knew that and he had learnt from it. It would never happen again. But the queen... Now, that had been unexpected. What had happened to her? They would let Elemtum go quiet, lull them into a false sense of security then strike because by then their army would be ready. Until then, they would let the Wolf king and emperor of Elemtum and his minions play their games. Then they would strike.

In Warriors' Rest, the assault army was nearing completion. They had word from Phina that she was alive and well and with the Omani people. She would lead the strike against the Dark at the arena the next day once the water team had cleared the approach.

Happy that all the preparations for the coming battle were complete, Kurt had everything under control so the king could concentrate all his attention on the search for his old friend, now mortal enemy, Gebhuza Septima, and his final destruction. It was blatantly obvious to Frederick that he was responsible for all the troubles that had befallen him, his family and people and he would not let it continue.

Row had convinced everyone that she was ready to go on the hunt for the Dark. Tristan knew she was more than capable but Hollie and Kurt would be close at hand. Hollie was not particularly pleased because the king himself had asked her to act as personal bodyguard for his daughter. That meant someone else would lead her water team, for a while anyway, until she could get rid of the princess babysitting duties. Somehow she saw it as a snub because of the death of Prince Karl and the capture of Phina; that's how she saw it. This was not the actual case. The king had asked Kurt for a warrior he could trust to look after and protect his daughter. It was, in fact, a great honour, but she did not see it like that.

The force would move out in the early morning once the water team had cleared the route but the king's mind was not on that. He had been told that Gebhuza Septima had been spotted on Earth in a place called Louisiana. He had been told it was a swamp in the United States of America. He was in the process of finding out more about the place, the people and their attitudes to strangers. This could affect his possible intervention on his mission to capture Gebhuza

Septima that might occur in the very near future. Not that that really mattered. God help anyone who got in his way. He did not want to kill humans but if he had to, he would. He was aware that the worlds were connected but, apart from, that he was sure that lives were not connected. Now that he had his normal face back, he would fit in with the rest of the Earth's population. He would be noticed because he was a big strong man but at least he looked the same as the humans which would make his mission easier. In his mind it was easy; it was a search and destroy mission and that was it. In fast and out fast.

The king had a contact on Earth. He was a Scotsman, part of a canny family that had discovered one of the portals to Elemtum and had travelled there for a better life, fitting in well in the rugged area they now lived in which was north of the red mountain not far from the ice capped mountains and the snow wilderness. This Scotsman by the name of Billy Mullen somehow ended up in the American swamp and he liked it so he stayed there. His brothers, the clan leader, Robert, his brother David and sons Allen and David and a fiery redheaded daughter, Fiona, now lived in what can only be described as a castle. They fought well and drank well when and whenever their services were needed. They had come in very useful more than once at the side of the king and his brothers. The king was a friend of theirs as were Kurt and Tristan who liked to visit them whenever they could as they were great company. On top of that Robert's wife, Linda, made the best food in the whole of Elemtum which they had enjoyed on every visit. Fiona had joined the water team at the same time as Hollie and they were great rivals but also very good friends. In fact, it was Fiona who was leading Hollie's team in her absence. Knowing that had put Holly's mind a little at rest. Frederick had never met 'Mad Billy' who had decided to stay on Earth in the Louisiana swamps. That was one reason they called him mad, the second was his temper and the red mist that descended on occasions. The king knew all about Billy from his family. So much so, he felt he had known him as long as he had his family. Bill lived on Earth and the swamp supplied all he needed and that's the way he liked it. He wrestled with alligators as well as some of the locals, who he could outdrink. He was very proud of the fact that he even had his name above his local bar for drinking whisky with the strongest Louisiana hot sauce which would have killed a normal man. That was his reputation. Billy was rarely seen, once every six months if they were unlucky. He could not be missed as he always wore a tartan bonnet on his head under a mass of red hair and a long red beard. He was the man Frederick would be looking for help from when he arrived on Earth, and Billy was a man he knew he could trust because his brothers had told him so. Frederick had decided to go to Earth once the assault on the arena had been completed.

After an uneventful flight, the eagles landed at Great Porum, the capital, which had been cleaned up since the last time Karl and Tom had been there. Arn went to rest and have some food while Karl and Tom, now back in their people form, went to find someone they knew. The royal guard were amazed to see Karl and Tom, more so Karl as they believed him to be dead. Believing it to be a Dark trap, they called for backup and put the boys through the scanner. Karl protested fearing that, now being one with Alerio, he would be frozen again or worse, but his fears were unfounded and both he and Tom passed through without a problem. One of the guards escorted them to the strategic centre which, compared to the last time they had been there, was positively desolate. Only a few warriors manned the consoles that buzzed and crackled with the odd picture appearing on screen. They searched the faces only seeing one person they recognised. Samee.

She saw the boys and approached them, smiling. 'Well, we had been fearing the worst for you, boys. Tom, you disappeared and, Karl, you were reported dead but here you both are.'

'Indeed, we are, Leslie,' answered Tom with a grin. He was taking a liberty by calling her by her first name. She never used it and did not care for it; it was too personal, in her view. She let the cheeky little Wolf warrior get away with it because she had a soft spot for the little tyke.

'Where is everyone?' Karl asked.

'Warriors' Rest,' she replied. Then she told them everything thing that happened since they had been away, including his death.

'Attack? What attack?' Tom asked. He was told about the attack that would be going on that morning.

'Well, we thought you were dead and Phina had been taken...' she told them.

Tom butted in. 'Phina taken by who?'

'Well, what I mean is "taken". Well, yes and no. She was and she wasn't. What I mean is, she's safe... back now. Okay?'

'Okay. So, where?' asked Karl, so Leslie told them about the Omani people.

'We have to get to Warriors' Rest as fast as we can,' Karl told her

'Wait a minute. Your father would have my guts if I let you go and something happens to you,' she told them.

'It's okay. We won't be swanning around anywhere, we are going to Warriors' Rest to be with our family,' Tom said in a very mature manner.

'Okay. There is a sail craft leaving in twenty minutes. I will inform them to wait for you, so you had better get moving. 'And go straight there, no mucking about,' she added.

'Thanks,' replied Karl and they both ran off, heading for the sail craft dock.

On the way, Tom called Arn and told him to join them for the journey to Warriors' Rest. The sail craft left Great Porum with Tom and Karl and some specialist teams that Kurt had asked for, as well as Arn, inside the craft. Tom had felt sorry for him after all the flying he had done so he had coaxed him into the craft via the large cargo bay ramp where he settled down. The boys nestled into his feathers and they all fell asleep after a hectic couple of days.

The craft was twenty minutes from landing when one of the crew had the courage to wake the big eagle and the sleeping princes. After leaving the craft, they were met by a familiar face that flew down from above. Andor the Eagle warrior greeted them with a smile. 'It's good to see all the rumours of your demise were wrong, young prince.'

'Thank you, Andor. It's good to see you and be back in Warriors' Rest,' Karl answered, then they all flew to meet their family. They landed close to Kurt's home where Andor and Arn left them and the boys entered Kurt's home. The first person they saw was Raif who took a double take when he saw the boys. Raphina was behind him and put her hand over his mouth to stop him screaming out. The others were all sleeping and she did not want Raif to wake them. Raif had been told he could not go with the others when they attacked the arena. He had not been trained and his father would hear no more of it, so he was not in a good mood but that changed when he saw the boys. Raphina was still awake because she had been helping Tristan in the operations room. She had only returned to ensure Raif was fed. Raphina was overjoyed to see the boys fit and healthy and, after a hug, kisses and general talk of their wellbeing, they all sat down. The boys told the story of what had happened over the last few days.

They talked for hours until a sleepy looking Row wandered into the room still half asleep. 'I heard the strangest thing... I could hear Karl and Tom in my sleep.' She opened her eyes and stared. 'I'm still asleep aren't I because I can see Karl and Tom?'

'It's no dream, sis, we are back,' said Karl.

'No, you're not. It's a cruel dream, you're dead!' She turned to walk back to her room when Raif stood up and turned her around again so she was face to face with her two smiling brothers. She blinked and rubbed her eyes. 'Pinch me, someone.'

Tom went up to her and hugged her. Then she screamed. 'It's you! But you're dead?' she said, staring at Karl. Then she looked at Tom and squeezed his arms. 'You're real... You're both real, aren't you?'

'Yes, we are,' said Karl, as she grabbed him, kissing him, hugging him and crying.

'You're both never going anywhere without me again… Promise me!'

'It's okay, Row. We promise as much as we can. You know what this world is like.'

'Yes, I'm afraid I do. Now sit down and tell me everything.' She pulled them down onto the long comfortable seat and waited eagerly for their story.

'I can't sit through this again. Goodnight, everyone, see you all tomorrow,' said Raif, who then left them as did Raphina who had to go back to the strategic centre to relieve Tristan who was due a break. The boys relived their last few days for Row's benefit and the next few hours were spent with wows, no way, you're kidding, really and oh my gods until they heard movement from the area of the sleeping quarters. Kurt, Salina and their father appeared, the previous scenes were revisited and, for the third time, their story was told.

At the end of the story, their farther commented, 'Alerio saving you when he and you are so young, well, I have never heard of anything like that ever happening before. Either you are very special, Karl, or someone is looking after you and, by the sounds of it, Phina owes you her life.'

After all the excitement of the last few days and the reunion with their family, both boys were becoming very tired so their father suggested they go and have a sleep.

'We don't want to miss anything,' Tom told them as they left.

'You won't,' Kurt told them. 'I will wake you so you won't miss anything.'

Both boys were happy, happier than they had been for some time since coming to Elemtum and trotted off to their beds. Once the beds engulfed them, they were fast asleep. Kurt then set the beds for a day's sleep and left to go to war.

The boys awoke and could hear Tristan and Kurt talking. They were a little disorientated because they could see light streaming in through the windows. They thought it would be dark when they would be woken to go with Kurt to the arena but here it was brilliant sunshine. Tom and Karl sat up, stretched and looked at each other.

Tom asked, 'Thought we were going to fight the Dark?'

'I don't know,' replied Karl, 'maybe something went wrong or changed.'

They got up and went through to the room they were in previously where they were greeted by their uncles and Raphina.

'What's happened?' asked Karl.

'Nothing,' replied their uncle, 'absolutely nothing… Sorry, I decided after everything you have been through lately to let you have a good sleep to get your strength back and let your bodies relax and recover. You have been sleeping for two days.' Kurt was expecting the boys to protest but they didn't.

'Okay, cool,' replied Tom.

'Okay,' was the only reply from Karl.

'Are you both okay?' asked Tristan.

'Yes, fine,' they replied.

Kurt went on to explain they had, in fact, not missed a thing. The water teams had recced the arena and its approach, finding no sign of the Dark. Plenty of signs that they had been there and a couple of dead Dark warriors who looked like they had been executed for some reason. Phina had gone to the cells to look for Detor Eosin's body but that had gone although the bodies of the drunken guards lay all around. The local area was searched and nothing found. There were, though, signs of movement deep into the jungle to the south.

'Is anyone hungry?' asked Raphina. By the reply, everyone was so they went over to the great hall where they met Raif, Salina and Phina. After initial greetings, they got their breakfast and sat down, swapping stories of recent events, laughing and joking happily. This went on for a couple of hours until Tom asked where Row and their father were.

'Come back to the operations room and we will let you know what is happening and, Raif, you can go off for your training,' said his father. With reluctance, Raif left them but he was happy that Detor Eosin was dead. He had never liked him and had always thought there was something wrong with him. The others made their way to the operations room where Raphina explained to the boys about the letters Row had found on the blue moon in the cookbook. Also, that the king had been told and later given intelligence that Gebhuza Septima was on Earth and that he and Row had now gone there to find him.

'I hope Dad kills him; I knew there was something wrong with him. I could feel it in my bones when I met him. Do you remember, Raphina?'

'I certainly do, Tom. You jumped out of the window and flew away.'

Tom laughed. 'I didn't know I could fly until I jumped out of that window, so some good came of meeting him.'

'Apparently, he is hiding in a swamp in America, in Louisiana,' Raphina told them.

'Yes, I have heard of it but I don't know anything about it,' replied Karl.

Tom butted in. 'Well, it is the third biggest state in the USA and they are famous for catching catfish, shooting ducks and jambalaya.'

'Really?' asked Karl.

'No, I just made it up,' laughed Tom who received a punch on his arm from his brother for his pains.

'Idiot,' replied his brother as the others laughed.

'So, what are we doing to help them?' asked Karl. and was told about them being helped by Mad Billy Mullen.

'We have also decided... that is me, Salina and Phina will follow the king and Row down to Earth to make sure they are okay because, after all, we are the king's bodyguard and our brother does not know Earth and it's people like we do,' Kurt told them.

'If you're going, then so are we,' replied Karl. 'After all, we have lived on Earth most of our lives and you will have a better cover with us being with you. so that's that... no discussion.'

'Okay,' answered Kurt.

'Really?' replied Tom.

'Yes, really, we have already talked about it,' answered Phina. She went on to explain that they would be a family group touring the USA; they had passports, money, the lot. 'Even a Universal Studios baseball cap for you, Tom.'

Both boys were happy. They could feel another adventure and they knew this time they were with good friends and family.

They left and collected Earth clothes, passports, mobile phones for communication, money and some receipts from theme parks and restaurants, just as an added insurance policy if they were stopped by a diligent cop. They would be travelling back to Linasfarn to see Zuzza Zell who knew of a portal to that part of America. One of the sail craft was taken from its normal route to the blue moon and was rerouted to Linasfarn for their passage to the Zells.

Chapter 19
Louisiana

'This must have been the same route that Gebhuza Septima used to get to Earth, so I don't think he will be too far away from here and I am sure Billy Mullen will have his trail by now.'

From inside the tree line, Row and her father observed the bar that was across the road from their hiding place. 'It looks like a dive,' Row said.

'What do you mean by dive?' asked her father.

'A place frequented by roughens, scoundrels and women of ill repute,' she replied.

'Sounds like the sort of place I went to in the capital in the old days before it was all cleaned up… when I was young,' he added quickly. 'I learnt how to fight in a place like this.'.

'So, why are we here again?' she asked.

'This is Mad Billy's drinking hole; this is where he comes out of the swamp. This is where we are going to meet him.'

'If you have never met him, how are you going to recognise him?'

'He has red hair, a red beard and always wears a Scottish bonnet, whatever that is?'

'You mean ginger hair and beard,' replied Row. 'How will we know if he's here?' she asked.

Just then, the front door to the bar burst open and a man with wearing only jeans flew out and landed in a bloody heap on the ground. Row was just about to say something when another man in similar attire followed the first, landing on top of him with a grunt.

'Should we go and help them?' asked Row.

'Why?' answered her father. 'Neither of them has red hair so I assume our man is still inside and responsible for them. Let's go and have a look, shall we?'

'You first, Dad,' Row answered. They darted across the road and stood to the side of the open door. They left the comatose bodies where they lay. Frederick listened. There was not a lot of sound except some country music playing in the distance somewhere within the bar.

'Shall we go in?' Frederick smiled. 'Stay behind me, just in case.' He smiled once more. They entered the dark bar. A few orange lamps flickered, spreading light around the bar. As their eyes became accustomed to the light there were two people sitting at the bar and a bar lady behind it but no mad Scotsman. Row thought it odd that there were no windows and also realised the people were as far away from the door as possible, at the end of the bar.

'Hello, folks, I'm Maggie and this is my place. Would you like a drink? You old enough, young miss?' she asked. Then added, 'We have to be careful. The law pop in now and then.'

'She's fought in a war,' replied Frederick.

'That's good enough for me, sweetie. What do you guys want?'

'Whisky for me please and a coke for my daughter.'

'Beer please. I'm thirsty, Dad,' Row asked.

Frederick nodded and Maggie poured one beer and a whisky. 'What happened here, Maggie, the two blokes outside?'

'That's nothing, honey. That's just Mad Billy. He ain't mad by the way, just very sensitive,' she laughed.

'What do you mean?' Row asked.

'Those fellas out there dissed his skirt thingy,' she replied.

'It's a kilt,' came from the corner of the room. 'It's a kilt. How many times have I got to tell you people?'

'Okay, honey. Kilt, no problems. Do you want another drink?' Billy nodded and walked to the bar where Maggie handed him a whisky.

Frederick lifted his glass and said, 'To you and your kin, the Mullens... good health.'

'And to you,' Billy responded. They lifted their glasses and swallowed the whisky, putting both the glasses back on the bar at the same time. 'You must be Frederick. So, who is this beautiful young lady?'

'Yes, I am Frederick. Pleased to meet you.' Then turning, smiling, he introduced Rowena. 'And this is my daughter, Rowena.'

'Row,' his daughter corrected him.

'It's a pleasure to meet both of you; my brothers have told me a lot about you, Frederick, but not about you, young lady. You will have to be careful if my nephews see you, they will be fighting over you,' laughed Billy. 'You know what, I don't even like wearing the kilt but I'll no have any Yank take the mick. Another please, Maggie, and for these fine people, then we must get going as we have a wee walk to me house.'

Row asked for a coke and the two men downed another whisky. After a short while of general talking, Billy told them it was time to leave. On exiting the bar, they noticed the two bodies had gone.

'Off to lick their wounds, no doubt,' Billy mentioned as they crossed the road and made their way back into the swamp. Some hours later, Kurt, Phina, Salina and the boys came out of the swamp and crossed the road towards the same drinking establishment that Frederick, Billy and Row had left earlier. As they approached the door there was a short siren bust from behind them. They turned round to see a sheriff's car with its lights flashing in front of them.

With a very southern accent, a voice boomed from a speaker on the car's roof. 'Now, you boys, keep your hands where I can see them until my partner arrives.' Then the officer got out of his car and stood behind his door, hand on the top of his holstered weapon. Phina called over to him, 'What's the problem, officer?'

'You folks aren't from around here, are you? I can tell from that English accent, young lady.'

'You're right, officer. We are on holiday and a little lost, I'm afraid,' replied Salina, smiling at the officer. The officer visibly relaxed, took his hand off the pistol and walked around the door towards them.

'Mam, sir, boys, I won't keep you. My partner has a couple of guys in his car that claim they were assaulted by a big man wearing a dress. Now, that don't seem to fit any of you folks.' At that point a second sheriff's car arrived and they could see two heads in the back seat peering towards them. Several seconds later, the second officer got out of his car and walked towards his partner.

'Nope, Henry, none of these folks was the perpetrator that assaulted the Jones boys so I will take them back to their momma who no doubt will whip their hides for getting a beating.'

'Okay, Jerry, I will see if I can help these folks then I will be getting back to the station to write the report,' he replied as Jerry returned to his car then drove off with the two rather sorry looking Jones boys.

'Okay, guys, where you all from?' asked the officer.

'England,' replied Tom.

Laughing, the officer walked over to Tom. 'No, son, I meant where have you just come from? Is one of these folks your dad?'

Kurt stepped forward. 'I'm his father and this is his mother,' he said, pointing towards Phina who smiled.

'We were in a boat that has broken down a few miles inside the swamp. We've tied it up and headed inland to find somewhere to stay before it gets dark when we will let the owners know what has happened.'

'You did well getting here. Many people have gotten lost and died in the swamp, including locals.'

'I'm ex special forces,' Kurt told him.

'I can see that. I was in the rangers during Desert Storm and I know someone from special forces when I see one. Put it here, sir,' said the officer, then extended his hand towards Kurt who responded with his big hand and squeezed the officer's hand tight.

'My god, sir… that's a hell of a grip you got there.' Then the officer offered them his assistance. 'My cousin manages a motel a mile down the road. It's always got rooms and it's very clean and I would be happy to run you folks down the road if it helps you out?'

'That's very kind, officer, we would be much obliged,' Kurt told him, so they all got into his patrol car and drove off down the road. Karl and Kurt smiled at each other. 'We will get some rest there tonight then set off for Billy's in the morning,' said Kurt. Karl agreed. He was eager to get to his sister and father but he had a feeling that finding Gebhuza Septima would not be that simple, especially if he was, and it most definitely looked like he was, linked to or was the leader of the Dark forces.

The officer reappeared and took Karl and Kurt into his cousin's motel. It was clean and the officer's cousin was very friendly. He took all their passports for safe keeping telling Kurt that they must talk later after seeing a NATO stamp in Kurt's passport, explaining he was a Vietnam vet and had lost his foot over there. He then promptly came around his counter and showed Kurt and Karl the stump at the end of his left leg. 'Don't stop me getting round,' he told them, waggling it at them. Kurt told him he would love to talk about old times but they had been up since dawn and were all getting a little tired so he made a date for the next day which kept the cousin happy. They got their keys and left the Vietnam vet in his office and went to find the others.

They soon came across two opened doors. Inside one room were Phina, Salina and Tom sitting on a big double bed. It was double beds all round. Tom and Karl had one each as did Phina and Salina and Kurt had two in his room to himself. They went to freshen up in their respective rooms then met back in Kurt's room. Half an hour passed and there was no Karl or Tom so Salina went next door, knocked on their door and entered. Inside the room, Karl was lying on one bed, Tom on the other, both watching cartoons on the big forty-two-inch TV, transfixed to the screen.

'Karl, Tom, you not playing then?' Salina asked them.

The boys looked up. They had lost track of time watching the TV. To them, it had seemed like years since they last saw a programme but they quickly jumped up and turned the box off, apologising to Salina and again to Kurt and Phina when they entered the room. They all understood what the boys must have felt, for not too long ago it was their life.

They settled down around a map on one of the double beds and Kurt orientated it to where they were then indicated where Robert had told him Billy's log cabin was located, deep into the swamp with no visible path or road to it.

'That's where we will be going tomorrow,' he told them. Their kit had to be ready for early in the morning because they would be setting off while it would still be cool. Kurt gave them bearings for the heading they would be following and divided them into groups just to be on the safe side. He did not want them all getting caught as one big group. Phina and Tom would be one, Kurt and Karl another and the final one would be Salina and Tristan who by then was spending the night out in the swamp making sure their route was clear and that there would be no surprises when the others entered. He would meet Salina inside the swamp after the two other groups had passed him. After everything was set, everyone knew the timings for the next day. They had had a call from the sheriff; he and his daughter had invited them all to his home down the road for a real southern barbeque. He would collect them from the motel at seven in his big Dodge minibus. He would even ensure they got back to the motel afterwards. 'Don't you think it's odd that we have all just turned up out of the blue and these people invite us for a meal? It seems like they are being a bit too nice,' Karl asked.

'You've been away too long; you're getting too suspicious, Karl,' replied Tom.

'No, your brother may have a point. We are here to help the king and track down Gebhuza Septima. I will tell the motel manager that one of the boys is not well and one of us will stay with him. The rest can go to the barbeque. If it's okay then so be it but if not, at least we have separated our forces. If it seems safe, we will call you both forward. As long as we are all on our guard, we should be able to deal with anything these people can throw at us. Phina, you stay here with Tom and the rest of us will go. Everyone ensure you have a concealed weapon with you, just in case,' said Kurt.

Half an hour later Kurt went down and spoke with the cousin, the motel manager, who told Kurt his brother's housekeeper was a ex nurse so she could help the boy. Kurt declined the offer and went back to the others, now a little more suspicious than he had been before. It could be a coincidence, he thought, but very unlikely.

He returned to the motel room and they all rested until half an hour before seven when they all got ready to go, concealing weapons so they would all look unarmed which would give them a chance if it turned out to be a trap. Karl and

Salina promised Tom and Phina that if it was all genuine, they would let them know and get someone to come back for them. Tom was not too worried about going because there were some programmes on telly he wanted to watch; Transformers, GI Joe and wrestling, things he remembered from his previous life. Everyone was ready. They said their goodbyes, leaving Phina alert and Tom watching telly lying on his bed.

The others went down to the reception where the sheriff's van was already waiting. The motel manager joined them and they all got into the vehicle, as of yet no danger signs had emerged. The vehicle left the motel and travelled down the swamp-lined highway with no incident. After twenty minutes, they turned into a long drive that was lined by oak trees bent over making a tunnel to drive through. At the end of the line, after about half a mile, a grand white southern mansion loomed ahead. The van drove in an arc along the gravel drive to stop at the front, adjacent to the grand front doors. As they came to a halt, the doors opened revealing a grand hall with a white staircase sweeping up to an unseen destination. Standing in the door was the sheriff in a white suit with a white stetson upon his head but most notably of all were the red shirt and snakeskin cowboy boots.

'Oh my god, what does he look like?' laughed Karl who was nudged by a grinning Salina who put her hand to her mouth to stop her laughing. The motel manager either did not hear Karl's comment, pretended not to, did not care or just did not want to react. He opened the sliding side door. After a quick look round, Kurt stepped out on to the gravel followed by Karl and Salina. The motel manager indicated for them to follow him up the steps. Without making it obvious, both Kurt and Salina indiscreetly scanned around looking for any signs of danger; there were none. As they reached the top, the sheriff welcomed them to his home and hoped Tom would feel better soon. Kurt thanked him for the invite and shook his hand warmly, as did Karl and Salina. The sheriff took them along the hall under the stairs through an arch into a large drawing room. At the other end, two large doors opened onto a patio with stairs that led down to an immaculate green lawn. On the lawn were what definitely looked to Kurt and Salina law enforcement officers and their families. Seeing them, Kurt and Salina started to relax but Karl had his eye on something else. At the bottom of the steps was a row of ninety-gallon drums that had been cut in half and turned into barbeques; six of them in a row and covered with all sorts of fat dripping meat, sausages, chicken burgers, large corn on the cobs and several other things Karl did not recognise. But he did recognise that two of the barbeques were covered with four massive ribs and one was covered by the biggest prawns and lobsters he had ever seen. His mouth began to water and, without realising, he said, 'Real food.'

'You're right there,' replied Kurt as he slapped Karl's back bringing him back to life. He hadn't even noticed the other tables with salad, bread and all sorts of exciting food and goodies as well as every sort of drink known to man.

'Ladies and gentlemen, I would like to introduce some new friends of mine all the way from England in the United Kingdom. Hey, Kurt, what part of England are you from?'

'Suffolk, East Anglia,' Kurt replied.

'From Suffolk, East Anglia' the Sheriff replied to his guests. 'He's a god damn war hero like my pappy so make him, his lovely wife Salina and their son Karl most welcome.'

'Oh, and don't worry. They don't have any warrants, I checked.' The sheriff laughed as he shook Kurt's hand and walked him into the gathered crowd, Salina and Karl following. Kurt was handed a beer, Karl a coke and Salina a wine, then they mingled with the crowd, answering questions from folk about England and Kurt's war service. Several veterans made themselves known and shared their experiences.

Salina was gathered up by some envious women who asked her how she kept so young looking and how she kept her figure. Salina put it down to lots of exercise, running and being young. Being wicked, she also told them that Kurt who was a lot older than her and that they had married when she was eighteen. This got a few mutters from the assembled women so Salina added, 'It's legal where we come from,' keeping the smile from her face. The women seemed to be happy about that.

A young lady took Karl by the hand and lead him to a group of young people on the edge of the crowd. 'Guys,' she said, 'this is Karl from England, where the Beatles, David Bowie and the queen come from.'

'Cool,' was the reply from most except one who said nothing.

'Don't mind her,' said the young lady. 'That's the sheriff's daughter. She's always quiet until she gets to know someone.'

The youngsters talked about human things that Karl found quite refreshing after being on Elemtum, although he was already behind the times for new films, music, and entertainment, but he had never been quite up on those subjects anyway. All the time he kept glancing over to the solitary girl on the fringe of the group talking to no one but who, every now and then, looked at Karl and smiled.

Eventually, everyone was called to the barbeque stands to get some food. Karl left his group and returned to Salina and Kurt. 'Everything okay?' he asked them both?'

'These women don't half talk some rubbish,' replied Salina.

'This beer is going down well,' said Kurt, but he had still only had one glass since arriving. They helped themselves to a bit of everything, then went and sat on the grass together. As they talked, the solitary girl came over and asked if she could sit with them. They were all happy for her to do, so she sat down next to Karl and Salina. None of them noticed the figure in an upstairs window watching them, joined by the sheriff's cousin, the motel manager.

'It's strange. I feel connected to you,' said the solitary girl. 'It's strange. Since you arrived I felt like I know you all. Isn't that strange? I'm adopted you know. The sheriff is a good man and I think of him as my father but there is always something else, something I can't explain.'

'Don't all orphans feel like that?' asked Salina.

'I don't know,' the girl replied. 'I don't know any other orphans.'

'Fair point,' Salina replied just as the sheriff appeared.

'So, you folks have met my daughter, Erline. She's the closest thing to a boy that I have and she don't mind me saying that either, do you darlin'?' said the sheriff.

'Nope, papa, I don't mind one bit I'm not all girlyfied like Amy Lou who loves her dresses and things.' That's when it clicked in Karl's mind. she's a beautiful girl but in boy's clothes, that's what it was, he thought.

'Nothing wrong with that. I hate wearing dresses,' Salina thought back to him.

'Sorry, Salina, I didn't realise I was thinking to everyone.'

Salina smiled at him. 'Just be mindful of what and how you think, Karl. It could get you a lot of trouble one day,' she thought back.

The sheriff asked if everyone was having a good time. Just then Kurt noticed a movement in the swamp undergrowth some way off. The sheriff stayed and chatted for twenty minutes. Kurt was convinced someone in the swamp was trying to contact him; either that or they were very bad at concealment. When the sheriff and his daughter left them, Kurt told the others of his suspicions so he could disappear and turn himself into a wolf to find out if there were any grounds to his suspicions

He made his way around the big building, telling any that asked that he was heading for the toilet. When all was clear he turned into his wolf form and dashed into the swamp. He was making his way towards the area he had seen the movement when he came across another wolf; Tristan, he knew his wolf form anywhere.

'So, you saw Billy's attempts to get your attention. We believe that Gebhuza is in that building. I am sure I saw him watching you all. He was with a human at one point, the one who came with you from the motel. The king believes it was him too. Keep your wits about you. If they ask you to stay, don't. We will keep watch all night to ensure he doesn't leave. Go back to the barbeque, I will contact you when we have a plan. I will let Billy know to keep hidden. He is only distracting you.'

'Is the sheriff involved, do you think?' Kurt asked.

'We don't think so,' came the reply.

Kurt went back and mingled with the crowd and found Salina and Karl. They had talked a little more with Erline who had told them her story. She had been found by some Cajun swamp dwellers twelve years before, she believed, but wasn't sure. She had been found in an abandoned cabin inside the swamp and taken to the sheriff who had tried to find her parents but to no avail. Eventually, the sheriff adopted her. That was about the same time his long-lost cousin had returned from Vietnam. Everyone had believed him to be dead but he had been in a prisoner of war camp and eventually released, she had told them.

Tom sat up from watching the TV and noticed Phina watching something through the motel window. 'What are you looking at?' he asked.

'Nothing, Tom, just making sure there is nothing to worry about. I'm going to take a look about just to be on the safe side.'

Then it hit Tom. 'You're a human, Phina!'

'No, I'm not, Tom.' She smiled.

'You know what I mean,' he replied. 'I never thought about it until just know as I was watching you looking out the window. You're on Earth and you're not a wolf. How come?'

'Paccia was working on something to stop she wolves turning straight to wolves when they get to Earth. One of the forward scouts tried it after Salina returned from Earth with Kurt and Tristan. Apparently, it supresses something. It's all beyond me,' she told him. 'The only side effect we know of is that it makes me more inclined to eat young boys,' she told him then went over and tickled him on the bed, until crying with laughter he gave in. 'They are working on a theory that it has something to do with threads or time pathways that change a female's insides. I don't know what they call it... DNA thingy?' She smiled.

Gebhuza Septima was looking out of the upstairs window with the sheriff's so-called cousin who was, in fact, a Dark warrior; one of the very talented Dark warriors who, in Gebhuza's eyes, would go far in his new world on Earth'. He had fooled the sheriff and all the townspeople into believing he was the long-lost cousin. The great survivor from Vietnam, who now looked down upon the happy gathering with Gebhuza, was worried. The sight of Kurt, Salina and the queen's child, Karl troubled him; they were unexpected and that made him nervous. He would deal with them. The more he thought about it, the more he started to smile; this could actually work in his favour.

Phina left Tom and the motel room after instructing him to close and lock the door behind her. She would be no more than ten minutes, she had promised him. Along the landing and down the steps at the far end, Phina walked, senses heightened, looking for any sign of danger. At first there were none but as she became attuned to her surroundings, she began to notice things. In fact, it was the lack of things, no sound, no movement, something was wrong. As she turned the corner into the car park at the front of the motel, she noticed nothing; no cars, no vans. nothing. There had been at least six cars and a van the last time she had looked out the window. Then out of the corner of her eye she saw movement. An assassin was now on the landing, heading straight for the room she had just left, and Tom. Then, from behind her, the air was full of movement and sounds. She turned as she called a warning to Tom. She instinctively swung her fist around, impacting the side of another assassin's head, making its legs buckle at the knees. It dropped the dagger in its hand. That's when she ducked as a dart flew past her head from a third assassin coming out from behind the door of a motel room at the end of the building. She grabbed the unconscious assassin at her feet and lifted it up as a shield. Several more darts impacted into it from the assassin now closing in on her who threw away its blow pipe and pulled two knives from beneath its robe. Behind it, she noticed a Dark lancer coming out of the room, not even trying to conceal its presence from this Earth.

Tom had heard Phina's call and was getting off the bed as he heard a key pass slide into the door lock and the handle started to turn. He ran at the door as it opened, barging whatever was opening the door against it. He saw a black robe and a rat face as a knife slashed after him as he leapt headfirst over the first storey balcony towards the car park below. Then he was gliding, beating his wings and climbing.

For a second Phina's heart leapt as he flew over the balcony but now he was an eagle, twisting and heading towards her. The assassin's eyes widened as Tom swooped over Phina's head then hit the him full force, his talons lifting the creature off its feet, both its knives falling to the ground. Phina dived for them, grabbing one as Tom beat his wings and climbed into the sky with the screaming assassin flaying beneath him, tight in the eagle's grip. As she rolled, she let the knife fly at the fast-approaching lancer who fended it off with this lance. This was all the time she needed, throwing herself at him her elbow striking him in the jaw with as much aggression as she could muster, twisting and snatching the lance from his grip, rolling to a standing position with the tip of the lance close to his face. Milliseconds passed before the lancer realised he was dying. Then she was sprinting up the stairs towards the now fleeing assassin on the landing of the motel but the dagger Phina had retrieved from the falling lancer struck its back with such force that the creature bowled over and sprawled onto the landing floor. Phina stamped her boot on the back of its neck, breaking its spine instantly just to make sure it was dead. Then she stopped and took stock, looking left, right, down, then up as the third assassin fell past her to impact heavily on the tarmac car park ground below. Above her, Tom was circling after releasing the assassin.

'I'm going to get these bodies out of the way. Keep an eye out for any more trouble,' she told him.

'It's all clear at the moment,' he replied from above. Quickly Phina collected the bodies and placed them in the room the lancer had come from. The room was bare. There were no clues about how the Dark had known they had been there. Then she collected their things from the room and took them to the motel reception, placing them in a back room which she then locked, taking the key. There was still no one about, no sign of life. 'There's a van of some sort behind the motel,' Tom informed her.

Phina checked it out. It was the motel's van so she checked and found the keys in the reception, luckily hanging on a peg labelled 'Van Keys'. That's when she noticed she was bleeding.

'Phina, there's blood running down your arm.' She lifted her T-shirt sleeve; there was a two-inch gash on her upper arm.

'It's only a scratch, Tom. There should be a first aid kit here somewhere.'

Tom gave her a teacloth he found near a coffee maker. He told her to sit and he would find the first aid kit. He placed an absorbent dressing on the wound then wrapped it tightly with a bandage. 'There, that should keep you going till we get it stitched.'

Phina smiled at him. 'As good as new, Tom, thank you'. She let him get involved to keep his mind off what had happened. She knew the wound would stop bleeding soon.

Phina took the van and headed in the direction the others had gone to the sheriff's barbeque. Above, Tom looked ahead for anything that struck him as a sheriff's house. In the distance, surrounded by swamp Tom could see a big white house with green lawns and people milling about on it.

The sheriff's cousin lifted the sniper rifle and aimed it at Kurt. Just at the edge of his vision he noticed something move in the swamp so he readjusted his view to look at it. It was a large man with red hair and a dress waving his arms towards him. 'What the hell is that?' Gebhuza lifted the binoculars from around his neck and looked on in astonishment as the bear-like man turned his back to them, bent over and lifted the dress showing a bare arse to them Braveheart style. Then, turning to look at them, he placing a middle digit in the air before disappearing into the swamp.

'What do you make of that, sir?' the cousin asked.

'I don't know but I don't like it. Take out Kurt and the boy then we will deal with the rest,' he replied. The cousin went back searched the faces for his targets.

'Where are they?' He looked up from the sight for a better all-round view. His targets had gone. He looked around; all looked normal except that his targets had gone. He turned but where was Gebhuza? He was no longer in the room. Damn, damn. The cousin felt a sense of foreboding that his perfect life was slipping away and he did not want it to; he didn't want to go back to life with the Dark, he was someone here. What was he doing here?

Gebhuza was now in the swamp, heading for his salvation. The door to the top room opened. The cousin turned sharply from his vantage point. He had not been concentrating, his mind on other things.

In the door stood the sheriff, 'What's going on, Dwain? The English fella saw you in the window with a rifle. You having flashbacks? You okay?'

As Dwain looked at the sheriff, thoughts went through his head. He was happy here. This world was different but, deep down inside, he knew it would not last forever because other people would not let it. The cousin lifted his gun as he saw Kurt appear behind the sheriff.

'Get down!' he shouted as he waved the barrel of the gun, indicating to the sheriff move aside.

'You can't escape, you piece of dirt. Give up now and I won't kill you straight off, I'll give you a chance,' shouted Kurt.

A shot rang out and the sheriff fell back into Kurt, knocking him off balance back into the attic corridor with the sheriff on top of him. In seconds, the cousin was next to them gun, pointing directly at Kurt.

'You bastard, you're not going to ruin this for me, you bastard.'

'All I want is Gebhuza, I don't give a damn about you.' Another shot rang out, but this time the cousin flew backwards, hitting the attic floor with a thud. The side of his face missing, lifeless as the rifle clattered to the attic floor. Kurt looked behind him to see Erline standing there with a shotgun in her hands.

'Pupa! You okay?'

'Yes, darlin'. He got my shoulder.'

'What's going on?'

'Here, sheriff,' said Kurt as he helped him stand. 'You okay to stand, sheriff?' he asked as Erline approached them, concern and worry etched all over her face.

'I'm okay damn it. I was special forces in Iraq, I'm okay. Takes more than that to put me down. Now, what's going on? I take it Dwain ain't Dwain?'

Kurt turned to see Karl behind Erline. 'Everyone okay? What about Gebhuza?'

'I just saw Erline leg it to the house, so I followed. I got a bit worried when she ran to the police car, pull out a shotgun and follow you up here.'

Billy had seen a figure dart from the big white house into the swamp. He told Row and the king who then told Row to stay with Billy while he tracked the figure. Billy and Row did not agree. Billy knew all the dangers and the local area. He had trapped and hunted here for many years and Row was not going to leave her father, not now, not after all they had been through. It was decided that they would all go together because the king agreed that Billy knew the swamp like the back of his hand. So, it was agreed. 'Sense prevails,' said Row smiling at everyone. The three of them would track the fleeing Gebhuza.

Outside the white house, Phina had arrived with Tom circling high above, keeping watch for any unseen danger. The people on the ground could not see him. He could see all the people from the barbeque at the back of the house all now gathered on and around the back steps to the house.

After hearing the shots, a couple of the deputies who had been amongst them, were now taking control with pistols previously on display to reassure the innocent and warn any potential villains.

Inside the white house, Karl and Erline looked after the sheriff, doing what they could to comfort him and stem the bleeding. He had been lucky. The bullet had gone through his shoulder without seemingly hurting any main vessels or bone.

'You're lucky, Pa, clean wound,' Erline told her dad.

Karl picked up the rifle and removed the magazine because that's what was done to stop anyone else using it. He was now happy that everyone in the room was friendly, but there was one thing he had learnt in the last few day, you could trust no one. He lay the rifle on the floor, threw the magazine in to the furthest corner of the room, then he went over to the dead body. From what he could see it was definitely now extinct, dead. The side of his face was definitely gone, the rest of that side of his head had gone too. The basics Karl knew of anatomy told him that wasn't a good thing. Karl looked around and, near where he had thrown the magazine, he saw a corner table with a tablecloth over it. He had noticed Erline occasionally glance over at her dead uncle and he could see the horror and disbelief in her eyes. He went over, removed the cloth from the table, carefully replacing the plant pot that was on it back on the table. He then took the cloth over to the dead body and placed it over the head and shoulders. Erline looked up at Karl, smiled and nodded her head in thanks.

Kurt helped the sheriff into a sitting position with his back against the wall. Karl noticed Erline had gone and Kurt was talking to the sheriff.

'Sheriff, we have been tracking this man all over this world and finally tracked him here to the US. He has been trying to build an army to overthrow the world and change it from what we know to a dark and sinister place that suits his ambitions. And I am sorry to say the man you thought was your cousin, returned from being missing in action in Vietnam, was, in fact; a plant from this man's army, one of his henchmen. For what purpose, I am not sure at this point. I don't think his ultimate goal was to kill you. I believe our arrival may have forced him to try and kill us,' explained Kurt.

'You can't be talking about the doctor? He's been here on and off for many years; a well-respected man in these parts.'

'When you say on and off, do you know where he has been when he has not been here?' Kurt asked.

'Well, no. He always said he was doing humanitarian work all over the world.'

'And nobody suspected anything?'

'Why should we? We had no reason to. He seemed a good man.'

'Yes, I know him well so I can understand why you think that. It has only been the last couple of days when we started to suspect him after some information came to light. Before that he was a trusted medical leader who had done some great work for us,' Kurt told him. Then he continued, 'In fact, we suspect he is the mastermind behind thousands of innocent people's deaths, soldiers and civilians alike, as well as women and children.'

Wincing slightly as he moved, the pain from his shoulder injury shooting through his body, the sheriff slightly moved his position to try and get a bit more comfortable. Kurt put another dressing over the wound, careful not to remove the ones that had been placed over it initially. 'How come I have never heard of this guy or his army? I mean, I'm ex special forces and I still know some guys who are still in my old outfit. We chew the cud over a few beers now and then and talk shop. But this lot, not a word,' said the sheriff.

'He's been known by a few names and linked to several dictators and terror organisations,' replied Kurt as Erline reappeared with another medical box.

She spoke as she approached 'Here you go, Pa, all those years in the wilderness girls is finally going to pay off. Where did those dressings come from? she asked, seeing the dressings now covering her father's shoulder.

'I always carry a small trauma first aid kit with me, just in case,' said Kurt smiling. 'It comes in very useful now and then, as you can see,' he said.

Just then one of the deputies came into the room. 'Everything is under control outside, sheriff. Medical chopper is inbound and we will have you out of here pretty soon... You okay, boss?' he said with a worried look on his face as he looked at the sheriff.

The sheriff smiled. 'Don't worry, Jeff, you won't have to hold the fort for too long. I don't intend to be holed up in a hospital bed... Ahh.' He winced as a sharp pain shot across his chest.

Kurt told the deputy to go and ensure the helicopter could get in okay then bring the paramedics straight up to the sheriff. The deputy departed and Kurt asked Erline to watch her father and ensure the blood was not seeping through the bandages. Then he took Karl over to the corner of the room. 'I think there may be some poison on that round that hit the sheriff. He's a strong man and should not have that much pain across his chest. It should be more localised around the wound. I'm a little concerned.'

Erline called over to them. 'What are you whispering about? If there's something I should know about Pa, I should know.'

'It's okay, Erline. How's your father?'

'He's fallen asleep. Is that normal for a gunshot wound?' Kurt and Karl walked over to her and supported the sheriff on either side to stop him falling over.

Kurt then whispered to Erline. 'I think he may have been poisoned. It's one of the Dark's favourite tricks' he said.

'Dark...? Poison...! What are you talking about?' she replied.

'I will explain later. Let's make sure your dad is okay first.'

In the background they could hear a helicopter circling around above them. Tom could see and hear it approaching so he climbed a little higher and watched it just to make sure nothing funny was happening. The helicopter circled twice then spotted the deputy sheriff raise his arms and point in the direction of where he wanted the helicopter to land. The other deputies kept the guests away from any danger from the approaching helicopter. The deputy lowered then raised his arms in a flapping motion, indicating to the pilot to descend and land. She neatly landed then quickly stopped the rotor blades but keeping the helicopter's engine running. Tom watched two paramedics leave the helicopter carrying bags and heading for the deputy waving to them from the steps of the white house steps. Then they were gone inside, rushing with purpose towards the sheriff to administer aid.

Inside the house, the deputy ran up the stairs, the medics close behind. They entered the room to find Kurt over the sheriff, injecting him using a small vile with an attached needle. Erline was watching over her shoulder, worry and concern etched all over her face. The deputy stood to one side and let the medics pass. Erline stepped back to allow them access to her father. Kurt explained to them what he had done medically for the sheriff and about his suspicions of poisoning which was why he had been injecting the sheriff as they entered. He too then stood back to allow the medics full access to the sheriff as a second deputy entered the room with a folding stretcher and went to their side. No sooner had they arrived then they were leaving with the sheriff strapped into the stretcher, a drip hanging from his arm being held by a medic.

'I think that guy may have saved your Pa's life,' one of the medics told Erline, then they were gone. Erline went with them leaving Kurt, Karl, a deputy and the body alone in the now quiet room.

'Is that the sheriff's cousin under there?' The deputy asked.

'Not quite,' replied Kurt.

'Oh, because part of him has been shot away you mean?' the deputy said.

'No, he means everyone thought it was the sheriff's, even the sheriff, but it wasn't. It was an evil man working for a very evil mastermind,' said Karl.

'Oh… Well, guys, thank you for your help, but I must ask you to leave the room as it is now a crime scene.'

Outside, Kurt and Karl met Phina who told them Tom was watching from above. They turned to watch the helicopter lift and speed away. Karl wondered if he would ever see Erline again, then sadness tugged at his heart.

'Who are you folks?' The question came from behind them. They turned to see another officer. This time he was not a local deputy but a state trooper, a sergeant to be precise.

'Who, may I ask, are you, sergeant?' replied Kurt.

'I, sir, am Sergeant Naffzeger, from the state police. We handle all murders here in Louisiana, unless it's a federal case then the FBI boys step in. Now, what happened here and, I ask again, what are you doing here?'

'I'm a friend of the sheriff. This is my son Karl and my daughter Phina. We were invited here for a barbeque.'

'Mam.' The officer nodded to Phina and smiled, totally ignoring Karl.

'Officer!' said Kurt.

The officer returned his attention back to Kurt, his face going a little red. 'Oh yes, well… as I was saying, what happened here? Were you involved at all? Did you see anything?'

'We were having a nice time when I noticed a man in the attic window pointing a gun at us. I told the sheriff then we both went up to the attic to find out what was going on. We confronted the man who turned out to be the sheriff's cousin who was acting very strange then he shot the sheriff. Luckily his daughter...'

'Erline. Karl butted in.

'I know, kid, I know the family,' replied the sergeant.

Karl was going to react to the 'kid' reference but decided to stay quiet.

High above them, Tom circled out of sight of everyone, unnoticed.

'Erline shot him with a gun from the sheriff's car,' finished Kurt.

'Must have flipped. All those years in 'Nam, it can't have been good going through what he did. You never know what they did to them guys. Where are you guys staying in case I have to get hold of you?' asked the sergeant.

'Here with the sheriff,' Kurt replied.

'Well, it all seems quite clear to me. I will let the shrinks figure the reason out. By the way, for my records what's your full name?' the sergeant asked.

'Smith, Kurt Smith. My daughter Phina and son Karl,' replied Kurt. 'Oh, my wife, Salina, is around here somewhere, probably with the other women I imagine.'

'German?' the sergeant asked.

'English, of German descent,' Kurt answered.

The sergeant nodded. 'Figures. I mean Kurt and Karl.' Kurt nodded.

'Okay, folks, I will let you get on. Have a nice day, if you still can,' the sergeant added. 'If I need you, I will contact the sheriff or Erline.' He smiled. He thanked them for their help, tipping his hat to Phina and smiling as he did. Then he left them.

Around the corner of the house, out of sight of everyone, Tom came swooping in, flaring at the last minute and touched down. As he walked to them, he changed back into a boy.

'That was good, got rid of the cobwebs,' he told them.

'Show off,' said Karl, smiling at his brother. Tom smirked back. They continued around to the back of the house where the last of the guests were having their names taken before they left. Soon only the four of them were left. Tom went over to the barbeque, retrieved a chicken drumstick and started eating. Soon they all tucked in, suddenly feeling very hungry.

Once finished, their thoughts turned to Row, the king and Billy who were still tracking Gebhuza, still fleeing at speed away from them, the person they believed to be behind all that was going wrong in this world and theirs.

Billy could see the man was in some hurry, not even trying to conceal his tracks; vegetation was smashed and broken, clearly showing the direction he was travelling. Eventually in front of them was a bayou. On the far bank was swamp and the vegetation on either side was the same. It was quite thick. Billy did not believe he had got through it. But there was no Gebhuza Septima, only eyes looking at them from the water.

''Gators,' Billy told Frederick. 'Swamp's full of them. Maybe he's inside one of them now. If he went in there and they attacked him, he would probably be dragged to the bottom and kept there until he died,' Billy added.

'Let's hope so,' said Row.

'My thoughts exactly,' replied her father. 'The only trouble is if that has happened then all the information he has and the answers that we want would all go down with him. We were hoping he could answer a lot of our questions.'

'And don't forget, Dad… having the satisfaction of seeing him die,' said Row. Her father agreed. They decided to search the local area just to make sure he was not lurking around or had headed off along the bank in either direction. Frederick and Row went in one direction and Billy the other after a warning from him to keep a sharp eye out for 'gators or anyone that could be helping their quarry. They decided to come back to the same spot after half an hour; the thinking being if they could not track anything in that time then he was probably in the water.

They met up again after finding no sign of anyone fleeing in either direction. 'Perhaps there's a passage down there leading to Elemtum or somewhere else,' commented Row.

'You may be right,' said her father. Turning to Billy, he asked if he could get hold of any diving gear for the three of them and whether Billy could find this place again. The answer to both was 'yes'. In fact, 'nae problem, sunshine' were his exact words.

It was decided that the king would stay and watch the bayou in case Gebhuza reappeared thinking all was safe and Billy would take Row back to the white house to meet up with the others. Billy would then get the diving gear and bring it to the white house. He knew Gina the housekeeper.

Back at the house they had gathered up all the leftover food and put it in the biggest fridge any of them had ever seen with the help of Gina the resident cook and housekeeper. After that Gina had taken them to a large room, which she told them was the bar and games room. It had the biggest TV Karl and Tom had ever seen. She made them comfortable then left so Tom turned on the TV and started to flick through every channel which annoyed Karl who snatched the remote from Tom's hands. Tim did not react because he had noticed a cabinet full of small figures from the civil war through to modern times, so he was quite happy and left Karl to the TV. Salina had escaped from the local women and was now flicking through some of what she presumed were Erline's magazines, occasionally laughing at some of the pictures showing what Earth women were wearing at the moment.

'I honestly don't know why she is bothering to wear anything... It's not as though it's covering anything. A waste of material if you ask me... She may as well walk round naked.'

'Let's have a look,' shouted Tom, momentarily distracted from the military figures in the case. 'It's only a bikini, Salina,' Tom laughed. 'It's for swimming in.'

Kurt returned to the room after speaking to Gina who was going to make some rooms up for them. She was sure the sheriff and Erline would want them to stay as they didn't get many guests, especially as well travelled as they were. If only she knew.

'We are good to stay here tonight so I will be going to find my brothers and Row. I want you all to stay here in case we miss each other or Erline and the sheriff return', said Kurt.

'I'm not letting you go out there on your own,' Salina told him.

'That's wise, Father. I will stay with Tom and Karl. I can look after them here. I have just been out scouting around. It all seems quiet out there,' said Phina as she re-entered the room.

Gina entered the room. Smiling, she told them that a deputy would be bringing Erline back from the hospital because Erline had phoned to say that she would achieve nothing by staying at the hospital now. 'I'll make a special dinner for us all,' she told them. 'Clam Chowder.' It was her own family recipe from just down the road, she told them all then hurried away to get things ready. Then she came back. 'I forgot to say. Don't worry that you have just eaten. Chowder ain't quick to make so you will build your appetite up by dinner time.' She clasped her hands together, laughed and left the room.

Kurt and Salina left them, crossing the big hall to the front door and out. He headed into the swamp at the same point as Billy, the king and Row. After ten minutes, he sensed people approaching. Listening, he guessed two people only, then he heard Billy's distinct voice. Billy approached, followed by Row. They explained the plan to Kurt also telling him that the king would be along in due course after he had ensured they had not been followed or that anyone had come out of the water back at the bayou.

Back at the white house it was agreed that they would do nothing now until the morning so Billy left them after grabbing some of the spare barbeque bits, giving Gina a peck on the cheek and getting a smack and a smile in return. He would be back just after first light with diving equipment then he melted away. Kurt had introduced Row to Gina who was more than happy for the added guest. She did not bat an eyelid when she was told there would be one more, his brother, if that would be okay.

Heading back into the swamp, Kurt turned into his wolf form and tracked his way back towards the bayou meeting his brother after ten minutes. They then headed back towards the house. They talked about the events of the day and Kurt brought the king up to speed about the next day's plans.

In the meantime, a deputy had pulled his land cruiser up to the front of the house. After reassuring him that she would be okay with Gina and their new friends, Erline left the vehicle, waved and smiled to the officer before entering the big doors to the house to be met by Gina. They hugged, then Karl approached her. 'How is your dad?' he asked.

Tears welled up in her eyes. She let go of Gina and walked with them to the others. 'I need to sit down,' she told everyone. Gina sat next to her holding her hand. She gathered herself, facing everyone she said quietly, 'My pa, the sheriff, is dead…' Then she began to sob. Gina held her close. Everyone else was quiet. All were totally surprised at what she had said. For what seemed like an age, everyone stayed quiet, in their own thoughts. She then kissed Gina's cheek, stood up and excused herself. 'I need a little time just to take it in. I will meet you all back in the snug in a little while.' Then she left.

After half an hour Karl went into the kitchen where Gina was now finishing the preparation for the evening meal. 'Is it okay if I go and see Erline? I just want to check she is okay' he asked. Gina thought that would be a good idea and told him where her room was. He knocked on the door. After a couple of minutes, just as he was about to leave, the door opened.

'Sorry, Karl, I was in the shower. I wanted to get the smell of the hospital off me.'

'How are you getting on?' he asked her.

'Come in,' she said then her eyes filled with tears. 'I just can't stop crying. It's stupid, I know.'

Karl did not know what to do or say so he went up to her and held her. She did not move away but held him, nestling her head in his shoulder and gently sobbing for what seemed an age until she pulled away from Karl's tender hold.

Looking up she said with a sniff, 'Let's go into the snug. I could do with sitting down and being with people.' Then she moved closer to him once more. 'Thank you, Karl.' She kissed him on the lips.

'Look at me. I must be in a state. I'm kissing you and I don't even know you... sorry.' She smiled then stepped back looking at him.

'It's okay, I don't mind. You can hug me as much as you want.'

'Thank you, I will. You can be my go-to hug... that's if you don't mind?' she said smiling at him. Then she took his hand, not waiting for a reply, and walked back with him to the snug. On the way she asked him if he could tell she had been crying.

'No,' he replied, lying.

As they entered the snug, everyone looked up. They could all see she had been crying. She sat down next to Karl, still holding his hand. She took a deep breath then she began to speak. 'They started to lose him in the helicopter and by the time they had reached the hospital he had died. Once in the helicopter but they managed to revive him. They were great.' Tears started to build up in her eyes. Phina stood up and handed her a tissue from a box on a side table.

'Take your time, there is no rush.'

Erline gathered herself, took hold of Karl's hand once more, then continued. 'We moved into the A and E trauma area. I had hold of his hand, then he died once more. He never regained consciousness after that. I didn't even say goodbye!' She sniffed. 'They said he was a fit man; it wasn't the gunshot wound that had killed him but most probably something else. They are not sure what it was. They will do tests to find out what killed him. Most probably blood poisoning, they said. But I think your dad might know what it was?' She looked at Karl, not with malice, but with a desire to know the truth.

They heard the main door open and Kurt's voice call out, 'We're back.'

'In here,' Salina called out. Moments later Kurt and his brother were standing in front of them. They guessed by all the sad and solemn faces that something terrible had happened; Kurt had a good idea what it was.

Erline was introduced to Frederick then she recounted her story from leaving them in the helicopter until her return. All the time she clutched Karl's hand. Finally, she asked Kurt, 'Do you know why and how my dad died?'

'Yes, I believe I do, Erline, but I'm not sure you would understand.'

'Try me,' she answered.

'Go on, Uncle Kurt, we owe her that at least,' said Karl.

'Okay, we do owe you that much after what has happened to your father. We have been tracking this man by the name of Gebhuza Septima. He is a wanted man. Wanted all over the world. I work for Interpol and we just happened to be on holiday here in the US with my family and brother. It was by pure chance that I heard Gebhuza had been seen down in this area where we have been travelling. He is a very dangerous man with many followers, one who we believe was posing as your uncle. We believe this area has been a safe haven for him for many years.'

'That makes sense. It's just mad because he has been our family doctor for years. He did keep going off on what he called humanitarian missions for months, so that could explain what he has been doing in that time,' Erline told them.

Kurt continued. He could see Karl glaring at him. 'It was total coincidence that we were invited here for the barbeque and a total surprise to find Gebhuza has been and was, in fact, here when we arrived. I think I was meant to be the intended recipient for the bullet your father took. The poison on the bullet is a trademark of his organisation, but I must admit I was surprised at the lethality of it especially as I had given your father the antidote. Now we must track him in the morning and put an end to him once and for all. He has done so much damage.'

'Well, thank you for being honest with me and I do thank you for your efforts to save my father and the friendship you have shown to me. And I do mean all of you,' she said smiling directly at Karl. 'Now, if you don't mind, I would like to go and get a shower and change, I won't be long.' Erline left. Karl knew she just wanted to be alone for a bit as he knew she had already showered; he went straight to Kurt.

'Why! Why did you lie to her?'

'Because we don't know her, Karl. Even if she is who she says she is, do we really want to put her in any more danger? What if she was to tell someone?'

'What then!'

'She's alone, Kurt… she can come with us.'

'Not so fast, son,' said his father. 'Kurt is right. We don't know the girl and she's not from our world. Look how hard it has been for you and you have family. She would be better here with her kind.'

Annoyed, Karl turned and stormed from the room and went and sat on the back steps where the barbeque had been, his head in his hands and elbows on his knees looking out across the immaculate green lawn towards the swamp. He sat there for several minutes until he heard someone approach from behind. Ready to pounce, he turned to see Salina standing there with a smile on her face.

'Can I sit?' She indicated next to Karl. Karl nodded and sat back down.

'I'm so mad with Kurt and my dad,' he said.

'Why? Because they are right and you don't like it?' she replied.

'No! Well, maybe,' he replied. 'It's not fair.'

'When has life ever been fair, Karl?'

'But I like her, I really like her,' he told her.

'Now we are getting to the bottom of it, aren't we? You more than like her, don't you?'

Karl turned his head and looked at Salina. 'What do I do, Salina?'

She put her arm around him and pulled him closer.

'You wait. If it is meant to be it will be. There are bigger forces than us out there, you must realise that by now,' she told him.

'You're right, you know... Should I apologise to Kurt and Dad?' he asked her.

'No, I don't think there is any need for that. Who knows what will happen next? Let's go back inside.' Salina stood and Karl followed her. She held his hand and they walked back inside to the snug where everyone just smiled.

Kurt nodded. 'You okay?' he asked.

'Me? I'm fine thanks,' Karl replied and smiled back.

Gina brought some iced lemonade in just as Erline reappeared. 'You are all staying tonight, aren't you?' she asked.

'We would be honoured. If you don't mind?' replied Frederick.

'I don't mind one bit. Now, let's take the drinks into the dining room. It's a better place to talk around the table. I would like to know where you have all been. I have never left this county. It's sad, I know to you globe trotters, but there has never been a need before.'

As they walked towards the dining room, Karl asked her, 'That sounds like you are leaving.'

'Yes, I've decided I don't want to stay here anymore. Gina can have the house. I'll come back and see her, she's the only mother I have. I have a good bit of money in the bank so I think I will see the world for a while.'

As they sat down, Karl asked, 'What? On your own? A girl alone?'

'Shut up, Karl,' shouted Row. 'We don't need men, you know. Isn't that right, Salina?'

'Too right, Row. Me and Erline could kick arse all over this world.'

'Yeh go, girl,' shouted Erline as Row clapped.

After the laughs died down, Frederick spoke. 'Why don't you tell us a little about yourself, Erline. How you ended up here with the sheriff. Have you always lived in this part of America?'

'Pa, you mean. I have never left this state. I have good memories here. I was rescued from the swamp after my real mother had died it was the bad doctor you talked about that handed me over to Pa who was the sheriff back then too. He had just lost his wife and young daughter in a tragic car accident.' She went on to tell them how the sheriff and Gina had brought her up with more love and laughter than anyone should have. Then recently her uncle had reappeared after being missing in action (MIA) in Vietnam. Her father had been a little dubious but it all fitted together. Back then, her father was not long out of the army Delta Force. 'He says he was a ranger. He was but then he joined the Delta Force, Gina had been his housekeeper. She said that he left after returning from Africa after a rather nasty operation out there. Anyway, after that he became the sheriff, the rest is history,' she told them.

Gina walked in. 'There's something we have never told you, Erline. That doctor told us he had been in the Amazon. I thought it was strange that no one round here had ever heard of the woman he said had died and was your mother. Billy knows all the people that live in the swamp and he ain't ever heard of them folks. If I was to bet, I would bet on you as having been a love child. My theory was you were the result of a doctor and nurse in one of those aid camps getting it on, then they gave you to him to stop a scandal. That's what I think,' Gina told them all.

'Gina, you read too many of those romantic novels, you're terrible.' Erline laughed.

'There, I knew that would get you smiling,' Gina told her.

Everyone was smiling. It was a good distraction from what had happened. But something stirred within Row. 'How old are you?' she asked. Erline told her. Row started to think as they all talked. Dates started to thrash around her brain, flashes from the notes found in Gebhuza's home on the blue moon darted through her brain. She felt like she was having a migraine; if she hadn't been sitting, she would have fallen over. The room started to go bright white. She felt dizzy then made a concentrated effort to focus on where she was and the people around her. The conversations going on around her started to make sense again but something kept nagging at her brain. Erline was beautiful. The pictures she had seen of her mother; she too was beautiful and the more she thought the more her mind went to work... No, she was being stupid. 'You know you're right,' she told herself.

Someone touched her arm. 'Who's right, Row?' Phina asked her looking at her with concern. 'You didn't realise you had thought that to everyone did you?'

Row looked around. Karl, Tom, Kurt, Salina and her dad where all looking at her.

'Is everything okay?' Erline asked because the room had suddenly gone quiet.

'Yes, err, sorry, sometimes I drift off in my own thoughts and everyone makes fun of me,' laughed Row.

Salina squeezed her hand and smiled at her then she thought to her, 'It's okay, we can talk later.' Row smiled and Tom said something stupid that made everyone laugh taking the tension off Row. She was grateful for that and gave him a discrete wink. Things seemed to fit in her brain now but she would say nothing now until she had proof. They chatted and laughed until early evening when Gina left them to check then serve the dinner. They all ate with renewed hunger, probably because they were now all very relaxed even after the dreadful events of the day. Erline was happy and seemed carefree to everyone. She even flirted with Karl who tried his upmost to respond but not make it too obvious. He failed miserably to everyone's delight. After the lovely meal, they all went to the kitchen and helped Gina clean up. They tried to get her to go and relax but it was her kitchen and she was in charge. Once complete, they all moved outside and sat in the patio chairs on the lawn. Gina brought out some Jack Daniels and proposed a toast to Erline's dad, a good man tragically killed and sorely missed.

'A good man,' she said again, as tears rolled down her cheeks and the words became hard to say.

'A good man,' everyone repeated, each lifting a glass and taking a sip before sitting back down.

Erline went over and hugged Gina and whispered, 'This is all yours now; I will look after you now.'

'No, child, I will look after you. I promised your pa if anything was to happen to him all those years ago and that's still extant today. my girl. So, none of this nonsense from you.' Erline smiled and gave Gina a tight hug. Gina kissed the top of Erline's head then held her shoulders and looked her in the eye. 'You'll be fine, mark my words, your pupa will be watching over you.' Then she looked up and spoke to everyone. 'Well, I'm about all whooped now and, as much as I would love to stay and converse with you fine people, I will love and leave you. These old bones need their rest. Goodnight, everyone and may god bless you all this night.'

'Old bones, get out of here!' shouted Tom in his best southern accent to everyone's amusement.

'If I had met you fifty years before, young man,' laughed Gina. Then she turned and, with a wave over her shoulder, left them to go to her room.

'Goodnight, Gina, and thank you,' they all called out before she reached the door. All went quiet for a moment as people were left with their own thoughts and the sound of the southing swamp which was eventually broken by Row.

'Do you remember your mother, Erline?'

'My mum...' She paused for a moment, reaching back into her distant memory. 'I have memories mixed with things I may have heard when I was young, so whether they are real or not, I'm not sure,' she replied. Everyone was quiet. 'She was beautiful. I don't know why, but she was also strange. I remember the kids when I was young saying she was a voodoo queen. Their parents had told them she was also a junky, always out of her head. I don't like to believe that though. It's not nice to think about anyone in that much pain. What I can say though? That has never been proven and I put it down to jealousy. You know how some people can get around beauty. My mother, I mean, not me.' She blushed. 'Someone told me she had died from a snakebite. I don't know who told me. It just sticks in my brain. Gina's sister, who was very religious, said my mother had been taken by an angel. She had seen it but no one really knows because after that Gina's sister died and I was found in her house in the middle of the swamp when Gina went to take her some food. You see, she was a hippy, a throwback from the sixties. She and Gina had come over from Ireland then. Did Woodstock, all that jazz, but her sister met someone and got into all kinds of nasty shit. Gina had a thing for a young soldier so she went on a different path to her sister. Gina ended up marrying the soldier but he died in some war back in the day. His best man was my dad so he took Gina in and she has lived here ever since looking after the house and my dad. Then, after her sister unexpectedly died, she looked after me.' Erline smiled. Something inside stirred a good memory. 'That's what I think I remember, but I don't remember being handed over by the doctor. That's what everyone else said. My dad and she had a thing back then. He said she could have been the lead singer of a band, like Stevie Nicks out of Fleetwood Mac. Gina's sister, I mean. Gina has a great voice too... still does,' she added. 'That's it. They looked after me. That's it, my life, now it's all over. Time to start again somewhere new, I think... Europe. I always wanted to go to Europe, England, the royal family, all that jazz, Penny Lane, The Beatles, the Berlin wall, the Kremlin.'

'Very sad and romantic as well I think, Erline,' Row told her. 'Like you said, it's a new chapter in your life.'

Erline nodded with a determined smile on her face. 'Yep, I reckon.'

'Never forget where you came from and what your life has been so far,' Frederick told her. 'It's what we are and why we become what we will be, either good or bad.'

'Thanks, I will remember that.'

Then Tom jumped in. 'Have you got any films we can watch? It seems so long since I have watched a film.'

'Yes, Tom, in the snug there are lots of films. You pick one and I will show you how the system works; surround sound and all that...'

'Jazz!' Tom finished her sentence for her.

'Exactly.' she laughed. They all went to the snug; Tom chose a corny film from the eighties, *Big Trouble in Little China*. They all watched it, making fun of some of the clothes from the period, but it was good to laugh together and relax. After the film, Erline showed them to their rooms, telling them all they could stay as long as they wanted. The lights went out and all went still apart from the three wolves that crept out and kept watch till dawn. There were no out of the ordinary events so the wolves sneaked back to their rooms.

Chapter 20
A New Life Begins

Gradually everyone woke and drifted down to the smell of bacon and sweetness in the air. They all had a very American breakfast; sausage, patties and bacon, scrambled eggs, pancakes, whipped butter and maple syrup, fresh orange juice and coffee. After breakfast, Kurt told Erline and Gina that they were going to dive the bayou they had found the previous day. They believed that was where they would find the man they were looking for. The only one Gina and Erline could think of was the one close to Gina's sister's old house. The house was long gone, reclaimed by the swamp, but Erline knew where but suggested they didn't dive the bayou because it was full of alligators and very vicious snakes that had populated it about fifteen years ago.

Gina explained to them that one night there was one of the worst storms the area had ever seen. 'That fool Danny Summer had gone down to the bayou to catch himself some catfish but never came back so they dredged the water and his body popped up covered in snakebites but no sign of alligator attack. When they did an autopsy, they even found a live snake in his belly. That scared the shit out of the pathologist who was only saved by the sheriff shooting the snake's head off as it went to strike the doctor.'

'Some shooting,' Kurt commented.

Erline then told them about the snakes. 'It's strange. They are a type of Taipan snake, reputedly the world's deadliest snake. The problem is they are not natural to this area and they aren't water snakes. But they are here. The authorities believe someone in the past had one and released it into the swamp and over years it has adapted itself to living in the water. That's what they think killed Roisin, Gina's sister,' Erline added.

Frederick and Kurt both thought it strange that the snake could adapt that quickly to the swamp environment.

'Nature is a strange thing,' Gina told them which they all agreed. Erline also told them that they had a lot of dive kit in the shed that they could use. There was enough for everyone. They had all been keen divers, even Gina, and often went to the coast to dive. But she still thought they were mad to dive the bayou. They also had spear guns and shark prods they could use. She took them around to a shed which was more like the size of the average house than a shed. Inside they did indeed find all that they would need and some things they never even thought of.

Row left them to go and get a shower. She made her way upstairs to Erline's room. Checking up and down the hall to ensure she was alone, she went in, headed straight to the dressing table, picked up a hair brush, removed some of the hair and put it in a small sealable bag in her pocket. Then she went to her own room and had a shower.

In the shed, Erline had convinced Kurt, Frederick and Salina that it would be a wise move to take her with them to the bayou. They had never used the dive gear and she was very experienced in case they got into trouble. She also knew the dangers and the bayou. They decide that Frederick, Kurt, Salina and Erline would dive. Row, Karl, Tom and Phina would stay top side just in case they got into difficulty and needed help. They would be mad to dive without top support. They knew Karl would not be happy. After telling everyone the plan, Karl was not happy and, in the end, Salina, who was not ecstatic at diving, was quite happy to give Karl her place and stay with the top side team. The next two hours were spent in the pool. They practised and practised diving drills until they were all happy using the kit. Even the top side team trained.

After a quick bite of the last of the barbeque food, they set off with everyone carrying their own kit. They had the latest lightweight diving tanks courtesy of US special forces which was a great help even if they were all very fit. Gina stayed behind to sort the house and prepare the evening meal. After diving they would all be very hungry, she had told them. They set off and after only a short time stopped by the road. 'Why are we stopping here?' Erline asked.

'We are waiting for an old friend who will be joining us,' Kurt told her.

'Local?' she enquired.

'Yes, you might know him. Billy.'

'What? Mad Swamp Billy! My dad has arrested him a couple of times; normally for fighting when he comes out the swamp. He likes his whisky, he's from Scotland, England. He has a couple then beats up the local idiots. Dad lets him sober up in the cell then drops him off with his supplies near the swamp and off he goes.'

'Scotland is not in England, it's in Scotland; it's a country in itself, part of the United Kingdom of England, Scotland, Ireland and Wales,' explained Tom.

'Yeh, I know. I'm just being a little dumb,' replied Erline.

'He's an old family friend from the old country,' Frederick told her. They sat down and waited for Billy. After an hour he had still not appeared. They chatted, and Tom fell asleep in the sun. An hour on and Billy still didn't show. They decided they would have to go on without him; it was a good job Erline was with them.

'We will have to check on him when we come back. This is not like him,' commented Kurt.

'He might have had a drink,' said Erline. 'I've seen him drink at eight in the morning and by eleven he's throwing people out of the bar.'

'I know. I've seen it too,' added Row.

'I know he's got a reputation but he's a good man from a good family. He knows when there's a time to stand up and this is one of them. Something must be wrong, but we can't wait around any longer, we must get on.'

They set off after the delay and made it to the bayou in good time, if a little sweaty into the bargain. They checked the area and created a safe area so they could see any approaching dangers, by making a small clearing which took them another hour. Everyone put their dive gear on, even Tom, Selina and Phina as the top side team just in case they were needed.

'Everyone, get down!' shouted Erline, but instead of getting down they all looked at her, puzzled. 'Grenade!' she shouted and showed them it. 'To keep the snakes and alligators away,' she told them, then lobbed it into the water.

'Did you take the pin out?' asked Karl. Erline lifted her hand showing the pin and ring on her forefinger, then she hit the deck. Everyone else followed suit. Seconds later the grenade exploded, sending plumes of water into the air. The breeze sent a light drizzle over them that was quite refreshing if not a little smelly. Slowly, debris, a couple of snakes, some fish and an alligator floated to the surface.

'Right then, in we go.' Kurt told them and waded in, shark prod at the ready, quickly going underwater to see what was about. Slowly the silt and debris settled, and the water cleared. The others joined him, thumbs up all round, and they set off. Very quickly the riverbed dropped away into deep water free of entanglements, unlike the surface they had started at.

Soon they made out what looked like some old buildings. Erline held up a message board. Written on it was: It could be the little hippy settlement that disappeared after the big storm when the bayou got bigger.

They all nodded and continued to dive. So far, no sign of snakes or alligators; the odd fish and turtle went by but nothing dangerous yet. As they got closer to the bottom, they could now clearly make out buildings in a small cluster of five brick hulks. Karl then motioned to a small building hidden inside one of wrecked brick buildings. As they got closer, they could make it out through the silt, algae and kelp that covered it and the other buildings. There was door on the far side that was relatively clean. The building looked intact and, from the outside, it looked in a good condition.

Erline drew their attention to the gathering alligators and snakes above them, floating, still, all of them looking down at them. Frederick pointed to the door and they all swam towards it. The alligators and snakes began to circle above them in what seemed to the divers as perfect harmony. They reached the door and opened it with ease. The small building was the size of an old-fashioned outside toilet minus the toilet and in the floor was a hatch with a circular locking wheel on top to enable it to opened and closed tightly. There was only room for one person at a time in the small room so, while the others kept watch on the circling menace above, Kurt opened the hatch. It was wider inside and could accommodate two divers at once but only one diver could enter through the hatch at any time.

Kurt and Frederick went in then the hatch closed and the wheel was turned until it locked. As soon as it had locked, the water began to drain from the chamber. As the water got down to their shoulders, they took their masks off and let them hang round their necks.

'So, what's the plan, Frederick?' his brother asked.

'Get out of this deathtrap hole and see what we have here. I think would be the best idea, don't you think?'

'Roger that, your highness,' Kurt replied.

'Cut that crap now,' he told Kurt. Kurt nodded and smiled, and the king smiled back.

'Our way out, I think,' said Kurt as the water drained from around their feet revealing another hatch. This one had a lever, not a wheel. 'Shall we see what adventure lies behind this one?'

'Let's' replied the king. Kurt pulled the lever as they stood at the edge. The hatch slid sideways revealing a dark hole with a ladder running down in one corner.

Above them in the water, Karl prodded an alligator that had come directly towards them from the encircling creatures above. The shark prod touched the 'gator and it changed direction and swam away. Erline tried the hatch and it opened. She tapped Karl's leg and he looked down to see Erline entering the chamber. He followed, keeping an eye on the creatures getting closer above them. He was in the chamber pulling the hatch down when a Taipan darted at them, its jaws millimetres away from Karl's face. He slammed the hatch down, severing the head which floated to the floor snapping its fangs at them. Karl and Erline backed as far away from the head as they could which wasn't far. They could see vile coming from the fangs until Karl stood on its head. The water drained away, as it had done with Kurt and the king, revealing the second hatch. Karl removed his foot from the Taipan's head, its eyes stared up at them menacingly which made them both shiver, but it did not move again. Karl kicked the head into the corner of the chamber then removed his mask which fell around his neck. Erline did the same.

'Bloody hell. that was close. I thought I was a goner then,' said a very relieved Karl. Erline pulled him close and kissed him on the lips.

'What's that for?'

'Just thanks. That was a quick reaction, thank you.'

He smiled, a little surprised. 'No, thank you,' he said then added, 'That was a stupid thing to say, sorry.'

'I know what you meant, Karl, and you're welcome.' Then she kissed him again and he kissed her back and for a moment they weren't at the bottom of the bayou with creatures trying to kill them. In the moment they were Karl and Erline were having their first romantic encounter, it could have been on the corner of a Paris street or in a night club or on the sofa at home but no, it was at the bottom of a snake and alligator infested bayou. The kiss stopped as they came back to reality. 'Best we get out of here, hey?' said Erline. Karl agreed.

Below them, Kurt had taken his flippers off and dropped them down the hole. Seconds later they slapped onto a solid floor that echoed slightly so it was a bigger room, probably empty, they both thought. 'Only about ten feet down, I guess,' Kurt communicated to his brother who agreed. Kurt pointed the spear gun down and dropped through the hole into the darkness. As soon as he hit the floor, lights came on illuminating a bare, nearly empty, ten-feet square room. Nearly empty because it had six chairs along one wall and that was it. Kurt stepped to one side and called, 'Clear.' His brother dropped down beside him, shark prod at the ready. Above them, the hatch closed automatically.

Karl pulled the lever and the hatch slid to one side. Light came up and they could see the ladder leading down to a concrete floor. 'Kurt, Dad, you there?'

'Yes, come down. It's safe,' replied his dad.

Erline went first, dropping her flippers then going down the ladder, meeting Frederick and Kurt at the bottom. Karl followed her then they were all together again and safe for the time being. 'What is this place?' asked Erline.

'I believe it is an escape route, somewhere that a certain person can go to either to hide or travel to another destination,' said Kurt

'I don't quite understand. What do you mean? It's just a room under the bayou. What good could that be to anyone trying to escape, apart from a fool that may not know any better?'

'Don't judge a book by its cover, Erline. I have learnt that what you see is not always what you get. This may look like an empty room but I'm sure it has a few hidden secrets or surprises,' Karl told her.

'It's hard to explain. There are things you wouldn't understand yet,' said Kurt

'Try me, I'm a big girl,' replied Erline.

'Okay,' said Frederick, 'I think we can trust her... What if I said we come from another world? Would you believe me?'

'Of course not, that's just stupid.'

'Really? What if I said this room could lead to Europe or even to another planet?'

'Now you're shitting with me and I don't think I like it.'

Karl went over and held her hand. 'Don't dismiss anything, Erline. We are your friends. We just want to prepare you for what might happen,' said Karl.

'I don't understand,' replied Erline.

'I didn't either at first, but, just remember, we will look after you and protect you. With our lives, if need be,' Karl added.

'That's reassuring but... can you hear something? Listen.'

They all stayed quiet... There was a sound coming from behind the furthest wall, a scratching. Kurt walked slowly towards the wall, spear gun raised and ready, Frederick behind him to one side, spear gun also ready and raised, facing the wall. Karl stayed back with Erline, their eyes fixed on the wall. As Kurt neared the wall it suddenly slid sideways until it was flush with the adjoining wall. There in front of them stood a Dark warrior holding a demon dog that was straining on a chain, fierce red eyes with saliva dripping from its jaws. Erline flinched and held Karl at the sight of them.

'What the fuck's that?' she screamed.

A spear left Kurt's gun, piercing the dog's skull right between the eyes. The dog slumped straight down, its head making a hollow cracking thud as it hit the concrete floor. The warrior ran, exhaling a demented screaming from the bottom of his lungs which turned in to a gargle as he too fell to the floor. The sword in his hand crashed with a metallic bang onto the floor beside him. Kurt quickly retrieved it then he checked the warrior. His neck had a spear from Frederick's gun and a second in his chest from Erline's which had been more of a reaction than an aimed shot. They were lucky it hit the warrior and not the king or Kurt.

'Sorry,' she told them, a little embarrassed just as a gurgling came from the warrior. Bubbling blood was foaming from his mouth. He was still alive! Kurt thrust the sword into the warrior's head, ending his torment.

Erline turned her head away. She had never seen anything like that before.

She had heard some stories from her dad but they were only stories, not real like this. Karl held her in his arms as she tried to wipe the sight from her mind.

In front of them, a corridor disappeared at right angles; the walls bare and bright white. Frederick went forward and peered around the corner. In front of him was an Earth gate. 'Kurt. come see what we have here,' he shouted back. Kurt had just finished checking the warrior. He found a small knife that he gave to Karl and a rayzor on his back which he took for himself. He also pulled the spears from the warrior's chest and the dog's head, wiping them on the warrior's clothes. He put one in his gun, cocking it, and handed the other to a startled Erline who had just lifted her head from Karl's shoulder, and was staring down at the dead warrior, oblivious to anything else.

'Well done, Erline. We will make a fine warrior out of you one day, I'm sure,' said Kurt as he walked to wards Frederick.

'What?' replied Erline who looked up at Kurt's back walking away then down at the spear in her hand.

'Kurt gave you it and said well done, Erline. You shot the Dark warrior.'

'Did I?' she replied.

'Yes, you did,' said Karl as he took the spear from her and picked up the spear gun from next to the warrior's body where she had dropped it.

Looking at him, Erline asked, 'What just happened? Was that something from this other world you were talking about? It's true, isn't it? You are aliens.' She waited for his reply, but Karl was little taken back by the question for a second. He did not know what to say but Kurt and Frederick, who had returned from around the corner, did.

'Yes,' replied Frederick, '… and no. You see, we are from both this world and ours because once they were the same world. So, we aren't really aliens, just from another place not on this world, you might say.'

'Oh, that makes sense then… no!' said Erline who walked over to one of the chairs and sat down. 'Can I have a minute to take this in; I think I may have a few questions.' She looked up. All three were smiling at her. A caring smile and not a demented smile, that was reassuring, she thought to herself. Karl sat next to her and went the take her hand but she pulled it away from him, turned to look at him and kissed him on the lips. 'I think my life just changed and I think it will never be the same again. And you know what? I'm excited.' Smiling, she kissed him again then she stood up. 'Right, what do I really call everyone then?'

Karl stood. 'I'm Karl, this is Frederick and Kurt.'

'Oh, it's the same,' she said, surprised. 'I thought you would be called Zarton, Zorn or something.' She laughed.

'Really?' replied Karl.

'I don't know,' she answered. 'It's all a bit strange, finding I'm friends with people from another world.'

'Well, that's a start,' said Frederick. 'At least you didn't call us aliens again.' They all laughed, and it felt normal again, the tension of the last twenty minutes had gone.

Karl added, 'My last name is De-Callen, I am the king's son.'

Erline looked at him. 'Really?'

Karl nodded.

'Yes, really, again.'

Erline smiled. 'Sorry.'

'This is my uncle, Kurt De-Callen.' He pointed to Kurt who smiled then bent his head as if meeting royalty. 'This is my dad, the king. King James Frederick De-Callen of Elemtum, our world.'

'Wow! Really? There I go again, sorry. Wow!'

'Right, let's head back to the others and make some decisions. I think we have to come back, all of us, but a little more prepared and find out where this Earth gate goes. It's definitely never been mapped,' said Frederick.

They got ready and went back through the air locks in a repeat of how they got there. Karl warned his dad and Kurt about the snake, so they had better be careful when opening the hatch. The king and Kurt went first. In the last chamber, as it filled with water, the snake's head went passed them, Kurt pointed it out to his brother. The king nodded and lifted the shark prod that he had swapped with Karl for his spear gun. When the chamber was completely full, Kurt turned the wheel, but it would not budge so his brother added his strength and it began to turn slowly. Once unlocked, he heaved the hatch, but it only moved slightly. Frederick helped and they managed to lift it enough to see that there was an alligator lying on top of it. Opening the hatch wide enough, Frederick prodded the alligator with the shark prod which did the trick. The alligator swam away, a little indignantly, then the hatch was opened. Carefully, they swam out. Above them were a few alligators and the odd snake, but nothing seemed threatening now. They closed the hatch and stood guard, occasionally having to ward off an inquisitive alligator and, more worryingly, a Taipan which was stunned and speared to stop its aggressive attack as the hatch opened to allow Karl and Erline to vacate the chamber. They closed the hatch behind them to stop any unwanted creatures getting in and jamming the wheel to stop any unwanted guests getting out. Slowly, they ascended, prodding and stabbing anything that got too close. At one point a Taipan struck Frederick, striking his air tank before it was struck by a spear and floated down, chased by an alligator which was after an easy meal. Eventually they reached the surface and were helped from the water by the others.

Billy was now with them, a gash on his face and a banged hand newly adorned his body. 'What happened to you?' asked Frederick as he took his mask off.

'Assassin tried to take me out this morning. It and a lancer are now both dead and buried in the swamp. It was close. I thought at one point I was a goner, but they didn't count on one thing.'

'What was that, Billy?' Tom asked him.

'I'm a Scot, laddie, and no push over. Ken?' They all laughed. 'See you have dive gear. A good job because I raced back to the white house to tell you about the demons, but you had all gone. Gina told me you had left. That's a fine woman,' he added.

'Hey, that's my mum,' Erline told him.

'I'm sorry, lass.' Billy apologised to everyone's amusement, including Erline. They gathered their stuff and made their way back to the white house telling the others what had happened under the bayou. Reaching the house, they sorted and stowed their gear, filling the air tanks ready for the next job.

Gina had prepared a nice fish platter with fresh salad, crayfish, lobster, crab, all the sea creatures you could imagine, and it looked and smelt beautiful, all laid out in the big kitchen. They all hurriedly went and got cleaned up, even Billy who was invited to stay by Gina. They sat outside and ate their feast in the sun then Gina went to clean up and the others were left alone. The talk turned to the next day.

It was decided that they would all stay together and go through the world gate to wherever it took them. If it turned out that there was something bad at the other end then they would get back in and return to their starting point. nothing lost, then another plan would be made. Erline took them to her dad's armoury which was under the house; they were amazed at the type and quantity of weapons the sheriff had. Erline told them he was also a colonel in the National Guard so some of the weapons they could not take because they belonged to the government but that still left a shed load of weapons, more than they would ever need. They selected their weapons and placed them in neat piles depending on whose they were. Erline picked her selection and was asked what she was doing by Row.

'I'm going too,' she told her. 'I know who you all are.'

Row turned to Karl. 'What have you said?'

'It was all of us; Row, Dad and Kurt too. She was great down there. She killed a Dark warrior. The least we could do was explain what was going on. She's cool about it.'

'Erline, Row is my sister and a princess. Tom is my brother and a prince.'

'At your service, my lady,' Tom said. then bowed.

'Salina is my cousin along with Phina and Raif, who is not here. He is Kurt's son and Salina and Phina's brother. They are Wolf princesses.'

'Great. So, I don't get a say then?' said Row.

'Don't be like that, Row, the more the merrier.'

'Karl's right, Row. Erline will be safer with us now and, like she said, there's not a lot left here for her.'

'Suppose,' Row replied. 'But you will have to put up with a lot of boy smells and sometimes they're quite disgusting, especially when they are wolves.'

'Wolves! No one told me about wolves,' said Erline.

'Ah sorry. Have I said something I shouldn't have?'

'And eagles,' blurted out Tom, as massive smile covered his face.

'Yes, well, we may as well tell you everything now that it's come out,' said Kurt.

'Yes, let's,' came a voice from the top of the stairs, followed by footsteps as Gina came into the room with Billy.

Billy explained he was just coming down with Gina to let everyone know he would not be going with them but would be staying to look after Gina and Erline, but it sounded as if things may have overtaken that.

'Right then. Best we go somewhere comfortable and I will explain all,' said Frederick. An hour later they were all sitting in the snug. They told her all that had happened since they had left Earth the first time. Now Gina and Erline were fully in the loop.

'Well, I never expected that,' Gina said. 'But, to tell you the truth, I'm not that surprised either. As a young hippy with my sister, we had dreams of another world and she always said she had had an affair with an angel from another world. Now, that could have been the mushrooms or the LSD talking, who knows? I take it you do want to go with them, darling?' Gina was now staring at Erline who went over and hugged her. 'I know, girl, you don't have to say anything, but you just remember where I am, and you come and visit me and this old fool occasionally.' She meant Billy. 'This will always be your home.'

'I will, Gina, you can count on that.'

'We will leave you three together for a while. I'll go through some weapon drills with the boys,' said Kurt.'

'Yes!' shouted Tom, punching the air.

'Drill, Tom, not play,' Salina told him. Tom got up and ran off in the direction of the cellar armoury, the others followed him leaving Gina, Erline and Billy to talk.

Chapter 21
Leaving Home and Going Home

The Louisiana sunrise brought drizzle which left everywhere cold and damp; water dripped from every beam, roof and tree. Gina commented that she had never felt such a damp cold Louisiana morning for years. When she said years, she meant many years. Not since in her hippy days when she slept in a tent had she experienced such a cold and damp morning in the winter. Not at this time of the year.

'A strange morning to part!' she said as she fed them all her famous American breakfast with all the trimmings, freshly squeezed fruit juices from the garden, fresh American coffee and European coffee, a special buy from the local store that morning before anyone was up. The store was open twenty-four-seven. She was an early riser, much to Billy's dismay who had gone with her to the store that morning. It was all appreciated by the departing group who thanked her at every opportunity through mouthfuls of the delicious breakfast. Then came the time for them to leave. All the delaying tactics Gina could think of finally came to nothing. Billy told her, 'Let the girl go. She will be back. She is growing up.'

Gina finally accepted it and, after saying goodbye to them all, especially the little boy Tom who she felt was far too young to be going out on a day like this. Erline was young but the boy was younger. She even offered to look after Tom until he had grown up a bit more. Frederick thanked her but declined, thinking she was joking, but she was deadly serious. She had visions of the little boy going into action against some unseen enemy that would even make the special forces on Earth flinch. She rationalised her thinking and let it go, she was being stupid. If only she knew. She said goodbye, then watched them all trudge off under their weight of their loads which included weapons and ammunition.

Through the early morning mist they went. The younger ones had their shoulders up, pushing their necks further into their jackets to keep the damp out as they entered the swamp. She was about to scream to them to stop when Billy's comforting arm went around her shoulder as he pulled her closer for a reassuring hug. She let them go until Salina disappeared into the mist. Billy was ready to join them but the sobbing Gina pulled him back to reality. It was time he stopped his fighting ways and settled down. Now he had his chance. He knew he would see them all again and have a chance to renew his youth but that would be another day and this was their destiny, not his.

After trudging through the swamp for a while, the chill of the morning air had gone, heat and sweat replacing it. To Erline's surprise, Tom had turned into an eagle and disappeared though a wide opening they had reached twenty minutes into the journey. Karl had also told her that Kurt had gone ahead, scouting as a wolf. She would have liked to have seen that as she had images of the film about a werewolf in London that she had seen recently with her dad. A classic, he had told her. It made her smile then she remembered the agony the character had gone through to become a werewolf. This was totally the opposite to their transitions which were a peaceful release from the restricted human form. 'Like being naked on a beautiful beach then diving into the water and being free,' Karl had told her.

They finally reached the bayou with the clearing they had made the day before where they met Kurt who had been joined by Phina and Tristan. They proceeded to put all their kit and weapons into waterproof bags, then they heard the sound of the eagle above. Tom swooped down low over the water, his wing tips making ripples in the water until an alligator snapped at it and took a couple of feathers. Tom stopped showboating and glided in towards them a little higher than he had been before. At the last minute he came in. Everyone rushed to the edge of the clearing. Tom was just about to land but then pulled back into the sky with an amazing manoeuvre. He seemed to bounce off the ground, turn almost on the spot, going back out over the water. Everyone watching realised he had a Taipan snake in his talons that he had grabbed just behind the head so it could not move to strike him. He ripped chunks of flesh from it as he flew until it was dead then he dropped it into the bayou where a watching alligator devoured it. He made another approach, this time not so close to the water. He had learnt his lesson about his approach height. Flaring at the last minute, he landing gracefully in the clearing, the wind from his wings gently blowing into the spectators' faces.

'He's a natural bird,' his brother told Erline who was fascinated, watching Tom transform back into his human form.

'It's all clear,' he told them, then added, 'I'm not looking forward to getting into the water.'

'Don't worry, Tom, I will watch after you,' reassured Phina ruffling his hair, then she threw his waterproof sack at him which contained his kit that she had been carrying for him when he had taken off as an eagle.

'Thanks, Phina. When I'm fully grown, I will marry you and you will be queen,' he said smiling.

'Okay, Tom, that's a deal. I will take you up on that when you're a handsome strapping warrior, but we have to survive this madness first.' Then she winked at him. Tom went red, smiled then delved into his bag s everyone around him laughed.

'That was amazing. Can you all do that?' asked Erline.

'No, Tom and I can, the rest are wolves. I think it's something to do with our mothers.'

'Amazing,' she said, as they all donned their dive gear and put everything else into their dive bags. After a rehearsal, they were ready to enter the water.

Kurt lobed in two grenades then they all entered the water. Once under the water they went into order. Kurt, Frederick, Karl and Erline, Tom, Row and Salina with Phina and Tristan protecting the rear. They dived in a diamond shape for better protection. They reached the little building with no incident. The bar jamming the wheel was still in place, so Kurt removed it and opened the hatch. It was clear so, once again, they entered the chamber.

After half an hour they were all standing in the room with the now smelly bodies of the Dark warrior and the demon dog in exactly the same places as they had left them the day before. Kurt knew this because he had balanced shavings from one of the chairs in the room on the bodies, knowing one or, maybe, two might fall as the bodies decayed and the gases moved the bodies. Only a full movement of the bodies would have displaced all of them which, after inspection, were very much intact. That indicated to Kurt that no one had been back since they left so that could possibly mean that this gate was not used regularly and may only have been known about by Gebhuza. He determined that the warrior and demon dog had been put there as guards to slow anyone who may have found the gate.

There were now seven bags of diving kit piled in the corner of the room with a nice little booby-trap that only they would know how to defuse in case they were forced to come back.

The gate did not speak to them which was a little worrying but it was an unknown gate so they put it down to it not being part of the major system. Once inside the gate, there was no way of knowing how long the journey would be so they took it in turns to guard while the others relaxed. Only Frederick, Kurt, Salina and Phina took part in guarding while they travelled. This could be a long journey if it was to Elemtum but quicker if it went to somewhere on Earth which Kurt had now ruled out. They had been travelling longer than it would have taken to get to the other side of Earth through the gate, he surmised. So, all the more experienced travellers now knew the final destination was not on Earth.

After a couple of hours, it was not Elemtum either. Row had guessed it could go on to the blue moon, otherwise it would be some unknown destination which did worry them. They could end up in a viper's nest but if that happened then so be it. They would deal with that when and if it happened. Finally, the sensation of moving slowed then stopped. Weapons ready, except Tom because he was wedged behind everyone, they waited… Then the gate opened.

They were in a room; a cellar to be precise. They came out slowly, carefully listening for any sound. Then a laugh rang out coming from the direction of an air vent high in a wall. There was also a set of stairs leading up to a door. The small air vent where the laugh had emanated from erupted with another laugh.

'I know that laugh,' said Karl.

'Me too. It's Clomp, I would recognise that laugh anywhere. Clomp!' shouted Tom. 'Clomp, it's me.'

'Me who?' came the reply down the vent.

'Me, Tom… Row, Karl, the king, Kurt, Salina, Phina and Tristan.'

'Don't be daft. How can you all fit in that vent? It's not big enough.'

'Where are you, Clomp?' Kurt shouted.

'Here, sir,' came the rather puzzled reply.

'He's having us on, isn't he?' said Kurt.

'No, I don't think so, it's just Clomp.'

'We are in the armoury at Great Porum,' said another voice.

'Who's that?' Frederick asked.

'Sir, it's Presario, one of the royal guard.'

'Presario, go to the command centre and find out where the vent in the armoury leads to. We can't be far from you. We are going to try a door near to where we are,' the king told him. 'Get everyone on alert. There may be Dark warriors around the capital.'

'Yes, sir,' came the hurried reply.

Karl went up the steps and opened the door that had a handle. 'That's novel, using a handle in this world, the good old-fashioned way,' he said as the door started to open. It was forcibly shut from the other side which took Karl by surprise, making him lose his footing and stumble backwards. This may have just saved his like because, seconds later, the door was in pieces, sending wooden splinters flying around the room, one of which embedded in Tom's thigh causing him to scream out in pain. Another was thrust into Erline's shoulder, sticking out her back, making her crumple to the floor. A second sliced her cheek open. Karl was stunned and not sure what was going on. Salina dashed over, covering both Tom and Erline. With her back to them, she pointed her weapon at the hole where the door had once been. The others, extraordinarily, were not touched.

Karl had pulled himself against the wall where he slumped forward, his chin resting on his chest then his eyes closed. Salina looked at him, seeing blood trickle from his ears and nose.

'You have thirty seconds to comply otherwise we use deadly force,' shouted a forceful voice from beyond the blown door.

'Steven, it's Kurt De-Callen. I have the king with me, the two princes and Princess Row, Tristan, Salina, Phina and a friend. What are you doing?'

'One of you come to the opening. Any sign of betrayal and you will all be eliminated. Do you understand? I will not ask you again.'

Kurt went to get up, but Frederick pushed him back. 'He will not shoot me,' said the king.

Phina got up and rushed up the stairs. 'He won't shoot me either, he has a thing for me.' She smiled, then shouted out, 'Steven, it's Phina. I'm coming to the door. Don't fire.'

Slowing down, she walked through the hole where the door had been with her hands high in the air.

'Stop where you are. Stand still!' shouted Steven. Phina did as instructed. The others listened in anticipation. Kurt was now at the bottom of the stairs, ready to assault if need be. Then there was the tell-tale sign of a scan; light streamed through the door opening.

'Okay, she's clear,' someone shouted from behind Steven who was the head of the king's security in the capital.

'Get some healers. The princes and a companion are injured down there,' Phina calmly shouted to them.

Steven went up to Phina. 'What are you doing down there? We had a report of infiltrating Dark warriors.'

Kurt was now at the top of the stairs. 'Steven, where did this report come from?'

'Gebhuza Septima… he told us not more than twenty minutes ago that he had been down in the quarantine storage facility and that Dark warriors had broken in, but he had managed to shut them in the store but warned it would not hold them long.'

'Well, my friend, he nearly managed to wipe out the entire royal family. Where is he?'

'Going to the infirmary to sort out an emergency response team in case of any casualties,' answered Steven.

Two healers rushed past and down the stairs. They went directly to the now unconscious Karl, slumped on the floor against the wall. After a quick scan, one of the healers called out, 'We need to get the prince to the infirmary immediately.' Between the king, Salina and a healer they gently carried Karl up the stairs, past the guards into one of the basement rooms next to the armoury. The second healer was quickly joined by a third who attended to Erline and Tom, who was now quiet.

'Get the capital shut down, Steven. I will be with the king in the command centre. Gebhuza Septima and his daughters are to be apprehended on sight and brought directly to the holding cells. Do you understand?'

'Yes, sir,' replied Steven before ordering a section of guard to protect the king as well as two to guard the princess in the infirmary. Then he went to arrange the close down of the capital. Tom and Erline walked, aided by healers, to the top of the stairs then along the corridor past Kurt.

One of the healers stopped and pulled down her mask. 'Do you want to clap me in irons now, Kurt?' she said and put her arms out. 'I heard what you instructed Steven,' said Nerilla Septima. 'While you are at it, you may as well arrest Paccia who's operating on an Eagle warrior to save his wing, or Theon who is on a ward recovering from a spear wound while saving a Wolf warrior after a skirmish on the Gransdon Plains.'

'Uncle Kurt, there is no need for this, is there?' said Row who was now holding Kurt's arm looking directly into his face.

'No, you're right, Row. Sorry, Nerilla, please see to Erline, then when you and Paccia are free, could you come and see me in the command centre please? I will rescind that order.'

'Thank you,' she said then pulled her mask back up and escorted Erline towards the infirmary.

'Damn it, Row, we nearly lost all of them and you. I've failed you all.'

'No, you haven't, Uncle Kurt. No one could have known this would happen,' said Row.

'But I should have thought more about the great risk we were taking with you, the king and the princes.'

'The king was with you, Uncle Kurt, it's nobody's fault except Gebhuza Septima. Now, let's go find that son of a bitch and try and sort this mess out.' Kurt agreed with her he, thanking her for her maturity and common sense then he gave her a hug and a smile.

They made their way to the command centre where they met Clomp who was frantic after hearing the explosion and Tom's scream. He didn't know where the vent went to, so he was going to find Tristan to get some explosive to blow it open.

'Good job we found you then, Clomp, otherwise you may have killed us all!' Kurt told him with a laugh and he patted Clomp's back. Clomp then ran off to the infirmary to check on Tom and Karl but not before he found Steven and re-briefed him on Kurt's original order about Paccia, Nerilla and Theon. They made their way down to the command centre which was a hive of activity. Tristan was poring over a map with Steven at his side along with Raphina, Phina, Zuzza Zell, Lord Barra, Leslie Diocesan and Abla from the desert Omanian tribe. The king and Salina were already there. The king noticed Kurt and Row enter the command centre.

'Come over, both of you, and listen to the briefing. A lot has happened since we left, but before that have a minute with Raphina. She has some news about Raif.'

Kurt went over to Raphina and kissed her. He noticed her face was very serious and strained, deep black bags under her eyes. Looking at her face, he noticed, for the first time, a wound that had been crudely stapled together. It went from behind her ear, down her neck and underneath her stained, ripped and bloody combat suit. 'Warriors' Rest is no more; our son is missing, and the Dark are, as we speak, crossing the plains heading for Great Porum burning every settlement they come across, enslaving or killing everything they find,' Raphina told him. Kurt was stunned. Phina and Salina went to their mother and father and all embraced.

After several seconds, Kurt looked up. Sorry, Frederick. Please continue.'

'Steven, please restart the briefing,' the king asked.

'As most of you know what has happened, if you wish to leave and attend to your duties, this is mainly a briefing for the king and those that have been away.' Zuzza, Lord Barra, Abla and Leslie bowed to the king, telling him they would just go and get some food then they would all be back. They then left leaving the others around the map table.

'I am sorry to hear about the princes and their new friend. I had not heard from you since you left. We did send two warriors to find you but I'm afraid I have had reports that they were both killed in an ambush at the Earth gate by the Dark. We received a coded report that the Dark were planning to attack through a secret gate beneath the capital and the coordinates given were beneath the armoury. We could not communicate with the gate. We were even told what time the gate would open and when the attack would happen. That's why I and my warriors were down waiting to destroy whatever came out. That was further reinforced when Gebhuza Septima told us he had just come from Earth after finding a new thread that already had a gate attached. He said he had fought with the Dark and managed to get into the gate. He told us the Dark were on his tail and would be with us in about a day. So, we prepared for their arrival, preplaced the charges to blow the door then kill all inside, then we were going to blow the gate and seal it. Why would we not believe Gebhuza? We had no reason to. I think we may have been set up in a bid to kill you, lord, and as many of your family as possible.'

'Good, I don't blame anyone but myself for Gebhuza, I had intel and was acting on it on Earth. My failing was not informing my command team about it,' said the king. 'We will find him but, first, what has happened at Warriors' Rest?'

'The morning you left the first attack happened. The listening posts along the edge of the Dark quarter were over run and everyone was slaughtered. Then, with great speed the Dark pushed from the Dark quarter to within a mile of Warriors' Rest in one day. On the second morning, they attacked. They had been helped by people unknown to us at this moment, but we believe they came from within Warriors' Rest. Two defence towers were destroyed. Some inner walls and two gates were destroyed by charges that had been set and detonated from within Warriors' Rest, then the Dark hordes rushed in. A magnificent counterattack was organised, but they seemed to know exactly how we would react. They had countermeasures for every assault we threw at them. By the mid-afternoon, it was clear we would not be able to hold Warriors' Rest and a decision was made to evacuate everyone as quickly as we could. A very brave rear-guard action was put into operation organised by Hollie and her teams as well as Andor and three squadrons of Eagle warriors with one hundred Wolf warriors commanded by Raphina. Less than a quarter of them made it out and only then by a cat's whisker. Andor gave his life to ensure Raphina could escape with some of the warriors. I'm afraid to say there has been no news of Hollie and her water teams. Also, reports came in of a band of young warriors from the warriors' academy that had made it out of Warriors' Rest and were making their way behind the rear of the Dark warriors' column of reserves heading to Warriors' Rest. By all accounts they harried the Dark warriors, making some of them run away… then no word of any of them, they simply disappeared. The good, or bad news however you look at, it was that Raif was leading the young warriors. His and the other young warriors' whereabouts are unknown at this time.' As spur of pride went through Kurt's heart and soul; his son, by all accounts, had acted with great courage. A true leader, leading his teams with guts and intelligence. He could be no prouder than he was at that moment, that would only be overtaken by having his son at his side safe once more.

'It broke my heart when I found out he and the young ones had not made it out onto the transports. I will never forgive myself for leaving them behind. I was unaware until we had reached Great Porum. They never reached the airship before it had to leave or else it would have been lost. I might add the crew of that vessel stayed and saved a great deal more warriors long after they should have left. They should be commended,' Raphina told them all.

'Raphina, that ship went back and has not been heard of since, I'm sorry to say,' Tristan told her. Tears welled in Raphina's eyes, which shocked Kurt; he had only ever seen tears of joy in her face before. The last few days had taken a great toll on her. He looked into everyone's eyes around him. He could see the distance in their eyes, their minds and souls were somewhere else.

'Do you need some time, Raphina?' the king asked her.

'No... you will not see these tears again, lord. They have been shed and now there are no more in my heart,' she replied, then she whipped the last tear away. Before he could console her, she had gone back to the map and asked a question, 'So, when do we strike back?'

'Steven in our absence, along with the others, have come up with a counterattack that we will go through, when the others return from the dining hall.'

While they waited, Paccia and Nerilla appeared and briefed them on the boys' and Erline's conditions. They were all in healing chambers and should all make a quick recovery. Row took the two healers to a side room along with Salina to explain to them their fears about their father. The reaction was one of shock; the looks on their faces told them all they needed to know. They could be trusted.

The king entered the room along with Kurt, Phina and Raphina.

'It would not surprise me,' Nerilla said. 'He abused both of us when we were younger. He lived a secret life. We had no knowledge of what it was or what he was doing but sometimes when he returned from his travels, he had a strange smell about him and he would spend hours cleaning himself before he would go near a Wolf warrior.'

'He changed too. As a young healer, I had known happiness with him and Nerilla, then he went to Earth and did not return for two years. He had changed his looks, which is natural for male healers of that age, but then the abuse started. He changed; he spent more time away from us and more on Earth. We would stay away when he was home then we started at the healing university, we hardly ever saw him, the abuse stopped and our lives went in different directions. I hated him,' said Paccia.

'We are so sorry for what he has done to you and your family. You should have told someone,' the king told her and her sister.

'I'll break the healer's code and take retribution on him if I ever see him again,' Nerilla told them.

Row hugged both of them, telling them they had nothing to be sorry about and that there was no need for either of them to break their code because she would kill him first if she ever came across him.

Meanwhile, in the other room, everyone had reassembled and were busily talking about recent events. Tristan told everyone to quieten down. Once everyone was settled, he went and got the king and the others. The two healers went to leave but the king called them back. 'You are now in charge of the healers. If you would take on that responsibility, I would be eternally grateful to you both.'

They took it as a great honour to be asked. They agreed straight away. The king asked them to stay as they would have to make a plan for the medical services support for the future operation. He told them Tristan would be at hand to help them with the logistics. Then Steven went through the forthcoming plan involving many of the planets leading tribes. Eagles, Wolves, Omanian, Surviyns, Romonia, and Zell People would all be taking part in the forthcoming operation. Tactics were discussed and tasks were handed out to the various units.

Two hours into the planning, one of the operations people caught Steven's attention. He went over to him, listening intently to what the intelligence operator had to tell him. Thanking him, he returned to the planning group. 'I have just received some intelligence that may change our plan. I have received the same information from three different sources. One of the reconnaissance eagle flights has noted Dark warriors leaving Warriors' Rest. This has been verified by Sentar as well as some scouts from the Omanian. They are not heading towards Great Porum but in the other direction back to the Dark quarter. It seems they are being recalled… but why, I don't know.'

'We need to watch this very carefully to ensure this is not a trap. It just doesn't make sense. Why take a prize then give it up without a fight? We must prepare to strike once we have more intel. Ready your forces to deploy at a moment's notice. If we can destroy some of this force while they are retreating it may save us casualties and another bigger battle another day,' the king told them.

Tristan added, 'Once your forces are ready, rest them. I will be sending out fighting patrols to test the Dark's defences in that area. They will report back to me in the early morning when a go, no go decision will be made. Good luck, everyone. May Atta be with you.'

The majority left, leaving the De-Callens together. 'I'm worried about this; it's got to be a trap or one of the biggest military blunders of our world's history. We were close to being on our knees, they could have taken the capital before all our forces could have been assembled. Why wait a day, then retreat? … It doesn't make sense,' Frederick told them.

'Steven and I will take shifts in the control room tonight. Everyone else get some rest, sleep if possible. I will wake you all if anything major happens in the meantime,' Tristan told them. 'And that means you too, Frederick,' he added, patting his brother on the back.

Everyone was left with their own thoughts that night. They were all in the same dark room adjacent to the control room, all thinking different thoughts about what had happened and what would happen the next morning.

Karl, Tom and Erline slept, unaware of what was going on. Clomp kept watch over all three as did the royal guards assigned to them who allowed Clomp to help or, at least, let him think he was helping. The night dragged on, the healing continued, and the night dragged on… There was a lot of tossing and turning as minds raced that night. By daybreak, not a lot of sleep had been had by anyone but there must have been some because no one had seen Kurt leave the room. Kurt had left not only the room but Great Porum; he was heading south in his wolf form. He was being carried by an eagle; not just any eagle but Fedora the Eagle queen. She had felt the pain in Kurt's heart when he had been told about Raif and now she carried him to the last place anyone had seen him alive near Warriors' Rest. Fedora and Kurt had both gone to the warrior academy in their youth. As youngsters, they had grown up together, so they were as close as brother and sister, if not twins.

The light came on in the room where everyone was resting. Tristan walked looking as fresh as a daisy. 'It has been quiet all night, so you can go and get yourselves cleaned up in your rooms. If I need you, I will call. There are also some clean clothes in each room. Raphina, Phina, Salina, can you come with me, we need to talk. Oh, Frederick, there is also good news about the boys and Erline. Tom and Erline are awake and fully healed. Paccia has been at Karl's side all night. She tells me he is doing well and should be back with us either this evening or tomorrow. They are being careful because it was a head trauma, but he should be fine.'

Frederick was relieved. He made his way over to the infirmary to see Tom and Erline then check on Karl. The others left with the king, leaving Tristan, Raphina and Kurt's daughters.

Tristan told them about Kurt leaving to go to Warriors' Rest. Raphina had expected as much when she had awoken without him by her side. Raphina and the two Wolf princesses made it clear to Tristan that as soon as they had got themselves clean, refreshed and fed that they would also be leaving for Warriors' Rest. Tristan knew better than to talk them out of it. Above all else, Wolf families looked after each other in times of trouble and this was probably one of the worst situations to come across this family since the king's attempted assassination. This was a little different, this was a young wolf, a son and brother in trouble. The more Raphina thought about it, the more she cursed herself for not going back the minute she had realised Raif had not been evacuated from Warriors' Rest, but they were confusing times and she had to make sure before risking more lives. However, she still regretted that decision. She prayed to Atta that she had not made the wrong choice. Quickly they showered and changed into their combat suits, then ate with the others before going to the armoury to collect their personnel weapons and rayzors.

Tom and Erline had left the infirmary with Frederick to be greeted outside by Arn who swooped down from upon high to land in front of them as they walked through the courtyard towards the command centre. Startled to see this giant eagle arrive in such a manner, Erline had cowered behind Frederick, physically shaking with terror. It had been a frightening couple of days and these birds were the last thing she expected to see after coming out of hospital.

'Arn!' shouted, Tom who sprinted towards the bird. As he did, to Erline's astonishment, he turned from a boy into an eagle.

What next? she thought to herself. Tom darted past Arn, almost daring him to chase after him as he fled away skyward. Not one to miss a good chase, Arn followed the smaller eagle and lifted into the sky. Erline looked on in terror. 'Frederick, you must do something. That big bird will kill the little one. Err, Tom, I mean. Won't it?' As she watched, the two birds dived, twisting and falling then climbing again to swoop down. She realised they weren't fighting but playing. Her fear turned to amazement as Frederick put a comforting arm around her shoulder.

'They are friends, soulmates. Don't worry, Erline. Come over and meet Arn. I will call them back.' Frederick called to them, asking them to land which they did immediately. Tom turned back into his people form, walked forward and stroked Arn's head, telling him, 'Arn, this is Erline, our friend.'

'Good to see you again, my king, and your young friend. I smell you are wolf too, but I have never seen you before why is that'?

'She is from Earth and has never been here before,' Frederick told him.

'I think I am going mad. I can hear you talking to the bird and the bird talking back.'

'You can, which is quite unusual for a human. Arn also smells wolf in you. That could be why you understand him and me when we communicate that way.'

The beaming smile had returned to Tom's face, for a split second he looked like a little boy again. His face changed when he saw the three figures emerge from the command centre in combat gear, armed to the teeth. 'What's going on?'

he asked.

'It's good to see you well again, Tom, and back with Arn. You must be so happy,' said Raphina.

'What's up Raphina, Phina… Salina? You all look so pale and unhappy. What's changed?'

'You don't know, do you? It's Warriors' Rest. It's been overrun by the Dark and Raif is missing.'

'So, what are you doing?' he asked them.

'We are going to get him back,' said Phina.

'Then me and Arn are going with you,' Tom told them.

'Not this time, Tom. You need to stay here with your father and brother. It's important that you stay safe,' Raphina told him.

'That's right, Tom, you have to stay,' added Phina.

Tom looked at them, feeling their pain. He turned to look at his father, quickly glancing at Erline, then back to the king. He did not have to look at Arn because Arn knew what was in his and Tom's heart. They were going to look for Raif with or without anyone's blessing. 'Dad, you need to stay and look after things, Erline, Karl, Great Porum, the eagles, the wolves, the people, the tribes, the creatures of this world. And I… and Arn are going to help to find our friend with his family.'

'No, Tom, not this time,' Phina told him.

'Yes, Phina, this time more than any other time. You have looked after me for years, forsaking your family for me. Well, now I am going to help you and your family. I will never forgive anyone that stops me. Do you all understand?' he told them all.

'Yes, son, I do understand. I agree with you, now is the time for you to cast your own destiny. You have been led long enough; you can go with my blessing on one account.'

'What's that?' he asked his father as Erline looked on and listened, not quite understanding what was going on. It was Tom growing up. 'You go with Arn and you do what Raphina, Phina and Salina tell you to do because if you don't you will have me to answer to. And remember, when you first saw that scary half man half wolf? Well, I will be that creature again if you muck up. Understand?' Then the king went up to him, bent down slightly and hugged his young son, almost taking the wind out of his sails. Then he put him back on the ground. 'But first, say goodbye to your brother. He might not respond but he will remember and that will mean something to him when he wakes. I am sure these warriors will wait for you, won't you?' he said looking at the three of them. They smiled for the first time in a while and Raphina nodded at Tom. Now happy, Tom ran off towards the infirmary.

'Are you really going to let that young boy go off into danger? You're his father,' asked Erline.

'It's because I'm his father that I am going to let him go. When Karl awakes and finds his young brother gone, he too will try and go but because he is the eldest son, I will not let him go and he will hate me for it. He will see sense one day, with your help, Erline,' he said smiling at her.

The three warriors left them to sort their transport out with the help of Arn; only the best eagles would do for this mission. Tom ran to the infirmary, passing the guards with no problem, up to his brother's room. Inside the machine was his brother Karl. The machine was healing him. He saw his brother sleeping peacefully, no differently from the time before all this happened when he would quite happily have thrown a pillow at him to wake him up, ready to pounce on Phina. But those days were over. He had gone from a little boy to a warrior in a matter of days. Looking down at his brother now, it did not feel strange or unusual. He had become very accustomed to the healing vessels now; he knew they would make Karl as good as new.

'Karl, it's me, Tom... your brother,' he added then regretted it straight away knowing Karl would remember everything he had said. The machine would store all the information it gained while the patient was asleep then it would send it back to him when he awoke recovered from his wounds. 'I'm going with Raphina, Phina and Salina to rescue Raif because he is trapped in Warriors' Rest that has been captured by the Dark. Oh! A lot has happened since we have been away. Dad and Tristan I am sure will fill you in when you awake. Not Uncle Kurt because he has already gone to rescue Raif. He sneaked out last night while everyone was asleep. I have only just woken up myself by the way. Oh, and by the way, Erline is fine. She's with Dad so you will see her when you wake up. Well then, mate....' Tom thought. 'Brother, I mean, take care and I will see you soon. Don't worry, I am being well guarded. See you later.' Then he left, saying hello once again to the warriors guarding his brother. Then he was out of the infirmary, running back to where he had left his dad, Erline, Raphina, Salina and Phina but there was no one there. He stopped and looked around. No one. They have left me, he thought with a sudden range until he felt Arn above him.

Arn was now sweeping down towards him. Above Arn were the rest. Raphina, Phina and Salina were all on eagles circling above him, as well as several other warriors all patiently waiting. Arn landed next to him. 'Your combat gear and weapons are with your father. Go and get them. He is waiting for you in the command centre. Hurry, I will be waiting,' Arn told him.

Tom ran to the command centre where he was let straight in by the guards. The sensors had all been shut down knowing Tom would have blundered straight through in his haste to get back to Arn and start his next adventure. The guards opened the final door to the command room where his father and Erline were waiting for him.

'Quickly, son, the others are waiting. They are keen to find your cousin. Don't forget stay with the others and do as you are told, be a good warrior, obey your orders. This is not a game. You are going to a place where many brave warriors have died. I am sure before this all ends many more will die. I don't want one of them to be you. Understand, son?'

'Yes, Dad, I mean, king.' Tom gave his father a cheeky smile but before he could do anything else the king stretched out his long powerful hands, grabbed his son, squeezing him tight then he put him down.

'Go, young warrior, stay safe.'

Tom rushed off into the map room where his combat suit was waiting for him along with his Tom-sized rayzor, helmet and personal weapons. He changed quickly and made his way back to the command room where his father and Erline waited for him.

'We will walk you out to Arn. It must be good to be back with him?' his father asked.

'It is. I've missed him,' Tom replied.

'You look older dressed up like that, Tom, like Rambo. You're going to fly that big eagle to who knows where,' said Erline with a small tear in her eye. 'Take care, Tom, I really want to get to know you better so come back safe.' Then she kissed his cheek and ruffled his hair with her hand playfully.

'I will,' he replied as he clipped his helmet to his belt. Tom started to run towards Arn then stopped, turned around and waved at them. Then he was on Arn's back. They left the ground, heading up towards the other eagles and their riders waiting above. In front of them, two Eagle warriors scouted ahead while six wolves ran off below them in the direction of Warriors' Rest, a great distance away. They would not reach their destination for several hours. Before long, they had all disappeared.

The king and Erline were left looking up into the cloudless sky above them. 'What a strange land I have come to. I'm not sure if I like it here or not. So much has happened in such a small amount of time. I feel alone again, just like I did when my dad died,' Erline told the king as they headed towards the infirmary.

'You will never be alone again,' he told her. We will all look after you now. I think your path is intertwined with this place and these people. I have a feeling,' the king told her.

Unbeknown to all of them, Row was now in the king's study leafing through some of the historical accounts about the recent history of her family, Elemtum, and particularly the goings on around the disappearance of the queen. Also, the travels she had made to Earth, with whom and for how long. She had a theory and it was all coming together especially after reading Gebhuza Septima's diary entries that she had gone and retrieved. This had been more enlightening than anyone had realised and now she believed she was ready to tell everyone.

Chapter 22
Raif and Tom

Tom nestled into the feathers on Arn's back and fell asleep. The others, fully alert, flew on and the wolves ran without a break. They would land to the west of Warriors' Rest where there were some small fruit trees that would mask their approach. They would rest there until the evening when it would get dark. Then they would move in. By that time, the wolves should be with them and they too would have had time to rest. They did not need much, they would rest fully later on; an hour was all they needed plus some food and water and after that they would be ready to go again.

Karl awoke… It was now early dusk. Erline and Paccia were at his side, he was a little dazed and unsure where he was. Seeing Erline, he thought he was still back on Earth then seeing Paccia the blue healer and Erline together he felt he was dreaming. He closed his eyes for several seconds then opened one at a time. Erline and Paccia were still there and both were smiling.

'Where am I?' he asked.

Paccia told him then handed him a drink and a small tablet. 'This will stop any sickness. I think you have come out of the healing vessel too early in my opinion, but it must be okay otherwise you would not have been allowed to waken.'

Karl thanked her, took the tablet and drank the drink.

'Are you ready to stand?' she asked him.

He pulled himself onto his haunches, then the room went white. He felt like his eyes were crossing and he felt faint, lying back down.

'No, not just yet,' he told her. Now his face was pale and waxen. Paccia told him it would be best for him to stay there for the night and rest. The healing vessel would finish the healing. He had obviously, somehow, come out of the healing sleep early. He should be fine in the morning after a few hours more.

'Try not to run before you can walk. There is no rush, Karl,' she told him. Slowly Karl faded away once more after muttering sorry to Erline.

'There is not much point in you staying around here for the rest of the night. Go and refresh yourself, have a good meal and chill a little. The royal guards will look after the prince. You can't do anything until he awakes,' Paccia told Erline.

'I don't know this place. I don't know where to go,' Erline told her.

'Then you will come with me. You can get refreshed in my quarters, then I will show you the sights and find out where you are staying.'

The door closed behind them, leaving Karl recovering in the healing vessel guarded by two royal guards, one inside and one outside his room. The king would not take any chances now that Great Porum was not the safe haven it should have been for his son.

Tom woke as Arn started to descend. Following the contours of the ground low along a ridge and into a valley that led towards Warriors' Rest. Twenty minutes later they were amongst the fruit trees; they landed and waited. Raphina and Phina had scouted ahead to ensure their approach had not been detected and that there would be no surprises waiting for them. One of the Eagle warriors circled high above them, out of sight of any Dark warrior might happen to look up.

They all waited... Minutes went by, then hours. Suddenly the hairs stood up on the backs of the necks of the waiting group! Wolves approached Raphina and Phina? No, it was the six Wolf warriors who had run from the capital. They had made excellent time, without any incident, but they were exhausted and needed to rest. It would take them at least an hour until they were ready to run again; two would be better, their bodies needed rest. But being descendants of Atta Wolf, an hour would be enough before they would be ready for battle. Even Atta would be proud of them for running so fast and far. The wolves lay down amongst the group, tongues hanging out, panting away in time to their chests that heaved up and down with every breath. They would regain their strength and energy quicker as wolves than they would as people. The others watch on guard as the wolves recovered. From the hidden vantage point, they searched in the distance for any movement, friend or foe but so far there had been none.

One and a half hours had passed when Salina noticed movement very close by. Then she smelt them, wolves, three of them, Kurt, Phina and Raphina, no mistake. Turning back into their people form, Kurt spoke, 'I have scouted the whole of Warriors' Rest. All I have found are the dead, ours and theirs. More of theirs, I might add. The defenders did very well, I guess at least six Dark warriors for every one of ours as far as I can see. But what is puzzling is that there are no living Dark warriors in Warriors' Rest. They have all gone. Everything has been looted or destroyed, but, don't be disheartened, we will rebuild and this time we will keep an eye on who comes in or out. It is blatantly obvious that everyone here was betrayed and when I find those responsible, I will kill them without mercy. I swear this, now, by Atta,' he told them.

'And what of Raif and the young warriors?' asked Salina.

'No trace,' Phina replied. All went quiet. At least two of the six Wolf warriors that had recently arrived had sons at Warriors' Rest going through some of their final training along with Raif. It was decided there was no time to bury the dead, that would come soon enough when reinforcements arrived. Now was the time for the living. They guessed there were at least twenty young warriors out there somewhere. Their main goal would be to get them back to safety. They all ate quickly because they needed the energy for what was to come and the sooner they departed, the sooner the young warriors would be found. Once the six Wolf warriors were ready to go again, they scouted ahead. The rest combed through Warriors' Rest on their way to the main front gate which was now guarded by burnt out desolate towers betrayed by someone who recently had been a supposed friend. Once outside the gates of Warriors' Rest it was clear which way the Dark warriors had gone. There was a trail of dead bodies and discarded booty that the warriors could no longer carry due to the heat of the desert which they had entered. It was turning into the hottest part of the year in the desert, so it was decided to wait for help. Some Eagle warriors were on the way to them who could lift high into the sky away from the soaring heat on the ground. That's why the Omanian people lived underground. It was plain for all to see now as they waited at the edge of the desert.

Before the Eagle warriors arrived, someone else did. Sentar and his fellow Surviyns had met the Wolf warriors and given them shelter from the harsh desert. The warriors had told them of what they had found in Warriors' Rest and the plight of the young warriors so the Surviyns would do all they could to aid their new friends. They had a keen sense of smell, so they could track their pray, and they could travel much faster underground using their deep tunnels under the sand, away from the heat. They would take them all to the Omanians at the furthest edge of their land where Phina had been found by Princess Abla after her escape from the Dark, days earlier. So much had happened and so much had changed since that time. Forty-five minutes later they were in the Omanian capital. They were all underground, thundering towards Abla who was now waiting for them with some of her people and a number of Romonia warriors who wanted to help as thanks for all the assistance and help they had been given by the king and his people over many years.

Back in Great Porum, Karl woke feeling fresh, full of energy and life, unlike the last time he had awoken. It was as though he had never been hurt. He checked his arms and legs; they were all still there. Then he noticed Erline sleeping in a chair next to him. She was sound asleep in beautiful silence. He lifted himself from the healing vessel and stood in front of her watching her sleep. She began to stir, sensing someone was nearby. Opening her eyes, she saw Karl standing in front of her. She smiled, and he smiled back.

'You're awake. How do you feel?' she asked him as she adjusted herself, rubbing her stiff neck caused by the position she had been sleeping in. Karl knelt in front of her, taking her hands and holding them softly.

'I'm fine. Couldn't be better. It's not my first time in one of these things. I'm getting quite used to them… Are you okay?'

'I can't quite believe what has happened. It all seems unreal. I think I will wake up in a minute and I will be back in Louisiana with Dad… but I won't, will I?'

Karl held her hands tighter, but still gently, more comforting. 'No, you're not, Erline. You're stuck with me in this crazy world …But if you want, I can get you back to Louisiana and a normal life?'

'No, there isn't anything left there for me now. I feel I belong here… with you, is that okay?'

'That's more than okay, that's great,' replied Karl. He helped Erline to her feet where he held her tight and kissed her cheek. 'I will look after you,' he told her.

'I know you will,' she replied, then kissed him back on the lips just as Paccia came into the room.

'I see you are lot better, Prince Karl.'

'Less of the prince, please,' he asked her.

She nodded and smiled then checked the readings on the bed. He was back to his normal self; she could see that from the display and the way he now was.

They left the infirmary, walking across the square to the dining hall where they waited for his father and Tristan. Soon the door that led to the dining hall from the command centre opened. In came the king and Tristan, both smiling on seeing Karl and Erline together, happy with no sign of any injury between them. Karl and Erline stood as they approached. Karl and his dad embraced, then Tristan shook his hand.

The king went to get them both some food while the other three talked and laughed until he returned. 'You have some catching up to do, Karl. Warriors' Rest has fallen to the Dark. Many brave warriors have been slaughtered. Kurt and the girls along with Raphina and your brother are now in Warriors' Rest. Raif is missing along with around twenty young warriors from the training academy. We are very lucky. Initially we thought it was around forty young ones but since that estimate we have found the other missing students. Unfortunately, three have died.

All signs so far are not too bleak for the recovery and rescue of the missing with Raif. Unfortunately, many of our friends are also dead.'

'I can't wait round here for them to come back; I need to be with them!' Karl told them.

'I'm not going to stop you, Karl, but you can't go until I know Warriors' Rest is secured. Then you can go and join up with the others on one of the reinforcement vessels. You have got about two hours so, if I were you, I would go and get cleaned up, put some new clothes on and, for what it's worth, teach Erline how to use the weapons. That may come in handy,' his father told him.

'Hey, I don't need anyone to show me how to use a weapon, sir. My pa taught me when I was a young 'un,' she told them all, rather offended.

'Sorry, Erline, I didn't mean to infer you don't know how to use a weapon, just that ours are a little different that's all,' the king told her. Just then one of the command staff walked in.

'Excuse me, your majesty, we are getting a message from water team one. Hollie is alive and transmitting.' They all left the dining room and went down to the command centre.

On the big display screen a blurred image of Hollie spoke to them. 'This is a delayed message from commander Hollie and what is left of water team one I have lost most of water team one. I only have four of the original team of twelve left alive. I lost most on the initial storming of Warriors' Rest. We have followed the Dark since they suddenly started to retreat form Warriors' Rest just as they were about to take the whole city. Something is going on, tactically it does not make sense. They are up to something. This could have all been a diversion otherwise I have no rational reason for why they would have attacked.'

Karl was looking at the big map on the table in the middle of the command centre, Erline was with him. He pointed out all the places he could remember that he and Tom had been since arriving on Elemtum. At every point he described the place and told Erline of the adventures they had had there, including Great Porum and the Dark attack leading to the encounter with Tanibeth who he now did not know where she was or what had happened to her. He also told her of Phina's escape from the Dark, his death and revival by the Eagle mother atop the great red mountain. Erline could not believe he had died and been brought back to life.

'That's amazing,' she told him.

Then a message arrived from Kurt who was now with Abla and the Omanians. They had news of the young warriors. They had received reports the Romonia scouts had seen them being guarded by the Dark as they entered the swamp lands not far from the coliseum where Phina had been held captive. They had also seen four warriors from Great Porum who they had assumed were following them into the swamp, but they did not know who they were as they were all wearing suits and helmets. They described the type of uniform they wore. It was definitely Hollie and what was left of her team. A couple of minutes later, Hollie came back on the screen. 'We have followed them back as far as the arena where Phina was held captive; I believe they are using it as a prison camp because we saw them herding some of the young warriors in there as we arrived. By the look of them, they were very angry because the young ones had cost them many hundreds of warriors going by the trail of dead we have come across. It looks like they have been deploying hit and run tactics on the Dark since they left Warriors' Rest, but I think they pushed it a bit too far and have were caught. I don't believe there are many Dark warriors guarding them, but there are more than my team can cope with. We can't make a dynamic entry and free the prisoners yet, not without support. I am asking most urgently that you send reinforcements to my position as soon as possible. I am setting up two observation points and a safe RV point for support troops. If you could give me an expected ETA as soon as possible that would be good. One more thing to add… the Dark suddenly left Warriors' Rest just as I thought my team and I were going to die. They just turned and left. They are still retreating past the arena south to where I can only presume they came from. It… it just doesn't add up, as I said before.' She began to fade out then she was gone.

'There's a massive storm that has just reached that area so I think that's why we have just lost Hollie,' one of the operations staff said.

'See if you can send her a reply… maintain current position, do not engage the enemy unless you are threatened, reinforcements will be with you as soon as possible. Kurt and a small force are currently with the Omanian people. Once established, they will come to your support. End it with well done, JFD. I will be sending warriors to defend Warriors' Rest and to back up Kurt and Hollie. I want the first two sail craft to leave within thirty minutes to be followed by two more fully loaded with battle-ready warriors who, if asked, will be ready for action immediately.'

The command centre came to life. Messages were sent out informing all commanders of the king's intentions. 'I want you on that first craft, Tristan, I need a forward command centre set up as soon as possible. Warriors' Rest will become a staging post for the warriors going forward to engage with the Dark as soon as possible. I also want a field hospital set up there for fast treatment of the wounded. Paccia, can you handle that?'

Paccia, who was standing behind him, said, 'It will be done. I will go and oversee preparations. We will be ready within two hours. I will lead the battlefield infirmary myself.' She turned and walked towards the exit.

'Thank you, Paccia, I know this is a difficult time for you and your sister. We're here for support if you need it. I do trust you and your people.' the king told her. She could see he meant it which made her smile.

'We will be on the first craft as well, Dad, Erline and me. Come on, Erline, we don't have long,' said Karl, taking her hand and pulling her towards the same door Paccia had left through. Once out of the command centre, Karl and Erline ran towards the accommodation block where their new rooms were situated. Once inside Karl's room he explained the toilet to her so she could get a quick shower. Karl waited until she had finished then gave her some clothes. He then also went for a quick shower.

Within half an hour they were racing towards the sail craft port where they could hear the gentle throbbing of the craft's engines at it prepared for flight. They boarded the craft, going directly to the commander in the flight deck where Karl asked him to inform him when they were halfway to Warriors' Rest because he was going to leave the craft and fly. At that point Tristan walked in, just catching the last sentence.

'What's this about leaving the craft, Karl?' he asked.

'I'm only going to fly outside the craft with Erline until we get to Warriors' Rest. I feel I need a stretch and Erline has never flown with me before.'

'Okay, but no aerobatics, do you understand Karl? And stay close. If you stray too far, I will have you shot down. Do you understand?' he said jokingly. Smiling, Karl agreed, then took Erline to see the rest of the craft. Soon there was a small shudder and the next time Erline looked out the window they were high in the sky.

'Wow, this is amazing! I can't believe it, and this thing puts my little Cessna back home to shame.'

'You can fly?' asked Karl

'Sure. Dad taught me when I was ten. I had been flying since six but not properly until then.' She smiled. 'What are we going to fly?' she asked.

'An eagle,' Karl replied. 'My good friend Alerio will be with us, he's always with me now. Let's go up to the top gun position and I will tell you about it. It's also the best view in the whole craft.' The top gun position was automatic, but it did have a clear dome around it, so it could be manually controlled. 'Look there, Erline, just past the tail above that big cloud, do you see?' Karl pointed him out to her.

There was a formation of eagles following them. 'Isn't that fantastic? How graceful they look, don't you think?'

'Are they some of the eagles we will be flying? I'm a little scared. We are quite high,' Erline asked him.

'No, I will be flying with my soulmate. He saved my life. In fact, he brought me back from the dead, nearly killing himself in the process.'

'Wow, I have so much to learn. How long was it before you felt part of this?' she asked him.

'I am still learning. I have only been here less than a month, so I am learning all the time,' he told her. She looked surprised but remembered what she had been told back in here home before they left Louisiana.

'We will learn together,' she told him.

Settling down back in the cargo bay, they talked and talked until they fell asleep to the humming of the crafts engines, Erline's head resting on Karl's shoulder.

Meanwhile, down under the desert, the Surviyns had left Kurt, Tom, Phina, Salina, Raphina and their small party at an underground cavern. In the centre of the cavern was a large clear green tinted pool which was illuminated by a single ray of light coming from somewhere above them, a single point cascading down upon the surface of the pool. They looked into the clear water. It was very inviting after the dry air and dust of the tunnels they had just raced through. They peered down to see if they could see anything lurking below. They did not notice the figure standing in a dark corner at the edge of the pool until it spoke. 'It is good water, safe to swim in and safe to drink.' Then out of the dark came a figure completely covered in robes. All that could be seen behind the black hood and the red scarf that covered her face were two striking light blue female eyes staring at them.

'Hello, Abla, I would recognise those blue eyes anywhere. Everyone, this is Abla, she is the princess warrior of the Omanian people. This is the woman that saved me from the harsh desert above us after I escaped from the Dark,' said Phina, smiling at seeing her new friend once again. Abla walked towards them. As she did, she released the cloth from around her face revealing the beautiful bronzed face of the princess who was smiling as brightly as Phina. The two princesses embraced warmly then Abla bowed gracefully to the others.

'You are all most welcome to our lands. Come with me and I will take you to where you can all get freshened up then we will have some food and drink. I am afraid we will not be going anywhere until morning because above us there is a mighty sandstorm rolling across the desert. The scouts have told me it's one of the worst they have seen in living memory. Not only that, it is turning into a vicious rainstorm as it leaves the desert and hits the area around your intended target. Your warriors on the edge of the jungle have moved further in to get some shelter from the storm. I might add they are all well. My warriors have contacted them and helped them build shelter as well as supplying them with food and water. Our scholars are predicting the storm will pass by early morning, so I suggest we move then. Your Wolf scouts are also safe. I will take you to them.' Raphina thanked her.

Just then there was a joyful scream as Tom leapt high into the air, pulling his knees to his chest and bombing into the water, the spray hitting some of those still standing next to the pool. They all turned sharply to see what was happening. Tom came to the surface with a gasp and a smile. 'My god, that was cold!' he gasped then pulled himself from the water feeling very refreshed and joined the others who looked at him enviously. 'Go on, jump in. It's great, go on!' No one moved then Abla took Phina's hand, pulling her to the edge. They both jumped in. Soon all the weapons and outer clothing were in piles and everyone was in the cooling refreshing water.

'I wish I had a camera,' Tom said to himself as he looked at everyone laughing in the water. Then he forced himself to jump in once again, knowing the cold would hit him as he entered the water. But this time it seemed warmer. Sooner than everyone wanted they were out of the water, back in the real world, as Abla led them, dripping, through a passage that had not been visible to them due to the dark shadow that had obscured it from their view when they had first entered the lagoon.

As they walked down the passage, Abla told them of the preparations that the Omanian and the others who had gathered in the city had made to help the king against the Dark. Twenty minutes later they reached a massive cavern that had ornate carvings all over the walls and roof. Along two of the walls were some ornate balconies with large wooden and glass doors behind them. She explained that behind the walls were some living quarters for single males and females. At the end furthest away from them was a massive gate, open but guarded by six very aggressive looking Omanians in long robes with face masks designed to kept sand out of their eyes, nose and mouth. In their hands they held curved swords, the blade resting on their shoulders. At their side was a fighting dagger and, on their backs, they could see the barrel of some sort of rifle. The guards nodded to Aba as she passed them with her guests.

'We have gone through four layers of defence to get this far and I might add we have never been breached,' she told them as they entered a large well-lit tunnel which they walked along for two minutes. Tom was sure every now and then he saw eyes watching him. He told Abla, but she just laughed.

'Very observant, Prince Thomas,' she told him, making him cringe.

'I'm not Prince Thomas, I'm Tom,' he corrected her. She smiled at him, then told everyone that there were reports of a great eagle with a woman landing in the northern desert. 'The Surviyns are contacting them as we speak.'

Alerio had landed, then Karl was next to Erline in his human form. Just then, the sail craft they had been travelling in went overhead. It had received coordinates for a rendezvous with the Omanians.

'How was that?' he asked her.

'That was amazing. I was a little scared when I was on your back and you flew out of the sail craft... but then I felt safe with you and I think I even fell asleep on your back for a short time. I can't wait to do it again. So, what now?' she asked him.

'I'm sure we will be contacted soon. Don't be afraid when it or they turn up, they look very vicious, but they are my friends, so everything will be okay.'

'What do you mean?' she replied. Then Karl pointed towards a slight ripple in the sand then it came out. Erline backed into Karl, nearly knocking him over. 'Are you sure?'

Karl held her until the giant creature was out of the sand.

'It's Sentar, I would recognise him anywhere.' As Karl let go of Erline and ran up to the Sentar, its tongue came out and wrapped round him.

Karl laughed as Erline screamed, 'Karl!'

'It's okay, he's being friendly,' Karl said as the tongue unwound and disappeared back into Sentar's mouth.

'I had to check. You all look the same to me,' the big creature told them.

Karl beckoned Erline to come closer. Carefully she slowly walked over to Karl, grabbing his hand for reassurance. The tongue came out once more. Erline looked at Karl as it approached her. Smiling, Karl nodded at her as the tongue wound round her. She closed her eyes, taking a deep breath. Then her eyes opened. 'It's not tight, it's really gentle.' The tongue unwound.

'There you go, he knows you now. You're safe. He basically told me you smell nice which is better than saying you taste nice, I suppose,' laughed Karl.

'I've never done anything like that before. It was amazing but also terrifying at the same time. I'm glad he's on our side. What now?'

'Now we ride,' replied Karl. 'How did I not see that coming?'

Behind them they could see a big bank of sand forming which hurtled towards them. In front of the approaching sandstorm, they could see lighting. Behind the upper most cloud was an even-blacker cloud rolling towards them. They were smack in the centre of where the storms would meet.

'Time to go I think, Sentar.'

They both got on Sentar's back as Karl had done previously. Before they could blink an eye, they were hurtling through tunnels just big enough for Sentar to pass through as the storm crashed above them.

In the jungle, Hollie and the surviving water team members had set up two new observation points where they watched for any activity from the Dark. They had eaten and cleaned as best they could, then while one watched the other had some much-needed sleep. They would alternate the watch all through the rest of the day and night. Above and around them the rain thundered down, smashing against vines and leaves as the storm howled. At times the rain was so heavy it obscured the watchers' view as sand mixed with the thunderous rain.

At Warriors' Rest, the sail craft had landed. It had to turn back from its original planned rendezvous with the Omanis as the storm had proved to be too large and dangerous to fly through due to the lighting and wind speed. The teams left the craft and started to sweep through Warriors' Rest as Kurt and Raphina had done earlier. This time a more thorough search was completed by the sections in every part of Warriors' Rest, room by room. Once that task was complete, a third and fourth sail craft had landed, offloading warriors, healers and supplies before returning to Great Porum. This operation would go on for the next few days as long as the storm they were tracking did not turn and head towards them.

Engineers were now in the towers rebuilding the defences and battlements. In the city itself there had not been too much damage to the infrastructure. There had been a lot of looting and vandalism which was easily fixed but the headquarters and command and control elements had been totally destroyed. Someone had known where to go and how to get in those structures and that looked like the work of Gebhuza Septima, they were sure of that. A message had been received from Lessi Zell; she and the rest of the Zells would be ready to help whenever they were needed. Along with that, messages from all the clans of Elemtum adding their support had been received with specialists from many of them now descending on Warriors' Rest to give assistance. In the meantime, Tristan busied himself with locating an alternate command centre.

Soon Karl and Erline were with the others and, for a short time, they were all together, safe and happy. A message had been sent back to Warriors' Rest informing them that they were now safely with the Omani. They had been fed and shown quarters where they could rest. Phina and the others had all gone to briefings that lasted well into the night. Karl, Tom and Erline talked about everything; their childhoods, what had happened since leaving Earth, even what might happen in the morning. They had taken Erline to the makeshift supply area so they could all be fully kitted out for the next day. As yet, they did not know what part they would play in the forthcoming events.

The morning came quicker than anyone wanted; they all gathered in the main hall and even after having some food it was still early. Phina and Abla were not amongst them.

'Probably at some meeting or other,' Karl said.

Then they both appeared. Abla and Phina walked towards the group,

'We have a plan,' said Phina then began to explain the plan of action to everyone that had not attended the battle planning. Karl, Tom and Erline would be with the reserve force; they would help any part of the battle plan that needed it. Phina could see the disappointment on Karl's face so she explained to him how vitally important his task was to the success of the operation and that it could be the difference between victory and defeat. Karl brightened up once he realised this, then he took Tom and Erline to meet the troops he would be commanding while the others carried on with their preparations.

Hollie and her four-man team had moved closer to the old arena, keeping eyes on it as the bad weather rumbled away across the desert in the direction of Warriors' Rest. They noted that eighty Dark warriors had left and gone south, deeper into the jungle. From where they were, they could see around ten guards patrolling the outside of the arena with another four mingling and talking at the main gate. They had a demon dog with them that constantly sniffed the air and pulled at its handler's chain every time a Dark warrior passed on their patrol.

Hollie reported this back to the main command centre. Soon she would be relieved, she was told, but Hollie would have none of it, not until the forthcoming battle had ended either with victory or her death. It did not really matter which to Hollie at that point.

Karl, Erline and Tom now stood amongst their troops, some of whom Karl and Tom knew but most they did not. There were Wolf warriors, Eagle warriors, some Omanian warriors. Then at the back of the assembled warriors, Tom noticed movement; black, fast, and weaving between the assembled crowd. 'Look out,' he shouted but he was too late. The black beast was on top of him, its head rubbing against Tom's. Karl started to move then, after a delay, he started to laugh. Not sure what was going on, Erline stepped back almost behind Karl.

'Blacky, you old dog!' Tom cried out as he tussled playfully with the now fully restored black panther. The gathered warriors laughed and smiled, light relief breaking up the thoughts of what may lie. Eventually, Tom, Blacky, Karl and Erline stood in front of the warriors.

'I think I should say something, don't you?' he whispered to his brother.

'Yep, I reckon, as you're the boss,' Tom replied.

'Thanks for that bit of wisdom, Tom. Right then,' he said loudly but meaning for himself. 'Right, guys, I mean warriors, hopefully, you all know why we are here. We are the reserve which, as you all know, is an important task. We could be the difference between victory and defeat. I know I can depend on you all to do your best in whatever is in store for us in the following few hours. I have, I mean, we have been in battle before and I can see some trusted faces in front of me. I am only young so if some of you older wiser warriors, I mean friends, see me doing something stupid by all means give me a kick. Me and my brother will fight with you side by side to whatever end comes our way.' He quickly added, 'I mean our victory today. If anyone wants to come and talk, I will be here. I know I don't need to tell you to make sure you and your kit is ready, so I wish you all the best of luck and may Atta be with you this day. Thank you that's all.'

'Good luck to you, princes,' someone shouted from the crowd then a wild roar erupted along with stamping feet and the waving of weapons. Slowly the warriors moved away to the areas and groups they had been in previously. Warriors from every part of the planet mixed with each other. This is one united force, Karl thought to himself, then he turned to see a smiling Tom and Erline.

'Well done, bro. Not sure about the "I'll be here if you want to talk" bit, Karl, they are all hairy scary warriors.'

'Yes, a little over the top that bit but, altogether, a good speech. Well done,' said Erline, affectionately rubbing his back then kissing him on the cheek.

'The speech of a future king, I thought,' Blacky told them all.

'Thanks, Blacky!'

'Karl,' came a voice from behind them. 'Prince, excuse me, but there is someone to see you all. Follow me,' said the Wolf warrior. He led them out along a dimly lit passage then onto a shuttle that took them speeding along underground for five minutes. It came to a stop and the doors opened. In front of them was a massive well-lit cave with huge doors at one end. 'This way please,' said the warrior and they walked towards the doors. Along the side of the cave there were Omani warriors staged at strategic points to defend the doors if needed. Stopping in front of the door, a shout came from behind them, 'Open the doors.' Slowly, with much effort and the occasional screech of metal on metal, the doors slid open. As they did, light streamed in illuminating the dust particles that could not be seen before. They all blinked and tried to focus in the bright light.

'Hello, boys. Miss me? I couldn't let you have all the fun, now could I?'

'Karl, it's Row,' Tom shouted then started to run towards her. She opened her arms and met him with a big sister's hug and kiss.

'It's good to see you, Row,' said Tom.

'Yes, very good,' added Karl, joining in the hug, leaving Erline standing by herself feeling a little awkward.

'Oh, where are my manners? Boys, don't leave Erline standing there by herself.

'You know Erline, you remember her, she's my... err, friend,' replied Karl.

'Girlfriend,' added Tom.

'Really? You have been moving fast since I last saw you. It's only been a day, remember. Hi, Erline, nice to see you again. I did not recognise you when I first saw you in all that combat gear. Jeans and checked shirt with trainers the last time I saw you. How are you finding our new world?'

'I'm not sure. It's very dangerous from what I've seen, and I thought Earth was bad but at least there I wake up every morning and can walk around without getting killed. Actually, I will amend what I just said, most places on Earth you can wake up and walk around without getting killed,' she laughed.

'I do know what you mean,' Row replied, 'but it will get better, I'm sure of that. A few bad apples, if you know what I mean.'

'I certainly do,' she replied.

Then Tom heard a clicking sound from above. He looked up to see two huge claws which grabbed him, then he was spinning in the air; one minute on the ground, then sky, then black fur. Then it stopped. He saw the back of a head with large bat shaped ears. 'Tearmoss!' he shouted then he was startled by a hand on the shoulder from behind. His head shot round to see the beautiful face of Zuzza Zell.

'I couldn't leave you boys alone to fight these vermin, could I?' She smiled at him as Tearmoss landed. They both got off his back and Tom went around to his face and rubbed his nose. Tearmoss lowered his head so Tom could scratch his ears as the clicking increased. Tom would swear he saw the Zell smile.

Zuzza walked up to Karl and bowed gracefully. 'Prince, we are at your command. My Zells are in the jungle hiding as only Zells can. No one will know we are there, and we are ready to strike fear into the Dark creatures at your command.' She bowed once more.

'You have no need to bow, Zuzza. You and your Zells are equal to me and my kind. I am happy to have you with me. Come with me and I will show you the plan and our part in it.'

Zuzza thanked Karl for his kindness. Then she turned and spoke to Tearmoss, telling him she would be going with the prince to study battle plans and that she would call him when they had finished. She also told him to ensure the Zells were all properly rested and fed, ready for battle. Tearmoss clicked his reply then gently returned Tom to the ground, nudging him with his talon towards his brother and the others. Then, with a few beats of his wings, he was gone and the dust settled around them.

'I like him,' said Tom as he walked back to Zuzza and Karl.

'He is very fond of you as well, prince. He thinks you are funny and brave after watching you fight on our last encounter,' Zuzza told him which brought a broad smile to Tom's face.

They all walked away as the big doors shut behind them and headed back to the command centre. Karl explained the plan to Zuzza as the others watched on. He explained their part in the operation and what was about to happen. It was to be a three-pronged attack. One element would take the arena, two other elements would do pincer movements behind to cut off any forces trying to escape. That was stage one. Once that phase had been consolidated, there would then be a search and destroy mission to destroy all Dark forces encountered as they pushed deep into the jungle. This phase would continue until the Dark stronghold was found and destroyed. How long that would take, no one knew. A lot depended on the enemy and what they found as they pushed deeper into uncharted territory. Karl's job was to back up any part of either phase that needed it.

Happy with the plan, Zuzza returned to her Zells along with a communication device Karl had given her so she could communicate with them if needed. After that, everyone prepared and checked kit and equipment and waited and waited. Then did it all again; sleep, eat and wait. Waiting was the hardest part, knowing other warriors were in action while they waited.

But Karl knew differently. He stayed in the command centre. Phase one had been completed with no enemy sighted and the arena had been cleared again. They had all somehow disappeared during the night as the storm rolled by. Hollie had seen Dark warriors but had lost sight of them as the storm intensified. She had been the first into the arena with her water team and found nothing. Nothing dead, nothing living and no prisoners, no Raif.

After a short break for food and drink, phase two started. Karl asked the Zells to help search ahead of the main body of warriors advancing deep into the jungle. Their keen eyes and sense of smell would detect any Dark warriors ahead of them and give early warning. The Zells were now doing as asked and six hours into phase two nothing had been sighted. Command were getting worried. No one could move that fast and not be detected in this jungle.

It was decided to airlift Karl's force several hours ahead of the main body to set up observation points and killing ground to catch the Dark. It reminded Karl of the grouse shooting he had seen on TV back on Earth; the beaters pushed the grouse towards the gun line that would then shoot them down. Karl's force was the gun line. He was happy that they were now involved in the operation. Before he knew it, he and his force were ready and were dropped by giant gyrocopter gunship transports that were still on their test flights, but the command thought the scientists had had long enough to produce and test them. Now they were needed, and they worked well, quiet and fast carrying over fifty warriors each, all without a single hitch apart from an inquisitive Zell that nearly got too close to one.

Now Karl was on the ground, receiving updates from his commanders as their warriors got into killing positions. Tom, Row, Erline and Blacky were all together, slightly behind the lead force in a very old decaying wooden hut that was being used as a makeshift command post for the killing force that Karl now commanded. Everything was deadly quiet, the silence only broken by the odd wail of some jungle creature nearby.

Reports came in about the progress of the three elements as they pushed deeper into the jungle, hopefully forcing the Dark towards Karl's force. The Zells reported no movement on the ground or in the air by anything other than the elements advancing and Karl's killing force. Where were the Dark? Something was not right. The longer the operation went on, the more commanders began to think they had missed something. But what? Finally, the elements met up with Karl's killing force. The only Dark found were no more that twelve dead bodies that looked like they had been executed. Where were the rest?

A base camp was set up around an old temple complex that had been discovered several years before but had been abandoned when the Dark had started to appear. While the warriors and Zells rested, the commanders gathered to debrief on the day's operation and discuss their next move to establish what had happened to the Dark.

Meanwhile, Tom, Row and Erline sat under a tarpaulin under the jungle canopy. 'Did you find anything out, Row, after you read those letters you found?'

'Yes, I did, and it may have some bearing on why we can't find the Dark,' replied Row.

'What are you talking about?' asked Erline, so Row explained about the letters she found in Gebhuza Septima's house. She explained it as only a woman could, with lots of exaggeration, colour and mystery to enhance the story, as if it ever needed enhancing as it was quite unbelievable in the first place.

Tom was getting bored with the whole story. 'Come on, Row, get to the point...'

'Shut up, Tom, it's just getting interesting,' Erline told him.

'Yes, shut up, Tom, and go and do something somewhere else,' interjected Row.

'Right then, I will. I'm going for a walk to see what I can find,' he said but neither of the girls heard so he stomped off. As he did, he picked up his rayzor and slung it into its sheath.

Meanwhile, in the command centre… ''We must have missed something. I can't believe they could slip by us unnoticed,' said Karl.

'I agree. Hollie saw them. The during the storm they disappeared. We will have to go back and methodically check everything from here back to the arena, leaving no stone unturned,' added Raphina Both Tristan and Kurt, who had arrived from Warriors' Rest for the meeting, agreed.

Tom wandered off, a bit disgruntled; he felt alone. Row had a new friend and Karl was busy being in charge of his army… so Tom wandered. He wandered through the camp and chatted with the warriors he met, then he came to the camp's edge, where sensors pointed outwards protecting the camp. Tom walked past them. In the camp headquarters an alarm sounded; the operator saw the figure going out of the safety of the camp, so he looked at the ID displayed on the screen. It was the prince, so he called him on his intercom. But there was no answer. Tom had left his helmet with Row and Erline. Row answered the inquiry and told the operator she would go and find the prince. Tom wandered on, unaware of any possible danger.

He came to a clearing in the jungle. At the furthermost corner was an ancient archway partly covered by vines. Tom could see markings and sculptures on the exposed stone, so he walked up to it. As he approached, he could see a waterfall beyond the arch. The water was illuminated by a ray of light from above. As he looked, he could see something glistening behind the water, so he went closer, fascinated by what it might be. There was a well-trodden path around to the left of the waterfall. It was muddy from a great deal of use by many people walking behind the waterfall, but he did not think about that as he squelched through the mud mixing with the spray from the waterfall. In front of him, a little way ahead, was a stone doorway; no door, just black. All around it were vines that had crept over the entrance, partly obscuring passage, so Tom took his rayzor from the sheath at his side and hacked the vine away. Then he took a torch from his utility belt and shone it into the dark….

Row and Erline were directed by the command centre to Tom's exit point from the camp. On the way, they gathered several warriors who were eager to help locate the prince having just been speaking to him. One of the helpers was Blacky who could smell the direction Tom had taken. 'Dogs aren't the only animals that can smell well,' he informed those assembled. He took them to the same entrance behind the waterfall that Tom had found and entered. The vine had regrown but everyone noticed the rayzor lying in the mud just inside the entrance. A little way beyond was a torch still partly illuminating the blackness... but no Tom.

'This does not look good,' Blacky told them. Row reported back to the command centre who told them to secure the area and wait for backup which they did apart from Blacky and two warriors who ventured into the black, searching until they came to a rockfall stopping them from going any further. It had not been long since it happened because the air was full of dust from the freshly fallen rocks and boulders.

Kurt, Raphina, Hollie, Tristan, Karl, Row and Erline, along with many warriors, were now outside the cave.

'Hollie, maintain a guard around this position. Let me know if there is any movement in the area; this could be a trap to pull us into an ambush,' Kurt told her. Hollie selected some warriors and started on the task. 'Raphina, can you man the command centre and track down some miners ASAP? I don't want to blow the rockfall as I don't know what's behind it.' Raphina took Tristan and the girls with her as they would be more use than standing around the cave entrance.

Kurt set up a listening post next to the rockfall which Karl took charge of. 'It's a matter of hurry up and wait until the miners arrive, I suppose, Uncle Kurt'?

'I'm afraid so,' replied Kurt. 'I will go and let the king know. I will be back soon. Inform me immediately if you hear anything from the rockfall, Karl.' Karl nodded as Kurt left.

Blacky sniffed the air. 'I can smell them. They have been here and not too long ago, Karl.'

'Can you tell what sort of Dark warriors they were?' Karl asked.

'Not really. The smells are all intermingled, they all smell as bad as each other. I can smell Tom as well as some other wolf smells.

'I will let Kurt know. That at least gives us hope that there may be some others still alive. Well, at least, for a couple of hours anyway.'

Tom awoke after a gentle nudge. As he opened his eyes, he saw a rather battered and bruised Raif, as well as a handful of cadets that had been training with him but nowhere near the number that were missing. 'Raif, you're alive! It's so good to see you and the others. Where are we?'

'I don't know, Tom, but I don't think we are in Elemtum anymore. It just all smells different.'

Tom took a sniff. The pain in the back of his head hit him; he winced then felt his head. There was a large bump just behind his crown and it was damp. He pulled his hand away, then looked at it. A small amount of fresh blood as well as dried blood was visible.

'Let me have a look,' said Raif. He parted some of Tom's hair. 'That's a nice lump, mate. The skin is broken but it's not bad. It won't need stitching or anything, but we will need to keep an eye on you just to make sure you don't have concussion!'

'Earth! That's where we are. I can smell it. Definitely different to Elemtum. We must have been moved here for some reason?'

'Yeah, because our warriors are obviously making it difficult for them at home,' said one of the other cadets. Tom and Raif nodded in agreement.

'You know Earth, don't you, Tom? That could be to our advantage.' Raif smiled.

'Don't get your hopes up too much, Raif, I was only a little kid when I was last here.'

'You were a goat?' replied a puzzled Raif.

'No, nutter, a child. That's another name for a child here on Earth.' Tom laughed. His head hurt. 'Bloody hell, I don't even remember anyone hitting me. They must have been behind me in the dark, I wonder why they didn't kill me?'

'That's what we are all thinking. They killed some of us but not the others. No doubt they have a bigger plan for us. Knowing the Dark, it won't be very nice, I'm sure,' said Raif.

'Then let's not wait around to find out,' said Tom.

'It's not as easy as that, Tom. We have tried many times to escape but they are watching us like hawks and every time we try… they kill someone to teach us a lesson,' said one of the cadets.

Back on Elemtum, word had come in that little Terry and some of his miners would be with them in around two hours, so things were starting to happen. Not only that, Leslie had contacted the command post from Great Porum. She believed they would find a link to Earth behind the fallen rocks and, if that was the case, she also believed it would have been destroyed and there was no knowing if it could be re-opened. So, Kurt and the others now believed all they would probably be doing was looking for Tom's body or finding out that he was no longer on Elemtum. The atmosphere was now very subdued; plans would have to be drawn up to deal with either outcome.

Two hours passed, and Terry and the miners turned up and got to work watched by Karl and the complete command team. 'We're going to blow a bit of the rockfall away,' Terry told Karl and Kurt. Everyone moved back and waited for the explosion. 'Three… two… one… heads down!' Terry shouted. The explosion followed, not the big bang everyone expected but a low thud and some dust. As it cleared, weapons were raised and aimed at the entrance just in case it revealed some hidden danger. It became apparent very quickly that there was still some rockfall to move so the procedure continued several times until Terry told them the rockfall was most probably all the way to the link to Earth terminal that would most probably had been destroyed.

Kurt left a section of warriors to protect the miners until they got to the terminal then they would know. Kurt and Karl went back to the command post to make some decisions. First call would be Leslie to see if she could pinpoint the nearest link to Earth that the destroyed tunnel would have gone to if that was possible.

'Raif, how many of you are there left?'

'Exactly nine,' Raif replied.

'How many of the Dark guards come into the cell and how many stay outside?' Tom asked.

'Normally two come in; one with a whip or knife, the other covers him from the door with a weapon which I have never seen before. It fires metal projectiles that tear a person apart.'

'Sounds like a rifle or machine gun from Earth,' replied Tom.

Tom gathered everyone around him, getting one of the cadets to watch the door. 'I have an idea. I want to run past you all… a way to get out of this cell and maybe escape. If we don't escape, I don't intend to live,' he added. He continued, 'There are ten of us, including me. How many Wolves and how many Eagles do we have amongst us?'

'That's no good, Tom, we can't transform here on Earth.'

'Said who?' replied Tom.

'It says in the ancient text that no Wolf or Eagle shall show himself to a human on Earth so as to keep the balance of the planets,' replied one of the cadets.

'Crap. One, these aren't humans and two, has anyone tried?'

'Well, no… we can't, it's useless,' said Raif.

'Okay, let's see, shall we?'

In front of them Tom became his wolf form, then returned to his human form. 'Now do you believe me?

'There's eight wolves and one eagle, actually nine wolves and one eagle including you,' said a cadet.

'Don't forget, I can be an eagle or wolf if need be,' replied Tom with a smile.

'Right then… what's the plan?' asked Raif.

'Is the door the only place they can see us in this cell?'

'Yes,' came the answer.

'Okay then, I will stay in sight of the door... the rest of you will transform and hide either side of the door. When it opens, we will attack in three groups. Three go for the lead, three go for the Dark holding the weapon and three rush through the door and confront whatever is there. I will join the last three and rush through the door once I have transformed into a wolf. Who's the eagle?' Tom asked.

'I am,' replied the smallest cadet standing in front of him. 'My name is Kee and I am a falcon, not an eagle. I'm small so I will be through that door and looking for an exit or the enemy before a fat eagle can blink,' he said, smiling.

'Falcon? How?' replied Tom.

'It's a long story, prince. I will tell you one day if we all survive,' said Kee.

'First thing, Kee. I'm Tom, not prince, and second thing, I look forward to seeing you fly and hearing your story. Now, is everyone happy with the plan?' Tom waited... No one had any objections. 'Right then, sort yourselves into three teams. You know each other's strengths and weaknesses, then let's get ready. It could be a long wait.'

Leslie contacted the command post where Karl and the others were assembled, poring over different plans and considering a covert operation to go to Earth without Earth ever realising. It had never been done before. That's wasn't quite true; warriors and academics from Elemtum had travelled to Earth for centuries, without Earth's knowledge, and of course, Gebhuza Septima had been dabbling with Earth unofficially for who knows how long or what damage had been done by him.

'We have made some calculations; we believe the point on Earth where the tunnel led to would be somewhere in Mexico. Near an area called Cancun. We looked up the area for some likely places and one especially ticks all the boxes. It's an old Mayan city called Cobá which was once a great city for the Mayans. We have found some text about the Mayans in our library. It talks about warriors from Elemtum making friends with the Mayans who then revered them as gods when they turned into wolves and eagles. Because this could have changed human history, contact was broken with the Mayans and the warriors returned home. After that, we don't know why the Mayan civilisation collapsed. Some of our scholars said it was because of our intervention in the Mayan civilisation, but others put it down to invaders from other lands on Earth. Like the Spanish or British had some of the biggest empires at the time but I'm not sure about that period in the human history. Not that it matters at this point.'

After some time, the lookout warned everyone inside the cell, 'There's someone coming, two as usual, get ready!'

'You all know what to do... good luck, guys,' Tom added.

A face peered through the small barred hatch in the door. 'Time for a beating,' the Dark warrior growled with delight at the forthcoming pain he would inflict on the young prisoners.

'Come on then, you filthy scum, if you think you're hard enough,' shouted Tom with a taunting laugh.

This immediately infuriated the warrior who, now in a rage, fumbled with the key in the cell door lock. 'You're going to get it, you little shit. Prince or no prince, I don't care what my orders are, you're going to get it and get it good,' he screamed as he pushed the door open with force which slammed against the cell wall. He stepped in, eyes fixed on Tom as he lifted his club ready to commence the beating. The second warrior stood slightly back from the door, his weapon at that point aimed at the first warrior's back. The first warrior lifted the club above his head when something clicked in his small brain,

'Where's all the others, you little shit?' It was too late. In front of him, Tom was now a very angry looking wolf, teeth bared, saliva dripping from his jaws. The warrior's pupils enlarged as he started to realise the trouble he was now in; he didn't even notice the falcon dart past, heading straight for the second warrior, talons raised ready to gouge his eyes from his face. Then it all happened very quickly. Two wolves had the tendons from the first warrior's legs, making his knees buckle. Tom leapt over him, heading for the throat of the second warrior who was now screaming, trying to fend off the bird gouging at his eyes. His weapon had fallen to the floor; the first warrior was now a bloodied mess on the floor, his jugular now missing, two wolves on his back keeping him down as the last drops of life seeped from his body. The second warrior fared no better; he too was now on his back with four wolves ripping him to pieces.

Then it was all over... everyone realised how quiet it now was! Kee was nowhere to be seen. The wolves dragged the second body into the cell. Tom, now a boy again, pulled the cell door shut. 'That went well, better than I expected,' he said with a smile.

'You had doubts?' asked Raif, now back in human form.

'Well, a little. We only guessed there would only be two guards... but it all turned out okay, didn't it?' replied Tom with his usual smile. 'Best we vamoose as quickly as possible.'

'What?' replied a puzzled Raif.

'Get the hell out of here, quickly.'

'Oh right… now I understand. Do you know what, Tom? It's amazing we speak the same language, but half the time I don't have a clue what you're saying.' Laughing, they all ran down the corridor to a stone stairwell going down which had dim lights on the sides.

As they cautiously went down, step by step, Kee reappeared. 'There's an entrance about twenty metres down. No door, but there is a Dark lancer standing guard. I could see past him, there is a jungle outside, but all I could see are what look like temple ruins, very old looking. We must be somewhere south because I could feel the heat coming in from outside. It's definitely not like anything I have seen on Elemtum. The only good thing was that I could only see one guard. Do you want me to go out and scout around before you go out?'

'Yes, that would be good. We will stay at the top of the stairwell where we can protect ourselves best and wait for your return,' replied Tom.

In a flash, Kee was gone, darting past the guard at the entrance who just looked up at the bird darting away from him and thought nothing of it. This place was full of those creatures flying around. I wonder what it tastes like? he thought in his boredom.

Kee was up above the pyramid shaped structure which was surrounded on three of its four sides by jungle. Then he made out paths leading from one structure to another. He also saw one of the paths led to a great many tents where Dark warriors lay around or sat in groups as warriors do when they were idle. Close to them was another pyramid-type structure which towered above the jungle below it. On the crumbling steps leading to its summit stood four Dark warriors, each surveying a side of the pyramid. Halfway down, four more warriors did the same. At the foot of the steps to the right was another doorway, this time guarded by two Dark warriors with demon dogs straining at their chains whenever anything got too close, including Dark warriors who made a detour to avoid them.

That must be their headquarters, Kee thought, or something very special. He then flew on.

Chapter 23
Life's Destroyed

Kee flew back to the structure that the Dark lancer was guarding; he flew fast and low, shooting past the lancer before he even noticed. Up the stairwell he flew to where Tom, Raif and the remaining cadets waited.

'How did you get on, Kee'? Tom asked.

'Good,' he replied. 'There is a Dark lancer at the foot of the stairs. Apart from that, there is no one close enough to see us escape. We will have to distract him somehow, then dash out and go round to the left of the building. If we go straight or right, we will encounter enemy soldiers, particularly if you go straight on. That leads to a well-guarded headquarters of some kind, so avoid that at all costs.'

'Okay, thanks, Kee, that is valuable information. We can make a plan now. First thing is dealing with the lancer at the bottom of the stairs. Any ideas?'

'What about shouting to him to come up?' said one of the cadets.

'Don't be stupid,' said Raif, 'he's not going to come up here because we ask him too. He's going to run straight to the nearest Dark warrior and get help.'

'No, Raif, listen to what he has to say. We don't have to shout to him. We can annoy him so much he will lose his temper and run up here, where we attack him like we did the other two.'

'Tom's got something there,' interjected Kee. 'I can fly down there, scratch him with my talon or even shit on his head. He would not be happy with that. I fly back in and he follows me in a rage and we do what we did to the other two.'

'That's a good plan, Kee. Agree, Raif?'

'I suppose, as long as it all goes to plan,' he conceded. That was the plan. They all agreed they would turn into wolves and wait at the top of the stairs, ready to pounce as he came up the stairwell. Kee would fly down, scratch his face, then fly back up to the waiting wolves. Hopefully, the lancer would follow. Then they would finish the job as they had with the two other guards. They all got ready then Kee left.

In seconds, he was out of the stairwell and in the air. He turned and dived at the lancer; one talon hit his face, the other the top of his head. The lancer dropped his lance and started waving his arms to get the bird off. Kee let go and climbed out of his reach. 'I'm going to kill you, little bird,' he shouted, as he picked his lance up and hurled it at Kee who easily dodged it. He dived and then pulled up as he released some bird dropping that smashed into the lancer's face… That was it, the lancer grabbed his sword and started to wave it at Kee who dived as close to the lancer as he dared then shot up the stairwell. The lancer turned in a rage, ran after the bird shouting to his comrades who should have been at the top of the stairs. 'Grab that bloody bird. I'm going to eat that thing after I dissect it alive,' he screamed as he ran up the stairs. He didn't even realise his companions did not answer him. He got to the top step just as one wolf went for his throat, one for each for his legs and arms, the rest waiting for him to crumple to the floor then they all pounced… he was dead in seconds. All went calm and the wolves listened, no sound at all. They had got away with it.

'Kee, go down and check there is no one about then we will all leave as wolves. Run round to the left and keep running. Don't stop until we are well away,' Tom told them all.

Kee was gone in a flash. Before they knew it, he was back. 'It's all clear, go for it,' he told them all. Then he was gone and the wolves raced down the stairs and out into the bright sunlight which dazzled them for a second. Then they were off running round the side of the ancient structure and along a wood line. High above, Kee watched the wolves ran as hard as they could. Tom brought up the rear, continually looking behind him to make sure they were not being followed. Raif led the way, darting between some of the spread-out ancient buildings, until they reached the edge of the ruins where they entered the woods and ran. They eventually reached a road that was a dual carriageway. Some cars and lorries were travelling along on both sides so they all stopped in cover and transformed back into their people forms. Kee joined them and sat on Tom's shoulder.

'Right, a new plan is needed, I think,' Tom told them all.

'We can't stay here. We're too close to the Dark. We need to cross and cross soon before those bodies are found,' Raif told everyone.

'Okay, let's split into three teams of three plus Kee who will stay as he is. Raif, you lead the first group. I will bring up the rear with Kee and two others.'

The groups divided. Raif and two of the cadets checked the road, then at a break in the traffic they were gone, stopping at the central reservation until the far lanes were clear, then they were off across the road and into the scrub on the other side. Once hidden, they turned back into wolves and waited for the next group to cross. The traffic seemed to get heavier; it was probably that time of day when everyone leaves work. After another twenty-minutes' wait, the second group crossed, just missing being run over by a truck and a taxi but they made it safely to the other side and went into cover where they too turned back to wolves. Tom was a bit worried about the last group to cross; he had heard the horns sounding and he was sure he saw one of the truck drivers get on his radio.

Now, it was their turn. 'I have another idea,' said Tom. 'I will turn into my eagle form, you stay in your falcon, Kee, and you, Sam,' he said to the cadet with them, 'can get on my back and we will fly over. Then, I will come back for you, Malek. That way we will dodge this mad traffic.' So, that's what they did.

Tom lifted with Sam on his back and Kee flew ahead. They flew high so they would not be noticed by the drivers below. On the other side, they joined up with the group. Then Tom went back for Malek. Once back with the group, they heard sirens and the screeching of brakes from the carriageway behind them. Then there were shouts in Spanish.

'Go, go!' communicated Tom and the wolves ran again. He lifted into the air as the wolves ran. Kee soared high and looked down on the road.

Police cars had blocked the road and officers were milling about, searching for something in the scrub. Someone must have called the police after the near miss on the road with the running boys. Tom and Kee lifted high from where they could see the coast and its brilliant blue sea. They headed there, which they communicated to the wolves below.

Soon, Tom and Kee were there, and landed on a beautiful white sandy beach, turned back into their people form and waited for the arrival of the wolves. Half an hour later, Raif and the wolves arrived. Now all back in their people forms they lay on the beach and soaked up the sun. They were all now mentally and physically exhausted after the trials of the past few days.

Several hours later. Tom opened his eyes. It was dark. Raif and his group had gone. Tom woke the others to find out if anyone knew where they were? Then he realised Kee was also gone. No one knew so Tom decided they had been on the beach long enough and that they had been lucky not to have been caught. They moved back into the dense undergrowth that was on the edge of the beach. They went in a short way and waited.

'Tom, Tom.' The quite calling woke Tom; he had fallen asleep again, as had the rest of the group.

'Raif! In here,' he called.

Raif and the others came in with a sack of food. 'We got it from the locals. They were happy to help us out; fruit, two cooked chickens and these things in the bags. There is one for each of us.' He lifted one bag up and showed Tom.

'Crisps, Raif, they're crisps. You open the bag and eat the contents. They're cooked potato chips with a flavour sprinkled over them; you will like them.'

Raif opened one bag and handed it around. Everyone took one crisp.

'Go on then. Put it in your mouth and eat it.'

'But what if I don't like it?' replied Sam.

'Then spit it out,' Tom told him as he put the crisp into his mouth. 'Hmm, that's nice. it's a while since I had one of these.'

'What's the flavour?' asked Raif as he did not recognise it.

Tom took the bag and looked at the packet. 'It's paprika.' Then he looked at the other bags. 'There are two more the same, plus two sea salt, two cheese and onion and two salt and vinegar.'

'They don't last very long, do they?' Kee said.

'That's because you are meant to eat the whole packet!' Tom laughed then dished the remaining packets out. He had had loads in his time so he let the others enjoy them. Some of the reactions on their faces as they tasted the different flavours made Tom laugh, but before long the packets where all empty. Then the chickens were shared out and finally the fruit.

'What a feast,' commented Raif, as he rubbed his now bloated belly after the food had all been finished. They all agreed it seemed like a long time since they had eaten such nice food.

A couple of minutes went by then Tom spoke. 'Okay, guys.'

Raif interrupted him: 'You're doing it again, Tom. What does "guys" mean?'

'Sorry. Okay, team. Is that better, Raif?' Raif nodded and Tom continued. 'Okay, we need to work out what we are going to do next. We can't stay next to the beach for the rest of our lives. It won't be long before people start talking about the lost boys living on the beach, so we will have to move. Not only that, I'm sure the Dark will be searching for us soon if they haven't already. Any ideas?'

There was silence, then Kee piped up. 'I remember during training one of the trainers told us something about if we were ever lost on Earth and what we should do. Does anyone else remember that?' he asked. There was silence once more as everyone racked their brains.

Eventually, Tom spoke, 'What we need is the internet to search for Gina and Billy. If we can find them, we could contact Billy and get him to tell his brothers where we are then they could contact my dad and let him know where we are. How does that sound?'

'We all know about the internet here on Earth but none of us know how to get it started. Apart from that, it sounds like a good idea. Unless anyone else has come up with something?' Raif told them all. All the faces were blank.

'Right then, all we need to do is get some money. There must be somewhere round here we can go on the internet; an internet café they call it. We just need to get the money to pay for it...' All was quiet once again. 'I've got it. It may be a little risky but if we are careful, we can do it. We will go and find a beach with a lot of people. Then we will pretend we have trained Kee the falcon to fly between two of us. We can pass the hat around, even get the people to pose with Kee. We could make a mint. Enough to get on the internet anyway.' Tom stood in the middle of everyone looking pleased with himself. 'Well? he said looking at all the puzzled faces 'What do you think?'

'I don't know,' replied Raif. 'How will that get us the money we need for the internet?'

'Really, you don't know what I'm talking about?' They all looked at Tom like he was from another planet... Well, to be fair, he was so he broke it down into bite size pieces for his audience. 'Right. Later we will scout a beach with a lot of people on it. That would be best done by Kee as he won't stick out. Then me and one other with Kee as a falcon will go on that beach and Kee will fly between us and perform tricks and have his photograph taken with people on the beach. Then the people will give us money for entertaining them, which we use to get on the internet and contact Billy. Everyone understand'? Everyone nodded except Raif. 'What, Raif? What don't you get now?'

'Why would anyone want to give us money for watching Kee fly around? I just don't get it.'

'Right. These people are on Earth for one. Second, they are tourists on holiday here, in a different country, having fun. They most probably have never seen a falcon before so it is something different so they will pay us for showing them, entertaining them while they relax on the beach. It's what humans do. Okay?'.

'Okay, Tom, if you say so, you know humans better than us.'

'Good, I'm glad we have got that sorted. Now, down to the nitty gritty, who is coming with me?'

'I will, Tom,' said Raif, 'that way I can tell my father and mother I looked after you.' He laughed.

'Okay, good, Raif. Now, we need to make these clothes look more like human clothes or we steal some. Anyone got anything sharp?'

Raif smiled and pulled out one of the guard's knives. 'Thought it might come in handy.'

'Good thinking, Raif. Now, let's cut the legs off these combat suits or what's left of them anyway.' Tom took the knife off Raif and started to cut the leg off his suit. It was harder than he thought. He had to take the suit off and get two people to stretch it so the knife would cut it more easily. It was not easy but, in the end, Tom and Raif had a pair of Bermuda-type shorts each. There was no hope for the tops and none of them had footwear on so that was not a problem. 'We could use a T-shirt and possibly a hat. It's going to get hot out there.'

Kee had seen some washing hanging up behind some houses on the beach and he was sure he could get some clothes from them. 'One at a time,' he emphasised, 'I'm only a little bird.'

They all laughed but that would do the job. 'Be careful, you are the main attraction, remember,' Tom told him.

Kee smiled, then he was a falcon and gone. Half an hour later, he was back with a T-shirt. Twenty minutes later, a baseball cap, then a panama straw hat. Task complete. They put the tops on. Tom had the panama hat and Raif the baseball cap.

'That's it, we are ready for plan A,' Tom told them. 'The rest of you wait here. If we are not back by last light, something has gone wrong so use plan B.'

'What is plan B?' Sam asked.

'Someone take command and come up with another plan,' Tom told them.

Tom and Raif left the group and headed down the beach with Kee the falcon on Tom's shoulder. They continued along the beach until they reached a spot where there were lots of tourists. This had taken them a good hour's walk and the sun was now beaming down on them. 'You stay here, Raif. When you see Kee flying towards you, hold your hand up and, Kee, you land on his shoulder. Everyone happy?'

Raif nodded so Tom and Kee walked along the shore. Every now and then, Tom dipped his feet in the sea as it lapped the shore. He walked twenty metres away then he stopped and turned. There were people going in and out of the sea between him and Raif but that did not matter. He took a deep breath then called out to all on the beach, 'Ladies, gentlemen and children, be amazed as I fly this falcon for your entertainment today. Any donations for the upkeep of the falcon, me and my brother,' he pointed down the beach to Raif who waved his hands, 'would be gratefully appreciated.' Then he put his hat down on the beach so people could throw their coins in.

'First, Kee, that's the name of my falcon.' He pointed his arm at Raif. Kee lifted high into the air. The people paying attention watched him go.

'That's the last you will see of him, my lad,' said a rather large man on the beach with a beer in his hand.

But then Kee dived straight down towards Raif, slowed and landed on his shoulder.

'Well, I never,' said the man.

'Now, Kee will fly back to me.' Tom lifted his arm and Kee responded. He did three loops on his way back and landed on Tom's shoulder. Everyone clapped.

'Has anyone got a small ball that you could throw in the air and Kee will retrieve it for you?'

He looked around then a young girl shouted, 'I have,' and she held the little yellow ball in the air. 'It's from my bat and ball set,' she told Tom.

'That's just perfect. What's your name?'

The girl shouted back, 'Lucy.'

'Great.' Tom replied. 'Now throw the ball as high as you can and Kee will bring it back to you.'

'That's called gravity, lad. That's what will bring the ball back,' the beer-drinking man shouted out then laughed. No one else did.

'Shut up, Pete. You're making a fool of yourself. Let the boy be,' a lady with blue hair shouted at him from the sunbed next to his. 'Don't worry about him, Lucy, throw the ball in the air!'

So, she did and Kee shot after it, grabbing it with his talons, then flying back to her. She held her hand out and Kee dropped it into her hand, then landed next to her. The gathering crowd all started clapping and cheering. Lucy stroked Kee's head.

'Careful, darling, that's a wild animal,' her dad told her.

'Give up, Frank, it's trained,' his wife told him.

'You can't be too careful in these countries,' he replied.

Lucy continued to stroke Kee until Tom lifted his arm and Kee returned to his shoulder. the crowd clapped and cheered once more.

'What now?' Kee asked him.

Just then, a man dropped some coins into his hat then someone else. Tom even saw some notes go in. He beamed and kept saying thank you as the money rolled in. Even Pete and Frank coughed up. Lucy walked up and asked Tom if she could have a photo with Kee so Tom said out loud, 'Kee sit on the girl's shoulder, there's a good bird.' When he did, everyone clapped and more money hit the hat. After that, there was a queue of people all waiting to have a picture with Kee, all of them had money in their hands.

Tom waved Raif back and he started to collect the money in the hat as he told Kee to sit on people's shoulder. After the last person had had their photo taken Tom told them all they would have to leave as the falcon was getting thirsty and hungry. They left, telling everyone they would return the next day.

With Kee on Tom's shoulder and Raif, stuffing as much money in his pockets, by his side they left the beach and headed towards some shops on the street behind the beach. Tom took the remainder of the money and put it in his pocket. They walked along the street as Tom looked out for an internet café. He could not see one, but then he saw an English book swap shop with a café attached.

'Let's get a drink, I'm parched,' he told his companions who agreed. They all went and sat on a table outside the shop. Kee hopped onto the table then a nice woman came out with a bowl and put it next to him.

'What can I get you young gentlemen?' she asked.

'Two glasses of cola with ice and a two burgers and chips with all the trimmings. You'll like these,' Tom told Raif. 'Could I also have some raw meat for the falcon?' he asked the waitress.

'That's on the house I watched you on the beach. That bird is well trained,' she told them then left to get the drinks. Forty-five minutes later they had been fed and watered and life was good as they sat in the sun.

'I suppose we had better get back. Oh! I forgot; I'll ask the waitress if she knows where there is an internet café. Kee, you fly back and tell the others we will be back soon. Take care and don't take any risks.' Kee was gone when the waitress came back out.

'You guys want anything else?' she asked with a smile then she added, 'Your bird's gone.'

'Yes, he's gone home, he was getting tired,' Tom told her'.

'That's amazing. You can tell that, can you?' she asked.

'Yes, I have known Kee since he was a young chick, I can tell when he gets tired. By the way, do you happen to know where the nearest public internet café is?'

'There's not one in this area, but I have internet in my apartment above here. You are welcome to use it.'

'That's great, I am trying to get hold of a family member. We need to get home.'

'I've got a car, hun. I could drive you if that helps?' she told them.

'That's very kind of you but we live in another country so we need them to come and get us. There was a mix-up and we were left behind.'

'That's terrible. Anything I can do to help just let me know. You need some where to stay?'

'No, we're good. We only live down the beach a bit. We will be fine. By the way, what's your name?'

'Jenny, my name's Jenny. I'm from England, too. I can tell from your accent. I came here about four years ago; I just love the way of life here. Anyway, I'm waffling. Come with me. I'll take you to my apartment.'

They got up and followed her into the back and up some stairs past the book shop.

413

'Won't your boss mind?' Tom asked her.

'I am the boss. The book shop and the little café are all mine. I used to be a dancer at a big night club, saved all my money and bought this place. I don't make a lot of money but I get buy and I'm happy here, that's what counts,' she said. She showed them the laptop she had at a small desk in her small living room. She logged on for them and told them if they needed any help to let her know, then she went back downstairs.

Tom thought for a minute. 'I wonder if Gina is on face page? I know Billy won't be.' So, he put her details on his face page account, a site where you could contact friends and family. Raif looked on amazed; he had never seen the internet working before. There were about fifty Gina Tios. Tom had remembered her last name because it was different and easy to remember. He looked at the faces of the fifty people, one by one, then he found her,

'Got it. The only trouble is, I don't know how often she checks her account for messages. Can you go and ask Jenny if she has an email address we could use to receive a message from America?'

Raif went down and asked Jenny even though he did not know what he was talking about. She was serving a customer so she wrote her email address on a paper napkin and gave it to Raif. He went back up the stairs and gave it to Tom. He did not notice the local police officer watching him from across the street.

Tom put the details on the email. And wrote: Dear Gina, I hope you are well. It's Tom De-Callen. We are stuck in Mexico after being abducted. We are near a place called Tulum. We need to contact my family and let them know we are safe and where we are. Can you help us? This is the email address of Jenny at the English book shop and café that is helping us. P.S. there are ten of us. Love, Tom. 'That should work, Let's hope they're not too busy and she checks her messages. Now it's just a matter of waiting for a reply.'

Tom and Raif went down to Jenny who was just cleaning a table and told her she should get an email soon from a woman in America called Gina. If it was all right with her, they would come back and see her later. They said goodbye to Jenny. She told them to wait there as she rushed away and came back with six pack with bottles of cola and a pile of rolls and sandwiches which she gave them to them telling them she would only throw them away as she would be closing soon. They thanked her and wandered back to the beach.

They were followed by the police officer who went on to the beach, watching the boys from a distance. They headed down the beach, away from the public. When he got closer to them, he shouted, 'Stop! Police!' The boys turned round because of the loud shout but they did not know what the officer had said as it was in Spanish. Tom realised it was a police officer but he was unsure whether he should go to him. Raif just waited for Tom's lead. The officer walked closer.

'I don't understand,' Tom told him in English.

'Ah, gringo.' He laughed.

'No, English,' Tom replied.

'Sí, I understand a little English,' the officer replied. 'You must come with me, someone knows you and is looking for you, you understand? Your father, Frederick!' he told Tom.

'My dad, Raif, he must have come for us.'

'You sure, Tom? How does he know who you are?'

'Come, come, yes. Your father is waiting at the police station, please.' He indicated for them to go back in the direction they had just come.

'What have we got to lose?' Tom told Raif as they walked. Raif had a worried look on his face. 'We will be okay,' Tom tried to reassure his cousin. They got back to the street where they had met Jenny and continued past her shop; Tom looked for her in vain but he did not see her.

The officer spoke into his radio then he ushered the boys onto the next road. There, waiting for them, was a police van. As they approached a second officer got out, opened the side door and directed the boys in. The first officer sat next to them. The van then drove off down the road.

Kee had seen the boys get in the van because he had flown back to see where they were as they had been longer than they had said. He flew directly back to the other cadets still waiting in the shrub by the beach.

Jenny was at her computer responding to an email from Gina. Hi, Gina, Tom and his brother are in Tulum, Mexico. They are fine. They will be back later to see me; my name is Jenny and I own the Bookshop Café. It is situated at the bottom of the Calle Playa Maya.

Back at Warriors' Rest they had received a message from Robert Mullen who had been in contact with Billy on Earth. He, in turn, had been in contact with someone called Jenny in Mexico who had seen Tom and Raif. But they had not returned that afternoon to her as they had promised.

'Right, we need to get to Mexico as soon as possible,' Frederick told his team. Leslie was on it, looking for the closest gate which she thought might be Louisiana. The one they had come through to get back to Elemtum.

'It may be quicker to get Billy to fly there,' she told the king. So, Billy was sent a message to get to Tulum as soon as he could. He and Gina were now waiting to fly a chartered plane to Cancun. They were waiting for clearance from the Mexican Government which normally did not take long. The pilot had the aircraft ready while Billy and Gina waited in a private lounge.

Tom and Raif were now in a police station; not under arrest but as close as could be. They had been given some drink and food and were sitting in a room with a television playing Spanish children cartoons that Raif found funny even though he did not understand a word the fast-talking characters were saying. Tom just sat there getting more worried as the minutes passed. They kept getting told someone would be there for them soon. At one point, they said it was their mama which Raif thought would be Raphina as Tom's mother was dead.

It was starting to get dark when one of the officers walked into their room. 'Okay, boys, your mother and father are here for you. Follow me please.' They walked through to a different room where another police officer put handcuffs on them both.

'This is just to stop you running away again. Your mother has told us all about you two.' The door opened and a man they did not know walked in.

'Boys, you're safe. Your mother is waiting in the car; we will get those cuffs off you when we get you home. We don't want you running off again, do we? Especially as we are going home tomorrow.'

The boys looked at each other, confused and getting frightened now. They went out to a top of the range limousine with dark windows; they could not see who was inside. The man opened the door and forced the two boys in with the help of the police officer. The door slammed shut and they heard the door lock. Outside they watched the man hand the police officer a brown paper bag. The officer smiled and shook the man's hand, saying something in Spanish that neither of them understood. Tom looked at Raif. 'I think we are in trouble,' he told him.

The man got in the limo and the slid the hatch between them and the driving compartment. 'Your stepmother is waiting for you, prince, and you, wolf boy.' He laughed and slid the hatch shut, then limo set off as Billy and Gina landed at Cancun international airport.

Kee had followed the limo, staying quite low as it was now dark. He followed it out of Tulum, down a highway. It turned off down a dirt road for about two miles then stopped at the gates to a big villa in dense vegetation that had a sea view and a helicopter pad to the left. Two men with weapons opened the gates and ushered the vehicle in. It drove down a winding road to the villa where it stopped and another man came out of the building. Kee recognised the face but he could not say who it was. He landed on the roof and watched the limo.

The driver opened its door and told the boys to get out. He and the other man pushed the boys into the villa. They went along a brightly lit hall, past a very opulent and comfortable looking living room, through a very large kitchen that looked out to the beach and the sea where the moon was glinting of its surface. They headed for what looked like a cleaning cupboard but when the door was opened it led to stairs going into cellar. After being manhandled down the stairs, the boys were put in a very bare room with a single bulb hanging from the ceiling. In the corner was a sofa that the boys were thrown on. The boys were left alone and the light was switched off. They still had the handcuffs; they were starting to chafe their wrists.

'Well, I think we are in the crap again,' Tom told Raif. 'I wonder if Gina has replied to Jenny yet? Otherwise, we are on our own.'

'Not only that, Tom, we haven't even got a fighting chance with these chains on our wrists. We can't change and fight them with this metal on, it could end up anywhere in our bodies.'

'Won't it just disappear like our clothes do when we change?'

'I don't think so because our clothes are designed especially for us and these are made by humans. I don't think it would be a good idea to try. It might kill us.'

'If it's our last change and things get desperate, I will try,' Tom replied.

'Me too,' Raif added.

They sat there in the dark with their own thoughts for what seemed to be hours, which, in reality, it was.

Kee had flown back to the cadets and told them what he had seen. They were all ready to turn back into wolves and try and rescue their friend and the prince but Kee told them he would go and see the kind lady who had helped them and see if she could help. They all agreed with that so Kee left and went back to see Jenny. He stopped on the beach. There was no one around so he turned back into the boy Kee and went round to the side door of Jenny's building and knocked on the door. To his surprise, the door was opened by a big man with bright red hair. 'Can I help you, young man?' the giant said in a strange accent that Kee only just understood.

'I'm Kee. I was with Tom and Raif earlier. I've come to see Jenny.'

'You had better come in then. I'm Billy, a friend of Tom and his family.'

They went into a room that was obviously in the inside of the small café. Sitting at a table were Gina and Jenny. Behind them, the chairs and table they had sat at earlier in the day were all stacked up against the front door and window to the café. 'Well, who's this young man, Billy?' Gina asked in her southern accent'.

'This is Kee. He was here with Tom and Raif earlier.'

'That's the same name as the falcon they had with them,' Jenny told them.

'I am the falcon,' Kee told her.

'But you're a boy? I didn't see you this afternoon.'

'You did,' he replied and turned into the fin front of her, then back into the boy.

Jenny was speechless, all she could do was say, 'But, but you.'

Billy went round and held her hand, Gina held the other. 'It's okay, Jenny. I had the same feeling when I saw Tom change from an eagle to a boy back when I first met them in Louisiana,' Gina told her. 'They won't hurt you. He is friendly, we are all friendly.'

Jenny looked at Gina and Billy. 'Are you birds as well?'

Billy and Gina smiled. 'No, I'm sorry to say we are just humans like you,' Billy told her.

'But how can they? I mean, why can they, where do they come from?' Jenny asked.

Gina replied, 'Have you seen those X-Men films? Well, they are like the Mutants; they have been on this earth for centuries. The ancient people of this world thought they were gods. They are calm peaceful people that the modern world does not understand. There are people in this world that, if they knew, would want to enslave them and do experiments on them. We are here to save them and take them back to safety where they can live in peace... You can never tell anyone of this.'

'I won't. That's wonderful, I had no idea... no idea at all. So, how can I help?' she said, now smiling. 'Is any one hungry or thirsty? I can get you a drink and something to eat.'

'Yes, that would be good,' Gina and Billy told her.

'And you, Kee?' she asked.

'Please, but we will have to be quick. I have something to tell you.'

Jenny told them to go upstairs where it was more comfortable. She would get the food and drinks and bring them up.

'That was quick thinking, Gina, I was well impressed about the X-Men,' Billy told her.

Kee told him and Gina about the seven survivors on the beach, what he had seen and where the limo had gone. Jenny came up with a plate of sandwiches, a can of pop for Kee, then went back down and brought three coffees up. As they ate, Kee told Jenny about the boys on the beach and Billy told her they would have to go and rescue Tom and Raif as soon as possible. He also asked if she knew where they could get a couple of guns just in case. She did and had one in her bedside table that a friend had given her for her personal protection. She would phone him because he trained the police to shoot so she was positive he would have a couple more if she needed one. He had a soft spot for her. She told them they were close and had a no-strings attached relationship so there would be no questions asked. After that, she would go and get the seven boys from the beach; they would be safe in her home with her and Josh her friend. She made the call and within ten minutes, Josh was round with an assault rifle and a powerful handgun that, once satisfied they were not going to rob a bank or kill police officers, he handed them over to Billy. Jenny had told him the X-Men story, so he was happy, especially as he was helping Jenny. Jenny went and got her pistol from the bedside table.

'Bloody hell, Jenny, it's a magnum!' Billy exclaimed. 'That will knock a hole in a wall, we should get the boys back with no problems with that on our side.' Gina was used to guns after being with the sheriff for many years and she was a good shot as well.

Billy had hired a 4x4 at the airport so he, Gina and Kee left for the villa that Kee estimated was just over an hour away. Jenny and Josh went to get the boys; Kee had told them a couple of names to shout out when they got close so they would not run off.

Back at the villa, Tom and Raif had fallen asleep but were woken by the sound of a helicopter starting up close to the villa. Minutes later, the light came on and the door opened. Standing in front of them was a beautiful woman dressed in black. Tom had seen her picture before. 'Queen Labatina, what do you want with us?' he asked her.

She could hear the fear in his voice and it made her smile. 'You, Prince Thomas, will be coming with me and you, wolf boy, will be left as a message to your father and his brothers.'

'Don't you mean with a message?' Raif replied.

Labatina could hear the hate in his voice. 'No, Raif son of Kurt De-Callen, as a message.' She went over to Tom and went to touch him but he flinched so she said something to him and he stopped and looked into her eyes. 'Follow me, prince,' she said as she turned and walked out of the room. Tom followed her. 'Take those things off him,' she told the guard who was with her. 'He won't need them anymore, he won't change… he's mine now.'

'What about me?' Raif yelled. 'Tom, come back; change, you can get away!'

Tom kept walking, not looking back at his cousin. As Labatina went past the guard, she said quietly, with menace, 'Kill him.'

The guard walked past her as she began to climb the stairs with Tom in tow. Raif had heard what she had said but did not believe it until the guard was next to him with a hunting knife in his hand.

'No!' Raif cried out as the knife entered his chest with such force it knocked him back on to the sofa; the second blow killed him. As his eyes closed, a tear ran down his cheek. The guard turned, threw the knife on the floor and walked out of the room.

The guards in the house all left in their 4x4 police vehicle, leaving the front gates open.

Labatina, Tom and Arthfael departed, leaving the villa with all the lights on and the doors open and boarded the waiting helicopter. It lifted into the air as Billy turned the 4x4 into the gate surprised that there were no guards. Guns at the ready, they got out of the vehicle. They heard the thudding of the blades and the whine of the engine as it turned and flew over the sea away from them, out of sight.

Billy ran through the villa out onto the beach to see a distant flashing red light as the helicopter flew away. He walked back inside where Gina and Kee were now searching the villa for Tom and Raif; they found nothing. Billy's eyes went to the door in the kitchen; he could see it had steps going down. 'Stay here,' he told them as he lifted his assault rifle and descended the stairs.

He walked into the room with the single bright bulb to find the slain boy lying partly on the sofa. He went over and felt for a pulse. There was none... He took his jacket off and placed it over the boy's upper body and face. He turned and went back to the others with tears in his eyes.

'What is it, Billy'? Gina asked, concern etched all over her face.

'A dead boy. He hasn't been dead long, he's still warm. It's not Tom, so it must be Raif,' he told them as a tear ran down his check. Gina held him. Kee went to see but Billy grabbed him, 'No, son, you don't want to go down there.'

Kee pulled away. 'I've got to see, it might be someone else,' he cried and ran through the door, down the stairs and into the room. He stopped in front of the body, too scared to lift the coat. He took a deep breath and lifted the coat off the head, looking at Raif's peaceful face. He felt comforting hands on his shoulder. He replaced the coat and turned round and hugged Gina who also had tears in her eyes. They turned and followed Billy up the stairs.

'It's Raif!'

Chapter 24
Rescue

Billy and Gina decided the best thing now was to use the building as a base. They found some keys which they tried in all the doors, locking the place up, securing it as well as Raif's body. The plan was to take the 4x4 back to the town, get the remaining cadets and take them back to the villa. Then they had to somehow contact Kurt and let him know what had happened. Then find out what the next move would be.

Back on Elemtum, unaware what had happened on Earth, Karl, Row and Erline were now back together in the command centre at Great Porum mulling over their options or, to be more precise, the lack of options they had before them. That was until Phina and Salina walked in with smiles all over their faces.

'What are you two looking so happy about?' Row asked them.

Phina reached them. 'We think we have found the location of Tom, Raif and the cadets. Steven the guard commander is looking for Leslie or Tristan. He has an idea. He remembers something from his training. He remembers reading something while studying ancient history; a bit about going from Elemtum to Earth through a gate that was eventually closed because at the time they thought the people from Earth might be changed by their intervention in their world.'

'So, what's that got to do with finding Tom and the others?'

'Sorry, I did not make myself clear, Row… The gate was around the area Tom went missing near the arena in the jungle. The thing is they used to travel to Mexico… the old Mayan empire at Calakmul, from that gate, he believes. Steven is just trying to get that clarified. He said his memory is a little vague about the detail, but he is certain he's right.'

'That would be great, the first lead we have had. Does anyone else know yet?'

'No, we want to be positive of all the facts before we start telling everyone,' Salina told them.

They decided to go and get some food. Hopefully by the time they got back there would be an answer for them. When they returned to the command centre, both Steven and Leslie were waiting for them. 'Wow, Leslie, you look amazing in a combat suit, but why?' asked Row.

'I'm coming with you to Mexico. I've always wanted to visit the ancient ruins in Mexico and this is my chance, so I decided to look the part.'

They all looked at her and smiled, even Steven. Then Phina spoke, 'One, do you know how to use that suit? And two, we won't be going to Earth in combat suits, we aren't going to war.'

'That's a shame. I was looking forward to kicking some ass in this thing,' she replied as she stroked the suit.

'Really, Leslie? Kick ass, you?' Salina remarked with a smile.

Leslie was quick to answer her. 'Come on, Salina, you and Phina must remember in our basic training I was pretty good at all that ninja fighting stuff,' she said with a wry smile.

'I will give you that, Leslie, but you also have to remember that was a long time ago and we are not spring chickens anymore.'

'Excuse me, Salina, I am a lot younger than you. If you remember, I was put in to the training because I was bright and had a glowing future ahead of me.'

'I certainly do, Leslie, but putting all that aside, the mission will not be to invade Earth but rescue Tom, Raif and the other cadets, so no kicking ass.' Phina coughed, then added, 'I wouldn't say no kicking ass... you know what the Dark are like, they just invite it.' Everyone laughed just as Kurt and the king walked in.

'What's so funny? Have we missed something?' asked the king.

'Just talking about training and how good Leslie was. Do you remember, uncle?' Phina replied.

'It depends who we are talking about. I remember you and Salina were joint top of the class for the first time ever.'

'Bloody typical that's all anyone remembers about our training,' Leslie interjected.

'We have a plan, Dad! We need to get to Earth, to Mexico. That's where we think Tom and the others are.'

They all sat down. Karl and the others went through their plan with Kurt and the king. 'I agree that this is the only plan we have that is feasible with the possibility of success,' the king told them.

Then they went down into the detail and several hours later they had a plan. It meant getting to America then across to Mexico, which in itself was no easy task, but it was doable. Several small teams would make their way to Mexico where they would have to try and find the Dark, Tom and the others. This was helped by the fact that Erline had some contact details for Gina that they could use to get some help once they had arrived in America. They were blissfully unaware of the part Billy and Gina were now playing in this story.

The teams were sorted. Kurt, Salina, Erline and Karl would go first and contact Gina. Then Hollie and her water team would go, followed by Phina, Leslie, Steven and another royal guard as the third team. Then two more teams of warriors would back them up. That was quite a potent force to send to Earth on a rescue mission, but, as everyone knew, the Dark could not be underestimated and they did not know what they would be facing but they had some old friends in Mexico that would help them if needed.

Plan 'B2' was also put into action; the preachers had thrown into the works that they may able to build a replacement pathway from the damaged gate in the jungle where Tom had gone missing. That plan was being worked on as they spoke; they had estimated two to three days before it was fully functional.

Row decided to stay with her father and Tristan; she would follow later once the Earth pathway was finished. She was up for a bit of peace and quiet.

A day later the first team was in Louisiana at Erline's home which was locked up with no sign of life. Erline knew where the spare keys were hidden so she let them in, then she went about contacting Gina. If Gina was away, which was only very rarely, she would have her mobile phone on her. It was a very old one, but she found it easy to use. It was just a phone with no other gadgets. Erline did not know that it was not the original phone as that had given up and lost the signal many years ago, but it was the simplest basic phone she could find and it worked just as she liked it to, to make calls. Gina always put all her numbers in an address book and Erline knew where that was. She retrieved the phone number and called her from the house phone. On the second attempt, Gina answered. She was surprised and delighted to hear Erline at the other end of the phone. She told her that they were all safe in a villa in Cancun waiting for help to arrive. Gina asked who was with her then she asked to speak to Kurt. Erline told everyone the good news then handed the phone to Kurt. After the initial hello, Kurt went silent, his face changed and everyone watching knew whatever he was being told was not good. 'Thank you, Billy, we will fly out as soon as possible. I will contact you when we arrive.'

Kurt put the phone down. With a shaky voice, he told them, 'Raif is dead, killed by the Dark. His body is with Billy and Gina in Cancun. They have the cadets, but Tom was taken away by helicopter as they arrived. They don't know where he is… I need a minute to think,' he told them, then he turned and walked out to the patio where they had had the barbeque that now seemed like a lifetime ago. Salina, Karl and Erline stood in silence, taking in what Kurt had just said. Salina hugged them both.

'I think my dad needs me.' She walked out to him.

'Oh, Karl will all this killing ever stop?'

'I can't answer that, but I hope so one day.'

They hugged. Both had tears in their eyes. It was probably the saddest day of Karl's life, he thought to himself. Some time passed then Kurt and Phina returned.

'Are you two okay?' Kurt asked. Karl got up and embraced his uncle. 'I'm so sorry, Uncle Kurt.' Kurt nodded then Karl hugged Salina. 'So, what now?' he eventually asked.

'We go to Cancun and find Tom,' Kurt answered.

'Did Billy and Gina see the helicopter?' Erline asked.

'I don't know,' answered Kurt.

'Why?'

'Because if we know the helicopter type, we can work out how far it could go on a full tank of fuel. Then we would have an area to search.' Erline called Gina and asked the question. From the brief look that Billy got it was quite a modern helicopter. Sleek looking, black, it could have been an Augusta, but he wasn't sure. He had only seen something like that on the TV when he had been with Gina. It was a starting point so Erline went on the computer in the house and started searching.

'It says on this site that with full fuel and no reserve tanks that a normal Augusta has a range of 648 km. So, that's a starting point. Let me just look at a couple of other sites to see if there is any difference,' Erline told them. 'Three hundred miles, 932 km. So, three hundred miles is around 482 km so that's well less than the new Augusta's range of 932 km and that's without any added tanks. So, if we put the search out to 1,000 km maybe? ...'

Everyone agreed it was a starting point at least. Erline went into the one of the drawers in the table she was sitting at and pulled out a drawing compass set in a leather box. 'It's what I used to use when I learnt to fly. It should give us a rough estimate.' She worked out the distance she needed using the scale on an aviation map of South America which included Mexico, pinpointed the compass on Cancun and drew a circle, 'There we have it... that's a big area to cover.' she told them.

The mood in the room sank. Everyone was a little subdued as they realised the enormity of the task ahead of them. 'I think we may have to change the plan,' Kurt told them. 'We will get to Mexico, evaluate what our options are when we get there. It may be that we will have to wait until we either get some information from our sources or the Dark contact us.

'Why would they take Tom? He's not Labatina's son...'Karl asked.

'He may just be a bargaining tool for you and your sister, Karl. That could be a possibility. If that's the case we should hear from Labatina fairly quickly, I believe,' Salina told them.

They packed their kit, then headed to the nearest airport where they would get a flight to Cancun international airport. In the meantime, Gina and Billy had gathered all the surviving cadets at the villa and waited for a call from Erline to say they had landed in Mexico.

Labatina was now with Tom, Arthfael and Gebhuza Septima in Brazil. They had flown to Havana where a private plane had been hired to take them to a roughly cut airstrip north of the Amazon river around one hundred miles west of Manaus deep in the Amazon jungle where the Dark had a camp with a sizeable force of local men and some Dark warriors. The local men had been seduced by the promise of wealth beyond their own imagination. There were also a number of dubious mercenaries, more criminals than soldiers. Once at the camp, some of the locals had been turned by Gebhuza with the same powers he used to control the rest of the Dark and Labatina, his queen.

Salina was right. The plan was to get Karl and Rowena and use Tom as the bait but it was not Labatina's plan, it was Gebhuza Septima's. He had started to notice that his love Labatina, with whom he was infatuated, was starting to break the connexion he had with her. He had started to notice it when her son Karl had died, she had broken the attachment with him and the Dark then. Luckily enough, he had managed to turn her back in time. It nearly did not work because his new arch enemy Arthfael had interfered. Gebhuza knew he had feelings for the queen. That was where Arthfael's loyalty lied, not with Gebhuza and he knew it. He could not be trusted anymore so he would use him as long as he could then kill him. He would not destroy his dream of building a new world with Labatina by his side. An empire on Earth without the interference of Elemtum; it would be a new Rome, a modern Rome, with all the glory and ruthlessness of the old but brought up to date. He would not stop until he had control of the whole world. Earth would be his empire and one day he would return to Elemtum and destroy it. He hated the wolves and eagles that he saw lording it over their world; they would not let him live in peace with his beloved Labatina. It was as simple as that. Love! Or was it his megalomania? The head of all the health systems policies and medical personnel on the blue moon and Elemtum was a megalomaniac and, apart from Row, no one had realised... not until now anyway.

The camp in the Amazon jungle was surrounded by high barbed wire fences, pits filled with stakes, watch towers and gun emplacements. There were even observation points, strategically positioned around the camp for some distance, to detect any inquisitive humans or wolves or, for that matter, anything from Elemtum that Gebhuza and Arthfael were expecting to make an appearance once they had contacted them about an exchange for Tom. Even though the exchange would not be at the camp they both knew nothing had ever gone to plan when dealing with the king and his minions. They were not stupid enough to know that someone, most probably a local, would inform on them even though they did not know the location of the camp.

Arthfael was confident the camp would not be found as he had developed a cloaking device that would hide it from any preying eyes. He had developed it, or it should be said, a brilliant young inventor from Earth did. He had been heading for a great career with some intelligence agency or the highest paying government. The only problem was that he was now dead so no one would learn of his great invention. Arthfael made certain of that, he wanted no leaks. So, they sat there in the Amazon jungle waiting for the next move.

Tom was in an underground cell that had been built with great effort; a concrete cell with a steel door, no window, a single light and a bed was all Tom had. Tom roused from whatever spell Labatina had used to take control of him back in Mexico; he had no idea where he was, why he was there or that Raif had been killed by Arthfael's man.

Kurt, Salina, Erline and Karl were now at Cancun international airport. They charted a private light aircraft from a family friend of Erline's who let Erline take control of the aircraft and navigate it to Cancun. That would give her the last tick in her flying log she needed to go solo. All she had to do now was send it off to the Federal Aviation Administration in the USA and she would get her private pilot's licence. They had all seen what an advantage that could be, especially if they had to keep coming back to Earth in the future.

They cleared customs with no problems. The people at the airport did not seem bothered about the Americans after they had been shown a document saying they were archaeologists who would be studying the ancient Mayan civilisation that had dominated Mexico centuries before. This was quite a regular occurrence for the customs people, so they made their entrance as easy as possible for the team of archaeologists and their two students. The team back on Elemtum had done a bit of research on Mexico and had concluded that this would be the quickest way of getting them into Mexico. They had sorted out the correct paperwork and passports that they would require for their journey and, as usual, it had worked perfectly.

Erline contacted Gina as soon as they had landed so Billy was now on his way to the airport to pick them up. Some time later, Billy arrived, collected them and the 4x4 was now on its way back to the villa. Billy briefed them on what had happened and how he and Gina had come to be in Cancun. Thankfully, the 4x4 had air-conditioning as the day was becoming very hot and eventually, they arrived at the villa.

When they went inside, all was quiet. They went to the back of the house where they could see everyone was in the sea, apart from Gina who was watching them. Gina told them that the boys needed a bath so they might as well have a bit of fun while they got clean. They had been through quite an ordeal and needed to blow of a bit of steam. The boys noticed the new arrivals, changing to wolves as they left the sea as their clothes were all with Gina, except Kee who had been sitting with Gina. Over the last day, he had become very fond of her and would not leave her side. She told them he would not go back into the house because Raif's body was there.

After talking to the cadets, Kurt, Salina and Karl went down to the cellar to see Raif. Kurt and Salina discussed what the best options for the body would be. They came to the conclusion that the best thing would be to build a pyre and send him back to his ancestors. Raphina and Phina would approve of that as Raif had been in the cellar for a couple of days and he needed to ascend so Atta could then look after him until the rest of his family ascended.

In the cellar, they had no need to clean the body. Billy and Gina had already done that and he was now wrapped in several blankets; only his face could be seen. Karl looked down at his cousin and friend. He looked so peaceful; he did not look dead. He touched Raif's forehead to say goodbye and was shocked at how cold it was. This would haunt Karl's dreams for days to come, he had thought. 'I will leave you with him for a while,' he told Kurt and Salina.

Salina smiled at him and then kissed his cheek. 'He will be okay. Soon we will get him back to his family. We will see him again,' she told him as she gently held his hand. Karl smiled at them both then left.

He went upstairs and spoke to the boys. 'Okay, guys, we need to collect some wood for a pyre for Raif. Get as much wood as you can. I'm not sure how much we will need.'

'When Gina and I travelled around India, we helped build a pyre for a friend of ours who died so we have a good idea how to do it,' Billy told him.

'We all know as well, Karl. We're taught it at the training centre. All wolves and eagles, as well as most people, on Elemtum are cremated so we are taught how to build one.'

'Really? You're taught that? That's so morbid,' he told them and laughed. The boys were a bit puzzled at his reaction. They told him it was what happened. There was nothing morbid about it, you were going to meet your ancestors and start your next journey.

Karl suddenly realised what they were saying was true. His mind went back to when he had died. He remembered dying and coming back to life with help of his mother. Yes, he remembered. He had never really thought about it until now. Even though he had died, he was not dead, he was waiting for the next stage of his existence. They were right, that's why Raif looked so happy. He was sure of it now. 'Right then, let's crack on with it. It's only a couple of hours and it will be dark.' The boys looked at Karl. 'Okay, crack on means let's get on with it right now. Everyone happy?' They smiled at him then split into two teams; one would go one way along the beach, the other would go the opposite. Erline went with Karl and a couple of cadets, the remainder would go the other way.

Billy stayed with Gina and Kee to build the pyre. Billy went to the side of the villa where he had spotted some pallets when they had first searched it. He retrieved them then went to start the pyre on the beach but Kee stopped him. The family needed to place the first piece and locate where they wanted the pyre to be, he told Billy and Gina. So, he just piled wood on the beach until Kurt and Salina reappeared.

The spot on the beach that Billy had originally decided on was 'perfect' Kurt told him and Salina placed the first bit of wood to start the build. The wood went on thick and fast. The pyre was nearly finished as it started to get dark. Kurt and a couple of the cadets went down and retrieved Raif's body and placed him gently on to the pyre, his face was now covered.

Billy disappeared for a while. When he returned, he had some whisky, rum and beer with him that he placed to one side. 'We can't have a wake without a little drink, now can we? We will have to toast the lad off, now won't we?' he told everyone assembled. Kurt and Salina agreed. They all stood watching the sun go down. As it hit the sea, Kurt lit the pyre. Everyone was transfixed as the flames took hold,

'It's so beautiful,' Erline told them as the last rays of sun danced with the flames of the pyre on the white beach. Then it was dark; the shadows of the flames danced on the beach and the wall of the villa. Billy passed around the beer to each cadet, Karl and Erline. Kurt, Salina and Gina all held a whisky tightly in their hands.

As Raif's body disappeared from view, Kurt lifted his glass. 'My son, have a safe and quick journey. We will join you soon. Atta will look after you now... Raif, and the ancestors,' he told everyone, then swallowed the whisky.

Everyone responded, 'Raif and the ancestors.' Then they all took a drink

It all went quiet except for the sound of crackling wood as the fire took hold. They were all left with their own thoughts as the fire danced in front of them. The air was warm with the occasional cool refreshing breeze blowing in from the sea. They all sat. No one talked. The wood crumbled into the centre of the pyre. The cadets curled up and, as wolves, they slept next to the fire. The rest had gone back into the villa, picked up some beach chairs and were now sitting watching the fire. Eventually, by the time the sun rose and all that was left were some dying embers on the blackened sand, everyone was asleep, except Kurt and Salina who had watched over the fire and the sleeping souls around it. They noticed that Karl and Erline had lain close together, holding each other all night. Billy had been the last to fall sleep after the last of the rum had left the bottle.

'That was nice... I hope when I go it will be as peaceful as Raif's passing,' Salina told her father.

'Yes, I agree. Unfortunately, now, life must go on and we are no closer to finding Prince Thomas,' her father replied.

Back in the control room, Row had been contacted by Paccia. Her father had contacted her through another healer who had found a message in the infirmary addressed to Paccia. After reading it, she took it straight to Row. It was what they had been waiting for, contact from the Dark about Tom. It read: Paccia, I know you do not know what is going on but one day you will, I promise. I am making a better world for us all away from the grasp and rule of the Wolf king.

As you know, I have Prince Thomas. I do not care for the wretched animal, but the queen wants to swap him for her son and daughter, Karl and Rowena. She wants them to reign at her side as we build the new world. Please tell the Wolf king this is non-negotiable and the exchange will happen as described below. There will be no deviation from this, no interventions from Elemtum, Wolf, Eagle or any other beast. I will make this very clear. If there is, the prince will die. It is as simple as that. Make sure the king and his ape, Kurt, are aware of this and understand there will be no negotiations about this.

This is where the exchange will take place.: Park Shopping Centre next to the horse. You will find it on an internet map of Brasília. SAI/SO Área 6580, S/N, Smas Trecho 1 – Guará, Brasília – DF, 71219-900, BRAZIL.

Prince Thomas will stay by the horse for one hour, then you can collect him. He will be watched, so no games. Rowena and Karl are to leave the shopping centre and walk directly east into the Parque Guará (the Guará park) where they will be collected. Again, they will be watched all the way, so no funny games. I make that very clear. They will be killed if anyone interferes. These are our terms. If we do not hear anything back within forty-eight hours, the prince will die.

Emperor of Earth, Gebhuza Septima

The note then went on to give a letter drop in Rio de Janeiro in one of the favelas called Rocinha. All the reply had to say was a time and date for the exchange. It also added if no one turned up, the prince would die.

'Thanks, Paccia, this is what we have been waiting for. It doesn't give us much time, but it is doable.'

'You're not actually thinking of doing this, are you Row? It's madness if he thinks this will happen. The king will never allow this!'

'You leave the king to me, Paccia. I not going to let my little brother die at the hands of that maniac and his band of misfits.'

She left Paccia with a kiss and hurried off to find the king. Her father was in his rooms with Tristian going over some old maps of the known worlds' pathways. They looked up when Row walked in.

'This is a nice surprise, Row, I haven't seen you for a while.'

'No, we seem to be on different paths at the moment, Dad, sorry, Uncle Tristan, I forgot myself. Sorry, real Dad,'

'It's okay, Rowena, you lived with my brother for a long time. It's an easy mistake to make. What brings you to us?'

'Not good news, I'm afraid. We have received a communication from Septima and its quite straightforward. We do what he says or Tom dies!' She handed the note over to her father who read it then passed it to his brother.

'It's not going to happen; I'm not handing you or Karl over to that deranged individual!'

'Dad, think straight for a minute. This is the chance to end this. I am no fool, neither is Karl. We can look after ourselves. He says we are going back to our mother. She won't kill us. Then we can see what's going on, escape, give you their location and we can wipe them out once and for all. To top it all off, we get Tom back unharmed. Win, win I say!'

'No, Rowena, it would not be as simple as that. It may take years to get you back. Minds change after so long as a captive. I won't risk either of you.'

'Think logically, brother. It makes sense what Row is saying. It's the only option we have at the moment and as Row says, the queen will not allow anyone to harm her son and daughter.'

'It makes sense, Dad. As Uncle Tristan said, it's the only option we have and I'm willing to give it a go… and I bet Karl will be as well.'

'Okay, let me think about it for a while then I will let you know. That's fair I think?'

'Okay, Dad, but remember we don't have long. We must have an answer soon. Tom's life depends on it!' Row left the room with Tristan and the map which they were going to use to find the nearest gate to Brazil, if there was one.

Back where Prince Thomas had disappeared, there was a breakthrough. Terry and the miners had found the entrance to the old gate. All they were waiting for now was a technician who could reopen the gate, then someone to test it and see where it would come out. Leslie had been informed; she deduced that it was most likely the gate that led to Mexico and the old Mayan ruins, she was sure of it. Some of the Wolf and Eagle warriors along with some of the Omanian royal guard volunteered to go down to Earth. They would be given an Earth mobile phone so they could contact the Earth woman Gina who was in contact with Kurt. One of the knowledgeable preachers was briefed on the gate and how to realign it to its original destination. The only bit they did not know was what was waiting at the other end. There were enough experienced warriors that could deal with most of the possibilities that could be waiting for them at the other end. The command team were happy that these warriors could handle anything that they knew of anyway.

One hour later the gate was functional. The preacher told command there were no problems on the system. The warriors were cleared to go down to Earth. So, they left, armed to the teeth, and estimated they would get to Mexico in six Earth hours.

In the command centre, Tristan and Row had found a gate going to Bolivia, near Santa Cruz. It had an airport with flights via Sao Paulo Guarulhos then on to Brasília which took around seven hours. It could be done as long as there were no problems with the team who were travelling to Mexico as they spoke.

'Karl will have to fly from Cancun direct to Brasília. Kurt could fly to Rio to get to the letter drop so our answer would be there in time. It will be bloody close,' Row told Tristian.

'Not just that, Row. When was the last time anyone travelled through that gate?' Tristan replied.

'Where does it go from?' she asked him.

'Well, I never... you will never guess... the same gate that came from Louisiana. I never realised there was more than one destination from a gate.'

'Nothing surprises me in this world anymore,' she laughed.

'I will speak with Leslie. If anyone knows, she will,' Tristan replied just as Leslie and the king walked into the command centre.

'Speak of the devil, here she comes.'

'Are you talking about me, Tristan?'

'Yes, we need some advice about a gate. Can one gate go to two or more places? he asked.

'I believe they can. I remember reading something when I was studying. It

431

was from around the time of Atta. It was an old handwritten text about when he first found a gate. The gate here at the capital. That's one of the reasons it became the capital. Anyway, I digress. He asked the gate to take him to Earth. He thought it was going to the highlands of Scotland but it took him to the Harz Forest in Germany, Europe. Well, it wasn't Europe back then, anyway,' she answered.

'Interesting. I wonder whether you could tell the gate where to take you?' Row asked.

'I don't think so, otherwise I would have read about it,' replied Leslie.

'Very interesting, I wonder. By the way, Row, I have seen the sense in your idea. You can go but I don't like it. I will not be able to protect you or Karl but, as you said, Labatina would not hurt you. We will brief you before you go, and we will keep an eye on you for as long as we can. That's as long as Karl agrees to go with you.'

'Thanks, Dad. Some good will come from this, I am sure of it; you never know, we may be able to get Mum back. After reading those diary entries from Gebhuza Septima, I am positive that he is holding her against her will by drugging or manipulating her somehow. That's one of the reasons I want to go to find the truth.'

'You are a brave young woman, Row, and I will miss you around here. I know we have... I have not had my family around me very long, times have been difficult and I... we have lost a lot of good friends and family. I don't want to lose you, Karl and Tom, but I can see the sense in it. The spirit of Atta will be with you. He will protect you all, I am sure of it. Now, we must get on we have no time to waste; we must get ready.'

Things started to move at pace. The problems surrounding the exchange were solved, tickets were produced and plans made. The clock was ticking. The most important thing now was getting the message back to Gebhuza Septima and arranging the exchange before time ran out. They had to contact Kurt and quickly.

Back in Mexico, everyone was now awake and eating when the call came through to Gina's phone; the warriors had arrived and were now at the Mayan ruins. They had scouted the whole area and found signs of the Dark. Two bodies were sent back the same way they had arrived through the pathway back to Elemtum.

One thing the preachers had been working on for several years now was communication between worlds. They had come up with an idea, very similar to what happened on Earth with mobile phones but a lot more powerful and a lot smaller. The only thing they did not know at that point in the tests, and the newly arrived warriors were the guinea pigs for that, was if the authorities on Earth could detect the signal it emitted. They did not believe so; they had cloaked the signal just to be certain. The preachers had fixed a device to one end of the thread and the warriors had a second device that they had been shown how to attach to the exit end of the thread. They also had two more devices that they could place on any gates they found. It worked using a small device placed in the helmet of the warriors that transmitted and received coded signals that were then scrambled, sent through the thread back to the device at the start of the thread at the gate's entry point. This signal was then sent back to the command centre in Great Porum. It was a powerful system that had been put into service quicker than the preachers had wanted but it was now a device to communicate with Earth that would be very useful in the coming days, weeks, or even years.

The lead warrior, Snordor, made the first call back to Elemtum. 'Hello, gate one, gate two calling Andor. Do you receive?'

A minute later a reply came back. 'Snordor, nice to hear from you on Earth. It's Tristan. Proceed with the plan and contact Kurt. We must speak to him urgently. Carry on and may Atta guide you.'

A minute later Tristan received, 'Is that all?'

Listening next to Tristan, Row suggested, 'Maybe if you introduce a system on Earth so you know when you have finished speaking, like the communicator in the helmets here. Over and out? Just a thought,' she told Tristan.

'How stupid of me. It's the same thing, isn't it? Dah! Snordor, use this device as you do your communicator here in Elemtum. Use hello, over and out, so we know when the communication starts and finishes. Okay? Over.'

The reply came back, 'Roger, out.'

'Dah! Tristan, you're starting to sound like me,' laughed Row.

'I know! I've been around you too long. I will miss you, Row. Don't take any stupid risks, promise me, Row.'

Row gave Tristan a big hug and whispered in his ear, 'I promise... Dad!' Then she kissed his cheek and smiled. 'I must get ready and find some human clothes. I don't want to stand out now, do I?' Then she went off to her quarters to get ready.

Below her at the Louisiana thread Leslie was trying something out. 'Are you ready to travel, Preacher Leslie?' the gate asked.

'What? To Louisiana?' she asked.

'Yes,' came the reply.

'Can you take me anywhere else?' she asked.

'No one has ever asked me that before. Yes, where would you like to go, lady?'

'Linasfarn,' she answered.

'Route changed.' Then they left Great Porum. Seconds later she stepped out of the gate on Linasfarn to the surprise of one of the warriors nearby.

'Preacher Leslie, I did not know there was a world gate here?'

'No, neither did I. This will change everything we know about the world gate and the threads.' Then she was gone and back at Great Porum.

She rushed to tell Tristan and the king. She was very excited; she had discovered something no one on the planet knew. She would go down in history. She burst into the command centre. Everyone inside looked up.

'I've got some exciting news,' She told the king, Tristan and anyone else who would listen.

'So, she was right,' replied Tristan.

'Who are you talking about? I found it out,' she told them, a little upset that she was not the sole discoverer. 'Are you talking about Row? ... Well, she did put the spark into my brain and light the fire, as it were,' she replied.

'Yes, thank you, Leslie, you have discovered something that may help us immensely once we have tested its potential. Can you get a team together and start testing right away and tell us where we can go and how we use it? This is ground breaking.'

'Right away, Frederick' she replied with a smile. She made her way out to get the team together.

As she left the room, she heard the king say, 'She's a clever girl.' She continued out with a beaming smile on her face, but not realising the king was talking about his daughter Row, not Leslie. 'I agree, brother. I think she and Karl will do well down on Earth. They both have something about that's different from the warriors here. I think Earth has added something to their character.'

'I totally agree. You and Kurt have brought them up well, I am very grateful. I think what they have been through in their short lives will serve them in the future. That's one of the reasons I have agreed to Row and Karl going on this perilous journey. That and the fact that I don't believe Labatina will hurt them and, as Row said, their being there may even change things for the good. Only time will tell.'

Kurt, Karl and Billy went to speak to Snordor and his warriors after receiving the call sent to Gina. Snordor immediately put Kurt on the communicator back to Tristan who explained everything to him as well as what was to happen next. There was no real need for Snordor and his warriors to stay on Earth so they would accompany the cadets home. Karl was happy to go on the mission with Row and a plan had been hatched to get them together.

Billy went back for the cadets and brought them back to the warriors who promptly left after showing Kurt and Karl the communication devices and how they worked. If they found the nearest gate, they could communicate through it as long as it had been prepared with the two devices either end of the thread. Kurt had taken the communicator from Andor's helmet as well as the two gate devices in case he came across another gate.

Billy, Kurt and Karl returned to the villa where Erline and Gina had prepared some food. They ate quickly, then Kurt told them the plan. Billy and Gina would go back to Louisiana via Cancun Airport from where Kurt, Karl and Erline would catch a flight to Rio in Brazil. They would drop the note off at the favela then get a flight from Brasília where they would meet Tristan, Steven and Row at the airport. They would all then travel to the area where the exchange would happen and find some rooms for the night. Twenty-four hours later the exchange would happen. After that, it was in the hands of Karl, Row and the Dark?

They all said good bye at Cancun Airport; Billy and Gina caught a flight to the USA while Kurt, Karl and Erline flew on to Rio. Meanwhile, Hollie and her water team had been stood down along with every other team that was meant to go to Earth to back up Kurt's team. Instead, Hollie and four of her team, now in civilian clothing along with Steven, the head of the royal guard, would escort Row to Bolivia, then onto Brasília to meet with Kurt and the others and then escort Karl and Row to the designated exchange point. There they would wait out of site, observe, then retrieve Tom and return to Great Porum. That was the plan. Whether it would all go as planned was another matter, but now only time would tell if it would be successful.

Eight hours later, Kurt, Karl and Erline got a glimpse of the famous Sugarloaf Mountain as the plane circled on approach to Rio Airport. 'It's a shame we don't have longer. I would love to go to the top of the mountain. The view from there must be amazing. You could get some good pictures at the top,' Karl told the others.

'Never mind, we can come back and see it once all this is finished,' Erline whispered to Karl. then she kissed him on the cheek.

'Yes, fingers crossed,' replied Karl. Then he smiled and gave Erline a kiss on the lips.

Tears filled her eyes. 'I'm not happy about what is going to happen. I might never see you again.'

'Don't worry, Row and me can handle ourselves. After all, we will be with our mother. What could happen?'

'You might never come back. Or be killed. After all, it's the Dark we are talking about… I could lose you; we have only just met. It's not fair. Why do you have to go? We could land and just run away!'

'I have to support my sister… I am the prince of a world. It's my duty… I have to save my brother.' There was a short pause. 'Then we will be together for ever, live a normal life, but I have to see this through otherwise I could never be happy knowing I let my brother die.'

'I can't do this, Karl. I love you, but I can't watch you go off to possibly die. When we land, I am going to get a flight back to the USA and stay with Gina and Billy in my home. I will wait for you but I won't sit here and wait for you to die. I'm sorry.' As tears once again filled her eyes, she looked away out of the window. She tried to wipe the tears with the sleeve of her sweatshirt but the tears kept coming. 'Look at me. Look what you've done to me, Karl De-Callen.' She laughed and cried at the same time. Karl did not know what to do so he held her hand.

Kurt watched on, then told them both, 'It's a wise decision, Erline. You will be safe and happy with Gina and Billy. You know, Karl, that will be one less thing for you to worry about. I will sort it out for you when we land. I can't say for certain any of us will see each other again but, in my heart, I know you two will, the connection between you is too strong. This a calculated risk, the odds are in our favour. You have to trust him, Erline. He will return and this will all end.'

Erline looked at them both sniffed and smiled. 'I hope so.'

The announcement came over the intercom telling everyone to attach their seat belts for landing at Galeão International Airport. The aircraft landed safely and they passed through arrivals and made their way to departures and found a flight going to Alexandria International Airport in Louisiana, where they bought a ticket for Erline. Kurt left them to say goodbye.

It was a very emotional parting. Karl's eyes filled with tears as did Erline's. A thought went quickly through Karl's mind, am I doing the right thing! At that point he was not sure if he was making the right choice. Was he ready for this, was he old enough to deal with this? Then he saw his brother and sister in his mind; he could not let them down. He did not tell Erline what he was feeling so they hugged and kissed, then she left, not looking back. Karl's heart sank. He had not felt like this before. It was as if something was being ripped from him. Would he ever see her again? He was not sure. He wiped the tears from his eyes, sniffed, then went to find Kurt as Erline's figure disappeared.

'You okay, Karl?' Kurt asked him as they met.

Karl nodded. 'Let's get on with this. The sooner we get this done, the sooner we will all be together again.' Kurt put his arm around Karl's shoulder and they left the airport terminal.

They took a taxi to the area for the letter drop. It was a house where the occupant had been paid a great sum of money to pass the reply back to the Dark, but he was unaware of who he was dealing with. It was easy money that would get him and his family out of that place. It took about half an hour to get as close to the area as the taxi driver would go. They left the taxi and walked on foot until they came to a run-down children's play area where several teenagers were hanging out. Some of them were heavily tattooed, even at their young age; they obviously belonged to one of the gangs in the area.

'Leave this to me, Karl.' Kurt walked up to the gang, who shifted involuntary as the big man approached. 'Hola,' he said to them in perfect Spanish. Karl looked on amazed; he never knew his uncle could speak other languages. Kurt went on to explain to the gang that if they delivered the note to the address written on it, he would pay them a lot of money; ten thousand Brazilian Real which worked out at around two and a half thousand dollars, a lot money in the favela, money they could not refuse for such a simple task. They asked him what the catch was? He told them there was no catch, he would pay them up front. He also told them he would know if the note was not received. If that turned out to be the case, he would come back and kill them all. That was a promise. They all looked at him. His eyes told them that he was not bluffing so they agreed, took the money and the note then they were gone. He could do nothing now, he hoped he had made the right decision. He walked back to Karl who was amazed by his uncle; he never knew he could speak Spanish, something new every day.

They walked out of the district and got a taxi back to the airport. It was their lucky day; there was a flight to Brasília in two hours, giving them enough time to have some food and drink before it departed. They now had forty-eight hours before they would meet Row and find the shopping centre. Kurt was happy that it was all achievable. As they ate, Karl spoke to his uncle, 'You're a dark horse. I never knew you could speak Spanish, Uncle Kurt.'

'Spanish, French, German, Russian, several oriental dialects and Japanese. I had a lot of free time bringing you and Tom up. I had some long nights and days when you were at school.'

'That's very impressive...' Karl paused and thought for a while. 'Do you think I am ready for this? It's been on my mind.'

'I have been very impressed by you. I have no doubt in my mind that you are both strong enough to do this, both you and your sister. I would not have agreed to bring you here if I had any doubts.'

'But I had back up before. I will be on my own this time. If I am honest, I'm a little scared!'

'That's only natural, Karl, we all feel like that at times like this. Row will be feeling the same. But once thing starts happening you will both come alive. I've seen it in you before. You are a born leader and warrior. You will be okay, trust me.' Karl did. He was now filled with a new vigour. He had a feeling inside. Was it his wolf and eagle taking over, he wondered? They finished their meal, then went and boarded the aircraft to Brasília.

Row and her team had now arrived at the airport in San José de Chiquito. They were boarding the flight for the first part of their journey to meet Kurt and Karl. Row had had the same doubts as Karl. She too had had a similar conversation with Hollie who reassured her she would find her inner self once it all started. What Hollie meant about inner self, Row was not sure. She had not turned into a wolf or eagle like Tom and Karl but she did feel happier about what was coming and she was looking forward to seeing her brothers again. It seemed like a long time since they had all been together. In reality, it had only been days.

Finally, everyone was together in a hotel on the outskirts of Brasília. Kurt and Karl had been to the exchange point and seen the horse in the shopping centre. They had also walked the route Karl and Row would take from the shopping centre to the park. Karl was now happy with the route they would take the next day. While they were in the shopping centre, they had also bought three sports watches; one each for Row, Karl and Kurt so they would all be on the same time. This was important because if Karl knew when the hour was up after leaving Tom then they could try and escape if they had the chance, knowing Tom would be safe. Karl had asked Kurt why they didn't inform the local police; they could help. Kurt had dismissed the idea. He did not want to chance the local police knowing. They might ask too many questions and he also did not know if he could trust them. Kurt had decided to get one of Hollie's water team, Ado, an eagle, to fly high above the park. With his superior sight he could observe the pair when they walked from the shopping centre. Karl saw a problem with that as the eagles were a lot bigger than eagles on Earth. He could be noticed. Kurt agreed so that idea was shelved for the moment. They would speak to Hollie on their return to the hotel. If only they had Kee with them, Karl thought.

In the park, Karl had noticed a few areas that he could run and hid in with the possibility of changing either into a wolf or eagle and try and escape. By that time, he would not care about being seen as long as he could get away. His only problem at that point that he could think of was his sister. Could she change?

If not, he could not leave her. Maybe he could fly with her on his back.

Back at the hotel, Kurt got everyone together, briefing them about everything they had done and seen. Then he asked Hollie her opinion regarding the eagle. She agreed that if the eagle flew high enough, he would not look big, but would he see anything on the ground from there? Secondly, did they have eagles in Brasília? If they did not, it would draw unwanted attention and that was something the Dark would pick up on which could jeopardise the whole exchange and the prince's life. Hollie and her team would go out that night and find some observation points that might help for the morning's exchange. She was unhappy that they would only have a small Earth weapon called a pistol, but at least they would have eyes on whoever picked up Karl and Row. That could be helpful, after that it was down to Karl and Row.

They decided to stay in the hotel for dinner that night after which Hollie and her team along with Steven would depart. Everyone else would try and relax and get some sleep because no one knew what would happen the next morning.

The shopping centre opened at seven in the morning. The exchange would be fifteen minutes after that before the place got too busy. Hollie with her four water team members and Steven made their way to the area of the park and shopping centre where they divided into three teams. Hollie and Steven would find an observation point overlooking the entrance to the shopping centre. The second pair would go to the park and pick a location that would give the best view of the park and the last team would watch the road leading from the shopping centre and the park. This was the route Karl and Row had been briefed to use to walk to the park. Her team all had pistols concealed on them as well as a mobile phone for each group; not ideal, but it was all they could get and at least they would be able to keep in contact with each other. They got into their concealed positions without any problems. All they could do now was wait!

For them, the night was long with nothing happening apart from the odd inebriated individual staggering along the road when the local bars kicked out. One team got close to being discovered by a young couple looking for somewhere hidden to make love but the team made a scary noise and the couple ran from the park.

Back in the hotel, it was also a long night for Karl and Row. They could not sleep; they both tossed and turned all night, falling asleep what seemed like only minutes before Kurt woke them up. The new day had started all too quickly. They ate a breakfast of cereal and fruit then waited in Row's room until it was time to leave for the shopping centre.

Meanwhile, Hollie and her team had observed their allotted areas all night; nothing suspicious had caught their well-trained eye. As it got light, cars started moving along the road, but nothing stood out as unusual.

On arriving at the shopping centre, Kurt escorted Karl and Row to the horse statue. Again, nothing unusual caught their eye. 'Well, this is it. You can still pull out and no one will feel you let your brother down. It took a lot of courage to come this far. I will take you back to the hotel no questions asked. All you have to do is say the word.' Kurt told them.

It was Row who replied almost immediately. 'Thanks, Uncle Kurt, but I am ready to do this. It's the only way we will get Tom back. I'm sure Karl agrees with me.'

'Yes, I do.'

'In that case, it's time for me to leave both of you. Take care and don't be the hero, Karl. Look after your sister!'

'I think it will Row looking after me!' Karl replied with a smile. Kurt shook his hand, then gave him a hug. He kissed Row on the cheek and gave her a hug then left them alone.

This was spotted by a cleaner who spoke into a small microphone under his lapel, 'Okay. They are on their own. The big man has gone, you should see him leave any minute.' A voice at the other end confirmed the big man had left the shopping centre and got into a car that had driven off. A car further up the street would follow it and let them know when it was far enough away to pose no threat to the operation that was about to take place.

Kurt quickly spotted the car tailing him; the driver had obviously never been trained like Kurt had. He let it follow him taking it away from the area to a more desolate spot. He had a plan for the driver.

Row and Karl waited at the horse; the time was ten past seven, all seemed quiet. Meanwhile, Kurt had driven to a rather deserted industrial area. He slowed down so the car following him could keep up then he turned a corner and parked. He got out quickly, leaving the driver's door open. He made sure he would not be seen by the following driver, who turned the corner and slammed his brakes on to avoid hitting the abandoned car. 'He's gone!' he told his controller.

'Well, bloody well find him and kill him. Do you understand?' the controller told him.

The man got out of the car and walked towards Kurt's abandoned car. He bent down and looked inside. That was his second mistake, his first was getting out of the car. As quick as a bullet, Kurt was on top of him, kicking his legs away causing the man to collapse onto the driver's seat and hitting his head on the steering wheel. Quickly, Kurt put the man in an arm lock, pulling him out of the car and slamming him down onto the bonnet. The man smacked his head, dazing him. Kurt restrained him so he could not move. He was now in a lot of pain.

'What's the plan, friend? Why are you following me?'

The man replied in Spanish, 'I don't know. I was only ordered to follow you. Let me go. I'm a police officer. You are in big trouble, let me go!'

'Tell me the truth or I will kill you right now!' Kurt replied in fluent Spanish. This put the man on the back foot. As the pain increased, he buckled.

'I am only doing what I was ordered by my captain of police. He told us it was a drug gang that was using children to smuggle drugs to other children. He said it was a special operation and that we would all be paid three times our normal week's salary for one day. A bonus from the government, he told us. That's the truth, I swear it on my children's lives,' he pleaded.

'Sounds plausible so I won't kill you but if I cross you again I will. All I am trying to do is rescue a family member, a child who was abducted in Mexico. That's all, no drugs involved. Understand? All I am trying to do is protect my family.' He loosened his grip on the policeman but did not let him go. He searched him and found a concealed police issue revolver and a badge. 'I am going to take the gun, just for my own safety. You can tell the rest of the police officers your boss is probably bent, working for the gang that abducted my nephew. Tell them if they get in the way they will be taken out. Do you understand?'

'Yes, I do,' the officer replied.

Kurt released his hold on the much-relieved police officer who stood up and stretched his arms that had been held in a tight lock by the big man. Kurt then went over to the car and pulled the radio from its mount just for a bit of insurance. He did not want the cavalry to come running, whether they were good or bad. The officer made sure the big man did not feel threatened, so he walked away from his car and sat on an old plastic deck chair that was propped against a warehouse wall. He sat and watched Kurt drive away. He was in no hurry to follow the big man.

As this was all going on, Hollie and Steven observed a 4x4 pull up outside the shopping centre but no Tom. His vehicle had dropped him off with his minder around the corner and they were using the service entrance into the centre. The 4x4 promptly left after doing nothing which they found unusual and reported the fact to the group.

A door behind Row and Karl opened and Tom wandered out. They turned to look and there was Tom in the doorway behind one of the Dark's henchmen standing menacingly. Tom walked slowly to them. There was no expression on his face, it was blank.

'You okay, Tom?' Row asked.

Tom did not answer. He just sat down on a bench next to the horse. It was as though Karl and Row were not even there. Karl walked up to him.

'Tom, it's me… Karl. Are you all right?'

Tom just stared ahead as though he was not there. Karl shook him by the arms.

'Tom, look at me, answer me… Tom!'

Tom looked up at his brother; his eyes were empty of any emotion. Then he looked ahead as though no one was there. Behind them the door was ajar, and the menacing man was still standing watching them. This time they caught a glimpse of a weapon, some sort of automatic rifle. The man grinned and thrust his weapon forward as if to say get going.

'We had better make a move, I suppose,' Row told Karl then she kissed her younger brother on the cheek.

'We will see you later, little man,' she told him then ruffled his hair. Still no reaction. 'Will he be safe here on his own? Why don't we stay and see what happens?' she asked Karl but as she said it, they suddenly became very aware of a lot of people staring at them menacingly. None of them looked like they belonged in a shopping centre; more like a prison, some even would be at home in a zoo. They started to move towards them. As quickly as they had appeared, the menacing mob disappeared. They took one last look back at their brother still sitting by the horse seemingly oblivious to his surroundings. They stepped out into the bright sunshine that made them momentarily squint until their eyes became accustomed to the bright light of the day.

'It's left we have to go, towards the park,' Karl told his sister. They headed along the road. From his hidden observation point, Steven reported to everyone that they had left the shopping centre and were now heading along the road to the park. All around them now the city was coming alive. More cars were now moving along the street, more than any of them had imagined. In the park, more people were using the paths as a quick way of cutting off the main road to get to their place of work or the shopping centre, that and the fact that it was a lovely day and why not wander through a beautiful park if you could.

Hollie decided they could be no use to Row and Karl stuck in their observation points, so she ordered everyone out to mingle with the people going about their daily business. As they got ready to leave, Steven spotted a fast-moving vehicle.

'It's okay, it's just a police van. It has it's lights on and its siren. I can hear it now,' he reported.

Abruptly the van skidded to a halt right next to the Karl and Row, the side door opened, and four police officers jumped out. Two of them had tasers in their hands which they stuck into Karl and Row who immediately fell to the ground, helpless. Seconds later they were tumbled into the police van which shot off down the road, siren blaring and lights flashing. Then, they were gone.

In their earpieces they heard Kurt who was now back in range. 'The police are in on it. They are being paid by the Dark. Keep an eye out for any police officers. They are not friendlies.'

He was immediately told what had happened.

'Damn, they have had us over a barrel. How could we have been so stupid?' They heard him say over the air.

To the shock of the people walking through the park, a giant eagle had appeared and was now soaring high in the sky. By the time people had got their phones ready to video or take a picture, the eagle was high in the sky and looked like any normal eagle at that height. Some people took pictures or videoed the bird as this was the first time they had seen an eagle that wasn't in a zoo. The remaining warrior reported that his partner was now an eagle looking for the police van.

'Great thinking. We will deal with any consequences later if anything comes of it. If they have got their act together, that van will be long gone. Row and Karl have either been put in a building or another vehicle,' Kurt told everyone. 'I will go in and get Tom from the shopping centre before the Dark can change their plan and try and take him as well. Hollie, Steven, follow me in. We don't know what we will find in there. Hollie, get the guys left in the park to meet us in there too, the more the merrier.'

They entered the shopping centre by the main entrance. All seemed quiet, nothing out of the ordinary. Walking towards the horse, they could see Tom sitting at its feet on a small bench made from white painted concrete. He looked very alone. His face held a stare that was out of this world. He did not even acknowledge their approach; something was not right. 'Tom, it's me, Kurt. Are you all right?'

Tom looked up at him with a blank expression and said nothing. No emotion showed on his face whatsoever. His body was there but his mind was not.

'What have they done to him?' Hollie asked, very concerned with his appearance. 'This is not like the Tom I know,' she said.

'It's not the Tom I know either,' replied Kurt. 'Steven, give me a hand and we will get Tom to the car and get out of here.'

Back at the hotel, they made preparations to leave. They had booked two more nights but there was not a lot they could do now with Tom so it was decided Hollie and one of the water team would escort Tom back to Elemtum. They had noticed that her female voice calmed Tom; he would do what she instructed him to do. She did not like the idea of babysitting the prince; she wanted to stay here where she would be useful finding Karl and Row. But she did see the logic in it as she seemed to be the only one Tom would listen to. She handed over command of her water team to Steven. She knew he was a good warrior and would lead her remaining team well. She was driven to the airport with Tom and the water team warrior by Steven who saw them off safely before he returned to the hotel.

At the hotel, Kurt decided they needed to move to the centre of Brazil to a villa with its own land that was out of the way and secure so they could plan their next move in peace without any outside interference. He started to reach out to some of his Earth contacts.

Everyone was very disheartened; moral was down as they sat around in the hotel. Kurt knew he had to get out of there and re-motivated his team.

Kurt was right. Karl and Row had been transferred into a camper van which was now heading out of the city on its short journey to a small makeshift helicopter pad where a black Augusta waited for them. Both Karl and Row had been sedated and a bracelet had been placed on their wrists that would prevent them from turning into an animal form and escaping. The devices had never been fully tested but Gebhuza Septima was sure they would work; he had done trials on prisoners they had captured in the past.

Theon returned to the hotel several hours later, he had landed out of sight away from prying eyes, then made his own way back to the hotel. He had had no luck with his search. All the police vehicles he followed ended up as false leads, but he had seen a black helicopter lift off from somewhere south of the city. It flew too fast for him to catch but he had managed to get a tail number for it as it headed north very quickly. Apart from that, he had nothing else to put forward.

'It could be a coincidence that it was the same type of helicopter used in Mexico to abduct Tom. So, we either need to confirm it's the same one or eliminate it and look somewhere else,' Kurt told them all.

It was late afternoon when Kurt got a call from an old friend from when he had attended the English military college at Sandhurst when he was much younger. He had been placed there on the pretence that he was an overseas student. He had done well and been awarded the sword of honour as the best officer cadet of his intake. He had found the experience interesting and a little challenging. At first, he hadn't understood the logic in the endless room and kit inspections but he got it in the end and the whole experience had been fun. If the college had known how overseas he truly was, things might have been a little different. It had given him a good insight into the thinking of the Earth's military leaders; well, some of them anyway. His friend was an overseas student too who was already an officer in the Brazilian army and was also there for the experience. Sandhurst was known as one of the best military academies in the world. The young Brazilian officer was called Dave, not a very Portuguese sounding name. His mother was Scottish, from Glasgow, his father Nuno de Oliveira Gonçalves from Brazil. They were both training to be a doctor when they had fallen in love, much to the disgust of her father who thought she should have married a rich Scot and settled down in Scotland. But Dave's mother had a better idea. Along with Nuno, she would go back to Brazil and bring medicine to the people that could not afford it at that time. David de Oliveira Gonçalves, or Dave to his friends, was the result. He had been very sporty in his youth and not at all interested in medicine like his parents. He had eyes only for the up-and-coming Brazilian army. He was a born leader and was only beaten to the sword of honour by Kurt De-Callen, his mysterious friend from the Cayman Islands, an autonomous British overseas territory in the western Caribbean.

David replied to Kurt, telling him he had a farm in Bahia which is located in the north-eastern part of the country on the Atlantic coast. It was being sold so David was more than happy for Kurt to stay there for as long as he required. Kurt phoned David and they spoke at length for an hour. David told him that he was now in command of the Brazilian Special Operations Command who dealt with direct action, airfield seizure, special reconnaissance airborne and air assault operations and personnel recovery. The last operation, personnel recovery, made Kurt listen harder to his old friend. Kurt told him he was in the country to track down his niece and nephew who had been abducted. The only lead they had was the black Augusta helicopter. He gave David the tail number which he said he could track down for him. He also told him to go with his men to the local army base and he would arrange a military helicopter to take them to his farm in the east. He would make up a story so no questions would be asked.

David was as good as his word and two hours later they were being ferried to the east of the country by a special forces' Chinook helicopter. David personally greeted them at his farm. He also brought them some equipment to use; pistols, helmets, fragmentation vests, coveralls and boots of various sizes.

They sat down and talked about what David could officially offer them and what he would actually unofficially offer him with regard to resources and help. They talked well into the night with the help of some beers and a few good bottles of the very strong national drink, Cachaça.

David stayed the night with one of his trusted lieutenants, a big intelligent capable strong man who went by the name of Danny. His friends called him Dan the man because there was nothing he could not do or had not done militarily. He had started his life in the French Foreign Legion and had served twelve years

445

before he went home to Brazil and joined David's crack unit. H had done a tour with the British SAS and the American Delta forces. He had taken all that he had learnt back to his own unit which enhanced it greatly. He was a big hard, but likeable, man. Kurt and his men bonded quickly with him.

In the morning, everyone awoke to the sound of three 4x4 land cruisers being dropped off by some of David's men who, while the others got up and washed, made everyone a mouth-watering brunch of salad, fresh fish and Brazilian beef. One of David's men even made some bread for everyone. They all sat down around a long table under the veranda with a view over the massive farm that sprawled out in front of them, in the distance they could even make out the sea.

David, Kurt and his men all had sore heads except Danny who seemed to absorb the alcohol all night with no adverse effects, not outwardly anyway. The big lieutenant, full of life, told Kurt and David that they had tracked the helicopter. It had been leased by a third party who would not give the name of the customer due to client confidentiality, the young woman at the management agency that had hired the helicopter for the client had told them. Danny told his boss and Kurt that the company would be their first port of call. David knew the commander in the area would get the information for them one way or another. They should get the details in a couple of hours.

Before David and his men left, he and Kurt talked. He had told Kurt he was happy to help his old friend; officially it would be put down as mutual team training with overseas friendly forces, namely a contingent from the Cayman Islands even though David knew Kurt was no longer in the military. He also offered any further assistance they may need to find his abducted family. Dany would stay with Kurt as his liaison officer for any future help they might need.

Chapter 25
Rescue

Kurt was not the only one who had woken that morning with a bad head. Karl and Row had both woken with sore heads and dehydration. They were in what one could only call a posh yurt. It had comfortable beds, not that they could remember their sleep or how they got there. It had electricity with a TV on the wall and a fridge stacked with food and drink that they both remembered from Earth; soda, fruit, and snacks including chocolate. They drank and ate before thoughts of where they were entered their heads. Feeling bloated by the soda and chocolate they had consumed, they sat on the very comfortable chairs that were placed around a wood burner in the centre of the yurt.

'How do you feel, Row?' Karl asked his sister.

'My head feels a bit better but I still feel a little tired. I have no idea where we are or what this bracelet thing is for. Are we prisoners? I don't know.'

'Well then, sis, let's find out, shall we?' Karl got up and tried the big wooden door that he assumed led out into the world. To his surprise, the door opened into bright sunlight. He looked around. It looked like they were in a jungle; the area they were in had been cleared of all vegetation. In front of him he saw some wooden shacks, some looked like meeting houses or living quarters. In what looked like kitchens he could see people working. There were more yurts and tents as far as he could see; the area was very big. He could hear vehicles moving about and a couple of helicopters in the air, but he could not see them. Row went to his side.

'Not quite what I was expecting,' Row told her brother. 'Are we prisoners? It doesn't feel like it at the moment,' she asked Karl.

'I'm not sure, but someone has gone to a lot of trouble to get us here. Is this all for us, I wonder?'

'Good morning, sir, madam, I am Maria. I will be looking after you for your mother who will be down to see you in a while,' a bronzed middle-aged woman told them. She had been sitting in a chair in front of their yurt.

'God, I didn't see you there!' Row told her, a little startled.

'You seem normal.' Karl said. 'Not like the Dark at all.'

'Dark? I don't understand, sir,' she replied, a puzzled look on her face.

'Karl!' Row scolded him, with a look that would have made a sailor blush.

'What?' he replied.

'You can be such an idiot sometimes… Hello, Maria, I am Row, and this is my idiot brother.'

Maria nodded and smiled. 'Who sent you here to wait for us?' Row asked. D

'Why, your mother sent me. Lady Labatina. Did you not know?' she asked.

'No, we did not. We have only just woken up after a long journey to get here,' Row told her.

At Marcão Management Services, the young lady at the reception was not having a good day. Two rather large military policeman were grilling her about a helicopter that had been leased to a client.

'I don't know… I only answer the phone,' she was telling the soldiers who did not care what she did. They wanted answers or they would close the place down.

In tears, the woman ran into the manager's office where her manager and boyfriend was sitting at a big mahogany desk surrounded by phones and computer screens. 'What's wrong, Belinha?' he asked. Before she could answer, the two soldiers pushed her to one side and bodily manhandled the manager up against the wall behind his desk.

'Tell us what we need to know, or we will arrest you for withholding vital information pertaining to a kidnapping,' one of the soldiers screamed into his face. Petrified, the man told them he could not disclose confidential client information.

'Okay,' said the second soldier, now playing the good cop.

Behind him, Belinha was crying. 'Tell them what they need to know, Paul.'

'Listen to your receptionist, Paul, or you will be arrested for withholding evidence in connection with a child kidnapping case we are investigating,' the good cop told him.

The bad cop, still holding him, added, 'We will beat it out of you if we have to,' as he banged Paul's head against the wall.

'Okay, I will tell you whatever you need to know. You should have told me it was about children. I love children. I have a boy and two girls myself,' he replied.

'Paul, you never told me you had kids!' his girlfriend screamed.

'He's probably married!' bad cop told her.

She stormed out of the office, then they heard the front door slam. Paul rifled through his filing cabinet, found the information and handed it to the soldiers who promptly left. Paul closed the office and raced after his girlfriend, hoping to catch her before she did any damage.

The information gained was passed to Danny minutes later. He thanked the two military policemen, then hung up and informed Kurt and his team.

'The helicopter was tracked to a medical team setting up a field hospital in the Amazon for the native peoples of the area. Part a UN project apparently.'

'What's the name of the person or the company that hired it?' Steven asked.

Danny looked at his notes. 'Here we are. Professor Samuel Hastings MD, plus some other rubbish that I did not write down. More qualifications than you can shake a stick at,' Danny told them.

'Does not ring any bells with me,' said Steven, 'what about anybody else?' Everyone had blank faces, even Kurt who was good with names.

'That's a blank then,' replied Kurt.

'What about the company name?' Steven asked.

'Let's see.' Danny rifled through his notes once more… 'There we have it… Gebhuza Medical.'

'That's it, we have them!' Kurt punched the air. 'What a conceited idiot. Did he think we would not track him down? Do we know where the company is setting up?'

'The military police are looking for that information as we speak. By the time we have packed the vehicles, we should have the information,' Danny told them all.

True to his word, minutes later the camp's position was sent to them. 'That position is in the Amazon jungle. We will need helicopters and boats to get near. I'll call David now and ask for some help.' Danny rang his boss with the information. He also asked Danny to let him know if they came into any contact on their recce to let him know and he would personally bring down more special forces to deal with the bandits.

After speaking to Danny, Kurt told his men they would be moving to a new camp by helicopter. Then, depending on the situation on the ground, they may have to travel by boat. They would be setting up the next camp in the Amazon jungle. David would supply all the kit they needed which, as he spoke, was all being moved to a rendezvous point along the Amazon river not too far from the supposed field hospital, but not close enough for the bandits to know they were on their trail.

In the helicopter, Kurt told Danny that the so-called bandits were a bit more than bandits; they were a small army of ruthless killers who followed a psychopath. Danny sent the information back to David who reassessed his plan and added more troops and equipment to deal with them. The only thing they did not know was the size of the forces they would be up against. This was a vital bit of information they needed before any rescue mission could be launched. They decided to fly one helicopter over the site, using one of the medivac helicopters for the job as it would not seem too aggressive to the enemy on the ground.

Maria gave Karl and Row some clean clothes to put on after she had shown them where the shower blocks were. After showering and changing, Karl and Row met Maria back at the yurt. They sat outside in the sun and talked. Maria told them that she had been hired to help a lady who had had mental health problems, their mother Labatina. She enjoyed working for Labatina but every now and then she would descend into total madness and viciousness. That's when she would hide from her and wait for the doctor, Septima, to arrive so that Labatina could be calmed down. The doctor told her it was because she had been separated from her children and that would soon be resolved. She was not happy anymore nor were a lot of the local workers as they had been promised good money to come and work for the doctor. However, all they got was abuse and bad treatment from the guards who were evil people with disfigured faces who would not let anyone leave.

'I don't know what has happened to my son and husband. Why has nobody come for me? Where are the authorities? They must know something is wrong here,' she told them. Row told her not to worry as they were being held against their will as well; they had been taken from their family and friends too. They would escape and take her and anyone else with them that wanted to leave. Just then one of the Dark warriors turned up. He was in Earth clothing which made him look odd to Karl and Row, but it still did not hide the smell of the warrior. It was enough to make you barf, as Row told Maria. Maria's soul was lifted and she was smiling once more.

'Leave these children alone, you animal,' she cursed at him and got whack with the back of his hand for her trouble. Maria fell to the floor; Karl went to help her but was pushed away by the guard.

'Leave the bitch. She won't be around for too much longer,' he snarled at them. Then he kicked her on the ground. Maria screamed! Row swung her fist with such force it caught the guard on his cheek and knocked him to the ground. Row and Karl were amazed at the strength of the punch; the guard had been knocked out cold.

'Help me drag him into the yurt, I will tie him up there,' Karl asked Row.

'Not so fast, kids. I thought you might try something like this. I said you would be more trouble than you were worth. I should have just killed you and especially that little brat, Prince Thomas,' said a man, now standing in front of them. He had a white beard, neatly trimmed, and he was wearing tan combat fatigues. On his head was a pith helmet with a mosquito net wrapped around it so it could be pulled down when required.

'Gebhuza Septima… You scumbag!' Row said, then brought her hand back to take another punch.

'Now, now, daughter, that's no way to treat your father! Yes, Rowena De-Callen, you are actually Rowena Septima. I'm quite surprised you're not blue like my other daughters. It might have something to do with the pigment tablets I was taking when I slept with your mother sixteen years ago.' He smiled, put his arms out to hug her but she pushed him away, stepping back against the yurt's canvas wall.

'You're a horrible man!' she screamed at him. 'You liar, I'm going to kill you!' She took a step forward as did Karl, both with looks of sheer disgust and anger on their faces, when from behind Gebhuza two massive Dark warriors appeared and stood at his side.

'Now then, daughter, it will take a little time but you will come to terms with it. You will be a good loving daughter to me and your mother, my queen,' he sneered at her.

Next to him on the floor Maria had taken a hair pin from her tied up hair. She thrust it into the side of his leg, right into the calf muscle. He screamed and crumpled to the floor. Maria screamed something in Portuguese as the warrior closest to her grabbed Gebhuza as he fell. Karl ran at the second warrior. With all his force he rammed into him, bowling him over, punching him in the face as he fell. He hit the ground with a thud. Slightly dazed he lay on the ground. Karl turned into a wolf, ripping at the warrior's neck. He screamed out in pain and fright as he tried to push the wolf off him, but it was no good. The warrior's fight stopped, and he went limp, dead. Gebhuza looked over to Karl, now a boy again, on top of the deceased warrior. Maria grabbed Row and pulled her away from the warrior now helping his master.

'Come with me, Row. I will get you out of here.' She pulled Row away from the chaos in front of them. Row briefly resisted.

'Karl!' sshe shouted, and put an arm out to grab him but he was too far away.

'Go!' Karl shouted at her. 'I'll be okay. I will meet up with you later.' Then he was up on his feet and off. He ran around the build in front of him as Row and Maria ran the other way.

'Go after them, you fool! Get the children, you idiot! Go!' Gebhuza screamed at the warrior who was trying to help him.

'But you are hurt!' he replied.

'I'm a bloody doctor, you idiot. Now get after them, I can look after myself,' he screamed as he pushed the warrior away from him. The warrior ran after Karl.

'The girl, you idiot… my daughter. I don't care about the boy, you buffoon,' he screamed after the warrior who turned, confused, and ran the other way after Row.

Maria and Row ran on. Maria knew the camp and she ran holding Row's hand. Row was not really aware of where she was going, her mind was spinning with what Gebhuza had said. It couldn't be true, could it, she kept thinking. She didn't see the old man waving to Maria who ran towards him, looking around all the time to make sure no one was watching them.

They ran into the shack that the old man called home. He shut the door behind them and ushered them into the corner of the single room. There was a bed which Maria and Row helped him move to the centre of the small room. Then he scraped some of the mud floor away to reveal a wooden hatch. He pulled on a bit of rope attached to it and the hatch opened, revealing a ladder going down into a black hole. 'Climb down the ladder. When you get to the bottom, you will feel a light switch directly on your right. There are good people down there who will help you.'

'Thank you, Samuel. Come with us!' Maria pleaded.

'I am old and do not have much time left, I would rather stay here and help people escape. Someone needs to sit on the bed and play infirm. It stops them dragging the bed away. Now, go please. You don't have much time. Hurry, they will start searching soon… Go! Go! Please.'

Maria momentarily tenderly squeezed Samuel's hand just to let him know she was thankful for his help. 'Take care, Samuel, and thank you.' She smiled. Row smiled too and gave the old man a kiss on his cheek that brought a smile to his face.

'Go, go, please!' He ushered them into the hole and down the ladder then closed the hatch, kicking the dirt back to hide it. Then he pushed the bed back, removed the scrape marks from his mud floor, then sat on the bed. A moment later his flimsy door was wrenched open and a Dark warrior in all his disgusting glory stood in the opening staring into the insignificant room with a bed, a small table and a chair with a bucket in the corner for his ablutions. A single uncovered light bulb swayed gently from the wriggly tin roof.

The warrior grunted. 'Where are the children, old man?' Then he walked into the hut, taking up most of the space.

'I don't know, sir, I have been asleep; I have seen nothing.' Samuel lifted his thin arms to emphasise the point. The warrior picked up the chair and smashed it over the table which collapsed into a heap.

'That's what will happen to you if you be lying.' The warrior snarled at the old man then turned and left, not closing the door on his way out.

Why do those brutes always smash the table and chair? Oh well, it gives me something to do, he thought as he got up and closed the door.

Below him Row and Maria had frozen to the ladder in the darkness when they heard the Dark warrior above them. In the darkness, they strained to hear what was going on.

Karl was not having as much luck as he sprinted through the camp. He was not sure where he was going. As he turned a corner, he ran straight into five Dark Mangoul warriors. He was knocked to the ground by one who then lifted his big knife and was just about to skewer the boy when a voice screamed at them, 'Leave my son alone or you will suffer the consequences!'

They all turned to see Queen Labatina walking towards them. The Mangoul warrior who was set on skewering the boy, now lifted him to his feet, brushed him down and pushed him in the direction of his mother. Karl was transfixed by the beauty of the woman who was walking towards him.

She walked to him and embraced him. He could smell her beauty and feel her comforting arms embracing him. He closed his eyes. It was strange, he was happy for the first time in a long time. The embrace seemed to go on for ever, he did not want it to ever stop. Everything around him disappeared. Then she let go and pushed him to arm's length.

'Well, look at you, my child, you're all grown up... It's been so long, my darling, I never want to let you go again' She pulled him to her in a second loving embrace then kissed his head. 'Let's go somewhere we can talk. Are you hungry?' she asked.

She did not wait for a reply, she took him by his hand and walked away from the warriors who just stared. One was very thankful that he had not skewered the boy.

She took Karl to an inner camp with very luxurious surroundings. Karl noticed they were coming up to a large marquee with two Dark vengeance lancers guarding the entrance. They pulled their lances in as a salute as the queen and Karl walked past them into the marquee. He could see in front of them were some ornate steps going down into the ground. 'These are our quarters, Karl. There are rooms for all of us. Follow me' so Karl did.

It could have been a room in any five-star hotel. How they had managed to do it, Karl did not know. Even though it was underground, there was no lack of light. She guided him into a very plush living room with comfortable chairs, a music system and even a large TV.

'Would you like a drink?' she asked him. Then she went over to a wall, pushed a dark square and the wall opened, revealing a bar. She poured herself a drink then got a bottled coke for Karl. She indicated for him to sit which he did. She sat next to him. 'What's that on your arm?' she asked.

'I'm not sure. It was on my arm when I woke up.'

'Do you want it on your arm?'

''No, I don't think I do,' he replied.

His mother got up and walked from the room. Seconds later she returned with one of the lancers minus his lance. The lacer produced a very sharp looking knife and cut the bracelet from Karl's arm. 'Thank you,' he told the lancer.

'You don't have to thank him, darling, that's what he's here for.'

The lancer left and his mother sat back down next to him. 'Now then, what have you been doing since you were a baby?'

Karl proceeded to tell her a brief history, omitting the bits about killing her warriors. Every now and then she asked him a question about something he had said, enquiring about his uncles, the king and the family. She was interested in the role Phina and Salina had played in their upbringing. Karl watched her face as he spoke. It was almost as if she was remembering people from her past. She would go quite for a moment then return to the present. The calm was broken by Gebhuza entering the room. He hobbled in, headed for the bar and poured himself a whisky.

'He's here, I see. Where did you capture him, my darling?'

'I did not capture him. I saved him from your creatures that were going to kill him. It was only pure luck that I happened to be walking that way or he would be dead now.'

'Pity,' he said under his breath.

'She's not your darling. Where's Row?' Karl stood up and went closer to him in a threatening manner. Gebhuza stepped back after noticing Karl no longer had the bracelet on.

'You've taken the bracelet off... Why? He will escape, my love.'

'Don't worry, Septima, I will not be going anywhere, not until I have killed you!' Karl spat the words in his face then returned to sit next to his mother.

'Now, Karl, there is no need to speak to your father like that. Things are going to change. We will be a family again.'

'He's not my father and we have never been a family, Mum. Don't you realise that?'

Labatina looked puzzled. 'What are you talking about? You know he's your father.' She looked up at Gebhuza who changed the subject quickly,

'Did you get your daughter and the bitch that did this?' He pointed to his bloody trouser leg.

'My daughter, I totally forgot. Where is she, Gebhuza? You were going to get her. What happened?'

'That bitch of a maid of yours stabbed me in the leg then ran off with Row. My men are looking for them now… they can't have gone far. I'm going to get my medical kit and dress this wound in the bathroom. Make sure he does not escape while I'm gone.' He pointed at Karl to make his point then, with Karl watching his every move, he walked out of the room.

Once he had gone Karl turned to his mother. 'Why are you with him? You know you have a husband on Elemtum. He still loves you; do you know that?'

'Who?' she asked.

'My father, Frederick De-Callen, the king and emperor of all the people on Elemtum. Don't you remember?'

'I do' He is evil. A threat to all of us.'

'No, Mum, you and that sociopath Gebhuza Septima are the evil ones. You and your Dark army that has been terrorising the planet for years. Why do you think you haven't seen me since I was born? I've been hidden away. Me, Row and Tom, hidden from you! You and that monster in there.' Karl flung a pointed finger towards the door Gebhuza Septima had left by. 'What has he done to you?' Karl shouted with frustration then stood up. 'Where's my room? I want to be alone for a bit.' He walked to the door.

Labatina got up. Her face was white. Something had hit a nerve, she remembered something familiar about what he had said, something in her memory. She got up slowly, without making a sound, and showed Karl where his room was. She opened the door then closed it when he walked in. The room had pictures of aircraft and ships as well as Karl's favourite films on Earth, Space Wars posters.

Gebhuza had finished patching himself up. He walked into room and saw Labatina sitting there quietly. He could see she was deep in thought and did not want to disturb her, so he looked for Karl making sure he had not escaped. He opened Karl's door and saw him sitting at a desk with some headphones on; he had found the music. He had not heard music for so long. He did not hear the door open, close then lock from the outside.

Gebhuza walked into his makeshift medical room and picked up a loaded syringe, then walked back to Labatina and stuck it in her arm. She flinched and looked up. 'What was that for?'

'A little something to help you relax. You're a bit stressed, I can see. That will calm you down, my love.'

'Am I your love? I'm not sure now? Oh, I feel a little lightheaded. I may just have a little sleep here.'

'That would be a good idea. You rest while I go and find our daughter.' Labatina's eyes closed and she fell asleep.

In the dark, Row and Maria had now reached the bottom of the ladder, Maria reached out with her hand and found the light switch that was where Samuel had said it would be. The light illuminated a long tunnel with cable lights all along one side giving just enough light to see by. They had to crawl along after a couple of feet from the ladder which was not hard going as the ground was dry and there was not much dust. After five minutes they came to a junction. Someone had put signs on little plaques giving directions. They were all in a language Row did not understand but Maria understood Portuguese, so she translated. 'This one says to the river, this one to the jungle and the last one says to the store. Where would you like to go?'

'I don't know. What do you think would be the best direction to go in?'

'The river, I think. I know a village a little distant from here. My husband bought our fresh fish from there.'

'The river it is then.'

They hurried of in the direction they thought the river would be. They did not meet anyone until they got halfway to the river, they knew this because the guard and their new guard their told them so. He was a cheerful young man who was helping anyone trying to escape from the camp. His grandfather was the old man who had helped them. His grandson had tried to persuade him to come out, but he had told him that he could help people better from inside.

His grandson said, 'He was doing something good in his last days of life.'

The grandson, whose name was Pedro, showed them to the exit of the tunnel. He popped out to make sure all was clear then called them out. He also showed them a spike trap. 'If you come back and I am not here the spike trap will be set so don't go in' He smiled and then shouted after them, 'Don't trust the local police. They are being paid to help the bad men inside.' He waved them goodbye and wished them luck.

Row and Maria made their way down to the river's edge just inside the jungle so if they had to hide, they could. Parts were hard going until Maria realised where she was, then things got better. They made their way to the fishing village and approached cautiously, looking out for any signs of the unusual. On the outskirts of the village, Maria pulled Row back. 'Police. Look.' She pointed to the centre of the village. A police 4x4 vehicle with a policeman manning a large machine gun scanned the area.

Row and Maria ducked behind some of the houses. As they crept along, they were watched by a young boy who went and told his grandmother who walked out the back of her house.

'Maria,' she whispered, 'come over here. Come inside with your friend.' The old woman waved them over. She ushered them into a room that could not be seen from outside. She told the young boy to sit on the porch. If the police came near, he was to run in and tell her. The boy went and did as he was told. 'Have you come from the camp? Have you seen my husband and son?' she asked.

'I saw your son the other day, He was, well, cutting back the jungle. I don't know why,' Maria told her.

'My husband?'

'No, I'm afraid not. I was not allowed to go everywhere on the camp so he could have been in any part of that. I do know there were lots of work parties every day; he could have been on one of them.'

'He's a fisherman. What good would he be on a work party?'

'I know they been catching their own fish. Maybe, if they have any sense, they would use him for that, don't you think?'

'Yes, I suppose you are right. No point in worrying if you have no bad news, is there? ... Where are you going, Maria? Hiding in the shadows?'

'We have been told not to trust the police!'

'These people are not police. Half of them aren't even Brazilian. I don't know what has happened to the local police. I used to know them all. Nice lads.'

'I am going back to my village. Me and this young girl have escaped with the help of Samuel and his grandson Pedro.'

'Maybe they can help my boy and find my husband?'

'Don't worry. This young lady has connections that will bring this camp and all the monsters inside to justice. We need to get going.'

They made their way back outside again and the woman told them the best way to get out of the village in the right direction that would lead to Maria's village. Just then an army helicopter with a big red and white cross on its belly, denoting medical, flew over the top of the village, then down the river.

'You don't see many of them in this area of the Amazon,' she told them as they were leaving.

That got Row thinking as they made their way away from the fishing village. 'I wonder, Maria... I wonder if my uncle Kurt had anything to with that helicopter? I know he will be looking for me and Karl. Karl! She had totally forgotten about him. 'My brother is still in that place; I must go back for him.'

'You can't. It's too dangerous. We only just got out alive, young one. We will get to my village then you can call your uncle and we can rescue everyone.'

Row stopped and thought. 'Yes, it makes sense, Maria. He is good at looking after himself. He will probably be more worried about me. I do want to see my mother though. I'm sure that time will come.'

They carried on for several hours until they reached Maria's village. She had been away for six months, but she did not expect to see what she saw. Nothing! No one! The village was completely empty. She started to cry; Row held her.

'It's going to be okay, Maria, I promise.' Just then two more military helicopters flew overhead, descending into what looked like the jungle. These had come from a different direction to the medical helicopter.

'They must be heading to the football pitch we cut out of the jungle for the kids. We use it for medical emergencies as well. The doctor normally lands there if he is needed.'

'Let's go and find out who they are, Maria. They may be able to help us. We won't show ourselves until we are positive they are not part of the Dark.' Maria agreed, wiped her eyes and together they headed off for the football pitch in the jungle.

Tom had arrived back at Great Porum with Hollie and the escort. There had been no problems throughout the journey. Tom seemed to perk up a bit; he recognised Hollie and even spoke to her. She thought he was getting back to his normal self. They were met by a healer who gave Tom a once over and found nothing wrong. Hollie took him to see Phina and Salina who he recognised straight away, giving them both a big hug. After eating, the princesses escorted Tom to see his father, the king. Frederick was in his rooms getting a follow-on check-up from Paccia and Nerilla, the medical sisters. Phina walked in and announced she and Salina had someone to see the king.

Tom walked in. The king turned around, a beaming smile across his face. 'Tom, my son, you are here and well, thank Atta.' He stood up and stretched his arms out to Tom who ran into his father's arms.

'We will leave you alone,' said the two healers. Phina and Salina joined them and they all left together. If they had not, they might have seen the change in Tom's eyes as they stared at his father's face. There was no emotion at all on his face.

'Thomas, my son, are you okay?' The king had seen the change on Tom's face. Tom's hand slid down to his trouser leg and removed a spike from a sheath strapped to his leg. Instantly, before the king could react, Tom plunged the spike into his father's heart. The king staggered back, not breaking his stare at Tom, disbelief etched all over his face.

'Why, Tom?'

Then he collapsed, dead, to the floor. Tom stood there, no expression on his face. A sly smile crossed his face for a second, then the realisation hit him.

'What have I done?'

Then he screamed for help and started to cry. He ran over to his father's body and lay over him, sobbing.

Seconds later, Salina, Phina and the healers found him. They stood over him, trying to sort out what had happened.

'I killed my dad!' he sobbed to them, 'I don't know why!'

Phina and Salina took him away from the room his father lay in. The two healers tried their best, but the king was dead. Tom was inconsolable, uncontrollably sobbing in Phina's arms. Salina spoke to the healers who showed her the spike they had taken from the king's body. It was crudely made but deadly, the king's body was testament to that. Tom was taken to the infirmary and placed into a healing vessel that would put his brain back to its original state; they believed he had been brainwashed while in the custody of the Dark.

The king's body was recovered by the royal guard and lay in state for twelve hours before, as was tradition, he would have a state cremation. Messages were sent around the world notifying everyone of the king's demise at the hands of the Dark. That was who they were blaming, not Prince Tom. Deep sorrow was felt for the king and his family; they had suffered more than most at the hands of the Dark.

Row and Maria had made their way to the edge of the football field, out of view of the three helicopters and soldiers that had landed. Row looked carefully. She did recognise anyone at first. Three soldiers, all big men, walked from behind one of the black helicopters. One face she did not know, the second looked familiar. The third she recognised straight away; it was her uncle Kurt. 'That's my uncle Kurt,' she told Maria.

'Are you sure?' she asked.

'Yes, I would know him anywhere, and he's smiling. That has to be a good sign.' She stood up and shouted to him and waved. Uncle Kurt, it's me, Row.' Then she started to walk from behind cover. Maria called to her, 'Be careful, little one.'

'It's okay, Maria. I will give you a wave when I know it's good to come out.' Row walked towards the group of soldiers who had turned to look at who was calling. Some of the soldiers instinctively lifted their weapons in the direction of the shout. Kurt looked over.

'I don't believe it, it's Row, the girl I am looking for. Tell your men to stand down, Danny, it's okay.' Kurt ran to her, lifted her off the ground and twirled her around. 'Are you okay, Row? Have they hurt you? Is Karl with you?'

'Hi, Uncle Kurt. Just let me call Maria over.' She waved and shouted over to Maria that it was all right and that everyone was a friend. Maria came out, smiling, thankful that their ordeal could nearly be over. They welcomed Maria then one of the medics checked her and Row out. Apart from being a little dehydrated they were both in surprisingly good health considering what they had been through. Then they gave them some food and water and talked to them about how they had escaped, what the disposition of the camp was like and the quantity of enemy they may have to deal with. Kurt and Danny were very interested in the tunnel, Samuel and his grandson Pedro. They were also a little puzzled about the position of the camp as the medivac helicopter had not found it when it flew over the area. A camp of the size Row and Maria had mentioned should have been easy to find. Danny brought a local map out and asked Maria to pinpoint the area of the camp. When she pointed to the camp, Kurt told them it must be using some sort of cloaking device. Row had told Kurt that Karl had run off; she was almost positive he was still in the camp somewhere as Maria told them that no one could escape, or had escaped, that she had known of anyway. It was decided they would do a recce of the area, find the tunnel and Pedro and see if that could be of any help.

Maria told them she thought there were probably one hundred people in the camp who were bad and about one hundred and fifty who were normal people like her, been forced to work there. Most were fit; fishermen, farmers and their families. She was sure if they could they would help the soldiers defeat the bad guys.

'This will be a big ask, Maria. Would you come with me and Danny back into the camp? we will protect you with our lives. What we want to do is speak to as many of the people in the camp as we can to prepare them for our attack. Once we have recced the camp, we will know the best place to blow a hole in the fence to allow most of the people to escape. If need be, we'll blow two holes if that mean we can get most of them out before we take out the others.' Maria thought for a second, then said she would do it. Row also told them she would be going in as well and that her uncle Kurt knew how good she was with weapons. Danny said she could stay with the medics. Row agreed, but Kurt saw the mischievous look on her face that the others did not. He would have to keep an eye on her.

It was all agreed. They would start with a recce through the tunnel by Kurt, Danny and Maria. They did not want too many going in because it would be harder to hid if they needed to. Row thought she should go but Kurt would not have it. He had only just found her, and he was not going to lose her again. Danny communicated the plan to David and asked if they could get some support from a couple of gunships. David agreed. He told Danny that he would get some of the federal police commandos to back them up as well. 'They should all be with you in a couple of hours,' he told Danny.

Danny informed Kurt who agreed that by the time the recce was over a plan would be finalised. 'As long as it all goes to plan,' he told him.

They would leave the helicopters at the football field with a small guard, namely the crews who would be on standby to help out with casualty evacuation if needed. It was only be a short flight, but for Kurt and his men, as well as Danny and his men, it would be a minimum of a two-hour slog with all their kit to the fishing village where they would take out the mercenaries posing as police. They set off at around 1600 hours so any recce of the camp would be done in the dark. That suited Danny and Kurt.

As they approached the fishing village, the teams fanned out, creeping forward, telling each other when they saw one of the bogus police officers. In the end they located eight men. One was manning a machine gun on the back of a 4x4, three others were talking, standing around the bonnet of the vehicle, two were patrolling down by the river, and the last two were standing on the wooden porch of a hut at the entrance to the village. None of them were aware of the danger they were now in.

Kurt, Danny and their teams all had silenced weapons. Once they were in position, they would all shoot on command. Minutes past until all the teams were ready. One by one the teams called in until everyone was ready. They had identified their targets and were ready to shoot.

Danny spoke to everyone, 'On my mark. Three! two! one! Go!' Eight precise shots were fired, seconds later eight mercenaries lay dead, each shot through the head, silently, deadly. They all waited. Nothing else happened so the shooters carefully and silently made their way to the bodies, first removing any weapons then checking the bodies while their partners observed the area. Nothing else moved. Danny gave the command and everyone else made their way into the fishing village. The bodies were moved out of sight and placed in an abandoned hut. Then they deployed guards at the entrances to the village. Maria went from house to house as the sun set, letting the villagers know the bad men had been removed. The people of the village were so happy and thanked the soldiers before their thoughts went to the loved ones that had disappeared. Danny spoke to everyone as Kurt got the kit for the recce of the camp ready. Danny told the villagers the plan. Nothing would happen until the men from the recce returned. He implored them to stay quiet and not to leave the village. Their families would be home soon. The villagers, mainly women, young children, and old men agreed. Happily, they went back to their homes and waited. For the first time in a long time, they had hope.

Danny, Kurt and Maria made their way back to the tunnel that had been guarded by Pedro. As they moved closer, Maria told them to stop. She could see that a trap had been set. Pedro was not in the tunnel.

'Hey, you, don't move. I have you covered. One false move and you will be dead.'

Danny and Kurt turned around. Behind them was a small teenager with a rather large machete in his hand and a determined look on his face. Maria came from behind the two men,

'Pedro, it's me, Maria. It's okay, these are friends. They have come to help us!'

'Maria, it's good to see you. Sorry, I have to guard this tunnel with my life. it's the only way people can get out.'

'Not anymore, kid, that's our job now. You can stand down,' Danny said as he walked towards him and went to take the machete from his hands. Pedro pulled away from him.

'No. It's my only weapon, I need it!'

'Not any more, kid. How old are you?' Danny asked him.

'Fifteen. I am the man of our house since my brother and Grandad were taken.'

'Well, Pedro, the man of the house, we will get your family back. Do you know how to use this?' Danny showed him a pistol he had taken from a holster on his hip.

'Yes, my brother was in the army, he showed me. I know about the safety catch and not to point it at anyone unless you intend to kill them. My brother was a good soldier.'

'Good. You can look after this for me until we return, you can be our rear guard. You could not do anything with that big machete in that tunnel,' Danny told him.

'I know. That's why I have this!' He pulled a fighting knife from his belt, jabbing and slashing the air with it to show the two men he knew how to use it.

'Good lad. I can see you are more formidable than I first thought.'

Pedro replaced the knife then hid the machete in its concealed hiding place near the entrance to the tunnel.

Danny handed him the pistol. 'This is a SIG P320 M17. It's loaded with a 17-round magazine. Here's another magazine just in case.' Pedro put the second magazine in the pocket of his raged shorts then gently felt the pistol. He held it in his hand, finding its balance then checked where the safety catch was. Danny and

Kurt could tell he had handled weapons before. 'Are you happy, young man?' Danny asked, putting a reassuring hand on Pedro's shoulder.

Pedro smiled, nodding his head as he slid the pistol into his belt at the back like an undercover cop on a TV drama series. Then he went and disarmed his trap at the entrance to the tunnel.

'Follow me!' he told them, then led the way into the tunnel. Kurt and Danny had to take their tactical vests off and hold them and their assault weapons in front of them. They were both surprised and happy to discover the tunnel had light and got wider and higher as they got further in. Pedro told them that it was his idea to make the entrance tighter as well as three more areas further up. This was to slow anyone following him at speed, a bit of insurance he told them as they stood up. Halfway in they found Pedro's hiding place where he had first met Row and Maria the day before.

'Just keep going forward. Take the first right you come to. One hundred metres along you will come to the exit ladder below my grandfather's bed. Knock four times and he will open it for you. Oh, I nearly forgot, before you knock, listen for a minute. You will be able to hear if anyone is in the room with him. The enemy tend to talk loudly.' They thanked him and moved on.

Eventually they reached the space next to the ladder. They put their kit back on, switched the light off and listened… they could not hear anything in the room above, so they knocked four times. After a short time, the hatch opened, an old man ushered them in. Danny went first and watched the door then Maria, who hugged Samuel on the way out. Kurt moved into the room which was completely dark. With their night vison googles on this was not a problem.

Samuel was told the plan; the bed was pushed back into its original position and Samuel adopted his usual position with a big smile on his face. He adjusted his one dirty pillow, rested his head and closed his eyes. 'I will be here waiting like a coiled spring!' he joked with them.

Danny opened the door slightly. It was dark but there was some ambient light coming from the lights on the perimeter fences that were one hundred metres away. 'How on earth did the medivac helicopter not see this place?' Danny whispered to Kurt through their intercom.

'I think I know why. There has been talk that a cloaking device was being experimented with; I assume the Dark have cracked it. We will have to find its source or we might not get any support later.'

Danny agreed but first they had to find their way around the camp and find the people being held captive. Maria took the lead. She told them most of the men were being held in a big shed, on the opposite side of the camp, with the women in another one. 'There are towers directly opposite the huts with search lights and machine guns. A tall electric fence surrounds each one, that's why not many people have used the tunnel. During the day, they are closely guarded when they are working and at night they can't get out!'

'We will have to find the electricity supply to the fences and cut it off without the Dark realising,' Kurt told them.

Maria touched his arm gently. 'I think I know where that is. There are two brick buildings near each hut. They have lots of wire coming from them and pylons that go to certain parts of the camp.' She pointed one out to them. It was slightly standing apart with the light from the fence highlighting parts of it.

A lot of the wooden huts in the camp were on small stilts. It obviously rained a lot here, Kurt thought. There was a lot of drainage around the brick buildings as well. Maria guided them around the camp to the areas that the guards rarely went to, they seemed to stick to their routes like clockwork. They turned a corner. In front of them was a man puffing on a cigarette who seemed more shocked than they were. It did not last long. Kurt raised his silenced pistol, the man fell to the floor, dead. They dragged him into a dark corner then waited a short while… no one else heard anything. They moved on towards the electrical station for the men's hut. It had a fence around it; the gate had a big brass lock on it. Danny quickly dealt with that and the lock on the main door then they entered the building, closing the door behind them. In front of them was an array of dials and switches. Fortunately, someone had put stickers on each switch naming the area it controlled. They quickly found electric fence 1 so turned it off and waited. Nothing! Danny took a timed pack of explosives from his pack and placed it on the side of the control panel. Anyone entering the room would not see it unless they looked hard for it, which at this point they had no reason to. They cautiously moved from the building. They would not be able to open the gate to the hut without taking the guard in the watch tower out.

It was decided Kurt would go up and neutralise the guard. Maria and Danny would enter the hut and let the men know the plan for later. The sign would be an explosion, they would be told. They waited under the tower as Kurt climbed the ladder. Once he reached the top of the tower, he carefully lifted his head over the wooden floor, his pistol at the ready. He saw the guard sitting with his hand on the searchlight. He was fast asleep, so Kurt entered the watchtower. Drawing his knife, he covered the guard's mouth and dispatched him quickly. Then he took his place. He could see the other tower in the distance. There was no movement in that one either, so assumed that guard was asleep too. He spoke to Danny telling him it was all clear, so he and Maria made their way to the compound gate where the lock was easily opened by Danny. They made their way to the hut entrance. Making their way in, they were confronted by row upon row of three-tier bunk beds. At the far end were some ablutions. They made their way to the first bed and woke the sleeping occupant who was a little startled at seeing Maria in the men's hut. He was told to quietly wake everyone because the soldier needed to speak to everyone. The man indicated to Danny that there was a snitch in the hut. Everyone knew who it was so Danny went over to him with some of the other men. They woke him, tied his hands with some plastic cuffs he had in his sack then put some tape over his mouth. As Danny did this, a couple of the men got a punch in on the man. They did not care; he was a snitch and now his time of reckoning was coming. Once everyone was assembled, they were told the plan and the signal that would start it all off. Excitedly, they all went back to their bunks. Outside, Kurt met them. He had propped the dead guard up to look like he was awake and on guard. No one would see his shut eyes until the morning when the sun came up. They moved and took out the second guard in the tower as well as the electrical building, setting the explosives as they had before. The women were told the plan and they too waited for the sign that was to signal the start. Maria then took them to the entrance to Labatina's and Gebhuza's quarters. They had been told by the women that's where they had seen the boy being taken to. Maria pointed the entrance out to Kurt and Danny. There were two Dark vengeance lancers outside the entrance as well as two Dark Mangoul warriors with two demon dogs straining on their chains. 'What the hell are they?' Danny asked.

'They, Danny, my friend, are humans and guard dogs that have been modified by a mad doctor I have been chasing for years now. This is the Dark I have been speaking about. We can't really take them on without stirring up a hornets' nest. Let's set a few timed charges around the place. Then we will get out of here as time is ticking on.'

Danny agreed they had done what they had come to do. Once the charges had gone off, hopefully the cloaking devise would be disturbed and the support would find the base. They had taken the position of the centre of the camp on their GPS so that would help the teams find the place. They also took the position of the two explosive devices they had set on the outer fence near the two huts containing the local people. The explosives had been set for first light so they had to move to get back to their teams and brief them then get everyone into position for the attack. Time was tight but both Danny and Kurt knew it was achievable if they hurried. So that's what they did without any of the Dark finding out they had been there.

Back in the fishing village, everyone was briefed and the GPS positions sent to David who was now in the air with some more of his men and the commandos as well as two gunships that would be overhead fifteen minutes after the first explosions had gone off. Danny split his men into two teams who made their way to the two positions that they had fixed near the breached areas in the fence they had set up earlier. Kurt, Steven and the water team would make their way through the tunnel and go straight for the quarters of Labatina and Gebhuza. Once the explosions had gone off, if needed they would fight their way to the quarters and dispatch the guards and demon dogs before storming the quarters to rescue Karl. Once the locals had escaped, Danny and his teams would clear the camp then meet up with Kurt.

Chapter 26
Closure

They were all in position ten minutes before the explosions were due to go off. There was not enough space in Samuel's room for all the water team so some of the warriors had to wait in the tunnel; it would not take them long to get out of the tunnel and into battle. Last minute checks were carried out by all the teams. Everyone was ready. 3-2-1 bang! Bang! Two simultaneous expositions rocked the camp as two large holes were blown in the fences, followed a second later by two more explosions as the two electrical buildings were blown apart. As hoped, the cloaking field disappeared around the camp. It was not obvious to Kurt and the water team, but Danny and his teams reported that they could now see the camp. David and his team would have no problems finding them now.

Kurt and his team were out of the door and heading for Labatina's quarters, Danny and his team emptied the male and female huts and sent them through the holes in the fence. There were a few encounters where the teams took out some of the mercenaries who came out of building but there were not as many as anticipated.

Kurt and his team reached the entrance to Labatina's quarters. The two demon dogs and their handlers had disappeared but the water team dispatched the two lancers. As they fell, the door to the quarters opened and Gebhuza stuck his head out. He saw the water team and Kurt descending on him and pulled the steel door shut just as bullets hit the door. Kurt reached the door. It was shut fast. He reached into his bag and pulled out a breaching charge that he placed around the door.

Inside, Labatina had got up wearing her nightgown, pulling a robe around her to break the morning chill in the cave. She unlocked the door to Karl's room that Gebhuza had locked the night before; she had no memory of that time and only just remembered that Karl was there. She stepped into his room as he got up; he had fallen asleep in his clothes. She went over to her son and hugged him. 'What's that for?' he asked.

'Because I can and it's been a long time since I last held you. Where is your sister?' she asked.

Karl was going to explain when Gebhuza rushed in with a machine pistol in his hand. 'Come on, we have to get out of here!'

'Who's here?' Labatina asked.

'Kurt and his men. I heard some explosions so I went to the door and they were running at it. We must go. There is another way out,' he screamed and went to grab her. A quick as a flash Karl was a wolf and grabbed Gebhuza's arm. With a scream, Gebhuza dropped the pistol and tried to fend the beast off. His arm was bleeding and the pain was excruciating.

Labatina shouted at her son, 'Karl, leave him!'

But Karl was not listening; he hated this man and he was not going to let him go. They did not see Arthfael, the Dark lord, enter the room carrying a rifle. He lifted it up and smashed the butt down on to the wolf's head. Karl fell to the floor, not moving. Labatina picked up the machine pistol and aimed it at Arthfael who pulled Gebhuza in front of him.

'You killed my son!'

Gebhuza screamed 'No!' as the pistol barked, sending a stream of bullets into his body.

As Gebhuza fell to the floor, Arthfael grabbed the gun from Labatina's shaking hand. He then grabbed her and pushed her out of the room along a corridor to the last room on the left. As he opened the door, the entrance exploded, throwing the heavy steel door three feet into the room, crashing to the floor. Arthfael looked back and saw Kurt entering the corridor, weapon at the ready in his hand. Arthfael pushed Labatina further into the room then slammed the steel door behind him and bolted it. They would not get the door open in time to save her, he thought.

Kurt ran to where he had seen Arthfael. The door was shut tight but he did not have any more breaching charges. While his men cleared the rooms, Kurt called Danny. 'Do you have any more breaching charges?' he asked. In the background he could hear shooting and grenades going off.

'Sorry, Kurt we are under it at the moment… We got all the locals out. We started to clear the camp when rows upon rows, I reckon about fifty plus of those Dark dudes, the ones with the fucked-up faces, and those dogs appeared from the back of the camp. I think they came from the jungle. Anyway, I have casualties, but we are holding our own. I just hope the support arrives soon. We could do with it.'

'We will be with you as soon as we have checked these quarters out. Will you hold that long?'

'Yes, we giving better than we are getting. Out!'

One of the water team came to Kurt. 'We have found the prince. He's out cold. We are giving him first aid; he should be okay.'

Through the breached door they heard approaching helicopters; was it was David? No... it was the medical helicopter that had been called in by Danny for his wounded men. It landed near the camp. A couple of medics ran from it towards the gun fire. Following was Row with an assault rifle in her hand. They reached the area that had some shelter and a field dressing centre set up in it. Row asked the men running it if they knew where Kurt and his men were. They indicated the direction but told her they would be here soon to help Danny once they had finished clearing their area. Row did not hear the last bit and ran off in the direction the medic had pointed. She saw the open entrance that he had indicated but the from a building in front of her just as two Dark foot warriors appeared in front of her.

'Look what we have here; a princess all on her own. Get her!' They ran towards her. One had a spear and one had a sword, both dripping with blood. As they got closer their eyes filled with terror as the white wolf pounced on them. Its fierceness was unequalled. A third warrior ran round the corner, saw what was going on so turned and ran in the opposite direction as quickly as he could. Row could see what she was doing but did not believe it was her. She trotted off towards the entrance by the time she reached it she was Row the human again, not even realising she had changed. Inside she was met by a disapproving Kurt.

'You have blood on your face, are you okay?'

'Yes, I'm fine but the two out there will not hurt anyone ever again.' She smiled. 'Have you found Karl?'

'Yes, he's in there. He's got a bit of a headache, but he will be fine. He was next to the dead body of Gebhuza Septima; he has been shot several times. I don't know who by but I'm sure Karl will tell us.'

Row walked into the room and saw Karl sitting on a bed looking sorry for himself. On the floor was a dead Gebhuza Septima who looked like he had been attacked by a wolf then shot. She kicked him and there was no sound or movement.

'He's dead, Row,' Karl told her.

'I'm glad about that. How are you anyway? I was worried about you. I did not know where you had gone.'

'I'm fine. I met Mum. She was a bit confused last night and that sod,' he pointed to Gebhuza Septima, 'did something to her, then he locked me in here. I saw her again this morning. She was lovely, just like I imagined a mother would be then he turned up with a gun, so I attacked him. He dropped the gun, but I was not going to let go of him, then the world went dark and here I am. No idea what happened after that. Then you walked in. You've got blood on your face. Ae you okay?'

'I'm fine… in fact, I have never felt better, I feel exhilarated. Alive!' she told him.

'You've turned, haven't you?' he said.

'How do you know?'

'I felt the same,' he told her.

'I don't even know I turned.' She smiled. 'But the Dark I tore apart do. And do you know what? I'm not upset because they are bad people.'

'Welcome to the Wolf family, sis,' Karl told her then stood up and hugged her. 'This could finally be over, wouldn't that be great? Mum and Dad, me, you and Tom, Salina and Phina, Kurt and his wife, Tristan. Peace.'

'That would be nice, Karl, but there is still a lot to do here. Queen Labatina is in a room we can't get into at the moment and she's with that traitor Arthfael, so it's not happy families yet. Not only that, the Dark are coming out of the Jungle attacking Danny and his team, so we need to help him. I will leave a couple of guards on the door so Arthfael and the queen can't escape.' Kurt had heard Karl and Row talking as he entered the room. 'And you, young princess, why are you here? Did I not tell you to stay with the medics?'

'I did stay with the medics. They are here. I just came to find you.' She smiled.

'You will be spending some time with Salina and Phina when you get back. It sounds like you need a bit of control when you turn, but that's for another day. Now, stay close to me and the water team.' He looked at both of them, big broad smiles on their faces. 'I mean it!' He was being serious, and they knew it.

They left with the water team and made their way to Danny and his team who, at times, were fighting hand to hand as the Dark kept coming from the jungle. It was blatantly obvious that they had been fighting hard because of the bodies piled up all around them. Behind them, the medics were fighting hard with the casualties. Five of them had six soldiers to look after at that point.

Kurt and his team took up positions and started fighting the Dark which helped Danny and his teams out immensely. They did realise that David and his men had arrived. The first they knew was when a killing rate of fire came from their right, decimating the Dark, but they still kept coming.

Then they heard the helicopters above them. The beating of the rotors and the downdraft told everyone they had arrived. The Gatling guns started as the door gunners raked the advancing Dark warriors. Slowly the Dark started to wither. The amount of fire they were receiving was taking its toll. The warriors with the firing weapons had stopped. Now it was only lances, swords and axe-type weapons that they held as they charged.

'This is becoming a blood bath. Why don't they give up?' David asked.

'They have been trained not to give up. They would rather die. Running is not an option for them.'

David sent some of his team to flank the Dark from the right. Kurt sent the water team, led by Steven, to the left to try to find out how many more were on the way. The two forces would join up to split the attacking force, then Danny and Kurt would take the battle to them. The two helicopters had to return to the football field for fuel and more ammunition; they would return as soon as they could. Their departure did not affect the rate of fire still coming from the remaining forces. Every now and then a Dark warrior would make their way through the fire then hand-to-hand combat would take place but one on one they were no match for the special forces opposing them. Steven's and David's teams cut the attacking force in two and now had the new defensive position. Kurt and Danny's team now moved forward, cutting down the now panicking Dark warriors. Danny observed two big wolves running past his teams attacking the Dark, one was brilliant white.

'What the?'

'It's okay, Danny, they are with me. Someone has let them out, I did not intend to use them,' Kurt said.

'I'm just glad they are on our side. Look at them go; they're killing machines!'

'Yes, I know. They are young and stupid,' he told Danny.

'If that's young and stupid? Give me young and stupid any day... Do you want to sell them?'

'Sorry, Danny, they're family.'

They fought their way to Steven and David who were holding their own. In front of them now was a much smaller force of Dark warriors coming from a tented camp two hundred metres away. Above them, two of the reserve helicopters arrived from the football field. Hovering low over the jungle canopy, they started dropping boxes of ammunition to the troops below.

'I guessed you might be needing this by now,' one of the pilots told them over the air. 'We will be back with more soon.' Then they were gone.

And the two gunships reappeared. 'We can't make you out through the canopy. Can you throw smoke to illuminate the targets for us?' one of the pilots asked. Danny got one of his men to fire a smoke grenade to the edge of the camp. There was a pop as the round left the tube of his weapon then a yellow burst of smoke exploded on the ground before rising through the canopy.

'Only fire forward of the yellow smoke. Friendlies are behind it under your position,' Danny told the pilots.

'Roger that. Firing now,' came the reply from above. Then the Gatling guns started again; the rounds tore through the jungle leaves impacting amongst the tents. Light started to stream down through the new openings to the sky. The ground forces and the two wolves, now replenished, moved steadily forward until they reached what was left of the tented camp. They used classic fire and manoeuvre tactics which worked well to keep the enemy's heads down.

Danny called over the airwaves, 'All callsigns, hold your fire.' A deathly quiet filled the jungle, occasionally broken by a bird call or the sound of a dying warrior calling out. 'Okay, teams, clear the camp. Take extreme care. If you can, take prisoners, but don't put your lives at risk.'

The two helicopters retuned to the football pitch where the casualties had been evacuated to and were now being readied for the journey to the nearest medical facility that could deal with them. They got off very lightly; only one soldier had a serious injury, the others were not life-threatening wounds. Eight in all had to be evacuated.

The teams, led by the wolves, searched the camp. They found a few cowering Dark foot warriors who were easily detained, and also came across two chained up demon dogs. They were ferocious, so had to be shot. They also found some human bodies that showed signs of torture in a tent. Next to that were six young women, all chained to posts; they had to be calmed by the soldiers as they were petrified when they had entered. Row joined them along with one of the female medics who successfully calmed the women down then cared for their minor wounds.

Outside, the soldiers blew a clearing with explosives so one of the helicopters could land. This all took time, so everyone tucked into their rations, sharing them with the women. The searching continued but nothing of any significance was found. The camp was obviously just a holding area for the Dark warriors with the limited facilities they had needed. A medical helicopter arrived and took the women away. It was decided to burn the tented camp to the ground. It was well alight when they left and returned to the initial camp where more troops had arrived along with a grave registration team that David had asked for due to the large number of dead Dark warriors. A digger was airlifted in to start digging trenches for the bodies.

Karl reappeared so they all went back to the room Arthfael and the queen had entered. The water team outside had heard no movement from the room since they had been stationed there. Two Dark warriors with demon dogs had appeared and were dispatched quickly by the water team. Apart from that, it was all quiet. Karl and Row with some of the water team that were not needed for the breach waited outside in the sun.

Danny walked up to them carrying a breaching charge. 'Where are your magnificent wolves? I haven't seen then since we entered that camp in the jungle?'

'They're exploring!' Row told him.

'Funny. I didn't even notice them when we flew over here.'

'They are very good at hiding,' Karl told him.

Danny accepted that and carried on into the quarters to give the charge to Kurt. It was fixed to the door. Everyone stood back, ready to breach. 3-2-1 go! Bang and the door fell away from its hinges. Flash bang grenades were immediately thrown in. After they went off, the team rushed in to find Arthfael dead on the floor with his throat ripped out. In the furthest corner away from the body sat a beautiful white wolf with piercing blue eyes. It was no threat to anyone and happily followed them out when they left the room. Outside it ran to Row and Karl and made itself-comfortable next to them. They tried communicating with it but it seemed just to be a wolf, no other thoughts whatsoever.

It was decided to blow the quarters up with Arthfael's body still inside. The assault troops then left the place to the engineers who would dismantle the camp, help with the burial of the dead and then help the local villages restore fresh water and electricity.

They met Maria who had not found her family, so it was assumed they had been killed. She had decided that Pedro and his grandfather could live with her in her village; it would stop her being lonely. She had also been inspired to go back to nursing by one of the medics. David had also told her he would sponsor her to do a bit more advanced training that would complement what she already knew and would also help the local community. She agreed and was looking forward to the future.

They all said goodbye. Danny told Pedro he was now the man of the house and he could keep the pistol he had been given. They had not found Pedro's brother, mother or father. So, Maria would be his new mother; he liked her. They all boarded the helicopters and departed.

The helicopters took them back to David's farm where they could have a bit of R&R before returning home. At the farm, David and Danny bid them a fond farewell telling them all they would be welcome back any time. The helicopters left.

Kurt, Karl, Row, Steven, the water team and the white wolf had a relaxing three days before they would return to Elemtum and the king at Great Porum. Before they left David phoned Kurt and told him that DNA samples had been taken from some of the dead Dark warriors, but the strange thing was that they did not have human DNA. The scientists believed whatever experiment that had been conducted on their poor souls had totally changed and made a new strain of DNA that had never been seen before. That was the only explanation they could come up with. A story would get out about what had happened so David released a counter story; mad drug-fuelled scientist belonging to a devil worship cult aided by mercenaries had abducted local Amazon villagers in order to expand their cult with a misguided view that they could take over the world to build a new society. The federal government had become aware of the killings and abduction and had sent military forces to apprehend the suspects. They would not surrender so fifty of the cult members were killed in fierce fighting with the special forces sent to deal with the situation. Several prisoners had been captured who were now in a secure mental establishment and would never be released. The villagers were rescued and returned to their homes and would be looked after by government agencies for the near future. No mention of Kurt or the wolves was made, and David told Kurt that the numbers of dead were reduced otherwise the public would not understand why so many had been killed. And it would be described as a massacre by his troops, which it was, but everyone who had been there realised it had been a necessary evil.

Back in Elemtum, the planet had been told the king had been killed by a Dark assassin, which, in theory, he had. Tom was now out of the infirmary with no memory of his part in his father's death.

The party from Earth returned to the sad news that their king was dead. Karl and Row took it better than everyone had thought. They had not really had a bond with their father, and they had their mother, even though she was still a wolf. It was decided that Rowena De-Callen would be crowned Queen of Elemtum, Kurt De-Callen would be emperor and her adviser. A grand ceremony was planned for the week after the dead king's cremation.

Erline was sent for. She re-joined Karl, now happy that they could have a safe life together. Every living soul on Elemtum would be invited; the Zells, Omanian, and even the Surviyns, to name just a few. There would also be a search for Tanibeth – the Taniwha green-haired girl, the last of her race. It was decided there would be a week of celebrations to formally end the war between the Dark and the peoples of Elemtum. Everyone hoped the peace would last.

Lastly, for the first time ever in the history of their world, humans would be invited to attend. Billy and Gina would be honoured guests. It had not been decided whether the invite would be given to David and Danny. Kurt would go back to Brazil and test the water with them.

After the ceremony, it would be decided by the queen and princes if the white wolf was to be taken to the blue moon to see if she could be returned to her human form,

But that was for another day.

Now was to be a time of happiness and peace for everyone on Elemtum, especially the new Wolf queen and the two Wolf princes who had only briefly known peace and happiness before. Their time had come!